I0822425

Incredible praise for the world of BLOOD OF TITANS

Smoke and Rain

International bestselling fantasy and winner of NewApple Literary's 2015 Excellence in Independent Publishing Award

"Holmes weaves a tapestry of the forthcoming events with the skill of a thaumaturge…In [the] seductive opening few lines so much of the nidus of this fantasy tale is hinted...Wade deeply into these waters for a fine curtain raiser for REFORGED. V.S. Holmes quite simply demonstrates that she is an artist of significance"

- *The San Francisco Review of Books*

"A well developed and subtly-layered world...filled with compelling characters and dangerous magic"

- *Aurealis Magazine*

"The very first page hooked me with the simple yet elegant narrative…The characters' dilemmas were revealed in perfect timing yet kept me wanting more, and Holmes didn't disappoint with dropping tidbits of emotion, character growth, and internal struggle among all the the action and war-time maneuvers."

- Kathrin Hutson, author of *Gyenona's Children*
and The Unclaimed Trilogy

"I couldn't put it down to save my life and I couldn't turn the pages fast enough. The plot line was incredibly unique ... Holmes gave me a lot of the things I look for in a wonderful story and so much more."

- Cassandra Carpio, *The Bookish Crypt*

Lightning and Flames

"The atmosphere surrounding this saga is intoxicatingly real...Very highly recommended… This REFORGED volume elevates the reader even more, adding to the obvious stature of V.S. Holmes' literary presence. Very Highly recommended."

- *The San Francisco Review of Books*

"Holmes' prose perfectly illustrates the incredible, world-shaking horror unleashed when Alea and Arman's magic clashes with that of the gods."

- *Aurealis Magazine*

Madness and Gods

"...This tale focuses on the political struggles of its characters with few traditional trappings of the fantasy genre...it takes fantasy's ability to explore complex issues such as gender, mental health and human rights through allegory, and refocuses back on the issues themselves...while new and secondary characters now take centre stage. The new protagonists are interesting and richly drawn..."

- *Aurealis Magazine*

"Following this fantasy experience is addictive and thoroughly satisfying."

- *The San Francisco Review of Books*

Blood and Mercy

"The series excels in using allegory to mirror contemporary issues and explore them in a unique, thoughtful manner. Frustration, hope and the transformative power of righteous fury ooze from the...The underlying optimism of the series, balanced with unflinching realism regarding the difficulty of change at personal and systemic levels, is a testament to the possibilities of the fantasy genre—and a worthy read for our times."

- *Aurealis Magazine*

Books by V. S. Holmes

BLOOD OF TITANS

REFORGED
Smoke and Rain
Lightning and Flames

RESTORED
Madness and Gods
Blood and Mercy

REBEL
*Treason's Tears**

STARSEDGE: NEL BENTLY
Travelers
Drifters
Strangers
Heretics
Fugitives
*Emissaries**

SHORT FICTION
"Nowhere Fast" (*We Came to Dance*)
"Starfall" *(Vitality Magazine)*
"The Tempest" *(Out of the Darkness)*
"Disciples" *(Beamed Up)*
"Familiar Waters" *(Love and Bubbles)*
"Mere Primordium" (poem, *Mystic Blue Review)*

**forthcoming*

RESTORED

V. S. HOLMES

AMPHIBIAN PRESS

This is a work of fiction. All of the characters, organizations, and events portrayed in this novel are either products of the author's imagination or are used fictitiously.

None of the material within was created, in whole or in part, using AI technology.

RESTORED

MADNESS AND GODS Originally Published in 2015
BLOOD AND MERCY Originally Published in 2020

Amphibian Press
www.amphibianpress.online
www.vsholmes.com

Cover art by Ben R. Donahue
Cover design by Amphibian Press
www.bendonahueart.com
Printed in the United States of America

ISBN: 978-1-949693-34-8

RESTORED I

To all those who shouted into the void
and heard it answer back

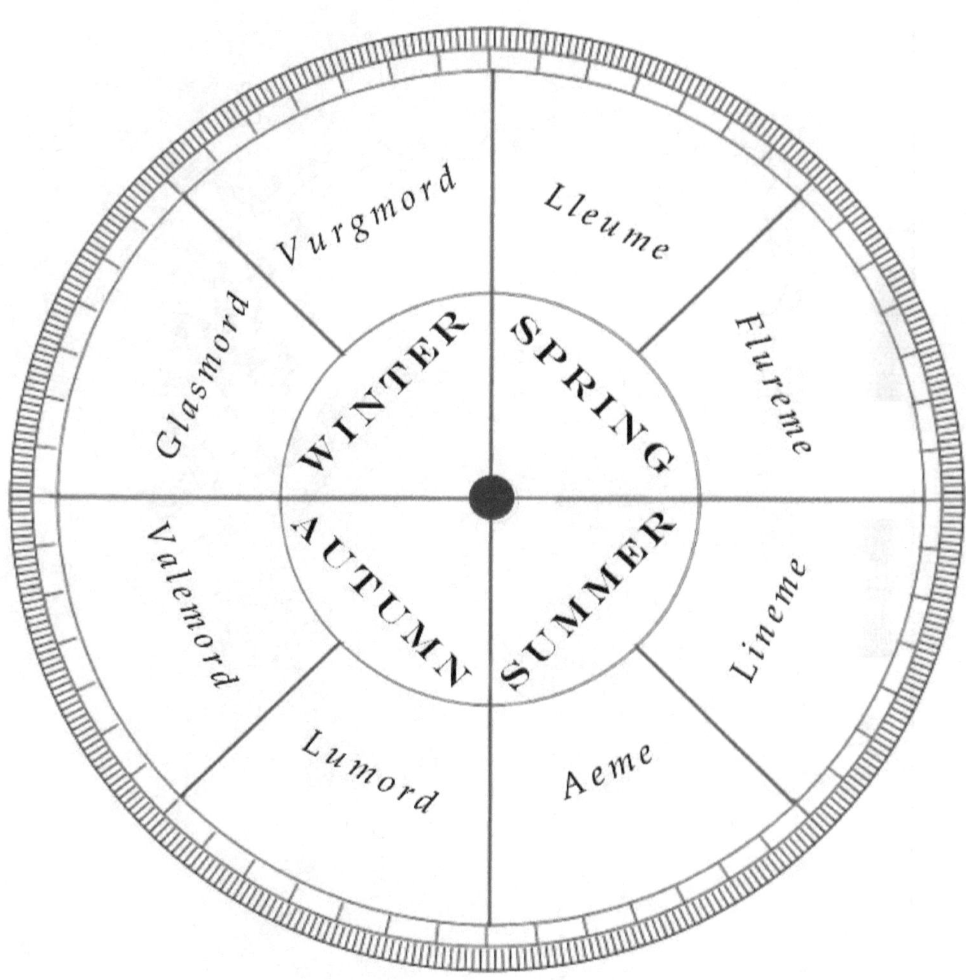
WINTER
SPRING
SUMMER
AUTUMN
Vurgmord
Lleume
Flureme
Lineme
Aeme
Lumord
Valemord
Glasmord

The World Of
BLOOD OF TITANS
N
The Icelock
NORTHLANDS
Neneviir
The
Ilmar
MIRIK
Mirik
Claimiirn
Eastern
Ocean
Ceir
Felden
Iron Sea
Ceir
Athrolan
Fort
Stone
Fort
Shadow
Arc of Zunu
Zunu

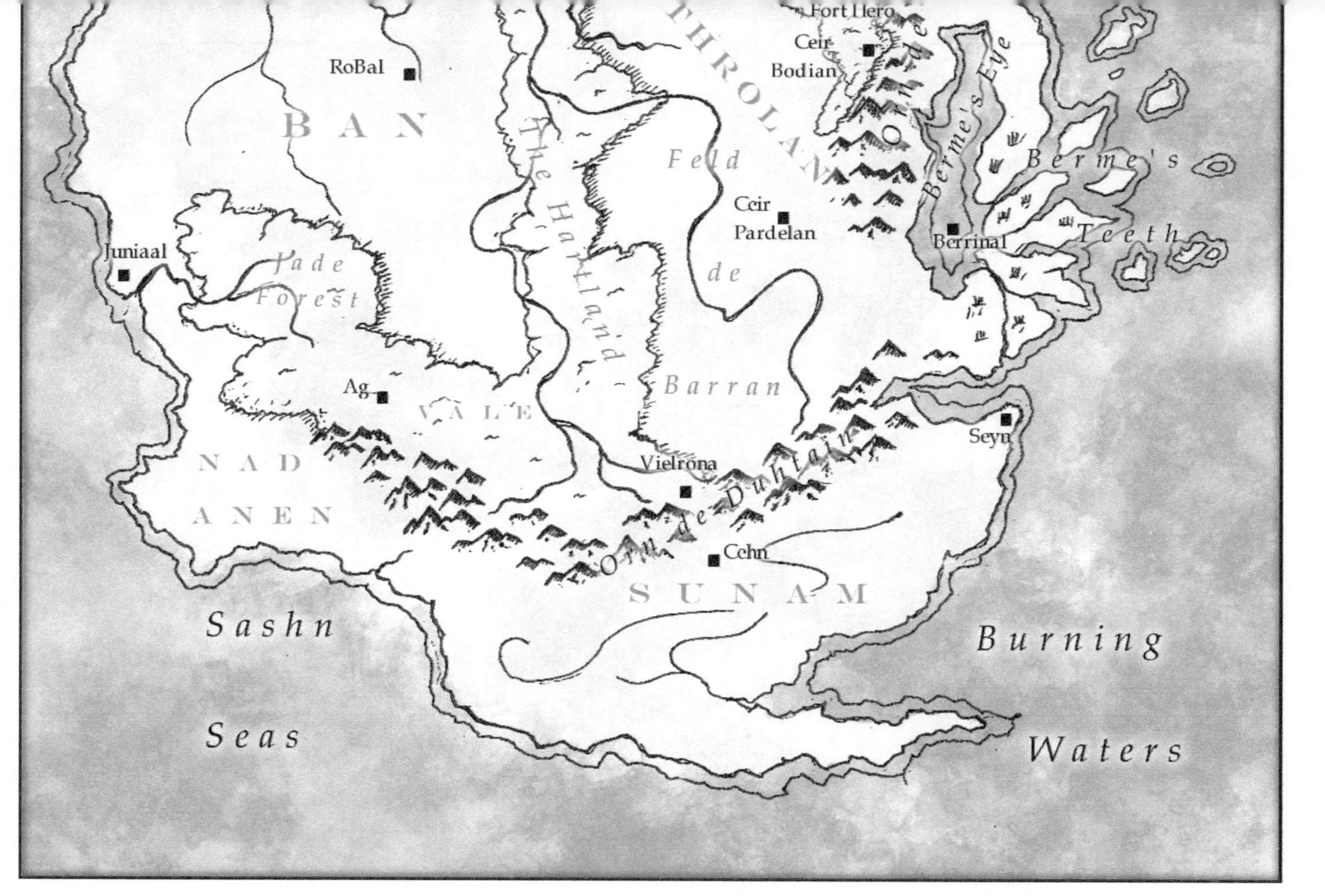

Fort Hero
THROLAN
Ceir
Bodian
RoBal
BAN
Feld
de
Barran
Ceir
Pardelan
Berme's Eye
Berme's
Teeth
Berrinal
Juniaal
Jade
Forest
The Hartland
Ag
VALE
NAD
ANEN
Seyn
Vielrona
Orn de Duhtain
Cehn
SUNAM
Sashn
Seas
Burning
Waters

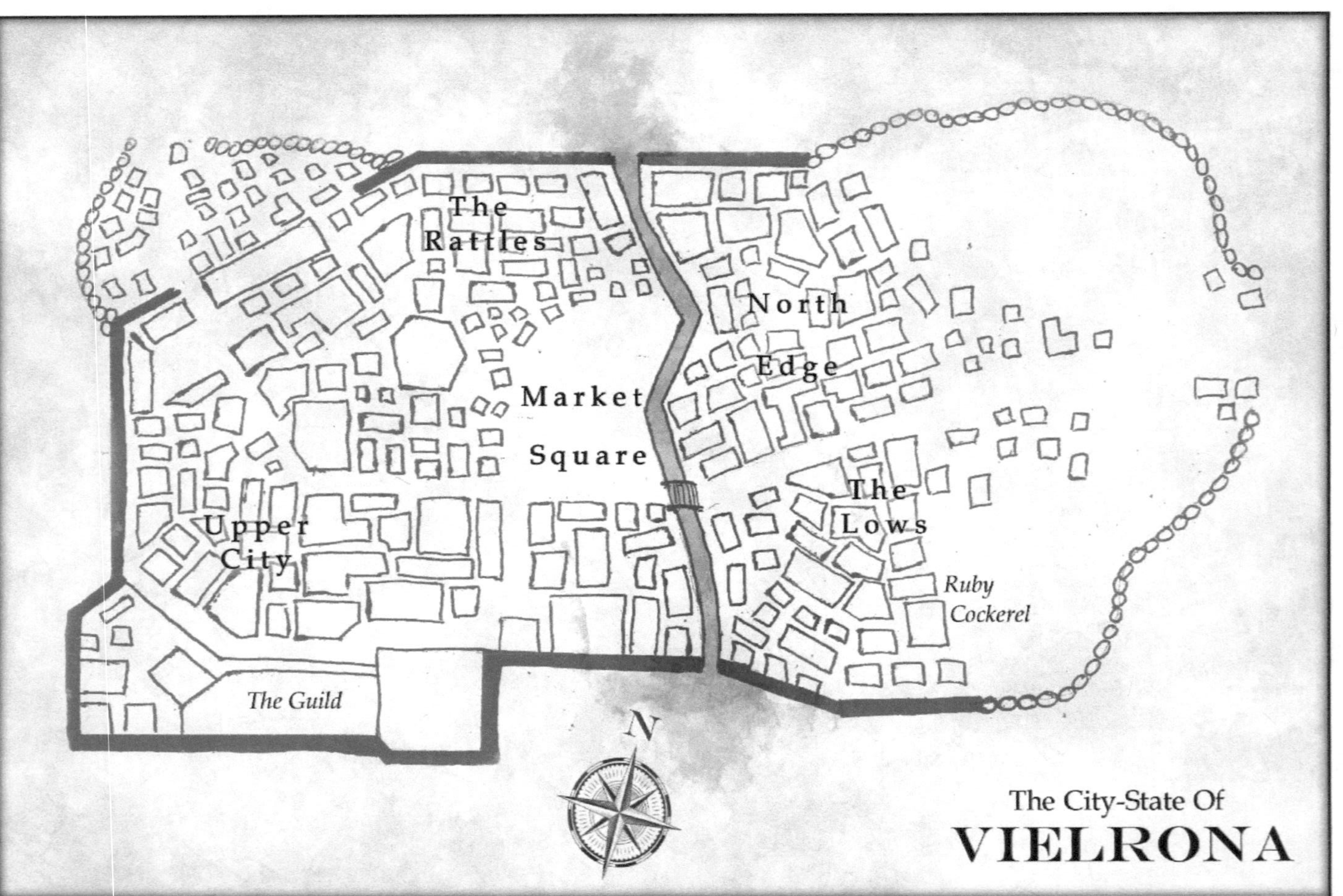
The Rattles
North Edge
Market Square
The Lows
Upper City
Ruby Cockerel
The Guild
N
The City-State Of
VIELRONA

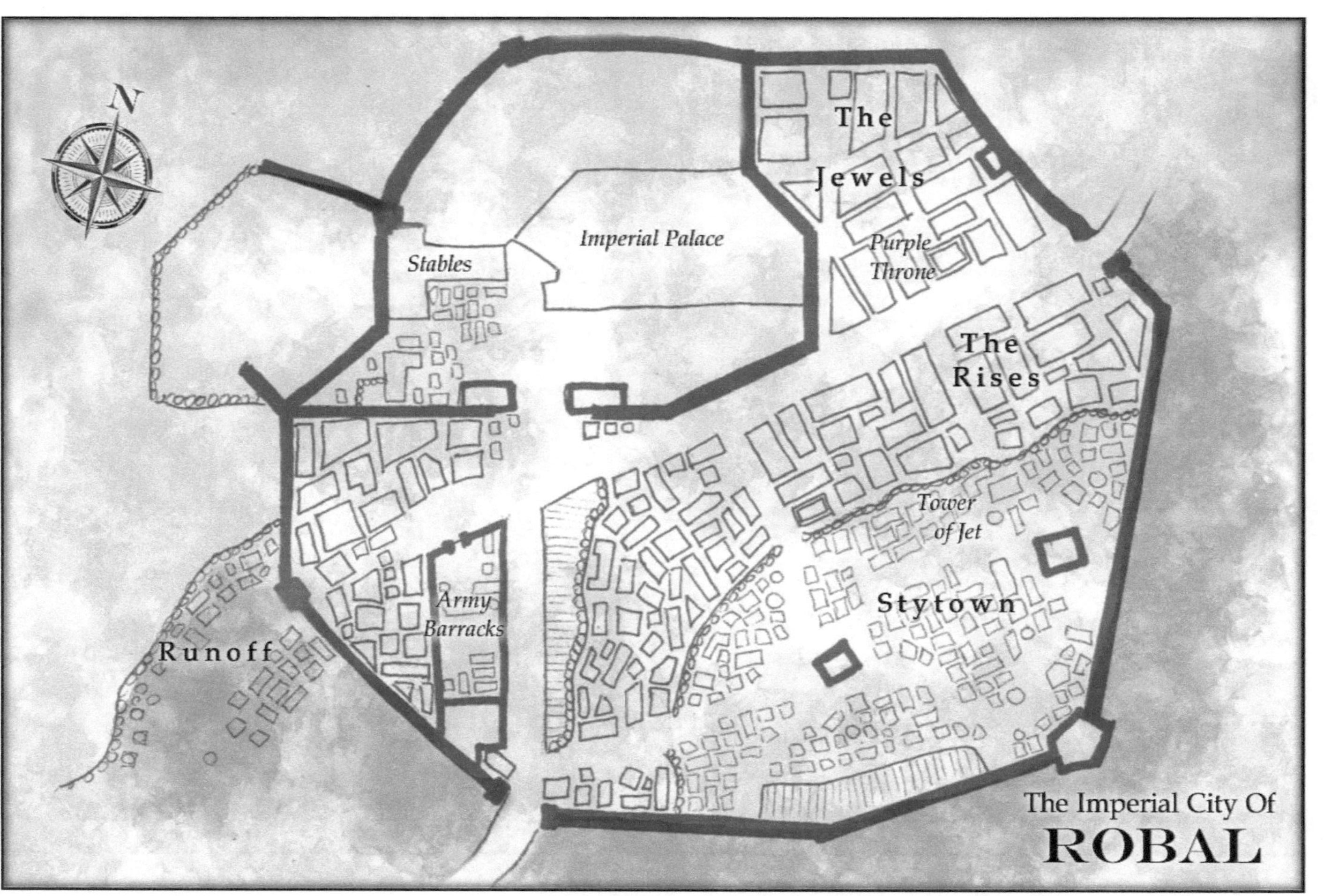
N
The Jewels
Imperial Palace
Stables
Purple Throne
The Rises
Tower of Jet
Stytown
Army Barracks
Runoff
The Imperial City Of
ROBAL

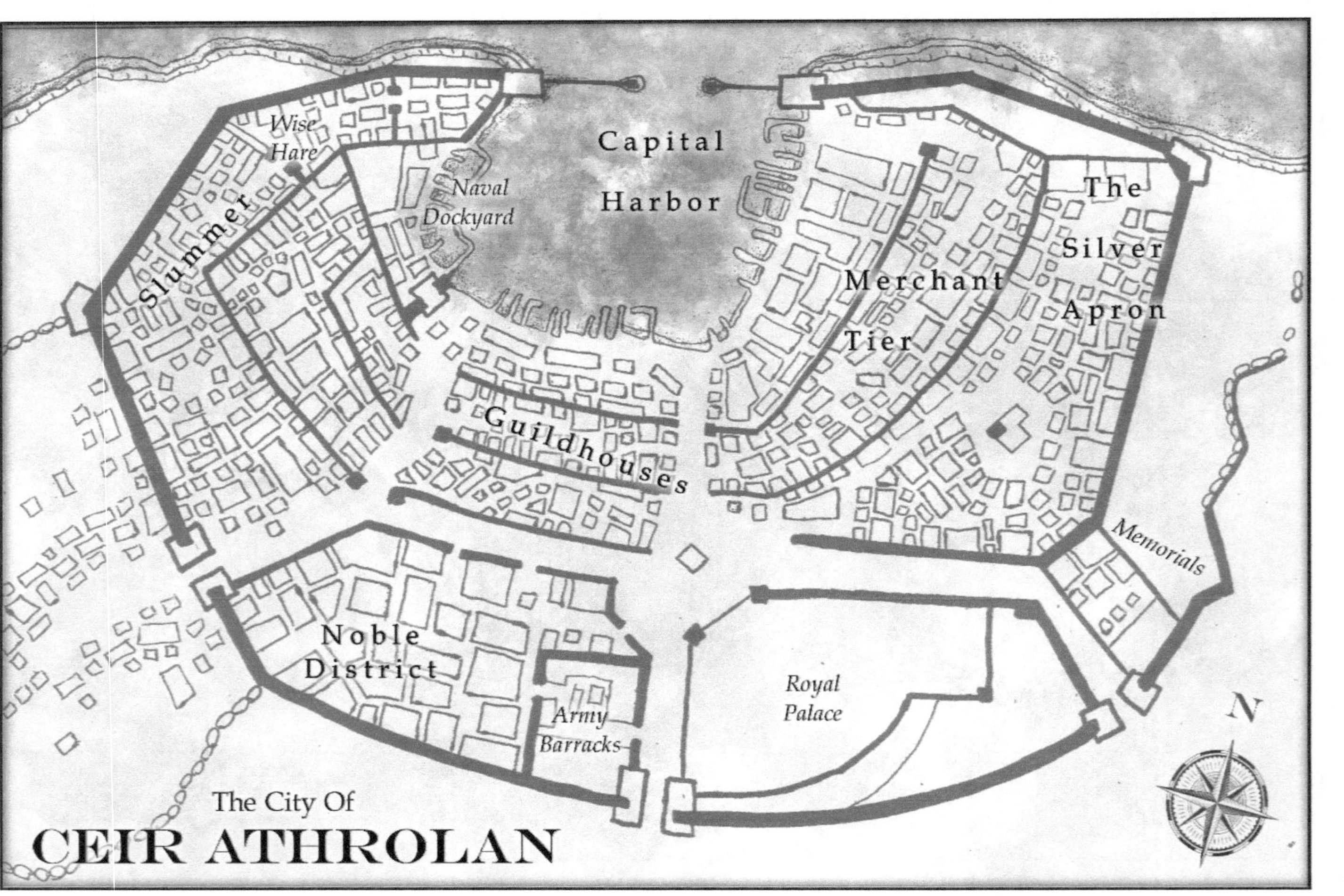

Capital
Harbor
Wise
Hare
Naval
Dockyard
Slummer
Guildhouses
Merchant
Tier
The
Silver
Apron
Memorials
Noble
District
Army
Barracks
Royal
Palace
N
The City Of
CEIR ATHROLAN

THE MARKS OF
VIOLENCE

CHAPTER ONE

The 27th Day of the Month of Rainfall, 1272
The Forest of the Hartland

THE ROOM WAS DESERTED. Arman felt the absence before he opened the door. His gaze roved from the made bed to the hook by the door that no longer held breeches. *It's all wrong.* They kept the truth of their bloodlines from their son, hoping he would live the life they could not. One of peace. Of anonymity. *Perhaps it was a mistake.* Pain gnawed at Arman's gut. He thought Alea would panic, and he would comfort her. Instead, it was his body thrumming with fear and guilt.

He wavered on the threshold, unwilling to allow the last person to enter be someone other than Keplan. The part of him that heard too many legends expected a note on his son's pillow, explaining he left for some adventure. There was none. The ragged parchment protruding from the desk drawer spurred him into the room. It was a letter, but not one from his son. It was one he had kept secret, even from Alea. Underneath lay a series of sketches, drawn in Keplan's quick, haphazard hand.

Arman took both and retreated to the kitchen. His eyes remained fixed out the small, soot-stained window above the kitchen washbasin, waiting for the water to boil. Soft footfalls sounded behind him as he took the muttering kettle from the fire and poured two mugs of tea.

"Has he come back?" The circles under Alea's eyes spoke to how well she had slept. "It's not like him to spend a night in the forest without telling us."

He jerked his chin at the teacup waiting on the table before her. Concern erased his usual compassion. "I don't think he'll come back for a long time."

"How can you say that?" Her voice rasped with tears and fatigue.

Arman heaved a sigh. "Alea, when I left home I packed my bag, made my bed, swept my floors. Trust me when I say I know what running looks like." The words replaced his despair with understanding. Fear, though, still burned through his body. "I found something. Though perhaps you should finish your tea."

"All the tea in the world will not help if my son is missing."

Arman winced. *He's my son too, Alea.* Instead, he set the letter and sketch between them. "I received a letter on my last visit to Namus. I hoped ignoring it would work. I realize, now, I was wrong."

Darkness filled Alea's eyes, an expression he had not seen in years. Decades. "What does it say?"

"It's from An'thor." He held the letter up.

> "'*Alea,*
>
> *I don't know how this letter will find you, in all senses of the words. I've spent precious amounts of what's left in the kingdom's treasury to find you. I think, finally, that I might have. Namus. A tiny town, unremarkable save for its proximity to the Hartland.*
>
> *I understand the value of peace, more than many, I think. You've looked in my eyes and you know this to be true. I remind you of this, so you understand the gravity with which I write this letter.*
>
> *She is dying. Perhaps she will be gone by the time you read these words. She never revoked her dismissal of Daymir. Instead, she named your child, should you have one.*
>
> *We need you. Ceir Athrolan needs you. Just once more. This is my last resort.*
>
> *I won't beg, though I want to.*'"

He swallowed. It explains the news we've gotten, the patrols we've seen. I knew Ban was on the verge of war with Mirik, but this is different. This is our fault."

"He uses no names—"

"That was to prevent rumors of the queen's death should this letter fall into other hands. You and I both know to whom he refers. This was in Kep's desk. Fates know what he thought. I assume, like us, he left looking for answers. And I don't think our power ended with us."

Her winter-chapped hand touched the ragged edge of the sketch. "You found this with the letter?"

Arman let her regard it in silence. He already knew the scene. It was a battle, their battle, above the cliffs of Clai'miin, half a dozen armies locked in a divine fight of lightning and fire. It was not just accurate. It was perfect.

When she looked away, he cleared the emotions from his throat. "Somehow he knows. Maybe not all of it, maybe nothing but this, but he knows."

"You told him?" There was as much confusion as accusation in her tone.

"No! You all but forbade me. I may have disagreed with your choice, but I respected it. That sketch, it's not him drawing a story I told him. It's as if he reached into our memories and drew exactly what he found."

She rose, tea forgotten, and paced the tiny room. "How could he know?" It was a question, but they both already knew the answer. The power that drew lightning from her skin, pulled fire from his hands now told him, unwavering, their son was not human.

"Alea, we denied him the truth. You did exactly what your mother did to you."

"I was trying to protect my child!"

"So was she!" Arman's hand shook, but it was no longer from panic. It was rage. *Our son ran from us because he couldn't trust us to tell him the truth.* Arman was tired of secrets, tired of protecting. "Keplan may not know what we were, what he is, but he damned well knows someone wants him in the capital. And I'm willing to bet he knows they won't lie." Arman's fist rattled the counter. "There are thousands of leagues between here and Athrolan. I'm damned if I know where he is."

Alea trembled, eyes frantic. "Arman, what have we done?"

Her words made him pause as he tugged on his cloak. "I protected you both. You blinded him." The words he threw over his shoulder bit sharper than the draft blowing past him. "You better hope he forgives you." He slammed the door. "I'm not sure I can."

CHAPTER TWO

The 35th Day of the Month of Rainfall, 1272
The Banis Prairie

GRASSES HISSED IN THE wind, rolling in waves of green and gold as the air scuttled across the hills. Keplan drew up at the crest of the hill. But for the dark line of trees far to his right he could have been anywhere. The prairie had a sentience, a quiet draw that threatened to swallow him if he met its eyes for too long. Still, the adrenaline and confusion that drove him from home still echoed in his limbs, and he could not help the laugh that bubbled from his throat when the wind tugged his long brown hair from its tie. "Pity Ma and Da had no true maps, eh Moly?" The gray horse flicked one fuzzy ear back then forward again, cocking one hoof as if to remark that she was confident they would find their way.

He pulled out a tattered piece of deerskin and held it open against the wind. His penmanship left much to be desired, and his knowledge of geography came only from his own mind and stories pieced together from childhood. His gaze traced the woods stretching north from his home. The rocky fields in the east were Athrolan, and while the capital was his goal, the Banis plains were a shorter road, he hoped. "Besides, Da was always touting their beautiful horses. Don't you want to see your cousins?"

Moly's snort drew a smile from him. He preferred animals to people and preferred Moly best of all. He pushed away guilt that his parents would search for him. He realized now, the sanctuary of his parents' house became isolation. His mind was quieter since leaving. The barrage of information and voices had not come again. *I still won't turn about.* Hard choices must still be made, even if they hurt.

The steady rattle of insects heralded the dry season on the plains.

Keplan looked up from the map, tucking it back into his bag as he scanned the sky. *There.* Sullen smoke inched upward from a hollow in the plains. It was too thin to be a grass fire, too regular to be a cloud. His heart hammered, fingers tightening in Moly's mane. The Hartland forest received fair few visitors, and though he occasionally rode into the neighboring town with his father, the idea of other people still sparked his imagination. "Campfire. Or a house." *Rel. Banis houses are called rels.* It may be quieter, but his mind was far from silent.

He shook the unsolicited information away and nudged Moly faster. He was hungry, and though he could use the bow strapped to Moly's rump, curiosity lit in his gut. Waving grasses hid the curves of the prairie, smoothing them into a featureless plain. In another hour he paused atop a hummock. The *rel* squatted in a shallow cleft below him. The roof barely reached Moly's withers, the door leading into the dark depths of the sunken dwelling. A low shed served as shelter for some animal. Keplan lifted his nose to the eddying breeze. *Oxen. Maybe a goat.* Smoke curled from the hole in the peak of the round roof's shallow curve.

His stomach muttered to itself. Keplan urged Moly down to the bare, hoof-trodden area that served as a yard. He cleared his throat, unsure. He knew serviceable Banis, but was unfamiliar with their customs. "Hello?"

The silence sharpened, and after a breath the form of an old man appeared in the shadow of the doorway. The black eyes rested calculatingly on Keplan's gangly form. "Ho, the traveler."

Relief washed over Keplan. "Evening, Farmer. I've been riding alone for a time. Might I share your fire? Perhaps I could tend your animals for the night."

The man's eyes flicked to the hills behind Keplan, to the beaten track running north. "Just the night. I'm not a rich man."

Keplan smiled brightly. "Then I would be happy to share the grouse I caught earlier."

The farmer's smile was faint, but warmed his eyes. "Get your mare stabled and clean the stalls. I'll have supper ready when you're through."

The heat of the stable was comforting, as was the familiar smell of animal. Tending their horses had always been Keplan's favorite chore. Now it was a bittersweet reminder. *Before things changed.* He shook away the shadowed thoughts and slid the stable's door home. The chill of winter was almost absent here, echoed only in the dampness of the ground.

He ducked under the eaves and trotted down the few stairs to the sunken door. The house was warm and smelled of a sweet spice. *Cinnamon?* He shucked off his boots and stepped down into the tiered single room. The farmer crouched by the central hearth, watching the grouse sizzle. His robe was stained and tucked up into a tattered rope belt.

"What is your name?"

The man's eyes flicked over, but he did not turn his head. "Hi-taln."

"Well, Hi-taln, you have a fine house." He offered his hand. "I'm Keplan. Have you lived here your entire life?"

"I was raised just east of the Vale. I came out here after the revolution."

Keplan nodded, though he had no idea to which revolution Hi-taln referred. "I was born east of here, in the Hartland." He suspected it went by a different name in Ban, though it was not one he knew.

"And you're traveling north? Times being what they are, I'm surprised a man of your color would brave it."

Keplan looked down. It was obvious his pale skin was far from the warm brown of the Banis. He had not thought to look into the political state before traveling. *Did I tumble into a war?* "An old family friend asked me to visit. This was simply the quickest route." It was not, strictly, a lie.

Hi-taln hummed in response. "I suppose your coloring could be Athrolani. Besides, your accent speaks of the south, not Mirik." The man tested the meat with one calloused finger, then tugged the grouse off the spit. He handed Keplan a wicker plate and a wooden stick with a prong on one end and a blade on the other.

"Thank you." Silence fell, interrupted only when they tore meat from the bones. Keplan struggled to master the dual-ended utensil, managing to barely shovel the meat into his mouth.

A wry smile hovered over the older man's mouth at the display, but he said nothing. When the food was gone, Hi-taln snugged a broad pan into the coals and removed the lid. He jerked his head at the thick mixture when it began to bubble. "Some tea there, if you'd like."

Keplan eyed the pan warily. Tea was thin, black and bitter in his house. This looked closer to something left over from frying meat. "Perhaps just a little."

Hi-taln's chuckle rolled low and soft, but he poured a single ladle's worth into a clay mug and handed it over. The drink was both savory and sweet and rolled down his throat like gravy. A night bird trilled outside, echoed by another, closer. The man's eyes narrowed on the small window, then glanced at the locked door. "I'd best be off to bed. You can sleep here." Hi-taln nodded to the rush pillows left a few tiers higher. His brown eyes refused to meet Keplan's. "I'll be out by dawn, and so should you."

"Thank you." Keplan curled his back against the earthen step, face to the fire. Uncertainty fluttered in his chest, and he missed home. Images and words flickered on the edge of his own thoughts. When the breathing from the other room was even, he opened a scrap of parchment from his bag.

An'thor, Daymir.

The only two names mentioned in the letter. He had not meant to snoop, but found it tucked in his father's writing kit while searching for charcoal to sketch the alien images bombarding his mind. Nights of poring over the words before leaving helped him memorize the lines. "*Ceir Athrolan needs you. Just once more.*" So Athrolan's capital had needed his parents before. Maybe more than once. *Were they warriors? Spies?*

Keplan knew Ceir Athrolan, but there his understanding stopped. He did not know what he had been named, or why this person would choose him. Perhaps his parents had owned a business. Stories of his father helping in the inn as a boy were always his favorite. *I could do that.* He hoped, too, the city might hold an answer as to why he saw things not his to see. In a place as great as Athrolan, a city as perfect and legendary, surely even a madman could find peace.

Φ

The 36th Day of the Month of Rainfall, 1272

The wealth of Ban was not in the gold of the empire's fields, or the jewels glittering on the hands of the nobility. It was in the sleek muscle of horses and the long strides of the army. Rih crouched in the grasses, her brown fingers tracing tracks in the rain-softened ground. The prairie in spring was always her favorite. It bore a potential that the summer sun burnt away in later months. She picked out the nuances of the trail through the grass. The prints were those of a heavy horse, not one of the Banis beauties. Boots, not sandals, marked the ground where the rider had dismounted.

Rih flipped the camouflage of her woven hood back and scanned the scattered soldiers. The patrol numbered eleven women if she included the two trainees. Captain Gali was wrapped in what seemed a fervent conversation with another soldier. Rih tucked her head down to blow the clay whistle tied to the shoulder of her leather breastplate. She wondered, briefly, how annoying it was for her fellow soldiers to hear it. From the little she could hear, it was the same tone as theirs.

The older woman glanced over and nodded an acknowledgment. A moment later she jogged over and knelt beside Rih. Her gnarled fingers curled, her head tilted. "What?" she signed.

Rih pointed at the track, hands twisting in the same language. "One horse, not ours, with a light rider."

The captain traced the tracks herself, following the direction toward a dip in the hills. Rih watched her mouth as the woman called orders to the others. This close, Rih picked up enough voiced words to make lip-reading easier. "Pack up! We move northwest in five minutes. Ji-alt and Yana, flank us, Rih-elte: take up the fore." She turned, catching Rih's eyes and switched to signing. "Front."

"I saw, thank you." Rih fell into place at the head of the group. Her long legs stretched easily to keep stride with the other soldiers. While the male generals and commanders might be mounted, as were the male cavalry, the female infantry relied on their sandaled feet and the steady endurance built by years of training.

She traced the grasses with her eyes, picking out tiny depressions the others might miss. She rarely envied them their speech and perfect hearing now, though it might have made her life easier. *Stronger shoulders may make the dart fly further, but they lack the flexibility for precision.* She honed her vision to find tiny nuances in faces, to read mouths and features as well as any other could hear tonal differences. Now, as a soldier, that skill made her an unparalleled tracker.

The grasses thinned, and the soft earth was trampled into hard mounds. Rih slowed and raised her fist. An old rel was tucked into the hills. By the barn and tracks surrounding the buildings, it belonged to a farmer. The captain gestured for the others to fan out, surrounding the home.

She sent Rih and two others into the barn. It smelled sweet and dusty, the way a barn should. The two oxen stared at them, brown eyes distant. A Banis horse watched them curiously, golden head bobbing as he scented the air. The stall at the end, however, held a pony. It was not the beautiful gold or cream of a Banis horse, and it lacked the tell-tale dorsal markings.

Rih glanced over the half door at the hooves. *Unshod. Small.* She snapped her finger to get her captain's attention and jerked her chin at the foreign horse. The older woman's lips pursed, and she slipped outside. Rih followed, watching the other women circle the house. She crept up to one of the windows. The smell of smoke was faint, and the air eddying from within was only slightly warmer than outside. *No one is up yet to tend the fire or start breakfast.*

She drew a steadying breath and peered inside. As she had guessed, the central fire was low, sullen embers shedding orange across the tiers of the main room. A boy sprawled a step above the fire. He lacked the coloring and height of a Banis man. His pack pillowed his head. His fingers flexed in his sleep, and a strange expression crossed his features. Rih met the eyes of her captain who crouched just outside the house's door. The captain held up a finger and tapped it on her wrist, held up another and tapped her throat. *One prisoner, one traitor.*

Rih sat back on her haunches to watch. She was too much of a liability in ambushes, her captain claimed. The woman raised a fist, then brought it down. The soldiers swarmed the house. The door broke, splinters flying. Rih leaned against the clay. She felt the reverberations as a body fell. She closed her eyes. Their orders were clear. They were always clear. "*You are to hunt down any who might betray the Banis Empire and by extension, His Eminence the Emperor. Any who seek to spy upon us or bring ill will through our borders from our Eastern neighbors shall be detained and questioned. Any who aid them are to be slaughtered without delay.*" Acrid smoke billowed across her face as blood doused the fire.

Φ

The sky was still dark and bruised when the door exploded inward. "Ji-alt, check the stables!" Keplan scrambled to his feet, adrenaline scouring sleep from his mind. The tall figure of a soldier was silhouetted against the blue of fading night. Leather armor scaled shoulders and chest, tassets swaying over a silk tunic. Hi-taln appeared in the bedroom doorway, hands peacefully open beside him. The soldier thrust her spear into the fire-lit room, drawing a knife from her sash. Her dark eyes pinned Hi-taln against the far wall. "You're the master of this house?"

Keplan strained his ears. He heard the Banis words, but understood them, or at least the essence.

Hi-taln jerked a nod. "I am."

Three more soldiers entered, similarly dressed, but without the crimson wrap around their skullcaps. The first soldier's eyes flicked to Keplan. "And who is this?"

"He is a guest, a traveler, Ma'am."

"He's Mirikin."

"I'm not. I'm from the south," Keplan interjected. *I should have looked into the politics.*

The soldier descended the tiers in two strides. Brass rings on her left hand split the skin over Keplan's cheek when she smacked him once, twice. "Silence, barbarian!" Her brown lips curled in a snarl, and she glared down at Hi-taln. "I ask you again: who is he?"

"I just met him today—yesterday. He offered to tend my animal in exchange for a fire and bed."

"You let a foreigner touch your horse? Idiot," the soldier scoffed, large black eyes rolling. She kicked Keplan's bag dangerously close to the fire. "Check this."

A subordinate crouched, upending the bag onto the floor before rifling through the contents. "Change of clothes in the eastern style. A personal letter written in Trade. Old bread. Half a dozen coins—old, but Mirikin."

Pain bloomed across Keplan's face with her third blow. He was too frozen to protect himself, or even panic. His teeth gouged the inside of his cheek, and blood flooded his mouth. "Ma'am, I'm just a traveler."

"You're a damned barbarian spy." Her hard fingers bit into the back of his neck and shoved him to the floor.

Behind him, Hi-taln's shouts of protest guttered into wet silence. A thick trail of blood dribbled down the stairs and hissed against the coals. "Bind and drug him. He's coming to the capital. Burn the rest." The earthen smell of the floor was replaced with that of an acrid rag that stank of urine. Keplan's vision narrowed then went black.

CHAPTER THREE

The 38th Day of the Month of Rainfall, 1272
The City of RoBal, Ban

KEPLAN WOKE TO DARKNESS and pain. He blinked rapidly, focusing his mind as much as his vision. It was dark, the kind of dark that pressed against his eyes.

"Moly?" Pain bloomed in his lower left ribs. *Broken ribs, bruised collarbone.* Blood matted his hair, and his temples throbbed. *Concussion.* What puzzled him was the stinging in his right palm. He tried to flex the hand, but the skin was tight and stiff. *I must have scraped it when I went down.* He gently felt the walls with his other hand. It was not a room, but a cell the size of a coffin. Straw stuffed in a bucket served as a privy. He returned to his curled position and cradled his hand against his chest. He was hungry, but not painfully so, not yet. *Must have only been here a day.* Keplan rested his head on a scuffed knee. *Where's Moly?* The past weeks seemed like a lifetime.

Three weeks ago his woodsman's life melted with the snow.

Three weeks ago I went mad.

The images were like remembering pieces of a dream, but these were things he had never dreamed. Some events he recognized from stories, recalled with such detail it was as if he witnessed them. Now he need only focus on a topic or place, and fragmented information tumbled into his mind. He closed his eyes, focusing on the city around him. *Ban, empire to the west of Athrolan. The only kingdom that rivals its size. Civil to its neighbor.* He swallowed hard. *Apparently close to war with Mirik.* If only he had checked, if only he had stuck to the winding road through Athrolan's rocky fields. *If only I had left a note.* His thoughts fled at the sound of a key in the lock of his door.

Light poured in. After the darkness of his cell, even the dim hall lights were blinding. He shrank back against the wall, away from the rough hands. His back met stone, however, and he was hauled out. His adolescent frame had not filled out, and even his best attempts to flail free did nothing. He caught glimpses of stone floors and dark, wooden walls, but nothing else. The way was short, and after a moment he was pulled into a small office at the end of the hall.

The guards shoved him into a seat, standing just behind him. Keplan's vision finally began to return. The desk before him was utilitarian and covered with papers. A small rack of wooden rods held a collection of the stone, metal, and clay beads of Banis currency.

"Banis?" The man behind the desk was lean, his brown face lined from a life on the sunny, dry plains.

Realizing the man was asking if he knew the language, Keplan nodded, ashamed of his obvious trembling.

"Name?"

Keplan swallowed the dryness from his throat, but his voice was still a croak. "Keplan Wardyn, sir." He was still curious enough to note the planes of the man's face. Besides the few trips to Namus with his father, he rarely saw people other than his parents and the face that stared back from the tarnished mirror in their kitchen. Like Hi-taln and the soldiers, these men were brown and their hair black. Their eyes were large and wide, like his own, but darker.

"Height?"

Keplan opened his mouth to answer, but a sharp rap on his shoulder stopped the words.

"He's a hand under two paces."

"Coloring?"

"Sickly."

"I asked for coloring, not constitution, El-Jak."

"Pale. Hair brown, like dead grass. Eyes colorless."

"Features?" The man behind the desk looked up, eyes narrowed. "Birdlike. His journey here must not have gone to plan. He looks like a wretch."

Keplan glanced up. He had never been muscled or wiry like his father, but neither had he cared or questioned it.

"Nationality?" The man's eyes pinned Keplan.

"What do you mean?"

"Are you an idiot? Nationality—to what nation are you pledged?"

"I don't know—I grew up in the Hartland. My father is Vielronan. I'm not sure about my mother."

"See, this is where we disagree." The guard leaned forward. "You are a spy sent from Mirik. You traveled from the capital through Athrolan—perhaps you did come from one of the southern cities. And you came to what? Bring down our slave trade? Free our property?" All composure evaporated from the man's eyes at Keplan's stammering attempt to argue. "Well, I'll tell you what—you're our property now, and if you don't die in the next three weeks, you'll wish you had."

Φ

The 40th Day of the Month of Rainfall, 1272

Swollen wood screamed as the guards jerked the door open. Keplan scrabbled toward the back of the cell, but a pace of space was precious little for escaping. Sleep was a generous term for the drifting state of mind he adopted in the cramped, dark space, but it was dear to him. Landmarks slipped from his exhausted mind when he tried to memorize the turns down a set of stairs. The room they dragged him into was low, beneath the street level. Locks clicked shut when the door slammed.

A barred tunnel at the top of the wall opposite the door shed light from a window far above. He whirled, dropping into a crouch, but the two guards were broad and practiced. They dropped him into a heavy chair bolted to the stone floor. His wrists were shackled to the arms. His heart thundered as if trying to escape the cage of his ribs.

One of the guards, the one with several bronze earrings, bent to look Keplan in the eye. "What is your purpose, son of Mirik?"

Mirik? They still don't believe me? "I have never been to Mirik. I am a traveler from the south." A misunderstanding, a perceived small crime, those were easy to rectify. This was different. He heard the other guard moving about behind him, and he craned his neck to see. The man laid out tools that looked like those used to carve wood. *Not wood. My skin.* He glanced down at his shackled right hand, only now seeing it was not scraped, but newly tattooed. The design was a red handprint over his palm. *Enemy. Slave.* Dread was the cold spread of frost in his stomach.

The session was short, and while it brought little pain, there was the promise of much worse. He guessed less than an hour had passed when he was returned to his cell. He did not rise from where the guards dumped him. He curled in on himself, hoping he would wake, and it would be a terrible dream.

CHAPTER FOUR

The 42nd Day of Lleume, 1272
The City of Ceir Athrolan

AN'THOR'S HOBNAILED BOOTS CLACKED against the flagging of his room, the buckles clinking softly in the silence. Outside, the servants' shoes were muffled and the conversations whispered. *As if the queen will recover if her sleep goes undisturbed.* In truth, he wished she would wake. Her eyes had not opened in a week, and hitching gasps replaced her breaths. An'thor knew the signs. A soft knock paused his steps, and he jerked the door open. The queen's lady of honor stood in the hall, trembling hands hidden in the folds of her skirt.

"General, sir. The healer says you should come."

An'thor did not even dare nod. The knot tied around his chest tightened and sank to somewhere beneath the flagging. He followed her to the royal wing in silence. A single, dim lamp lit the royal chambers, where Raven waited. The commander was pale.

"Raven, is she—?"

The commander's glare cut the Ageless man's words short. An'thor ducked under the curtain across the door, Raven close on his heels. The bed was in the center of the room. Incense fogged the air and, save for the crackle of flames in the hearth, silence reigned. The doctor leaned on the mantle, staring at the fire.

An'thor stepped up to the bedside. The queen was still, her skin yellowed and waxy. Someone had brushed her hair across the pillow in a thin, snowy fan. He laid a hand on hers. "When?"

"Not five minutes ago," the doctor answered.

Raven dropped to his knee in the doorway, jaw clenched as his fist met his brow in a salute.

An'thor ignored the dramatics. "Who else knows?"

"Her Lady of Honor, Countess Fiena of Felden. That is all. Servants gossip, of course, but no one has been in." He wavered for a moment. "And I will say nothing, of course."

"I will expect to see you here tomorrow morning to discuss things further. Send the countess in when you leave." An'thor's gaze did not waver from the queen's face. He finally turned when the curtain's rustle announced the countess's arrival. "Have you told anyone?" When she shook her head he asked again, black eyes pinning her. "Anyone, even your husband?"

"I have not left the room save to fetch you, sir. I met no one in the halls."

"You will keep this from everyone—including family—until I say. I don't have to explain what this will do to the country. Do you understand?"

She nodded, but An'thor crossed the room and gripped her hand, splaying the fingers so the firelight caught the wedding band on her middle finger. "Swear on your country."

"Sir, is this necessary?" the doctor interjected.

An'thor loosened his grip, but only slightly. "You understand me, Countess?"

"I do. I swear on my country, my life and that of my family, I will tell no one." When An'thor released her hand she tipped her head toward the door. "Now if I may go? I haven't seen my family in days."

"Of course."

"What should I tell them, sir?"

An'thor glanced back at the queen's body, half-expecting her to stretch and wave away his dour mood. *Tell them the world has ended because she no longer graces these hills.* "Say the doctor has brought his own nurse to help care for the queen. You've been given leave as thanks for your dedication to the Xain house." An'thor paused, unable to meet her eyes. Alcohol and a century of heartbreak had cauterized his heart, but Fiena was his queen's dear friend. "Thank you for your care of my lady queen, may her spirit rest with those—" his voice faltered. "Good evening, Countess."

When she was gone, An'thor glanced at Raven, and his mouth thinned. The man still kneeled. "Get up."

Raven stared at the flagging. "She was as precious to this kingdom, and to me, as she was to you. Have some mercy."

"You realize we face civil war." An'thor's boots rattled against the stone as he paced from window to hearth and back.

"Write to Daymir, to Brentemir, even." His face twisted in scorn. "You don't still hold hope for Dhoah' Lyne'alea's promise that Athrolan will not fall?"

An'thor jerked his head at the door. "Out. I can't think with your nationalism hanging over my thoughts."

"You're an ass."

"Raven, please, not in front of—"

"She's dead, you fool." Raven lurched to his feet and stalked from the room without another word.

An'thor sank onto the window's broad sill with a ragged sigh. Uncomfortable emptiness filled the room without Tzatia's sharp wit and quiet laughter.

Or her breath.

"I wrote to Alea already, your majesty," he spoke to the air, whatever faint energy was left of his queen. "She never replied. There are no gods, no Laen, no Rakos."

Φ

The 45th Day of the Month of Rainfall, 1272
The City of RoBal, Ban

Stagnant air lay in the bottom of Keplan's cell, but the close space was no longer maddening. Instead, it was a sanctuary. Pain shot through his palm when he felt his face for stubble. His cheeks never boasted a beard like his father's, but it was his only way to judge passing time. Images of Moly, free on the prairie filled, his mind. It was less painful than thoughts of her put to work or imagining his parents searching. *Do they know? Did they search the road to Namus or follow my trail here?*

His empty stomach clenched. He kept careful stock of his injuries thus far, but hunger clouded his thoughts. *Five meals since I arrived. Is that two days or five?* He pressed his bruised face to the cool relief of the stone floor. Faint light under the door showed him two rats hunched at the edge of his plate. Loneliness made him imagine they were the same ones each time.

"That piece looks far too rotted, Aud." He named them after heroes in his father's stories. "There's far better food on the prairie. Seeds and grasses and places to burrow down by the river." He barely recognized his own voice. The scratching of his throat aged his tone. A laugh hitched and bubbled between the words. *If I wasn't mad before, there's no doubt I am now.*

Morose thoughts clattered to a halt as the door jerked open, bringing a flare of torchlight. Weakness made his struggle little more than a jerk of the shoulders. He recognized the gray in one guard's brown eyes, and the other's lock of beaded hair. As much as he tried to force the questioning from his mind, he noted the guards were always the same two. His eyes closed when the belts tightened over his limbs. He hated the weakness, the exhaustion. Each time he planned escape he was met with the same dilemma—in the middle of Ban his pale was a beacon, and all the knowledge in the world could not lend him the strength to run.

"Why are you here?"

"What have you learned?"

"Who are you informing?"

"What are their plans?"

"Why did you ride from the south?"

Keplan understood now they were not seeking the truth. They were seeking a confession. Burning pain followed a blade down his sternum. The world tipped. Roaring blood muffled any other sound. It was as if he stumbled in a dream, but he did not fall into wakefulness.

A city burned, perched on soaring cliffs. Survivors clung to boats, to debris bobbing in the harbor below. Above, the clouds themselves ignited. Keplan searched the ruddy faces and copper eyes. These are the gods. *Wind gnawed his cheeks as he spoke, but it was not his voice, just as his hands and body were not his own. "This is where we end. This is where we must end." Time unraveled before Keplan's fading vision.*

Long grasses and gentle wind brushed his mind. It was silent. Pain still writhed, persistent, into his unconsciousness. Aching pounded the tattered skin of his chest, thumped in his bruised bones.

"Hooves of Faco-il, you killed him."

Rough fingers pawed at the boy's eyelids and he slid back from wherever he had been. The face before him lurched into focus through the bruised skin and blood-laced tears. He met the guard's gaze. *A rel burning to the ground. Mirikin soldiers dancing atop the smoldering wreckage. Receiving commendations from the Lord Interrogator. Pride. Frustration. Terrible dreams of his sister dying in the fire. Honor. Confusion. A storm approaching.*

Keplan's pupils blew wide, and he was promptly sick all over himself. *I don't have a sister.* Somewhere, thunder growled a warning. His eyes found the copper square pinned to the guard's sash. "They killed your sister."

The guard straightened. "Excuse me?"

"The Mirikin took your sister." Clotted blood splattered the floor with the effort of his words. "But I'm not Mirikin. Doing this to me won't fix your dreams." Foreign memories flickered between memories of peace, of pain.

The man with the gray-laced eyes scoffed from his perch on the countertop. "Now he speaks?" Another boom of thunder rolled through the city.

"Quiet." The guard's eyes narrowed on Keplan's for a terrible minute, then he spun away and rummaged through a drawer.

"What're you doing?"

"The rains were over weeks ago."

"Your meaning?"

"I trust my gut, and it's a warning. We are through questioning him." He unclipped the wooden lid of a squat jar and drew a thin stick from a toolkit. *Poison? More pain?* Adrenaline fired up his arms, but it only gave him the strength to strain the straps.

The guard with the light eyes pursed his lips, muscled arms crossed. "The Lord Interrogator will have your hair for this."

"Then let him take it. You know this is a fool's chore. If this boy were a spy, he'd be the worst I know." He dipped the needle on the end of the tool into the pot and spread Keplan's left hand out. His gaze flicked to Kelplan's face, then returned to his task.

Blood and pearls of dark ink followed the pricks of fire across Keplan's palm. His head flopped back onto the hard wood of the chair's headrest. Red blood and green ink dribbled down his wrist from the new handprint on his palm. He did not smile with relief or at the meaning of the new mark, or its irony.

Innocent.

Φ

The 47th Day of The Month of Rainfall, 1272

At least this cell had a window. Keplan followed the pool of sunlight across the earthen floor. Stillness in the wake of agony was its own kind of pleasure. The ache in his chest could not be described as homesickness. It was grief. His mind drifted on the piece of knowledge he earned, rather than inherited: he had power. *I looked that man in the eye, and whatever he saw there stayed his hand.* He did not understand it, not by a league, not yet, but it gave him hope. If he kept his head he might just survive Ban.

The door scraped open, and the guard with the braided hair entered, then shut the door behind himself. His hand rested on a long knife, but he did not draw. He would recognize the large, dark eyes for the rest of his life.

"What are you doing?" Keplan's weakened heart thrummed against his ribs, loud enough the man must have heard. His mind screamed at him to fight back, but the guard was armed. *And he hasn't been starved for days.*

"How did you know?"

The question lit something in Keplan's mind, something too hot to be fear, too large to be anger. *How did I know?* "I just did." He swallowed hard. "I know things. Nothing useful. You said yourself I'm not a spy."

"Then what are you doing here? Pale boy, in the middle of war? That's got to be the worst mistake you've made." His tone was not friendly, but curious. "My mother was in the war. The Gods' War. I know the gods are dead." It was his turn to swallow. His eyes darkened, hand relaxing its grip around his knife. "What you said made me wonder, though, if that were true."

"I'm not a god." If Keplan were on level with the man, he would have rolled his eyes. He only dared a sigh. "I'm just a madman."

The guard did not answer. Instead, he tossed a woven sack on the floor between them.

"Put that on."

"Why?" It did not seem like death was imminent, but Keplan was in no mood to gamble.

"I don't care what you are, cursed or touched or something else entirely. But I'm not having it on my head."

Something burned in the man's eyes, but it was not hate. Keplan would not even say it was fear. Keplan hauled himself to his feet and pulled the sack over his pounding head. The two days since his ordeal did much for his spirits, but walking was a chore. Locks clunked, and the door creaked open. Dry hands twisted both arms behind him and guided him out. A stumbling march up two flights of stairs and a winding path through a cool, still hall brought them into a muggy space that smelled of dust and urine. The bustle of the streets was strange after the peace of the forest and the cloying stillness of the cell.

The first step was faltering, sunbaked brown clay burning Keplan's tender feet. Shouts arced through the crowd. Slapping sandals beat dust from the red road. Thundering hooves sent Keplan cowering, but the guard's hands tugged him forward. Cooking meat and overripe fruit overpowered the baking smell of the prairie grasses. The guard was quiet for the twenty minute walk, speaking only to warn Keplan of a stair, or swear at a poorly driven cart. After several minutes, neighing and bustle replaced the clamor.

Someone tugged the sack, from his face and stinging sunlight flooded his eyes. They stood in a stableyard, tucked in the shadow of the looming palace. The guard and another man conversed just out of earshot.

Run. Trembling legs told him he would only make it to the street before someone caught him. The sun was almost at its zenith, and he had lost all concept of east or west. The short walk taxed him enough. He already knew that a single false step would at least send him straight back to the interrogation room. *More likely I'd be killed.* He lowered his head, colored palms tucked close to his body, and tried to get his bearings. The massive mound of the city dropped away to the right. Roads switch-backed up the red earth. Slatted wooden rooftops and brightly dyed silks were an apron around the crooked towers and bridges of the tiered palace behind him. It was as if the city climbed to the clouds. Keplan was impressed in spite of himself. *Whatever their customs, this is beautiful.* RoBal was stunning as it was cruel. Gold and crimson opulence dripped from the hungry, grandeur built over suffering.

Shrieking of an angry horse shattered his thoughts. As much as he loved Moly, the creature in the stableyard was wind made into flesh. Banis horses were a legend, one his father mentioned often. Their build was closer to that of the prairie gazelle, and their dorsal stripes and markings seemed like royal signets. His heart twisted at the thought of his pony. He missed her mutter and the tickle of her coarse whiskers.

"Come on, we'll get you sorted."

Keplan whirled, dizziness clouding his vision at the movement. The other man held a hand out. He was of middle years, and his stable uniform bore an insignia on the chest. The interrogator had already disappeared back into the street.

He caught Keplan's glance back to the street. "I wouldn't. Come talk with me, and I can get you fed and clothed." He gestured to an office built between the stable's two broad aisles.

Even if I made it out of the city, I have weeks of travel on foot. He had no horse, no clothes, and no food. His body ached, and desperation gnawed at his bones. This was a better chance than any he could have planned. The adrenaline drained from his limbs, and he staggered into the office.

The stable master settled himself behind a broad desk and motioned for Keplan to take the chair across from him. He did not speak for a moment, taking in every inch of the false stable boy before him.

Keplan forced himself to keep the man's gaze. If he was someone who believed in luck, or anything at all, he would have prayed.

"The filth will wash away, but you look starved. And we'll have to do something about your hands and the Kisses."

Keplan frowned. "Kisses?"

"The marks on your face. We call them Interrogator's Kisses."

Keplan looked down at his palms. "But green means I'm innocent."

The man sat back with a snort. "You must know by now 'guilty' and 'innocent' are meaningless here. Everything is at the discretion of the Interrogator. Green simply means they've released you. We'll find you gloves."

"Sir, I'm sorry, but why am I here?"

"You will work for me. I don't know what you said to my nephew, but he was adamant. I don't often take released prisoners, but we have a few indentured. You will work for me for six weeks. In return, you will receive clothes, a place to sleep. Food. After you have served your time, should you wish to stay, you will be given wages."

Keplan stared at his bare feet. The offer seemed too simple, too perfect. "The last man—other than your nephew—that showed me kindness bled out into his own hearth."

"I'm not showing you kindness. The care of our horses costs much. I'd rather not spend more on labor than I must. You're doing me a favor in exchange for your life." The words were hard, but his eyes were steady and soft.

He's kind. Keplan forced words through his abruptly tight throat. "Aren't you afraid I'll run? That I'll escape?"

The stable master's mouth thinned, but his displeasure did not seem directed at Keplan. "No one escapes." He briskly drew out a wax tablet. "You'll find clean, suitable clothing in the room beside the bathhouse, which you will visit first. The yellow shelves should suit if you fasten the sash tight enough. You'll be a mucker, and only handle the drafts in the evenings." He etched a few more marks onto the tablet before brushing ink over the wax and pressed a thin piece of cloth over it. After a moment he drew the cloth off and passed it to Keplan. "Read and sign, please."

Keplan glanced at the symbols. They were curled and riddled with hard stops. "Would you mind reading this?"

"You cannot read Banis?"

"Only speak it. My father knew some but had never learned to read it himself."

"You speak it well, for a foreigner." He peered at the paper and read the words aloud. It reiterated the details of the contract with set dates. "Any questions?"

Keplan signed where he was told. "Only one. What happens to the horses of those taken by the Lord Interrogator?"

"Ah." The stable master's expression closed. "If you give me a description, I'll do my best."

"A mare—a barbarian mare—red roan and old. She's just over 14 hands of stubbornness with tufted ears and nose. Her name is Moly."

The man jotted down the description, glancing up at Keplan when he was through. "Anything else?"

"Why are you doing this?"

"This city is complicated." He pulled a cord hanging on the wall behind him. A gong rang outside.

A moment later a boy not much younger than Keplan himself stepped through the door. "Afternoon, sir."

"Afternoon, Fer-hil. I have a new mucker here who needs to get washed and outfitted. I trust you can show him to the bathhouse and then to the stock-shelves? He will need gloves."

The boy frowned, tucking a loose strand of black hair behind his ear. "He's a barbarian, sir."

"Fer-hil, I do not pay you to be either political or rude." The stable master had already turned to a pile of scrolls awaiting his attention.

"I'm sorry, sir. I'll show him about."

Keplan pushed himself to his feet, suddenly conscious of his bare chest and legs. He followed the silent Fer-hil down the broad aisle. Keplan caught a few curious stares, but nothing that made his skin itch with fear. The entire building smelled of horse sweat, leather and grasses. It was a safe smell, Keplan decided. Still, the longer he stayed in the city, he could not shake the feeling he was crawling down the gullet of a beast.

"Are you even listening?"

Keplan glanced over and realized Fer-hil had been speaking. "I'm sorry, it's a very impressive stable. What did you say?"

"I'll take you to get your bath and uniform first, then we'll talk about the schedule. It's still early enough we have time before the afternoon rides. Most of the rich folk go for a jaunt after they have lunch, and the stable is busier than a brothel at midnight."

Keplan frowned at the analogy, but did not comment. The long, low barracks hall ran along the rearmost wall of the stable, like an afterthought. The bathhouse sat at the end.

"I'll wait out here." Fer-hil settled on the floor and pulled a set of game tiles from his shirt.

Keplan ducked into the dim bathhouse, blinking in the humid, scented air. Brown stone slabs covered the floor surrounding the yellow tiled bath. Oily lanterns hung, unlit, from the low ceiling. Keplan stripped off his tattered loincloth and plunged into the warm water. He kept his still-tender right hand as dry as he was able and took stock of his other injuries. Scabs covered all but the shallow line down his sternum. A few were angry and ached with heat, but none oozed with infection. *A small mercy.* He allowed himself a moment to drift in the comfort, swallowing his relief past the lump in his throat. Only when the blood was gone from his matted hair did he haul himself from the water.

He dried quickly and peered through the door. Fer-hil appeared to be losing his solitary game. "I'm done."

The boy glanced up. "You really are pale."

Keplan looked away, embarrassment burning on his cheeks. His own nudity did not bother him, but without the layer of dust and grime, his wounds and emaciation were a stark reminder.

A narrow room beside the bathhouse was seemingly comprised only of shelves. Fer-hil paced up and down a few times, shooting a critical glance at Keplan's body. "Start with these." He tugged a pair of knee-high sandals from a low shelf and tossed them over.

Keplan held them up. The shins and toes were reinforced with wood, held against his skin with leather straps. Manic laughter bubbled from his chest at the thought of sauntering through the stables naked save for a pair of boots.

Fer-hil looked over and finally cracked a grin of his own. "There's more to the uniform." A loose brown tunic joined the sandals, and Fer-hil found a red sash that would denote Keplan's status.

Keplan cinched his pocketed leather work belt a bit tighter and caught a glimpse of himself in the copper mirror by the door. The face that stared back was unrecognizable. Something burned deep in the ice-chip blue of his eyes, and it seared his gut. He shook himself and stepped quickly out into the hall. "Did I forget anything?"

Fer-hil stepped back to give his uniform a cursory glance. "Seems fine to me." He jerked his head at the curtained doors of the barracks. "You'll get one of these later. We get up at dawn, dress and eat in the mess hall across from our rooms. Slaves take away the night soil, but we tidy our own space. We take rolling lunches—a third of the muckers and stable hands at a time, so the stable is never left untended. You'll be in the third group with me."

Fer-hil frowned suddenly. "Where are you from?"

Keplan's heart thundered into panic. *Why are you here? Where are you from?* "The south. In the forest. The Hartland."

"You're not Mirikin?"

"No. Never even seen it."

The other boy hummed in response.

Keplan pointed vaguely up the aisle, desperate to change the conversation. "What are our duties?"

He barely listened as Fer-hil detailed the mucking in the mornings. Keplan knew how to clean a stable. The only part that seemed complicated was the afternoon handling requests for renting draft animals. Like the rest of the city, everything was built of wood and leather. There was no metal, not even in the hooks for the horses' harnesses. Two main halls connected with the lower one that housed the drafts. *Four hundred horses. Maybe more.* He hoped, if Moly had been taken, she was in a stable half as nice as this.

Keplan stared at the warren of halls. This was not the life he wanted. This was not how he pictured leaving home. *One step at a time.*

CHAPTER FIVE

The 2nd Day of Flureme, 1272
The City of RoBal, Ban

IT WAS WARM IN the barracks. The winds and rain of winter had finally dissipated, with the exception of the sudden storm two days before. Rih eyed the square of light on her wall. It was just below the darker board halfway to the ceiling from her top bunk. *Almost time for breakfast.* She rarely joined the other soldiers in their mess hall. The atmosphere was too close, and keeping track of even one conversation was exhausting.

She rose with a soft breath and stretched, shoulders popping as she rolled them. Finally, she shucked off her blankets and swung herself off the bunk. She landed easily. Though her muscles were stiff, she was strong, and the warm weather did wonders. She grinned as she jogged, naked, through the halls. Morning was one time she had no need to make excuses or find an interpreter. She was gloriously alone.

The bathhouse was empty, save for the afternoon training master. The older woman stood before the broad copper mirror, peering into a cleared space on the fog-hidden metal. She scraped a straight razor over her scalp. Wiry gray hairs dusted her shoulders and the tiles around her broad feet.

Her eyes met Rih's in the mirror, and she lifted the razor to nod good morning.

Rih signed a greeting, punctuating the gesture with a brief smile. Il-fald was her favorite of the trainers, a woman she hoped to one day become. *Perhaps by the time I'm old enough, another will have ascended the Holy Emerald Throne of Emperor and the empire will have changed.*

She shoved the private wish into the tiny, secret place of her heart before sliding into the hot water. It was a luxury to bathe twice a day, and she knew it, but there was no better way to awaken her body. Sudden waves lapped at her back, and she turned to see who had entered the pool.

Il-fald smiled and dunked her hair-covered shoulders into the clean water.

Rih wrinkled her nose playfully and made a show of escaping the floating clippings. She flicked a finger up her right jaw. "That's disgusting."

The training master tilted her head back, shoulders shaking with mirth. Even with just the two of them, the room's tiles reflected and altered what little Rih could hear.

"Will we practice the staff today?"

Il-fald shook her head and flicked her wrist. "Atlatl."

"I'll practice before then," Rih promised. After a quick scrub she stepped out of the bath and moved to the adjoining dressing room. Atlatl was her favorite weapon, but not one at which she excelled. If she was ever going to become proficient enough to train anyone older than a child, she would have to learn.

The training court was deserted for another hour until the morning training began. Rih would rather stay for the entire day. She felt the twang in the atlatl's supple wood when she released a dart properly. The darts were of two sizes—the standard hunting darts and the larger, heavier war darts. Her body was lean and long. At twenty, she already reached close to two paces in height. Still, her range on the hunting darts was poor, and her control of the war darts was laughable.

She collected a quiver of each and went to stand at the throwing line before the central target. Her back straightened out of habit, her shoulders rolling back and her eyes closing. She drew a breath and cleared the dark thoughts. *A warrior has a single mind. She wakes for the Empire. She rides for the Empire. Her blood and heart and mind are Ban, breathing and alive. A warrior has a single mind.* When the litany was through, her spirit was steady and her hands sure.

She settled one of the war darts into the notch at the end of the atlatl. Most soldiers started with the lighter missiles to warm their muscles, but Rih preferred the foundation of strength the heavier ones provided. Her hand curled around the handle, forefinger and thumb steadying the dart as she drew her arm back. Her left arm rose, guiding her sight to the center of the target. Warm air filled her lungs as she twisted. Her arm coiled past her shoulder, loose and smooth until the last moment when her wrist tightened, launching the bolt into the air. It was a clean throw, the wood passing through the target's edge and skittering over the ground behind for several paces.

She raised the next dart, but a hand pressed against her shoulder. She suppressed a gasp and turned. Enif raised a hand. She was a palace guard of middle years, tall and with an angled face. "You're summoned to the palace where you will be honored by His Eminence's presence." Her fingers were deft, and she knew most of Rih's signs, as several of the Emperor's male cousins were also born unable to hear, either completely, or, like Rih, only under the most ideal circumstances.

Rih watched the lines on the interpreter's face, hoping for any clue as to the nature of the request. Nothing. She had not made it so far in the palace by being careless. "Is he angry?"

The guard pursed her lips. "Always."

Rih would have smiled, had it been a joke. Instead, she drew another breath. Most of the emperor's many children were brought before him yearly. This was several months too early. No amount of reciting the Woman's Code would prepare her for a meeting with the Emperor. She put the atlatl and darts away and followed the interpreter at a jog. Her tassets tapped against her legs, and she was glad she donned her full uniform early, instead of practice clothes. *This will present better before His Eminence.* She momentarily wished she could wear the silk-bordered cap of an officer, carrying her head high under the weight of duty. *Perhaps then I would be taken seriously.* She scoffed at that thought, as well.

A woman was never taken seriously.

The road sloped up to the massive arched doors. The city was picked out in the reds and browns of the earth from which it was built, but the palace itself was a vicious green sore at the capital's peak. Green tiles and verdigre decorated the doorway. A winged horse leapt with emerald coat and hooves across the black jungle wood of the door. Enif's mouth moved, but Rih's angle was poor. The other guards seemed to understand, however, and stepped aside to let them pass.

The palace was a warren Rih never understood. She seemed to take a different route to the throne room each year. This time they took a winding stairway she was certain she had never seen. The windows were open to the air, save for a picture made of colored glass suspended in the center of the opening. The grandeur was sickening. Enif led her down a dark, richly painted hall and to a set of double doors made of the same dark wood as those at the main entrance. These, however, were emblazoned with the emperor's crest.

This is his personal receiving room. Rih heard the room beyond was filled with more riches than all of Ban combined. She straightened her shoulders and lowered her eyes, waiting for the press of the guard's hand on her elbow before she stepped through. The floor trembled when the doors shut behind her. She knelt, hands spread on her bare knees. She never caught more than a glimpse of the emperor—it was forbidden for someone not of the court to look higher than his jeweled feet.

Her eyes found the copper surface of the gong at the foot of his dais, however. In the gleaming metal, his image was reflected from the mirrored surface of the doors behind her. He was a warped sea of jade and emerald silks and golden jewelry. The black draping his shoulders told her his long hair was down.

Enif reminded the emperor which soldier stood before him and began to sign his words to Rih. "We have allowed you to entertain the role as soldier for these years, but the farce has gone on long enough. You are unable to be a proper soldier, and you are useless to the army. If anything, you are a liability."

Rih's face flamed with anger. *Useless? I've patrolled. I brought in that Mirikin boy. My tracking is some of the best in the army.* "I've bled for you!"

Enif laid a hand on Rih's knee, gaze piercing the younger woman's. She shook her head. Even though the words were Rih's, the punishment would fall on them both. "The Mirikin barbarians might consider a treaty to avoid war. Though defeating them on the battlefield would be easy, treaties look better to our Athrolani neighbors. You are my blood. You will be the bride in this peace marriage."

Rih's shoulders slumped. *No.* Before, he never acknowledged he sired her. *Along with a quarter of the officers and court women.* It was no coincidence so many bore the same striking high and wide nose of the emperor himself. "I don't know anything about court," she argued, forcing her trembling hands to form the words, "let alone the court of a foreign kingdom."

The guard grabbed her hand to halt the tirade. "You cannot speak, so you cannot betray Ban by telling secrets."

Rih's stomach heaved, then tightened somewhere near her lungs. She was just a tool, a replaceable factor in a very long equation. The lowest soldiers were always female, for women were disposable. This was different. She did not watch whatever the interpreter signed for the Emperor's closing statement. Her tiny, silent world curled tighter on itself. In Ban she had people who understood her language. In a barbarian country she would have nothing. She did not even know enough of their tongue to read their mouths.

Φ

The 5th Day of Flureme, 1272
The City of Mirik

The wind off the sea bore too many teeth for summer, but its bluster was now mostly show. Brentemir shrugged deeper into his cloak with a sigh. Twenty years ago his body would not have noticed the change in weather. *Now I run for the hearth at the balmiest of winds.* He leaned on the ramparts, eyes narrowed on the open ocean to the west. The island of La'yne still glowered across the channel, its shores barren. He refused to meet the caverns in its black cliffs that seemed like the isle's eyes.

War. He had avoided it for twenty achingly beautiful years. Now it slavered at his doorstep again. He scraped a hand through the stiff gray-brown of his receding hair.

"Pa, the steward says there's a warrior here to see you." The young man was as tall as Bren, with a slighter build.

Bren glanced over his shoulder. "Can it wait, Al?"

Alleanthus shrugged and jogged up the remaining steps to lean on the wall beside his father. "Is it the war?"

"I'm not ready to go back to that life."

"You're an ambassador, not the Military Commissioner. You don't have to."

Bren laughed softly. "You were always as direct as your mother."

"Don't call her that."

Bren's mouth tightened, but he allowed the retort. "I don't fear war just because I think I'll be called back. I know I won't. Your Ma will do fine. War destroys things, things you don't see or miss until it's far too late to reclaim them."

"If I wanted dark thoughts I would have written to An'thor."

Bren snorted wryly. "Insolent boy."

"Old man."

Bren smiled at the familiar banter. "Where's your brother?"

"Training. He's got it into his head he'll be champion at the head of an army."

"Toar, I never should have read you both those legends."

"I doubt it was the legends in the books that inspired him." Alleanthus leveled his dark eyes on Bren. "It's the ones you lived." He shoved off of the wall with a sigh and ran a hand through his thick black hair, his fingers echoing the path of his father's. "Best not keep them waiting."

Bren followed his son down into the modest manor. "When Azimir's through with training I want to see both of you over lunch." He waited until the young man had disappeared before stepping into the study. The light was stark, but strong. He smiled at the warrior perched on the window sill. "I wondered if it was you."

Reka answered his tight embrace with her wiry arms. "And I wonder if you're mad. Last summer in Athrolan you seemed set on peace." Her eyes, one dark, one clouded, narrowed on his gray ones when he finally pulled away. "I leave Mirik for two months, and you start a war."

"I didn't start this one. And it's been five. Azimir is almost sixteen."

Her features softened for a moment. "Are they well?"

"Yes, though you don't seem to care." As long as they were trading barbs, he would start their old argument again.

"Bren, they're your children, and the children of your wife, even if she couldn't birth them. I only bore them for her. I care about them because you do, but I'm not their mother." She slid off the window sill and sank into the chair across the desk from his. "Please, I'm not interested in this argument. I actually came to bring news."

"From Athrolan?" Bren shucked off his cloak and propped his head on his clasped hands.

"Partly. I'm hungry, though."

"Toar, of course." When Bren had ordered food for her and drinks for them both, he returned to his desk, a battered officer's log open before him. He maintained an extensive intelligence network, many branches of which were unaware of others. Reka would always be the best of his officers, though she hated her title of Spy Master.

"Athrolan's shifting. The queen's illness changed things. There's violence and darkness on those streets I haven't seen before. I have a theory, but it is just a shadow." She fingered the faded butterfly tattoo on her scarred nose. "I think Tzatia is dead."

Bren gaped at her, dark brows advancing on his graying hair. "You can't be serious. She wrote me just two weeks ago. It wasn't as keen as her usual letters, but she's weak. Surely we'd know if the city was suddenly grieving."

"Bren, I don't think the city knows either."

He sat back, arms crossed over his chest. "Explain yourself."

"I saw An'thoriend often. He is a drinker, but his habit is usually nursed in privacy. It was late in the evening, close to midnight. The queen's Maid of Honor—the one attending her night and day for weeks—was dismissed. She looked frightened, not worried. Not even an hour later, An'thoriend emerged. He was drunk and weeping. He sat on the stoop of the Royal mausoleum until close to dawn."

"And that told you Her Majesty had passed? I think An'thor just fears it. From what little he shared, they are quite close."

"Brentemir, you pay me to understand people, to see into their minds without a single word shared. Trust me, what I saw was not fear, not anxiety, but cold, fathomless grief."

Bren frowned at his log, thin lips twisted. He did not look up when Reka's meal was brought, or when his serving man delivered a steaming mug of tea. "I hoped they would back us," he finally murmured.

"In a war against Ban? They will be pressed to stop civil war, let alone a pretentious argument over another man's business."

"Slavery is not another man's business."

"When you blunder in and kill most of the people who are slaves, it should be. But you and I will never agree on politics."

Bren smiled at the softness in her eyes. "I'm glad you keep me focused. I never could do this without your friendship. You said 'partly,' do you bring news from Ban?"

"No, and I won't until Yun reports back. He's already three weeks overdue, and I fear the worst. I bring news from the south."

"South?"

Reka put her fork down and leaned forward, her eyes holding his unwaveringly. "Bren, I think I found them."

Bren wordlessly reached into his desk drawer and poured a generous portion of wraith into his tea. He took two deep sips before meeting her eyes. His heart hammered with something between betrayal and relief. "You 'think.' If you say you found Alea, you damn well better have spoken to her yourself, or I'll never believe it. You've thought you found them twice before. My heart can't take another."

"This time I'm certain, Bren."

"Where?"

"There's a village a day's ride from the Hartland. Townsfolk mentioned a man who trades with them a few times a year. I waited for weeks, but he finally arrived. I did not speak to him, but I saw him. It's Arman. He seemed healthy and happy. Old, like the lot of us. He shared banter with several shop-keeps. He bought a beautiful pin, one fit for a woman with gray eyes."

Bren scrubbed his face with his shaking hands. *Twenty years. Twenty years without her and now I've finally found her.* His pulse clattered in his neck. "Toar, she's alive. After so much time I had started to fear...."

"There's more." Reka's mouth curled. "They have a child, and he's on his way to Athrolan."

Φ

The 7th Day of Flureme, 1272
The City of RoBal, Ban

Keplan was already late to breakfast. He hoped to avoid the ordeal all together, but going without food until the afternoon made him irritable and fog-minded. Now he risked making a spectacle of himself by entering late. The din was caustic. Boys from ten to eighteen shouted over each other. Insults and jokes were tossed with food and coins to pay up bets from the week before.

Keplan edged up to the table. Several bowls held honey-covered fruit and oats. Two vats steamed with porridge, and another held a thick tan substance that many of the hands and muckers drank by the mugful. He collected a small portion of everything onto a wooden tray before finding a quiet table. He knew better than to try and find Fer-hil in the chaos. The boy was his guide, not a friend. The table's other occupants glanced at him, but said nothing and returned to their rapid conversation. He wondered briefly if he would get lonely. It was a familiar, but comfortable emotion after growing up alone. Now he was too focused on surviving the next few weeks.

Peppery spice followed each bite of the sweet fruit, and the plain porridge reminded him of the kind his mother cooked in winter. He wiped fruit juice from his chin and pushed the tray away. Confident they took no notice of him, he watched the boys carousing at the end of the table. They were mostly muckers, and their hair was long, like his, braided or held back in wooden and leather clasps. His eyes found the wide ones of the current speaker.

A family of close to a dozen children, raised on a farm. Hot days spent on the prairie, evenings by a river. Too poor for any masters' craft training, save for the eldest boy. Five sisters, all sent to the military or neglectful marriages. He loved the stables, the loud boys like his family, and the importance of working with horses in the capital. He had dreams to travel to the rainforest in the southwest as a horse trader.

Keplan's head ached at the barrage of information. His trembling hands spilled the thick drink as he bent to take a sip. Sweet butter rolled over his tongue, replacing foreign memories with those of Hi-taln's rel. *Somehow, I can see their lives.*

His own childhood was spent learning survival, history, and legends from his father. His mother taught him nature, politics and economics. Neither mentioned anyone having such an ability. He stumbled on a second realization. *They never discussed their own past.* He knew the antics of his father's childhood friends, the names of his mother's sisters and brothers, but nothing about how they met, or when, or anything of their adult lives before his birth. *Who were you?*

A distant gong rang. He scrambled up, discarding dishes and tray on the stack by the door before grabbing his pitchfork. He preferred to be early, to pick his hall before the others. It gave him the illusion of control. He opened the first stall, blocking the door with his barrow before stepping inside. "Hello there," he murmured to the horse within. Like their people, the Banis mounts stood impossibly tall and proud. This one had a cream coat, her markings a warm beige. She muttered at him and shifted the weight on her rear hooves.

Accepting that as a "good morning," he set about his work. He told her about his breakfast and a story about Moly. He continued down the line, stalls emptying as the morning wore on. The gong for third lunch startled him from his discussion of the weather with a placid brown draft.

Lunch was similar fare as breakfast, cold fowl stew replacing the porridge. By the time the sun hung low over the city, staining the walls of the stable red, his body ached and his mind sputtered with exhaustion. Supper was disinteresting, and he ate little before slipping off to the bathhouse. Most of the boys had yet to return from their meals, and he had the baths to himself. It took the past few days to fully work the mats and blood from his hair. He took cursory stock of his wounds, as he did every time. Scabs were becoming dry, preparing for scar tissue. Hooked marks on his cheeks stiffened his expressions.

Before the others arrived, he was tucked in the curtained sanctuary of his room. The hammock in the corner was comfortable, and he lay watching the candle on the shelf beside his head.

"Oi, anyone seen my tunic? I lost it days ago." The voice drifted over the curtained walls, answered by a series of puzzled or disinterested negatives.

Keplan grinned, hoping the banter would keep him awake. Exhaustion dragged at his eyelids, but nightmares were only a matter of time. He sat up after several precarious moments drifting on the edge of consciousness. When he struggled to sleep as a child, his father would play tiles with him by the hearth.

"If you win, you can stay up." Keplan always won the first two games, but at the third Arman would try moves that Keplan had never been taught and invariably beat his son in the game.

Keplan's eyes fell on the broad woven slats of wood that made up his wall. A piece was loose in one corner. He slid off the hammock and bent the strip away. His knife was in the Lord Interrogator's drawer, but the edge of the shelf made a decent fulcrum over which to break the strip. In a minute he had the 17 pieces of a basic tiles game. The pin from his sash scratched the symbols and soot from his candle turned them black.

He lay back in his hammock, pieces laid out haphazardly on his thin chest. He was asleep by the third game.

Φ

"Ah, that's a good move." Keplan's eyes narrowed on the tiles spread across a bare path of floor among the stray. "Someday you'll have to tell me where you learned to play so well."

The horse puffed air at him as if in promise.

"Of course, you must have studied hard. It would be difficult to play with hooves." He slid a tile over and tapped another. "I've got you in four counts if you're not careful."

A whistle shot down the hall, and the horse's head popped up, ears flicking forward. She was on her feet in a moment, dark hooves scattering the carefully laid game Keplan had played by himself for the last half hour of lunch.

"That's a dirty trick." Keplan pocketed the tiles and rubbed a gentle hand down the horse's neck. "I'll get you for it tomorrow." He ducked out of the stall and jogged down the hall. He was supposed to meet Fer-hil at the lower halls.

Sure enough, the boy leaned against a door in the main hall. His brows curled together as Keplan approached. "You were supposed to be here a minute ago."

Keplan ducked his head. "I'm sorry, I got caught up in a game of tiles."

The boy's eyes brightened. "I didn't know you played. Most barbarians don't." His expression faltered at the slur, but he did not apologize.

Keplan ignored it. Being called "barbarian" was a small price to pay for conversation. "I'm not a master, but I enjoy it." He hoped for an invitation to the games the other muckers and stable hands began in the dining hall after supper, but again, none came. "You are teaching me about the drafts?"

Fer-hil jerked his head and took off at a jog. One of the side halls led out to the east of the stable. The double doors were smaller and plainer than those in the main courtyard. Racks of painted wooden beads hung against one wall. Most were slid to the side, but others had been arranged carefully in some pattern Keplan could not decipher. "Are these codes?"

"They're requests. Someone will come in and slide the beads explaining how many drafts they need, for what, when, and for how long. They ring a gong, and one of us will come to check. We collect payment upon their arrival."

"No one ever steals them?"

"Horse-thieving is punishable by torture and slavery. Few have been so foolish."

Keplan's shoulders tightened at the thought. He glanced over to see if Fer-hil had noticed. The other boy's eyes were fixed on the beads. "Looks like we've got a request coming in shortly." He took a stone disk from his belt and hung it on a peg above the rack he indicated. "This shows that I'm taking care of this specific request. It can be competitive since most of the renters tip well."

He pointed to the colored beads. "Can you figure out what this says?"

"One yellow—one draft. Two red?"

"Pulling a ware's load."

"Two plain—this afternoon?"

"Yes, morning is one, afternoon is two. Three is tomorrow morning and so forth."

"Four of the green—is that rented for two days?"

"Yes. Follow me, I'll have you harness him up."

Φ

The 20th Day of Flureme, 1272
The City of Ceir Athrolan

"I think we're past the point of claiming this is political, An'thor." Raven glared at the locked door of queen's bedchamber. "This is sick and born only of your own selfish ties."

An'thor glared at the other man. "You were worse when Eras died."

Raven's face twisted into an ugly sneer. "She was my lover."

An'thor's brow quirked. "Only sometimes." He brushed a hand over the empty desk before him. They announced the queen's worsening illness the week before. The city knew any day might bring news of her death. "Death and illness can look so similar, but yet the greatest gulf lies between them. Odd that. She has not spoken to her subjects in a month. If I told them today that she was dead, everything would fall into chaos."

"Maybe in your eyes."

"And what do you mean by that?"

"I mean you're on this pathetic search for a murderess' spawn when there is a man of Tzatia's blood who spent thirty years training for the position."

"She disowned him, Raven."

"She was scared."

"And so are we all." An'thor jerked his head at the door. "I'm upholding her last wish."

Raven rolled his eyes. The stress showed in the thinning of his hair at the crown and the white streaks in his formerly dark beard. "Daymir has more support than you realize."

"This fanatic, Peraan?"

"Contact him. Just hear what he has to say," Raven reasoned.

"I have no idea who he is."

"He has influence. Several of the lords—most those who worked closely with Daymir when he was Treasurer—have made it known their swords are for him."

"How many is 'several?'" An'thor's shoulders tensed. Whispers in the city were dangerous. Lords who commanded troops were worse.

"Five at least. And I command the navy."

An'thor's white brows shot up. It was a blatant threat, and one he hoped to never hear. "It won't come to that. Fates, Raven, don't make it come to that."

"Get your head out of your arse, and it won't." The commander slammed the queen's chamber door on his way out.

An'thor slumped against the desk. He thought finding their child would be the most difficult piece of the complicated puzzle Athrolan had become. Putting down dissenters was not what he wanted, but he could handle the task. *A war between Athrolan's navy and army would rip the kingdom apart.*

He checked that the main chamber entrance was locked before going to the bedroom door. Dust already lay thin over the sigil. He wiped it carefully clean. Over-sweet rot drifted from under the door. It was insidious under the thick incense and bowls of dried flowers he placed in the foyer each day. He had wrapped her tightly and dressed her in her best robes. The room was far from the rest of the palace, and her windows faced the forest. His morning ride told him the windows were still shuttered tight. He pressed a hand to the door hiding his gruesome secret.

"I'm sorry, Tzatia. You deserve so much better than this. And you'll receive it, I swear. Just a few days more. You'll have the finest funeral anyone has ever seen."

Inside, he heard the buzz of flies.

Φ

The 25th Day of Flureme, 1272
The City of RoBal, Ban

The clattering gong echoed through the stable. It was the rougher, low sound calling a mucker to tend a draft animal. Keplan propped his pitchfork against the wall and hurried up to the lower entrance to check the request. *Two drafts to pull a military wagon for two days.*

A hand stopped him as he turned to fetch the horses. The soldier was tall, even for a Banis woman, and Keplan stumbled back a few paces. His skin crawled at the sight of her. He preferred an arm's length between them. "Is that your request?"

She jerked her head at something down the road. Her fingers curled, and she tapped her badge, pointed at the sky then made a complicated gesture around her throat.

"Excuse me?"

"The soldier Rih-elte says she will return for the mounts shortly. She needs a harness for both that will fit a flat two-wheeled cart." A youth stood a pace behind the soldier, watching her flicking hands carefully.

"Of course. Right away." Keplan left the courtyard at a jog. His nerves still ignited at the soldiers' shaved heads and brightly wrapped helms. This was only the second time he dealt with them directly, but it was two times too many in his mind. He grabbed harnesses from their hooks and found two of the larger animals, both well fed and alert.

He clipped the animals to the cross-ties in their hall and set about grooming them and settling the harnesses over their worn, striped skin.

Keplan waited outside the lower gate when the soldier returned. He accepted her payment and signaled thanks before rushing from the building. It would be another few minutes before his absence was noticed. His body buzzed with the memory of pain, and his heart seemed determined to crawl up his throat and lodge itself between his clenched teeth.

Large paddocks bordered the rear of the stable, surrounded by high wooden fences. The side of the building there was low, and Keplan easily pulled himself up onto the flat roof. Blazing sun warned of summer's heat. It was far from silent, but the sounds were distant, softened across the rooftops.

He was not given to panic, not before Ban, at least. Now his blood screamed in his veins, every inch of his flesh crowing for movement, to run, to scream, to do something, dammit! His father suffered explosive rages. Once, when Keplan was five, his mother went missing. Though not old enough to understand, he heard rending wood as every chair and table in the house broke and burnt before Arman's fear and anger. She stumbled from the woods close to midnight, shivering and with blank, too-dark eyes.

"I took a walk."

He understood his father's anger better now. The need to go, to move, the surge of energy commanding he break something. He could not stand a world continuing on when so many were broken down to their very souls. His hand groped at the space beside him, searching for Moly's warm flank.

The Hartland and Athrolan seemed a world away. It occurred to him that, were he to die in RoBal, his parents might never know. He scrambled down, stumbling back through the stable.

His fist almost split when he pounded on the stable master's doorframe.

"One moment." A muted conversation wrapped up, and then Hi-et's voice came again after a new mucker emerged from the office. "Enter."

Keplan could not school his hands into stillness or remove the quaking in his voice. "Master Hi-et."

"You look ill." The man gestured at the seat. "Before you fall down, please."

"Forgive my suddenness." He swallowed some of his fear and perched on the chair. "I was wondering how one might send a letter."

"A letter?" Hi-et's glanced at the doorway as if someone might hear. "To whom?"

"My parents. They've not heard from me since I left. I told them I was going to Athrolan. They don't even know where I am."

"I'm sorry, Keplan, but I can't help you."

"What do you mean?" Keplan's stomach was a yawning chasm threatening to swallow him.

"The Lord Interrogator will see it as correspondence to your masters, whoever sent you here. And don't even think about asking me to send it in your stead. You said yourself they killed the last person who showed you kindness."

"But I'm innocent. I work here. That must count toward something. Please." It was hopeless, and he knew Hi-et was right. *I have to try.*

"You are a mucker now and under your gloves you have a green palm proclaiming your innocence." He leaned forward. "But you bear a white face. Your eyes are as blue as King Azirik's himself. And your other hand is red. You may not be a spy, but under the Banis sky, you will always look like one."

Φ

The 30th Day of Flureme, 1272

Summer heat drifted in through the window. It was cooler than outside, but the air was stale. Rih watched the bustle of the courtyard outside the captain's office window with longing. Last year at this time she was returning from the Emperor's Progress March across the nation. Now she waited for the next decree that would further cripple her future. *And outside, my sisters are the wheat before the millstones of war.*

Air wafted past her, heralding a door opening. The captain entered with a nod, followed by a soldier Rih had never met and a woman swathed in silks.

Rih caught the captain's eyes and signed, "What is this?"

The captain motioned for the robed woman to sit. "This is Ki-elte, Mistress of the Hall of the Purple Throne. She is here to take you to your new quarters."

Though the captain tilted her chin so Rih could better make out the spoken words, it still took far more effort than she realized, and often much was mistaken. "I thought I was to remain here until a suitable marriage was arranged."

"I'm sorry," the captain said, switching to signing, "His Eminence has decided you should learn your role as a wife before you are wed."

Fear flooded Rih's mind. *I thought he would forget about me. I thought I would have months, perhaps a year, to prepare myself.* "No."

"I'm sorry." This time the captain used Rih's signs. Her eyes flicked to Ki-elte, and Rih's gaze followed.

"We should leave now, so we have plenty of time to get her settled." Ki-elte spoke quickly, which was not always a problem, but she spoke to the captain, and Rih had trouble deciphering her voiced words.

Rih's fear and anxiety flashed into anger, and she reached out, snapping her fingers before the woman's face. "You will be teaching me. Learn to talk to me, not over my head."

The captain hid a smile and relayed Rih's words to her new tutor. "She's not stupid or touched, Ki-elte. She just cannot hear or speak the way we do."

Rih's anger faded for a moment. It was nice to be defended. She assumed her captain was indifferent to her existence. *Frustrated, if anything.* "May I say goodbye?"

"I don't think you have the time, but if you give me names I'll pass along your farewell."

"Just Il-fald and Jih-alan." Her chest ached. It was like she was a tumor, an infection they neatly excised from the world she inhabited for so long.

"I'll let them know. Gather your things. As of now, you are dismissed from duty." The captain rose, shoulders rolling back, and touched her fingertips to her breastbone. She waved them upward, a salute to an equal. Her dark eyes bore into Rih's, brighter than Rih remembered them ever being.

"Thank you, Captain. It has been an honor." Her feet took her to the barracks. She was aware of Ki-elte beside her. Perhaps the woman tried to speak, to comfort her, but Rih could not bring herself to look at the woman's face. She threw open the chest at the head of her hammock. Most of her belongings were on loan from the army. She tied her few personal things into a bundle and slung it over her shoulder before turning about the room. It was deserted, but she had few enough friends that it did not matter. She closed her eyes, fingered the rough, worn fabric of her hammock, and turned to Ki-elte. The woman's calm face would have looked expressionless to anyone else. Rih caught the tension around her eyes, the clenched jaw.

She did not bother to ask why the woman was worried. *She wouldn't understand me, anyway.* Instead, she jerked her head toward the door and followed her out.

She expected to be brought to the palace, or the hall for dignitarys' wives and daughters. Instead, Ki-elte turned right as they exited the barracks. She expected a male guard, or to be stopped and asked her business. No one even looked at them twice. *With anonymity comes freedom.* The barracks and training halls stood across from the trade markets. Downhill, the lower city was a tangled mass of color and smells. Through the haze of midday, Rih picked out the red clay guard towers looming over the piles of buildings and throngs of people. *Not so much to keep us safe, but to keep the rabble from rising.*

They skirted the edge of the city, winding through the larger buildings of state and commerce. It was not the most direct route, Rih was certain, but the mess of carts and traffic, with war approaching, were easier to avoid than navigate. She glanced at the woman leading her. She afforded her grudging respect—Ki-elte hardly broke a sweat, despite the nearly hour-long walk. A massive building rose before them, the center of a smaller square. Like the others, it was mostly clay and built in rising concentric circles. Instead of the baked red and orange, however, the clay was washed with a deep purple. She collided with Ki-elte's silk-covered shoulder. "Forgive me, I was distracted by the building."

Ki-elte watched her fingers, but looked back to Rih's face and shrugged. "I can't understand your hands. I'm sorry."

Rih slowed her breathing as if preparing to launch a dart. She gestured for them to continue on. Instead of heading toward the women's wing of the Dignitary's Hall, Ki-elte turned into the courtyard of the burgundy building. A small stable curled around one side, and a gilded door led into the bulk of the building. There was no emblem on the larger door or hanging over the arched entrance to the courtyard. There did not need to be. Heavy pungent flowers, undulating tiles on the ground and walls—everywhere Rih caught glimpses of purple. *Hall of the Purple Throne.* Ki-elte pointed toward another door. It, too, was built in a pointed arch, but the pillars and vines afforded some privacy.

Ki-elte pulled two circular keys from her sash and fit them into the large locks on the door. It swung inward, and she stepped aside., gesturing left. "This way."

Stepping through the door was akin to emerging from the cool training hall into summer's heat. Still, warm air brushed Rih's bare arms. Musky jasmine underlay sharp sandalwood, echoed by eucalyptus. Instead of windows, glass sconces shed rich light across the dark draped walls. She followed the woman down the low hallway and up a series of stairways. Each woman they passed nodded to Ki-elte and offered Rih a smile or greeting.

After the third, Rih stopped to stare. Their faces were not lined with soldiers' creases. *Their eyes bear the wisdom this life forces upon us, but their mouths are framed by smiles, their eyes by laughter.* She glanced back to Ki-elte, stopped at the top of the stairs. *Even Ki-elte carries herself differently.* It could have been lack of soldier's training; it could have been the layers of silk wraps and robes. Rih suspected it was something else.

They arrived at a room at the end of the third-floor hall. The rolling silk screen bore wooden lattice and a simple lock. Ki-elte handed her a silver key hung on a braided purple cord. Rih ran a calloused thumb over the bright metal circle.

"You can read my mouth?"

Rih nodded, though the reality of her actually understanding was more complicated, especially as Ki-elte was not used to accommodating Rih. *We'll start small.* "Yes."

Ki-elte watched her hands and then mimicked the gesture. It was clumsy, but correct. "Yes?"

Rih nodded again.

"Bathe, change, unpack your belongings. I will be by in a few days for your first lesson, but for now, you may adjust in private. Someone will bring you supper at sundown. Clothes and books will arrive tomorrow perhaps. You have a tub, but the bathhouse is downstairs."

Rih twirled a finger, asking her to repeat several phrases. When she was sure she understood, she smiled. "Thank you."

Ki-elte cocked her head. "'Thank you?'"

"Yes."

The other woman smiled. "Good night."

Rih slid the door shut behind her and rotated the lock until she felt something click. The room was dark but boasted a shuttered window. Deep shelves ran along the left wall, flanking a mirror. Behind the desk on the right were empty racks for scrolls and tablets. A straw-filled mattress in the far corner was larger than any she had slept in, since her mother's death. She slumped onto the bed and tucked her face into the soft sheets. Other women might speak her signs, and she hoped to find them soon. It would be a long few months if she could not talk to anyone. The room was still, and the fresh straw of the mattress smelled of freedom.

CHAPTER SIX

The 34th Day of Flureme, 1272
The Forest of the Hartland

DARKNESS WAS SOOTHING, A lack of sensation enveloping Alea's mind. Her lungs billowed silently. Thoughts slid through her mind like a leaf on the surface of a placid pool. This was where she escaped from the war.

A face blossomed from the darkness. It was a woman's, lined with an impossible tangle of wrinkles and scars. Eyes too bright silver to be anything but Laen rolled with madness. "Gods' blood!" The words were furtive, whispered. Her gaze locked with Alea's, and the woman screamed. Her lips cracked, bleeding, as the sound went on and on.

Alea hauled herself out of meditation with a gasp. Sweat drenched her back and chest. Her pulse thundered in her throat. *What was that?* She raked a hand through her graying hair, wincing as chapped fingers caught in a tangle. Only the wind hissing through leaves broke the silence. The house was far, out of shouting distance. The war was distant enough for her to feel safe, even out of earshot. She put a shaking hand to her mouth, wondering if nausea would do more than threaten.

Arman stood at the clearing's edge when she looked up again. "What happened?" Resignation, rather than fear, lined his face. Since Keplan's departure they had spoken little.

"How did you know?"

His features softened, brows relaxing. "It's you. I'll always know." He gestured to the grassy patch under the largest of the beech trees. "May I?" He rarely came to her meditation spot and never entered.

She leaned back against the beech's trunk, nodding. Her limbs were heavy and her eyes ached, but she did not yet trust the darkness when they shut. "I'm afraid, and I hate it."

Arman sighed as he sat before her. His rough palms scratched at her breeches when he placed his hands on her knees. He did not speak, only rubbed circles on her legs with his thumbs.

"I was happy here. It was beautiful and peaceful and ours. Even when Keplan was small it was perfect. I feared for him, but only in the usual ways—I feared he would trip, or find an animal in the woods. I feared he would fall sick. Now I am afraid of everything." She raised her head from the trunk and looked at him. "You were right. We should have told him."

Arman looked down. "I know. But I had just as much a part in his raising." He squeezed her hand. "Are you having dreams, too?"

"Dreams of pain and fear. And every time I see this woman's face."

"Laen?"

"Yes."

"I thought they were all dead."

Alea shrugged, staring at their entwined hands. "I'm not. The world is whole, and yet the winters grow colder, the summers shorter. After the war something powerful and beautiful was supposed to replace the Laen and Rakos, the Gods. I fear I missed something. What if I was supposed to die?"

Arman's hands tightened on hers. "Please don't walk that road again. After the war was terrible. Neither of us knew how to live without fear and pain and running. Please don't go back there." He brushed a strand of hair away from her clammy cheek. "Have you thought about what the woman wants? Does she say anything?"

"She says 'Gods' blood.' Sometimes she says that it's everywhere, or spilled. It doesn't feel like she's damning me or threatening. If anything, it's a warning."

"Gods' blood. In your reading, where did the gods come from?"

"There were as many theories as there were books. The Laen created them. The Rakos created them. They were the children of the Rakos and the Laen." Her eyes met Arman's, silver and gold luminous in the shade of the clearing.

"What if they were right?"

Φ

The 42nd Day of Flureme, 1272
The City of Robal, Ban

"Keplan?" Hi-et's voice cut down the hall.

Keplan glanced up to see the stable master silhouetted against the brightness of the main doorway. "Yessir?"

"When you're through with that request, I need to see you in my office."

"Of course, sir." Perhaps it was the man's refusal to help him send a letter, or maybe the four military requests he filled that day, but his stomach flipped at the words. *What did I do wrong?* He shoved the thought into the back of his mind and headed to the man's office. Keplan hovered in the doorway until the Stable master gestured to the seat across the desk. He forced his legs into stillness as he sat. "What did you need, sir?"

"You know what today is?"

"I believe it's the 42nd day of the month, sir. The final week of Flureme."

He slid a scroll across the desk.

Keplan unrolled it, frowning at the symbols. His gaze fell to the date beside his signature at the bottom. He could read the numbers now. "Oh."

"Your servitude is up, should you wish to leave. We also found your horse. She was set up in a stable in the lower streets. She is thin, but otherwise unharmed."

Keplan stared at his feet. Surviving did not include thinking of freedom.

"Will you stay?"

Keplan glanced up. "I can't. Not here."

"Collect your things, then. Your horse is in the seventh draft hall. You may leave in the morning."

Keplan did not rise right away. "I wish I could have learned about your city in a better way. I feel there are beautiful people and customs."

"There are. Perhaps one day you'll return. Keplan," Hi-et's voice stopped the boy on his way through the door, "I had a brother. There was a misunderstanding. He was dragged from our house, and I never saw him again. That is why I agreed to hire you. I don't want more innocent men to meet the same fate."

Keplan looked down. "I'm sorry." When the stable master said no more, Keplan bid him a good night. Excited relief exploded once he turned down the side hall. Sawdust skittered from under his sandals as he took turns too quickly. He stumbled to a halt outside a dim stall. His heart hammered between his ribs.

A familiar gray and red head bobbed over the door. Moly's face was thinner, but she looked healthy. She nosed him once, then again, letting out soft whickers of happiness as she lipped his tunic.

"I missed you too." He swung over the door and wrapped his arms tightly around her neck. "Tomorrow, girl. Tomorrow we'll be out of this place and on the road to Athrolan." Moly must have slobbered on his face because his cheeks were suddenly damp.

Φ

The 47th Day of Flureme, 1272

Dawn broke slowly. Sunlight bloomed through the haze already clouding the horizon. Keplan was awake before the sky was fully light. The hammock creaked as he rose and donned his mucker's uniform. He buckled on his sandals, folded his blanket and pillow. There was nothing to pack. His bag was taken, perhaps destroyed when he was captured. Now his only belongings were borrowed from a man too kind for Ban.

The stable was just coming alive. Night Hands made a final round before bed, extinguishing the dangerous lanterns and unlocking the side doors. Moly's ears perked when he arrived at her stall. He handed her some dried fruit from his pocket and checked her over. "Tomorrow we'll wake in a new place."

She bobbed her head at him, and he smiled before leading her down the hall. The rear door of the stable opened into a dimly lit and poorly guarded area of the city. The road leading past wound down and through the eastern gate. Fer-hil and the other muckers had not considered Keplan a friend, but it was odd not to say good-bye. Leaving was easier, more joyous, with good-byes, even if it was from a place of pain. *I never said fairwell to my family.* He promised himself he would write when he arrived in Athrolan. "Though what could I possibly tell them?"

Moly snorted and nosed his pocket. He scratched the bristles at her poll. Dawn bleached the sky when he pulled his stiff body onto her back. He did not pause at the gates and nudged her into a trot as he passed the guard house. Something rose in him as he left the city, cracking the thin, numb shell helping him survive. Anger roiled in his chest. Ceir Athrolan was a terrifying unknown, but it was a fear he welcomed.

Keplan stopped to rest Moly often, but there was no way to put the endless waving grasses behind them swiftly enough. Wind that seemed a thoughtful hum when he first emerged from the Hartland was now a sinister hiss. Despite her own weeks of work in the city, Moly was strong and the pace affected her little. The dark band on the horizon became a brown smudge and soon grew into the green tangle of a forest. Left with his one-sided conversation with the mare, Keplan was uncertain which were his own thoughts and which were the strange new memories collecting in the corners of his mind.

The crack of an ax jolted Keplan from his stupor. Moly's ears perked with curiosity. A cluster of sunken houses abutted the dense copse. Raw wooden stakes ringed the village, jutting out at an angle. Keplan shuddered. *Perfect height for riping open the bellies of attacking cavalry.* With the majority of the Banis military consisting of infantry, most cavalry would be an enemy. He counted almost two dozen houses. Cooking meat sparked his hunger into an audible growl, but he could guess the nature of his welcome.

He swallowed hard and glanced about. It was almost dusk. Snares were simple, and Keplan knew how to make a snare and shoot a bow, but he had neither the materials or patience to make them. But a growing man could survive only so long on bruised fruit and dried berries. He urged Moly off the road and into the shelter of the trees to wait until dark.

Birdsongs he recognized rose from the black tree boughs. Lanterns bloomed in the village. Furtive talk and hurried steps told Keplan he must be close to the border. What seemed like an inn at the edge drew his attention. Rough walls encircled the rear yard. *Inns mean trash, trash means food.* He slipped through the crossed stakes and moved along the fence, listening to the pattern of the noises and talk within. Adrenaline stung in his veins at each crunch of soil under his sandals. Music swelled as a group of young men emerged from the inn carrying a drunk companion. Keplan ducked behind the privy. When they stumbled down the street, he edged farther.

Compost filled the corner furthest from the building's door. Most of the food was rotten, but a few fresher pieces dotted the top. He stuffed half an eggplant and a bruised pear into his shirt before the door behind him banged open. He pressed his back against the wall, hoping the shadows would hide him. Newly sawn wood dug into his back, and the scent of spoiled meat threatened to make him sneeze.

A boy stood on the steps, dark eyes wide. After a moment he stepped down. One brown hand gripped a bucket full of scraps. His free hand trembled, raised. "I'm just getting rid of these. I won't tell, just don't hurt me."

Keplan realized he looked like a thief, one much larger than the boy. He cleared anxiety from his throat. "I'm just hungry."

The boy inched closer to dump the bucket over the pile. "There're some good pieces in there, just stay clear of the pork." He peered into the dark, as if waiting for Keplan to emerge, before turning back to the inn. "If you're here in the morning, I'll leave a bag of food by that tree."

Keplan murmured his thanks but waited. No shouts or running feet indicated betrayal. He grabbed what he could and dashed back to the safety of the trees to examine his finds. Spoiled parts were easily pared away, and his red sash made a good sack to hold the leftovers. With the promise of a breakfast in the morning, he settled in for the evening. He curled against the dip between roots and closed his eyes.

A nightbird's warning shriek sent adrenaline burning down his limbs. Then Moly's hoof falls as she grazed shook him awake. He untucked his hands from his chest and removed his gloves to peer at his palms. Moonlight turned the red of the right into a rich purple. The left was still tender in a few places, where the needle pierced too deep. The green ink was nearly black. Both were already marred with callouses. If someone asked, he would have denied thoughts of vengeance.

Φ

Keplan's stomach drove him to the village just before dawn. Gold bled across the wooden slats of the low rooftops. Keplan hung back, crouched where the shadows still clung. The boy emerged. He was younger than Keplan first thought, perhaps twelve. He slipped across the yard and tucked a parcel from beneath his arm into the compost pile.

Just as he turned to leave, Keplan stepped out and raised a hand. "Thank you."

Whatever the boy's response, it was interrupted as the door to the inn swung open.

"I thought you were Banis, Kola-ih." A young man strode down the steps.

Kola-ih's shoulders fell. "He was just hungry."

"Da said he saw a stranger last night. You taking the Mirikin side? Traitors are worse than barbarians. They're not even human." His lilting speech was calm, almost friendly, but his words cut. "You want to be a dog, brother?"

Kola-ih had not moved, save to close his eyes. Now he looked up at Keplan, and his hands fisted. Keplan wanted to grab the food and run, but his feet rooted to the earth. The mocking tone echoed the words of the interrogators and Kola-ih's tiny rebellion burned in Keplan's chest. *That's right. Fight him.*

"You eat like a dog, you're no better than one." Kola-ih's voice was small, but his mouth snarled the words an instant before he leapt forward.

Keplan's eyes widened. This boy showed him kindness. Now his small fists rained on Keplan's head and ribs. His sight darkened. Pounding filled his ears.

A groan drew him back to the confrontation. He crouched in the dirt, the boy's face pressed to the ground, his impossibly bent wrist gripped in Keplan's bony fingers. He blinked and staggered back. The older brother seemed too stunned to act. Keplan ran. A whistle brought Moly racing through the grass. He kept pace with her for a few staggering steps before dragging himself onto her back. It would take minutes for the village to muster. Even if they never gave chase, he held Moly at a run.

Φ

The 1st Day of Lineme, 1272
The City of RoBal, Ban

Footfalls rarely shook the floor. Though Rih could not hear the press of silence, she noted the stillness of the air. At first, she relished the space to stretch and bathe in private. After several days, however, the solitude felt more like isolation. An alcove by the window boasted a wooden tub hidden by a dressing screen. In the army she shaved her head once a week, less if they were on patrol. Now it was every other day, mostly out of boredom. Rih swept up the tiny hairs from that morning and smoothed the coverlet across the surface of the straw-stuffed cotton. The cords of muscle in the small of her back bunched and cramped. Adjusting to a mattress after almost two decades of military hammocks played havoc with her body.

Sunlight through the lattice of the window painted plaid across the ceiling and down the opposite wall. The light warmed her naked skin. Ki-elte would arrive after breakfast, and Rih was unfamiliar with traditional women's clothing. *I am a warrior, not a wife.* She perched on the dressing stool and fingered the silk shift and draping wraps. *My mother made dressing look like a dance.* Each morning Valin-elte would scrape her scalp bald with deft fingers, thread jeweled wires through the half-dozen holes in the shell of her ears and brows and nose. White and lavender, sometimes pink, wraps drifted down on her shoulders like gossamer. *Like wings.* Rih sighed and just donned her kalas.

Ki-elte arrived with a smile and a wooden tray of fruit and yogurt. She set the tray down as she caught Rih's eyes. "I thought our first lesson would be best over food. Are you hungry?"

Rih nodded and sat at the desk—the only surface large enough for two in the small room. She piled her plate high with fruit and took several deep sips of the thick tea. She wished there was time to eat before concentrating on Ki-elte's distracted speech. The tutor had a habit of talking through every action, and it was impossible for Rih not to miss most of the words. Now Ki-elte discussed Rih's outfit, it seemed.

Ki-elte settled in the seat across from Rih and looked up expectantly. "I hope you will teach me some gestures so we might better understand one another."

Rih smiled. The offer seemed genuine, but teaching others her signs was an endeavor. Whatever else the woman had said was a mystery.

Ki-elte winced. "Can you read and write? It would make this easier. I'll try to speak slowly."

Rih pushed her food away with reluctant hands. She found a wax tablet from the desk drawer and carved hasty marks into it.

> *Yes, I can read and write, any soldier can. Long phrases and not seeing your face are worse than speaking quickly. Long speeches are almost impossible. What I speak is a language – not gestures to punctuate speaking, and it will take time.*

Ki-elte's smile faded at the rebuke, but she took the advice. "I'll try my best, and please, stop me when I'm being unclear. Writing will help until I know enough to read your hands." She helped herself to breakfast and settled into the chair across from Rih. "Do you have any questions?"

Rih looked away. She had hundreds. Some she simply did not like the answers to. *I'm here because I'm the smallest liability to the Empire. I will never see my friends, and when this marriage is final, I will never see my home again.* She scratched another line onto the wax, pointing at each word and showing Ki-elte the signs for key words. "You, and the others, you look happy. How can a woman be happy in an empire such as Ban?"

"Perhaps we should start your lesson now." Ki-elte's eyes burned, an expression Rih saw in her training mistress's eyes more than once. "Do you know why you are here?"

Again, Rih wrote and then signed her answer. "Because His Eminence believes I can't hear plots or speak secrets."

"Because we are at war. His Eminence wanted to send one of the women trained here because we understand politics like we breathe air. He considers us well-trained. We consider ourselves soldiers of a different war. The way you dress tells the world something, whatever you wish. Just as armor protects you in battle." She finished her food and pointed at Rih's plate. "If you're through, let's begin."

Rih cleaned the last of the fruit from her plate and tucked it under the others on the tray. As much as Ki-elte tried to liken dressing to armor and battle, Rih hesitated to believe her. *Armor protects against blows, against darts and arrows. There is nothing that protects against words.* She brushed a hand over the shell of her ear. *Not even being deaf to them.*

Ki-elte rummaged through the shelves beside the dressing screen. Often she turned and repeated whatever comment she spoke first into the baskets so Rih could see. Rih refrained from rolling her eyes, but only just. "We'll have to do something...only soldiers lack rings and studs." At Rih's wrinkled nose, Ki-elte laughed. "Just like with clothes, each one means something. We'll find something you like, and you don't have to decide right away." She straightened, a stack of folded silks in her arms. A pile of fine, gleaming chains topped the fabric.

Rih smoothed the front of her kalas. It was longer than her thigh-length soldier's tunic and made from lighter cotton. There were short sleeves, and bright blue bordered each hem. Ki-elte babbled again, and Rih grabbed the tablet.

> *Show, don't tell me. It might be easier if you write too, unless you are sitting, looking at me.*

"Of course, I'm sorry." Despite her distracted energy, she seemed to genuinely want to do better.

> *The pieces don't change, but the colors you wear say much. Several bright colors make one statement, while shades of a single tone make another. The first implies passion or mirth, the latter control, dedication.*

She draped a shorter lavender wrap across Rih's front and back over her shoulders where she fixed it with a pin. The second, gray wrap crossed only one shoulder and folded at the waist to create a pocket before falling to the floor in front and behind. Ki-elte stepped back so Rih could look at herself. "What do you think?"

Rih plucked at the twisted belt holding everything in place and shrugged. *I don't look like a wife either.* She glanced at Ki-elte's gleaming head, stained a deep rose to match the woman's usual color palette. A burgundy silk net stayed in place with delicate chains clipped to the woman's ruby studded earrings, and the weight of the tiny gems hung at the edges. "I like your net." She added extra gestures to help convey her point.

Ki-elte's eyes crinkled at the corners. "I can find you some." She pointed at the outfit. "You like blues?"

"And purple." Rih brushed a hand down the lavender wrap and turned to see how the fabric fell in the back. *I'll snag on everything I walk past in this.* She heaved a sigh.

Ki-elte frowned, began to speak, then wrote instead.

> *I know this is a change. I'll try to take things as slowly as our time allows. We're also going to meet with one of the ambassadors to learn the politics and customs of the kingdoms you might marry into.*

"I thought it would be Mirik?" Rih leaned over to repeat the question in writing.

"Probably. But we aren't certain they'll listen to reason."

Rih winced. "I don't want to marry a barbarian on a salt-stained pauper island. At least our other allies know our tongue." *I don't want to marry at all.* "I want control over something, even if it's only my own body." She didn't bother to write the second half. Sometimes she appreciated the privacy of speaking a language few understood.

Ki-elte gestured for Rih to take a seat by the window, her expression bare of its usual playful smile lines. "I am Mistress of the Hall of the Purple Throne. You know what this is?"

Rih's gesture was rude, borrowed from the barracks, but unmistakable.

"Yes, a brothel. The palace brothel, to be exact. We are paid in amenities, rather than beads so we can keep up this lifestyle." She repeated a few phrases before continuing. "There may be shame in being a woman in Ban, but whores are the best off of all."

> *Why did they send a Mistress to train me? And one who doesn't even speak my language?*

Ki-elte looked down for a moment before meeting Rih's eyes. "You're being traded in negotiations as a wife. I cannot guess to whom, or when, but you will be married. You do understand a woman's role as wife?"

Rih slashed the air with her hand and made the rude gesture again.

"It is unlikely you'll have a choice to bed him."

Rih squeezed her eyes shut. Being sold to a foreign man was frustrating, but she could study another culture, learn to read another language. She could not replace her body. A gentle hand settled on hers.

Compassion brightened Ki-elte's dark eyes, and Rih realized the woman was not much older than she. "I know what you feel. I felt it too. We do not have a choice in this, but you must remember you have power."

Rih rolled her eyes. Her only power now was whether or not she wore a blue robe or red.

"Listen to me." Ki-elte winced at the poorly chosen word. "I'm sorry, I misspoke. I need you to understand. A man might—"

Rih handed her the tablet.

> *A man might bed whom he wishes, but you will be his wife. You will bear heirs. I will teach you skills to impress him, to control when you bear a child, but more than that, I will teach you how to navigate court, how to manipulate the people around you without them seeing. The Language of colors and dress isn't just to pass the time. The right dress will force people to listen, even if you don't speak.*

"Tell me, who rules the people of Ban?" she asked.

"His Eminence," Rih replied.

"Yes. And what rules him?"

"He is as a god here." The answer was one they all memorized as children.

Ki-elte stared out the window for a moment before rising. "I'll bring you a net tomorrow. For now, there is someone you must meet." She nodded toward the door. "We're meeting him in the Lapis Room."

Rih fell into uneasy step behind her teacher. There was something she missed, something between Ki-elte's question and her answer, but she could not place it. Now her fingers trembled with nerves. The Hall's corridors twisted through rooms lit with low screened lanterns, and the heavy scent of flowers clung to the myriad draped silks. Ki-elte paused at the top of a flight of stairs and swung open the heavy door that separated the women's personal quarters from the Hall of the Purple Throne itself. "We are meeting an ambassador. He will help explain fashion and dances of the kingdoms you might marry into."

Rih forced her pace into calm, steady steps, rather than the strides she trained to do in her sleep. Anxiety fluttered high in her stomach. Even the windows were covered with dark blue and lavender silk screens. Each door bore elaborate inlays of specific colors and stones. Ki-elte directed Rih to the Lapis Room.

I could buy enough horses for my entire patrol with the gems on this door and still retire in a palace of my own. Rih shook the dream away and watched Ki-elte unlock the door and slide it aside.

The room beyond was awash with blue silks. A broad bed sat in the center, draped with more curtains and pillows than Rih had seen in her entire life. The window shades were thrown open. Ki-elte's tap on her shoulder brought Rih's attention to the man seated on a shelf beside one of the windows. His face was smooth, but his eyes held a spark that said his patience took effort. His gaze slid over Ki-elte and fixed on Rih. His lips flew into action too quickly for her to catch more than a few words.

She turned away and waved a hand at Ki-elte. Some bothered to learn her gestures in the army, but there her future had not been at stake. Now the isolation tasted bitter in her throat. She remembered the faint condescension in Ki-elte's eyes the week before. A warm hand touched her shoulder, and she turned.

The man lowered his head, dragging her gaze up to his black eyes. "Forgive me. I did not know." He made a few halting signs. "You, I young play." He offered his hands, palm up, in greeting and switched back to voicing. "I am Ambassador Mosil-ten-Ebal, third nephew of His Eminence."

Her eyes narrowed on him. There was something in the thick brows, the angle of his eyes and cheeks that tugged at her memory. *A boy, when my mother still lived in the Women's Wing.* Warmth burst in her chest, swelling out to her fingertips as they flew into action. She could not keep the smile from her lips.

"Yes! You were my mother's friend's son," she shrugged, "and, I suppose my cousin."

He raised a hand. "Slowly, please, I am out of practice." He glanced at Ki-elte. Rih realized she must have spoken. "I can understand it, yes, though I speak it poorly." He gestured to the two chairs by the window seat. They did not match the rest of the decor. "Please, both of you, sit. We have much to cover." There was a shadow to his face, something another might have missed.

Rih trained herself to learn how faces changed. It helped when she inevitably missed their spoken words, but, moreover, she found it useful in navigating the complicated Banis hierarchy. "You seem sad."

"I did not know you were the bride I was to brief. It makes this more complicated." Mosil's chest hitched in a laugh Rih could not hear. Though his lips curled up, his eyes were still dull. "Politics make slaves of us all." He turned to include the teacher in their conversation.

Rih took the chair closest to the desk, perched on the edge. As a boy, Mosil was kind, and judging by the lines about his mouth he was a man who still smiled often. "Do you know whom I am to marry?"

"There are two possible matches. One is the son of Ambassador Brentemir Barrackborn—the man descended from Azirik." He paused to clarify the latter to Rih before continuing. "The other option is a man of forty, a son of a wealthy former lord across the island. Of course, both will fall through in the face of outright war."

A shred of hope fluttered in her stomach. "Could I return to my duties as a soldier?"

"If we're at war, we will need allies more than ever. Our eyes will turn to Athrolan perhaps. Maybe Sunam."

"What do you need to teach me?"

"I have books you are to read. Brief histories and etiquette I can teach you myself. For now, we will focus on Mirik." He looked to Ki-elte and began discussing their teaching schedules. "I regret that I'll only be able to teach her every fortnight—the very work that makes me a perfect tutor also pulls me away."

Rih looked away, unwilling to process more. Her future stood on the auction block like an underfed heifer. After a few moments, Mosil turned back to Rih. "Perhaps we might write, so your questions are answered more readily." He unrolled two scrolls and opened a rare book, clearly bound in the east. "Mirik is a small kingdom, but not without its traditions." He detailed the government, the lack of king, and the roles of the commissioners.

It must have been close to an hour later when both Ki-elte and Mosil turned to the door at some unheard interruption. The former opened it after a moment. A wide-eyed woman stood outside, her face pale. Rih could not follow her rapid speech, but Ki-elte's face sobered further. The teacher turned. "There's been an accident. I'll continue my half of your lessons tomorrow. In the meantime, I'll have someone bring you two scrolls to read." She flashed a faint smile and disappeared down the hall.

Rih turned back to Mosil, determined to learn. She would never command armies, she would never rule an empire. *But I might influence the man who does.*

Φ

The 5th Day of Lineme, 1272
The Banis Coastline

Brown rocky fields surrounded him. Here, the unbidden flood of information did not scare him. Athrolan was still barely more than a precocious city-state to the north. Building clouds darkened the horizon behind him. The ground broke apart ahead, and a city rose up, stark and sinister. A man stood at the gates, swathed in green and bone white. Dust rose from the pile of bones on which the city perched. The trim of his tunic was deep red, dyed with blood seeping up from each footfall.

Keplan tried to turn Moly about, but her steps continued, unchanging. He glanced down. Her fluffy coat shed, changing into the stripes of a Banis mount. The stripes became ribs and spine. Putrifaction burnt in his nose. The skeletal horse brought him ever closer. Nausea rose, and the world spun. Ahead, the man's face split into a gaping chasm that swallowed him whole.

Cold, damp wind hit Keplan's face. Salt and something else he could not name tickled his nose. He groaned and blinked. It was dark, and the air held a chill that was absent in Ban. Warm breath and long whiskers brushed his cheek. He sat up. Moly stared, as if puzzled why he had chosen such a strange way to dismount. The sound of water rushed nearby. His sore hands clenched, dry leaves crunching between his fingers. Stars glimmered through the trees' canopy and a thin smattering of clouds. He smiled at the sight.

"Apparently I need to rest." Rain whispered louder on the leaves, and he noticed they were like those from home. It took a moment for him to gather a few branches overhead and brush damp leaves away from the still-dry ground. Moly settled with a graceless thump behind him, and he leaned back on her flank. His gaze roamed the sky.

His dream was strange, but he supposed it was just that, a dream. "You know," he began softly, "in RoBal they think of their horses as great wealth. Like a gold vase or intricate tapestry. They aren't friends like you are to me." He reached up and brushed his colored palm against her downy chest. "It was strange, down in the dark. I never knew the time or when to expect food or pain." His words faltered as he recounted imprisonment and the weeks that followed. Her ears flicked forward and back, large eyes lidded and content at his voice after so long.

Dawn showed him the stream he heard the night before was, instead, a large cobbled river, running north from the hills. The water was clear enough to see the pale rounded stones littering the rocky sand of its bed. He sniffed the air. *Salt.* Keplan brushed dirt and leaves from Moly's burr-like coat and mounted up. The river's edge was broad and gentle on his side, sloping easily down to the river from the trees. He guided Moly carefully, watching ahead for places she might turn her hoof. Summer made the waters shallow, and the other bank grew farther as he rode north.

The trees dropped away to his left and they stood amid the waving beach grasses of the ocean. He sat back, and Moly stopped at the change in his weight, her ears flicking back to listen for a further command.

Keplan patted her shoulder absently. He could not find the words worthy. Green waves lapped at the rocky strand. The horizon was a vague gray strip where the water merged with the colorless summer sky. White birds swooped at fishes in the brackish water of the delta, black speckled counterparts dappling in the foam with earnest, pattering strides.

The noon-day sun struck orange and gold from the white-caps, smarting Keplan's eyes. He raised a hand to shield them as he looked a moment longer before dismounting. He stripped and tied his sandals and clothes into a bundle on Moly's back before leading her out into the delta. The tide was just beginning to turn. The crossing took the better part of an hour, Keplan, then Moly losing the bottom for several minutes in the middle channel. The far bank was steep and higher than the other, but Keplan kept his footing. He was glad for the warm summer as he spread his clothes on the hillside to dry. He lay down beside them, staring at the wisps of clouds scuttling past. Moly nosed his wet, salt-thick hair then turned her attention to the grass.

"This is it, Moly. That was the border. We're in Athrolan." His heart fluttered with something too pained to be happiness and too resigned to be relief.

CHAPTER SEVEN

The City of Mirik

"ANYONE HOME?" THE DOOR rattled closed as Kemmer stepped into the foyer.

Bren emerged from the parlor, mug of tea in his hand. His brow furrowed as it often was in the past weeks. "Hello, love. How did the meeting go?"

She hung her cloak on the hook on the wall and heaved a sigh. Her smile was exhausted but genuine. "Long. And we spoke in circles for about three hours. Please tell me Janna saved some supper."

Bren nodded his head toward the parlor. "It's in here. I was keeping watch, making sure Azimir didn't eat any."

Kemmer snorted, kissing him on his bristled cheek. "You'd be as likely to eat it as he. You look as tired as I feel. How was your day?"

He followed her into the parlor without answering. He leaned onto the long table that held a collection of alcohol. Wraith splashed into his cup. The shaking in his hands gave away that this was far from his first drink of the evening.

Kemmer allowed him the dramatic silence as she set about eating. After a minute she pointed a piece of chicken at him. "Brentemir, you haven't been my commanding officer for seventeen years. I'd like an answer." Her brown eyes softened, and she leaned forward. "What's wrong? I've scarcely seen you in the last week. Is it the war? You missed the meeting tonight. I know an ambassador doesn't need to be at every one, but this is a perilous time. It's not like you to miss a war council."

His bloodshot gray eyes flicked up to hers. "So, it's war then?"

Kemmer sighed. "It has been for a while. You know that. I hope to hear from Athrolan within the week on an alliance."

"But for certain? Mirik can't go to war again, not so soon after the Gods' War. I just finished rebuilding her."

"Oh, for fate's sake, Brentemir. You did not single handedly swing each hammer and write every law. Mirik going to war is no longer your decision. It's actually mine."

He glanced up. "You're acting queen?"

She sighed, twirling her empty glass by the stem. "Yes. Tonight the council named me Hetmir."

He turned away. His chest hurt, and his head already pounded. He was too old to drink this much. His hangover started before being tossed. The thought of Kemmer as queen so soon after Reka's news of Tzatia made his skin crawl. It was stupidly superstitious, but he could not shake the unease.

"Do you wish you were in my place?" Her voice was suddenly hard.

"Yes, love, but for an entirely different reason than the one you imply. Reka came to visit."

"When? I never saw her."

"That's rather the point. She'd be a rubbish spy elsewise." His wife did not laugh. "Right. She brought news from Athrolan. Her Majesty Tzatia is dead."

Kemmer's glass shattered against the far wall. "When were they planning on telling us?"

"They don't know. An'thor and the Commander are keeping it from the kingdom to stall potential civil war. Reka happened to see An'thor's reaction and made an astute deduction."

"I supposed we can't expect an alliance for a while, then."

"No, but I do have some hope. I'm sailing for Athrolan in the morning. Alea's son should arrive there soon."

Kemmer fell silent, her face unreadable. "So you're leaving us in a time of war to chase a nephew you've never met."

"Don't make it sound like that. I'll bring him here. Having the son of the Dhoah' Laen on our side will make the Banis think double before attacking us. They were there. They saw what she did at Claimiirn."

"You don't even know if he has abilities, let alone whether he wants to be roped into a war."

"He's her child. There is no question."

Kemmer slid her half-eaten plate away. "I'm going to bed. If you're not too preoccupied, perhaps you could spend some time with your wife before you leave."

Bren hummed in response, but did not follow when she swept from the room. After a moment she called down the stairs to him. He did not hear, staring into his drink long after the hall lamp was extinguished.

Φ

The 9th Day of Lineme, 1272
The City of Ceir Athrolan

Bells shook the earth. Moly's head bobbed up, ears pricked at the sound. Keplan drew up at the crest of the hill, pulse thrumming. Afternoon light bathed the city pink. The road wound through the villages and farms smattering the surrounding foothills. Buildings crowded against the city walls as if to press themselves into the protection. Keplan kept his jaw from dropping, but only just.

Rolling foothills replaced the broad river banks from five days before. White cliffs plunged hundreds of paces to the ocean, and Ceir Athrolan perched on the edge, an ancient white bird protecting its harbor. Legends betrayed him now. It was easy to run from home seeking a stranger based only upon a cryptic letter. With Athrolan's vast capital sprawled before him, how could he hope to find a man with nothing but a single name?

"Move along!" a guard barked.

Keplan dragged his attention back to the packed street and pressed forward through the tide of color and noise. Massive gates stood open, their archway muffling sound before he emerged into the city din. A square opened from the main road, boasting performers and stands of finer wares. He stayed firmly seated on Moly's back, wincing each time a shoulder brushed his leg or eyes paused on him over-long. Damp stone and salt underscored the scent of timber and lantern oil.

"The General will force our army against us!" The shout came from just beside him. He whirled, heart hammering. A man of middle years perched atop an overturned crate. His clothes were tidy and bright, worn to catch the eye. "The greatness of Athrolan will fall to these foreign warmongers. Already she rots from the top! We will be fodder for Ageless war machines if we do not take our rule into our able palms. Prince Daymir, rightful heir to our throne was exiled when the general arrived!" The man brandished a sheaf of papers. Catching Keplan's eye, the barker raised a fist. "You, capable Athrolani, do you not agree Lord Daymir is your true king?" He shoved a paper into Keplan's shaking hand.

"I'm not Athrolani." Keplan pulled Moly away. *Is Athrolan under martial law?* Tension tripped along Keplan's spine. He shoved the drawing into a pocket of his sash and searched for a quieter street. Tiled roofs of manor houses jutted above the wall to the right. Most streets angled down to the harbor and crisscrossed the tiers. The chipped and rust-stained palace dome reared above the rooftops.

By evening, his eyes were tired and his back ached from his stiff stance. *I'll need a place for the night.* A street to the left skirted the city wall and curved around to the towers above the naval barracks. It was dirty and its storefronts dark and poor. He headed down the narrow road, relieved when the bustle lessened. A few establishments made his stomach churn with their cleanliness, or the haggard eyes staring from stained windows.

"Copper for a bag, silver for a box." The croak twisted from a stoop in the shadow of an aqueduct's pillar.

Keplan edged away. "What?"

"Dust, lad, it'll turn your nightmares into nothing."

He gripped Moly's reins and shook his head. "I don't have nightmares," he lied. He was about to turn back when a small inn caught his eye. It sat at the end of the street, tucked between a derelict cotton mill and what may have once been a brothel. Stale alcohol and the bite of rotten food hung in the air.

Old wood had faded to gray, but the windows were clean and the lantern out front polished. He dismounted by the door, fiddling with the reins. He loved the woods, but his body ached from so many days sleeping on the ground. *They might take Banis beads, or know where I could exchange.*

"If you're looking for a place for the night, you can shack your pony around back. We've got a barn of sorts."

Keplan's hands tightened in Moly's mane. A bearded man peered from the ally beside the inn. His clothing and body matched the condition of the inn—worn, but clean.

He jerked his head down the alley. "We've no stable boy, but I trust you can care after your own. Elsewise you can find a place more to your liking." He flashed another smile before disappearing up the narrow stairway on the building's side.

When he was gone, Keplan led Moly around the back where a dingy barn haphazardly hung off the rear of the inn. It allowed for barely enough space to dump the rubbish. He put Moly into one of four stalls, avoiding the vicious teeth of the draft horse beside her. He checked her coat, fingers running over and over scars and rough patches he had long since memorized. It was only when he smoothed his hands down her legs for the third time that he admitted he was nervous. *You blend in here, at least more than in Ban.*

He wished he had the letter to vouch for him, but in a city of thousands, he doubted he would stumble into an inn that knew the sender. He straightened his tunic and swung open the door between the barn and the inn. It moaned audibly, but the three patrons in the corner did not look from their mugs. Keplan slid onto a stool at the end of the bar.

"What can I get you?" The woman paused beside him was a darker, female version of the man from the alley.

After weeks of communicating solely in Banis, his native Trade was almost awkward in his mouth. "Just water, please."

Her lips pursed, but she brushed past him without another word and ducked into a room that, by the heat and smell, had to be the kitchen. He leaned back on the wall. His gaze flitted from corner to door, to patrons, to door. One leg bounced soundlessly on the wooden rung of the stool.

The low ceiling was swaybacked as a nag's, and the fireplace shed more light than the dim lanterns. Carved pillars caught his attention. They were made in the shape of rabbits in scribes' garb, some holding outstretched tomes and maps serving as tables and shelves. One's raised iron quill held a cloak by the door. Most bore marks of hasty repair from bar brawl damage. Despite himself, a smile tugged at Keplan's mouth.

"I don't trust a man who orders nothing but water in a tavern, noontime be damned." The man from before leaned on the bar and slid a mug over to Keplan.

Keplan gestured at his clothing. "The only money I have is Banis." He took a slow sip of the water, wishing his stomach was not so empty.

"So you came here to rest from the sun?" His brown eyebrow arched playfully. "You staying in Athrolan long?"

Keplan lifted one boney shoulder in a shrug. Who knew how long it would take to find the man who sent the letter? "For a while, yes."

"If you sweep up the place in here, and tidy the back you can stay the night and have some supper. And nevermind Mirrel. She bites a bit at first, but that's just her way."

Keplan watched the dark-haired woman bustle from the kitchen. Her green eyes shot a hard look at the two of them. "She's your sister?"

"Older by two years." The man stroked his thick brown beard. "I'm the prettier though."

The joke startled a laugh from Keplan, and he looked down. "I'd like to stay the night." His stomach punctuated his words with a low rumble.

"When was the last time you ate, my man?"

Keplan paused, counting back. "It's been a bit. I was traveling, for a time, and lost my bow."

The man's eyes darkened only for a moment, and Keplan wondered at the expression. "I'll fetch you something now. We can talk clean-up details when Mirrel's through. She works mornings, I do evenings. I'm better at bar-talk anyway." He patted the bar before Keplan with a smile. "Firas."

Keplan frowned. "Excuse me?"

"Firas Smytheson. My name."

"Ah. Keplan Wardyn."

Firas's grin broadened before he slipped into the kitchen. "Well then, welcome to Athrolan, Master Wardyn."

"Thank you." Keplan looked away, nervous at the attention and the kindness. He wished trust was more durable, wished it took more than weeks in a cell to rip it from him. He smoothed the barker's paper on the bar, eyes scanning the crude sketch. Two military figures grappled, one with horns, the other broad and gripping a ship's tattered flag. They stood on a pile of dead officiates. At the top of the mound lay an older woman with a crown.

"Here you are. Not much, but Mirrel would be ticked if I gave away our best." Firas slid over a bowl of greasy sauce and a plate of toasted bread and meat strips.

Keplan glanced up. "Thank you. Might you have a fork?"

Firas snorted. "Not from Athrolan, eh?" He jerked his head at the other patrons. "Fingers are fine."

Keplan flushed and looked away. "Forgive me."

"Nothing to forgive." Firas's hand tapped the parchment. "I see you've met Peraan's group."

"Who?"

"The barker who heads this train of thought that General Domariigo plans to destroy the nation."

"Is Athrolan at war?"

It was Firas's turn to shrug before pushing off from the counter. "Not yet. Who knows what will happen when Her Majesty passes?" He waved at the food. "Eat up before it gets cold."

Keplan shoved the paper away and set about eating. His parents told him of Athrolan, of her might and beauty. Her palace's glittering pearl of a dome, the queen's grace, the joy and bustle of her streets. *Can that much change in twenty or thirty years?* He fingered the tattoos on his gloved palms. He supposed it could.

Φ

The crowd grew in the evening. Lanterns bloomed with the setting sun, and it seemed every moment the door banged open again. Keplan sat on the rear stoop for a moment, broom in hand, and looked up at the stars. Ban was interesting for its differences, but Athrolan fit around him. It was not the people or the language, for he imagined under different circumstances Ban could be beautiful. *This is familiar.* The purpose of his journey seemed so distant in the dark Banis cell, in the dim heat of the stable. With every borrowed memory from those inside the inn, he felt a step closer to whatever set his feet on the path to this city.

He rose with a silent sigh and finished sweeping the makeshift courtyard and alley. Disused tools and hay filled the barn, which he set about tidying. It was close to midnight when Firas coughed politely from the doorway.

"I was beginning to think we'd scared you off." His eyes lit on the state of the barn. "You did well in here."

"I worked as a mucker for a bit." The words slipped out, startling Keplan.

Firas did not seem to notice his embarrassment, nodding instead at the door. "Most of the patrons are gone to bed if you want to start the common room."

Keplan followed his host inside, closing his eyes for a moment to enjoy the flood of firelight and swell of warmth. It took a few minutes to straighten unoccupied chairs and stack dishes and mugs by the kitchen door. The last customer left by the time the common room was clean and Firas dimmed the lanterns. The bearded man leaned on the counter with a tired smile. He pushed a full mug over to Keplan. "Have a drink. You earned it."

"I only earned the one meal."

"Nonsense. You earn what I say you earn." He tugged off his apron and tossed it onto a hook by the door to a narrow stairwell. "So, what brought you to Athrolan? Your clothing says you're from the west, but your coloring and accent certainly don't." His eyes narrowed in mock suspicion. "Are you a spy?"

Blood roared in Keplan's ears, drowning whatever else the bartender might have said. "*Worthless barbarian spy!*" He choked down a gulp of whatever was in his mug, but it tasted of blood. "I'm not a spy." He spat the words, ale misting the bar before him.

Firas straightened, hands still planted on the counter. His brows met over his green eyes. "I'm sorry. Mirrel's forever saying my mouth is too fast for my head."

Keplan glanced up, and the whirling of his thoughts slowed. "You meant nothing by it." He took another deep sip of his drink. It was too acrid for his liking, but filled his gut with pleasant warmth. "I'm from the south. I came here to find someone my parents knew before I was born."

"Ah. Many come here looking for something and never leave. Maybe they find something better." His smile was softer this time, kind and shadowed with patient curiosity. "You probably just want some quiet. I can show you to your room."

"I would appreciate that." Keplan drained his mug and trudged upstairs after Firas. Half a dozen rooms lined the narrow hall above the common area. Keplan took Firas's smoky candle and ducked through the door with quiet thanks. The room was as bare and small as his barrack in the stable, but in the style of his room at home. A low window sat above the bed. He crawled across the thin coverlet and pushed open the shutters. Cool air brought the sounds of sailors, ships, markets, the smell of lanterns and fish and old stone.

The neighborhood may have been poor, but the view was spectacular. The row of houses across the street were low and Keplan could see over the brown battered tile of their rooftops to the bowl of the city. Glinting lanterns painted the twisting streets and outlines of buildings in golden light. Aqueducts ran through the city like ribs. The reflection of dock lamps swelled like starflies with each wave in the black mirror of the harbor. Torches cast guards' exaggerated shadows on the dome of the palace.

Keplan stripped off his Banis clothes and let the air cleanse his body of prairie dust.

Φ

The 11th Day of Lineme, 1272
The City of Robal, Ban

Summer's heat was a cloying blanket. Overripe fruit covered the scent of sweat and baking soil. Rih flung open the wooden slats of her window with a sigh. It was a useless gesture, hopeful of a breeze that would never reach so far within the walls. The Hall was tucked into the heart of the city, away from any proper prairie wind. She unrolled the scroll in the stand on her desk and paused at an image. It was a dance. Mosil gave her instructions to read accounts of his time in Mirik before the threat of war. He expected her to memorize every move and phrase of introduction. Today, when they met in the heat of afternoon, she would learn to dance. *At least the first part was easy.* She neither knew the language nor could she speak it, so her introduction was entirely reliant on her cousin or another state official.

She ran a finger down the detailed painting. Mosil was taller, but something around his eyes and the set of his mouth told her it was intended to be her cousin. Traditional loose pants and a silk wrap covered him. The knots and draping of the fabric were the same as Ki-elte taught her and she smiled. *I'm learning.* Beside him was a young man she presumed to be Mirik's king wearing a quilted orange vest layered over a longsleeved gray-green shirt. Tight breeches were tucked into high boots. She shook her head. Mirik may have been a more eastern nation, but she could not fathom being cold enough to warrant so many layers of wool and leather. *If it's so cold, then why do the men cut their hair so short?* She glanced at the caption:

Ambassador Mosil-ten-Ebal of RoBal meeting Alleanthus A'hane of Mirik, son of Military Commissioner Kemmer A'hane and Ambassador Brentemir Barrackborn.

Her heart raced. Everyone knew of Brentemir Barrackborn—Azirik's son and the brother of the Dhoah' Laen. That meant Mirik's Military Commissioner was female. Did that change negotiations for the Banis Emperor? *Does it irk His Eminence to sit eye-to-eye with a woman?* She pushed away the ache in her chest. A soft breeze brushed her cheek, and she turned.

Ki-elte stood in the door, bright smile in place. Her usual pink clothing was pale in an effort to ward off the heat. "Good morning!" Instead of joining Rih, she gestured to the door. "You can take lunch during a break in your lesson. Dancing takes time even when...." She tried to hide the falter with a smile, but Rih saw.

"Even when the student can hear the music?" Rih signed.

Ki-elte paused and mimicked the gesture of a bow on strings. "Music?"

"Yes." Rih tried to use signs Ki-elte recognized. The woman was a fast learner when she focused, but often fell back on writing out of impatience.

Ki-elte smiled, made the gesture again, then signed crudely, "Yes. Even when hear music."

Rih grabbed her tablet and asked:

Couldn't they just tell the Mirikin boy I cannot dance?

Dance is a part of so many Eastern rituals, especially for a figurehead of court. I can't imagine them agreeing to a marriage with a woman who couldn't dance.

Rih sighed and followed her teacher through the Halls. It soured her stomach that she was learning dance before Trade. *Teach me their language. Teach me to read their mouths, their songs, their legends.* As it was, most myths she knew involving the Eastern lands were of the Dhoah' Laen and the asai. When Ki-elte knocked at the door to Rih's lesson, fatigue dragged the other woman's movements.

Rih touched her shoulders. "Are you alright?"

Ki-elte smiled again, but this time Rih saw the shadows underneath. "I'm tired," she signed before switching back to voicing. "The threat of war is heavy. Its weight falls on us first."

Rih rolled her eyes. She knew about war. Ki-elte had never seen the true frontlines of battle.

I'd think it falls on the soldiers' first.

Ki-elte's chin jerked in a derisive snort. "Then you haven't been listening." She waved the conversation away when Mosil opened the door. "I have other things to take care of. I'll return to show you back to your room." A rare frown curled her thick black brows, and she wrote on Rih's tablet.

> *War kills the nobles, the rich last. But the soldiers are never first. You want to see whether war will come? See if the poor are dying, if the invisible are dying. War isn't coming, Rih. It's already being fought.*

She smoothed her words from the wax once Rih read them. Her honey-colored eyes hardened to amber, and she disappeared down the hall.

Rih stared after, wondering why her stomach had turned to stone. A hand on her arm startled her from the dark mood.

"Morning, Rih-elte." Mosil punctuated his signs with a frown. "Is everything alright?"

Rih offered a false smile and pointed to the room. It was clear in the center with a small dais for musicians, meant for private gatherings and performances. "You are going to teach me to dance?"

"I will. Usually, I can just say 'it will make sense when you hear the music.' Today will be a learning experience for both of us." He paused. "Can you hear at all? I know many can only hear certain tones."

"Only very loud noises or in a very quiet space. Often, I simply know something made noise, but it's not clear. A ballroom is neither of those. I can feel, but with dancing, my steps will cause more disturbance than a faint tremor from music." She repeated some signs, exaggerated, for him, but it was a relief to use her own language. "If I can see the musicians, I can read their rhythm and that of other dancers. And my partner." She stopped. "Do Mirikin dances have partners?" Banis dances began as great patterns with partners growing closer and closer, the music ending when hands finally touched. If the pictures were any indication, formal Mirikin—and most Eastern dances—were often paired.

"These are paired. You can follow your partner, but be sure you don't trip over his feet." He held out his hand and switched to verbal speech. Standing so close, face to face, she could see enough of his words to understand. "Let's start with positioning and steps. We can worry about music later." He moved her hands, one against his and the other featherlight on his chest. "Feel the pressure in my hands and body as I move." The steps were mostly back and forward with a few rotations returning them to where they began, albeit facing the opposite direction. The count seemed to be of three.

When they paused for a drink, musicians filed in. Two were white and bore the marks and clothes of slaves. Rih frowned. "Where are the cellos? The violins?"

He laughed. "Mirik has none. Eastern lands rarely use them, though some of their songs adopted our instruments." He made a face. "They play them poorly. Instead, there are drums and wind."

She resumed the starting stance. Over his shoulder she watched the musicians bend into their first notes, one man tapping the drum. Mosil's hand pressed on hers, and she tripped over the beginning step.

His lips thinned, and he waved for the musicians to start again. "The first steps are the most important. The rest just follow."

Another hour passed before Rih mastered the first half of the dance to music that she could never hear. Her cousin called a stop and dismissed the musicians with a sigh. "We'll meet again soon to do more. There are four other dances you'll be expected to know. For now, that's enough for you to think on and practice."

Or you're too frustrated to continue. "I'll practice."

"Good." He gathered his things, his guard falling in step behind him. "I'll see you soon."

Rih laid her glass aside and turned to look for Ki-elte. The seat in the corner was empty. She checked the hall, but only a guard stood beside the sliding door. Long shadows stretched outside the window. It was afternoon, and their lesson ran late. *She should be here.* Rih waited a minute longer, then slipped out on her own. The hall was crowded, but she managed to find her room without mishap. It, too, was empty, the lamp unlit. She settled in to read more while she waited. The sun set and her supper arrived, but Ki-elte never came.

Φ

The 14th Day of Lineme, 1272

The letter arrived with breakfast. It was one of the three days of the week Ki-elte spent teaching her, but the woman was already late. Rih helped herself to a bowl of fruit and tea, one hand peeling the seal from the scroll.

R-

Forgive the sudden nature of this letter and my absence. News came from the west, news that bodes poorly. I will elaborate further in person and when I know more. I hope to return to the city in time for our next meeting, but until then, please study your books. I asked, too, for some advertisements on fashion to be sent to you from the city jewelers. I thought you could decide on which style rings you wanted.

I wish you well,

-K

Something churned in Rih's gut. This felt like the hour before a raid, pulled from sleep to creep through the darkness, for once, her companions as silent as she. Despite Ki-elte's words during their first lesson, Rih did not consider the woman any sort of warrior. *She was called away on an emergency, something about politics and war, no doubt.*

Ki-elte was as much a soldier as any who carried an atlatl or armor.

Rih pushed her food away, stomach a knot of nerves. War was less terrifying when she bore a weapon. She fingered the edge of the reed cards on her tray. They bore images of impossibly beautiful women, each dressed in intricately patterned robes, bedecked in skull nets and gemstones.

The figures' expressions were vacant, faded eyes gazing at some distant point. The women in the Hall of the Purple Throne, however, were different. Rih had been contemptuous of the life of a courtesan or prostitute over a soldier's. She realized, now, she missed a large piece of the story. Her gaze slid to the doorframe. A silk thread bedecked with wooden beads hung through a small hole there, presumably attached to a bell somewhere on the other side. She tugged it firmly and turned back to the cards on her desk.

When a serving woman arrived a minute later, Rih handed her a roll of paper.

The woman scanned the words. "You want someone to come pierce you?" She glanced up at Rih's bare face and ears and smiled. "She will be by shortly."

Rih offered a nervous smile and returned to perusing the variety of rings on the cards. She thought the decorations were pretty, if impractical. Curiosity sparked in her mind the more she learned how much women conveyed without speech. Body language and expressions were universal, even for her. This was new. *And something men may not even notice.*

A hand touched her shoulder, and she whirled. The serving woman stood behind her and a woman, tall even by Banis standards, waited in the doorway with a box in her arms. Rih penned a quick explanation for why they would communicate through writing. The woman smiled in response and gestured for the serving girl to be on her way.

When the door shut, the piercer turned. She bore laugh lines and gray in the stubble on her head. Her hands flew into motion. "I'm Hi-alan-Kan. I do most of the ring work at the Hall. I understand you're new here?"

Rih's heart thundered at the signing. "I was a soldier before I was chosen to marry. My teacher tells me each ring means something."

"Yes." Hi-alan opened the box. "Unlike with clothing, where color carries the most obvious meaning, rings are more about placement." She laid a sheet of silk on the desk and unpacked a series of needles, a bottle of dark liquid, and several tiny boxes with jeweled rings. "A ring in the nose indicates strength, in the brow, intelligence or power. Lower in the ears shows kindness, empathy. Higher is for philosophy. Some women prefer a bead, like the one in my nose, here." She tapped the tiny pearl stud on the right side of her nostril. "These are often seen as playful, rather than elegant rings."

"And left and right—do those have meaning too?"

"Wives and teachers tend toward the right side, while courtesans prefer the left. The gems are chosen to match our outfits." She turned to look at the shelves of Rih's clothes. "Blue?"

"Purple, too." Rih pointed to the deep purple wrap Ki-elte brought the other day as a gift.

Hi-alan opened one of the boxes and handed it to Rih. Inside were rings and studs of varying sizes, each bedecked with amethyst, lavender chalcedony, or lapis.

Rih grinned. "These are beautiful." She peered into the small mirror Hi-alan produced. Her features were strong as it was, and she did not want to damage what little she could convey to others who did not know her language. *This is just another way to communicate.* She pointed to her left brow, both her nostrils and her left earlobe.

"Both sides?"

"Is that wrong? I'll need all the strength I can muster."

Hi-alan smiled. "I think it'll look good on you."

Rih eyed the needles while the other woman cleaned her skin with the dark liquid. Pain from a pulled muscle or twisted ankle was familiar. Pain by choice was entirely different. The first punch through her ear burned. The second ached. Pinching accompanied the hoop through her brow. Tears flooded her cheeks, and she glanced down at the bloodless knuckles of her hands on the chair's arms. The needle through her nose was a hornet's sting. The ground disappeared, her body falling forever, leaving her stomach far above. Darkness receded from her vision a moment later.

Hi-alan's smile was kind, if amused. "The first time I received my rings I fainted dead away. Ripped my lobe in half." She turned her head so Rih could see the fine white line bisecting the flesh.

Rih shuddered, stomach still flipping in the aftermath of the pain. She checked the mirror. Though red and still dotted with blood, the new jewelry was striking on her face. "Thank you." Her eyes met the reflection of Hi-alan's.

"Keep yourself clean, and take care with your new hoops. You'll forget and catch them on all sorts of things if you aren't careful." She set about cleaning and packing her tools. When her box was fully packed, she touched Rih's shoulder, expression soft. "This life is hard. We are expected to be everything and ask for nothing. Be perfect without the respect. It isn't easy. I wouldn't know how different the soldier's life is, but I know the fire in your eyes, in mine, is the same in most women in this city. Ki-elte is a good teacher, but she only sees the happiness it seems sometimes. Perhaps she has to, to survive this." She paused and finally met Rih's eyes properly. "You did not ask advice, and I don't know if you need it, but my suggestion is to learn. Learn everything you can. What we know is our power." She squeezed Rih's arm and bowed her head. "Good luck."

Rih caught Hi-alan's hand. "Thank you."

The woman smiled. "I wish more women spoke your language. Some men know it, but not many. It'd be nice not to hide half of what we say anymore."

A frown bloomed on Rih's brow as she watched her go. She always viewed her lack of speech as a frustration to others—if not always herself. Silence was often isolating. *I never thought it could be freeing.* Her body hummed, wanting exercise, wanting to jog the open prairie with her patrol beside her. Energy filled her limbs as her body countered the pain of piercing. Instead, there were scrolls to read if she was going to do things properly.

She heaved a sigh and went to the cluster of scrolls beside her desk. Half a dozen were those Mosil lent her. During their first week together, Ki-elte urged her to read a smaller, darker one. Rih tugged it from the vase and settled herself by the window.

> *There is a colorful history to Ban. Drenched deep with red blood from wars and slavery and the betrayal of emperors. The darkest blood, however, the coldest drip of gore across the pages of our people is what we have done to our own. There was one day when we were as city-states—warriors and warlords eating upon one table. Women commanding beside their men. But there is one way, the easiest way, to command an army, to drag warlords under a single banner and make them think it is for their own good.*
>
> *To command the horse, you break its will. To turn its road you rein its head. Humans are no different than horses. Bloodier, perhaps, but just as simple. The empire was not always an empire. There was a time when we were but cities, sisters and brothers to the Vales. The men who ruled were not always great or even good. The first emperor broke his people and cut the will from their hearts. He reined their generals, killed those who opposed until the only officers were loyal.*
>
> *But even a horse may break free when he learns the whole of his will and the might of his body is greater than the strength of the man who seeks to ride him.*

Rih sat back. What did Ki-elte mean? If the people of the empire realized they were stronger than the emperor, than the generals and nobles, it would destroy Ban. *He must live in fear of that, for to have power is to fear its absence.* She grinned and scrabbled from her seat. The tablet from her first lesson with Ki-elte lay nearby, where she read it before bed, hoping the answer would arrive in dreams. *What commands the Emperor?* She rummaged through her desk until she found her stylus and scratched one word across the wax surface:

Fear.

CHAPTER EIGHT

The 10th Day of Lineme, 1272
The City of Cier Athrolan

SUN POURED THROUGH THE open shutters, dripping over the coverlet and onto the floor. A particularly insistent ray crossed Keplan's face. One hand flopped over his face, and he groaned. His eyes shot open when the noises of a city registered. *Not at home, then.* He rolled from his bed and stretched. The city was beautiful in the morning, though not as magical as the night before. The folded tunic brought a frown to his brow. Looking out of place was dangerous, but a new set of clothes would be expensive. He needed food and a room too. *I need money*. The common room was quiet, and as he feared, Mirrel perched behind the bar, dark head bowed over a tattered ledger.

When she did not look up, he cleared his throat. "Miss?"

She ignored him a moment longer before glancing up. "Why are you still here?"

"Your brother let me stay."

She snapped the ledger shut with a disgusted look. "He's worse than a dock-whore. I couldn't count the number of times he's tupped patrons, not even if I used my toes."

Keplan blanched. "No, I mean in a separate room. In trade for cleaning up the common room and courtyard."

She snorted at the term. "You mean the alley?" Her expression slipped from annoyance to contemplation as his words registered. "You tidied up?"

"Yes."

Her eyes scanned the room before returning to him. "You did well. Better than Firas ever has."

Keplan bit his lip, something close to hope blooming. "You own this inn?"

"I inherited it from our mother."

"I would like to continue to work for you."

"We can't pay you. I just looked at the ledger. Trust me when I say you'd have to pay us to make it worthwhile."

Keplan squared his thin shoulders. She was clever and, moreover, she was stubborn. "Miss, how many rooms are let at a time? Two? Three? You have six. I won't take up valuable space. This tier is above the docks—"

"As is the whole city if you hadn't seen."

"Right, yes, but I mean the naval docks. Do you have a courier? Do you have a proper barn? I'll help you. I promise I'm good with my hands, quick on my feet. I spent time fetching horses, so I know errands. You both are too busy to worry about those small jobs."

She did not turn, but she was listening. "You act courier and errand boy, tidy the place, mend things what need fixing. In return, we offer you meals and bed?"

Keplan glanced down. "And I'll need something to wear."

Mirrel's eyes fell to the ledger, her full mouth twisted in frustration. "I can run this business myself."

"Of course you can, sistermine, but for fate's sake, listen to the boy's sense." Firas stood on the last step, leaning on the doorway. His beard and hair looked wild, and fatigue narrowed his eyes. "If he helps, we could bring in a bit more coin. You're busy enough with cooking and the books."

"Two weeks. I'll give you two weeks, and we'll see how things go." She jabbed a finger at him. Despite her small stature, Keplan retreated a step. "You steal from me, boy, and I'll bake you into our sailors' pot pie."

Firas tossed Keplan a tired grin and nodded up the stairs. "Come on, I'll see if I can find something that fits you."

At the end of the second-storey hall, another set of stairs led up to the attic. The space was divided in two, the other side presumably for Mirrel. Firas's room was cramped, and Keplan ducked his head to avoid hitting the gabled ceiling. The view, however, was a fantastic one.

He patted the slight paunch from his nights of drinking. "Hard to believe, but I was once almost as slender as you. My shirts might fit, though I'll have to search to find suitable breeches." He dug through a chest at the end of his rumpled bed. He tossed two tolstovka over his shoulder. "Try these."

Keplan turned away and tugged off his tunic. He was not modest, but he did not want to discuss the obvious pattern of scars across his body. The shirts fit well, though the sleeves were shorter than the current fashion dictated. The cloth belt allowed him to tighten it over his narrower waist.

Firas's eyes lingered on Keplan's bare legs before handing over a pair of dark, loose breeches. "Your build does not lend itself to being that thin. I know Mirrel's a hard woman, but please eat as much as you need. I'd rather have a healthy bar boy."

Keplan's cheeks flamed, and he tugged on the breeches quickly. "I eat fine."

"Of course. If you wear boots over those no one will notice they're too short for you. Mirikin folk tuck their breeches still."

"I'm not Mirikin."

Firas frowned at the hard tone. "Well, no. Of course not. Neither are you Banis, but you wear that thing." He pointed at the discarded tunic on his floor. "Let me see your feet."

"Excuse me?"

"Boots, you idiot." His grin, bright through the brown beard, softened the mock insult.

Keplan flushed again and held out a bony foot. "My father promised I'd grow into them, but I haven't yet."

"You're what, sixteen? You've got some years left."

"Seventeen. I was born during snowmelt."

Firas laughed and dug deeper into the chest. "I was too, though I'd say a fair few years before you. I was a wartime babe." He drew out a pair of worn boots. They were old and far too large for the short Firas, but recently polished. "These were my Da's. His boots and armor came back from the battle at Claimiirn, but he didn't."

Keplan eyed the dead man's boots. "I don't want to intrude."

"Nonsense. I'm a sentimental man, but I'd like to see them used. They do no good collecting dust."

Keplan shoved his feet into the boots, almost toppling over in the process. He righted himself with a soft laugh and tucked the short legs of the breeches in. He glanced up at Firas, curious. "Think I'll pass?"

Firas nodded in appreciation and flopped onto his bed gracelessly. "Rather well. Now get down to the common room. I'd like to sleep for another two hours before I deal with Mirrel again."

Keplan found the man's kindness contagious and left the room smiling.

Φ

The 14th Day of Lineme, 1272

Stone buildings ringed the harbor, marked by crests and signs. Anvils, ships, coins, cloth marked their trade, but none were actual workshops. *Guildhalls,* Keplan realized. The largest bore coins and scales above the arched double door.

The cool room was dim, and he blinked to adjust his eyes after the sun-bleached city outside. A counter ran across the cool room, topped with heavy iron bars. It was quiet, despite the two dozen people in various lines. He found a shorter wait and clenched the paper in his hand tightly. Surprisingly, Mirrel trusted him, but he supposed she knew he would get nothing from stealing a delivery note.

When called, he approached the clerk and slid the note through the bars. "I'm here from the Wise Hare. Miss Mirrel Smytheson requests her coin retrieved on her usual day." Seeing the well-armed guards outside, Keplan understood why it was far safer to have the bank retrieve her money.

"You're a new face."

He glanced up at the clerk, puzzled.

"I've seen the Smythesons come in for years."

"They've just hired me to help out a bit." He took the stamped note stub with a faint smile and hurried out the door. The clerk meant well, but Keplan's skin crawled when singled out, even if it was just through common talk. The commotion in the harbor as he exited overcame his worries.

Fishing boats long since sailed, and the sparse docks were shadowed by a massive vessel. It was not the long, armed naval ships clustered near the harbor's entrance, but tall and fine, built to weather the storms of the open ocean, if not battle.

Keplan's steps stalled. He knew little about ships, but he enjoyed the way the hull slid through the water, the rigging swarmed with sailors as they made ready to dock. Deep green lacquered the wood, accented by vermillion rails, both shining with layers of resin. The stiff sails were bright white, save for the flying jib, emblazoned with a vermilion serpent and crossed keys.

Mirik. People swarmed the docks, but Keplan was heedless of the jostling. *Their flagship, no less.* He shouldered his way to the edge of the dock, clambering onto a piling. The ship was secured and the gangway lowered for the first wave of cargo and mail, including two horses fine enough to rival the Banis mounts. A man of middle years disembarked, flanked by clerks and guards. Faded auburn striped his short gray hair. An older boy followed, his darker features too akin to the man's to be anything but a son.

Something strange writhed in Keplan's stomach. Mirik's ambassadors should fill him with anger. *Shouldn't I be blaming them for what happened in Ban?* He hardened his eyes, leaning forward on the piling to catch a glimpse of the dignitary's eyes. They were a pale gray, almost colorless. No foreign personal history flooded his mind, however, only vague images from the war. The boy was the same. *Why can't I see?* One fact forced itself through his cluttered thoughts: Mirik somehow silenced his madness.

Φ

The 15th Day of Lineme, 1272
The Forest of the Hartland

Arman smoothed a hand over the rough countertop, staring into the distance. Alea believed hers were the only thoughts twisted with ugly darkness. He let her, but it was a lie. His mantle of protector was heavy after so many years. Anger was heavy too. She meditated now, and had been more often. It was a way to seek answers, but it worried him. *What if she sees only what she wants?*

A blank sheet of parchment lay before him. Writing to An'thor would seal Keplan's fate. The vague letter from the general was damning enough. Instead,

Arman carefully scribed Bren's title and name before pausing again. *What does one say after twenty years of silence?* He shook the dark thought away and set about his letter. It was long, but not nearly long enough to encompass all that changed. Black ink dried to charcoal while Arman wondered if he made the right choice.

Keplan's birth was unplanned. Alea thought she was unable to bear children, and Arman was content to love only her for the rest of his days. Their son was a beautiful surprise. Now he wondered if it was coincidence. Power begat power. They were the most powerful creatures the world had seen in aeons. *How could our child be anything but miraculous?* Alea predicted something came after the war, something she could not name or understand, but more powerful than she.

What if it's Keplan?

"What are you writing?" Alea leaned on the door frame, arms crossed over her chest. Her body was relaxed, but her eyes tired. "A letter?"

Arman stared at her, wondering how long he would lie to protect her from her own thoughts and fears. Should he even bother? "Alea, I don't think you missed anything."

She moved to sit across from him, brow furrowed. Her eyes lingered on the parchment, but made no move to read it. "What do you mean?"

"Whatever you saw predicted in that book. I don't think you got anything wrong. I think you just don't want to see it."

Her frown deepened, following the familiar paths of wrinkles. "I don't like your tone."

He closed his eyes and shed the weight of protector. "I don't like your blind idealism, Alea. You are the most powerful Laen in centuries. I'm an Earth Shaker."

"Was. Were. We're just people now, Arman."

"No, we're not. We never will be. Alea, we're barely human. What hope could we possibly have that our child would be normal? Something changed in Keplan. We both saw how preoccupied he was. Within a week he was riding north looking for An'thor. He realized something."

Alea looked away, lips in a tight line. "What are you suggesting?"

"I'm suggesting he's something incredible and powerful and alien that this world has yet to see. What if our son is what you saw?"

Her eyes flicked to the letter, head still turned away. "You're writing to him?"

"I'm writing to Bren. We tossed Keplan into the world without any tools, without the knowledge of what we are. Someone has to help him, and I don't trust An'thor not to make him a pawn."

Unreadable darkness filled her eyes. She had been simply Alea for so long, calm and quiet, writing poetry and gardening. The woman who looked up at Arman now was not Alea. Softness fled her features and shaking hands clenched. "Pack your things. We'll leave tomorrow."

Arman watched, incredulous, as she strode into their bedroom. Anticipation tightened his chest. "What are you doing? What if Keplan comes home?"

"You know as well as I do he won't. I'm finding Daymir and convincing him to take the throne instead. I'll find this woman who haunts my thoughts and learn what she means by 'gods' blood.'" She appeared in the doorway, fingers braiding back her gray hair. "I don't care if he's the most powerful thing this world will ever see. He is my son, and I'll be damned if he rides into this alone."

Φ

The 18th Day of Lineme, 1272
The City of Ceir Athrolan

Unlike Ban, Athrolan's summer weather varied. Heavy, fluffy clouds filled the sky, and breezes curled through the streets carrying trash and leaves. Travel's momentum kept his mind busy, but now uncertainty plagued him. Errands and chores filled his mornings, but his afternoons were free.

Now he moved along the edge of the market in the paved circle near the western gate. Each time he met someone's eyes, he cataloged the information to explore later. It was strangely intimate, and he struggled with the morality of his actions. *The man with the bead on his beard plans to leave his wife next week. The woman by the apple stall works as a half-dressed barmaid in a love-house. The smith across from me runs a smuggling and spy route to Mirik.* Keplan paused at the last one, peering closer at the man and memorizing his face. Information and discretion were good skills. He turned down a smaller makeshift alley between stalls. A young man admired the tooling on a leather sheath, tanned face lit with an open smile. It was the Mirikin dignitary's son.

Keplan's thoughts were silent.

Why is your family the one thing I can't see? He moved to tap the other boy on the shoulder. Hard fingers twisted his wrist, and he sank to his knees to avoid breaking the bones. White-hot pain burst behind his eyes. Ban flashed through his mind, and it took all his will to clear his vision and focus on his attacker's words. A burly, older soldier held him. "Sorry to disturb you, Master A'hane. This scum was angling for your purse."

The dignitary's son stared, confused, at the proceedings.

Keplan shook his head violently. "Sir, you have it wrong. I was trying to get his attention, not pick his pocket. I thought I knew him."

His last words were cut off as the other boy waved the soldier off. "Thank you, but I know this man. I was supposed to meet him here, but this knife smith's ware distracted me."

The soldier paused, his gaze going between the two. "Are you sure, Master?"

The boy pressed a hand to the man's shoulder. "Quite, Captain...?"

"Sousa," the Captain offered.

"Here, for your trouble." The boy handed Sousa a gold coin, one of the square ones from Mirik, before turning to Keplan. "Come on then, we ought to be moving on."

Keplan hesitated only a moment before dusting himself off and hurrying after. After rounding a few corners, the boy leaned against the stone of the building at the head of a narrow street. An uncertain giggle bubbled from his chest. "Were you really going to pick my pocket?"

"I was trying to get your attention." Keplan fixed him with a hard stare. "Why did you lie?"

"You don't look like a pickpocket. My pa always said I'm too trusting, but you looked horrified, not guilty. And I have few friends here who aren't nobles." He shifted his feet. "Why are you staring at me like that? Why did you want my attention?"

Keplan looked down. Lying came easier to him now, and truth did not bring safety. "I saw the snake pin on your shirt—I had a saddle blanket with the same mark."

The boy laughed, the sound light and loud. "Fair enough. Who are you?"

"Keplan Wardyn." He held out his arm in greeting, then remembered he addressed a noble, and tried to bow, only to realize he did not know which to use.

"I'm Azimir." His smile brightened his dark face. "Azimir A'hane of Mirik. My father is here on business and agreed to take me along." His eyes narrowed playfully. "I'm the son of an ambassador and the Military Commissioner of Mirik. How do you know nothing about me?" Without waiting for an answer, he rattled on. "Well, if you've never been here, would you like a tour? Where are you staying?"

Keplan stumbled over the stream of questions. *Nothing good comes from favors.* Yet something loosened in his chest, not strong enough to be hope or happiness, but it unfurled at the younger boy's words. He looked up at where Azimir waited with barely hidden impatience. Firas did not need him back for another few hours. "If you aren't busy, a tour would be nice. I'm staying at the Wise Hare in the slums."

Azimir jerked his head toward the east side of the harbor, grinning. "You have to see the Thread."

"Thread?" Keplan asked as he followed the boy's easy, confident stride.

"It's where all the merchants unload their warehouses for their stores. It's named for the silks and fabric they ship in, but they have everything there!"

Though Keplan knew many of Athrolan's streets angled down to the harbor, the city's plan was more complicated. The main streets did indeed lead from the highest points of the city to the docks, but on the tiers of buildings roads twisted, the whole looking like dozens of interconnected, tangled strings. Each "knot," Azimir explained as he hurried through the masses of people, was a district with its own name.

"The streets were built before anyone used carriages, so they're a mess. The three biggest streets are named, but most people navigate by tier and district. Waves' Crash is the street along the navy yards. Lane of the Sun connects the Guildhouses to the square where we met. Tzama runs straight to the palace, following the biggest aqueduct."

Azimir's excited chatter reminded Keplan of a squirrel. Though he could gain knowledge when looking at someone, he realized information was vastly different from understanding.

"What about yours?"

Keplan realized Azimir had been talking. "I'm sorry, I was distracted."

"I said my family comes here often. My father and brother at least. We're a small family. What about yours?"

Keplan turned sideways to let a two-team wagon lurch past. "Just my Ma and Da. I'm not sure if they ever visited."

Azimir turned to stare, but whatever questions were about to spill from him stopped when Keplan caught sight of the street before them. Ropes were strung between the upper storeys of the buildings, draped with fabric and skeins of thread. The colors were brighter even than the streets of Ban. The smell of dye and wet cloth hung heavy. The combination of metal, gems, silk, and carvings made the street seem like the hall of an opulent palace. Even the white paving stones shone from the boots, sandals, and slippers that polished them each day. City and private guards dotted each storefront. Sunlight filtered through wood screens and cotton awnings. Lanterns glowed from the warehouses of the glass merchants from Mirik, and the smell of oil and sawdust drifted from the ebony imports from western Val. Each stall of wares was an organized pocket within the general chaos. He grinned. "This is what my mind looks like."

Azimir's brows rose, but he did not respond, only going on to detail where each shipment hailed from. Keplan listened absently. They wound through the Thread, then up the Tzama and back across to the Market. Keplan learned each district had a distinct smell and sound as well as a name. By the time they returned, his stomach rivaled the rumble of the cartwheels on the cobbles.

"Would you like lunch? There are fantastic meat vendors, and I know a place to eat with a view of the harbor."

In truth, Keplan wanted to go back to the Wise Hare. His feet ached from pounding cobbles in his thin-soled boots, and his mind was exhausted from the press of people.

Azimir caught the hesitation and gnawed on his lower lip. "I'm sorry. Da says I talk too much. Did you want to do something else?"

"I'm tired, but food sounds nice. I don't have any coin, though. I eat at the inn where I work."

Azimir waved away Keplan's words and led him to a vendor on the corner. He bought them each a stick of rolled meat, bread, and vegetables roasted over a greasy fire. He handed Keplan the meal before nosing through the crowd to one of the aqueducts. A narrow, rusted ladder led up the side of the stone. The top was not much wider than a footpath, but it was cool, and the noise of the street below lessened. Keplan sat on the edge, enjoying the thrum of the water rushing beneath him.

"So, the Hartland, eh?" Azimir spoke around his large bite. When Keplan nodded the darker boy continued. "How long did you live there? What brought you to Athrolan?"

"My parents lived there since before I was born. I know my da was raised in a city called Vielrona. He says it's gone now. My mother never said where she came from, but her accent is different from his." He took a bite of the meat while he thought about the answer to the next question. The food was good, the spices more earthen and herb-based than the intricate flavors of Banis seasoning. "I came to Athrolan to learn."

Azimir glanced over with admiration. "You're young to be a journeyman. You must be talented."

Keplan stared at the stones. *I want to stop my mind from spinning and understand the images I keep seeing.* "I'm seventeen. I want to study history and politics."

"You're a year older than I am. The worms can have history, in my opinion. It's too slow for me, but I suppose if you like it well enough...." He shrugged, a gesture that accompanied the boy's every answer. Azimir stared off, silent for a rare moment.

Though he claimed to only be a year younger, his features were far more open than Keplan's. His nose was not as strong as his father's and his skin several shades darker. Warm brown highlighted his black hair. "Your father was in the war, wasn't he?"

"You want to study history, and you don't even know that?"

"My parents told me nothing of the war. I think it was a dark time for them."

"War's a dark time for most. The Dhoah' Laen was my Da's sister. Younger sister. She and the Rakos won the war, bound the world. She disappeared after that."

"My da had a book on the Rakos—they have the stone plates and the fire in their hands. She disappeared? The binding killed her, I suppose."

"No." Azimir's face was uncharacteristically serious. "She rode off and didn't come back. I never met her, but sometimes Da's face gets sad. I think that's when he misses her."

Φ

Warm purple bathed the sky, orange clouds scuttling after the setting sun. Keplan finished sweeping the courtyard and ducked through the rear door. His tasks were easier with daily maintenance, though the common room was always hopeless after the patrons got their boots and hands everywhere. There were still several hours before he would have space to himself, and he tried to sidle past the bar to his room.

"Keplan!" Firas grinned from his perch on a stool. "I was going to go dancing. Would you like to come?"

Keplan frowned. "I thought you work evenings?"

"Ah, but Mirrel does sometimes so I can go out and shirk responsibilities for a bit. Besides," he flicked a hand at where his older sister toiled in the kitchen. "I worked her morning today."

Keplan's brows rose at the lengthy response. The man was clearly well into his mug. "I'm afraid I have no knack for dancing." He grinned sheepishly. "Ma said I have crooked feet, and Da told me I was note-deaf."

Firas laughed. Drink flushed his cheeks, and his eyes sparkled with mirth. "You'd still probably dance better than most there, but suit yourself." He paused in the doorway, head tilted to the side. "Keplan, how long will you be staying?"

Keplan shrugged. Late at night, with the air soft through his window, he wanted to stay forever. "I don't know. I have no plans, no other place to be."

Firas's smile broadened, and in a whirl of blue shirt and patter of boots he was gone.

Keplan closed his door and flopped onto the bed. There was no use trying to nap. *Is this where I'll stay?* Home was faded and childhood gone. Returning would only be a jest of what once was. Firas and Azimir were so bright, finding happiness even in dark corners of the city. *How can they be happy? Is it as simple as ignorance?*

Keplan was still awake when the bartender returned hours later. Keplan was about to open the door to talk when he heard another, deeper voice laughing and muffled talk through the ceiling after the upstairs door shut. Other noises followed a few minutes later, softer ones, that made Keplan's cheeks flame.

When bells tolled midnight, he shoved on his boots and hurried down the stairs. The common room was warm, and the fire crackled in the hearth. He placed the chairs up on the tables and bar before thoroughly sweeping the rough wood clear. He had almost memorized which spots were burn marks rather than spilled food. The task cleared his mind. When Mirrel emerged to set out washed mugs he was already hanging the broom and mop in their place behind the counter.

"Do you need supper?" Her voice was low, more tired than usual.

He turned, unable to hide his surprise at the offer. "I ate in the city, thank you though."

Her brows rose. "With what coin?"

"I made an acquaintance. He bought me food."

Her mouth thinned. "Be careful, Keplan. Not everyone is out to pay you favors." Her face softened. "Though I imagine you know that better than most. I have a bit of cider leftover. Care to finish it with me?"

He sat wordlessly, afraid if he spoke she might change her mind. The steaming half-mug warmed his heart as much as his hands. "I like the spices you use. They're rich."

She grinned, the expression very like Firas's. "It's our da's recipe. He taught our mother to make it too, but it was never quite right."

"Firas said he was in the war."

Mirrel looked down at her mug. "He never met our da. I barely remember him. Both of us look more like my mother's blood. I miss him, sometimes. More, I miss what moments we could have had." She glanced over. "Both your parents are still about?"

"Yes. They lead a simple life, but I think they're content. They don't mention their lives before me, though. Perhaps that is what keeps them happy."

"I wish I knew their secret." Melancholy shadowed her smile. "It's lonely, working all the time."

"You have Firas."

"He doesn't like serious talk. Besides, he is scarcely still long enough for me to speak to him."

Keplan snorted into his cider. "I heard him come home before I came down to clean."

"I doubt he was alone."

"He wasn't."

She grinned at his dubious tone. "Now you know why I put you in that room. None of the paying patrons would be able to sleep with his ruckus."

"Perhaps I'll forget to mop tomorrow after having such a poor night's sleep." He twirled his near-empty mug slowly. "I wish I knew their secret too. Firas's and my parents'."

"Then I'd have no one to talk to." Mirrel nudged him with her shoe. "Go head up to bed. Perhaps they'll pause in their lovemaking long enough for you to catch some rest."

He rose with a soft groan and stretched the stiff muscles of his back. "Thank you for the cider. And the talk."

She toasted him before draining her own mug. "And you."

He wound his way quietly up the stairs and locked his door behind him. Loneliness still weighed on his heart, but his mind was still. He might have been alone, but he took strange solace in knowing he was not the only one.

Nightmares woke him just before dawn, sending his heart thundering with the echoes of pain. He rose, rough palms brushing the still-tender scars on his chest. They were bright red against the tawny skin. He tugged a shirt over his head, angry at the Banis and at himself. His mornings were usually quiet, but his mind needed distractions.

He hurried downstairs, nodding a good morning to Mirrel as he passed. Her scowl was back where it belonged, and she waved his greeting away. Trash and broken furniture and fates knew what else crowded haphazardly under tattered canvas in the stable. Keplan winced. *I hate messes.* He rolled up his sleeves and began with the bins.

Mist burned away as the sun marched up the sky. The sounds of the city changed. Constant wagon wheels and hooves on cobbles grew louder, replacing pockets of low laughter and conversation. Keplan paused to wipe sweat from his brow and perched on the stoop to survey his work. Moly wickered at him from over the stable's half door. The courtyard was clear, the bins neatly lining the small space behind the stable where they would be out of the way. He had untangled the jumble of leather piled by the rear door. It was an old harness for a horse-drawn rickshaw. The vehicle itself he had moved from a disused stall and parked beside the stable under the canvas. He brushed the wood with a hand, smiling at the smooth warm grain on his skin.

A young man with Firas's smile drove a woman home to the Wise Hare. Stolen kisses and a promise before war. He jerked his hand away with a frown. He glanced back at the rickshaw as he retreated to the common room. Objects had never given him memories before. He pushed the thoughts aside and found a thick piece of parchment behind the counter. He was bent over the bar, pen in hand, when Firas stumbled down the stairs.

The bartender's eyes were bleary, narrowed even in the common room's dim light. His neck was scraped red from someone else's beard, and love-bites dotted his collarbone. He offered an incoherent groan and tottered into the kitchen. He reemerged a minute later with a mug of something that looked better suited to a privy floor. He slumped onto the stool beside Keplan and peered at the parchment, only one eye focused. "What's that?"

Keplan turned the drawing so the older man could better see. It was a sketch of the rickshaw pulled by the bad-tempered gelding. A few lines topped the drawing.

"I can't read, lad."

Keplan's cheeks flamed. "I didn't realize. It's an advertisement. I found the little wagon in the stable while I was cleaning, and with some care the harness could be made usable again. If you provided service to the docks and markets, you might draw more customers. I'd be happy to be the driver."

"You cleaned the stable?" Firas's frown deepened, though Keplan did not know whether it was from a headache or thought. When Keplan nodded, the older man looked down at the picture. "That thing hasn't been used for years, but we kept it for sentimental reasons."

"It was a reminder after he died in the war." The words were out before he thought better of them.

Firas glanced up sharply. "Mirrel tell you that? It's not the kind of story she'd share unless she was warning you not to mess about with it."

Keplan grasped onto the excuse only to be interrupted by the inn door banging open. Visitors in the afternoon were uncommon, patrons not arriving until their duties elsewhere were finished for the day. Azimir leaned on the bar, watching Keplan with a bright smile.

Mirrel bustled out of the kitchen, glowering at Firas, who seemed happier to sit. "Welcome, lad, what can I get you?"

"I'm Azi, Keplan's friend, actually."

Her suspicious gaze eyed him from toe to top. "Will you stay long?"

Azimir glanced at Keplan. "I've got a few errands to run, and I thought you might want to come along."

"We'll head out, thank you, Mirrel. I'll be back for supper and to tidy." Keplan led the way out the door, breathing deeply when he was safely out in the street. "I'm sorry to rush you out of there, but I needed air."

Azimir glanced back through the window at Mirrel. "Why, when you have her to look at?"

Keplan stared at the younger boy, confused. "What?"

Azimir rolled his eyes. "That woman, she's a pretty one. Let's go to the markets. I need to find a gift for my brother."

Keplan snorted and fell into step beside him. "Her words are far from pretty. She bites worse than a snake. Firas is kinder."

Azimir glanced over curiously. "Do you prefer the saber to the shield?"

"Excuse me?" Keplan frowned.

Azimir's laughter bubbled from his chest. "Are you more for the menfolk? Are you courting your own?"

"Fates, Azimir, I understand now." The euphemisms tugged a smile onto his face, however, and he felt his steps lighten. "I haven't given it any thought."

Azimir stopped and stared at Keplan, incredulous. "You're seventeen and you've not had a lady or a fellow?"

"Azimir, I lived alone in the woods with my parents until just several weeks ago. What chance, really, would I have had? I wasn't about to jump into the trees with the squirrels."

Azimir doubled over at the thought, his raucous laughter drawing stares.

Keplan's nerves flamed at the unwanted attention, and he nudged the boy with his foot. "Come on, I thought you had errands to take care of."

Azimir's laughter trailed them to the market and Keplan scanned the crowd. Between Azimir's curious questions and his slip about the wagon with Firas, he felt exposed. His legs tightened with the instinct to run. Facts flooded his mind each time he glanced sidelong at the crowd, as if heightened by his anxiety. Azimir paused by a table of jewelry, and Keplan waited for him a pace away. His narrowed his eyes at his new friend's back. *Still nothing.* He shook the curiosity away and focused on his surroundings.

It was close to evening. Sailors and barmaids replaced housewives and children. Cooking meat and pipe smoke underscored ale and burning lamp oil. Keplan may have felt out of place on the streets during daylight hours, but nighttime brought security. He could be anyone. The scars on his cheeks were simply shadows in the low light, and he was one of many foreign young men.

A raised voice arched over the crowd, and Keplan glanced over. It was the same barker he had paused to listen to his first morning in the city. He stopped again. The litany was much the same, with added portions about how trade would fall and the city folk would starve. It was tailored to a poorer, working crowd.

"Azimir," he drew his companion back from his pursuit of a gift. "What is this talk of civil war?"

"I'll explain while we eat. I'm tired and Alleanthus is hard to buy gifts for." He insisted they eat at a bar stall, buying them both a mug of ale and platter of chicken to share before he spoke. "Her Majesty Tzatia is ill, and she disinherited her only heir years ago during the war. Many worry she'll pass without naming a new heir, though who knows who it could be. It would pitch Athrolan into civil war."

"Imagine being thrust into that fate?" Keplan shuddered. "If they do exist, I pity them."

CHAPTER NINE

The 20th Day of Lineme, 1272
The City of Ceir Athrolan

AN'THOR GLANCED UP WHEN Bren opened the door. The general frowned and shuffled his papers into order. "I thought there was another day before we met."

"I'm not here in any official capacity." Bren slid into a chair across from the Ageless man. His features were carefully schooled, but he was a soldier first and An'thor an observant man.

He's afraid. An'thor waited for the man to speak, pale fingers picking at themselves while his gaze did not move from the ambassador.

Bren's eyes flicked to the conspicuously empty chair at the head of the table. "I heard a rumor, An'thor. A distressing one."

"And I've heard one as well, Brentemir, but I doubt you are here to discuss the new brothel opening on Jen Corner."

Bren scraped his hand through his hair. "I'm tired of dancing. Speak plainly."

"The time for that ended when I became general of Athrolan and you were the Military Commissioner of Mirik. We're locked in this dance of kingdoms, and eventually the song will change."

Bren rolled his eyes at the flowery language. "You're a better warrior than poet."

"My legends won't write themselves, I fear."

"Tzatia's dead, isn't she?"

An'thor's fingers stilled. "That's a poor rumor to breathe life into, Barrackborn." He wanted to draw his sword on the younger man, to weep and confess all at once.

"It's a poor truth to keep from your own kingdom."

My kingdom. That is what Athrolan has become. If he had to burn to keep the city's flame lit, he would light the match with his own hands. "You came to ask if the rumor was true? If I'm hiding the queen's dead body from her own people? Denying them mourning and a new leader?" He shook his head. "She's ill. Her strength will leave soon. For now, though, she fights."

"Then you can tell her to renege her declaration about Alea's son." Bren's voice was hard, but it was with desperation, not sadness. "They deserve peace. They deserve freedom. There is still time to reinstate Daymir."

Certainty sunk its claws into An'thor's gut. "So there is a child."

"You know as well as I do that they disappeared. Who can say if they're even alive? But wherever they are, they deserve peace." Bren rose, clearly through with his demands. "I'll see you tomorrow. Perhaps then you'll have brought Her Majesty to her senses."

An'thor let the ambassador stalk from the room. His mind churned with Bren's careless words. It was only a matter of weeks before the truth of the queen's death wormed its way out of his careful plans. Now, however, there was hope. Brentemir had said "son." *He knows where they are and that she bore a child.* Somewhere, Tzatia had an heir. There was a time when he shared Bren's sentiments about Alea and Arman, but it was not now. Peace was a luxury heroes never found.

Raven would not give him the time. The fact that the secret lasted a month spoke to the commander's idealism and fear. *He wants this to work out.* No one wanted civil war. Not a man as nationalistic as Raven. An'thor heaved himself to his feet. Rumors were starting, and he would be damned if the truth escaped before he was ready.

He pulled on his cloak, though the balmy night did not call for warmth. He visited the queen's room each day, under the guise of tending the woman. The guards at her door rotated frequently. He was lucky that, from the outside, death seemed so similar to illness. *And that the queen isolated herself so much in the last year of her life.* He nodded to the guard. "Is the doctor in with her?"

"Yessir. He came an hour ago."

An'thor slipped into the foyer and carefully shut the door behind him.

The doctor sat at the desk by the door, a book propped on his knee. He glanced up. His face was lined and pale. His lips thinned at the sight of the general. "General Domariigo."

"Doctor." An'thor looked at the queen's bedroom door. "You've been well?"

"Well enough." He followed the Ageless man's gaze. "This is sick, you know. There are words for what you are, ones I won't utter in polite company."

"I've never been considered polite company." An'thor eased himself into the seat beside the man. "Ambassador Barrackborn told me he's heard the queen is dead."

The man blanched. "Are you accusing me?"

"Should I be?" An'thor's smile was bloodless. "I assume you love your wife enough to keep your mouth shut."

"I haven't breathed a word. I don't think it's any one man or woman who's let the truth slip, sir. The city's not blind. And there is the matter of the countess."

An'thor's eyes flicked to him. "You think she's given us up?"

"I couldn't say. And there is no 'us.'"

An'thor stood. "You may leave. We won't require your services until tomorrow. Thank you, Doctor." He waited until the man gathered his things and left before turning to the queen's chamber door. *Fates have mercy on me.*

The lock groaned as it turned. The door creaked inward, and he winced. The wave of sickly sweet rot buffeted him. He walked enough battlefields to control his roiling stomach, but his disgust at himself raged high.

The shriveled body on the bed no longer looked like Tzatia. It barely looked human. He slid the coverlet down, past the heaps of salt and sawdust packed around her body. She no longer rotted, her skin mostly leathered. The first week was the worst, before he thought to bring the salt to dry her. Unable to open the windows, for fear patrols would recognize the smell, he let the air stagnate between the stone walls. *At least the flies are gone.*

He smoothed her hair, covered her with fresh salt and a new, unstained sheet. "I'm trying to protect your wishes, I swear. I know I'll pay for this for the rest of my days, but please, wherever you are, forgive me." He pressed his lips to her brow. Her skin was stiff and acrid against his mouth.

"And there is the matter of the countess." An'thor's gut clenched. He smoothed the covers once more and stepped from the room. He refreshed the bowl of flowers and locked the door.

He did not bother to light his lamps. His hands found the bottle easily without light, and after draining a third, he donned the old clothes from the bottom of his trunk. The black breeches barely fit, and it took him a moment to fasten his jerkin over the paunch of alcohol. *Perhaps I ought to train with my officers more.* He pushed the thought aside and swung open his window. Spring mist shrouded the palace. The shadows of the guards were long, but he knew this particular window was rarely watched. It was why he chose it. He swung his leg out, then the other, dangling from his fingertips before letting himself drop. He hit the ground with a groan. *This must be why Bren chooses to rely on a sy network. We're too old.*

The houses of the noble district were ethereal in the backlit moisture. His feet traced the path to the tall manor belonging to the Count and Countess of Felden. He crouched at the rear gate and fumbled his lockicks out. It took a minute, many moments longer than it would have years ago, but he was in.

The small gardens were wilted and rain stained the whitewash to beige, though the front of the building gleamed white. Grass overgrew the stone path to the parlor's double doors. An'thor skirted the patio, counting windows. A lamp gleamed in the countess' study. He wedged the toes of his boots into the chipped mortar and hauled himself up. Waist-level with the window, he stopped. Countess Fiena was engrossed in a book. An'thor tapped at the glass.

Her eyes closed. When they opened, she was staring at him. She unlocked the window and stepped aside to allow him in. "General."

"Countess." He pulled himself over the window ledge and into the room. "Good evening."

She offered a chair opposite her own. The gesture was gracious, but she did not smile. "I wondered when you would come to kill me."

An'thor reared back. He had not realized it was his plan until he stepped into the garden, but somehow, she had known.

She must have seen the thought cross his face because her mouth quirked, and she said, "I'm not stupid. I've lived in this court my entire life—almost as long as you have, I would wager. I know when someone's days are counted. The moment I witnessed Tzatia breathe her last, I was as dead as she."

An'thor looked away. Despite all his paranoia and planning,this surprised him. "Why didn't you leave the city? You could be begging me, swearing you'll never tell. Why haven't you called the guards? Told your husband?"

"My husband is gone to our estates to meet with our son." She rose, moving to the window. The view from her study was of the city, just a sliver of one palace tower visible to the right. "I could beg or swear oaths. But I've already been questioned. That man, Peraan who is loyal to Daymir, he harasses me every day for information. Someone could blackmail me for the truth the way you've done to Doctor Jalmer—have you killed him, or am I the first?" She waved away his answer without turning to look. "Nevermind. Do you know what I learned, waiting on the queen?"

"I can imagine a lot."

"She was a phenomenal woman. Even weakened by war, she never broke. But what she taught me most was love. Not of family or men, for that I knew on my own, but the love of an idea, something intangible. When the gods were destroyed, Athrolan had already ceased its worship of them. Instead, Her Majesty taught me faith in Athrolan. You have your trust in the Dhoah' Laen. Commander Dorcal has his dedication to the Xain line." She swallowed audibly. "I have Athrolan."

An'thor's blood pounded. This was not how he planned it, if he truly planned it at all. The countess stood in the window, eyes harder than he bet his had ever been, and threw his faith in his face. "Fiena—"

"I'm not through, General. When I'm gone you will leave here, with these words ringing in your mind. It's not a condemnation, just a promise." She fixed him with her hazel eyes. "I'll die for this country, same as any of your poor soldiers. Not to keep your putrid secret, but because I know Tzatia would not want civil war. She believed in Athrolan more than anything. And she believed in The Dhoah' Laen's child. Her Majesty was old, but she was rarely wrong." She spread her arms out. "Stave off civil war for another few weeks. Bury her death with mine."

An'thor's hands shook. He stood. "I'll need you to write a note."

"Suicide? How poetic."

"Don't. Don't be like that. Cynical, harsh."

"No offense, but you don't know me." She went to the desk and drew out a plain sheet of parchment. "What do you wish me to say? I cannot bear to watch my queen pass, and I fear it will come soon?"

"Make it sound real, that's all." An'thor tilted his head, scanning the words as she wrote for treachery or code. If there was one, he could not find it. It was straightforward, the tone exhausted. His heart clenched.

"Satisfied?" She looked down when his eyes met hers. "As much as the city may think you're a traitor, a monster, I don't. I doubt you'll rest easy ever again." Her hand found his. "Get this over with."

He slid open the drawer of the desk, fingers feeling for her letter opener. The razor edge caught the chapped skin of his thumb. *Just as I suspected, a weapon hidden in plain sight.* He wondered if she saw the fear in the black depth of his gaze, the fear not mirrored in her own. "I pray I find half the strength you have."

Her lips quirked in the corner. "I think you will be disappointed."

He stepped close to her, shaking hand pushing the blade against her wrists. His heart hammered. Skin was more resisting than he remembered, and he stopped. Her face was smooth, even the lines from court life feather light in the face of death.

She met his gaze, expectant.

He bore down again. His grip faltered and he fell back. "I can't."

She grabbed his wrist, fingers hard, firmer than he would have imagined. She dragged his hand down, the letter opener sinking across her wrist once, twice. He grabbed her other arm and finished the job, his cheeks as wet as their hands. She staggered, hip crashing into her desk. The carpet turned from blue to burgundy.

An'thor guided her to the chair by the window. "Do you want me to stay? It'll be a few minutes."

Her breathing hitched. "No. Leave me. Let me die with my family's portraits around me. You are little more than a stranger."

He dallied another minute. "I'll remember this. Your family won't. Your kingdom won't, but I will. When the truth is finally known, when Athrolan is safe, I'll sing your praises. I'll sing them till the day I die."

"Always the poet." She flicked her hand, sending blood spurting down her skirt and across the arm of the chair. "Go." Her eyes, half-focused, roved up his face. "Love and luck go with you."

He swallowed the ball of lead in his throat and crawled from the window, pulling it shut behind him. A greased thread pulled the latch down from outside. He tucked the string away, eyes still fixed on the dying woman. *Go.* The last thing she saw should not be a shadow hulked in her window, but the scattered lights of the city she died to save.

He climbed down to the garden, locking the door behind himself. The streets were dark. Mist drifted, ghostlike, across the cobbles. He made it halfway across the district before the manor bells sounded the tragedy. The wall met his back, cold and hard. He slid down the stones, heedless of the gutter filth soaking his breeches. He had killed before. He would kill again. *Some deaths are harder than others.* He knew ghosts were only manifestations of guilt, but that did not stop them from haunting him. He dropped his head to his hands and wept.

Φ

The 25th Day of Lineme, 1272

Lanterns, hovering like starflies, rose in Keplan's mind. They flitted around the city, a hill of stacked earth huts. Keplan stepped through Ban's gates, laughing and calling greetings. Instead of greeting him in return, they stared, like Hi-taln. They pressed closer until he had to shoulder his way past. He could not stop his steps. Hands prodded him, grabbing his clothes until they dragged him down. Pain blinded him, white and burning. Acrid smells assaulted his nose – blood, a latrine, hot metal.

And then he was in darkness with only the sound of his breath. The space was silent. Something glimmered before him, a reflection of his own moon-pale face. There were differences though. The scars were deep, wet cuts again and his palms bloody. Salt and ink ground into the flesh under the abraded skin. It was far gorier than when he had received his tattoos.

"What is this?"

"Humans are terrible." Though his own lips did not move, those of his reflection did.

"Why are you showing me this?" Keplan's gut clenched in horror.

"You won't speak to me again." The words were quiet. His reflection's gaze was eerie and bright, almost colorless.

"How? You're a part of me."

"One of us has to die. They will kill you, and only I will remain."

His chest heaved, sweat cooling on his skin. His window was open, but he still felt trapped. The walls pressed in on him. He rushed through the door and down to the stables. Moly poked her head over the stall curiously, nudging him with her nose. She seemed more at home than she had in Ban. Keplan smoothed his hand over her flank, over the knots of her old Athrolani brand.

An Athrolani brand and a Mirikin blanket. Keplan's thoughts tore past the curiosity. A sharp breeze blew through the open door from the ocean. It carried the sharp smell of brine and smoke. His vision darkened, and images flickered across the backs of his eyelids. *Screams, crashing, the smell of ocean and fire. A woman's muttered words, answers in a deep, burning tone. And then he was suspended over a battle, incorporeal, as chaos reigned. It was a plain, or had been, but one side was covered in roiling black water, the other in towering white-hot flames. Again he heard the voices, louder in his mind than the sounds of death and fear.* The Dhoah' Faer, and the Earth Shaker, *he realized, as with each phrase the elements raged higher.*

Strong arms wrapped around him, rocking him. "Come back, 'Lan."

His eyes flew open, and he realized his throat was sore from shouting. He shook worse than before.

Firas held him gently, pulling away slightly as he came to. "Are you all right?"

They were still in the stable. Moly pawed at the corner of her stall, spooked by the noise. He nodded. "I'm fine."

Firas's brow rose. The usual jest and wry wit were gone. "You looked like you were having a fit."

"It was just a dream."

"You were asleep in the stables? I think not. I heard you run out here a minute ago."

"I wasn't asleep," he admitted before catching himself. He ran a hand over his face. "Never mind it. It's over now."

Firas seemed ready to say more, but his gaze fell to Keplan's exposed palms. "Keplan...." He took one hand in his, touching the tattoo carefully. When Keplan made a weak attempt to pull away, Firas's hand tightened gently. "Not everyone is going to hurt you, you know." He tilted his head. "One of my da's friends, who took care of my ma after the war, had nightmares. Sometimes he wasn't even asleep. When we see terrible things, our mind does that, as if it's trying to fix the memories, revisit them and somehow change what happened."

"I'm sorry I woke you."

"Nonsense. Let's get you back to bed. Dawn will come early." Firas helped him to his feet and followed him back upstairs. He waited as Keplan fumbled with his door. "I know Mirrel says I'm flighty, and never take a moment to be serious, but if you need to talk, honestly, I'm just upstairs."

Keplan smiled. The expression felt wrung out on his tired features. "Thank you."

Firas leaned in and pressed a kiss to Keplan's brow. "Feel better, 'Lan."

Keplan crawled back into bed, his sheets still warm from before. His body and mind were exhausted, but his thoughts refused to cease spinning.

Φ

The 30th Day of Lineme, 1272
The City of RoBal, Ban

Patrols doubled in beyond the Hall of the Purple Throne. It was evening when the floor shook with rushing feet. Rih flew to the window and shoved open the curtains. Women thronged around a wagon in the courtyard below, movements furtive. Rih's stomach knotted. The cart bore a wicker basket in the unmistakable oval shape of a coffin.

Please don't be Ki-elte. The woman was impatient and exuberant, but she was kind, and Rih appreciated their time together. They carried the coffin into the women's quarters, followed by the shaking driver.

A moment later Rih's door swung open. Ki-elte stood in the doorway. Summer sun tanned her face, and travel stained her robes. Her usually playful eyes were marred with shadows. "I'm glad you're awake. I'm sorry I was away so long."

"Has there been another accident?" She did not think much on the first time Ki-elte was called away, but the memory returned to her now. She repeated the question in writing.

The other woman's face was pale. "No, not really." She gestured to the ceiling. "The gongs rang for an assembly a few minutes ago. We're wanted in the women's hall."

Rih tucked slippers on her feet before following down the corridor. The women's quarters were built for privacy and contemplation, and so there were few large common areas. The exceptions were the baths and the low hall set into the basement of the building.

Like every room, silk draped the walls, cushions covered the floors, and even the table on the low dais in the back was rounded and richly patterned. The air was close, even for a summer night. Most of the seats in the front were filled.

Hundreds of footsteps shook the floor.

Ki-elte gripped Rih's hand. "I wish I could stay, but I have to speak." Her fingers clenched. "I'm sorry."

Rih watched her go, heart thundering, a thousand hooves on the battered ground of her chest. *Why is she apologizing to me?* Ki-elte ascended the dais and raised a hand. The crowd must have quieted, for the air stilled and her lips moved. At the distance, Rih barely made out a single word. A hand on her arm drew her attention to Hi-alan, two rows back. The piercer moved closer until she stood just beside Rih.

"I'll translate for you. She's talking about our negotiations with Mirik."

"Thank you." Even relief could not loosen the knot in her gut.

"Many of you know our role in the palace. Our role in the beds of our lords, our commanders. Some of us do not fight our war in the city. Many fight it in the distant small towns, in derelict army camps. And some fight it in foreign nations. Sa-at was one such warrior. She was traded out of the city and brought to Mirik. Hypocrites—they may not buy human flesh, but neither do they question how their exotic whores arrive.

"Sa-at reported to us, and we reported to the Imperial Inquisition. Four weeks ago her messages to us stopped. We were told of her death a week ago. It is not rare for us to be the first casualties. Around her wrist was a set of beads, symbolizing a single word: Hetmir." Hi-alan's fingers faltered as she spelled out the word. Tightness around her eyes told Rih the stumble was from emotion, not the guttural foreign title.

"Hetmir, a title assumed by the military leader of Mirik. And only during times of war. As of tonight, Ban is at war. Our sisters will march, to victory perhaps, but to their deaths. And in our way, we march with them. We will hold an appreciation for our sister Sa-at tomorrow at midnight. After, we go to battle." Hi-alan paused her translation to sign, "Ki-elte is asking us to recite the Woman's Code." She raised her arms, and around them the others did the same.

War. Rih's fingers trembled as they rent the words from her heart. "A woman has a single mind. She wakes for the Empire. She marches for the Empire. Her blood and heart and mind are Ban, breathing and alive. A woman has a single mind."

Φ

War barely changed the bustle of Ban. Poor still clamored for food, and stagnant water clogged with waste. The rich still lavished themselves with luxuries and gemstones. Dust rose higher beyond the walls each day, drummed from the earth by thousands of sandaled feet. Rih watched the red cloud drift across the tangle of Stytown. A gust of air told her the door had opened.

"You wanted to see me?" Ki-elte greeted Rih with shaking hands. Her expressive face was stoic.

"I did." Rih paused, her mission forgotten for a moment at the pain on Ki-elte's features. "You were close to Sa-at?"

The woman nodded, lapsing into voicing. She recognized many of Rih's signs now, but often forgot to use them herself. "When she lived here, we were lovers."

Rih looked down. "Then I grieve for you." She let the signs drift in the air between them for a moment. She pulled a chair out for the other woman and sat at her desk. It took a minute to shuffle through the scrolls and tablets before she found the right one. She handed it to Ki-elte without preamble.

"Fear," Ki-elte read.

Rih produced the larger tablet she used for conversation.

> *You asked me what commanded the Emperor. It is fear. I think I understand our role now, since Sa-at. We are invisible. We fight for Ban in a way the men cannot. We influence. We suggest.*

Ki-elte frowned. "Fear rules us all." Her hands knotted in her lap. It could have been a sign of weakness. The metal in her eyes, however, said it was determination.

> *But you are right. We are not allowed to be truly a part of this world, but neither are we spared its fate. War destroys so many plans, so many lives.*

Rih looked away. Ki-elte placed her anger on Mirik, and while she was not wrong, Rih did not wholly agree. "*Perhaps she has to, to survive this.*" She straightened. "I meet with Mosil today, correct?"

Ki-elte made her repeat the two signs, then nodded. Her face brightened as she dug a broad, flat box from her clothes. "I brought you this."

Rih flashed her a smile and took the offered box. It was the plain wicker of a market ware, but the grasses were painted in bright stripes designating the shop was in a nicer district. Inside, a silk net lay on a bed of silk. It was a deep burgundy, shot through with white accents. The weights were cloudy sapphires chosen for their muted pink. Rih brushed the gift with careful fingers. As a soldier, she wore only what she was given, and the gifts to commemorate her induction day each year were few and practical. For years she turned her envy of courtesans' finery into scorn. "Thank you, this is beautiful!"

Ki-elte smiled, and her rare signing was perfect. "I'm glad you like it."

Tears blurred Rih's reflection too much to fasten it.

Ki-elte's gentle hands draped the net over Rih's shaved scalp. Two tiny bronze cuffs clipped to the top of her ears, holding the silk in place. By the time she finished, Rih's emotions calmed enough to see the handiwork. Though it did not match perfectly, the burgundy accented her purple outfit. *The color of Ban. The color of blood.* She squeezed Ki-elte's hand and thanked her again.

"We should go." Ki-elte reminded her.

Rih gathered her tablet and stylus and followed Ki-elte through the halls. The Purple Throne was subdued since Sa-at's death; even in the height of the day the bustle lacked its usual playfulness. Rih looked forward to her cousin's smile and the distraction of learning.

When the door opened, however, Mosil waited in the center of the room. In place of his usual casual robe, he wore loose breeches tucked into tall boots, a fitted shirt with buttons along the forearms, and a thick brocade jerkin. His hair was scraped back into an ugly horsetail. Sweat beaded his brow despite the open window.

"You look uncomfortable."

"Address me properly." Despite the curt words, his expression was gentle, and he gestured to his attire. "Pretend I am your future husband. This is your presentation at the Mirikin court, such that it is. We still hope for negotiations."

This is a test. She stopped at the edge of the dance floor and bowed her head. She understood now why Ki-elte had encouraged her to wear her new net. *This is my armor now.* She tucked her foot behind and bent into an Eastern curtsey. She watched his spoken introduction then rose from her curtsey and signed her reply. *Will I be able to bring a translator with me?* Perhaps one of the women in her entourage would know enough signs to help.

When he extended his hand, she took it. When the time came would her hand tremble? Unlike during her lessons, his finger did not tap the rhythm against hers. She glanced at the musicians, counting as the drummer began the song. Her first step was uncertain, but Mosil's arm across her back tugged her left, and she fell into the movements. He made small talk, and though she only caught a few words, she saw he discussed the weather, the drapery, and the food they apparently consumed at their imaginary supper earlier. His smile was kind, if vacant. *I wish I could marry him. A man I know.* But baring impending war, she would marry the son of Mirik's Hetmir.

She almost collided with Mosil when he stopped. She blushed and gestured an apology.

He smiled and stepped away. "You did well," he signed. "A few steps out of place, but you will practice."

"How long until the negotiations are final?" *How long until what freedom I have is gone?* She followed him across the room to the tray of juice and fruit, watching his mouth curve down as he explained.

"It's difficult to say, Rih-elte. Negotiations are still underway, despite them declaring war. I wish politics were simple, but maybe then they would not intrigue me so. With luck, you will be married, and we will be at peace by the time the rains end."

"And what more do I have to learn?"

He glanced at Ki-elte but did not meet Rih's eyes. "What is left is not for me to teach. You will continue to meet with me, but only every fortnight. Ki-elte and the other mistresses will begin your tutelage in the carnal arts."

Rih choked on her juice, setting the cup aside before it shattered on the brown stone. *Of course. I am studying to be a wife.*

Ki-elte appeared at her elbow and motioned that they should leave. They returned to Rih's room, and Ki-ete ordered tea. If she spoke, Rih did not notice. Despite her usual restlessness, Rih was glad to be between four familiar walls again. She touched Ki-elte's hand to get her attention. "When does that teaching begin?"

Ki-elte's brows knit. Dullness fogged her eyes again. "Technically it already has. Everything we are, our understanding of our place in the world, and how we affect it, in turn, plays out as lovers. I fear a heavy heart is not appropriate for these lessons, but I will do my best."

Rih's stomach tightened. Giving her body to battle, to arrows or blades or to be trampled under the hooves of her own cavalry, as happened too often, did not frighten her. Sharing it with a man she knew nothing of, whose appetites were unknown at best, was worse than death. She hoped Ki-elte would reassure her. Now it looked like the woman shared her dread.

Tea arrived and Ki-elte prepared Rih a mug heavy with horse butter and spices. She drew Rih's tablet toward her.

> *To begin, we must be relaxed. Tea helps. Massage. Baths. If your husband is not interested in sharing such things, you do them for yourself. Have you lain with anyone before?*

Rih shrugged.

> *No man. Some of the soldiers, when we were in training, we would explore. It was more out of admiration for one another's bodies and urges than romance. Others preferred female lovers. Sex interests me very little, regardless of the partner.*

Ki-elte smiled. "Women are often different lovers from men. We make good teachers. Communication is the most important piece to lovemaking."

Rih winced at the words. Lover. Lovemaking. She doubted those were privileges she would enjoy. "Communication? I can neither understand Trade nor hear."

Ki-elte shook her head.

In this, you have the advantage. Our bodies speak volumes. The press of a hand, the tilt of a head, the nudge of a knee, these are all questions your husband's body will ask. Your body will answer. You will likely marry a boy. He's inexperienced. He may have developed tastes, but you will know more than his common companions. I cannot promise anything, but I can give you the tools to make it as bearable as I can.

Rih grimaced

I have heard about the horrors most women marry. Sex is like battle.

"In some ways yes." Ki-elte offered a faint smile.

I will teach you how to give him pleasure, but moreover, I will teach you control of your body – when and if you have children, and whether you are more likely to conceive a male or female child.

Her smile darkened. Determination slipped her into speech. "We will endeavor not to attack his field of battle, Rih, but instead, force him to fight on yours."

Φ

The 49th Day of Lineme, 1272

By Midsummer, Keplan could have told anyone the best places to buy sweetrolls, bacon, a flock of sheep or a barrel of fish. He knew which sailor had an affair with whose wife, what child was the bastard of the Duke of Pardelan, and the human-trading intent of certain merchants. Much like in Ban, his days took on a disinteresting repetition. He was certain Firas noticed, and perhaps Azimir as well.

It was mid-morning, and his chores were through. Summer was in its full, the sun bright and uncomfortably warm. He perched on the poles of the rickshaw, attempting to mend the hooks for the harness.

The *swish-bang* of the rear door was not yet as familiar to him as the wind through Hartland trees. "Morning, Firas."

The bartender's laugh was low. "You should join the air-tumblers with balance like that." He leaned on the stable door. "Tonight is Midsummer."

Keplan hummed in response, eyes narrowed on his task.

"There will be a festival with dancing."

Keplan finally looked up. He lamented over not having a normal childhood, a normal life. Now when one stepped up and asked, he almost refused. *What is wrong with me?* "Azimir asked as well." He sighed and climbed down from the rickshaw. "When you went dancing you wore a colorful shirt. Do I need something better than my usual?"

Firas's second laugh boomed. "Just don't smell like dung, and for fate's sake deal with your hair!" He returned to the kitchen, leaving Keplan to put a bewildered hand to his head.

Φ

When Azimir arrived just before dark, Keplan was glowering at the tolstovka on the bed. "In the woods, no one cared what my clothes or head looked like!" Keplan groused without preamble.

"That explains an awful lot," Azimir joked. "I rather think you haven't cared before now."

"This is different. And I was told I had to do something with my hair."

Azimir's laughter started as a snort. Soon he was howling, collapsing on Keplan's bed and the offending shirts.

Keplan turned his glare to Azimir. It was fine for a dignitary's son, who probably had new clothes for each hour of the day. He tugged the whitest shirt from underneath his still-chuckling friend and turned to change. Azimir's laughter died at the sight of the scars.

"I'm glad you came here," the younger boy began awkwardly. "After what happened. You're fine company if a bit odd."

Keplan finished buttoning the off-center breast of his shirt and fastened his belt. What did one say to that? He chose to smile. "Firas said to fix my hair," he reiterated.

"I should imagine. Most everyone wears theirs short now."

"I am not cutting it," Keplan stated. His room had a tiny copper mirror by the door, and he peered into it at the tangled mess of dark brown hair. He grasped at Azimir's favorite hero. "The Earth Shaker had long hair."

"He also shot fire from his hands. No one's going to tease you long when you can burn them to cinders."

Keplan ignored the comment and decided to leave his hair down and loose for once.

Firas met them outside the inn. The barkeep elbowed Keplan with a broad grin. "I hardly recognize you." He fell into step on Keplan's other side, arms swinging widely as they strode up the street. "Did you have celebrations at home?"

"My parents lit a fire on a few holidays. What about you, Azimir, do you have the same festivals in Mirik?" With the conversation safely off himself, Keplan focused on the thoughts racing through his head. They may have been uncomfortable, but details about those around him soothed his anxiety. *Knowing secrets gives me control.* It was the same reason he avoided telling Azimir or Firas anything more personal than his taste in ale. His mind grew louder the closer they drew to the crowd. Loudest of all were the small details trickling through Firas's firm hand on his shoulder.

The city ringed the marketplace with ropes and lanterns. Great metal barrels held cheery, crackling fires. Shadows hid emaciated dust-dealers and beggars. The disorder was different than during the day, and Keplan felt at ease. His father sung loudly and often, and made a small drum and flute to play, but Keplan never heard music like this before. Whistles accompanied various drums and cymbals. Once he thought he heard a Banis violin. Pockets of dancing sprang up, blending into each other and curving around stalls of food and wares.

He leaned across to ask Azimir over the undulating ruckus, how one knew the steps. "There doesn't seem to be any pattern." His words jerked to silent when Firas pulled him into a knot of stomping, twirling bodies. Keplan gripped the other man's hand, as much to keep from falling as to follow his path. Firas looked back, playful eyes glinting in the firelight. A thought, not Keplan's own, tumbled into his mind at the glance. "You want to kiss me?"

Firas's brows shot up, his voice pitching over the crowd. "I didn't think you were that bold."

"You were thinking it, not me!"

Firas frowned, and it was a moment before his smile returned. "I'll let you know." The music changed, and Keplan followed him back to where Azimir watched the festivities.

"Let's get some egg-breads." The noble's mind was, again, preoccupied with food.

"I'll find some if you wait here." Dancing and embarrassment still flushed Keplan's face, but navigating the maze of stall to collect food allowed him to order his thoughts. He returned with a full tray and an awkward grin. "Here we are."

Firas's face lit up and he gathered his portion into his hands. He leaned over to plant a quick kiss on Keplan's cheek. "Perhaps you were right."

Keplan busied himself with eating to hide his sudden blush. If Azimir noticed, or cared, he said nothing. The loaf in his hands was round, stuffed with eggs, onions, and mushrooms. "This is possibly the best thing I've eaten in my life."

Firas snorted. "Your standards are low."

"What did you discuss in my absence? How much better my hair looks than Azimir's?" *I'm apparently rubbish at flirting.*

"I think it might look even better than my own. But no, Azimir was ogling the women."

"I enjoy festivals much more now," Azimir defended. "I can appreciate the scenery."

Firas rolled his eyes and glanced over at Keplan. "So, is this sufficient to bribe you into staying here?"

Keplan stared at the crowd. It was a jesting question, but it had a more serious answer. The mass of dancing city folk was a great pulsing heart, lit with firelight. Swirling colors and winking jewels like stars shining through late evening clouds. *This could be home.* He allowed Firas to throw an arm around his shoulders as he grinned. "It might be."

Hours later, Keplan slumped against the back of a stall, holding a leather flask. "You're hopeless."

Azimir swayed gracelessly to the music beside him. Though Keplan did not dance again, his feet tapped along when Azimir spun with first one girl then another. Firas excused himself half an hour before, begging drunkenness and the press of responsibilities the next morning.

"What makes me humpless?"

"Hopeless, Azimir." Keplan giggled at the other boy's misunderstanding. At first, he disliked the bitter alcohol, but it seemed to improve the more he drank. "The girl with the dark curls, she has a fellow already. The navy captain with the thick brows."

Azimir groaned. "I thought she was giving me lover's eyes." He glanced over at Keplan. "So do you just notice more or is it some sort of...." He wiggled his fingers over his own head.

Alcohol loosened the hinges of Keplan's tongue. "I see secrets. Things you don't wish others to know. Whatever you think most, your history, it jumps into my head."

"Show me!"

"Pick someone." The game continued, Azimir choosing from the crowd. It was a fickle gift, if it was a gift at all, but he could read close to a third of the folk Azimir chose. He rattled off what sprung into his mind with eye contact. Dawn was closer than dusk when they meandered from the square. Azimir paused where they parted ways.

"What about me?"

"What do you mean?" Keplan suppressed a hiccup.

"What do you see when you look at me?"

Keplan glanced over. *I can't see much of anything. It's part of why I enjoy your company.* He pulled a grin onto his face as he lied, "You want to bed a city girl before you go home."

Φ

The 2nd Day of Aeme, 1272

Grit in the bottom of An'thoriend's mug added a certain authenticity to the topic at hand. Despite the rich robes of the council members, cheap candles lit the table, and the meal growing cold before them was meager. "This talk is fine," An'thor remarked, leaning back in his seat to the right of the empty throne, "but what of the civil unrest in the Slummer and Merchant Town? I would rather be in ill-graces than be hamstrung while paying my debts."

"Rabblerousers in the Thread or Slummer scarcely equal civil unrest, General, even with your dramatic touch," the senior consulate scoffed. The Athrolani Council was rarely called to meet in full, the two branches often functioning independently. Since word of the queen's failing health spread, the entire force of noble-representing consulates and commoner-elected House of

Guilds had all but taken up residence in the meeting halls of the Ceir Athrolan's palace.

"Consulate Eron, please remain polite," An'thor asked, rubbing the bridge of his nose. "What's changed? Last I knew, you hoped to encourage trade."

"You're right." One man leaned forward, shipyard's insignia glinting on his breast. "However, few want to trade with an unstable kingdom. And there is the matter of a noble woman's suicide. If even the nobles are that concerned we do, indeed, have a problem."

Raven's brooding gaze rested on the paper before him as he toyed with a dry quill. He finally broke his usual silence. "The army is disbanded, sent to guard at home. The navy still barricades offshore, prepared for war between Ban and Mirik. Many of my navy men are still in port, however. I can send them into the city to bolster the guard."

"You bring a point," another consulate mentioned. "We are not at war, yet the general and the commander sit here as if there is a queen to flank and blood to shed."

An'thor's ring clacked on the table as he slammed his hand down. "Were Her Majesty not ill, she would be seated here to punish your insolence herself." The words echoed softly and settled over the tense conversation. "She should not be troubled by this. I, or her doctor, would be happy to convey your concerns to her, but she does not have the strength to sit state." His gaze swiveled to Raven. "Send aid to the guard, Commander. Our debts will wait until another day. Those of the Xain house arrive within the month. Until a decision is reached—and it will be, before Her Majesty passes into peace—Dorcal and I will remain." His use of the Commander's name made it clear they were united on the matter. *Despite his threat a month ago.*

With the meeting dismissed, the consulates of the House of Commons returned to the city. An'thor watched as the rest broke into their factions. When the door shut behind the last, his black eyes flicked to the commander. "Your men will not stop a revolution, Raven."

Raven fixed him with an exhausted stare. "Let it rest. You've made your point that Athrolan is weak. Let a lesser cousin take the throne and allow the queen some dignity. You've poisoned this. Between hiding her body, whatever you did to force the countess' hand—"

"I did nothing!" An'thor paced to the window. He drew a breath, then another. When he spoke again, his voice was too sad to be bitter. "I want to believe Tzatia knew best. I have to believe it."

"Her Majesty is what's best! Her blood, her line!" Raven's normally reserved features were rabid, then anger dissolved as his face sunk into his palms. "Fates, I wish she were still alive. She would fix this chaos."

"If she were still alive, we would have no chaos. I know you want me to tell them, but we need firmer ground to stand upon before we announce her death. Please, give me that time." An'thor paused, seeing the Commander's shaking hands. "You meant Eras." He frowned, staring out at the angry sky.

"You think she would do differently than I? Goodness knows you and she agreed on precious little when it came to state matters."

"She was one of us, loyal to the queen."

"She was asai!"

"She was more Athrolani than you will ever be!"

An'thor had heard and said far crueler words, but the fatigue of ruling weakened him to breaking. "If you wish to watch our city fall simply because you are too stubborn to change, then you are a fool. My blood does not make me care for her any less." Slamming the door as he left was childish, so he let it click carefully into place, but his blood seethed.

Raven's pragmatic nature once balanced An'thor's idealism during their private meeting and during council. Now it opened chasms where there had only been lines. His feet found the worn path to the tombs without guidance, and he sank to the floor of the Vault of Heroes. His capped horns clicked against the stone of Eras' grave. Across the way, the white stone of the Royal Mausoleum glinted. He had not sat there since the night of the queen's death. Instead, he had an agreement with the stone sealing Eras away—he paid it in conversation, and it refrained from making him weep.

He had no such agreement with the blank stone that would mark Tzatia's grave. *When I admit she needs one.*

"Raven misses you," he told Eras. "He wishes I were in your place. He hasn't said as much, but he might soon." An'thor slid a hand along the floor absently. "All the blooded claimants are coming to the city. It's months away, and even if we announce it, I fear the city will consume itself. Already there are supporters—paid and volunteer alike—of each royal cousin, barking at street corners and in the square as if our capital is a damn village hall. Raven's close to begging Daymir to return." He rested a cheek on the cool stone. "He does not realize I already did. Daymir refused. Alea refused. Civil war is inevitable, but I fear Raven and I will fall on opposite sides."

CHAPTER TEN

The 4th Day of Aeme, 1272
The City of Ceir Athrolan

BREN SAT AT HIS desk, Reka across from him, when Azimir clattered up the stairs. The door banged open, and Bren glanced up with a wince. "If you had a fraction of your brother's tact, Azimir, it would be a miracle." His eyes brightened, however, when his son dumped a tray of honeyed meat haphazardly near the stacks of paper. "I dislike you spending this much time in the city alone, but if this is the result, I might turn a blind eye." He glanced up at Reka. "Begging your pardon."

She snorted and waved the comment away. "If I cared about my condition, I wouldn't be here." She offered an arm in greeting. "I don't believe we've met."

Azimir grinned and took her arm with youthful enthusiasm. "I'm Azimir A'hane of Mirik, second son of Ambassador Brentemir Barrackborn."

Reka's mouth twitched wryly. "I'd gathered. I'm Monareka Elang, a correspondent for your father."

"You're a spy!"

Reka glanced at Bren. "Well he's bright, I'll give you that."

"I doubt it was my doing." Bren flushed and looked down. He and Kemmer's arrangement with Reka was one he still danced around. As much as he wanted both his sons to know the woman who birthed them, Reka's wishes were just as valid. *Alleanthus discovered it for himself, but there's no need for me to ruin a good evening.* He pointed at the door. "Regardless of how bright you are, Azimir, we have state business. And I meant what I said about being in the city alone."

"I'm not alone, I'm with Keplan."

Bren's eyes narrowed. It was difficult to adjust to the threats that came with his station. The threats on his children, however, he took far more seriously. "And who is Keplan?"

"We met shortly after we arrived. I met him in the market when a guard accused him of picking my pockets."

Bren's brows shot up. "And I assume you didn't think he actually was."

"He really wasn't, honestly, Pa. He lives and works in one of the inns in the Slummer. The Wise Hare."

Bren's frown deepened. "I know the place." After a moment he waved the boy away. "Please use sense. And go practice in the training courts. You could stand to work on your upswing." He glowered at the honeyed meat. When his son was gone, Bren turned back to Reka.

Her thick black brow quirked. "Shall I look into this Keplan?"

"Please. This is the first I've heard of him, but I'd like to err with caution."

"I'll take care of it. In the meantime, keep your boy busy. Elsewhere. It could be a harmless friendship."

"Or a potential kidnapping."

Reka jerked her chin at the paperwork. "Pick this up in the morning? I find myself in need of a walk."

"Indeed."

Reka returned to her small room in the city only long enough to change into common clothes. A few practiced wraps of a *jahi* and a light cloak later, she passed for a Sunamen trader. Bren may have had soldier's roots, but he was naïve and Reka knew enough to never trust a man who befriended a noble's son.

She crossed the city in a winding route through busier areas. Her network of gossips and spies was irreplaceable, but she learned a lot from her own careful listening. She sighed with appreciation as she stepped up to the Wise Hare. Four years had passed since work last brought her to its bar, but the old inn had changed little.

She slid behind a small table and dissuaded any ill looks with a bright greeting to the bartender. Firelight filled the lively common room. Most faces she recognized as sailors, with a few traders tossed into the mixture. None were young enough to warrant suspicion. She was almost through with her meal and mug before she heard anything of interest.

A quiet figure entered through the rear door, brushing straw from a pair of breeches that looked both too loose and too short.

"How'd the errands go, Keplan?" The bartender slid a plate of food and drink to a seat at the corner of the bar.

Reka's curiosity piqued. Long hair told her he either did not know current fashions, or did not care. Hardship was evident in slumped shoulders. Scars on his cheeks spoke of time ill-spent in Ban. Her gaze fell to the gloves, still on despite both heat and being indoors. *I'd bet good money those hide a crimson palm.* He flashed a tired smile at whatever the bartender said and set about eating.

He cleaned his plate, motions precise, and turned to rest his gaze on her. Cold settled in Reka's gut. Azimir's friend may have been world-weary, but he was no more than a boy. Ice-chip eyes and awkward features echoed in her mind. His attention moved on as suddenly as it settled. After discarding his dishes, he whispered something to the bartender and disappeared upstairs.

Reka recognized the fearful nature. *Just because he's a victim doesn't mean he means no harm.* Unable to find the bartender, she left a silver coin and a handful of coppers on the counter and slipped back onto the street. She took a deep breath of the evening's cool air.

"What do you want with him?"

Her hand fell to her dagger's hilt. "I don't know what you mean."

The bartender leaned against the wall, tucked into the shadows of the alley. All mirth was gone from his narrowed green eyes. "You've visited us before, each time watching your fellow patrons. Usually one in particular. This time you were interested in our new boy."

Reka sighed. It was clearly too long since she last gathered information on her own. "He keeps the company of a friend's son. I was concerned his intentions were ill-willed."

The bartender laughed, though it was not a happy sound. "I wondered when milord's family would take notice of his slumming. Enough nobles lie about their birth for a night and spend time in places like this. I recognize the signs." His features sobered. "I don't know Keplan's full story, but the family need not worry. He's harmless."

Reka crossed her arms. There was no threat in the bartender's stance, but her nerves were wary. "Where is he from?"

The bartender shrugged. "The south somewhere. He speaks Trade as though born to it, but isn't accustomed to a city. He may be Athrolani, maybe not." His eyes hardened. "I haven't asked. It's his business." The accusation was sharp and hung in the air between them.

Reka had far outstayed her welcome. "Thank you for the food and your candor." She tucked her hands in her pockets and strode away. Her thoughts returned to the boy's face. The intensity in his eyes nagged at her. Somewhere, she had seen it before. Whatever it was, she lay it aside with her cloak upon returning to her room. Her report to Brentemir was quick and to the point.

-B,

I visited the inn tonight and caught a glimpse of your son's new friend. He's about the same age, though appears to have lived enough for twice the years. Though skittish, I doubt he has any ill intent. The bartender was quick to defend him, and that speaks to his character.

She paused, wondering what else to add. Her gaze paused on the portrait tucked into her writing kit. A much larger version hung in Brentemir's study depicting the Dhoah' Laen, her Rakos guard, Brentemir himself and the general and commander of Athrolan at the time. It was a contrived portrait, one that none shown ever sat for, but the likenesses were good. Upon her appointment as Bren's spy master, she received the much smaller copy, and one did not refuse a gift from the acting king simply because aesthetic tastes differed.

Her eyes narrowed on the painting. Lyne'alea stared back from the canvas. A few shades lighter and her eyes could have been the boy's in the bar. She tugged the painting into better light, eyes flicking from Alea's to her guard's. *Strong nose, dark hair. Sharp chin, cheekbones.*

"Deershit."

Keplan came from the south, far from people. Lyne'alea's son would be close to Azimir's age. "What are the odds you found your way here and befriended your own cousin?" Far stranger things happened. *Especially when your blood carried that much power.* Still, Lyne'alea could have passed for a striking Athrolani woman in her youth, and Arman's features were common enough in the south. She scratched another line before folding the letter neatly.

Perhaps you can ask to meet him.
-R

She did not add a postscript.

Φ

The 7th Day of Aeme, 1272

Steady tapping of summer rain woke Keplan just before dawn. Damp air gusting into his room brought the smell of soil and ocean. He reached up to fumble the shutters closed, but paused. Mist hid all but the closest buildings and muffled the normal city sounds. It reminded him of home, as if someone showed him their idea of what his childhood had been. He finally pulled the window to, leaving just a crack for fresh air. The closed space was all the more reason to begin work.

The stable was nearly clean when a knock sounded on the door frame.

"Were you planning on taking a trip to the market?"

He flashed a quick smile, vaguely disappointed to find it was Mirrel. "I hadn't thought yet. I could if you need something."

"Just the supplies for the week. The wagon would be easier. I'll make a list."

In another minute he was wrestling for the gelding's head as he backed the animal up to the rickshaw. Ragweed was used to the young man now, but nothing helped the horse's disposition. Keplan managed to get into the street with only two new welts from Ragweed's teeth. The market was less crowded, and Keplan silently thanked Mirrel for her timing as he moved along the stalls. Her formidable list set Keplan's stomach growling.

He turned back to the slums, but hauled Ragweed to a halt at the clatter of shod hooves in the mist. Riders approached from the west, heavy-boned mounts draped in yellow and brown. They were armed and armored, the figure at their center bearing a fur-lined cloak over his bare head. Keplan's eyes narrowed on the Athrolani insignia. He was so preoccupied, it took a moment to notice someone stopped beside him. Keplan opened his mouth to warn Azimir of

Ragweed, but his words came too late. The younger boy cursed as he dodged the next attack. "You attract foul-tempered animals as well as people?" Even rubbing a stinging forearm, his smile was bright. He gestured to the disappearing recession. "What do you think of that, eh?"

"I think that is a lot of weapons for their mother city. Who are they?"

"Personal guards and soldiers of County Felden. The Countess recently passed." He switched topics with the usual grace. "Care for a ride?"

"Meet me at the Hare?"

Azimir grinned in response and took off back toward his manor. It was a matter of minutes before Keplan unloaded the wagon and returned the feral Ragweed to his stall. Azimir waited in the street with his own mount by the time Keplan groomed the temperamental beast and readied Moly for the ride. Despite his noble upbringing, Azimir took riding in the rain well, and Keplan was quick to remark on it.

"Fog comes in every morning over Mirik. It's as if we're the only land in the world until mid-morning," Azimir explained.

Keplan's eyes fell to the cob between Azimir's knees. The animal was a blood bay, with a mane most women would envy. The tack, too, was fine, but little helped Azimir's seat. "Are you sure you've ridden before, Azimir?"

The boy laughed brightly as they crossed the square. "My Ma says I've footsoldier's blood. Besides, look at your pony—you can't tell me you can do much better!"

Keplan snorted. Azimir's explanation always involved something his parents or brother told him. Keplan shifted his weight as they passed under the city gates, and Moly broke into a jaunty trot. If there was one thing he knew, it was riding. "Moly may be dignified in her years, but I grew up on her back."

"Where did you grow up?" Azimir asked. "I know you said the Hartland," he waved off Keplan's automatic response, "but I mean, did you ever visit cities?"

Keplan chewed his lip thoughtfully. "We lived a day's ride from Namus. My father visited often, but I only went occasionally."

"You're strange." Azimir held a hand up in defense, causing his horse to pause. "Fun, but bizarre."

Keplan's brows arched, but a grin tugged his mouth and he urged Moly up the slope. The landscape was enough like home to make him miss the smell of his mother's cooking drifting through the trees. The rain hissed on the grass.

"So, you had no friends?" Azimir had caught up.

"You and Firas are my first. I'm not certain about Firas, though. I knew better than to make friends in Ban." He winced at the thoughtless words and waited for Azimir's usual barrage of questions.

"They thought you were a Mirikin spy."

As grateful as Keplan was for the lack of judgment, the pity radiating from Azimir's face was worse. Plenty of people assumed, and probably most correctly, what caused his marks. Having someone know, for certain, made him vulnerable. *Secrets give them power.* "You said you were good at tracking," he began, not caring the subject change was obvious. "Do you hunt often?"

"My father has a close Border friend. I've only actually met her once, but she taught my father a lot. My mother is a skilled fighter as well."

Scars crisscrossed the eyes of the woman in Keplan's thoughts. Only one seemed to still function. "Your mother is partially blind? From the war?" The knowledge startled Keplan as much as the words surprised his friend.

Azimir's eyes narrowed on Keplan. "That's my father's Border friend. Our ma is Kemmer, Mirik's Military Commissioner and current Hetmir. Did you see her leaving the house?"

Keplan made a show of peering through the canopy to see how heavily the rain fell. "Something like that." He pushed back his hood and closed his eyes. The forest brought him peace. This was earthier than home and had a sandy smell about it, just as he could always smell the stone of the city. Forgetting himself, he stuck his tongue out to taste the rain as it rolled from the leaves above.

Azimir edged up behind him, and Keplan's hand darted out. He shook a sapling, dousing them both with rain.

"It got you too, idiot!" Azimir laughed, wriggling on his poor horse's back.

"I'm not a noble. It's quite fitting for me to be rain-soaked—I was raised by tree spirits." He angled his gaze at the vegetation around them. "Not strange white ones, like these, though."

Azimir laughed again. "Sometimes I can't tell when you're joking." He made a face when Keplan began to chew a strip of bark from one of the darker trees.

Keplan offered Azimir a piece. "It settles the stomach. My father makes beer from it."

Azimir declined but asked about the beer. He led the way further into the forest while Keplan explained the process. Their horses' hoofbeats changed from soft *whump-thumps* on the loam to *whack-skriss* as they climbed higher into the hills. The light rain from the morning turned to heavy blue clouds.

Azimir drew to a halt, nodding his chin to the bare hilltop ahead. A plain stone stood amid blackened trunks. It was white, stained from two decades of rain. It had been left uncarved, its rough sides smoothed by erosion. "Have you seen the Rakos' tomb?"

The small hairs on Keplan's arms rose as gooseflesh peppered his skin. "The Rakos is dead?"

Azimir shrugged. "There are a few different versions of the story. It's not a tomb for him, exactly. It is titled 'The Tomb of Madness.' General Domariigo said when the Dhoah' Laen joined the worlds again, she thought the Earth Shaker was dead. She camped here, and in the middle of the night, a thunderstorm raged, and the Rakos came to her. With one touch she erased his madness from the war." Azimir shrugged. "No one comes up here much anymore."

Sweat bloomed on Keplan's palms. *Blood boiling through stone veins, dust and dried gore cloying his throat. Insanity and power sloughing from his skin, sinking back into his veins.* He shuddered, stomach clenching. Moly tossed her head and backed downhill until they were once again outside the ring of scorched trees. The scent of woodsmoke drifted between the blackened trunks. "I envy him."

"Envy the general?" Azimir's voice seemed to echo from a league away.

Keplan shook his head, as much to rattle his thoughts back into place as to answer. "What I wouldn't give to bury madness."

Azimir's dark eyes widened, and he gripped his reins with white knuckles. "Your secret-seeing."

Keplan pressed his brow to Moly's wet mane. "I came here looking for answers. All I have is a name from years ago, and too many voices that don't belong between my ears. So yes," he drew a ragged breath, chest still yawning in the wake of a fraction of the Earth Shaker's power. "I envy the Earth Shaker's madness, washed away in a storm."

Azimir looked at him for a very long time, silent. Then he shrugged deeper into his cloak and turned away. "I think our cook will be starting supper, and I'm getting cold."

Keplan counted the retreating hoofbeats, hands knotted in Moly's mane. He was not sure what made him toss his trust at Azimir with an awkward confession. Whatever it was, he regretted every word.

"Well, are you coming? I thought you could meet my father." Azimir waited at the head of the trail, face puzzled.

Relief exploded in Keplan's chest. He tried to hide it, but by the time he drew abreast of Azimir, he was grinning.

The manor houses clustered on the highest tier of the city, built neatly against the barracks at the city's southern gate. Stone walls separated each house, small turrets flying various pennants. Azimir drew up outside the gate of a narrow manor with a small garden in the rear. Sounds of stablehands and horses drifted across the empty courtyard from the stable along the right wall. Azimir's face brightened as he dismounted and led them inside. It was strange to hand Moly over, and Keplan made sure to thank the young boy who took her reins.

"My pa is back." Azimir nodded to the gleaming chestnut mare that turned to eye them with interest. "That's his Dawn."

Keplan reached a hand out to the animal with a broad smile. The horse was beautiful and clearly well cared for. "A lovely name for a lovely girl," he said softly as he scratched her poll.

Azimir snorted. "Her full name is Blood of Dawn, and she's a powerful warhorse. Sweet here, but vicious in battle."

Keplan's brows rose, but he gave her one more pat before following his friend to the private courtyard in the back of the manor. He expected the same opulence of the nobles in Ban. Instead, the finery was understated, the colors simple. Green and vermillion featured prominently, but muted. The boys threaded their way through a potted garden and up to a large wooden double door, one side of which was open. Azimir tossed his cloak and riding gloves onto a rack at the door. Keplan did the same, though he kept his gloves on.

A windowed room down the hall offered a small buffet of fruit and bread, upon which Azimir descended with alarming excitement. Keplan had a mouthful of pear when a face peered into the room.

The man was several years older than they, but had the same dark skin and black hair as Azimir. "Azi, did you just return?" As Azimir nodded, the newcomer caught sight of Keplan and stepped inside. "You must be my brother's city friend." He held out an arm. "I'm Alleanthus A'Hane of Mirik."

Keplan took the arm gingerly. "Keplan Wardyn."

Alleanthus turned back to his brother. "Da's busy. A missive just arrived from our mother. He wants you here for supper, though he will not join you. I'm off to meet with our clerks." He returned to the doorway. "Well met, Keplan." He left as quickly as he arrived, and Keplan stared after him.

"The nobles here are different from what I expected."

Azimir spoke around a mouthful of fruit-decorated bread. "You thought we would be pretentious?"

"In Ban anyone inferior is like furniture. Or worse."

Azimir made a derisive noise. "My father never shook free of his humble roots. I'm told we show his influence more than we ought. Athrolani nobles are more traditional." He scraped more jam onto a slice of bread and gestured to the stairs. "Come meet him."

"Didn't your brother say he was busy?" Keplan noted as he followed Azimir up the curved stairway in the front of the foyer.

"I think he will like you. Besides, he asked to meet you. He dislikes me spending time with people he doesn't know well." Azimir knocked on the closed wooden door at the top of the stairs and opened it before an answer came.

Keplan trailed behind, eyes wide. The study was plain and dark, with a large desk behind which sat Mirik's Ambassador. His thin lips pursed in a frown as he surveyed a thick document.

"Not now, Azimir. The breakwater took on some damage in that storm last week. This could slow trade to nearly half, and with the war...." He trailed off and scratched his head before continuing. "Ask Al if it's something important." He glanced up then, flashing a quick smile at his son and Keplan. "Is this the boy you met?" His eyes dropped back down to his work.

"Yes. Keplan, this is my father, Ambassador Brentemir Barrackborn of Mirik."

"Keplan Wardyn, my lord." Keplan bowed unsteadily. "Forgive me, I don't know the proper way to greet someone of your status."

Brentemir looked up, frowning at the introduction. "And where did you say you were from? I understand you were not raised in the city."

"He didn't, Da, and he's not a criminal."

"It's all right, Azimir," Keplan muttered. The questions made his skin crawl. "I'm from the south, the Hartland."

The ambassador's gaze swiveled to Keplan's face then fell to the boy's fidgeting hands. "Thank you for humoring me. I hope you and Azimir enjoy the evening." It was an obvious dismissal, albeit polite, and Azimir tugged Keplan away, calling a brief goodbye to his father. "He's been scatter-minded lately. There's a lot of busy talk about Ban."

Keplan glanced back as the door shut. Brentemir stared through the rain-streaked window seemingly lost in thought.

Φ

Keplan woke on the floor of his bedroom, back aching and a hen's egg on the back of his head. "Damn," he hissed, probing at the offending lump.

"Do you always run about in your sleep?" Firas's voice was gentle. He stood in the doorway, eyes still bleary. Gooseflesh dotted his bare chest and shoulders.

"There's not enough time in the day to get things done." Keplan's voice was so soft, Firas almost did not catch the joke.

He grinned finally and padded over to Keplan's prone form to tug the blankets from under him. It took a second to remake the bed, though Firas left the sheets untucked. Keplan wondered if it was out laziness or distraction.

The women in Athrolan were strong and curved, and his body responded to them often enough. Firas was different. His build tended toward stocky and he moved with careless ease. Keplan realized the bartender had spoken. "What?"

"I asked if you wanted to talk. Is it often? You can't tell me you don't remember them." He settled on the end of the bed, elbows propped on his thighs. A short dark curl fell across his forehead, but he made no move to brush it away.

Keplan pulled himself to his feet and slumped onto the bed. "I remember them. It's not every night, but more often than sometimes." He glanced over. Firas was not running. Keplan touched one curl with his long finger before pressing his brow to Firas's.

"Can I touch you?"

Keplan nodded, nerves singing under his skin. Firas's hands brushed shoulders, skimmed forearms, smoothed the small of his back. Featherlight but assured.

Keplan mimicked the gesture, his movements hesitant. He leaned back, blanketing his body with Firas's. Heat followed the scrape of Firas's beard against Keplan's neck, and the younger man shuddered. The bartender may not have had curves, but Keplan's body did not seem to care. He stopped Firas's hand as it moved further down. "Just this, please."

He felt the other man smile against his mouth. "Of course. I'm patient." He brushed Keplan's hair back carefully and pulled him closer. "This won't make you forget, 'Lan."

Sensation and the breath between them silenced Keplan's thoughts. *With one touch she erased his madness from the war.* He raised his chin and kissed the other man. "You do not know that."

It was not screaming, or fire, or pain that woke Keplan the next morning, but sunlight. The sheets beside him were still warm. He sat up with a yawn, running a hand through tangled hair. A love-bite marked his chest beside his scar. Keplan did not know what he expected, or whether Firas was just another piece of denial in his chest. He only knew that his sleep had been dreamless.

Φ

Reka had just hung up her cloak when rapid pounding shook her door. She sighed and slid back the leather flap covering the hole in the wood.

"Reka, it's me. Please just open up."

She jerked the door open. "Was I right about the queen?"

"What?" Brentemir blinked. "No. Perhaps. May I come in?"

She gestured for him to make himself at home. The single room was sparse, made for little more than sleeping. The kettle chuttered over the fire, and Reka nudged the coals with the poker before stripping off her wet clothes and hanging them on a rack by the fire.

She glanced back to see Bren was staring at his hands. Usually, her lack of modesty triggered a reminder from him that he was, in fact, married. *As if I'm interested. There are far too many emotions there for my taste.* She tugged on a dry shirt and breeches and set out two mugs. "Alright. Tell me."

"She was in my life for all of a year and then gone as quickly as she came."

Reka rubbed the knots of scars on her nose. "If you want to reminisce, I'd rather not do it at this cursed hour."

Bren looked up. "You're angry." His expression bordered on bewildered, and Reka wondered when he last slept. "I was waiting across the way since this afternoon."

She heaved a sigh. "When will you act like a noble?"

He looked back at the portrait. "I think Keplan—Azimir's new friend—is their son."

"Do you?" Reka leaned back. "He's a wretch and troubled by eight kinds of darkness, but I think he's just a boy."

"I met him. I was distracted, focused on the war and problems at home, and I did not look at him fully at first. His eyes are my father's, and he has the nose we are all gifted with. But his mouth and jaw could be Arman's exactly."

"And you're not seeing these things because you just found out they have a son? I saw him," she reiterated, "and he could have been any Athrolani mongrel." Bren winced at her words. Whether it was her chosen term or disbelief that offended him, she wasn't certain.

"His surname is Wardyn."

"I know. You had me follow him for three days."

"He comes from the Hartland."

She fingered the handle to her mug. "All right. Let's assume—for the sake of your desperation—you're right. The Dhoah' Laen's son has returned to Ceir Athrolan. What will you do? You claim him as nephew and An'thoriend will grab him faster than you can declare war."

"If he refuses the throne, then Athrolan will be at war—it might even if he didn't."

She glanced at the writing kit tucked into her desk. Brentemir finally realized what she knew for days. "If anyone is their son, it's him, Bren. But you're wrong to drag him into this. What if he refuses to be your child-champion and end your war before it begins? When we discussed the queen's choice we assumed their child would arrive well before the queen's death, on a foaming warhorse, lighning in one hand, fire in the other. This boy is poor and haunted and possibly mad. You claim him, you rob him of his future just as surely as Alea and your blood robbed you of yours."

Φ

The 8th Day of Aeme, 1272

Had Keplan been given to whistling, the rafters of the Hare would have rung. The sun seemed warmer on his skin and the day brighter. When Firas shot him a smile across the common room, he returned it tenfold. He sat, cross-legged, mending a table leg. A particularly vigorous whack from the mallet sent pegs skittering across the floor. One bounced off the highly polished boot of the man standing in the doorway.

Keplan's eyes met those of Mirik's Ambassador. "Fates." He scrambled to his feet and bowed. "Would you like to sit?" His eyes fell on the un-mended leg. "Though perhaps not here."

Brentemir held up a hand. "I am not here officially."

Is there any other way for you to be? Keplan's pulse thrummed. "Is Azimir all right?"

"Quite. He doesn't know I'm here. Perhaps we could speak somewhere privately."

Keplan led the way, opening the door wide and allowing the ambassador through first. The space seemed much smaller with the tall man in its center. Keplan did not know where to stand. He leaned against the wall, only to straighten when Brentemir politely accepted the offer of a glass of water. "It was not so long ago I frequented this tavern. Seems like lifetimes, though." Brentemir was transfixed by the glass in his hands.

"You've come to ask me to leave your son alone." Keplan was frankly surprised it took this long for the man to stop his son's slumming.

"Not at all." On less fatigued features, Bren's expression would look surprised. "No offense, but such a request would not warrant a personal house call." He gestured to the narrow chair. "May I?"

"Of course." Keplan continued to stand and crossed his arms over his chest.

"Will you tell me about your parents?"

What is he getting at? "Not much to tell. They came to the forest a few years before I was born. I'm seventeen now. They built their homestead with their own hands and rarely left."

"And their names? Wardyn like yourself?"

"My father's is. Arman Wardyn. And my ma is Alea. I don't know what her surname was before they married." He frowned. "Or whether they married at all, actually."

Brentemir seemed to make a study of Keplan's boots. He was the picture of patience but for the white knuckles of his hands gripping the glass. After a moment he drew out a canvas. It was in the style of a lover's portrait—intimate, discrete. Discoloration at the edges showed where a frame usually rested. "May I show you something?"

Keplan did not move to take the picture, forcing the ambassador to rise and reach across the distance between them. The young man waited until Brentemir sat again before looking down. He frowned. It was one he knew well. It captured a moment of joy on the road. A young woman was mid-step in a fire-side dance. She wore traveling clothes and her black hair hung loose. The man she danced with was serious, but his eyes burned even through the dried paint and canvas.

Keplan tilted his head at the image. "Where did you get this?"

"I thought you would recognize them better this way."

Keplan shook his head. "No, where did you get the painting? My parents have its twin in our house. They said it was from years ago, before the war."

"Not before the war, exactly. The night before the battle of Clai'miirn. By the time we all met, the war raged for over a decade."

Keplan glanced up. "You knew my parents?"

"We fought together for a time. Though they went by different names than they do now." Bren's face was casual, schooled into tense neutrality. "They went south after the war, and I received no word, not a letter, not a sign. I grieved for your mother as if she were dead. I began to think she was."

"Was she your lover before my da?" Keplan did not really want to know the answer.

Brentemir winced. "Certainly not. She was my sister. Your father, my friend."

Disbelief and anger reared in his head, drowning the ambassador's words. *But your sister is the Dhoah' Laen.* It was impossible to marry the fierce image with his unassuming parents, but the proof was burned into his mind. They were not hiding from the horrors of war, but the horrors of themselves. *They weren't protecting me.* "They were protecting themselves."

Bren straightened. "What do you mean?"

"The Dhoah' Laen and the Earth Shaker left this city, left Athrolan, to protect themselves, didn't they?" Everything he knew of himself crumbled in the face of truth. His mind filled with the inhuman reflection from his dream. "*One of us will die.*" "Your sister, her guard—where did they go?"

"I wasn't certain until recently. They built a homestead in the wilderness, a day's ride away from a town called Namal, I believe."

"Namus." It was a curse hissed through a trembling jaw. Mania coursed through his body, spurred by denial. "My parents are peasants. They live in the Hartland in a house they built with their own hands and leave only a few times a year to trade for supplies in Namus." Keplan's eyes flicked up. Rage thundered through him, and something darker rose in his blood, in his mind. Something that, until then, had no name. "I can't say how often she thinks of you, or whether she healed, but I can tell you she was happy. By running, by keeping their identity a secret from even me, they were protecting themselves."

Bren's neutral expression melted into surprise, into something close to horror. "You didn't know." It was not a question, but a statement, nailing every speculation into place. Bren did not wait for an answer. "I thought I'd come here, and you'd be grateful to have found family again, that you were keeping their secret for them. I thought you would be happy. All this time and you didn't know." He put his head in his hands. "If it's not because of your mother's promise to Her Majesty, then why are you here?"

"I came here for peace." A dam broke. Denial may have mentally blinded him, but now a flood of information tumbled into his head. "How can you sit here, a king in my barren apartment, hoping I'll end a war you've only just begun? You're a symbol of everything I could have had if they chose to raise me here. And I'm just a madman." His voice rumbled. He lifted his apron over his head and folded it, then placed it on the desk. His heart hammered, as if a single misstep would send the pieces of his psyche clattering to the rough hardwood. "When I return, you'd best be gone."

He crossed the city quickly, steps fueled with as much panic and confusion as anger. Early hours deterred all but the most dogged of city folk. Dew still sparkled on the worn, thyme-covered steps to the cemetery. Just beneath the white Xain mausoleum stood the Heroes Vault. Dried flowers crunched underfoot. Months had passed since anyone left offerings in memorial or gratitude. Mosaics ringed the black granite tower, scenes most of the known world could recite. *The Gods' War.*

He thought of the reverence and fear surrounding his parents. Heat roiled in his veins. The shell holding his emotions in check shattered. Ban would never have touched him. *I would have grown up with Azimir, with education and friends and safety*. His pal smacked against the cool tiles, against the tidy pattern of their faces.

The Rakos's body was plated with stone, his joints cracked and bleeding magma. His yellow eyes glared through Keplan. Breath caught in Keplan's throat. Familiar features flickered under the ferocity. Through the thunder in the titan's chest, he heard the voice that instructed him how to draw a bow and build a fire.

Keplan snarled. He would give anything for it to be a mistake, for his mind to be playing tricks on him. For once he prayed for madness. Dark stone bit into his fingers. "What did you promise the queen?" *The Dhoah' Laen's eyes blazed, striking sunbursts from her armor. The rush of power dragged a scream from her throat. Ageless, ceaseless, and the scent of salt.*

"I cleaned horse shite!" His scream broke, booming against the stones. "I was tortured and forced to eat from waste piles when I could have been raised here!" His hands hammered the stone depiction of silver eyes and golden hair. Riches did not matter, nor had he dreamt of being a prince. But he could have had peace. *They will kill you, and only I will remain.*

"Unless you want to be arrested for crimes against an official monument, I suggest you lower your voice." Threat laced the calm words. A milk-pale man leaned on a headstone, fully black eyes narrowed. Morning light glinted off the iron capping his chipped horns.

Keplan's eyes bounced from the horns to the signet on his tunic. *The general grieved alone, grieved for a queen that no one knew was already dead.* "You're the general. You keep the city from ruin. Barely."

The implied insult was ignored. "And you are a madman screeching in a cemetery. Don't bother trying to destroy that thing—it'll stand long after you rot."

Distraction dragged the panic from his limbs, leaving exhaustion in its wake. Keplan staggered, catching himself before turning back to the city.

"Who promised Her Majesty something?" The general's eyes narrowed. "I believe that's what you said. Your smacking fists made it difficult to hear."

Keplan froze. "General Domariigo. An'thoriend Domariigo. An'thor." The words clattered from his mouth like pebbles before a landslide. "'Instead, she named your child, should you have one. We need you. Ceir Athrolan needs you. Just once more.'"

"So, they did receive the letter."

"It's the reason I'm here. One of them."

An'thor extended his hand. "You said you wished you had learned, wished you had respect. You came here for knowledge. Come inside. Just come talk with me."

Keplan glanced to the cliffs, to the city behind the general. His instincts screamed that whatever the general offered, he did not want. "Perhaps another time."

"I could have you arrested."

"And I could tell the world that the queen has been dead for over a month." He stepped down from the monument and nodded to the stunned general. "Good evening." The destruction inside his heart yawned beneath him, pitching him into darkness.

Only I will remain.

Φ

The 10th Day of Aeme, 1272

Bordom made Rih grateful her shaved head prevented her from ripping her own hair out. Despite her morning stretches and practicing her dance steps, her muscles sang for movement. *And pacing really only does so much.* Every scroll she re-read. Every dance step was memorized. Every sexual nuance understood. *Or at least as much as I can stomach.* She wanted conversation. She wanted exercise. Loneliness clawed at her chest. When she was restless in the barracks she would practice her atlatl or bathe.

Her gaze fell to the tub tucked in the alcove by her window seat. Ki-elte mentioned there was a bathing hall, and, though never invited, Rih assumed she was allowed. She gathered her key and ducked out the door. The halls were empty at mid-morning, but a few carved signs steered her toward the baths.

Rih slipped into the room, offering a tentative smile to the woman at the foyer. She sat on a dais surrounded by silk curtains. The shelves behind her held the folded outfits and sandals of those already inside. Rih traded silks for a towel and ducked behind the row of screens. Lilies wafted on the thick air. Red and purple glass softened the lantern light filling the low room. The floors were tiled, like the bath in the barracks, but purple and gold designs patterned these. She sighed at the warmth under her bare feet. Three tubs descended into the floor, one steaming, the others still. While the barracks offered a razor and oil for sore muscles, the Hall had rooms for stretching and grooming. One row of alcoves held masseuses.

A long breath pulled tension from her heart. *I might be the chattel in an international negotiation, but perhaps it's worth it to spend a day here.* It was not, and she knew it, but for a moment she would pretend. She set aside her towel and slipped into the heated water. Minerals from the spring lent a tang to the water, and she licked the earthy taste from her lips after dunking her head.

A woman several years older paddled up to Rih. Her grin flashed the polished ruby replacing one dogtooth. "Hello?" The sign was uncertain and exaggerated, but unmistakable.

Laughter bubbled from Rih's chest. She straightened and repeated the sign. "How did you know?" She could count on her hands the number of women in the army who knew her signs. The language was far more common where her mother was raised, where close to a quarter of the male nobles were also deaf. She was lucky enough to have lived her first few years there. The capital, however, was different.

"Ki-elte told me about you. My brother was also born without hearing or speach." She bit her lip, searching Rih's face for understanding. "You can read lips, yes?"

"Yes, though it's not always easy." Knowing this woman had family like Rih made it easier to be honest. Reading lips was exhausting, but explaining was sometimes more effort than it was worth.

"I am Hamin." She spoke the name and allowed Rih to correct the hand sign for two of the letters.

"I'm Rih."

"Would you like some tea?" She brushed a finger past her mouth mimicking the path of a smile, then made a gesture as if she stirred spices into the tea.

"I'd love some, thank you!"

Hamin waved over one of the young girls who worked as an attendant. When she was done speaking, she looked back to Rih. "Do you mind company?"

"Please." Rih moved aside to give Hamin room on the tiled bench beside her. "I talk to few people."

"You are preparing for marriage?"

"I am, to the son of Mirik's Hetmir. Alleanthus?"

Hamin frowned. "You must mean Azimir. He's the younger son. Alleanthus was to be wed to Ambassador Jien's sister, but the engagement fell through in favor of another, to the daughter of an Athrolani noble."

"Azimir?" She did not know much about their second son, only that he was younger than she.

Hamin shrugged. "He's a boy, apparently hotheaded like his father. They're beautiful to look at though, both of them. Tan and fit, not sickly pale, like soured milk, the way half the east is."

Rih smiled at the description. It suited the few Easterners she had seen. "How do you know so much about Mirik? Have you visited?"

Hamin's face grew serious. "My sister served for a time for the ambassador, and she told me all the stories when she came back. She is the one that passed recently, Sa-at."

Rih's chest ached at the thought. She remembered comrades dying in battle. She could only imagine losing a true sibling. "I am so sorry"

When the tea arrived, Hamin's eyes were overbright, but she switched easily to talking about the drinks.

Rih took the hint and set about preparing her tea. The tray fit neatly over the edge of the bath and held the usual pot of spiced butter and cups of thick tea. Necessary to maintain energy on marches, the rich tea was a luxury in the Hall. She took a long slow sip and closed her eyes. When she opened them, Hi-alan had joined them. Her iron-gray hair was long enough to curl at the top.

"Your ears are healing well."

"Thank you, it's good to see you again." She gestured for Hi-alan to help herself to some tea before settling back into the water. Her muscles loosened, limbs settling. Peace eased through her nerves. Hamin and Hi-alan fell into a voiced conversation about a mutual friend, as far as she could see. Leather covering the tub's rounded edge pillowed her head. She smiled and let her eyes close. It was enough to have friends near. Rih drifted somewhere between dreams and waking for a moment. Water sloshed, startling Rih back to wakefulness. The other two women turned as Ki-elte rushed into the room. Her face was ashen. "I'm sorry to interrupt." She knelt, offering Rih a towel. "I need you to get dressed. Ambassador Ebal is calling for you." Shaking hand's made Ki-elte's rudimentary signs difficult to understand. "Quickly."

Rih frowned and hauled herself from the water. She dried too quickly, and the silk of her kalas clung to her damp skin. She ran a hand over the prickles on her scalp. "I should shave."

"No time." Ki-elte handed her a net as they wove through the halls.

Rih fastened it as they went. She was not sure if it was her teacher's urgency, or something more, but the halls seemed more crowded than usual. There were fewer smiles.

Now they did not meet in the opulence of the Lapis Room or the vast dance hall. Instead, Rih followed Ki-elte across the courtyard to the Dignitary Wing. An inlay of Mirik and the Athrolani coast decorated the heavy screen across the door.

Ki-elte barely finished knocking when Mosil slid the screen back. Wrinkles creased his clothes. Shadows clung like smoke to the undersides of his eyes. "Rih-elte, thank you for meeting with me." He gestured to their seats with an absent wave of his hand. "There has been a change in our plans."

Rih's heart was a bird trapped in the cage of her ribs. "What happened?"

"War. War happened. Rih, we are mighty, but Mirik's navy is their pride, and rightfully so. I do not fear our victory, only the cost it will require."

"We cannot negotiate?"

"Write it, please," he snapped. "I cannot think and translate too."

Rih stopped herself from pointing out thinking and translating were exactly what his role as ambassador entailed. She ordered all expression from her face and wrote the question on her tablet.

"Negotiations are tense. We're debating whether this war will become violent or just a show of power, with the only deaths those of messengers and spies."

And our women.

Muscles worked in his jaw, but his face was otherwise unreadable. He stalked to the window. She could not see his mouth, and Ki-elte's hands stumbled in her attempt to catch up with translating. "You're naïve, you're idealistic. Mirik is our enemy, and our hope at fixing this by throwing a faulty wife at their son is gone. I don't blame them. It was an insult. His Eminence was wrong in thinking they would see it differently."

Pain sparked in the heart of her anger, and though she wanted to look away, cut the cruel words off with the finality of closing her eyes, she needed to know.

"You will not marry Mirik's second son. You will be lucky if you marry outside Ban at all. I am meeting with His Eminence in a week to discuss our course with Athrolan now that we're at war with their ally. I cannot be bothered with matchmaking for you."

Rih's gaze moved to him when Ki-elte's hands stilled. Fury burned in her gut. "Faulty? Naïve? Idealistic?" Her fingers hardened around the signs.

Mosil rubbed the bridge of his nose, more tired than angry it seemed, now, and pointed at the desk. "Please, I asked you to write."

All Rih's carefully curated patience snapped. If her ribs could open and free the thundering wings of her angry heart, she would have cracked them herself. Clay shattered beneath when her hand smacked the tablet. She surged to her feet. "No! For once in your life, do your job and listen!"

His eyes widened before her violent signs, but for the first time, he did not turn to look at Ki-elte as she translated.

"I am not faulty, not any more than you, who clearly cannot think past yourself. I am not naïve. I've killed, I've seen my sisters fall in battle and at the hands of our own people, valued less than the horses our officers ride." She gathered her bag, leaving the tablet, with its accusation glaring on the desk.

"Wishing for freedom? For respect? Only someone who has never wanted for either would think that was idealistic." She slid open the door, but paused in the doorway. "Write if you find anything to teach me I don't already know."

She stalked from the room, hoping Ki-elte followed, hoping her cousin would not, hoping that guards would not arrive at her door in a minute to haul her away for her impudence.

By the time she reached the Purple Throne, she was running. She burst into her room, adrenaline hot in her limbs. The door shut, and she felt the tap as the lock slid into place. She pressed her head to the wood, hands splayed on the frame. *What did I just do?* Whatever path she might have had, the one she stared down now was darker. The wood under her brow shook with a knock, but her body was frozen. If they wanted to take her away, they would have to drag her. The lock shifted again. She caught herself on the doorframe as the door slid from under her.

Ki-elte was alone in the hall. "Are you alright?"

Rih collapsed on the other woman, hard arms gripping the softness of shoulders that never threw a dart. After a moment she pulled away. "I don't know." She backed into her room. "Will he call the guards on me?"

Ki-elte lifted a shoulder in a shrug. "I hope not." Her eyes narrowed on something out the window only she could see. "I think he sees the sense in your words. You might have shown him you make a better wife than he thought." Her mouth twisted. "But I hope he does not think too hard on what you said. We all have those thoughts, Rih, but they are for us, and us alone."

Rih turned away. Her heart was no longer thunder, was no longer a bird begging to break her chest apart. It fluttered, uneven, as panic faded to exhaustion. She dropped her hand to the other tablet, to the single word written across the wax. The Emperor was not the only one ruled by fear.

CHAPTER ELEVEN

The 12th Day of Aeme, 1272
The Feld be Baran

WARM AIR TUGGED A smile onto Alea's face, and she drew up at the hill's crest. She loosened her shirt front and folded up her sleeves. Green grasses rolled away on all sides , dotted with persistent white and blue wildflowers. A cluster of brown mounds on the eastern horizon marked a village.

"Enjoying the view?" Arman's voice was low, his face more serious than hers. His horse shifted its weight, as uneasy as its rider.

"I was thinking this was the first time we really traveled in good weather. Every other time, winter was either just beginning or just ending. It's beautiful."

Arman smiled. impish light filled his sidelong gaze. "I'll race you to that rock over there, the outcropping that looks like the Commander's awful haircut."

Alea nudged her horse into a gallop. Arman thundered down the hill a pace behind. Dirt spattered the roadside as they passed, and Alea let out a whoop. Her heart hammered as the air whipped her braid into disarray. Arman drove his horse up the embankment, cutting off the turn in the road. Her eyes narrowed, cheeks stinging from her horse's mane. She leapt a narrow stream and wheeled in front of Arman as he tried to rejoin the road. They arrived at the outcropping simultaneously, breath gasping with laughter and excitement.

"A draw." Alea's eyes were bright. After twenty years of solitude her veins missed adrenaline.

"Nonsense, I would have won had you not cut me off." Arman nudged his horse closer to hers and leaned out of the saddle to kiss her. "But I do love how competition looks on you."

She kissed him back before loping down the road again, trailing dust and laughter behind her.

The village emerged after another few hours of riding. Windows glinted with reflected sunset and newly lit lanterns. Several streets paralleling the main road and a low wall ringed the largest buildings. Alea nodded at a brightly painted sign to the left. "How does the Jumping Pebble sound?"

Arman snorted. "Like someone drank too much before they named it." Stablehands waited for their horses in the narrow courtyard and Arman unbuckled their packs. Alea watched as the boys joked back and forth on their way to the stables. They were young, barely thirteen, and moved with easy confidence. *What life would Keplan have had in a place like this?*

"Alea?"

She glanced over to where Arman waited on the stoop. "Sorry." She jogged up the steps.

He followed her gaze, expression sobering. "Every boy is going to remind us of him, I think. Until we hold him again." Rolicking music and the smell of bread and honey rolled through the door when he opened it. "We'll find him, love." He shouldered through the crowd, rough hand clasping hers. The bar was battered but ran the width of the common room.

Alea caught the innkeeper's eye and leaned over the bar to talk above the noise. "We need a room for the night."

"That'll be a silver if you want board with it."

"Please." Alea slid the coin across the table. It may have been a long time since she saw the inside of a tavern, but the price seemed steep. "You've plenty of business."

"Best inn in the province," the man boasted. "Supper's rabbit pies and honey." He handed her a key and turned away. Alea glanced back. The press of noise was a balm to her frantic mind. Most seats were full, but many were locals, come for the drink and conversation, but not stay for the night. "I'll bring our packs up—can you find a table?"

Arman nodded and wove toward a quieter corner.

Winding, narrow stairs curled up to the uneven floor of the second story. Wood smoke and ale brought a smile to Alea's lips. *Add a layer of moss, and this could be Vielrona.* Their small room was tucked between the roofs of the inn and the stable beside. A grimy window overlooked weathered tiles, a sliver of the Felds visible beyond the walls. Unpacking their few belongings was pointless for a single evening, but Alea took her time changing and rebraiding her hair. Gray strands outnumbered the black now; frown lines and gray lent better anonymity than isolation ever had. *We could be anyone.*

The music hummed under her skin, and the heat and smoke were dizzying. Arman perched on a stool by a tall table in the corner. She flicked the skirt of the only dress she brought in an attempt to remove the wrinkles and grabbed two mugs of ale. Arman's gaze wandered over the musicians in the corner. She slid his mug across the table with a warm smile. "I haven't seen you here before."

He took a deep gulp of ale before mirroring her smile with one of his own. "I'm just traveling through. You?"

"On my way north. Mind if I share your table?"

He bit back a laugh and shoved the other chair toward her with one mud-stained boot.

She sat, dipping one shoulder as she leaned on the table. "Maybe after you finish that ale, there, we could share a dance?"

"I'm afraid I'm not very good."

"Ah, surely you're just being humble. Give me a turn and I'll decide for myself." Mirth war with apprehension on his face, the latter slowly washed away with alcohol. Under the dim light of the common room, he was just a southern man, gray from a hard life, lined from long days. Boyish beauty was now quiet strength. She wondered absently what he saw when he looked across the table, across the years.

He knocked back the last swig of ale and shoved himself to his feet. "All right, missy, you get one chance at dancing with me. Up you get."

Φ

The 13th day of Aeme, 1272
The City of Ceir Athrolan

It was dark when the letter arrived. Rain peppered the glass, but the clouds seemed content to do little more than spit. Bren leaned his forehead on the window, The streets were busy for a gloomy day. *The whole kingdom is uneasy.* His eyes flicked to the palace. Reka was rarely wrong, but palaces gossiped, and a queen's death seemed too big a secret to keep. *Even for An'thor.*

A soft knock heralded his steward. "A letter, sir."

"From home?"

"No, sir. It's addressed to you by name, but they've gotten the title wrong. They call you the Military Commissioner." The man glanced at the envelope. "It's from a place called Namus?"

Bren crossed the room in two strides, almost tearing the letter in his haste to open the envelope. "Thank you, that will be all for now." Old travel stains and fresh rain stained the parchment. His hands shook as he turned it over.

Wardyn Homestead
Namus Township
Pardelan Province of Athrolan

He sank into the armchair by his window. The handwriting was not Alea's thin elegant lines, but the solid and crisp hand he recognized from his time in Mirik before the war. *Arman.* It was not what he wanted, exactly, but it was better than silence.

Bren,

I hope this finds you well. I cannot imagine what has passed in the last twenty years – twenty, can you believe it? Sometimes it feels like yesterday. I hope you found peace and happiness. We have. We both have. It seems foolish to write after decades of silence, but I have little choice. Something is changing. The world is not the blissful end we hoped. Alea has dreams, and I feel churning in the earth.

Moreover, our son is gone.

He is young, seventeen. We kept our power a secret, hoped he would live a normal life, one of simplicity and peace. One we only dreamt of. I see you shaking your head at our folly. Weeks ago he disappeared into the woods bearing a bow and some sparsely packed saddle-bags. He found a letter from An'thoriend. An'thor may be a hero, but he did not become one for his kindness. He means to make him the heir.

I realize this letter is scattered and makes little sense, but I am trusting you to keep our secret from the world, keep our son safe from a kingdom that would rip his future away. Find Keplan. Find him and bring him home. I do not care if he learns every story ever told about us. Just bring him back safely.

My thanks, and Alea's,
Arman

Bren's chest ached, and his throat burned. After so many years all he wanted was news. Now it came briefly as small talk and the request of a favor. Still, Alea had not written. Even if Keplan managed to live in anonymity, it was likely civil war would shatter the city about their ears before he decided to return home. Bren reread the letter, flipping it over, searching for anything else that might help.

He grimaced as another knock interrupted his thoughts. "What is it, now?"

"Sir, General Domariigo is here to see you. He says it's urgent. About the queen."

Bren's brows rose. Perhaps the man had not been lying about the woman's death. "Show him in." He leaned against his desk and dropped the letter behind him. His arms were firmly crossed when the general stepped in.

"Quite the summer we're having. This rain does not bode well for our crops." The Ageless man glanced out the window. "I suppose Mirik is used to this sort of weather."

"Rather. Why are you here?"

An'thor's lined face was unreadable, black eyes distant. "I met someone yesterday, a new friend of yours. He goes by Keplan, I believe. What was his last name again?" An'thor tapped thin lips with a battered finger. "Ah, yes," his gaze snapped to Bren's, "Wardyn."

"Toar, An'thoriend, cut the dramatics." His jaw tightened. "What did you do to him?"

"Nothing. I found him having a fit in the cemetery yesterday evening. He was pounding on the mosaic of your sister and her guard, apparently quite peeved he could have had a normal life. Frankly, I think he might be disturbed."

Bren shoved himself off the desk. "You saw his scars, didn't you? If you think he's disturbed, perhaps you should let him be."

An'thor shook his head. "There's something about his eyes. They see too much."

Bren threw a hand in the air. "Did you expect a normal child from their blood?"

"I expected a powerful answer to my every prayer." When Bren scoffed, An'thor slammed his fist on the table. "Gossip is all over the streets. I have people claiming I'm poisoning the queen. Colonel Hamacad is calling his men to the city and others bolster each fort. All the lords have drawn their personal troops home. This man, Peraan, rouses dissent in the lower city. He wants Daymir back, and he's not alone. Raven as much as proclaimed loyalty to him as well."

"And what of it?" Brentemir's skin crawled in the face of An'thor's obsession. He knew why Arman could not trust the man.

"You need to contact him."

"Peraan?"

"Their son, idiot," An'thor snarled. "Bring him to the manor, write him a letter, fates, sing under his window for all I care."

"And what happens when I return to Mirik?"

"I'll show him the declaration and hold a welcoming ceremony. He'll be Heir Apparent within the year."

"And his entire life will be forfeit. No."

Dim light made his unyielding eyes blacker than ever, and Brentemir understood why the Ageless were so often likened to predators. An'thor's hand found the discarded envelope and turned it over. He skimmed the sender's address and offered Bren a tight-lipped smile. "You claim him, Barrackborn, or I will."

Φ

Northern Clai Province, Athrolan

Even in late summer, mist rose from the river at dusk. Lovers would think it romantic. Peraan Goen of Littie's Green used it for cover. His forty-seven years showed in stiff legs and hard eyes. Night etched his features in blue. It was a good place—the center of the river emptying the Iron Sea. The rowboat bobbed on its mooring, but the slap of waves was quiet enough for Peraan to hear approaching oars.

"Ho," he called. "Does your ship fly the flag of Athrolan?"

"Aye, that of her king." The skiff drew close, and faint moonlight showed it had come from Meren. The viscount himself was seated in the aft, his emblem covered by his cowl. "May I come aboard, Master Goen?"

"Indeed, Lord Eier." Peraan took hold of the other boat, steadying his own as the lord stepped over the side. The skiff pulled away to moor further down river. Peraan turned back to his guest. "I'm glad to see you well. I trust your work is moving along?"

Eier fixed the man with an expressionless stare. "I haven't stayed in popularity for so long, even as my patron fell, without some pragmatism. You speak of Daymir's claim and yet make no move to send word to him about all that is done in his name."

"I think it wise to have strength before we show him our desires."

"Of what strength do you speak?"

"You are not the only lord with whom I meet. I have my own network. Others call their men back. It's no secret the country is wounded and howling. With your men, we would have a force to rival the army. Once you sign fealty to Daymir, we could move. Commander Dorcal, even, shows signs of supporting us."

Eier looked away. Though of equal years, he was in better form than his companion. "What do you offer?"

"A way to correspond with the true king without drawing suspicion. I still have contact with all his guardsmen."

"And what about the other rumor? I trust you have heard it."

"You mean the boy?"

Eier turned back, his eyes dark. "I mean the Dhoah' Laen's son, Peraan. I find it difficult to believe Ambassador Barrackborn to allow anyone else to wander about with his son so readily. The general is reportedly interested in him as well. The poor man clings to the idea that ancient powers could save us. I think we both know better." He raised a hand to signal his boat.

"I have seen him myself. He bears the marks of torture and distrusts others. I think there is something ill about him. Not evil, but broken beyond repair. I swear to you, he bears no inhuman blood."

Eier swung himself over the edge and onto his skiff. "Peraan, you forget many say Athrolan, too, is broken. Be careful."

Φ

The 15th day of Aeme, 1272
The City of Ceir Athrolan

Bren never found a place he loved as much as Mirik's cliffs. The manor in Ceir Athrolan was decorated almost identically to his private rooms at home, but it was not enough to keep homesickness at bay.

Azimir burst into the room with his usual careless assurance, tapping a belated knock on the door frame. "Have you heard from Keplan yet? Is An'thoriend coming? I wanted to ask him about his revolver."

Bren sighed. "Keplan did not respond, and I don't know if it's a refusal. General Domariigo will not be attending as I'd rather not frighten Keplan off." Distaste for difficult conversations was unchanged in his transformation from soldier to ambassador. "I'm having Keplan to supper with you and Alleanthus. Alone."

"He should meet the general—"

"They already met, and I imagine your friend would not like to repeat the experience." He gestured to one of the armchairs by the window. "Sit, and for

Toar's sake, listen for a moment." He sat on the edge of his desk and crossed his arms. It was as much to hide the shaking as to lend authority. "Do you remember when I met Keplan?"

"You interrogated him."

Bren squeezed his eyes shut. "I questioned him only after I heard his last name. It's one I haven't heard in a long time. I barely slept that night. Keplan looked familiar to me. I met with Captain Elang and she confirmed my suspicions, as did Keplan himself."

"You saw him?"

"Azimir, I asked you to listen. Before he went by Arrowlash, Arman's surname was Wardyn. When my sister rode off into the wilderness years ago, she did indeed take the Rakos with her. And now their son returned to Athrolan."

Azimir was silent for a breath, then a grin blossomed across his face. "Will he come to live with us in Mirik? Have you told him yet?"

"I thought he already knew who his parents were. I was wrong. He's scarcely an orphan whom we need to take in. He has a life here. This meal is, in part, to learn more about him. First, I need to ask you something." He fixed his son with a level stare. "You spend a lot of time with him. Is there anything different about him? Different from a normal seventeen-year-old?"

Azimir looked down, his open face showing an internal battle.

"If you know something, you are honor-bound to tell me. No one expects you to keep secrets from family." Uncertainty warred with hope on his son's face, giving away as much as his mouth tried no to.

"Anyone could see he's different." Azimir glanced up, jaw set with a stubbornness Bren recognized from the mirror. "But he's family now too." He rose. "Is that all? Could I go fetch him now?"

Bren waved at the door. "Fine. He'll take better to you than he would to me anyway." He watched Azimir leap down the stairs three at a time. Children were a beautiful trial. He could see himself young again. *But now I realize pigheaded and obnoxious I must have been.*

Φ

Bells tolled evening. Keplan paced his room. Now the thoughts kept at bay by work sprang to the forefront again. Rage still echoed in his veins, but it was distant. Everything he learned about his blood seemed like a lie, until he looked at the madness mapped within his mind. *And now the ambassador wants to have dinner.* It was late enough he could feign illness, but part of him balked still at refusing a nobleman. The decision was made for him when Azimir arrived with the last bells before nightfall.

The younger boy edged in after Keplan refused to answer his knock. Reservation shadowed his features, and he shifted from foot to foot as he stood by the open door. He cleared his throat. "Da told me who you were. That we're cousins."

"Shut the door."

Azimir did so, then leaned against the wood. "You could have told me."

Keplan raked his hands through his hair, hauling it back into a horsetail. "I didn't know." He hated being questioned, but it was worse only having half the answers. "When your father told me, I was in no mood to see anyone. Besides, you might have thought me angling for power."

Azimir snorted. "You can barely handle a crowd, let alone standing before one." He jerked his head at the door. "Will you at least come to supper?"

Keplan stared, unseeing, out the window. *I wanted to know why I'm mad.* "I suppose it would be rude to refuse the ambassador himself."

"Rather." Azimir's bright face still held a frown. "He asked if you had any of their power. If you were different from normal folk."

Keplan paused in lacing his jerkin, eyes flicking to Azimir's in the small mirror. "It's not a power. I can't shoot lightning from my hands or channel the sun. I can't even control whose secrests I see most of the time." Hissing rushed through his ears. "What did you say?"

"I said you were the one to ask. I wouldn't break confidence, especially since you're family now." Defiance lit his eyes at the words. "C'mon, we'll be late."

Keplan glanced around his room. In the wake of his world crumbling, he was a ship without a rudder or sails. With no way to steer himself, drifting after Azimir was as good as anything. Firas and Mirel's voices drifted from the kitchen, but the common room was empty. Before Keplan thought up careful answers to every question he might be asked, the manor eates loomed above them. The absence of Azimir's usual boisterous nature did nothing to help Keplan's anxiety. Wan laughter bubbled up, finally when he mentally likened the manor's white stone to a tomb.

"What is it?" Azimir allowed Keplan to walk through the gate first.

"This is a dinner, and I'm acting like it's an execution."

Azimir's grin was nervous, but there all the same. "You aren't much for state, eh?"

"Hardly." Keplan followed him into the foyer. Scents of peppered meat and wine drifted from an open door, and the ambassador's booming laugh echoed in the tiled hall. Conversation died when Azimir stepped in. "I brought him."

Keplan paused outside the door, slowing his breath in an attempt to steady the hammering in his chest. *Only I will remain.* The refrain wound through every thought now. This was not Ban. An ambassador requested his presence—practically begged for it. The dark part of him, the glowering half lurking in the dark, grinned. *They should beg.* Keplan rushed through the doorway before another thought surfaced.

"Good evening." He bowed to before taking a seat, wishing the only chair as anywhere but directly across from the ambassador. "Thank you for having me."

Steaming water sat in a bowl before him. After shooting a glance at Azimir, he tugged off his gloves and dunked his hands into his own bowl. He dried them swiftly and tucked them under the table. Awkward silence weighed on the room until Keplan looked up. Brentemir watched him, eyes thoughtful, and Alleanthus's gaze held open curiosity. Azimir stared at his plate.

Alleanthus offered a smile. "I imagine this is odd for you. And pretty miserable. We're a family of soldiers, and we don't do pomp well either. Would you feel better if you knew more about us?"

"Please." Keplan thought his cheeks might crack from disuse when he smiled. "I felt like I was walking to my doom the entire way here."

Brentemir choked on his drink and shot a dismayed look at his older son. "I told you I thought I frightened him off."

"That's because you always sound like you're delivering desperate or bad news." Platters arrived and Alleanthus leaned back. "I was born in Mirik, shortly after the war. Our Ma was a general then, and Pa, Hetmir. The city was in disarray still, I was raised by carpenters as much as warriors. Now I study state affairs so become an ambassador like Pa." His thumb jerked to the south. "Perhaps in Berr. I could stand to see more ships." Azimir added his own anecdotes, some of which Keplan already heard.

It was odd, eating around a table talking to men who grew up with servants, with manors. *With each other.* Keplan had not wanted a sibling until he met Azimir. Now yearning for family was a bright ache in his chest. *I should write them.*

"I remember your father played music—do you at all?" It was the first time Bren ventured a question.

Keplan picked at his shirt. His stomach was gloriously full and his eyes heavy. Alleanthus was quick-witted, but quieter than his brother, and put him at ease. "I have no skill with music—I can't carry a tune either."

Mead or memory misted Brentemir's eyes, and he looked down at the chalice in his blocky hands. "Your mother was a terrible singer. She loved it, but thank Toar Athrolan has no dogs, because she would have set them howling."

Warmth twisted in his gut. "We have a trader from Ban who used to stay with us when I was little. He traveled with a dog and my ma would sit on a stump outside with her and they'd cry at the moon." He met Brentemir's eyes. They knew two sides of the same woman—Bren the fierce, violent warrior, Keplan the quiet, wild mother. He might have missed home, missed his parents, but Bren had been without his sister for twenty years. *He tore the countryside apart searching for her, and she never spoke his name.* "Ma has a large garden—all our food is grown there. They taught me to hunt, to cook, they taught me everything. Though I realize now my history lessons have some large gaps."

Bren leaned forward. "When is your birthday?"

"Snowmelt. I left shortly afterward. I have questions I didn't think they could answer," he explained. The questions still made him vulnerable, but kindness and food and the sense of family steadied his nerves a fraction.

"What did they say of your time here, or in Ban? Did you tell them you found us?" Bren asked.

Keplan flexed his hands under the table. "I rode away in the night and have yet to write to them. I couldn't, in Ban. Now I don't know what I would say." He glanced up, hope a warm bloom in the pit of his stomach. "Perhaps you could tell them?"

"Me? Fates." Brentemir stared, incredulous. "They've had no word from you in months? Keplan, you ought to let them know you're alive."

"Some letters are more difficult to write than others," Alleanthus interjected.

"I just realized my world was a lie." Keplan picked at his nails. "Surely you understand the feeling."

Azimir's hand flew to his mouth as if this was nothing more than banter among bar friends, but the ambassador's jaw tightened. The words silenced conversation for a moment, and Keplan mentally kicked himself.

"I'm sorry, that was rude."

Bren sat back. "No, I see your point. I speak as a parent, and I know how I'd feel should Azimir wander off, silent for months."

The footman halted Bren's next words. "Ambassador, sir, General Domariigo is here to see you. Shall I show him in?"

"Toar." Bren surged to his feet. "Excuse me." Though he stepped into the hall, anger carried his words through the half-open door. "Dammit, An'thor, you told me to act, so let me!"

"Is the boy—"

Alleanthus snapped the door shut, but panic already burned through Keplan's limbs. Bren's words sucked the air from the room. Tugging his gloves over his palms, he made for the hall. "I'm sorry, Azimir, Alleanthus. Thank you for the visit, it was lovely."

He shut the door carefully behind him and turned to meet the general's glaring black eyes. "General." He turned to the ambassador. "Forgive me, I find myself ill." Measured steps brought him to the safety of the stables. Once he and Moly slipped through the gate he nudged her into a lope. Curiosity did not bring Brentemir to his door. It was plotting and whatever sick race he had with An'thor.

Firas was almost asleep when Keplan pounded on his door. The bartender peered into the dark hallway. "'Lan? I scarcely see you for days, then you beg at my door?"

"I need to talk." Keplan realized he was a hand taller than the other man. *We were almost at eye level when I first arrived.* "So much is changing."

His coy smile faded. "Come in, then."

"I don't know where to turn. I'm tired of running. I'm a damned coward, but fates, I'm so tired from running I don't have the strength to stand." Keplan slumped onto the bed head sinking to his gloved hands.

"Would it help to tell me what you're running from?" Firas's voice was quiet, so soft it drifted in the breath between them. "Why was the Mirikin ambassador here?" Firas brushed his hand over Keplan's gloves. "Does it have to do with these?"

"I'm not a spy for Mirik, if that's what you mean. He knew my parents during the Gods' War." His heart hammered for him to explain everything, each thought he had no right to know, all the history his parents never told him. "My parents ran from the war, and it seems now I'm running too. I'm pulled in so many ways and I scarcely know why."

Firas brushed Keplan's hair away, untying the horsetail with steady hands. "Is it something to do with the way you know things?"

Keplan moved away, eyes wide.

"Don't give me those big blue eyes of yours. You think I'd believe Mirrel told you about Pa's wagon? And you knew I wanted to kiss you during the festival. You see people better than you ought."

"I think it does have something to do with that. With who my parents were. I don't know who I am anymore." He had not even spoken it aloud to himself. "I'm so tired."

Firas's gentle hand ran down the bumps of Keplan's spine. "Tomorrow you can stand. Tomorrow you won't run anymore. But tonight, between these walls, you can rest. You keep me from drinking too much and tease Mirrel, and sometimes she even laughs. You work in the stables during the day and share my bed at night. Tonight, everything else is gone. The whole world can fit right here," he tugged Keplan's glove off and held their hands a hair's breadth apart.

Keplan pulled off his shirt with aching arms. Gooseflesh rippled over his abruptly uncovered skin, interrupted by smooth, pink scar tissue. "I know I said I was tired, but I don't want to sleep tonight."

Firas blew out the candle on his bedside. "I didn't plan on sleep." Even in darkness, Keplan heard the smile in the other man's voice.

The 16th day of Aeme, 1272
The City of RoBal, Ban

ADRENALINE STILL RACED THROUGH Rih's veins at every new visitor. No threats or retaliation arrived for her dangerous words to Mosil. It was as if he forgot her entirely. The rains would come soon, the dust and burnt brown of the grasses replaced by the sweet smell of new growth and moisture.

Rih checked the hoops in her ears, but stilled when she caught sight of her hand. Brown fingers tapered to short the nails marked with a pale crescent at the base. *These aren't mine.* Her calluses were all but gone, shadows left where hard skin once lay across the pad of her palm.

Greif flooded through her.

Ki-elte found her perched on her bed, hands loose in her lap as if detached at the wrist. Rih jumped when the woman touched her shoulder. She waved away Ki-elte's hasty gesture of apology and signed, "I must have lost track of time." Her back ached from stillness. Her neck was stiff, and her feet tingled with compressed nerves. It was evening, the sun almost faded from the sky.

"Are you—" Ki-elte faltered for the proper sign then shrugged and spoke aloud. "Troubled?"

Rih glanced at her desk. It was covered in scrolls and tablets of notes, most on etiquette and customs of Mirik. She half-expected them to bear a layer of dust. "We had aurpose in the army. Even if there was no war, there were skirmishes, raids from the Vales or bandits. If there were no raids, we trained, kept our muscles fresh, because there will always be war."

Ki-elte's smile was faint. "You are restless?" Her signs were smoother, but her vocabulary was a fraction of Rih's own.

"I feel lost." Rih began to write instead. She did not have the energy to explain herself half a dozen times.

> *I do not recognize myself. In the army, we were a piece of a mighty whole, a fraction of Ban. I can't remember when I was my own self. Now, I find I have interests outside of war, outside of weapons, outside of my lessons here. It is a strange feeling, meeting myself for the first time.*

Ki-elte sat back, expression thoughtful. "And what do you think?"

"Of what?"

"Of this person you are becoming, or have always been, but did not know?" Ki-elte voiced.

> *You spoke of how we are invisible, the unseen warriors and politicians of Ban. Yet I feel trapped in this room. I wish I could do something useful.*

Ki-elte shook her head. "We have a training hall, down below, but only a few dozen of us use it, and I'm afraid we don't have any teachers. It is more to help us in our other duties."

Rih's brow quirked. "I fail to see how throwing darts would help anyone be a better lover."

Ki-elte's chest hitched in a laugh. "Grace and stamina are hallmarks of a good lover."

Rih shook her head. "Throwing darts will not help me in this war, not anymore at least." She watched Ki-elte struggle to find the right sign. Rih grabbed her hand to interrupt. "I found some women who know my language. And you've been learning."

"I heard." Ki-elte smiled.

"If I asked, could you call several of the women together? A small group, no more than you'd have for a social gathering." Her heart pounded, unsteady but certain.

"Anyone in particular?" Dread shadowed the c in Ki-elte's eyes.

"Hamin and Hi-alan." She paused. This was the gamble, the dice that could end her life, end the faint plan uncurling in her heart before it ever bloomed.

> *You once asked me what ruled His Eminence. I responded with fear. Fear that we will see him as less than a god. Fear that we will see him as a man. Fear that we will be like Sa-at and realize we are more angry than we are afraid.*

She met Ki-elte's gaze. "Find me women who agree."

The other woman's eyes widened, but not with horror. "Would this evening be too soon?"

Rih's stomach flipped. Her limbs hummed with energy again, but now it was the flame of determination igniting her nerves. "It would be perfect. Thank you." She scarcely paid attention as Ki-elte began her lesson on herbal teas that would increase arousal or relaxation. After a moment she realized Ki-elte had stopped speaking. "What?"

The other woman's dark eyes rolled and she giggled. "If you are going to create a network of support and not be caught, Rih, you have to play the part. And these things I teach you, while not as exciting, I'm sure, are going to be vital for your life as a wife."

The long sentences were lost on Rih. When Ki-elte repeated herself, Rih insisted, "I was paying attention!" She pointed to the teas in turn as she listed off their properties. "Sleep, relaxation, stimulation, arousal, contraception—"

Ki-elte's waved hand interrupted her. "You've switched the last two around."

Embarrassment dampened Rih's excitement. "I'm sorry." She tapped the top of the box marked with a bog onion. "Contraception? How does this work?"

"Of course you'd be more intrigued by that." Ki-elte sat back and wrote the description.

> *It makes your body inhospitable to growing life. It makes you queasy in the mornings sometimes, but not terribly so. Other mixtures will cause miscarriage, but you have to be more discreet with those. I know your argument—a prison without bars is a prison still. An opulent palace can be a prison as terrifying as a dark cell. I know. Trust me, Rih, I do know.*

When Rih looked away, Ki-elte took her hand, drawing her gaze back to her face. "I wasn't always a tutor. Things happened that I would never wish on another. I think you see learning the rules to this mighty game as surrender."

Rih's cheeks flamed. Her chest and throat tightened. She knew nothing of Ki-elte's life. It was so easy to think soldiers were the only ones who saw death and war, who saw suffering. Silks could hide many things leather armor could not. "I know it's not the truth, but it's how my heart feels."

Ki-elte's hand covered hers for a moment before rising into a sign. "How can you break the rules if you don't know them as well as those who wrote them?" She tapped the teas again and switched back to speech. "If you memorize these and where they're from—by smell and look, not just their container—I'll let you leave early. In the meantime, I have your message to relay."

Rih nodded in agreement. When her tutor slipped out, she drew the first box toward her. *Chamomile. Harvested from the west and dried. Used to calm.* She was close to memorizing the second box's properties when Ki-elte burst back into the room.

"It's time."

Rih glanced out the window. Though the sun itself dipped below the horizon, warm gold still washed the cloudless sky. "I'm not through with the teas."

"Now you take your duties seriously. They're dried. They made it all the way from RoKetta. I promise they can wait a little longer." Her head tilted back in a laugh. "Most of our duties begin with nightfall."

Rih's eyes narrowed. "I thought chai was from the hills."

Ki-elte's smile broadened and an eyebrow quirked. "Good catch," she signed. Her warm hand wrapped around Rih's, and she tugged the other woman to her feet.

Rih felt the tremble in her teacher's body, the tension in her hand, watched the line of her shoulders bunch higher from nerves. She tugged her to a halt. "You're scared. I am too." She held her arms out in an offer for an embrace.

Ki-elte's expression softened, and she stepped into Rih's arms for a moment before pulling away. Her fingers curled and flicked in the first sign she had learned. "Thank you."

"They're waiting, come on!" Rih brushed past her and jogged down the stairs before she realized Ki-elte did not say where they were meeting. When she looked back, her teacher pointed to the bathing hall.

Rih wove through the foyer and into the main bath house. A woman in full robes—albeit lighter ones for the heat—raised a hand in greeting and raised the curtain to the largest exercise room. Rih froze when she ducked inside. She expected half a dozen women. Perhaps ten at the most. The dark gazes of twenty-seven women turned on her. A few she knew by name, several others by sight. Over half she had never seen. She offered a faint smile. Uncertainty replaced the excitement distracting her all afternoon was replaced with uncertainty. She never spoke to so many people at once. Watched them speak, surely, but never were so many eyes fixed on her hands, learning her words.

Rih settled herself onto a cushion at the front of the room. The women were restless, and she saw matching anxiety in many faces. The few words she caught on their lips were nervous. She raised her hand and Ki-elte called the crowd to order before settling into her own seat.

Rih found Hamin in the crowd. "Will you translate, please?" When the other woman nodded, Rih began to sign. "You are here because we are soldiers, and we are at war. We are the spies and politicians no one sees. You've known it better and longer than I. Just like with the army, though, we are the front lines. Women are the first to be called to action and the first to die. That will never change if we don't work as one." She waited while Hamin finished translating. Her soldier's eyes picked out distrust, women who seemed the kind of nervous that begat betrayal.

Rih leaned forward, pinning the uncertain women with her gaze. "I know what being invisible means. It's a prison, like these bodies we did not choose, but invisibility can break these bars. We already communicate silently—the colors we wear, our piercings." A surge of excitement filled her gut again. "I am here to broaden your vocabulary."

Hamin turned to them. "A few of us are fluent. Others know basic words and simple conversation. We can help you when you are confused."

"Are there questions?" Rih asked. "I know how easy it is to fall behind when communication fails."

A sea of head-shakes answered her. "Then let's start simply." She signed a polite greeting, fingers adding details and flourishes to the fairly universal raised hand and motioned for the others to mimic her. One by one they tried the sentence themselves. When most had the gist, she continued, Hamin translating. "When we first learn to read, those of us who are able, what do we learn?"

One woman raised a hand and replied, "The Woman's Code."

"Then let's start there ourselves." She fell into the memorized series of flicks and curls, letting the rhythm of her arms add cadence. It was her way of singing. "A woman has a single mind. She wakes for the Empire. She rides for the Empire. Her blood and heart and mind are Ban, breathing and alive. A woman has a single mind."

Rih's heart fluttered at the sight of two dozen women all gesturing back, all replying in her language. Most were clumsy, or signed in the wrong order, and it was more mimicry than fluency, but that was just a matter of time and practice. They went through the Code several more times, pausing for her or the others to clarify the nuances.

After an hour yawns punctuated the signs she and waved for them to stop. "It's late, and I'm sure you are all just as tired as I am. I hope you will return next week at the same time to learn more. And remember to practice!" She pointed to the women already fluent. "If you have questions or cannot come to my lessons, these women will help, too." She stepped down from the dais, nerves weakening her knees for a moment. She offered her hand, palm up, to the nearest woman. "Thank you for coming."

The woman repeated the goodbye with a smile and pressed her palm to Rih's. The former soldier moved down the line of her new students, thanking each in turn. Ki-elte joined her at the door when she was through, watching as they filed out. Without colored silks and sharp eyes the room was darker.

"You did well." Ki-elte clearly tried to avoid voicing. "I think this is a good thing. Learning is important. And community."

"I'm glad." Rih grabbed Ki-elte's hand. The other woman's pulse throbbed under her hard fingers. "I realized something about the person I am."

Ki-elte's smile broadened. "That you like her?"

"That I would want to be her when I was small." She was suddenly glad she did not have to speak through tears. "I'm proud of her."

Φ

The 17th day of Aeme, 1272
The City of Ceir Athrolan

Keplan woke alone. His mind was clear and his body sore. He rolled deeper into sheets that were not his. Sunlight struck his eyes, and he sighed. Days began despite how little rest he might have found the night before. He was checking his buttons in the mirror when his gaze fell to his hands.

Stop running.

A choice was laid at his parents' feet—join the war or let the world die. The clarity of that choice was enviable. Quests to save to world rarely happened. Instead, a multitude of dark paths twisted ahead. He could run, stay in Ceir Athrolan as a bar-boy and Firas's occasional lover. *Or I could make sense of the power my parents gave me.* Footsteps sounded in the hall and he peered out, hoping for Firas.

Mirrel's eyes narrowed on him. "I knew he was bedding you."

Keplan matched her glare. "Is he downstairs?"

"No, I left the bar unattended, so the patrons could rob us."

"Thank you." Keplan ignored her sarcasm and trotted down the stairs. He was fairly certain the patrons were honest folk, if a bit rough. Firas was serving breakfast to the few who stayed the night. Keplan found his usual seat in the corner, blushing when Firas shot him a coy wink.

"You're not usually one for breakfast."

"I was wondering if there was a library. I find I'll be in Athrolan for longer than I thought."

"You serious?" At Keplan's nod, Firas frowned. "The palace has one, but I doubt you'd be allowed in. There's a block of buildings down by the Guilds, though, along the docks. The Scholars' Hall. Scribes go there to work and learn. News barkers too. You certain you don't want something to eat?"

Keplan surprised Firas with a wink of his own as he ducked out the door. "Maybe I'll come back for supper."

Dust and the caustically sweet smell of cooking ink hung over the Scholars' Hall. Arrogance pinched the faces of many scattered about the rooms. Luckily, he passed without much notice, save for foul looks. The unfinished floor and walls cast everything from the tomes to the scribes in yellow. After several ill-received wrong turns, he found the library in the rear of the building.

Political and historical tests filled most of the shelves, peppered with philosophical works and sheaves of scribes' records. It was everything Keplan had been hoping to find. Replacing the knowledge his parents kept from him would take years, but he must begin somewhere. He settled on a sunlit window sill and laid a stack of older tomes beside him.

A Soldier's Account was riddled with narcissism, and *Gods and Men* seemed more intent on damning any but the human players in the war. It had been months since he read a book, but he did not remember the few his parents owned being so dry. A year ago he would assumed it was due to his mother's taste in poetry. *It's easier to keep the truth from someone when there are no histories on their shelves.* Frustrated, Keplan opened *Time of Faded Sun,* and found a world that worshiped his mother as a god, and feared the earth his father crossed.

The bells began at noon. Shouting followed, ringing from one tower, then another. Hooves snapped against the stone as guards flooded the docks. Fear exploded in Keplan's gut, twisting in a knot too tight to even be sick. It reminded him of Ban. Somewhere a horn sounded. Scribes traded bewildered looks as they flooded out the door, barkers grabbed wax tablets to record what they could. Keplan followed the press of people, shouldering his way through the door and into the street. People crowded the docks and square. Each time he caught someone's eye, his panic borrowed steam from theirs.

A gray charger thundered down the street from the palace, parting the crowd like waves before a prow. *An'thoriend.* Keplan ducked into the shadow of the Hall, but the general only had eyes for the bulky man by the docks.

"You fucking traitor!" The horned man flung himself from his horse's back. Fury twisted his pale face.

He batted An'thor away as the general tried to haul him from his perch on a piling. The emblem on his chest was Anthrolani, but Keplan did not recognize the black uniform. Other seemed to, however. Scribes fell back from the fight, faces white. In the harbor, sailors swarmed their ships. Black canvas cascaded from every naval mast. *Black uniforms? Black sails?*

Several paces away a barker clambered onto a crate. "Commander Dorcal brought news from the palace! Queen Tzatia is dead!" The words pierced the chaos like an arrow through fat. Keplan's heart faltered. *This is my home.* The only home he still clung to despite everything. Now war loomed over Ceir Athrolan's sun-bleached dome. Others ran to street corners to pass the news. Shouts rose across the city, and someone began to wail. Cannons fired in the harbor, bells booming from every tower. Cobbles shook with pounding boots.

Keplan could not move. His eyes found the general's across the churning crowd. Their blackness yawned, a void beneath Keplan's pitching heart.

INHERITING THE
GREATEST BURDEN

CHAPTER THIRTEEN

The 24th Day of Aeme, 1272
Marl Black, Glasden Province of Athrolan

AFTER TWENTY YEARS DAYMIR Blackhouse was used to the cold of the mountains. He still detested it. Exile for a noble was far better than for a common man, but the sweeping desolate hills surrounding the Xain manor—now known as Manor Black—were still a prison. Turning his horse's head toward home, his eyes narrowed on an approaching visitor. Mail and supplies brought company, but it was infrequent. *Anything to keep my mind from scattering even further to the winds.* The last visit brought a begging letter from An'thoriend.

Perhaps this time the news would be better.

Rocks clattered as he raced down the slope, weaving between evenly planted apple trees. Sixty years weighed only on his mind, rather than his bones. He arrived with enough time to drink a tall glass of water and be seated calmly in his study when the soldier stepped in.

"Captain Hylier," Daymir greeted with a smile. "I'm glad to see you."

"Master Blackhouse." The man bowed his head. Despite his soldier's uniform, he adopted the casual stance of a comrade. Pale hair and blue eyes spoke of southern blood, but he was raised in the Xain manor.

"You're two weeks late."

Hylier frowned. "Four weeks early, actually."

"I must have lost track of the days." *Again.* Daymir looked away to hide his embarrassment and gestured to the table between them. "Do you want something other than water?"

"No, thank you. I'll get something later for supper. I have news." Hylier's usually easy smile was absent. Doffing his hat, a nervous hand flattened the short cropped hair.

Daymir's heart sank. "Her Majesty?"

Hylier nodded. "Commander Dorcal announced her passing just a few days ago. She left this world on the 42nd of Llueme."

The exile stared at the place his signet ring once rested. The tan lines were long faded, but he still missed the weight. "That was months ago. Why am I just hearing of it now?"

"Because none of us knew until the commander told us. Ceir Athrolan is in an uproar." Pale eyes softened. "I'm sorry. That's really not what you want to hear right now. She was at peace, and with her attendant, Countess Fiena." He looked down. "Sadly, the countess took her own life not long ago."

A sigh slipped through Daymir's tight throat. "They were fast friends." He glanced up from his hands. "How long will you be here?"

"I'm set to return tomorrow. I thought it would be best coming from a familiar face."

"It is." It was not. *It's never easy to hear the woman who raised you, mentored you, disowned you, died without goodbye.* His eyes flicked up. "I need news. Not just what the scribes wish me to know."

"You want the barkers, the gossip. You want the truth."

"I want to know how close to war Athrolan comes."

Hylier bowed his head. "Of course. For now, I'll leave you to your thoughts. We can discuss details in the morning."

Daymir's voice stopped him in the study's doorway. "Thank you. We may have been estranged, but she was still family. You, at least, never forgot."

Φ

The 25th Day of Aeme, 1272
The City of Ceir Athrolan

Keplan's mind plummeted back into his body, and he lurched out of bed. His chest heaved, and his throat burned.

"Are you all right?" Firas's voice battered its way through the screams piercing Keplan's mind.

Keplan drew a breath. The screaming stopped. The air was still and close. "Just a dream."

Firas placed a hand on his shoulder. "From what happened to you before you came here?"

Keplan glanced back at him. Firas was an escape, a tiny world free from worry. That peace would shatter if he knew the truth. "I'll be all right." He glanced at the window. "How do you sleep with that closed? It's cloying in here."

"You don't like the smell of our passion from last night?"

Keplan made a face. "It's not that. I just can't breathe."

Firas sobered. "I closed it because of the smoke."

"Smoke?"

"You were resting, and I didn't want to wake you. Someone torched a warehouse."

Keplan glanced at the window again. "I was safe here. And now we're on the brink of civil war." He caught sight of Firas's sudden grin. "What?"

"You said 'we' like you're Athrolani."

"I'm not anything else, really." He sighed softly. "I haven't seen war."

"You're a bit young for that." Firas shrugged. "I haven't either. I was born of it. My da died in it, protecting the Dhoah' Laen."

Keplan froze. "He was her guard?"

"Well, not like the Rakos. Da ran with him for a time. Drinking buddies while she was off learning how to kill the gods."

"Did you ever see them? Afterward, I mean?"

"Not the Rakos. Mirrel saw the Dhoah' Laen. You could ask her about it."

Keplan snorted. "I'd most likely get slapped. We've had a few moments that weren't openly hostile, but that ended when she realized we spent nights together."

Firas's low laugh rolled through the dark room. "I only properly bedded you a week ago. It was all whispers and chaste kisses in the dark before that."

Keplan blanched. "Fates, she doesn't know that. I hope. I'd rather she not know any of it." He glanced back at the window. "Why was a warehouse burning?"

"I think we're all afraid of what will happen if An'thoriend can't produce his promised heir. Trade will plummet. Even Mirik can't be expected to help us with their own war brewing. One thing to be said about the Dhoah' Laen—she brought us together like no one else."

Keplan looked away. *Brentemir wants to use me for the same reason. Whatever inexplicable trait that made her a cavalcade of power has only made me see things that aren't mine to see.* "Do you think Athrolan will survive?"

"I think whatever happens she won't look the same afterward." He tugged Keplan's arm. "I love talking to you, 'Lan, but I also love sleep. I promise the city won't burn down around us in the night."

Keplan tucked himself against the other man's back, threading an arm around his waist. Now, even with the window shut, all he could smell was smoke.

Φ

The 26th Day of Aeme, 1272
Western Glasden Province, Athrolan

The road changed as they moved north. Soft brown soil turned packed gray dirt and rocks. Sweeping hills rose from the Borderland, too steep for trees. Here the wind was a funeral dirge. Perched atop the next hill was a weathered, crooked signpost at a fork in the road. Alea drew up and peered at the sign. Ugly black paint marred the carved wood. "Blackhouse?" She glanced back at Arman. "What is this?"

"It looks like politics to me, honestly. I think 'Blackhouse' is the surname given to exiled nobles. Perhaps it means Daymir." His eyes scanned the horizon. In the distance, a cluster of buildings clustered on the crest of a small mountain's root. A gray line of scree switchbacking up the sullen green of the slope served as the only road. Unlike the towns in the heart of the kingdom, this had walls. High ones. "There've been few traders on the road the past few weeks. A tinker yesterday and that was it."

"It feels like last time."

"It feels like winter," Arman suggested. He jerked his chin at the road leading from the mountain village. "That looks like a messenger." The rider moved swiftly along the road, helm glinting over the black of a tabard and the horse's trappings. Arman glanced at Alea, wordlessly agreeing to wait for the courier to pass. It took a minute for the rider to reach them. When she did, she barely slowed enough to hail them. "The queen!" she called when she was still several horse-lengths away. Her voice rasped, and shadows marked her eyes. "Her Majesty Tzatia is dead!"

Alea stared, moving aside as the woman thundered past, carrying the grim news south. Her eyes flicked to Arman. "No heir, and a dead queen."

Arman looked back to the crude word marring the sign. "It's not the winter, then, making roads deserted. It's war." He leaned an arm on his pommel. "Alea, what is this? We've avoided all the wayhouses and towns for the last week. If Keplan's written we wouldn't know, and there's no way to say which way he rode."

"I know what it looks like," she bit back. Worry for her son was a fathomless gulf in her chest, but the best way to protect him was down this new, dark path.

"It looks like running, Alea."

Her lips thinned. "I don't know where to begin. I can't just ask if anyone has seen a mad old woman. We'd be introduced to every grandmother between here and Berr."

"We need news, if for no other reason than to know the state of the kingdom we're traipsing across. What did you do during the last war?"

"Hoped I didn't die." She shrugged.

Arman rolled his eyes. "I meant besides the human bits you couldn't really help."

"This is different. That war revolved around me and you and the gods. We were the keystone in those battles."

"I love you, but that's nonsense. That war was about the world crumbling around all of us. Hundreds of battles were fought before either of us even drew breath. This war is the same—everything crashing down, orchestrated by the few who can escape the chaos." He sat back. "So—what did you do?"

She glanced up, finally. "I fought. I learned, I planned, I gathered allies. Mostly I fought."

"So fight. This is our kingdom. Well, at least more so than any other. Our son is somewhere out in this world, and our best chance at finding him is ensuring he isn't lost in the mess of the impending civil war."

"I have an idea, one I've been thinking over for days. You won't like it." Just as she knew the madwoman was the key to whatever was left of their power, she knew Daymir was the key to saving Keplan.

"I've liked plenty of your plans. Once I knew about them, of course."

Her brow arched in skepticism. "You've liked exactly one of my plans."

"I've liked all the ones that didn't include death and war and fire and lightning and madness and gods."

She allowed a faint smile to cross her mouth. "Those were most of my plans."

Arman snorted. "Well, our powers are gone, and the gods are dead. What is left to dislike about this one?"

"We need information. We need sanctuary and passage wherever we go next. One man can offer all those things." Her gaze swiveled to the vandalized road sign. "I want to go to Manor Black."

Φ

The 27th Day of Aeme, 1272
The City of Ceir Athrolan

"This should be different." An'thor's words sank in the silence of the Xain mausoleum. The half dozen personal guards on duty said nothing. There was nothing to say, truly, in the face of everything he had done. The queen's body lay in state on the marble slab in the center of the tomb. Behind her, past the graves of her father and daughter, the wall stood open, a black maw waiting for bones.

An'thor tugged the torch from the brazier and dipped it into the network of oil-filled troughs carved in the slab. The flames caught, clawing their way across the stone and onto the oiled shroud covering Tzatia's form. An'thor knelt and pressed his brow to the stone, headless of the heat raging over his head, the flames close to the capped stumps of his horns. If he had his druthers, he would pitch himself on the flames beside her. The shroud caught with a roar and the fire devoured hair and mummified flesh.

Bile threatened to crawl up his throat, but he clenched his teeth. It was not the smell or the sight. He had seen worse, done worse himself. *She's gone.* Mourning in secret was agony. But now he could not escape her death. Black hung from every rampart; a stone effigy would replace her body.

An hour passed before the queen was a pile of charred bones cupped in the hammered metal tray set into the slab. Decades of soot stained its bone handles. An'thor staggered to his feet. His knees ached, and his legs burned from crouching, immobilized with grief.

If it were not a time of war, Tzatia's commander, heir, and the Council heads would help him bear her body. Instead, he was joined only by his own few guards and Lord Henack of the House of Commons.

Hot metal groaned when they levered it from the stone and crossed the mausoleum. Bitter, sharp smoke wafted across An'thor's face. He lowered the front of the metal tray to the hole under her effigy. Blackened bones slid from the metal with a rattle and an inglorious puff of dust. Her name and title, the places and times of her birth and death graced the heavy stone lowered into place over the hole.

"General, sir there's visitors coming from the south. They fly the colors of Pardelan and Tetran."

An'thor squeezed his eyes shut. He hoped the war between Mirik and Ban would prevent travel, but the potential heirs to the throne were more dedicated than he thought. *Unlike Daymir, of late.* As it was, camps already crowded outside the gates as people waited to be let into the city proper.

"Sir, the men at the south gate want to know if they should allow them through," the guard repeated.

"Prepare another tent in the detainment camp for the Duke and Lady. And post a guard. I'm not letting nobles in, ally or otherwise until I know the details." An'thor brushed ashes from his suede tunic. Like every piece of clothing, it was black and gray. At least he had not needed a new wardrobe for National Mourning.

The small south gate wedged between the palace and the barracks, more often used for the military's comings and goings than anyone of state. Smaller meant easily controlled, however, and An'thor seized every inch of control he could. The streets were mostly deserted, but not quiet. Soldiers on street corners barked orders to those still out. An'thor glanced at the sky. Curfew would be called soon, and while safety was important, he did not want the army wasting slim resources on simple city folk late from their shops. When he reached the gate, the bells sounded the hour, loud and brassy, too demanding to sound joyous. "I'm here to see the Duke and his sister. Are their quarters ready?"

The soldier guarding a gap in the camp's makeshift fence relaxed from attention. "In a moment, yes, sir. They're at the edge, under the windows of the east barrack wing. You may escort them yourself if you wish."

"I'll let the captain handle that honor." He smiled at the sarcastic quirk to her brow at his choice of words. "I ought to survey the camp as it is. Thank you." He edged through the narrow opening. The tents were large ones used for infirmaries or groups of squires on training missions. Now lesser merchants and those unable to justify entering the city packed between the canvas walls. He counted at least a hundred cots, maybe more, not including the mess tents and those taking advantage of the literal captive customer base. What started as temporary delays now looked closer to a prison camp.

An'thor found the nicer, officer's tent tucked in the lee of the city walls. He nodded to the guard stationed outside the backlit canvas.

"General An'thoriend Domariigo of Neneviir and Claimiirn to see Duke Tzavanir of Ceir Pardelan and Lady Gella of Tetran and RoBal."

"Show him in."

An'thor ducked through the tent flap. A young man dressed in travel-stained finery paced along the rear of the tent. A woman, his double save for the long hair, stood in the center, a baby feeding in her arms. Their retinue gathered in separate tents outside.

"Sir Tzavanir, I'm glad you made the journey safely. And you, Gella, you must have had a long ride from Ban. How were the roads?"

"I know exactly what this is, general—" the Duke began.

"The journey was fine, if a bit long. My body tells me it grows longer each time I make it, but our carriage driver says it hasn't changed in length." Gella flashed him a smile. "Please forgive my brother. This entire unfolding of events took us by surprise. Even you, I'm sure." Her smile faded, and she shifted the baby from her breast to her shoulder. "But I agree this was not the welcome either of us expected."

"Of course." An'thor's stomach churned, heart sinking low enough to take root between his boots. "Of course. I understand. This may seem inhospitable, but it is for your safety. We cannot risk the only two heirs in a war-torn city. You should be comfortable here until we can fix this mess with the commander. I already have plans for negotiation."

"My sister has a babe in arms, and you consider this prison camp safe?"

Ah, there's the accusation I anticipated. "Tzavanir, this is not a prison camp. It's a refuge. You will have a cadre of my own personal guards at all times, and should you need to speak with me, you can contact me directly through them." He backed toward the tent door. "We will speak shortly, I am sure. For now, I will let you settle in and rest." It was a coward's retreat, and they all knew it, but An'thor could not bring himself to care. He needed to meet with Keplan, just long enough to shove a crown on the boy's head and put an end to the uncertainty.

After decades among them, An'thor's love for humanity was tinged with a father's disappointment, and an outsiders contempt. Tzatia's human heirs could not save them now. It was up to a boy in the slums, mad and lost, and brimming with power.

Φ

The 30th Day of Aeme, 1272
The City of Ceir Athrolan

Summer's end turned Athrolan gold. The hills flamed into yellow and orange, and the stone glowed in the still-warm sunlight. Crops ripened in the apron of fields to the west. Keplan's afternoons were spent in the Scholars' Hall, and crisp nights were warmed by Firas's body.

It should have been peaceful.

More fires broke out. Storefronts that withstood the last three wars were shattered and robbed. Even the impending harvest was not enough to distract the city from Tzatia's death. Firas rolled away, muttering to himself in sleep and taking most of the blankets with him. Keplan let him have them. Even with the window open, he felt trapped. The darkness in the tiny attic was too similar to his cell. There were a few hours before their duties downstairs began, but Keplan could not rest. He pushed himself up and padded across the floor, collecting his clothes as he went.

He was halfway to the docks when he realized the Scholars' Hall was undoubtedly locked for the evening. *I want answers.* Research often seemed to tangle his thoughts further. There was nothing groundbreaking, no sudden epiphany. Until he learned he was too old, he entertained training to become a consulate.

The streets were no longer cheery in the evening, and Keplan missed the noise. His feet turned him toward the Thread. In the colors and chaos, he was sure to find something, even if it was only distraction. He heard the district before he saw the glow of lanterns. Another two turns and he broke into the bubble of sound and color. Wares were much more expensive, and he shoved his hands into his pockets to avoid the desire to brush them over the shiny metal and rich cloth. He paused at a stall displaying curved blades. Some were simple, clearly practical. Others had only a raw tang for a hilt, ready to be worked to a buyer's specific needs. He lingered a moment too long.

"You interested in a blade?" The Banis smith's smile was broad. "We've got a variety, including some Anthrolani styles."

Keplan held up a gloved hand. "Forgive me, I'm afraid I can't afford such quality. I was just admiring. My father was a bladesmith." He winced at the revealing words.

"Ah, anyone I would know?"

Someone everyone would know, but not for his skill at the forge. "I doubt so. He worked far to the south, in a small city. I think he would have liked your work." He nodded a quick goodbye and stepped back into the crowd. Distraction made him careless, and he was not ready to claim the blood pumping in his veins. He lost himself in the flicking facts from the people he brushed past and the shouts of news from Ban, Mirik, Sunam, and countless other nations. The barkers were not all foreign, it seemed. A small crowd clustered around one brandishing an Athrolani poster.

Keplan's eyes narrowed on the man's grim face. It was the same barker from the market, a man dressed more finely than his battered box stool implied. The drawing depicted a dark-haired man imprisoned, the Ageless general holding the keys.

"Daymir's claim is rightful, Athrolani bred and born, even the queen's own declaration to support him! She only cast him aside when the horned beast arrived! He seduced her with his evil words until she knew no better. And when she disinherited her only heir, he poisoned her!"

Keplan heard little about the exiled heir, though the tomes accused him of moving funds about. *Most of the city wants you, Daymir, so why are you hiding?* Gossip would steer him in no useful direction, and he was due back at the bar. He heaved a sigh and shouldered his way back toward the slums.

"You're late." Mirel barked at him, tossing his apron over. Firas rolled his eyes behind her back. Exhaustion lined his face, despite his nap following their afternoon tryst.

Keplan shot an apology over his shoulder and set to work. The doors banged all night, despite the curfew, but the conversation a bitter rumble different from its usual levity. Between running mugs of ale for Firas and wiping tables between patrons, there was no time to rest. Sweat dripped down his back despite the chill creeping into the night air. He paused for a moment in the kitchen, leaning on the wall to catch his breath.

"You set, 'Lan?" Firas poked his head through the door.

"Yeah. It's just loud out there. So many people. Every single one angry." He shuddered at the insidious thoughts.

"I know. Hard times drive everyone to drink. It's a boon to us, but makes more work than we can rightly keep up with." He turned to shout a response to a patron before glancing back at Keplan. "Take a minute outside, then come back. I need you too badly to let you off for the night, though."

Keplan flashed him a faint smile. "Thanks." He shoved off the wall and slipped out into the courtyard. The walls seemed to encroach on him, and he jogged through the alley and out into the street. Cold freshened the stagnant city air.

"War makes things feel a bit close, eh?" The low voice grated from the shadows as if the words themselves bounced over the cobbles.

"War?" He peered into the darkness between the buildings across the street.

"You smell it. The grief on your face says as much. Same with the fatigue in your shoulders." A woman stepped into the street. She dressed like a ranger, in leather and layers, but it was black, not brown.

A spy, then. He recognized her from the corner of the Wise Hare weeks ago. "What do you want?" Facts trickled into his mind. *Azimir's mother. No, he's barely met her.* That was a puzzle for fiddling.

"A word, if you please, Wardyn." She shifted, her cloak slipping away from her hip and showing the set of various blades, all of which looked well used.

"You're threatening me. It won't work."

"I'm making you listen."

"You work from Brentemir." Keplan leaned on the wall. "The ambassador asked you to drag me across the ocean?" Keplan guessed.

"I'm not here for Brentemir. I'm here for all of us."

"Noble." Keplan looked away.

Reka offered a sheaf of paper to him. "Brentemir would be furious if he knew what I'm doing. Athrolan is Mirik's greatest ally. If we go to war without her, against a force as ancient and great as the Banis, we will be sent back in the very shackles we seek to break. Athrolan falling to civil war would jeopardize trade, our access to the southern lands, not to mention our business with the kingdom itself. You are a wise man, if barely out of boyhood. I trust you'll understand the duty and its necessity."

"The duty of what?" Keplan unfolded the parchment. Reka did not respond. He skimmed the words. It was formal speech, something he disliked but understood. Limp, crumpled ribbons hung from old wax. The first was a declaration of inheritance, naming Daymir heir after the death of Tzatia's daughter. The second was a more recent declaration, written just before the war. It proclaimed Daymir a thief from the crown and stripped him of various titles and honors. "I've heard what happened to Daymir. I don't understand why it's relevant now."

"The next one, Wardyn."

Keplan tucked the older documents away and peered at the most recent. It was another declaration of inheritance of the crown, drawn up years before. The queen's signature was almost illegible, but the words above were written by a scribe.

> *It is to be known that in the absence of a living direct descendant of Queen Tzatia of Ceir Athrolan and the Xain House, and in the event of the former heir, now known as Daymir Blackhouse, being exiled from the kingdom during the Gods' War, that a new heir has been chosen. The child of our closest Ally Dhoah' Lyne'alea and the Earth Shaker Aud'narman Arrowlash, known to have been born in the south, has been named by Her Majesty as her rightful and honored heir. Upon the arrival of the child and his or her coming of age, it shall be declared that he will ascend to the throne to rule after Her Majesty passes into peace.*

There was more, but the letters blurred before Keplan's eyes. There were a dozen seals on the paper—the queen's, the general's, various lords and a slew of clerks. *This is official.* Blood raged in his ears, drowning out the sounds of the city below, the hissing of the waves against the stone. He was cold. Now, more than ever, he needed Daymir to claim the throne.

"So, this unnamed thing the general mentioned in his letter was the Crown of Athrolan." He pressed his forehead against the stone wall. "Why do you all think a peasant boy from the forest will serve better than an exiled man? Better than a contested distant cousin? Is my parents' blood so powerful?"

"I imagine so."

"Domariigo's a madman."

"But he's not wrong." Reka pushed off the wall and gathered the documents. "If I were you, I would sleep on this. And then do what you know you ought. Good evening, Wardyn." She disappeared up the street.

Screaming filled his head, surging through his mind like thunder. He crumpled by the stairs.

"'Lan, I need you in the front!" Firas burst through the door, glancing down at the heap of his lover in the street. "Fates, you look ill."

Keplan could not look the man in the eye. Truth might tumble from his mouth. "No. I'm set. Just tired is all." He dragged himself up with Firas's offered hand. "I'll get to work." He wove into the crowd before Firas could ask more. Heat and conversation were overwhelming, but for once Keplan welcomed the cacophony in his head.

Later, he sat in the darkness of his room. Boards closed his window, shattered by vandals days before. The small space was stifling without airflow. His hands shook, and his mind skipped to the next thought before finishing the last.

Papers glared at him from the desk top. Most contained notes on what he had read in the scribes' hall. The parchment under his poised pen, however, was blank.

He began letters to his parents a dozen times, but never wrote further than "I'm sorry." He hoped this letter would be easier. *What does one say when they're asking a man to rule a kingdom?* He was certain many wrote to Daymir, people with far more influence than he. It did not matter. Before, Daymir's refusal to take the throne threatened Keplan's sanctuary. Now it threatened his future. Brentemir added the figures and discovered Keplan's heritage. It was only a matter of time before others did the same.

He had not written a word. He could not claim to be anyone important; the lie would be obvious. If he explained who his parents were, it would seem too far-fetched to be the truth.

Finally, he scratched out a few lines. He would not accuse or presume to offer advice. He would convince the man war was inevitable, and Daymir himself was the only man who could save them.

If that failed, he would beg, and hope to fate the man answered.

Φ

The 32nd Day of Aeme, 1272
City of RoBal, Ban

Rising wind brought the smell of burning grasses. Soon, rain would pound the flames into ash. Changing seasons filled Rih's body with energy. She paced her room. With her lessons on hold for the war, she had more time than ever, and nothing to do but read. There were only so many times a woman could bathe, and while she enjoyed teaching signs, teaching did not help her relax.

Luxurious robes and tunics gave her power, but now the silk was cloying, like smoke clogging the breath of her skin. The clothes pooled on the floor, and she stood naked, trembling with nerves, before the windows. Tucked in the dark of her room, she was certain few could see her. *I don't care. They don't know who I am.* Even she did not recognize herself any longer. She missed the strength in her limbs, the understanding with her body that she would ask and it would obey.

At least in the army there was always work. Always something to practice, to mend, to learn. Her gaze fell to the soldier's training gear folded, forgotten, in the basket on her shelf. Rih only walked past the training hall on her way to the baths, but she trusted it would be close to empty in the afternoon. Most of the women were with their clients or resting for the night ahead.

She broke into a flurry of motion, heart deciding before her mind. Training clothes were on in a moment, soft fingers remembering tasks from harder days. After a wrong turn she found the small training hall, narrower and more dimly lit than those in the barracks. *At least the weapons are serviceable,* she noted, pacing down the modest rack of atlatls, spears, and crossbows.

Lanky arms made her best at the spear, and atlatls were most challenging. Her fingers brushed the grip of a mid-length one. It lacked the rich patina from years of use, but it was still supple and strong. Her grip tightened around the leather-wrapped wood, eyes lidding for a moment. Waves of wind across the prairie. Smoke and sun-cooked grass. Powerful hooves under her the few times she was allowed to ride. *That was freedom. For a moment, a single moment, that was freedom.* She wondered if she would be punished for impersonating a soldier if she left the Hall this way, acted with purpose and fled the city, fled Ban altogether. *Where would I go?*

Shaking the treasonous thoughts away and let a dart fly. Running from the frontlines of battle was not an option, even when she swore they faced Toar himself. She had a job to do. It might be one she hated, it might break her heart, but these were simply new tactics, a foreign battlefield.

War was war, and she would not run.

Her second dart landed closer to the target's center, but still outside the wounding area. *I'm out of practice.* A breeze eddied across the room, drifting through the packed straw on the floor. She glanced over at the door.

Hamin leaned on the half-open screen, wearing a shorter, loose kalas clearly designed for movement. Linen wrapped her hands for combat and she was unarmed. "I haven't seen you here before. What's on your mind?"

"I feel soft." Rih shrugged, not sure if the other woman would understand. Hamin fell into a ready stance, then spun into a slow, graceful dance of blows and blocks. Rih's third dart zipped through the air, thudding into the target a few hands from her first two. It took another half hour before her muscles remembered the motions. She jogged back from fetching her darts and turned to see Hamin watching with narrowed eyes.

"You're good," she noted. "I was once the markswoman of the 103rd March."

"You were a soldier?" Rih's smile widened. "I didn't know."

"Several of us were. It's not common, but you aren't the first. I learned languages well, so they made me a companion for visiting dignitaries." Flurried blocks interrupted her signs, but after a moment she continued, "I didn't keep up with practice once I was here."

"I don't blame you—I didn't either. I just felt restless. I'll have little cause to practice once I'm married, unless I'm lucky enough to wed a Valen man," she joked. The matriarchal Vales were something of a legend among the Banis foot soldiers.

Hamin's face sobered. "You'd be more lucky to see a Valen raid than the inside of their bed chambers. They wouldn't accept a bride from Ban any more than Mirik will, it seems." Her hands stilled, and she watched Rih toss another two darts. Each was closer to the target's center.

Hamin held her hand out for the atlatl. "May I try?"

Rih handed the weapon over, eager to see a markswoman throw. Hamin settled the concave end of the dart on the spur. Her movements were unconscious, graceful in their certainty. She drew her arm back and brought it forward, the power in her shoulders sending the dart hurtling through the air. It split Rih's with a puff of shattered wood. She handed the weapon back so she could sign again. "I don't blame you for wishing to be married to Vale."

"It would be easier if they didn't hate us so."

"It's not hatred." Hamin's brows curled together. "It's enlightenment." Her head tilted at something unheard and her shoulders sagged in a sigh. "I'd best go. I just stop by here between visitors. Steadies my thoughts." She waved and slipped from the room.

Rih's heart thundered again, the same as when she stared down her cousin with all the fury she had never shown. *Enlightenment? If we are cousins, then how did things change so much?* Neither books nor Ki-elte would help. Questions led to trouble. It was the first rule of interrogation they learned in the army: find the source.

Replacing her atlatl and darts, she jogged back to her room. She did not bother to change before unrolling a blank scroll on her desk. It was one of the only times she used the pull by the door to summon a serving woman.

"What can I do?"

Rih wrote a quick line on her tablet.

I need to speak to Instructor Il-fald of the army. Tell her Rih-elte needs her advice.

"If you need a guard, we would be happy to send one."

"This is a personal call."

The woman bobbed her head in deference and slipped away.

Il-fald arrived with the darkness. Rih did not realize how much she missed the smell of leather until her nose was buried in the muscle of her former mentor's shoulder. She pulled away so she could sign, "I've missed you so much."

"You planning on sneaking back to our ranks?" Il-fald gestured to the training clothes.

"No, I was tossing darts and got distracted by some thoughts." She noticed, then, that the trainer's own clothing looked haphazardly arranged. "I'm sorry I interrupted your rest."

Il-fald's lined face broke into a rare smile. "I wouldn't say I was resting. She was pulled away by her own distractions, anyway." As usual she voiced and signed simultaneously. Her smile grew sad. "I miss having you at practice. You lent a certain humor that is lacking."

"You called me cynical," Rih countered.

Il-fald laughed. "Well, it wasn't unfounded. Have you learned much?"

"I did, but war slowed my lessons. I'm too still. And it seems my cynicism isn't as appreciated here as it was in the army."

"You said you wanted advice—is it about that?"

Rih looked down. *Why did I feel the urge to ask Il-fald to visit?* It seemed dire at the time, and now she felt dramatic, foolish, almost. "Part of it was loneliness," she hazarded, "and curiosity. My friend Hamin and I were discussing the likelihood of a marriage to one of their men. I knew you encountered them more than once and I wanted to know more. There's so little in the histories."

It was Il-fald's turn to look away. She ran a finger along the scar on her face. It began as a delicate line over her nose then widened across her cheek and ended at the missing tip of her ear. The Valen history with Ban was either erased or never written. Often the only accounts came from the few Banis women who survived meeting them in battle.

She was motionless for so long, Rih wondered if she would say another word. "They are ruled by a Queen." Il-fald's eyes remained fixed on the desk, the only movement her fingers and lips. "Unlike Athrolan's, though, she is a warrior. Their women are their warriors, like us, but they are also generals, strategists. Men stay at home and mind the children and farms. It's small wonder His Eminence hates them."

"I envy them," Rih interjected. "Hamin said they didn't hate us, rather they were enlightened." Fire hummed along her nerves and she clenched her fists before continuing. "I want to meet them." The words were signed before they were fully formed in her mind. *What good would meeting them do?* Teaching others her language, seeking advice from those who had overthrown their master—she saw what, together, those pieces made, and it was terrifying. *And liberating.* She glanced up, realizing Il-fald was signing while she thought. "I'm sorry?"

"Of course. I just said I am angry too. I promise you, I did not willingly give my body and soul to war, but this is our world. I see what you're doing, even if you don't realize it." Il-fald paused, eyes searching Rih's face. Her expression softened. "I think you just realized it too. But you must know a single woman cannot change something so ingrained."

"But she can be the catalyst." Now that she knew the secret lying in her heart, calm washed over her. "We are not the only women to be angry. I have a roomful of women willing to learn an entire language in order to speak freely. And like you said—the Vales are enlightened. We were once the same people.

And now we're not. They changed their path. I can change ours." She pulled a scroll from her desk drawer. "What's her name? This Queen?"

"Majilah Ag of Vale."

It took a minute before Rih knew how to begin, and ten more before she had something worth penning. In the end, she chose simplicity. She leaned over the desk and reread her words.

Your Majesty Majilah Ag, Queen of Vale,

You do not know me, but I am told our people were once the same. I am a daughter of His Eminence, the Emperor of Ban. I write because I have been sent from our army to learn to be a wife. I've learned more about the world, about our place in it as women, in the last few months than I ever did as a soldier.

And I want it to change. I want to know how you broke from us and took back your power. I hope you can help.

In confidence,

-Rih-elte

It was not perfect, but it was a beginning. *Everything I do now depends on beginnings. Everything started somewhere.* She needed to know where that place was. She rolled the parchment into a tiny scroll case and laid it on the table between them. Il-fald's expression was wary, but she made no move to leave. "You have informants, people who spy—on us as well as for us," Rih guessed.

"It's part of my job to know who to trust. The baniol might not think I'm capable, but I'm far from stupid."

"Could you to get this across the border to Vale?"

"Is it treason?" Il-fald pointedly did not read Rih's words.

"It's questions. It's hope." Rih shrugged. "Would it matter?"

Il-fald did not answer, but tucked the scroll away in her clothes. "Rih, this could kill you. Doesn't that scare you enough to stop?"

Rih's gaze bore into Il-fald's "If the gods still walked, they themselves could not stop me."

CHAPTER FOURTEEN

The 41st Day of Aeme, 1272
Marl Black, Glasden Province of Athrolan

IT TOOK A SECOND knock for Daymir to realize Hylier stood in the doorway. "I worried I'd find you cold when you didn't answer. Do you want me to come back later?"

"I was lost in thought." Daymir glanced over with a wan smile. After a moment before he remembered why Hylier was there. "I would rather not wait another few weeks for the mail. I trust the weather has not been too bad?"

"Not yet, though there are rumors of the first winter storm."

"I was displeased to hear the servants discussing snow yesterday." Daymir gestured to the chair across from him. "Please, sit. Tell me the news. I've seen a lot of traffic on the roads lately. Many swords."

Hylier sat with a heavy sigh. "Athrolan is in trouble. Everyone sees it, none acknowledge it, really. Each has a different idea about how to fix the problem." He handed Daymir several letters. "There are some new ones in there."

Though it was Hylier's job to keep Daymir from creating a revolution, his practice of reading the exile's mail stopped after An'thoriend's letter. Daymir knew he now straddled the chasm between exile and prodigal. "Reports, more reports, letter from that supporter, Peraan. Letters from cousins." Daymir put them all aside for later, peering at the last two. Neither bore a sender's address on the outside of the envelope. The dates were two weeks apart and the hand was the same. "Did you read these?"

"I'm not supposed to anymore."

"Doesn't mean you don't." Daymir slit open the older envelope and tugged the letter out. "Any idea?"

Hylier shrugged. "Shall I call for dinner while you read?"

Daymir's nod was distracted. Curious words scrawled across the page engrossed him. He turned so the light struck the page better.

Daymir Blackhouse,

I assume you get news from the city, whether by legitimate means or otherwise. You saw the Gods' War, and I assume you can imagine what the city looks like now. There are barkers on every corner that hold posters defaming Domariigo or you. Just as many cry for support. I am not someone you know, just someone with questions.

My first: What happened just before the Gods' War and how can we prevent Athrolan tearing herself apart? I promise you, she will.

Write to me at the Courier's Hall,

Lan Guardsen

It was not a familiar name. Something underlay the frank tone.

Hylier thumped into the chair opposite him with a sigh. "You look troubled."

"This letter's odd. The man—boy, perhaps, since he doesn't recall the Gods' War—writes only to ask me a question. Here, read it yourself." Daymir tossed it over and opened the next.

Daymir Blackhouse,

It occurs to me that mail to your estate might be slow. It also occurs you may not reply at all. War is nearing. How can a city save herself when her allies are caught in their own chaos? That is not my second question to you. Instead, it is this: which conflict is threatens us more—Mirik's war with Ban, or our own with our brothers?

Lan Guardsen

Hylier put the first letter aside. "I don't recognize the name, though the surname is common enough. He's to the point. Perhaps he's recording a history. What do you think?"

Daymir handed it to Hylier wordlessly and waited as the other man scanned it. "Or perhaps the name is false and he is a political figure."

"You're paranoid." The food arrived, and the guard made room on the table between them. "You think he's truly an ally?" He took a large bite of the bread and meat, allowing Daymir to consider his question.

"I have no motives for the throne, thusly cannot have allies. But I will answer him."

"You're that lonely?" Hylier's brows snapped up.

Daymir's smile was sharp. "I'm that curious."

Φ

The 44th Day of Aeme, 1272
The City of Ceir Athrolan

Rain splattered against the glass. To An'thor's eyes, it was the spray of Athrolan's blood. Pale hands clenched on the stone window sill. He listened as

Raven poured a drink from the general's well-stocked cabinet. "Why are you here?"

"Because you invited me for a drink."

"Don't be coy."

"I'm here because I hope you've seen sense. I'm willing to listen, willing to come to some agreement."

An'thor glanced over his shoulder, eyes narrowed. "You've never been willing to compromise in your life."

Raven stared at the drink in his hand. "For her, I would be."

An'thor wondered absently if Raven spoke of the queen or Athrolan. *Or Eras.* "So, what do you propose? I pay for your secret whores, and you'll allow Keplan to be king?"

Raven's growl was low. "I am trying to be an adult, Domariigo."

An'thor turned to lean on his desk. "And I'm trying to do what is best for our kingdom. Daymir is not a young man. His letters tell me his clarity is not what it once was. If he ascends, we have maybe fifteen years before we need another heir. The two cousins who are eligible have little training—"

"And you've trapped them in a prison camp while you stall negotiations."

An'thor sighed. "Gella has no interest in the throne, and her brother is next to useless. Keplan is young. He's who Tzatia wanted for king, and he is powerful. He's a symbol, Raven—one we need. Our ally is at war, and if you and I can't come to an accord, we will have larger issues on the table."

"Daymir will buy us the time to make this choice properly."

"We had twenty years, and we're still ready to throw each other into the storm."

Raven looked past An'thor to the portrait behind the desk. It portrayed the queen in her thirties. Eras stood at one hand, An'thoriend at the other. The commander's eyes were fixed on the former general. "She would hate us for this. She always loved Athrolan so much. She loved the queen and the city and every piece of this kingdom."

"Eras had allegiances higher than the queen, Raven, and you know it." An'thor rapped his knuckles against the rough wood of his desk. "Both she and the queen are dead, and it's left up to us. What is your compromise?"

"Allow Daymir into the city to speak with us."

"And what will you do in return?"

"I won't crown him the minute he steps through the palace gates."

An'thor rolled his eyes. "You don't have that power."

"With enough of the House of Nobles, I do. And you are a fool if you think they won't choose him over a power-addled pauper." Raven knocked back his drink. "Decide, Domariigo. You have five days. After that, you'll have no choice."

Φ

The 46th Day of Aeme, 1272

Marl Black, Glasden Province of Athrolan

Bitter wind buffeted the manor, whipping the mourning flags. Daymir sank deeper into his chair. Vaulted ceilings were beautiful but hardly homey. Even with a roaring fire, it was cold. He brushed dry fingers down the page of his book. Despite reading the words half a dozen times without comprehending them. Solitude may have become him in his youth, but now it chafed. Even for the mountains, a squall in Aeme was unexpected.

He slapped the book on the table and stalked to the window. Outside the world was white. Ice glittered in the churning sky. Fog swallowed everything beyond the head of the road. *If this isn't a metaphor for Athrolan's current state, I don't know what is.* Glass rattled under a blast of wind. Movement caught his eye as he retreated to the fire. A shadow moved through the whipping wind. It was faint, but approached up the road. Daymir's eyes narrowed. His servants sheltered in the town below, and he doubted he would see any before the storm retreated. Last winter he went an entire month without news.

Fifteen minutes passed before the shadow reached his courtyard. By then it formed the shape of two riders. He threw on his cloak, lacing it tightly before he yanked the door open. Snow spilled into the foyer. The riders dismounted, and the shorter of the two raised a hand in response to his.

"The stable's unlocked!" His battle-voice pierced the wind, and the visitors led their mounts inside. Unlocking the door between the manor and its stables, he headed to the kitchen, shedding his cloak as he did.

Pots of gravy and sweet sauce hung over the fire to heat, and Daymir collected bread and cold meat on a platter. Boots stomping snow from their tread interrupted his preparation of tea.

The hall was quiet as his visitors set aside packs and outdoor attire. Daymir stepped out of the kitchen as one rider rounded the corner. He froze. "Fates."

Alea's eyes still sent ice sliding down his spine. Lines mapped the history of her expressions, but her face was as striking as their last meeting twenty years before. "Good evening to you, too." She offered a tired smile. "Arman will be in once the horses are settled. We both thought it best if I greeted you alone."

"Indeed." *The Dhoah' Laen is in stocking feet in my foyer.* "Where have you been? An'thoriend would have a fit if he knew you were here. Fates, I might have a fit once I recover from the shock." He stopped himself from rambling further and resorted to simply staring.

Her dark brows arched as she waited for him to fall quiet. "I'll gladly answer everything. Might we stay a night, maybe two?"

"Of course. You're likely to be trapped here with this weather, though."

"We made it here. I'm confident we'll make it out."

The door to the stables shut softly, and Daymir heard a deep sigh as boots were shucked off. "Alea?"

"We're in the hall," she answered without taking her eyes from Daymir's. The kettle began to squeal.

"I've completely forgotten my manners. I set out some food and tea. It's not a feast, but it'll do until morning."

Alea followed him into the kitchen, and when he turned Arman stood in the doorway as well. The Rakos's ferocity was now an ember under steady might. His uncertainty was gone. Arman offered him an arm, which Daymir took.

"You grew older." Daymir raised a hand in defense of the obvious comment. "I know, we all did. I just never expected you to turn gray. Or, perhaps, I never thought I'd see it."

"We're as much human as we are anything else." Alea smiled. "Besides, now no one can say they thought the Dhoah' Laen would be older."

Daymir snorted. "Perhaps." He took the pots from their hooks and nestled them into their places on the platter. "As much as I was raised a noble and should make small talk well into the evening, I find I can't help but ask why you're here."

Arman looked down. "We started riding months ago. It seems we missed much being out of the world. We need to be caught up."

"So it's not for my witty company." Daymir shoved off from the counter with a sigh. "Well, let me bring these into my study, and I'll set a fire. There's a room at the top of the stairs, beside the black hall table. It should be warm enough. We can talk once you've settled your things there."

Quiet steps muted their conversation as they climbed up to the room. His shaking hands rattled the teapot. He did not know whether the tremors were from fear or excitement. He sat in a chair, then rose to stand by the door, and finally decided to wait by the fire. *No visitors for weeks and then the queen passes followed by a visit from the most powerful creatures in the world.* His mind tripped over the thought. Memories were dim more often of late, even erasing them entirely on occasion. He was happy that, at least for the evening, his mind was clear.

"You've got a lovely place here," Arman's voice rumbled from the doorway. He moved through the stacks of books, glancing at their titles.

"Yes. For a prison, it's quite lovely." Daymir looked down. It would not do to alienate his guests, however unexpected. "Sorry. I've been a bit restless."

Arman's brows rose. "I'm surprised you haven't returned to the city."

Daymir's gaze inched over the other man's face. He had no idea what Arman knew of Athrolan's current affairs. "Exiled is exiled. Perhaps news should wait until Dhoah' Lyne'alea joins us?"

"Perhaps." Arman's mouth curled with tempered mirth. "It's been a while since we answered to those titles. I'm not sure which is more uncomfortable, the fact that we forgot them so easily or that they still fit." He gestured to the seat. "May I? The way houses were full, and we've slept on benches more than beds."

"Of course." Daymir took a seat across from him. "The roads are busy?"

"Until we came farther north. The closer we get to the capital the few travelers we've seen." Alea breezed in. "This looks lovely, thank you." She collapsed into the third chair with a sigh. "You're taking this in stride. I'd almost believe you expected us."

"I've had my share of oddities lately. Before we dive into dark news, might I ask where you've been for the past twenty years?"

"Nineteen years and four months." Alea's voice was just above a whisper. Her eyes fixed on her untouched plate. "I've counted too, you know. I missed this world as much as I avoided it. I missed Bren, missed An'thoriend, even you at times."

Arman glanced at her. "Alea."

"I know. It was our choice. My choice. Doesn't mean it wasn't difficult."

"You've avoided contact, even with Bren?" Daymir leaned back with a sigh. "I correspond more, and I've been in actual exile." He twirled his cup thoughtfully. Alea knocked him off center, ripped his balance away. "Perhaps you ought to tell me what you do know, lest I assume and make an idiot of myself," his eyes flicked up to Alea's, "again."

Her smile was tired, but genuine, and after a moment she laughed. "Well, we've heard rumors of war—both between Mirik and Ban and civil unrest within Athrolan herself. Various nobles bolster their cities with personal guards. We've heard many shouting support for you from their windows. And support for another, a person An'thor promised."

"Do you know who it is, or are you hoping the rumors are wrong?"

"We knew An'thor's intentions, your aunt's intentions, if we ever had a child." Arman sighed, rubbing a rough hand over his weary features. "We had a son, and he's gone, after reading An'thor's pleading letter."

Daymir watched their expressions, eyes narrowed. "You came here to beg me to take the throne?"

Arman shrugged. "We came here to talk."

"No," Alea interrupted. "We wanted to look for our son, and I needed answers."

"Answers?"

Alea shoved herself out of the chair and wandered to the window. Outside the storm raged. "Something's coming, Daymir. Something more terrible than the gods, older, darker than what I faced. And I think I might have caused it. I need your help."

"How could I, possibly?"

"I keep having dreams, and this mad old woman tells me I'm poisoning the world. When I can make sense of it, she mentions a city in Berr. We need to go there."

"What's it called?"

"I don't know. It's in the mountains, tucked up above a plain."

"What's there?" A puzzle might keep his mind sharp for a little while longer.

"I don't know, but it's where the poison starts. In my vision, it's the place where something poisons the world. Where the blood turns black."

"Alea," Arman began, but Daymir cut him off.

"I think I have something. But why don't we let it rest for the evening?" He saw the mania in her eyes, the exhaustion in Arman's shoulders. "Tell me about your son."

Φ

Blood washed over the mountains, purple-red waves breaking on rocky slopes. The flow pulsed from a gaping hole where Ceir Athrolan once stood. Instead of ragged earth, a bleeding, tunneling wound, swollen flesh where bermed earth and towers should stand. Trickling blood stained the ocean black.

"You did this. You killed the gods, but you created something else, something mightier still, and now it strangles the world."

Alea sat up with a gasp. A sickly sweet metallic scent hung heavy over the bed. *Blood.* She scrambled free from the sheets. The privy's washbasin was full, and she dunked her face into the perfumed water. Still, the cloying sweetness clung in her nose. Raking back her hair, she peered in the mirror. The stress of the past month made her face closer to the woman in her visions than the Alea she once knew. "What do you want from me?"

Her reflection remained silent. She tugged on a dressing robe and left Arman sleeping. Below, a light told her someone else was awake. The library was warm, still, the hearth the only light in the room. Daymir slumped in a chair, a stack of books beside him. The one on his lap seemed full of outdated maps.

"Mind if I join?"

His eyes flicked up. "Not at all. Storm have you up?"

Alea shrugged and slid into the chair opposite. "Something like that."

Daymir's head tilted, and she was abruptly reminded of the calculating attitude he had been known for in court. "What of your power? Do you still wield it?"

"Only echoes."

He hummed thoughtfully and turned to look at the orange flames. "So, it passed to Keplan."

It was her turn to regard him carefully. "I didn't say that."

"Power like yours doesn't just fade." He ran a hand down the page of the book before him. "I'm surprised you never saw anything odd in him."

Alea sighed. "Arman would tell you we did him a disservice, raising him away from other children and without the knowledge of what monstrous things crouched in his bloodline."

"You disagree?"

"Children are complicated. It's so easy to forget they're human. Like parents, they are so often a symbol of something simpler in your mind. And then they surprise you, and you're forced to remember they're not an extension of yourself. I wanted a normal life. I wanted peace. I wanted simplicity and happiness. We've earned it, I think. But Keplan hasn't walked the paths that made him want those things." She narrowed her eyes. "What kept you up?"

He drew out the book of maps. "I was studying Ban's former borders."

"Ban?"

"Mirik is at war with them." He flipped to the front of the book. "The oldest I have of Berr is from 982."

Alea peered over his shoulder. "There." Her chapped finger tapped the parchment. "Except there isn't a lake in my dreams. But that's where it is."

"Tut Kunis." He frowned. "I know that name." He handed her the book and rose, muttering titles as he wove between the stacks of books. "*The Making of an Empire, Fall of Leaves, When Snow Falls in Summer.* Ah, here. *Matricide: The Death of Balance in the War Against the Laen.*"

"That sounds like something I'd rather not read."

Daymir snorted, flipping through the pages. "Here. A list of every Laen citadel and their guard cities. Look at the fourth from the bottom."

She tucked her hair behind her ear and bent over the book, tilting the page toward the firelight. "Citadel Lymorda. Guarded by Tut Kunis in the Orn de Galin in Berr, above the Ocean's Child."

Daymir measured the distance in finger-widths. "It'll take you three weeks if you ride hard. I can give you horses and food."

Alea turned away, scrubbing her face with her hands. "Am I truly doing this, again?"

"Saving the world?"

She shook her head, palms still pressed to her eyes. "It never feels that way, not to me, not inside my thoughts. It feels like I'm leaving peace in favor of war." She moved to the window. "There's something over in that city, maybe something left by the Laen, or even the gods. And in my gut, I know that this puzzle holds the answer to Keplan." She rolled her head on her neck. The world rushed around her, twisting, changing as they took each step. She did not like the sensation. "I think we'll leave tomorrow, at dawn."

"You can't stay longer? I could claim I want you both to wait out the storm, but truthfully you're the first new face I've seen in a long time." Air shrieked against the manor, punctuating his words.

"I wouldn't worry about the storm." Dreary weather followed them from the Hartland. "Something tells me it'll be gone when we are."

"Well, pack warmly. I'm sure I have things that will fit you. It'll be cold as this, colder."

She shook her head. "You spend enough time with my power, you wouldn't feel it. Besides, the Northlands were worse."

Daymir joined her at the window. "I didn't know you'd been."

"Just before the battle. And I intend to go again." She heaved a sigh. "Well, perhaps not as far, but a ways in. I'm happy to be on the road again."

"I'm sorry. You came here hoping for answers and found a pathetic exile who can't remember his mother's name half the time." He looked down at his hands. "Fates, how did we get here? This old, this jaded?"

"Speak for yourself." Darkness in her eyes shadowed Alea's small smile. "Hearing you speak, your careful, powerful words, it feels like yesterday."

"Since Athrolan?"

"Since I threw you from my room after you asked me to marry you." She glanced sidelong at him, imagining the dozen different paths her life would have taken. *Would I still have had a child? Would they have been Keplan?* "You were right—we would have made a powerful match. But we're far too similar for anything more romantic."

"It would have been a mess. I know that now. It's hard to see something so close sometimes." He reached over and took her hand.

After a moment Alea squeezed his fingers but did not answer. Her gaze was fixed on the iron sky and the cluster of thunderheads marching north.

Φ

The 49th Day of Aeme, 1272
The City of Ceir Athrolan

The kitchen smelled like home. Spices from breakfast breads and supper meats hung in the air. Keplan propped the pantry door open with a loose cobblestone and set about tidying. Mirrel eyed him from the stove but said nothing. It spoke volumes that she allowed him near her organized realm at all. He smiled and wiped dust from the shelves. The ground shuddered under him.

"Did you drop something?" Mirel snapped.

"You felt that?" He half expected it to have been in his mind. A second tremor shook flour dust from the rafters. Wood splintered in the distance. His eyes met Mirrel's, met the narrowed expression that so many mistook for anger.

It was fear. "I remember that sound. That's an attack."

Keplan shook his head. "We're not at war, Mirrel. I'll go look. Perhaps the aqueduct needs repair." The third cannon hit as he crossed the common room. Decades-old wood flew into slivers. The foundation shattered. Stone dust exploded around them. Rafters rent. Timber screamed and twisted under the impact. Buzzing filled his spinning head. Warmth trickled down his back and face. His vision pulsed between focus and blurry shapes. Mirrel was speaking, screaming, but he barely heard the words through the echoing in his ears. She was trapped, a fallen rafter blocking the kitchen door. Smoking coals spilled across the dry floor.

Her voice clattered into his mind. "The barrel outside!"

"What?"

"The rain barrel, you idiot! Get water before this place burns!"

Keplan's legs churned him to his feet, and he staggered through the rear door. Smoke already curled from the narrow window between the kitchen and their tiny courtyard. A bucket sat beside the rain barrel. His weak fingers trembled as he passed it through the window, dumping half the contents over his own head. Steam billowed from the window now, the hissing distant to his blown ears. "More?"

"No, I've gotten it."

"Can you climb through here?"

There was a pause, then scrambling feet on wood more accustomed to flour. Mirrel's head popped over the window sill. "I think I can manage. Grab a stool for my feet, would you?"

He did as she asked, glancing between her careful escape and the upper storey. "Where's Firas?"

Mirrel dropped down beside him, brushing the dusty hair from her face. Her eyes were bright. "You, sit. Here on the stoop. Away from anything that might fall on you. Keep your eyes and ears open. I'll be right back."

She disappeared into the inn and Keplan turned to the stable. "Moly?" He ducked through the door, wincing as something pulled at his back with the movement. The horses spooked, but fine, and the beams above looked undamaged. Navigating through new debris in the alleyway, he emerged in the street. The house opposite the inn was gone, a hollowed trench where the third cannon passed. Cannon fire still sounded across the city, puffs of dust rising into the clear sky. There were no Banis flags in the harbor, as Keplan expected. The Mirikin ships had yet to return.

The warships were Athrolani.

The pennants were the Commander's. Keplan's knees became water. He hit the cobbles hard.

A warm, rough hand brushed his hair back. Firas caught his gaze, peering into his face with worry. "Are you all right?"

"It's shock, Firas." Mirrel stood at the edge of what was once their neighbor's house. She drew a shuddering breath, then another, firmer one before she knelt by Keplan. Her hands were gentle on his cheek as she turned his face first one way then the other. "Close your eyes for me. Open." Her eyes narrowed on his. "You're all right." Her fingers found a stinging, sticky patch of scalp. "Just a gash. It'll mend." She sat back on her heels. "Shirt off."

He blinked at her. "What?"

"'Lan, love, you're covered in blood. We've got to get you patched." Firas offered him a smile, but the expression was weak. "What happened?"

"The third blow. I was by the door." Ringing in his ears lessened to an annoying whine. His thoughts still swam through honey. Mirrel snapped her fingers at him, but there was no contempt in her expression. "Keplan, shirt please."

He pulled it off, wincing at the stinging ache under his shoulder at the movement. Sudden exposure focused his thoughts further and he saw Mirel's gaze skim his scars. She turned him to look at his back. "This will be uncomfortable. Breathe in while I count to three."

Keplan did as she asked, scanning the building crowd and the soldiers racing through the upper city. Smoke and stone dust thickened the air filling his lungs. Mirrel reached two. Pain exploded across his back. Muscles seized, and his vision turned white. Hot liquid dribbled down his side and pooled underneath him. He glanced down, blinking his eyes clear again. Dark blood spread on the cobbles. It was more than he expected. He looked up at Firas. The older man's face was sickly white. "What happened?"

"A piece of our rafters found its way into the muscles of your shoulder blade." Firas seemed unable to look away from the blood. "Mirrel is a cold-hearted monster who never shies at injuries."

"If you saw your own blood every few weeks, you'd be cold-hearted too." Mirrel's fingers prodded the swollen flesh around the wound. "I got it all, I think." She rose, finally looking at the chaos roiling around them.

Keplan took Firas's offered hand and rose with a groan. Fading adrenaline left his body aching in strange places, injuries making themselves known. Turquoise flooded the road between the palace and the barracks. *This is my home.* Athrolan had been safe. Keplan's gut clenched.

The ground shook again, but not from cannon fire. Screaming metal pierced the smoky air. The towering white pillars spanning the harbor shuddered, and massive gates inched across the water. The rusted portcullis was taller than any city tower. Spikes several paces long fell outwards as the gate closed the harbor's entrance. *That will gut any ship brave enough to ram them.*

Athrolani battleships stretched to the horizon. Her army massed on the hills. *If they lay siege to either end of their own city, Athrolan will starve within a month.* Keplan's thoughts were quiet, for once, and his heart empty.

Φ

The 2nd Day of Lumord, 1272
The City of RoBal, Ban

Dust hung heavily under the layer of smoke. Rih tucked a fold of her scarf over her head and nose to keep the worst of it out. Still, though, it was pervasive. Since her time as a soldier, she had not navigated the streets alone. Hard cobbles bit through the thin soles of her sandals. Wagons trundled down roads usually reserved for foot traffic. Horses pawed new furrows in the packed dirt of the barrack courtyard as Rih slipped through the gate. Rough hands yanked her back against the wall to allow a march through. She pressed a hand to the letter folded inside her wrap. It was still there. The woman who pulled her out of harm's way waved a dramatic hand before Rih's face.

Rih frowned at the rude gesture. "What?"

Recognition filled the soldier's eyes, followed by scorn as she took in Rih's attire. "Oh, you're the simple one. I thought they traded you off?"

Rih swallowed bitterness with the hard words she wanted to use. A few months ago that scorn was hers, too. "I'm looking for Il-fald." She held up her tablet with the woman's name carved across the wax.

The soldier jerked her head at the barracks. "She's watching the formations."

Rih jogged up the stairs, forcing her expression into something between concern and determination. She could not risk looking fearful. She could not risk anyone questioning her. *Not with this letter on me.* A ladder at the end of the hall led to the ramparts. Rih hurried up it, shielding her eyes from the glare of the sallow sun. The dust was worst here without the shield of the city buildings or walls. Il-fald stood on the walkway, hands braced against the earthen wall. Black paint helped her eyes with the glare. Rih faltered, catching sight of the fresh green tattoos staining her newly shaved head. Il-fald always inspired her. Now she intimidated.

The older woman glanced over, and the lines of her face rearranged into a smile. "Rih. I'm glad to see you again. Do you bring news?"

Rih returned the smile, the expression deepening at the double-meaning. "I do." Her gaze lingered on the green designs on Il-fald's scalp. "I see you have been promoted."

"I am now in charge of the drill." Her fingers brushed the oil preventing the tattoo from forming scabs. It was a stylized horse's hoofprint with an atlatl crossing it.

Rih suppressed a shudder. The symbol reminded her of a skull crushed under a warhorse's hoof. "I need you to read this." She withdrew the letter and handed it to Il-fald. "It is vague, but I'm still fearful." Her former instructor's expression faded to neutrality as she scanned the letter's contents.

> *R-*
>
> *I was delighted to receive your letter. Your questions are good ones, but complex. I hope to answer them in person during my next visit to RoBal. I'll find you.*
>
> *-M*

Il-fald rolled the letter wordlessly and returned it to Rih. Her dark brows furrowed over the black smear of paint. "I didn't expect this."

"I wanted friendship, answers. I did not expect a meeting."

Il-fald hunched over the wall. "Why don't you speak with your tutor—Ki-elte? She seems like she would be a good source of support for you during this time of change."

Rih noted the change in demeanor and glanced over her shoulder. Another officer approached, male by the long lock of black hair braided at his neck. "We are friends, perhaps, but I worry I cannot trust her this far. These questions are difficult."

Il-fald switched to signing. "I cannot un-read that letter, Rih. You have my confidence, but be careful. You need women outside the army to help you. More than you need me."

"Ki-elte is willing to play at subterfuge, but I think this is too close to treason for her to stomach."

"This is treason."

The ground trembled, and Rih turned. It was rare a sound was loud enough to register for her. The sensation came again, and she caught sight of the woman at the tower just above the ramparts. Her barrel chest expanded, and she pressed her lips to the brass mouth of the massive horn. It was washed with copper, a tiny moon to the massive golden sun of the palace gong above the squalor of the city.

The plain below was not the rolling gold of the rainy season, the lush grasses carved with the black curves of the river. Instead, the undulating land was stamped to dust. Vegetation no longer hid the huts of the poor smattering the muddy banks of the Ninaket. She saw the prairie during the dry season before. That is not what made Rih's heart lurch its way between her teeth. She clenched her jaw to keep it from escaping.

There was no horizon. The mass of marching soldiers bled into the dusty distance. Bodies blurred into the sullen sky. "Il-fald, what is this?"

"War. You haven't seen it before. You've seen battles. You've seen death and the edges of what might become war. But this is its heart." Her shoulders heaved in a sigh and she voiced, "We're marching soon."

The older woman's mouth tightened around the words. Rih could not remember a time the woman was uncertain. Or scared. She remembered the earth vibrating through her boots, quaking under the might of thousands and thousands of feet, under the call to arms. She wished to grab Il-fald's hand, to have the grip of an atlatl in her palm. Instead, her fingers wrapped the rail before her.

"I cannot help but think how many won't return, their names forgotten, ground into the dirt with their bones and blood." Il-fald's hands were low, shaking as they signed. "Promise me you'll change it."

"I can't say it will look different at first. We'll still die. We'll still bleed, but this time our bones will make a bridge for us to cross. He has spent enough time winning wars with our bodies, throwing us into rape made legal by marriage, into battle made heroic by his cavalry. I'm tired of being tinder for his hateful fire." She clenched a fist. "If I'm going to burn, I will make it an inferno."

CHAPTER FIFTEEN

The 5th Day of Lumord, 1272
The City of Ceir Athrolan

AN'THOR'S HEAD ACHED, AND his back cramped from crouching over the council table. "I want every soldier we can spare to surround the nobles. Send word to each headman in the provinces and counties still loyal to us. I want our militia raised. Athrolan's military is coming here, and the towns and cities will have to fend for themselves."

"Sir, do you honestly think that's wise? Our neighbors are close to war."

"And we're already at war, Colonel." An'thor scrubbed a trembling hand over his face. He wanted a drink. He hated the weakness flooding his limbs every sober moment. "Squire, if you please?"

The boy bowed out of the room. An'thor remained silent until the boy returned with a thick glass brimming with wine. An'thor grimaced as the sweetness slid across his tongue. *It'd be ill form to knock back wraith in this company, I suppose.* He took another, smaller swallow and turned his attention back to the maps. Calm was returning already. "What are Dorcal's positions?"

"The Commander—"

"Dorcal, dammit! He's a traitor, and that's the only title he deserves." An'thor bit back the rest of his vitriol. He took another breath, another gulp, and wet his lips. "Forgive me. I hoped my camaraderie with Dorcal would prevent this disaster."

"We all did, sir. Many of us have kin in the navy."

An'thor looked down. Facing family across the battlefield was something he hoped never to feel again. "Let's begin with his ships. He's got the north and east fleets out there—" An'thor bit back a curse as another runner appeared in the doorway. "What is it now?"

"The warehouses are burning, sir. The Thread is unraveling, if you pardon the pun." When An'thor did not smile at the weak joke, the boy barreled on.

"The nobles are squirreled in their manors, each with their personal guard. Any who spoke of support for Daymir are gone, left in the night."

An'thor moved to the window. Smoke clogged the air, and soldiers swarmed through the barracks below. "Do not allow anyone else in or out of the city, save our own troops. The gates are closed as of this moment. Instate a curfew—two hours after sundown. Anyone out later will be detained. As for Raven—any ships arriving with his supplies are to be burned on sight."

Φ

Keplan ran a cloth over the counter, smoothing his hand after it to assure the sticky ale was indeed gone. The door banged open behind him. "Hey, Firas. We ought to make better use of this time while Mirrel's out."

"What?"

Keplan whirled, blood flushing his cheeks. A blond soldier stood just inside the door, long coat still wrapped around his shoulders. "Forgive me, I thought you were someone else."

The man's smile was quick and genuine. "I noticed. I'm sorry to disappoint." He jerked a chin at the empty, damaged common room. "I don't suppose you're open?"

"Not until afternoon, I'm afraid, unless you need a room."

"I've let a room in the Lily and Ahonsa." He slid onto a stool. "I'm actually looking for someone."

Keplan leaned on the bar. "They have a name or face I'd recognize?"

"Not sure about the face. I'm looking for a Lan Guardsen."

Keplan's heart leapt then clattered to a halt somewhere between his boots. "Who's asking for him?"

The soldier laughed, an easy sound, and patted his short hair. "No need to get your hairs up. I asked at Courier's Hall, and they said the letters were sent by a boy of your looks. Asked a bit more and they said you also delivered mail from the Wise Hare."

"And you've come to what, warn me? Threaten me?"

"You're quick to distrust. Though any man who doesn't use his own name must be running from something. Daymir's curious about you."

"Curious?" Keplan was too preoccupied with keeping his nerves in check to search Hylier's face for secrets.

"Aye. Said to give you this." He slid a thick letter across the counter.

"He could have sent it to me."

"And he thinks he has. He's a good friend, and I wanted some information for my own concerns. If you need to reply, I'd deliver it for you. Easier, with the city closed. Why the false name?"

Keplan shrugged. "I doubted the former heir would write a kitchen boy in the slums."

"I doubt most kitchen boys in the slums would write to him with the same articulation." He tilted his head. "You're clever. You claim to be an ally, claim to want answers, but never say why. You're a right puzzle. Who are you, really?"

Firas burst through the back door with a dramatic sigh. "Honestly, if one more urchin weaves me some tale about their poor baby sibling needing sup, I might just break down and try begging myself. It's far more lucrative than owning any inn." His brows arched at the sight of the man at the bar. "Keplan, really, I'm gone an hour, and you invite strange men in off the street?" The way the bartender's gaze lingered on the stranger's shoulders and forearms, however, told Keplan that, given the choice, Firas might have invited him in himself.

"Sorry, Firas. Master...." He glanced at the soldier.

"Hylier. Captain, actually," the officer offered with a broad smile.

"Captain Hylier was just leaving."

Hylier glanced between the two men before rising. "Right. Sorry to have imposed." He paused at the door and glanced back. "I hope you'll consider writing again. Good day."

Firas watched him go, gaze appreciative. "You have good taste, 'Lan."

"I wasn't flirting with him," Keplan protested.

The door shut. Firas's face hardened, and he turned to Keplan. "I know that." His eyes were dark. "I've welcomed you into this inn, into our family. Fuck, I welcomed you into my bed. I've comforted you when the world seemed on your shoulders and tupped you could sleep. I never once demanded where you came from or why you were running. Not once!" His quiet words rumbled into thunder, and he brought his fist down on the counter.

Keplan stepped back a pace. The captain's questions weaseled into his chest and lay there, a coal smoldering on the rug. Firas was the one person he opened himself to, and the sharp words burned. "I don't know why you're angry."

"Of course you don't. You're like a child sometimes. You see so much of the world you think everyone else about you is an idiot. You've had people asking after you. The ambassador's spy, with the scars on her eyes, came more than once, and I've seen others follow you home from the market. And now a captain?" He sank his head in his hands. "Oh, that life were as simple as you think it is for us. But you bring trouble after you, you bring it here."

"I didn't bring trouble, Firas. I'm a pauper's son from the woods."

"How does a pauper's son bear the marks of torture? How does a pauper's son befriend the child of the Mirikin Hetmir?" His voice lowered, and he looked down at the letter, forgotten, on the countertop. "How does a pauper's son write to Daymir Blackhouse? I can't read the words, Keplan, but I know that seal." He turned away. "Go upstairs, go walk the markets. For all I care, stowaway on a smuggler's ship. Just take your trouble with you."

Keplan waited a moment, but the man did not look at him or say another word. The floorboards turned to water and he was drowning. Tucking the letter into his shirt, he stumbled to the door. It did not matter which street he took or where he headed. He only wanted air and silence.

Chills already filled the void left by the other man's skin. Another cannon boomed across the harbor, and he winced. The battle might have started as a pointed dialogue between the navy and army, but with civilians caught between them, it turned deadly. The bodies pulled from rubble ranged from a few dozen to a few hundred, depending on who counted. *Civil war.*

His hands paused on the letter from Daymir. Even now his fingers faltered over the unbroken seal. Knowing the truth about why he was wanted in Athrolan changed things. *Daymir and I are equals, technically.* He paused in a pool of lantern light and pried the wax free. Richness was evident in the weight and smoothness of the plain parchment.

Lan,

I admit I'm curious about your interest in me. Not your stated concerns, but the root of it. I see the same warning flags in Athrolan as you. As isolated as I am, I see forces moving in the valley below Marl Black. I see them bristling with weapons, wearing provincial colors boldly. But when they stop in town, their faces are scared, not proud.

I've received many letters from supporters, but none as candid as yourself. Some are commoners. Others are officers and lords. I fear the numbers are equal on either side. When we went to war against the gods it was easier. We had a queen. We had allies. We had the figurehead of two titanic creatures. We have none of those things. You ask why I refuse the crown? The answer lies there.

My advice to you is this – do not turn to history. We never listen, and now is not a time to start. Look to the future. Ambassador Barrackborn did this when he reformed the Mirikin government as Hetmir. I'm not proposing reform – Athrolan is too large for that, and her government too complex, if unstable. Mirik's was nonexistent.

Let me pose a question to you in turn: which do you think would benefit Athrolan more – a mythical heir of the aforementioned creatures or an old exile of older blood? Let us pretend both were present and willing.

I look forward to your response.

-Blackhouse

Daymir's personal hand was clear, flourishes marking only the first letters of the paragraph and his signature. Anger burned in Keplan's chest. The man was born for royalty, trained for the throne. *So where are you when we need you? You're Athrolan's damned heir, and you've let her destroy herself, let her rot, slavering at her own limbs.* He caught sight of the manors on the highest tier of the city, and his thoughts tripped to an abrupt halt. Scarred eyes and the low voice of Mirik's Spy Master loomed in his memory: "*...do what you know you ought.*" Daymir was not the only one shirking duty.

Keplan looked again at the letter. He should write the nobleman, explain everything, confess to his blood, explain why he was unfit to be a monarch. The exile was clearly curious, enough to talk to a stranger. Keplan raked a hand through his hair. It would take months to convince the man of his birth, however, and Athrolan did not have months.

Athrolan did not have days.

What if we met? Adrenaline pooled in his stomach. Hylier's words returned to Keplan then. He did not need to earn Daymir's trust. Hylier already had it. He glanced up at the guards on the street corner ahead. Curfew would be in an hour. Soldiers were either tired from their watch or too busy to be bothered with a bar boy.

The Lily and Ahonsa was set in the heart of the Silver Apron. More expensive than the Slummer, it was a section of the city he rarely visited. Now it was a breeding ground for rebellion. He took his hands from his pockets and began to jog. If he was lucky, Hylier would not have left. He turned a corner, backtracked along a narrow road overgrown with leaning houses. The street twisted around an older smithy and spilled into a square. A building rose across the empty space. Pillars and arches told him it once was something official. Now it bore a sign with a white flower and a tattered green ribbon.

Keplan crossed the square and slipped through the door. Like every alehouse the past few weeks, it was both crowded and hushed. It was an unsettling combination. He slid onto a stool at the bar along two of the inn's walls. The bartender jerked a nod at him, taking two orders on her way to where he sat.

"What'll it be, sir?"

Keplan grimaced at the honorific. "I'm looking for Hylier."

She frowned. "He's out, but he'll be back within an hour if you want to wait and have a drink."

Keplan slid a coin across the bartop. "Fire-ale please, miss." Anonymity gave him confidence, and he turned to watch the musicians. He could not recognize a good tune if it spent the night with him, but the other patrons seemed pleased. The bartender delivered his drink, and he took several gulps without tasting the acrid flavor. It burned down his throat, a flame nestled between his ribs. His fingertips tingled when the glass was empty. Alcohol brought numbness, silence, but it was the silence of stunned ears, not peace. *Still, it's better than the cacophony.*

The barmaid delivered another without a word. When she was gone, a man stood in her wake. Hylier's hair looked greasier, though it was no more than a few hours since they met last. "You change your tune quickly, Guardsen."

Keplan grunted and pointed at the chair opposite him. "Sit, will you? I'm not used to looking up at people."

The soldier folded his cloak over the back of the chair and settled himself. His eyes did not waver. Keplan noted they were almost as blue as his own, albeit warmer.

"Where are you from?"

Hylier frowned. "I grew up on one of the Xain estates. It's how I met Daymir. Why do you ask?"

"Your eyes. Blue. Not the usual gray and brown of Athrolan. Your hair, too."

Hylier ran a hand across his scalp with a mocking look of horror. "My hair's turned blue?"

Keplan's lip curled at the bad joke. "Never mind. You said I could find you if I wanted to speak to Blackhouse. Said it'd be quicker, with the city under siege."

"Aye, mail's all but stopped. The only correspondence is military. I could get a letter through for you, though, if you convinced me it was urgent."

Keplan looked down at his half-empty glass. He barely convinced himself this idea was a good one, let alone whether it would work. The door banged open, wind blowing dead leaves and a cloaked stranger into the room.

The barmaid waved her dishrag. "Peraan, good to see you. I worried you were trapped outside when the city locked down."

"City this big, it's hard to watch every part of the walls all the time." He tossed her a bloodshot wink and asked after the business as he sat. Keplan's eyes narrowed on the thin beard, the deep-set eyes. *Arthritis from working the docks for years. He and his brother lost their parents in Capital Siege during the Gods' War.* More than that he wasn not sure. His gaze fell to the stack of posters the man dropped on the bar. They were propaganda, the familiar caricatures of An'thor and Daymir locked in a dramatic battle. *He's the barker who wants Daymir on the throne.*

Hylier followed Keplan's gaze, then rolled his eyes. "There's one on every corner. Barkers claiming one thing or another. Probably the same rhetoric about this mythical heir the general spews."

The man—Peraan, apparently—heard Hylier's comment and turned in his seat, raising a glass to them in solidarity. "This officer clearly knows the truth. Domariigo poisons the city, turns the people against us."

Keplan braced his elbows against the bar. As much as he disliked the general, he distrusted the bleary expression in the barker's eyes more. "What lies does he tell?"

Peraan's brows shot up. "What hole have you been living in?"

"A dark one. I arrived in the city just a few days before the gates closed," he lied, ignoring Hylier mouthing in silent confusion beside him. "It's hard to tell rumor from fact during a war."

Peraan's smile widened, no doubt seeing a new follower. "He's got this heir, right? Supposed child of the Dhoah' Laen and the Rakos."

The barmaid shuddered. "He was a piece of work, the Rakos was, let me tell you. Tried to take me to bed and burnt my sheets. I think he fancied I looked like his woman."

Keplan blanched. Those were stories he would rather not know. "And no one knows whether the boy exists?"

"Well, the general seems convinced, and the Mirikin Ambassador has been secretive enough lately. No doubt he has aims to take Athrolan over if she grows too weak." His thick lips pursed. "But the heir left us to rot, waiting to pick our bones when we're dead. A coward, running from duty like their parents." Peraan tilted his head. "You said 'boy'—you know something I don't?"

Heat bloomed in Keplan's gut. He wasn't angry, at least, not in the conventional sense. Anger was a flash as fat hit the fry pan. This was a caldera exploding. He hated lies. He hated questions. His gaze snapped to the barmaid. "If I took you to bed, I'd burn the evidence, too."

Her face tightened. "That's your last mug, boy."

"Fine. I'd rather not drink with idiots." He shook Hylier's firm hand off his shoulder.

It was Peraan's turn to glare at him. "Do you have a problem?"

"You're my problem, and people like you. Spitting lies like they're rote."

Peraan scoffed. "I think you ought to step outside."

Keplan knocked back the last of his drink and staggered to his feet. The alcohol burned truth into his tongue. "My parents weren't running from duty. They were protecting themselves. And you could call me a lot of things, but I'll be damned if I'm a coward."

The woman shouldered her way from behind the bar and grabbed Keplan by the back of his collar. "Out. Now."

The room whirled before Keplan's eyes. The mug in his hand shattered on the edge of the bar. He glowered down at the woman, mouth twisted in a grimace, broken glass held out. Blood thickened the air. Stinging in his palm told him the glass had cut through his glove.

Her eyes widened, and she let him go. "Fates. Those eyes."

His snarl curled further. "Thank you for your hospitality." He kept his eyes down as he swept from the common room. Once the door slammed behind him, he slumped against the wall. His body trembled in the wake of confrontation.

"Alright, I'll listen." Hylier stood just outside the ring of light from the tavern's lantern. "You were a passing curiosity before. Now you've got me properly intrigued."

Keplan's head cracked against the stone as he twisted to look at the soldier. "I'm tired of war. I've not even lived through one, and I'm tired of it. I need to talk to Blackhouse. I've got information that will convince him to take the throne."

Hylier's eyes remained fixed on Keplan's, but the boy sensed every inch was being memorized, every word recorded. "That information have something to do with what you said in there? They'll chalk it up to drunken rambling if you're lucky. But that anger looked like it has been brewing a while, and I know you weren't drunk." He watched Keplan weave himself upright. "At least, not that drunk."

Keplan shoved off the wall. "Say you believe me, now you know why they can't rely on this mystical heir to show up. Blackhouse has to take the throne. He knows you, trusts you, and you're a soldier—you can come and go as you please even with the city under siege. Get me to him."

Hylier glanced at the sky, then scanned the walls nearest them. "Watch will change in two hours. I'll send a bird to him. By the time he receives it, you'll be on the road. There's a small town; he'll know it and he'll meet you there a day after you arrive, two at the most."

"You're not coming with me?"

Hylier grinned. "As far as anyone's concerned, for the next week, you're Captain Hylier."

Φ

The 7th Day of Lumord, 1272
The City of RoBal, Ban

Shuddering gates shook the Hall as they opened, interrupting Rih's study of eastern eating customs. Despite the dust, she left her window open, sunlight filtering through the loose weave of a robe she hung over the wooden latticework. She pushed aside the cloth and peered down into the courtyard. It was late, and most of the visitors who could afford a carriage used tunnels from the lower levels of the palace instead. It was a cart, not a carriage, and the passengers filing from the benches wore chains, not jewels. Rih's hands trembled. All were female.

Most women who worked in the Hall were younger daughters sent so as not to burden families with no hope of wedding upward in the noble hierarchy. Some were common women, others who had few relatives chose the life themselves. *And some are slaves.* It wasn't common in a concubine house as prestigious as the Hall, but it happened. The soldier escorting them jerked a rope, and the women fell into line, entering through the rear door. Rih turned away, unable to watch any further.

She had no sooner returned to her study when Hi-alan appeared at the door. "Rih, a summons came for you."

"Is Ki-elte alright?" Her heart hammered, remembering when the news of Sa-at's death arrived.

"She's with a visitor right now." Hi-alan handed Rih a thin parchment. "This is from one of our sister halls, down in Stytown."

Rih skimmed the summons. It was a single line:

> *Requesting the presence of Rih-elte to discuss training logistics.*
> *-M*

The initial stilled her heart. *She's here.* "How do I get there?"

"There are wagons and carts, but if you're good at maps, it's not difficult. I'd walk you myself, but I have something to tend to."

Rih's lips thinned. "The new women?"

Hi-alan looked down. "I'm angry too. But change won't happen in a day, and it will not succeed without planning." She sought to meet Rih's gaze, her eyes warm. "Your outlook and methods are new. Your spirit is new. But you are not the first woman to have these thoughts. Many of us did as well. Many even succeeded for a time. But this isn't a place that fosters such things."

"I would think it was exactly the place that did." She knew what Hi-alan meant, knew she was not the first, knew she stood on the backs of a thousand women before her, just as a thousand women would stand on hers. *I'll just see to it that I stand tall enough for them to climb these prison walls.* She changed her wrap to her favorite sapphire blue. It was darker than the usual fashions, but it was evening, and even in the driest part of the season, nights were cool. "Can you pass on the invitation to learn with us?"

"I will. I'll even teach them a few words if they're willing." Hi-alan's expression was closed.

Defeat in the piercer's eyes burned determination into Rih's bones. "Where is this other Hall?"

"In the center, off of Ivory Circle. The sign is plain black. It's called the Tower of Jet. They can't even name something without being obsessed with their own phalluses."

Rih grinned and settled her net over her scalp, grateful she was bored enough to shave her head that morning. "I know the place. Wish me luck, then."

"It's just a meeting—they probably wish to make you a trainer if you can't be married."

Rih could not keep her smile from widening. "What is it you said? 'My methods and spirit are new?'" Before Hi-alan could ask, she ducked from the room. "Good evening."

The city was a different animal in the dark. Even with war looming, energy was high, a taut wire waiting to be plucked into the first stanzas of music. Colors were bold and bright now, replacing the pastels and whites of day. The brick street from the Hall ran north along the tall wall circling the palace itself. This close, she could only see the top tiers of the mounded structure. The road continued, but Rih turned right, down a broad street through the noble and merchant houses of the Rises. It was one of the only times she did not look out of place. As a soldier, she ran messages between the barracks and merchants requiring an official guard. Now she could have been any one of the wives or lesser courtesans in the district.

She slipped past a cluster of market stalls when she caught sight of the signing. A middle-aged woman leaned on the counter of her stall, mouth moving leagues a second as she discussed her daughter's upcoming wedding to someone named Kirka. Her hands, however, told another story. "She's close to war, there, close to the ocean where the Mirikin will attack. I must be sure she has allies, people who will help her come home if he's a monster, or when war erupts."

The other woman responded, but her back was to Rih and the signs hidden.

Rih faltered. Already people used her language to speak openly. She looked away, allowing the women their privacy, and hurried further down the road. She smelled Stytown before she saw the ugly, hulking walls. Human waste and the pervasive smell of rotting food hung low over the rickety, towering buildings. Lumps of hardened clay replaced the fired red bricks and the cleaned gutters. Rolling her shoulders back, she dropped her careful steps. A soldier's stride was impossible with skirts, but she raised her chin and walked as if she expected the crowd to part before her. In Stytown, it paid not to look weak, and for Ban, demure was weakness.

So was asking for directions. A looming guard tower marked the southern of the two central squares. She had only been stationed there a year, but it was enough to taste bitterness in the back of her throat at the thought.

Stytown was less of a city district and more a work camp gone feral. Most inhabitants were not allowed to pass through the towering walls. Those who did were only visiting for some seedy purpose, or to find someone disillusioned enough to trade poor freedom for indentured servitude in a place with less squalor. *Or to start a rebellion.* She winced, afraid to even think the words. A rebellion was not what she wanted. She wanted liberty. *And how do I expect to get freedom?*

The winding street dumped into the square. The two squares around the twin guard towers were the only cleared space, the dead area around a section of poisoned crops. *Except here the crops are people.* Those unaware, or desperate enough, to stumble close were rarely seen again, and if they were, they were not the same people. Rih had been stationed in Stytown long enough to know why they feared the towers.

In Ivory Circle, she found the Tower of Jet. The black monstrosity was dwarfed only by the guard tower opposite it. She slipped through the door unbothered and followed the widest hallway to a low, open foyer. It was not as fine as the Hall of the Purple Throne, but it was clean and lit with the usual soft lantern light.

The woman on the dais glanced up. "May I help you?"

Rih wrote her name and explained her presence was requested by a visitor. After a second she added a line about her lack of hearing and ability to lip-read.

The woman read it, then looked more thoroughly at Rih. "I'm Delan. My mother learns signs from you." Her smile was bright, and Rih realized she could not have been more than sixteen. "She says it's a good way to keep our minds sharp."

Rih nodded, not knowing what else to say. All learning kept the mind sharp, and she wondered if their mother felt that way, or if she was laying groundwork for a later conversation.

"You'll meet your friends down the stairs at the end of that hall, and it'll be the fourth room on your right." The girl gestured down the hall behind her.

Rih offered a wave of thanks and followed the directions. The stairs were narrow, the walls decorated with silks and pieces of velvet. While the colors above were deep blue and bright purple, like the Hall, down here the decor lived up to the Tower's name. Black silk, black velvet, scorched-black clay walls. If the bowels of a monster were picked out in luxury, she imagined they would look like the basement of the Tower of Jet.

Plain candles lit the lantern outside the fourth door on the right. She knocked. The door slid open to reveal a tall woman, dressed as a warrior. "Yes?"

Rih held up the tablet again. She wished she had a translator, but she did not trust anyone other than herself with this meeting.

"Come in, then."

Rih slipped inside. The small room was crowded with an entourage of a dozen women. Each wore armor; decorated beads denoted their rank. A large cushioned chair served as a throne. The guard turned back, frowning, and Rih realized she must have missed something spoken.

"This is Her Majesty Majilah Ag, Queen of the Vales," the guard repeated, this time for Rih's benefit. "Your Majesty, this is Rih-elte."

The queen was as tall as any Banis, with the same brown skin. Her black hair was long, though and kept back in a series of intricate tiny braids.

Majilah rose, hand outstretched like a soldier, not a queen. "I am pleased to meet you."

And I you. Thank you for meeting me.

"Is it all right if I speak, or would you prefer I write as well?"

Speaking is fine, though I find it much easier to read if it is more than just a phrase or two.

The queen gestured for tea, and waited for it to be prepared to her liking. She was compact, her body hard the way a soldier's would be. Majilah looked up and caught Rih's stare. She smiled, hazel eyes flashing. "I see you are a soldier too."

I am a bride. Once I was a soldier.

"There is no 'once' when one is a warrior. I see it still in you. In your walk. In your heart." Her eyes flicked to Rih's, dark and intense. "In your request to meet me."

Rih lifted a shoulder, but her gaze did not waver.

I was curious.

Majilah leaned forward to write her response.

If you were solely curious, my dear, then you would have been disappointed at the dearth of my people in histories and moved on. One does not invite the enemy of the Emperor to tea out of curiosity.

I did not invite you.

Rih corrected her with a faint grin. She liked Majilah.

The queen's brow quirked. "Didn't you?" Her eyes closed for a moment as she took a slow sip of tea. "I miss this. We have the spices, but our butter has little flavor, made without the rich palace grain. What did you wish to know?" She switched subjects as if she drew another breath, and it took Rih a moment to catch up.

Now the woman was before her, the task seemed insurmountable.

How did you become queen? Why do we hate you so? And why do you hate us – though my teacher told me it isn't hatred. I wish for freedom like you have, and I wish it for my sisters, too, and the slaves we keep.

"That's a large wish." Majilah leaned forward to elaborate.

Your teacher is right: we do not hate you. Pity, perhaps. Scorn sometimes if you refer to the upper echelon of society. But not hate. Hate means we fear, and that would imply you have power over us.

Rih frowned, trying to marry the image Majilah painted with all her indoctrination.

Our army is ten times yours. Three times the military of most other nations, save perhaps the Berrin navy. We have power over you. How did you manage to wrest power from them and escape? I read we were one people once. Not cousins, but brothers and sisters.

"So why have you never invaded us? You cannot say we have no resources—we have the rainforest. We have almost as many mines as Ban. So why are we untouched?" Her arched brow punctuated her next question. "What does a dog do with a snake?"

Rih sat back. *What commands the emperor?*

She avoids it. Leaves it lie. Barks, perhaps.

"Your emperor's propaganda against us? Barking. He does not dare to bite." She took another sip of her tea and continued her explanation in writing.

We didn't wrest power from anyone. They took it from us. Two centuries ago we had an empress. They never tell you that, do that? There were poor. There were rich. I am never going to say it was perfect. But it was better. She had a general who wished to be her consort. Some tales say they were lovers, others they never met. Regardless, she refused him. He did not take it well. You have seen a child throw a tantrum, yes?

It was much the same, except this was a man, with wealth and influence at his disposal. Like a tantrum, she ignored him. Our female generals began to die, were killed more often in battle, were poisoned while spying. By the time we realized it was him, it was too late. RoBal was once a broad and beautiful city, but the coup toppled it, and in its place was built this hulking mountain, built on our bodies, our bones. The women who could, escaped. Some with their families, some from them. They are my foremothers.

Rih's heart faltered. She heard the walls of RoBal were built over the bodies of their enemies. Now she wondered how literal that was. *It wasn't built on the bones of our enemies, but the bones of our mothers and grandmothers.*

And what of your men?

"They are strong, and often taller. So, we leave them home where they can build and protect." She shrugged. "It simply makes sense that way." Majilah leaned forward and touched Rih's hand. "I feel for you. I do. But no one will give you freedom, not in Ban. Just as they took it from us, you must take it back."

Rih's blood raced, the bird of her heart trembling against the cage of her ribs again. It was no longer a fledgling thing, all bones and no feathers. She took in the the warriors around her, the strength in their faces. Finally, she met Majilah's bright eyes.

I have a network of women, those who speak my language and who teach others. They share my same wish. I will take it. I'll take back the freedom of every woman in this empire.

Would you like to help us?

Majilah's grin was wolfish. "You said yourself you have an army ten times mine."

Yes, and they will help, but not all of that army is mine. You and your women would be a great ally.

Majilah beckoned her clerk over. "Draft an alliance, please. We will sign it now and not risk it traversing the city. I have two more days to conduct business. I visit once a year, but I fear war will keep me away for longer." When the scroll was written and decorated with seals, Majilah pressed her hand into ink then onto the broad, blank bottom of the parchment. She handed both it and the pot of ink to Rih.

Rih patted her palm with a damp rag then pressed her hand to the sheet of dye and onto the space beside the queen's handprint. She held it there, noticing the ridges and whorls that denoted callouses. Her head pounded with the weight of those handprints, with the rush of rebellion in her veins. The meeting itself lasted less than an hour, and yet her world changed. There was no returning. *I could be married off and never return, but this is in my heart now. I can't forget this.*

The guard leaned forward to whisper in the queen's ear. Majilah nodded and rolled the declaration into a plain scroll case before handing it back. "You'd best be getting back, Rih-elte. I have a few more things to attend to before the night is over." Calculations filled Majilah's gaze. "Who will sit on the throne when you're done?"

I assumed one of our male allies, someone within the Emperor's blood, but perhaps without his cruelty.

"Would you take a bit of advice?" When Rih nodded, the queen leaned forward, a prairie cat ready to pounce. "Dream bigger."

Rih wiped their conversation from the tablet before tucking it and the scroll case away. "Thank you."

Though the queen did not know the language, her response made it clear she understood. "Good luck. You will need it."

The words hung in Rih's mind for her return walk. It was close to evening, the streets crowded with a different sort of business.

Hi-alan ran into her at the woman's entrance to the Hall. Exhaustion hung on the piercer's eyes. "I have a message for you."

"Another? From whom?"

Hi-alan switched to signing. "The women I was tending, they're from the east. A town on the border that apparently was harboring alleged Mirikin spies."

Rih snorted. The definition of who was a spy depended more on the emperor's convenience and less upon actual evidence. "What of it?"

"One of them brought a message from a soldier stationed there, Jih-alan. Said she knows you."

"We were in the same patrol." Rih held out her hand, but Hi-alan offered her nothing. "It wasn't written?"

"No. 'We are on the frontlines of battle, and the women are tired of being fodder. Women here wish for liberty, women with allies and family across the border in Athrolan. We await your orders to us, and to them.'"

"Orders? I'm not their captain."

"No. You're their general. It appears your rebellion begins, whether you start it or not."

Rih's head spun, and she fell back against the corridor wall. "I can't command women to their deaths, to fight for me when I am holed up here in this cushioned, silk-wrapped existence."

"His Eminence does. They'll die anyway. They will fall before Mirikin blades regardless of who makes the order. You could help give them hope."

Dream bigger. "How do I get a message back?"

"She said the 213 March joins them in three weeks. You should talk to Il-fald."

"I'll think about it."

"You have allies. More than you realize. And more than women. I have close friends, men, who know we struggle, who hate to see the station we're relegated to. I'd trust them with this. I'd trust them with my life, with your life. We need people in higher positions, political ones, and ones of noble power."

Rih scoffed. "If they are so sympathetic to our cause, why haven't they used their power to help us?"

Hi-alan scowled at her. "Rih-elte, you don't know what they've done. You don't see it because no one is supposed to. I know men who have smuggled hundreds of women to better cities—and yes, there are better cities, better Halls than this, even within RoBal herself. Don't you go thinking you blaze a trail. There are highways you would never know exist."

Rih looked down. Hi-alan was right. "I'm sorry. If you vouch for them, I welcome their help, but please use utmost discretion. We can't afford to misplace our trust."

The older woman squeezed her hand. "You won't regret it. And talk to Ilfald."

Rih pushed off from the wall. For the first time in weeks, she sat in her room, without a lantern, and watched the light fade from the walls. The last, red rays crossed the tablet discarded beside her desk. It still had "fear" inscribed, her reminder of its power over her. She had the network. She had the language. Only details and allies remained. Allies who would do more than lie. Allies willing to commit treason. *Allies willing to die.* Her gaze rose to the sky, teeth bared in a grin. A single thumb stroke smudged the word away.

Φ

The 10th Day of Lumord, 1272
The City of Ceir Athrolan

Trash and bodies tangled in the streets. An'thor shifted on Theriim's back. Years passed since he wore armor. The few pounds he gained in the past decade chafed under the metal even through his leather jerkin. "Raven's a damn fool, starting a war when everyone's become old and fat," he growled.

Each district dissolved into factions, and violence rose on the edges. Deaths ranged from political assassination to desperate murder. Raven knew half of An'thor's moves ahead, those loyal to Daymir relaying information to the navy through birds and lanterns.

Burning war-oil filled the air over the Silver Apron, wind tugging it down to the warehouses through which he now rode. Excepting military personnel, the streets here were closed. Many merchants fled at the announcement of the queen's death. Now the vacant buildings held makeshift infirmaries and morgues. Rot was cloying even in the chill of autumn.

An'thor drew up outside the largest of the converted buildings and dismounted. Wool and silk from his layered headwrap kept out the worst of the stench. "This is a nightmare."

"Yessir, it is." An exhausted captain leaned against the building, her stance a mockery of attention. Like everyone, her face bore shadows of hunger. The harvest had been meager, and already a quarter of the city's stores for winter were gone. Most of what remained was set aside for planting in spring. Soon they would choose between starving this winter or the next. The captain jerked her head in the direction of the dead mounded inside. "We pulled three more from the rubble on the Merchant Tier."

"Any living?"

"None, sir. And there are rumors of a riot brewing down on Mossing Square."

"They have every right to riot." He heaved a sigh, mind pausing on Keplan. The boy was a burning distraction from the failures piling in his wake.

"General!" A squire skittered down the street, tripping over rubble from the harbor walls. He slid to a halt, bracing himself on his knees to catch his breath before remembering to salute. "Sir, the soldiers on the walls report the Commander is launching another assault on the harbor."

"Then tell them to answer it!" An'thor snarled. "I didn't order them there to sit with weapons up their arses." He wished for Nenev cannons.

"Sir, they said you'd say that. We're out of fire-arrows. Commander Dorcal took the last of the fire-goo. And the shipment from the south hasn't come in yet."

"Lord Eier's deliveries arrive every month. And it's war-oil, idiot—you'll be a gallant someday if you survive long enough. Learn the terms."

The squire seemed too tired to care about the castigation. "Lord Eier supported Dorcal, sir."

An'thor's eyes tightened in fury. This was not how he pictured ending his days, holed up in the city he loved most as he helped tear it apart. He jerked Theriim's head around and headed toward the palace.

The boy trotted after the warhorse's exhausted steps. "What are your orders, sir?"

"Fuck them all."

CHAPTER SIXTEEN

The 12th Day of Lumord, 1272
Marl Orna, Clai Province, Athrolan

THE AIR WAS SOFTER in the forest. Wind that shrieked through the city hummed between tree trunks. Even with winter glowering on the horizon, the weather retained summer's playfulness. Keplan followed the curve of the river, crossing via the ferry by noon. A few days brought him out of the trees and onto the rocky steppes that made up most of Athrolan's landscape. The mountains curved from the massive peaks near Fort Stone to the desolate hills behind Claimiirn.

Despite the nature of his time in Ban, the rolling prairie spoke to him. Barren fields here echoed with the same watchful emptiness. Now it made his hackles rise. Keplan smoothed the light jacket under his cloak with nervous fingers. Hylier did his job well—though his clothes were a bit long on the shorter Keplan, he was slim enough for them to fit. Dark gray and white, however, seemed too bright in the brown monochrome of the Feld de Barran.

Dusk cast the town ahead in yellow, a topaz set in the tarnished brown of the fields. He rode easily the last few days, giving Daymir time to receive the letter and set out on his own road north. How the man would escape from his mansion-prison was beyond Keplan, but Hylier had faith. If the soldier's math was correct, Daymir would arrive the next evening.

Exhausted and road-worn, Keplan reeked of horse. His borrowed mount may have been a well-bred pacer, but she still smelled like an animal. This far south, the town's gates were still open, at least until nightfall. He urged the horse faster, trotting down the hill to the gatehouse. Being a commoner might lend anonymity, but being a soldier gave him passage. When he raised a gloved hand, his cloak fell away from the captain's insignia on his breast. "Sir, I'm looking for The Hillock."

The gatekeeper hopped down from his post and peered at him. "You people never bring good news." His smile was rueful, and he jerked his head toward one of the only three-storey buildings. "The inn's up there, at the high side of town."

"Thank you." Keplan tossed the man a coin and headed across the town. Most of the streets boasted pairs of soldiers, more than a town that size warranted. Keplan shook himself. *The capital city is under siege; what did I expect?* The inn was large, made of timber and mud. He left his mount at the stable and ducked inside. Between Firas and Azimir, Keplan saw the common rooms of several taverns in Athrolan. Windows let in the sunset behind the hills, but there was only a single, narrow bar. A man with a face as gray as the mountains was the only patron. His head rested on the weathered wood, chest rising with an ease only drink would bring.

Keplan blinked away the sun-stains on his vision and raised a hand to the barkeep. "Afternoon."

"Captain." The tone was measured. "Welcome to Marl Orna."

"Thank you. I'm looking for a room for a night, maybe two."

The barkeep dug through a drawer behind the bar for a minute before fishing out a heavy key. "Food as well?"

"Please." He watched as the man tallied up his charge. It was strange to be treated with deference. A dark inner part of his heart reveled in it.

"It'll be ten, half now, half before you've gone." His mouth twitched in apology. "Travel's not as safe, so things are expensive. Time was I didn't even need a guard." He jerked a thumb in the direction of the soldiers standing in the courtyard. "Where you ride from?"

Keplan handed him the coin. "Ceir Athrolan."

The man's bushy brows arched. "Fates. No wonder you look like death. No offense, Captain."

"None taken." Keplan did not have to fake the sorrow in his eyes. "It is death there. Most of the city folk try to go on like normal, but it's not pretty. I have hope there's a lamp at the end of this dark, dank tunnel, though."

"I'll believe in hope when it does me good." He shoved off the counter with a sigh. "Supper is when you want it. If you wish to eat in your room, just ring, I'll send it up."

Keplan nodded his thanks and headed toward the stairs. At the landing he paused. "Master Barkeep, I'm expecting someone. I'm Hylier. He'll ask when he arrives."

"Very good, Captain."

Keplan found his room at the end of the hall and locked the door behind him. Perhaps it was the open air of the fields; perhaps it was the clarity focus brought, but his mind was quieter.

The room was a few paces larger than his bedroom in the Wise Hare, and the window faced the mountains to the east. It was a reminder of why he came so far. He upended his pack on the bed before stripping. The tub was a barrel sawn in half, and the water arrived just above room temperature.

It had been a long time since he was alone with his thoughts. As much as he kept his own council, Firas wormed into Keplan's heart. Even Mirrel, with her unexpected moments of kindness, had grown on him.

He scooped water onto his face to banish the thoughts with cold. Instead, he saw a face looming from the surface. The eyes were manic and blue, sunken cheeks marred with knotted purple scars. Trembling fingers traced the planes of his own face. The only thing missing was the battered black and steel crown.

His tattooed hands clenched, and he ducked under the water, eyes opening to look at the warped room beyond the surface. By tomorrow his future as an Athrolani commoner would be secure. *Even if it means relinquishing my parents, becoming a clerk or historian.* Tomorrow, Daymir would accept the throne, and Keplan would be free.

Φ

The 12th Day of Lumord, 1272
Marl Orna, Clai Province, Athrolan

Daymir's eyes narrowed on the road into Marl Orna. Only once in the last decade had he slipped from Manor Black, navigating the wood-walled tunnel between his root cellar and the house of Currow's widow. Currow was loyal, not to the Xain house, but to the man he served for the last fifty years of his life. As he drew up outside the gate, Daymir was grateful, again, for his steward.

"Who goes?" The gatekeeper peered into the dusk.

Daymir pushed his hood back from his gray hair. "Dam Ornsen." His former aliases were too well known, dragged through the mud of gossip when he was exiled. This one, though, was older still, almost unused since he was crowned heir decades ago.

"And your business?"

"Meeting an old friend who brings me news from home. My brother's unwell."

The man's face softened, and he stepped aside. "Sick's been going about, seems. World's not what it once was."

"You're right about that." Daymir offered him a wave and nudged his horse up the road toward the inn. The Hillock had changed since he last saw it—larger stables to make way for the popular stagecoaches, another storey perched atop the structure, expensive glass in the windows.

How much had Ceir Athrolan changed?

He left his horse with the stablehand and slipped through the rear door of the common room. Like all inns during war, it was swaddled in an uneasy, honest darkness.

The barkeep filled a mug with ale and slid it down to an in-stupored man before jerking a nod at Daymir. "Evening. Room for the night?"

Daymir shook his head. "I'm meeting someone, actually. He should have arrived yesterday, perhaps the day before. A Captain Hylier?"

"Ah. Quiet fellow. He's there, in the booth by the fire."

Daymir followed the man's gesture. Indeed, he could see the lanky gray-breeched leg jutting from under the table. The shoulders under the jacket were thin, and he never thought of Hylier as a quiet man, but civil war changed a person.

"What can I bring you?"

"Privacy." Daymir crossed the room and slid onto the other bench. Unless they started shouting, they were out of earshot. His gaze shifted to the man opposite him. Adrenaline sparked in his limbs. His tablemate was a boy, all man's height, but without the muscle to make his movements graceful. In place of cropped blonde hair was a length of brown tangles. "You are not Hylier."

"Just as your name is not whatever you said to get yourself through the gate." Wide eyes were colorless in the dim light. He extended a gloved hand. Like his feet and nose, it was too large for the rest of him. "I'm Lan Guardsen."

Daymir found his nobleman's ability to keep thoughts from his face suffered from disuse. "You're not what I expected." He examined the boy, who seemed tolerant of him doing so, if uncomfortable. The pale eyes darted from Daymir to the table then back again. Shadows on his cheeks could have been scars, could have been dirt. He pictured a middle-aged man with wit and steady eyes. Instead, Lan fidgeted, the kind of nervous more becoming of an addict. His eyes held manic intelligence that made Daymir's skin crawl. "I hoped to correspond with you again, but I did not expect a personal call. You wear Hylier's uniform. Tell me: 'what overcomes a black oath?'"

"'The red oath, for blood stains deeper than ink.'" The answer to the safe-phrase seemed awkward in the boy's mouth, but it was correct.

Daymir leaned back. "So, he found you?"

"Apparently it wasn't as difficult as I hoped. I asked to meet with you. He agreed my reason was important enough to warrant hauling you out of your luxurious prison. Perhaps we could discuss more over a meal."

Daymir's brows rose. Even stripped of his titles, the manor staff and townsfolk treated him with respect, albeit without honorifics. This boy seemed to either not care about such things, or not know any better. *You're only "master" now, and who knows his upbringing.* "You've got quite the set, meeting under false pretenses then asking for hospitality."

"I was led to believe you were curious about me."

Daymir snorted, but waved the barkeep over. When they had ordered, he turned back to Lan. "So you've come to discuss the war? The capital? My refusal of the throne?"

"All, hopefully." He frowned. "I'm most interested in your last point, there."

"I'd like to know whom I'm speaking to. I see no scholar's robes or medallions of mastery about your shoulders."

"I did not say I was a scholar."

"No, you didn't." His gaze lingered on the nervous hands, the old style of the boy's long hair.

Lan waved away the topic. "About this Peraan: how many of his rumors are true? About the support for your claim and about the general."

Daymir allowed the subject change, but noted it. "I'm told in the long run, most are true. Have you met the man?"

"Peraan? A few times, in passing. He doesn't take to me."

Daymir wondered if anyone did. "So, you beg me to take the throne, but you don't come from Peraan." The arrival of ale and a steaming mound of bread and meat interrupted Daymir's further speculation. When the barkeep retreated, Daymir continued, "If Hylier found you, I assume you received my latest letter."

"It's what urged me to meet with you in person." His expression darkened, and Daymir saw the boy under the thick façade. "Do you have any idea how bad it is there?"

"I heard there was civil unrest. Heard Commander Dorcal and General Domariigo are locking horns—if you'll excuse the expression—over who will claim the throne."

Lan lurched forward, his lip curled in a feral snarl. "It's not unrest, Blackhouse. It's war. Dorcal set a blockade of battleships across the harbor. Domariigo burns any ship sending reinforcements or supplies, just as Dorcal destroys any trade ships attempting to supply the city. I steer my cart around bodies on my way to and from the market. The House of Nobles' loyalty is split, and so whatever supplies the city could receive are divided. Cannonfire destroys buildings, lives every day. I pulled a chunk of beam from my back a week ago. It's a disaster."

Daymir frowned. Something nagged at the back of his mind, slipping through the weakening fingers of his memory. "You speak as if you're familiar with them. The general and commander, that is."

"No. I just have little respect."

"You aren't old enough to be that disillusioned."

He shrugged. "You wanted to ask me about my letters?"

Daymir drew the letters out of his coat and smoothed the paper before him. He made a show of peering at the words. "It strikes me odd that a common boy—forgive my assumption that you are, indeed, common—takes interest in who sits on the throne. Your actions, too, are odd. You write to me, ride here unannounced. But whatever you told Hylier, it was enough for him to give you the uniform off his very back. Perhaps you should include me in the secret."

"The throne is you blood. Your training, your experience makes you perfect. The queen exiled you—so? You're proud, but I don't think you're so petty as to let your kingdom fall to ruin over a false claim of treason." He tilted his head. "I'll tell you why I want you to wear the crown if you tell me why you refuse to. Don't say you know there's another heir, don't give me the tired line that Athrolan needs change. I'm offering you a trade—truth for truth."

Daymir's saw, now, his too-large eyes were blue, luminous ice glinting through bloodshot lace. His skin crawled, remembering another set of eyes, silver and black lace. The memories were so clear today. *And yet, a week ago I went the whole day forgetting how to lace my own shirt.* Dichotomy riddled the past year—days of confusion, and days of clarity made bittersweet by their increasing rarity. Now he sat across from a boy whose anonymity barely cloaked his mercurial character.

The exile played the cards of political intrigue enough to recognize the two ways this game could go. His common sense told him to keep his cards to himself, but the deeper burn of instinct told him it was time to fold. *Common sense and pride have not served me well of late.* "Do you know the stories of my grandfather? The king before Her Majesty Tzatia?"

Lan shrugged. "He was a fair ruler. He reign was peaceful. There's little about his later years, but I'm told he was still alive when Tzatia took the throne."

Daymir winced at the lack of honorifics, the brusque treatment of his late aunt's name. "Do you know why that is?" When the boy shook his head, Daymir looked down. "He lost his mind. Not in the bloody, maniac way some argue King Azirik of Mirik did, or the fragile paranoia of Her Majesty Tzatia. He literally lost it, left pieces of it along the way until he could not remember his station, his family, or even how to eat." He took a bite of the meat between them and wiped the grease from his fingers. "It's a madness that, it seems, is hereditary."

Lan's dark brows curled together, and his attention seemed suddenly fixed on his gloves. Whatever the boy expected, Daymir could see his response was not it. "And it cannot simply be because you've been isolated for too long?"

Frustration sparked through Daymir's hands, his fist rapping on the table top. "Dammit, boy, you think I don't wish that? I forgot I was exiled for two whole days. They found me wandering the hills south of Marl Black. I had to claim I was drunk just to save my dignity."

"Then I'm sorry. Losing your mind is a terrible thing." Something in Lan's tone made Daymir wonder what part of his own mind the boy no longer controlled.

"You have my truth, ugly as it is. Give me yours."

Lan stared at the table. "I am going to answer your letter's question with one of my own. What would destroy Athrolan faster: an heir of old blood slowly losing what makes him worthy of the crown, or a boy?" Lan's gaze slid across the table top, up Daymir's jacket, and stopped at the older man's eyes. "A boy whose parents never told him why he sees things that aren't his to see, hears thoughts he should not be privy to. Power is hereditary too, and is a kind of madness."

Daymir drew a breath. Lan's eyes did not waver now. The exile wondered if the boy even blinked. "I did not think Athrolan's throne would be decided over drinks in a country alehouse. Perhaps we ought to start again." He offered his arm. "Daymir Blackhouse, former treasurer and exiled heir of Athrolan."

Lan's mouth quirked, and something dark ignited behind his eyes. "Keplan Wardyn, son of the Dhoah' Laen Lyne'alea and Earth Shaker Aud'narman."

"And heir apparent to Athrolan's throne."

"Yes."

Daymir stared. Rumors hinted, but the floor still lurched under his feet. Weeks ago the Dhoah' Laen herself strolled through his door. Now her child sat across from him with the same intensity. *What are those odds?* He wondered if the boy knew his parents visited, but tucked it away for later. "You think you'll make more of a mess than I?"

"I'm untrained. I was never given a chance at proper teaching or knowing my heritage."

"You sound like a petulant child."

"And you are an incredible coward."

"Some of your father's teeth, I see."

"Not really." Keplan glared at a scuff mark on the floor. His gloved hands trembled on the table.

Daymir did not see destruction if Keplan took the throne. It was possible, surely, but Tzatia did not rule alone. Neither would the next monarch. There were advisors, officers, and the Council. Athrolan would not look the same, of that he was certain, but she sorely needed change.

"So, is this it? Civil war will decide what happens to her?"

"If it were easy, Wardyn, then we would not be here." Daymir gestured to the bar. "I need a drink. I've made my choice. You've got to make yours."

Φ

Keplan stared at the food, forgotten, before him. Across the room, Daymir ordered something and settled onto a stool. His conversation with another patron was low and meaningless.

Keplan's gut clenched in panic. The fickle ability to read others told him only enough to know Daymir did not lie. He expected to be awed by the heir, expected the older man's promise to take the throne. *An hour's conversation, no more.* Instead, he sat alone, trying to crush the insidious thought that Daymir was right. Keplan would make a better king. *Perhaps it wasn't he who needed convincing, but me.*

Another ache bloomed, but this one hunkered between his ribs. *I would miss Firas. And Mirrel.* He did not want to miss anyone. He did not want responsibility, the distance that meant never learning the particular sounds of someone's steps on the stairs. Loneliness clenched his heart. He thought of never seeing Firas's smile or watching Mirrel roll her eyes. Never listening to a third of Azimir's prattled words as they navigated the city streets. *Even if I give up my name, my heritage, the throne, I might never see those things again.* Civil war ripped happiness from the world in a way other wars only dreamed.

But he could end the war. He could assure Firas and Mirrel and Azimir stayed safe, stayed how he remembered. *I can't face them again. Not as their lover or friend or cousin. Instead they'll see these scars, these burning ideas, the son of the Dhoah' Laen, son of an Earth Shaker.*

I'll face them as a king.

His heart hammered loud enough for all Marl Orna to hear, he was sure. If he wanted the Commander on his side, he needed to arrive with Daymir in tow. *Give them what they want – both heirs.*

He crossed the room in four strides, as if he could outrun the voice that screamed he was making a mistake. He stopped at Daymir's elbow, his gloved hand resting beside the exile's drink.

Daymir turned to look at him, dark eyes unreadable beyond faint curiosity.

"Come to Athrolan. Meet with them, and with me. If you support me before Dorcal, he'll have no choice. Unless he's far less stable than we hope, it might just work." He glanced at Daymir. His stomach writhed from the noise in his mind and the shadow in the older man's eyes.

Daymir frowned. "I am an exile."

"I formally invite you, as," Keplan's voice faltered, "as Heir Apparent. Stay in the capital as Regent for a year, or advisor, or something, until I've learned enough to not destroy the kingdom. Your estate is lovely, but minds like ours do better in chaos." His skin hummed with the urge to move, and he flexed his hands. "I'm going to pack my things. I'll leave in an hour, at dawn. I can't do this without you. If you're willing to help, meet me outside." He retreated upstairs.

Dread stilled the quake of adrenaline. If he stayed the Wise Hare's bar-boy he and Firas would be as doomed as he was in his Banis cell. Keplan heard the hitch in his own voice at the title he would claim soon, the growl that accompanied "chaos."

His parents' power was his. The weight of their choices, their unfinished business, pinched his shoulders. *They don't ever tell you how much it scares us. How much we give up.* He swept the room a last time and found his cloak hanging by the door. Dawn swallowed moonlight as it crept up the sky.

His borrowed horse waited, head bobbing with anticipation. Keplan helped ready the animal, flashing the sleepy stable boy a smile with his thanks. Daymir's beautiful bay stood, unbothered, in his stall.

Come on, Blackhouse.

Rumbling boots heralded another patrol, and he looked away as they passed. It would take a single breath to scare him from his goal now, and he could not afford it.

Athrolan could not afford it.

I haven't earned the right to run yet. Keplan smoothed the horse's fur under the padded leather while he waited a minute, then another. In the courtyard, the sky was more gray than purple. He glanced back at the inn, mostly dark, not yet touched by morning. The disillusionment in Daymir's eyes, the fatigue, terrified him. Even if the man accompanied him, he could not stand in the former heir's shadow or the shadow of his parents. He drew a breath, reveling in the bite of cold air, and mounted up.

The inn door swung open. Daymir emerged, dressed in traveling clothes and bearing an old pack. He caught Keplan's eye with a smile. "I had to send word to my manservant." His eyes narrowed on Keplan. "You thought I wasn't coming."

"A bit, yes."

The exile snorted. "I don't miss the duty, but that house feels like a prison more each year. And you were right about our minds." The stableboy appeared holding the reins of the gelding and Daymir swung into the saddle. "You realize you implied your reign will be chaos."

Keplan's smile was sudden, and his heartbeat thundered just a bit slower. "Aren't they all?"

Φ

The 15th Day of Lumord, 1272
The City of Ceir Athrolan, Athrolan

Marching and shouted orders replaced the usual cacophony of the city. Spitting clouds blotted any warmth from the mid-morning sun. Keplan drew up on the crest of the hill. The grassy expanse between them and the city swarmed with troops. The detainment camp looked closer to a village.

"This looks like my nightmares." Daymir shifted his seat. "I assume we'll wait until morning?"

"We've little time, and besides—they've been expecting my parents' child to ride in on a flaming horse or some nonsense." He glanced over. Honestly, he would vomit if he stewed in anticipation any longer. "Do you disagree?"

"No, I'm just impressed with your...gumption."

"That sounds like a disease, not a compliment."

"More than one thing might be true, Keplan." Daymir frowned at the city. "Are we declaring who I am?"

"We'll deal with it if they recognize you. Otherwise, you're just my guest." Keplan nudged his horse into a trot and straightened his shoulders. Whatever Daymir labeled "gumption," Keplan knew was closer to impatience. Political dances already exhausted him. Silence filled the last minutes of their journey.

"Halt!" A soldier trotted up to meet them on the road. "The city is closed. You'll have to take your business elsewhere."

Keplan raised a hand to silence her. *I'll need to get used to being imperious.* "No need, Captain." He flashed his rank.

"I wasn't aware. You're free to go."

Keplan stuck to the damp shadows of the dark street. Firas's words, Mirel's promise, Peraan's threats, all rattled around his mind, the tinny tapping of distant war drums. Running from his past was fine, if the only person his cowardice destroyed was him. Now he was newborn, naked and squalling in the cold streets after the warmth and naivete of his months in the Wise Hare.

Torches bloomed against the stained white walls of the palace, and the guard tripled around the gates. *How, again, did I plan for this to work?* They stopped outside the walls, and he fumbled Daymir's letter from his pocket.

"You're breaking curfew!"

He shielded his eyes from the rain and shouted up,"I bring a message to General Domariigo. It's urgent."

The guard raise a hand and after a moment the speaking-door in the gate flapped open to allow the man to get a better look at Keplan. "Who's it from?"

"See for yourself." Keplan held up the back of the waxed envelope with its heavy black seal.

"I'll take it from here, Captain."

"I was told to deliver it to him personally." Keplan shrugged. "Could you tell him we've come? Say it's Keplan Wardyn." He stepped back from the gate, forcing himself to look unconcerned at both the treatment and the rain. Daymir simply stared up at the walls, hung with sodden, mourning black. Everything rode on the next hour. The palace doors opened, slammed. Rain sluiced from the walls, from the dome, forming tiny cascades through the gutters along the street. He supposed rain was the world's weeping and, like tears, came at transitions.

"Captain Wardyn?" The door opened in the gate, and the guard ushered him in. "General Domariigo asked to see you right away. Sorry about the wait."

"Not a problem, sir. It's good you're thorough." He caught the polite condescension in his voice and bit back other words. *Save it for when I know the way I leave An'thor's room.*

No bells sounded their arrival, no banners waved. Instead, the wet clap of hooves echoed against the walls, and the fresh tang of salt clung to the dew-drenched stone. The wind tumbled from the hills inland, sweeping the cloying smoke out to sea.

He glanced back at Daymir's quiet scoff. "What?"

"You'll have to get used to being known. The moment you're declared, you'll never go unrecognized again."

"You seem to be doing all right." Keplan snapped. He dismounted and followed the steward inside.

His thoughts stalled as he entered the inner courtyard. Gravel crunched under their boots. A birch pergola stretched the length of the entryway, the gray wood stained black from years of water. Scenes of the city's golden days inlaid the doors themselves. Above him, the dome loomed, a milky, glaring eye. The inner halls spoke of the same heritage—old and opulent, and long since faded. An entire wing to the north was boarded off. *What did my parents feel, riding into this city, heralded by parades, banners, bells? Did they ever grow used to it?*

"My mirror tells me the years took their toll." He scratched at the full beard left travel-long. "Besides, I'm exiled. People don't see what they don't expect."

"Perhaps we can use that to our advantage." They were ushered into a foyer and left alone. Fur and iron decorations told him it belonged to the general. Keplan paced to the window, twitching the curtains back. "If it wasn't too late, now would be when I rode for the fields."

Daymir hummed thoughtfully. "Smuggling the former heir into the city, staying long enough so he's not executed then escaping into anonymity? Not the worst plan I've heard."

Keplan's heart faltered, and he looked over at the older man. "I'd do it. In a heartbeat, I'd do it. I'd hand over the throne and the crown and this entire mess." He watched Daymir's calculating expression and the steel in his shoulders. *But I'm wondering if I should.*

"I'm not offering." Daymir's tone echoed the dust on the mantle. He moved to the window, hands clasped behind his back.

Keplan watched the man assemble his court facade, a warrior with armor unused during years of peace. How long before he had his own mask, before that mask was so familiar he forgot the face beneath it? He scraped his sopping hair back from his face. It would not do to look like a drowned gutter dog.

"May I offer you some advice?"

"That's why I brought you," Keplan reminded him.

"For the next days, months, years even, you'll need enough confidence in yourself to outweigh the uncertainty of the entire kingdom." Daymir glanced at him sidelong. "It doesn't have to be real, just convincing."

The door opened, and Keplan straightened, lacing his fingers. Perhaps he already wore a mask.

"The general will see you, this way." The guard opened another door and gestured for him to enter. Keplan stepped in alone and shut the door. Despite the fire in the expansive hearth, the study was deserted, stark. The few decorations showed the man's heritage and love for Athrolan.

"I didn't believe it was you at first." Domariigo's voice was ice cracking in bitter cold. He leaned on the darkened doorway to the rest of his chambers. By his easy stance, Keplan realized he stood there all along.

"Good evening."

"You avoid me for weeks, then show up to drip puddles on my carpet at midnight and all you offer is 'good evening'?"

Keplan smiled. "You don't have any carpets, Domariigo, and we're at war. I doubt you'd sleep as it is."

"You're late. A little later and we'd have burnt the place down. You brought a message from Daymir?"

"I had to get through the gates, didn't I?" He held up the letter. "It's from Blackhouse, but it's addressed to me, not you." He tucked the letter back into his cloak and straightened his shoulders. "I don't want the crown, you know. But I want war less. I'm here to accept."

An'thor's black eyes raked the boy's face with curiosity—Arman's jaw, Alea's nose, Azirik's eyes. "As much as I badgered Barrackborn, I was starting to disbelieve."

Keplan pointed to the chairs by the fire. "Might we talk?"

An'thor's chin jerked in an exhausted nod. "I'll call for some tea." He drew a bottle from his desk. "Unless you want something stronger?"

"Tea is fine." Keplan watched the general move about the room, lighting lamps and calling for tea. When he stopped and perched on the edge of his desk, Keplan held out his arm. "I won't pretend to like you, and you seemed uninterested in overcoming that."

"Perhaps." An'thor's tired mouth twitched. "I've supported you from the beginning, but others will need convincing. How do you plan to do that?"

"I need help—not just with that, with everything. I don't know what I'm doing. I don't know what it means to be noble or be a king. You heard from my own mouth about all I know is how to clean stalls. I'm mad as they come, but you're just as mad for supporting me. You've been ruling this city for months. I'll need a teacher."

"I don't think any would call what I've done 'ruling.'"

"Clearly. I wasn't speaking about you. Blackhouse will teach me."

"The fates themselves couldn't force that man to set foot in this," An'thor dismissed. "And I doubt he'd agree to teach you."

"Not the fates, just me." Adrenaline waned from Keplan's body and his hands trembled. Buzzing thoughts from the palace wormed into his head. Even the general's thoughts were a low, wordless murmur. He shook the sounds away and jerked open the door. "Ask him yourself, Domariigo."

The general's albic brows arched, and he peered against the brighter foyer light as the exile entered. An'thor's faint smile did not chase the exhaustion from his eyes. "Daymir." He moved across the room and offered his arm.

"An'thoriend." Daymir took the arm, but his gaze roved to the mess of soldiers visible outside the window and the chaos in the lower tiers of the city. "I can't say I like what you've done with the place."

An'thor's smile faded. "Perhaps if we'd had help, it wouldn't have come to this." He trudged back to the credenza beside the hearth and fished out a bottle. The glasses were the only thing in the room not covered in dust. "You've changed not a bit, I see. Still as much of an arse."

"Could we not do this right now?" Keplan drew a ragged breath. "Small wonder we war amongst ourselves, with Domariigo too drunk to hold his tongue and everyone else too tired of listening to it." He forced each word around the urge to vomit. "I'll walk out and let you ride this kingdom straight to doom."

An'thor looked like he wanted to correct the boy, but kept his thoughts to himself. "What do you intend to do, then?"

Keplan stared at the general. "I don't know the first thing about being king. I don't know what I'm doing. I barely know the details of Athrolan's government." He sank into the chair by the hearth. "A kingdom the size of Athrolan, she doesn't have one sole heir. There are lines, carefully tracked by clerks and historians. Daymir surely has cousins."

"I had a sister," Daymir offered. "She was next, after me. She's dead. There was my father's cousin's son and daughter Jaytian and Dirma, and their children. The first fell ill four years ago. The second was lost in childbirth. Truthfully, House Xain has been plagued by accidents and tragedy." Keplan watched the man's gaze flick to the general. "Much like the family of the Count of Felden, of late."

Keplan frowned. There was something there, an accusation, an admittance. He was not sure. It was a problem for tomorrow, someday when war no longer slavered at his future. "And those children, the cousin's grandchildren, they're unfit? Too young?"

Daymir faltered, but the general barreled on without noticing.

"Dirma's son, Tzavanir, is fit. He is Duke of Pardelan and nineteen. Jaytian's daughter, Gella married an ambassador from the Vales. Fit and of age is not the issue, Keplan. The queen declared an heir. One who is present." Daymir reminded. "Those alternates were in case no heir was chosen or found. Besides, they seem to have gone missing."

An'thor sighed. "They are currently housed with their entourage and every other visitor to the city since we locked the gates," An'thor looked away, "in the camps outside the walls. We could not risk them becoming the figureheads of further coup, intentionally or otherwise."

"Fates, Peraan's ramblings about your plot against the Xain house were true," Keplan remarked.

An'thor whirled. "If your parents hadn't shirked their duty, I wouldn't have had to plot, and plan, or play general and king and assassin to get you to this throne. Sometimes heroes make the greatest cowards." Glass rattled as he poured himself another. "But here you are. Let's forget how you got here and focus on wedging a crown on your reluctant head."

Momentum hurtled Keplan ahead, and each time he glanced back he saw the way closing behind him. As much as he dreaded what was to come, it was no mistake. Not yet, at least. *Perhaps I'm saving all those for when tens of thousands of people depend upon me.*

Daymir was an ally, but not a friend. An'thor's empathy barely glimmered through the tangle of duty and alcohol. Keplan expected loneliness. He had not expected it to bother him. He wanted Firas, wanted the escape and the warmth of the other man's bed. The ground seemed to collapse under his boots.

"Well, Wardyn?"

Keplan turned, realizing An'thor had been speaking for a minute. "I'm sorry." He shook himself back to attention. "I was somewhere else. What did you ask?"

"I asked if you wanted to meet Dorcal today."

He shrugged. "We don't even know what the Council will say. We can't call the Council without alerting the whole city. Whatever it is, we'll need the whole plan before we take a step." He looked at Daymir. "At least I can boast you as an advisor." Grinning felt false, but he tried at humor anyway. "Perhaps you'll remember the taste of power and take this hideous duty off my hands."

An'thor's eyes narrowed. "Whatever your reason for avoiding the throne, would this assuage it?"

"I would agree, yes." The former heir turned to Keplan. "I don't know if you'll be a good king, but I know you'll have a better chance than I do."

"What do we do about Dorcal? The Council?" Keplan looked between them. "Is there a vote?"

"This is a monarchy, not the damn town hall."

"Oh, stuff it, Domariigo." Daymir stalked across the room and poured himself a drink. "This stopped being a proper monarchy when you hid my aunt's body from her people."

Keplan pressed his brow against the cold glass of the window. Smoke drifted over the harbor from the latest attacks. If it would stop the death, the violence, he would march into the streets. "So, call a Council and announce my presence, announce my idea. If disputed, an heir needs backing by seven provinces, correct?"

"Or twenty lesser lords," An'thor added.

"How many provinces favor you? Us?" *Me.*

"Five and the Head of the House of Commons. Raven's got six and the Head of the House of Nobles."

"If I petitioned the council to see reason, I could win enough of them to gain favor. Then we convince Dorcal to stand down. He seems difficult."

"You have no idea." An'thor spat the words, and made as if to pour himself another drink. At Daymir's glare, however, he stopped.

"From what I've heard, he's a formal man. Adheres to tradition. His reasoning for his current course was wanting a blooded heir, I assume?"

"All true. He's also a superstitious and racist bastard," Daymir offered.

"So, my heritage was an issue." Keplan sighed. This was worse than he thought. *Give up while you're still free, still uncrowned. Let Athrolan follow the steps of Mirik and do away with the throne all-together.* "He's a warrior, though. He responds to strength?"

"He hated your mother most of all. He responds to whatever counts as right in his thick skull." An'thor ran a hand through his age-yellowed hair, black gaze following Keplan's pacing. "What are you thinking?"

"Other than diving off the harbor gates?" He swallowed hard. "If I gain favor, Blackhouse will request an audience with him. I'll go along. It would prove I was clever enough, strong enough to get backing."

"I cannot decide if you're a genius or a madman." Daymir's tone was dry but honest.

"Most geniuses are mad." Keplan's stomach interrupted his words, and he winced. Breakfast seemed years ago, and fatigue shortened his temper. It did not bode well for negotiations. "It's almost nightfall. Might we call the Council after supper? I doubt I'll gain any support by gnawing the foot of the closest councilor."

An'thor finally grinned. He tugged at the bell beside the door and issued orders to the servingman stationed outside before turning back. "We'll meet them in two hours."

Daymir rose "May I borrow your privy, An'thoriend? Marl Black has lower grooming standards than the palace."

"Of course." An'thor watched the man retreat into the private rooms beyond the study. His face was unreadable as ever. "I can't say I trust him, but I'm not sure I trust you either. You're both just better than war."

"Best come up with some better lines before you present me to the Council." Keplan picked at his hands, flesh peeling enough to bleed. The small mirror by the door helped him scrape his hair into further order. There was no question he had traveled for a week. "I ought to clean up too. I won't bother with a bath, because I might see sense and try and drown myself."

An'thor laughed. "I might not even blame you. I'll call for water and a clean set of clothes." He paused by the door. "I know you're scared. I know this doesn't feel real, yet. But you managed the impossible, bringing Daymir here. Remember that."

Keplan shook his head. "You just went about it wrong. I knew nothing less than both heirs would stop the war. The Council is welcome to fight over us, but they will damn well do it with words, not swords."

CHAPTER SEVENTEEN

The 16th Day of Lumord, 1272
The City of Ceir Athrolan, Athrolan

PERAAN CHECKED THE LOCKS on his door a third time before navigating the winding stairs of the Lily and Ahonsa. It had seen far richer days, but war made people drink. Moreover, this particular establishment was an unofficial headquarters of Daymir's, and by extension Commander Dorcal's, supporters in the city proper.

Peraan waved to the bartender. "I'll be out for the evening if anyone comes for me." He moved to the door, slinging his cloak over his shoulders. A group of armed men sat by the door. Though they played a round of blood-hand, the darting glances and arrangement of their seats said they were there to keep the peace. The pot in the middle held only a few rounds-worth of coin, and their mugs were still partially full.

Peraan nodded to the bearded one among them. "Jakim, I'll be back late. Keep an eye for that boy, will you? I don't want him back."

He ducked into the street, eyes roving from the alley beyond to where the side street spilled onto High Arch. Curfew and cannon fire cut Athrolan's usual bustle.

Peraan followed the arc of the side street. Keeping to the shadows was easy with every third lamp destroyed by cannonballs or riots. Another third were drained to create makeshift war-oil for the answering volleys.

He knew many of the militia and which roads were patrolled by his supporters. He raked a chapped hand over his face. War was exhausting. He was a boy when the Gods' War ended. Raising Daymir to the throne would hopefully not involve more bloodshed. *But we are men, and what can we do, but murder each other?* Glinting steel of army shields flashed ahead and he turned down a side street.

It took another half hour to reach the palace. Torches blazed, four dozen dying suns in the face of the yawning night of war. He skirted the wall, grateful for the decorative trees lining the stained white stone. He swung over the edge of the bridge to the gate and dropped. The gardens were quiet. Gravel crunched, mimicry of the city crumbling before Dorcal's volleys.

He upended the thick envelope from his cloak over his hand. Lilac pressed flat between the folded parchment. Only a time marked the parchment. A stand of lilacs encircled a bench beside the memorials' entrance. The trees bore only withered leaves, the ground cleaned of their brown, fallen flowers. He wondered, absently, when the bloom in his hand was collected.

"I thought you'd leave me waiting forever."

Peraan rolled his eyes at the saccharine tone. "Never, my dear." He caught the hand of the woman tucked against one of the twisted trees.

She let him keep a hold, but dropped the simpering act. "I don't have much time. They're calling us for extra shifts."

He held up his hand. "I shouldn't know any more about you." Poorly hemmed skirts aside, her bearing said she was a soldier. Her information told him which company. More details would be dangerous, and self-preservation extended to his network. *It has to operate with another man at the helm.*

She snorted. "Right. That why you gave me the false name, 'Vanabren'?" She exaggerated the name.

He extricated his hand from hers. Keeping up the pretense of romance if they were seen grew difficult the more they interacted. *Let them think we're quarreling.* "You wanted to meet tonight, so it must be important. Unless now you're dragging me out past curfew for conversation."

She made a face. "You're too old for me. And yes, it's important."

Peraan touched the gray at his temples with a wince before drawing out his thin notebook. "Go on."

"A boy entered the city this afternoon, from the east. He dressed as a captain. He went to the palace and demanded to see the general. Said he had a letter from Blackhouse. They wouldn't let him in until he said to give the general his name." She watched, disinterested, as Peraan jotted down her words, then continued, "A minute later they bowed him into the palace."

Peraan kept his breath level, but his mind churned. "Do you think Domariigo saw sense and sent for the true king?"

She snorted. "I'm not sure the man had any sense to begin with."

Peraan heaved a sigh. She was right, and he knew it. "What name did the boy give?"

Her expression settled between alert and conniving and Peraan remembered why he only trusted her with his brother's name and not his own. "That's why I thought you'd want to know. Keplan Wardyn."

Peraan frowned. "That supposed to mean something to me?"

She hiked up skirts she clearly had no use for and headed back toward the palace. "You'll catch on, Vanabren."

He watched her go without comment. No information she gave yet proved false, but he trusted her about as far as his arthritic shoulders would carry her.

Enough of the Royal Guard was disillusioned with the general that they would accept Daymir. He tugged his cloak closer and took off along the wall.

Ruined buildings and battered streets made his bones ache more than the night's chill. Soot and blood smeared Athrolan's gray cobbles. Trash and debris clogged the gutters. Though poor folk and the Slummer suffered most, war's teeth were long enough to sink into the merchants and clerks of the Silver Apron.

Fine houses were dark, small gardens overgrown and untended. Fountains ran dry. Smoke filled the streets even there, and Peraan tugged his scarf over his nose as he descended to the warehouses. Decay and sweat joined the acrid stench of creosote. Patrols lessened; other than the dead, there was little left to loot. Peraan paused beside the skeleton of a glassblower's stall and let out a low, trilling whistle. Behind him, the beams of the warehouse creaked. A muffled thump heralded his second informant.

"Peraan." The man's voice could have been further creaking floorboards.

"Luben." Peraan fixed the half-Berrin man with a glare. "You were supposed to arrive weeks ago."

"Didn't expect the city to lay siege to herself, now did I? Vinegar still burns my nose from the barrel I smuggled myself in."

Peraan shrugged. "If you were here on time, you wouldn't have had to. Besides, vinegar is an improvement. All your people smell like fish."

Luben sighed at the racism. "You're lucky the cause needs you. What do you have for me?"

"Something's stirring in the palace, I'll need to learn more. In the meantime, a man lives down by the docks, an old hand named Sar Salt-tongue. Fates know what name he was born to. He informs Domariigo on the Commander's movements and network here. Kill him."

"I didn't join you to kill the homeless."

"This is war, Luben. Or didn't you notice the bodies you walked over to get here? You bring any news from the east?"

"Daymir disappeared. My cousin in Marl Black sent word. The true king arrived in Marl Orna alone, and left with a scarred young man dressed as a soldier."

Peraan frowned. *Seems to be a rash of boys with scars.* "Any word where he's headed?"

"West. Treason, him leaving Marl Black. Whatever his reason, it's a good one." The man sighed. "Ready for this business to be over. Nothing good comes from a blasphemous heir. Nothing. My brother, still in Berr, far to the north, he tells me a new god's coming, and all that cling to the titanic forces of the past will come to see their err."

Peraan frowned. "Your cousin a madman?"

"No more than any other prophet."

He shuddered. Religion made him queasy. "Regardless of blasphemy, Luben, we will see this through. I don't suppose your cousin caught the name of this boy with the scars?"

"No. You think you know him?"

"Just information, that's all." Peraan shoved off from the wall. He needed to know more about Domariigo's visitor before he started passing information. "Take care of Salt-tongue, and I'll see you in a week's time. Same place." He waited for the man to disappear into the wreckage by the docks before turning home.

It was only later, in the dim light of the Lily and Ahonsa's hearth, that he drew out his notebook. He read over the information again, rolling it in his mind like he rolled spiced whiskey around his mouth.

When Nikola poured him another mug, she handed him a letter. "This came for you. Looks like it's from your old friend in the palace."

"I've not heard from him in years. Figured he died." He tucked it into his pocket to read in the privacy of his room. "Nikola," he stopped her as she turned away. "What does the name 'Keplan Wardyn' mean to you?"

"Nothing, really. Wardyn is common in the south, but it was the surname of the Earth Shaker."

"That was Arrowlash."

"Not when he first came. Aud'narman Wardyn. He's come up twice too much lately." She frowned. "Why do you ask?"

"Just adding to the puzzle." He looked back to his book, eyes narrowed on the name. *"until he said to give the general his name."* Whiskey no longer burned his throat. Ice in his gut told him the general's inhuman heir had already arrived.

Φ

"Tell me again why I'm doing this." Keplan swore when his hand caught in the decorative tie of his horse-tail.

"To save the kingdom," An'thor spoke as if to a child.

Keplan frowned at the mirror. "Fuck the kingdom."

"Wardyn."

"Right. Saving the kingdom. Easy." He straightened. The gray outfit turned his skin sallow and his eyes overbright. It did not fit. "I look terrible."

"You look like a symbol of youth and hope."

"I look ill, Domariigo." He clasped his gloved hands before him to hide their shaking.

The room beyond hummed with conversation, a mutter to the chaos in Keplan's thoughts. "I can't do this, An'thor. I wasn't lying when I said I might be sick all over the nearest councilor."

"Which is why I made you eat something."

Keplan rolled his eyes. He never felt more powerless. *Secrets give me power.* Beyond that door lay a dozen people with more secrets and power than most in the kingdom, Keplan would bet. He looked over at An'thor. "Let them ignore me. Let them work out their issues at the idea. Then introduce me."

An'thor rolled his black eyes. "You do love the dramatic entrance, don't you?"

Though he did not particularly care about An'thor's opinion of him, the observation was not wrong. Between his isolated childhood and the weeks of torture and invisibility in Ban, he was ready to turn the tables. *It's time someone listened.* "People expect heroes to arrive in a blaze from the sky. The least I can do is deliver some good lines. Besides, I want to observe them for a bit."

An'thor eyed him before tucking his tunic tighter around his thick middle and facing the door. He nodded to the squire.

"Sir An'thoriend Domariigo of Neneviir and Claimiirn, General of Athrolan's Army." The squire glanced, panicked at Keplan, but he shook his head and slipped into the room.

Three council men ranged about the table. War did away with formality, it seemed. Keplan scanned the room from the doorway, steadying his heartbeats by sheer force of will. Hair looked hastily done, and their eyes sank in shadow. Their squires clustered in the rear of the room playing what looked like a version of tiles. An'thor took his seat near the head of the table with a sigh.

The table was long and broad, with seating for the full Council—the House of Nobles and House of Guilds alike. Each chair bore a lacquered emblem of its user's position. The monarch's chair stood at the head of the table, flanked by the general's and commander's on the right and the two Head Councilors' on the left. Drapes hung between each window were the faded turquoise and black of mourning.

The other two Councilors presumably under An'thoriend's influence, entered a moment later, squires and personal clerks in tow. Keplan used the distraction to cross the room and stand by one of the wide windows. He eyed the latch on the casement. Perhaps, if he was careful, no one would notice him pitching himself out of it. *And then they'd have to crown Daymir.* He caught An'thor's level gaze. The man raised two fingers and tapped his brow, his chin and his collar in a subtle salute. Keplan drew a breath, then nodded a second time. *I did the impossible. I brought Daymir here. Alone. And now I have both his support and Domariigo's.*

The other half of the Consulates arrived en masse, eyes wary. Keplan noted they were accompanied by guards. Neither side looked pleased.

An'thor rose, cutting the mutters and speculation short. His black gaze slid from one Consulate to the next. When he made a silent visual circuit of them, he began. "Thank you for your prompt arrival, though my request gave little notice. Rarely do all of us agree, and our values are not something to take lightly. Indeed, that variation lends Athrolan her greatest strength. But this war has gone on long enough. There is a solution, but it requires cooperation and trust. This kingdom needs a king. Both Dorcal and I have reached out to Master Blackhouse without luck. The man has no interest in taking up the throne, and frankly, I can't blame him. We exiled him. But he was not the only man named the heir."

A noble rose. "We understand the situation with Blackhouse is complicated, but he is not the only blooded descendant of Xain."

Pardelan province's representative, a tall woman bearing a nose like a hawk's beak rolled her eyes. "He's imprisoned the only ones left living just outside our walls, Jantian."

"General, sir, Commander Dorcal will not surrender," another noble promised. "Your search for this mythic heir needs to end if we hope for peace."

Keplan's eyes roved from speaker to speaker, filtering through their ranks and names and opinions as quickly as he could. Some were prideful, others desperate, and, like An'thor, idealism and hope still filled another two. He filed what he could away for later consideration. One thing, however, lingered: every Consulate was exhausted and terrified of their kingdom's future—or at least their part of it.

"There's talk of madness, sir." A gray-haired man dressed in green interjected.

"Not to mention drunkenness—"

An'thor's fist slammed on the table. "Drunkenness—?"

"Enough." Keplan flexed his gloved hands and rose from his perch. Startled silence fell. A moment passed before the council traced the low, firm voice. He moved to the head of the table and rested a hand on An'thor's shoulder. "Your logic got us as far as it will. Let the legends do the rest."

Murmurs rose. He remained silent as An'thor returned to the seat to the right of the monarch's chair. It was not the introduction he hoped, but he would make it work. *I have to.* Terror rooted in his bones, a chill that steadied his gut out of sheer necessity. Slipping into the role of every Banis noble, every legend his father told him made it easier. "Bickering gets us nowhere. Athrolan tore herself apart these last months. I've seen a fraction of the war all of you lived through, and it's already exhausting. While you ripped this kingdom to pieces, I went to Blackhouse. You follow Daymir?" *Demand respect,* he reminded himself. "Good. Because he follows me."

This earned a narrow glare from the Duchess of Pardelan. "And you are?"

"Ah." He rested both hands on the tabletop and inclined his head a fraction. "I'm Keplan Wardyn, son of Dhoah' Laen Lyne'alea and Earth Shaker Aud'narman Arrowlash, Heir Apparent for the throne of Athrolan." He let surprise burble and die before rattling off their fears. "You don't know me, save my heritage. I'm young. There is no proof of my blood. I'm not noble, or even Athrolani, save by birthplace. But I have something no other claimant does. I have the support of both General Domariigo and Master Blackhouse himself." He hoped his faint smile looked kind and not manic. "Not to mention a writ in the queen's own hand declaring my right to the throne."

"Master Wardyn, we don't have—"

"Proof that Master Blackhouse actually supports me?" Keplan glanced at the door. "Squire, please invite Daymir in. You'll find him waiting in the foyer."

Daymir stepped into the room before the words left Keplan's mouth. The exile's white hair was trimmed to the nape of his neck and combed back. A small tuft under his lips was all that remained of his messy beard. Black clothes fit, but were a decade out of style. He nodded to An'thor before moving to Keplan's left hand and bowing. "Thank you for having me." The clear words were pitched to sound friendly, as if meant for Keplan's ears only.

He's a master at this game. "Of course." Keplan's gaze swiveled to the Council.

Daymir gestured to the seat. "If I may?" At Keplan's nod, he sat and directed his sharp gaze at the others. "Half of you promised to follow my wishes for the kingdom. You wrote your support to me and followed Commander Dorcal's attempt at revolution in my name. Yet here I am telling you to put your names behind this man.

"Your concerns were mine too, at first. He is young. He is inexperienced. He is not Xain blood," Daymir repeated. "And I don't care. He is driven and inspired. He is wise beyond most men twice his age. He does not have Tzatia's blood, but that of the most powerful creatures this world has known, and Her Majesty's own seal on his claim to the throne. It takes more than heart to rule a kingdom, and I have agreed at Master Wardyn's request—no, his insistence—to act as Chief Advisor to the Crown for a year's time. This will allow him to benefit from my experience and understanding of government, and you to grow the same trust in him."

A black-haired man with Tetran's sigil ignored Keplan and Daymir both, dark eyes narrowing on An'thoriend. "General, have you well and truly lost your mind? This boy is a child. He looks starved, scarred, and I doubt those arms could lift a sword."

An'thor turned on the marquess with a snarl. "I am trying to end this war, you piss-stained—"

"Did Tzatia raise a blade?" Keplan interrupted. "No, she had an army. Did Tzatia make every choice alone? No, she had us behind her. Did she choose to lead? No, it was chosen for her."

"What do you want? Coin for your acting? You are an overgrown shepherd. You ought to attend your flock before they get out of hand and destroy the countryside!"

"The way your civil war threatened to?" An'thor's face twisted into an ugly sneer.

"It was as much your war as ours, General!"

"I'd rather run into the woods." Keplan rose from his chair, pleased that the room settled into stillness. "I'd rather stay a bar-hand in the slums. It's easier. But your inability to end this war on your own forced my hand. You don't have to like me. My parents didn't have the time to earn Her Majesty's trust, but she followed them anyway.

"I know it won't be easy. I know I need you. But I'm not just the lesser of a poor choice. My parents raised me as a commoner so I'm new to state, but I'm clever, and learn faster than you could imagine. Mirik thrived under a soldier Hetmir. Let's see how far Athrolan climbs with a pauper king." He paused for a moment. "I will leave you to discuss this among yourselves. Cannon fire should be enough of a time limit."

An'thor and Daymir rose, the councilors hastily doing the same. Keplan kept his steps unhurried, as he left the hall and returned to the general's study. He sank into the chair by the window. Seconds, decades seemed to have passed in the span of the meeting. Already his back ached with the weight. The view of the harbor was so different from his room in the Hare. In place of cascading small Slummer houses perched atop the ordered navy barracks and offices, he was treated to the glittering Silver Apron and smoky ruins of warehouses. Midnight swallowed the expanse of graves and memorials.

"They'll be at it a while, you know." Daymir shut the door softly, face a neutral mask. "I can call for a meal."

Keplan frowned. "I don't think I could eat right now."

"By tomorrow afternoon you will probably be king. You need sustain yourself on more than stirring speeches. Even during the horrible, uncertain times."

Keplan hummed in response. He did not really care about supper, or breakfast, or whatever meal this was. He only cared how a shaggy pony fared without him, and what a Slummer bartender thought at that moment. *It's been a week.*

An'thor arrived with food and the ubiquitous glass of alcohol. Even considering his translucent skin, he looked wan. "State affairs are more tedious than I remember."

"State affairs haven't included four heirs and a civil war in many generations, general." Daymir watched the Ageless man pile meat and sliced potatoes onto a plate. "Remember to save some of that for His Majesty here. Can't have the boy starving to death before—"

"Don't," Keplan murmured.

Daymir handed a plate to the young man. "Don't what?"

"Call me that. Not yet. Not until you have to, and then, please, only in public. I've got less than a day before I sacrifice my life to this kingdom. Afford me some freedom until then."

They fell silent, only the sound of eating echoing in the small room. Bells clanged out the hour before dawn and An'thor rose. "I'd best see they don't wrest the kingdom from my hands now that they're all in one room. I'll call you both when we've decided."

Keplan rested his head in his hands. Buzzing conversation filled his mind from the Council Hall. Outbursts punctuated the unclear words. *I can't think about that, can't listen in until they've decided.* Instead, he focused on the thrum of his pulse and the bells counting down to the moment his future would be sworn to the crown or to war.

Thunderheads smudged the golden coin of the rising sun, changing faded blue sky to the vermillion of fresh wounds and the burgundy of bruises.

Keplan tugged his glove from his right hand and raised the palm. It was the same color as the clouds.

"What does it mean? That tattoo."

Keplan glanced back at Daymir. He could not find the energy to replace the glove. Instead, he removed the left as well. He spread his fingers, displaying the contrary marks. "They were given to me in Ban. The first, the red one, proclaims me an enemy of the empire. The second pardons me."

"I thought gloves were a quirk, some tic you inherited from your parents. Fates know they were odd at times. Or perhaps fear of touch, after what you suffered."

"I wear them to avoid the questions. Scars on my face will fade, perhaps not fully, but with time. These won't. They remind me what humans are capable of, what war does."

"When you say those things, I know you'll make a better king than I."

Keplan snorted, but the steward's arrival halted whatever retort he could devise.

"The council's finished." The man's expression was the careful mask of a servant, and unreadable. "They request your presence."

Keplan straightened his robes. "And?"

"Don't grill the staff, Keplan." Daymir moved past him and into the corridor.

The steward caught Keplan's eye as the young man followed the former heir. "I've spent a lifetime serving people, and they are still an enigma. If it were solely my choice, I would have crowned you at 'pauper king.'"

Keplan grinned down at his shirt as he adjusted it. "It wasn't the worst speech, was it?"

"No, sir."

"Thank you." Jogging to catch up to Daymir at the door to the Council hall, he half expected the palace floor to buck him from its flagging. He returned to the head of the table in silence. An'thor would not meet his gaze, black eyes fixed on some point out the window. Relief swathed the room. *Whatever it is, they've decided.* "You've chosen?"

"We have." The Head of the House of Nobles rose, folding her hands. "We would like to address the factors that led to our thinking. As leaders of our provinces, we have many concerns. You are young. You are inexperienced. You are not Athrolani. You are not of the Xain house."

Keplan's stomach fell. He did not want the crown, but their decision meant further war. Deeper, an unnamed part of him already wrapped bony hands around the Crown. He forced himself to listen.

"But there is a greater concern. One we all share, and that is for our future, our families, our people. We see you, too, have that concern." She gestured to him and to Daymir, a step behind. "Would you agree to sign a Regency order? It would ease this transition."

The floor stilled under Keplan's feet. "Whom did you have in mind?"

"Master Blackhouse. If he agrees."

Keplan looked to Daymir.

The man's expression softened, and he dipped his head. "If you wish it, I would agree."

Keplan turned back to the councilors and swallowed his heart back into its proper place between his ribs. *Short of them forcing Daymir into the role, this is the best of all possible choices.* "I accept." His voice was faint in his ears. He cleared his throat. "I accept your terms."

The Consulates stepped back from their chairs and knelt in a ripple, tapping chest, lips, and brow with their fists. The Head of the House of Nobles looked up. For a moment, Keplan thought he saw tears in her eyes. "You have our support."

Elation and terror exploded in his chest. Tears clogged his throat. *Do not weep.* Instead, he tucked his shaking arms behind him and bowed low. "I am honored." He straightened and turned to the clerk poised at the table's corner. "Draw up the necessary paperwork and have it brought to Master Blackhouse and myself as soon as possible." He turned to An'thor, still kneeling on the tiles. "My first command to you, General—call for a ceasefire and request Commander Dorcal's cooperation. Tell him the council wishes to negotiate tomorrow at dawn."

To a one they looked more exhausted than relieved. *That makes all of us then.* After an awkward nod, he slipped into the hall. It was odd not to be dismissed, and instead, be the first to sweep from the room. An'thor caught up at his door. Keplan sank onto a bench, head in hands. No one spoke until the locks clicked into place behind the new Regent.

"Are you all right?" Clinking of glass as An'thor poured wraith punctuated Daymir's low voice.

"I don't feel sick anymore." Keplan's words rasped and he leaned against the wall, as much for support as for conversation. "Tell me I didn't just make the largest mistake of my life."

"You didn't. It might have changed the entire course of your life, but as someone who made those same choices—the hard ones, the ones easier left to others, I promise you, it's the right one." Alcohol misted An'thor's gaze, but Keplan ignored its probable influence.

"You think you never made a wrong decision in your life?" Daymir scoffed.

"I didn't say that." An'thor bit back.

"So, what now?" Keplan attempted to redirect the conversation.

"Do you think you could sleep?"

"Maybe out of necessity." In truth, he wanted nothing more than to bury himself in blankets for a month. But voices and memories not his own chattered against the barricade of his mind. Sleep only brought nightmares and little rest.

"You could kip on the cot in my study. The next few days will not be easy," An'thor offered.

"I'd think they would give him his own quarters. Being the Heir—King—and all."

An'thor shook his head. "It'll take a day to ready chambers in the guests' wing. The royal wings are currently under repair."

"As they scrub rot from the walls?"

Another bickering match was the last thing Keplan wanted to hear. "The room can wait. I have to get Moly and some things from the Hare, and I don't feel like sleep yet anyway. We can meet in the morning for the ride to the harbor." He tugged his cloak on and edged out the door before they could argue. A guard fell into step behind him at the palace gate. After Keplan's second glance, the soldier smiled. "Hylier," Keplan greeted.

"Orders from the general and His Highness the Regent. You'll get your own guard soon enough, Your Majesty."

Keplan winced at the term. "And can I dismiss you?"

"That wouldn't be advised in the streets."

"Very well. Just until I arrive at the Hare."

"Of course, Your Majesty." The honorific was a heavy yoke around Keplan's neck. "I'll wait outside."

"I might be a while."

Hylier shrugged. "I've done longer shifts."

Keplan's steps were quick through the streets, but he forced himself not to run. There was enough chaos without him causing more. Gossip and news echoed from the winding rows of houses and storefronts. Keplan did not need to meet anyone's eyes to know their thoughts:

"...and thank the fates that the curfew's been lifted..."

"...but still the matter of the prison camp..."

"...I hear Blackhouse is back in the city..."

"...another heir, something about a farm boy...?"

He clenched his jaw and turned down the street to the Slummer.

Φ

Moly's acceptance, particularly in the face of tears, was something Keplan would never take for granted. She pushed her head against his tunic, muttering in her horse language, checking for injuries. He offered the apple he stole from the palace. "I'm so sorry. I did not know I was leaving until I was already out the gates, truly. I would have taken you if I could."

He ran a hand down her flank. Someone groomed her, and her already respectable girth had grown. "Mirrel always makes you fat."

"Apologies are easier to animals." The quiet voice cut through the cozy smell of the stable.

Keplan whirled.

"You left a letter." Mirrel's lips pursed.

Keplan looked down. "I know. I'm sorry." He tried to look behind her without making it obvious.

"Why ought I let you see him? It's not like him to get emotional."

"It wasn't a lovers' quarrel. He didn't like the attention I brought."

Mirrel's brows lowered, but for once it seemed out of worry more than anger. "I noticed too. More than once I've shooed people off. And now there's a guard out front."

His heart tightened. *She protected me*. The hardest woman he ever met, and she protected him. "I cannot thank you enough for that."

She lifted a shoulder. "Just come back. Between the lack of help and Firas pining, I don't have enough hands to do everything."

"I wish I could. I came back to collect my things and say goodbye, actually."

"You're leaving?" She paused in her feeding of Ragweed and turned to face him properly.

"You two are my home. Athrolan is my home, and I can't just stand by when I could stop a war."

Something dawned on her face, but it was not surprise. "The ceasefire. We heard the heir arrived, but I never thought— " She closed her eyes, and when she opened them again, they were bright. "Of course, it's you. When I realized you knew things you ought not, I wondered. I just never thought it would come to this."

"I'm so sorry for everything I caused you both, just being here. I don't understand why you let me in, but thank you." He swallowed past the seemingly permanent lump in his throat. "Why did you?"

"You worked hard and had no one else. Besides," she lifted her chin, "our da died protecting your ma, and I'll be damned if I don't carry on that duty." She rested her hand on the door latch and was suddenly back to being the business woman he knew. "I expect this is the last we'll discuss it."

"It is. I just need to find a way to explain it to Firas."

"I don't envy you, but do it kindly. I'm the one who gathers the pieces when you're through."

The door slammed behind her, and Keplan wondered if he was better running. Breaking someone's heart was more terrifying than any throne. *Besides, I'm breaking two.*

"A minute, you salt-head!" Mirrel's bellow to a patron cut through his thoughts as he edged up to Firas's attic bedroom. He was raising his hands to knock when the door flew open. A single greasy candle backlit the bartender. Hard arms wrapped Keplan's shoulders in warmth. "I recognized your footsteps."

"I wanted to come back sooner, but everything—I'm so sorry," Keplan began, but the other man's mouth was on his, and he forgot why he was there, forgot why he ever left. Keplan's smile faded when the man pulled away. Firas's eyes were bleary and bloodshot.

"Everything?"

Keplan winced. Saying it aloud to Daymir or An'thor was one thing. To Firas it was impossible. "I left a letter but.... Did you find someone to read it to you?"

Firas slumped on the bed. "I didn't know how sensitive its contents were. You could read it to me now, but I have something to say first." He turned so they faced each other fully. "I don't want you to leave. I'm sorry I said that, I'm sorry I distrusted you." He raked at his hair. "I thought I cared about who you were, before, but I mostly just care who you are now."

"Don't." Keplan's heart clenched. "Don't go down that path. I was a warm bed at night, help when the inn's busy. Don't make it more complicated than either of us want." It was a lie. Firas was more than a friend; he was solace, but solace was one luxury a king did not have.

Firas flung his hands up in exasperation. "Fates, 'Lan, I'm not talking love, I'm talking decency. I'm the first to admit I don't want to settle with one man. Doesn't mean I can't care about the one I spend time with." He held out his hand. "Whoever you are, whatever you did, it doesn't change the man I've come to know."

"You were right."

Firas peered into his eyes but moved back at whatever he saw in them.

"'A pauper's son.' I didn't mean to bring trouble, didn't know it followed me until I got here. And I lost the will to outrun it. I thought I could drown myself in work, in you, but I can't."

Sadness smoothed desperation from Firas's face. "The night you left, I told Mirrel everything, told her I knew you were a bastard of someone or a noble running. I might be daft, but Mirrel's not. She's got a bigger pair of stones than any man I've met. But the thing about older sisters is, they're never wrong. Said she knew who you were and she didn't care." He sighed, the sound catching in his throat. "And I suppose I don't either."

Keplan could not force words past all the lives he could never live. He cleared his throat, then tried again, "I think I should read you that letter now." Sooty prints and what might have been tears stained the letter. It looked how Keplan felt.

> *"Firas,*
>
> *I know this is abrupt, and for that I'm sorry. The city is crumbling around us, and while I was not born here, it's my home. You and Mirrel, you're home to me. And I would be a poor friend, a poor lover, if I didn't do everything in my power to protect you, to protect this way of life I love so much.*
>
> *I would rather stay here. But that would be selfish, and I can't watch you die when the walls crumble.*
>
> *I hope you can forgive me.*
>
> *I don't know if I can.*
>
> *-K"*

Keplan's stomach churned from too much adrenaline and too little sleep. He forced himself to look at Firas.

The bartender's eyes narrowed on some unseen speck on the floor. "Where did you go?"

"I went to Marl Orna, a town halfway between here and Marl Black."

Firas's jaw moved in thought. "But you came back."

"To explain things." Keplan frowned. "You thought I wouldn't?"

Firas shrugged. "In my family, when people ride off, they don't often return."

Keplan chewed on his lip. "I can't stay. I want to, but I can't hide here while your entire world falls apart at the seams."

"So your letter says. Doesn't explain why it's up to you. One man can't stop a civil war." Firas laced one muscled leg through Keplan's long ones.

Keplan wondered if the gesture was to anchor him to this world. He wished it would work. "The heir of a kingdom can. You thought I was a bastard. I'm not sure whether my parents ever married, but I'm fairly certain it doesn't matter when they're not human. The queen declared me the heir, not knowing who my parents' child would become, not knowing if I even existed. That takes a lot of faith. I'm not a man of faith, or legends, or greatness, but I can end this war. To protect you. To save Athrolan. I went to Daymir Blackhouse and begged him to take the Crown instead of me, but he refused, so I asked for his support. There can't be a war if the two of us agree."

"And he gave it? That's why the cannons stopped?"

"The general, the Council, they agreed at noon."

"You'll be gone. You'll be king."

"Just across the city," Keplan corrected.

"Lan, when you're in a palace, and I'm in the slums, 'across the city' is the same as gone." Firas's face was shadowed. "I don't know what to say. Part of me wishes you'd stay selfish. I'm not a one-man lover, but, fates, I could have been for you. I wouldn't mind war if I had you."

"Don't be dramatic. That's my territory." Keplan wove his fingers through the bartender's hair. "I have a few hours before I'm expected back." *Before I'm no longer a commoner. Before I'm no longer Lan.* "Do you think I can spend them with you?"

Φ

The Eastern Border of Athrolan

Arman crouched before the pile of tinder. New, deeper lines accented his frown. Cold gnawed his fingers and toes, a persistent predator. The wood got wetter by the moment. He reached out, willing fire into his palm. Nothing caught. Not even a line of smoke rose from the pile. He inched closer and tried again. Twisting roots of magma and fire were choked, the lava slowing, cooling into a sullen quagmire of not-quite-rock. Even with the silence and peace of the forest, his mind skittered over the earth's surface, unable, or unwilling, to puncture the crust. The only reaction was the pervasive scent of burnt bone and sodden creosote.

Alea trudged over the rise, arms full of rain-darkened twigs. "Fates, what is that smell?"

"The fire won't light."

"Tinderbox probably just got wet. Use your power." She dumped the wood beside their campfire and slumped down beside it. "I'm tired of rain as much as you. Can't seem to keep anything dry. Truly, what is that smell?"

"It's me, alright?" he snapped. "It's my power. I can't light the fire. I've tried, even with the tinderbox which, for the books, was dry as bone." He flexed his hands, chapped and cold for the first time in two decades. "Alea, I think I'm sick. Like, inside, in my mind, in my power. I can't access it like I used to, can't pull it from the earth. It's as if my connection to it atrophied." He swallowed hard. "Your dreams say anything about that?"

She sank to her knees beside him, colorless eyes searching his. The concern made his heart ache, but the fear was worse, a knife to his gut that said she did not have an answer. "Arman, I'm so sorry." She pressed her lips to his brow, and he heard the hitch of her breath. "You're cold."

"I know." The usual furnace burning in his chest, thundering between the ribs of his mind, guttered. "I'm scared."

"How did you overcome your fear during the war?"

"Which fear? War brings several."

"Any of them. Fear that you were going to die. That we might lose. Fear that I would die?"

"That last one I never overcame, Alea. I knew we could lose, at first, but when you returned from Le'yne so little could stop you. And when I saw you on the cliffs at Calimiirn, I realized there was no way we would lose. Die, perhaps, but not lose. When I learned I would die—granted that wasn't what I saw, but I was so certain that it still counts—it was trust. I surrendered to you, to your draw on me, to your power over me, to your faith we would win."

"You make me sound like this unfathomable being."

"You've never seen yourself from my perspective." He offered a smile. Complexities, carefully established roles defined their relationship. Sometimes he wished they could change, they could meet as they were now, without the weight of who they were before. He clenched his fist, willing his mind deeper into his power. Striations, glowing golden stains, marked the inner walls of his mind, high-water marks from when his power overflowed his magical body. Now the golden fire sloshed deep in the stagnant depths of his heart. "Alea, do you think we were supposed to?"

"Supposed to what, love?"

"Live."

She looked away. "I remember when I was in Le'yne. There was this tome. It must be somewhere in Mirik now if it ever made it out. But it was from when they predicted events—tapped into the power of the world and felt the ebb and flow like the tide. It predicted us."

"Doesn't mean it's right, doesn't mean we were meant to live into our middle years." Arman watched the lines of her face change, echo her fears. "You told me we were going to win, and whatever came afterward would be beautiful." He squeezed her hand. "Maybe we're just aging. Hold on to that faith." Something told him whatever was coming, they could not stop it.

Perhaps they were not meant to.

Φ

The City of Ceir Athrolan, Athrolan

News of the ceasefire spread through the city. The night was clear. Knots of soldiers on the walls and in squares stood down. It was not peace, but it was no longer war. An'thor propped his chin on his hand. "This feels too easy."

Daymir glanced up from his place beside An'thor's hearth. "Probably because you're not the one doing it. You're not Keplan, ill-prepared but determined to do the proper thing. You're not me, forced into a role I've avoided for the past decade. Walk in our boots a spell and see if you still think it's easy."

An'thor turned back to the window. "Why did you?"

Daymir sighed and laid his book aside. It was clear the general's mind was too busy to allow quiet. "Why did I what?"

"Avoid it. You spent your entire childhood—well, once Her Majesty's daughter passed—learning how to be a king. You forsook your dream of becoming a gallant to study finance and strategy. You were the best heir any monarch could ask for. When she exiled you, it broke your heart. Broke the kingdom's too, in a way." He fished a bottle of dark gray liquid from his desk. "And yet now that it could be yours, you've done your damnedest to avoid the throne."

"Can you get through one day without drinking? One conversation, even?" Daymir waved off An'thor's response before the words escaped the man's pale lips. "I'm not avoiding the question. Just observing. And that looks like gutter water."

"You're passing judgment, Blackhouse, and I'd like to remind you that, while I might not be able to do them sober, I didn't abandon my responsibilities."

"I didn't want it. Ever. When Princess Tzatte died, I was old enough to know I was next in line, to know it would be my duty, whether I wished it so or not." He fixed the general with a pointed stare. "What have I been known for?"

"Other than the unfortunate incident of treason, perhaps your determination? Cleverness?"

"I'm a perfectionist, general. I did not want the job, but I'd be damned if I didn't do my very best. What broke my heart was not that I lost the throne, it was that my aunt—more of a mother to me, truly—did not trust me. Losing her trust, my standing, the reputation and respect I had earned, it destroyed me."

"You could take it back now."

"I want it even less now, and honestly, Keplan will be better than I. Perhaps not at first, but he will." Sadness tinged with desperation tugged at the lines around his eyes.

An'thor could not bring himself to chase the truth. "You sound certain." Alcohol's slur softened the sharp words, but only just.

"For someone who sent the city to war over him, you sound awfully uncertain," Daymir retorted.

"You left me little choice, Daymir. He's the only thing that could stop this."

"The only person, Domariigo. He's a man, not a thing. And I thought the only person would be you or Dorcal, considering you started it in the first place."

An'thor slumped into the chair at his desk. "Forget I ever asked. I wish I hadn't."

"I told you he has the heart for it. I wasn't speaking thoughtlessly. He loves this city. It might have started as comfort and the place his lover sleeps, but it's become home. He speaks as if born here. And you ought to know what lasts in legends longest. It isn't tired duty or perfectionism."

An'thor pulled on his fur-lined coat. "I ought to see the Xain cousins on their way home. Camp was dismantled this morning." If Daymir responded, he did not hear. His head buzzed with despair and the drink drowning it. He wanted to believe a scrawny boy with scars and a battered heart filled with love could save their kingdom. Deep down, there was a part of him that did. A larger part, the part that drank, that cursed every morning he woke instead of died, told him that the war was not over.

Φ

The 17th Day of Lumord, 1272

Keplan slipped from Firas's bed without waking the other man. His room was as he left it. He folded his borrowed clothes and wiped the street grime from Firas's father's boots. Save for a handful of papers and a few collected knickknacks, which he shoved into his pack, the room was the same as when he first arrived. He ran a hand over the already smooth coverlet, checked the boards on the window. By some tiny mercy, the hall was deserted. He listened for Mirrel preparing breakfast, but the common room below was silent. Keplan's boots were heavier than ever as he crept into the cool morning. Fog cloaked the city, the clanging of the harbor bells with each swell somehow distant through the swaddling cloud.

Hylier waited in the stable and greeted him with a deep nod. "Where to, Your Majesty?"

"I need some time. Can you follow Moly?"

The guard glanced at the pony. "As long as she's better tempered than that yellow monster." He jerked his chin at Ragweed.

Keplan's laugh was fake in the early air. He took the long way through the city, passing through every district. War marred them all, buildings battered and no amount of sleep could remedy the fatigue on the residents' faces. Pre-dawn light turned the white stone ghostly, and Moly's hooves were muffled as they ascended. The palace was invisible through the fog, hidden until he paused in the street. The gates were shut, but the small door opened for him at his raised hand.

"Good morning, Your Majesty."

Keplan glanced at the guard, but there was no judgment in her eyes. "Good morning, Captain."

The steward appeared in the doorway as Keplan dismounted and handed the reins over. "Your chambers will be ready shortly, Your Majesty. And General Domariigo asked that I remind you to see him."

"Thank you." He paused. "I'm afraid I don't know your name."

"Master Valadai, Sire."

"Thank you, Master Valadai." Keplan rubbed the bridge of his nose and went to find An'thor. Light glimmering under the door told him the general had either been up since the night before or risen in the dark, early hours. He suspected it was the former. The door jerked open after a single knock.

An'thor's face was haggard, but his eyes bright. "Wardyn, glad to see you made it back. I was beginning to worry."

"Best get used to that. Worrying after me, I mean. I'm told people are supposed to worry about a king." He offered a smile he did not feel. "Any word from Dorcal? And have you eaten yet? I'm starved."

"Nothing yet. I just ordered mine, but they always send too much." The general's eyes lingered on Keplan's throat. "Did you rest a bit, at least?"

Keplan peered in the mirror. A love-bite marked the side of his neck along his collar. "Dammit."

"It's cold enough to warrant a scarf." An'thor did not meet his eyes for a moment. "I trust that was goodbye?"

Keplan raked a hand through his hair. "I suppose it has to be. I'm not an idiot. I know noble-commoner love stories are the plots of tragedies."

"I think one commoner is enough to grace the palace halls for now. I'm not doubting your discretion, but you will be watched more than most monarchs." The general finally looked him in the eye. "Let's keep the drama and scandal to a minimum, shall we?"

Keplan did not want to think about it. "Where's Blackhouse?"

"You need to start using titles. He'll be along shortly to go over the declarations. I'm told they found you a room."

Keplan hummed in response. He did not really care about new rooms or decorated writs. He wanted to be sure the commander agreed. He wanted to be certain civil war was through. "What did you do with the heirs in the prison camps?"

"Detainment, please. You make me sound like a savage."

Keplan looked up, ice-chip eyes boring into the black pits in An'thor's face. He smelled the tang of blood, felt the chill of night, heard the rasp of whispers. "Aren't you?"

An'thor's hand stilled its tracing of the desk's edge. "I don't know what you mean."

Keplan allowed himself a faint smile. "You'll learn it's very hard to lie to me. Most folk, if they think they've tricked me, it's because I allow them." He shrugged. "I'll figure it out, but it's nothing to waste my energy on today."

"Figure what out?" Daymir asked as he entered.

"Why our dear general smells of blood." Keplan offered a quick wave.

The new regent snorted and dropped a stack of papers on the desk. "You're probably mistaking the mixture of liquors coming off his breath."

Keplan laughed, but he felt the itch of An'thor's eyes on his back. *You've not shown all your hand, and there are many cards yet in this deck.* He shuffled through the parchment Daymir brought. The original declaration of Keplan's inheritance sat at the top. Below it were writs declaring Keplan and Daymir's new titles. "Do I just sign these? Like I'm buying a horse?"

"And seal them, with your signet," Daymir added.

"Which he doesn't have, Daymir," An'thor reminded. "The boy doesn't have a house or rank or anything really. Aside, of course, from His Majesty the King." The general sighed. "We'll deal with that later. The name and the Consulate's seals are the most important at this juncture." An'thor dipped a quill and handed it to Keplan. Metal scratching parchment was the only sound for several moments.

Ink's sheen became a matte black as it dried. Valadai's rasping voice interrupted the rushing in Keplan's ears. "Your Majesty, Commander Dorcal sent his response."

Keplan turned with a frown. "And?"

A soldier stepped around the steward and held his hand out to the young man. "We found this shot into the wood of the harbor barricade." Crumpled in his hand was a length of tattered, white fabric. It appeared to have once been a sailor's left sleeve. The wider edge was purple with blood.

Φ

Raven slumped against the rail of his ship. Everywhere he smelled the sea, the stench of unwashed sailor, the bitter tang of doom. He wanted to believe An'thor saw sense. He knew the general for too many years to actually think it was possible. He was as idealistic as the commander was stubborn. His battleship dwarfed the approaching craft, but the latter did not bear scars and stains from the last weeks. The boy in the bow raised his flags. *Come aboard.*

He shoved himself upright, head too heavy to lift. Pitching his weary voice over the snap of rigging and groaning wood grew harder every day. "Lower rowboat!" Raven tugged his helm on and gestured for two of his sailors to join him. They swung over the rail into a rowboat.

The mariner in the fore scraped her salt-caked hair into a horsetail. "How could Master Blackhouse get into the city without the general knowing, sir?"

"I don't think he could, Tzane. This looks like the outcome we wished for, but my gut tells me a piece is missing."

"They were blasting us a day ago. You don't call for ceasefire at dawn an hour after a fire-volley unless something changes." The Commander's squire was clever—sometimes too clever—but young.

"The smallest things can end war."

"And start one." Tzane shrugged into her cloak, brown eyes fixed on the small ship as they drew up alongside. There was the expected cluster of clerks and no small number of guards. Daymir himself stood by the cabin's door. He waited for Raven to straighten his stained clothes.

"Welcome, Commander Dorcal. It's been a long time."

Raven bowed. "Longer for some, I'd imagine. I'm glad to see you well."

"Thank you for meeting with me on such short notice."

"How'd you get into the city?"

Daymir's gaze moved past the commander, and Raven followed it. The two Head Consulates stood in the cluster of clerks both dressed in full state robes. "I was invited."

Raven's brows lifted. "I'm surprised the general came to his senses." *Or it's a trap and you've walked to your death.* It was more likely than he cared to admit. That an act of war during ceasefire was treasonous did nothing to calm his nerves. He had no doubt An'thoriend committed more war crimes than legends told.

"Please, join us."

Raven followed them into the cabin. It was brightly lit. The obvious difference between his battered clothing and their own was not lost on him. *He's making a statement.* The clerks and Head Consulates ranged about the desk. Daymir perched on the edge before gesturing to the chair before him.

"I can stand, thank you."

"Suit yourself." He held up a paper. "Do you know what this is?"

"It's a letter. Judging by the seals, one I sent to you declaring my side of the disagreement."

"It's war, Commander, call it by its proper name." Daymir stared at the paper, though his eyes were still, not actually reading the words. "A line here says: 'I swear to uphold your wishes for the crown, uphold the wishes of the true king.'"

"It's true, my lord." Something settled in Raven's gut. Every instinct told him this was not the peace he wanted.

"You swear to uphold my wishes for the kingdom, for the Crown and accept the king's command?" Daymir's eyes bore into his, darker than Raven ever remembered them.

"What is your command?" Raven hated the falter of his voice.

"Stand down." The voice was not Daymir's but another, much younger one. It rattled from behind the gathered officials. A boy waved aside the clerks. His clothes and long brown hair were older styles. His blue eyes were manic. He lifted his chin but did not stand. "Commander Dorcal. I don't believe we've met." He made no move to offer a hand. "My name is Keplan Wardyn. I'm told you knew my parents, even traveled with them for a time." The set of his face, the ice-chip glint in his eyes, spoke of something sickening in his blood. "My mother ripped the blood from her enemies, and my father opened the earth beneath their feet. Surely you remember."

Raven's stomach writhed. The boy before him was not human. *Run. Run while you can.*

"I see you understand me." Keplan jerked his chin at Daymir. "You requested Blackhouse's presence in the city weeks ago. You realize doing so is a direct violation of a royal decree. You would be an accomplice of treason. I doubt I have to explain the punishment."

"He's here now, without my urging. He, too, would suffer the fate of a traitor." He loathed the weakness falling from his mouth.

Daymir glanced at the commander, eyes narrowed. "You change your song rather swiftly, sir."

Keplan dismissed the impending argument. "Master Blackhouse was invited expressly by the Heir Apparent of Athrolan. His titles, the ones he still wished for, have been reinstated. Added to them, Regent of the Crown for a year's time. I repeat," all mockery disappeared from the boy's face, "stand down."

The commander faltered, dark eyes scanning the men before him. "What will become of me?"

"House arrest for the time being," Daymir explained. "Further orders will come."

Raven was a man of might, of battle. And he knew when he was beaten. Keplan's expression was stone in the face of Raven's frustration. He glanced at his two subordinates and gestured at the ground. "Lay down arms. Shipman Tzane, send word to the fleet." His raised hands shuddered and he dropped to his knees. "I surrender."

The 17th Day of Lumord, 1272
The City of Mirik

"A BIRD'S COME FROM Athrolan." Alleanthus shoved the door shut with his boot as he peered at the letter.

Bren glanced up curiously. "From Keplan?" He and Kemmer often shared her larger study. Their desks faced each other, separated only by a low bookcase.

"If it'll distract me from writing this missive, I welcome it." Kemmer rubbed her eyes. "I'll go mad if I have to explain how to start a war one more time."

Alleanthus expression tightened. "It's for Father, actually."

Bren frowned when Alleanthus met his curious gaze. "What is it?"

Kemmer glanced up, brows curling together as she echoed his question.

Bren recognized the plain seal as Reka's and grabbed the parchment from his son's hands. She never sent word by letter unless it was urgent. Word of mouth was far safer.

The words were a dozen leaded blows to his gut. "It's from Monareka. Keplan's King of Athrolan. Or will be." He met his wife's eyes across the desks.

"Bren, I am so sorry."

"I'll go. I have to. Not just as ambassador, but as family. Fates know he won't tell his parents." Bren scraped his fingers through his gray hair. He hated the relief he felt that Keplan was safe from being used as a tool of war, but he hated his disappointment more.

"You could write if you want," Kemmer offered.

"I don't want." He rose. "Where's Azimir? We're leaving on the next ship."

"You're taking him with you?" Kemmer frowned, putting aside her work for the first time all afternoon.

He glanced up at her. "I remember suddenly being in charge of a nation. What I needed most was a friend."

Her eyes softened. "Come say goodbye, please, before you leave."

He ignored Alleanthus's grimace when he bent and kissed her. "Always." He shoved his son's shoulder as he passed. "Soon you'll have a wife, and I will make the faces at your ridiculousness." The mirth fell from his features as he strode from the study. As much as he jested with his family and claimed to understand, the soldier's ideals in him burned at An'thor's plan, and Keplan had stumbled into it. He took the stairs quickly, though not several at a time as he once could. Distraction made him rude, and he shouldered into Azimir's room after pounding the door once. "Azi, get your things."

His son scrambled from his bed, naked despite the early evening hour. "Da! What'd you want? And can't you knock?"

"I did."

"And wait until I answer?"

Bren's gaze swiveled to the privy door, behind which came a muffled giggle. "Toar. Get whomever that is out and pack your things."

Azimir bundled the sheets around his waist and dodged about the room collecting his clothes and a green gown Bren assumed belonged to the resident of the privy. "Why?"

"Keplan's made a terrible mistake."

Azimir frowned and turned. "What did he do? Why am I packing?"

Bren stepped from the room, calling over his shoulder as he shut the door. "You can ask him yourself. We're going to Athrolan."

Φ

The 19th Day of Lumord, 1272
The City of Ceir Athrolan, Athrolan

Keplan watched night fall away. Darkness slid down the city's pale walls like rain sluicing from the hills. The palace rumbled into wakefulness, servants beginning the rounds of tidying halls and chambers. Across the palace he presumed the Council Hall was being prepared. Sheaves of paper filled the scribes' desks. Perhaps the monarch's chair finally warranted polishing. Double guards flanked the commander's rooms. Keplan drew a deep breath of the tiny corner of peace he found. The glass ceiling of the palace greenhouse afforded him a clear view of the mid-morning sky. The birds housed there were awake as long as he, it seemed. It was not the earth and trees of home, but the scent of wet earth and growth calmed his mind.

Bells tolled, and he forced himself to rise. He was among the first to arrive the day before. Today he would be the last. He rolled his shoulders and patted down the long coat. Mirik's tunic-and-breeches became popular among Athrolan's nobles in the last two years, but Keplan suspected he balked tradition enough for one week. *Besides, thousands of buttons make me look less like a starved common boy.*

He nodded to the guards he passed at each doorway. Nerves surged in his gut each time they responded with "Good morning, Your Majesty."

A young woman in the mourning black of the household staff greeted him at the door to the Council Hall before swinging open the door. "His Majesty the King."

Keplan breezed in, forcing his steps to be assured. "Good morning, consulates." He took his seat without preamble and gestured for them to do the same. "I trust you are as eager as I to begin discussions for the future." He folded his hands. "I would like to address, first, the current status of our divided military. Most notably, what to do with Commander Dorcal."

"'Do with' him? Surely you intend to strip his titles," An'thor suggested.

Keplan's brows rose. "I was hoping to hear each of the consulate's concerns."

"He sees reason, I believe. He was afraid—as many of us were," a countess argued. She addressed Daymir, her gaze unwilling to rest on Keplan for longer than a moment at a time. "He is a good man, one who always put Athrolan at the forefront of his concerns."

"Who are you implying didn't?" An'thor asked.

Keplan caught the sharp bite of alcohol and concealed his sigh. The general was as much a concern as the commander, but one that would keep. "One of the admirals would take his place, I assume."

"Unless you want to give the position to a little friend who's never seen aw a boat." The biting tone came from Delle.

Keplan did not bother to hide his laugh. "Yes, I see the metaphor, Duchess. While I'm at it, perhaps I'll do away with all of you and find new lords and ladies to surround myself with friends instead of enemies." His tone turned somber. "Considering I appear to be the only one taking my role seriously here, it might do Athrolan some good."

Silence followed his words and he gestured to the room. "Now, if we could continue without barbed comments, I would appreciate your thoughts on appointing a new commander."

"There is something to consider, Your Majesty." The Head of Guilds leaned forward. "Athrolan has relied on the trade of her wool and ore for generations, but with Mirik's navy growing, and Berrin exploration increasing, we might be pressed to find new commodities. Even in war, trade is lifeblood. Perhaps Commander Dorcal would be more suited to something in that sector."

Keplan hummed in response. The idea had merit. The room buzzed with opinions, and through the veil of fear, he caught a glimmer in their voices.

Hope.

After the last Consulate spoke, he rested the embroidered sleeves of his jacket on the table, gloved hands clasped before him. "I see we are working toward the common goal of Athrolan's safety. Dorcal's fear is a pebble perched on the mountain of his stupidity, forgotten until it begins a landslide."

Keplan shook his head. "I don't intend to have a Commander who starts civil war rooted in fear. That said, he is a valuable strategist, and I do not wish to exile the man, for he, too, has Athrolan deepest in his heart. I wish to have him under house arrest until the end of the year. We need to be certain he will not try to raise a new rebellion. After that time we will address his new role. In the meantime, I wish those officers supporting him also be removed from their stations and arrested similarly. Their subordinates will take their places for now. Any naval order will come directly from myself or Blackhouse." He looked to Daymir. "Do you agree?"

"I do, Sire. Perhaps we could address the next few months of your reign. A monarch goes on Progress his first year."

"Progress?" A snort rose from the table, but he could not pinpoint its source.

"A monarch travels the kingdom to meet subjects, see how the land fares. It boosts economy, morale, so forth." The Head of Nobles offered. "Something to look forward to, for the common folk. When your parents arrive to aid you, they would go too."

Buzzing filled Keplan's mind, and his mouth tasted of blood. "If you wanted them as monarchs, you will be disappointed. The regency ends in a year. If I went on Progress then, when I am fully King, would that be acceptable?"

"Yes, sire, however, we still must announce you, officially. We were on the brink of war. Half the time I don't believe we're through with it, and I imagine the cities to the south feel the same." The Viscount from Ceir Bodian rubbed a hand over his face.

"Many question the validity of your claim. They will need as much convincing as we did."

Keplan shook his head. "I understand this world in a way many do not. Perhaps that is what General Domariigo saw, and His Highness Regent as well. Each person has different doubts for different reasons, and thus I will address each as they come. We're to have the coronation in a few days. Use that as our declaration. You want something the city, the nation can see?" He gestured to the smoking, tattered city outside the window. "Lift the curfew. Remove the blockade. Send news that our war is over and announce the coronation. Other missives will follow with details, but I promise no one cares about those. Phrase it as happy news."

Admiral Fess frowned at him. "And is it? Happy, I mean?"

"I don't know what you see outside your windows, up late at night, unable to sleep. I don't know what you see in the rolling hills to the south or the vast forest between here and Ban. But I see sorrow. I see a kingdom that forgot what she was. And I see how far we could go if given half a chance and a little bit of hope." Keplan forced his hands into stillness. "War is over. A new king has come. In the legends, that is always happy. And, as it's been mentioned, I am born of legends." *Even if I don't feel it. Even if legends aren't ever as real as we wish.*

He turned to the Head of Nobles. "Lord Tevon, send writs to each of the cities and townships, along with invitations to the coronation. Most will be unable to make it in time, but please stress recovering from the past year is most important. General, open the gates and drop the watch down to single on the walls, double on the palace. Someone let the navy come home to berth. I think it is about time we let the city breathe. Tomorrow we continue our work. I look forward to hearing your suggestions." He nodded to them and strode from the room.

Daymir caught him in the hall, his quiet words drowned by the swell of voices in Keplan's wave. "That was perhaps the shortest first Council of a king's reign."

Keplan winced. *Did I forget something?* "It took the entire morning. You can't stay in there and keep them from plotting to murder me?"

"They won't murder you. Besides, An'thor is your ally as much as I am. This next month will be hard, for the Council and for you." He offered a smile. "I suggest you take advantage of whatever moments you have to yourself."

Keplan laughed and turned to find Valadai by the door. "Master Valadai, are my chambers ready?"

"Yes, Your Majesty. Would you like me to show you to them?"

No, I'd rather burn them to the ground and go back to bed in the Hare. "Please."

The palace's halls radiated from the dome of the central ballroom and throne room. The first floor, at level with the courtyard and entrance, held staterooms, libraries, training rooms. The lower storey, built into the ground on the level of the gardens and stables, consisted of higher officers' quarters, and those of the squires and pages. Valadai led Keplan to the third floor, where nobles', consulates', and highest officers' chambers were. *And those of the royal family and one stable boy.* The royal chambers themselves took up an entire corner of the palace, still boarded up by An'thor's orders. Keplan was led to the western wing. A set of guards stood outside the plain door and bowed when they appeared.

"I hope the rooms are to your satisfaction. Let us know if there is anything else you'll need, Your Majesty."

Keplan barely heard the man through the rushing in his veins. He turned the key waiting in the lock, slipping it into his coat as he stepped through the door. The first room was a foyer, decorated with portraits of nobles Keplan did not recognize. *What's wrong with a proper mountain landscape?* The first of the two doors led to a parlor boasting a tall window and several chairs and couches. Keplan doubted he could fill the room with all his friends and allies combined. The second room off the foyer was smaller, a rich study equipped with a broad desk and more shelves than Keplan knew what to do with. Here, at least, artwork was limited to a portrait of the late queen and a seascape.

Through the study lay his bedroom. The canopied bed crouched against the wall opposite a bank of windows. When he pulled back the velvet curtains, he realized two of the windows were doors to a narrow, planted balcony. Noon sun cast the barracks and Noble Quarter in white and gray. Warm autumn air muted the noise of the palace. Save for the distant clacking of training, even the city was quiet. His fingers combed the stiff vegetation of a potted rosemary. Here was his solace.

The deep bell atop the palace tower clanged, another joining it, and another, and another. Every clock tower in every square and circle of each district exploded into sound. Brassy fanfare announced a monarch returned from battle. Keplan braced himself on the balcony's wall, hands gripping the worn stone. Already the burble of speculation of the streets beyond trickled into his mind. *Let them gossip. Let them make a thousand stories.* Along the horizon, the ships' sails unfurled, billowed into fat bellies to carry them home. Patrols returned from along the hills, weapons cupped under relaxed arms. For the first time in weeks, the gates opened.

Perhaps it was in his mind, but somewhere, he thought he heard a cheer.

When wind had whipped most of the warmth from his body, he traded his fine coat for another, more simple linen one. His tiny garden may have brought peace, but he still took the longest route to Daymir's room.

"You have yet to run away," Daymir remarked when Keplan entered.

"I can't tell if you sound disappointed." He took the seat across from the regent. One leg bounced, and his hand tapdanced over the chair's arm. "Blackhouse, it takes years to learn to rule a kingdom. I have wisdom others don't and the weight of two terrible bloodlines, and I won't be on my own for another year. But all these people doubting my abilities—what if they're right? What happens then?"

"Then Athrolan falls into chaos."

"So, what was the point of An'thor finding me at all?"

"Because it might not." Daymir stared into the fire. "You're clever, you're powerful, and you have a good, honest heart. I've got to believe you'll succeed."

Keplan looked away. *Clever, certainly, and powerful, perhaps someday. But honest?* "How can I fit a decade of learning into a few months?"

"Even with the general and myself helping you, and all the consulates, you will need to focus, to hone your mind. Your priorities must shift to allow Athrolan to be at the top of the list."

"I know."

"I'll see about that." Daymir flipped open a canvas-bound notebook. "You and I will meet twice a week. We will find tutors for the subjects in which I am not proficient—dancing, music, history and such. Every two weeks begins with an audience. Do you know what that is?"

"When the cityfolk come to discuss issues?"

"Basically. You will hear them, as will the House of Commons and House of Nobles. Both are made up of a score of Consulates, some of whom advise you, and the Heads. The next day you meet with each House separately, and then the day after that you meet with the Council together, to come to decisions on the matters brought before you. Most can be decided during the audience and without any involvement on your part—the guards and District Masters take care of most small things before the complaints even reach the palace."

Keplan rested his head in his hands. "Fates, this is complicated."

Daymir chuckled, though the sound was far from humorous. "The other days you will take lessons in History, Government, Economics, and Politics."

"Will I learn a weapon?"

"Not unless you wish to on your own time."

Keplan massaged the dyed skin under his gloves. "Perhaps eventually."

"Have you any skill with one?"

"Bow, yes. For hunting."

"Then practice archery at your own will." Daymir's eyes paused on what looked like a letter. "Ambassador Barrackborn arrived this morning with his younger son. He's not pleased."

"I never thought he would be." Keplan looked away. "I did not know Mirik was so close."

"An ambassador's ship is swift, and I suspect the general sent his letter first."

"I'm certain the Ambassador has an extensive network that helps him acquire information." Keplan remembered the alleyway where he met the spy master. *I'll need my own network soon enough.* "Is that all?"

Daymir sighed. "One more thing—have you spoken to your parents?"

Guilt churnned in his chest. *What could I say? How do I explain the events of the past months?* "No, not lately. I know I ought to, but I simply don't know where to begin. And the longer it goes the more difficult the words are."

Daymir looked at his hands. "I don't have children, but I know they would be looking for you, hoping to find you, protect you."

Keplan caught an echo, something flashing across the regent's eyes. "Did they write to you?"

"No, but I think you will find they understand the inibility to write difficult letters." Daymir cleared his throat. "I'll see you tomorrow morning, before the meeting?"

Keplan nodded and rose.

"Speaking of your friends from before, and," Daymir did not meet his eyes, "the bar in the slums and the proprietors there."

"What of it?" Keplan was not aware Daymir knew of Firas.

"It'll need to end."

Keplan's chest tightened. "It already has. Don't worry." He turned back from the door. "I may not have been raised a noble, Blackhouse, but I'm quite familiar with loneliness." Keplan slipped from the regent's chambers without further farewell. He was already recognized on sight, and a guard fell in behind him. The time would come, he was certain, that every step would be followed by attendants and clerks and guards. He shuddered and buttoned the front of his coat before stepping into the chill of the road to the ambassador's manor. It would only grow harder to talk to them, and if he had an afternoon free of duty, it ought to be used for apologies.

Azimir thundered down the stairs when the footman announced Keplan's arrival. "I wondered when you'd come visit." He spared a glance for Keplan's clothes. "Since when do you like traditional fashion? Mirrel paying you more?"

Keplan laughed. The fact that Azimir thought palace finery could be bought with a bar boy's highest wage told him much about the boy's understanding of money. "Not exactly." He turned back to the steward. "Would you tell Ambassador Barrackborn I'm here and would like to talk at his earliest convenience?"

The steward bowed himself down the hall, Azimir watching him go. "What do you need to talk to Pa about?"

Keplan nodded to the parlor. "Mind if we sit down? I've had a long few days."

"I imagine. I'm surprised at the cease-fire. Part of me wondered if it would go on forever. If this was the new war, stacked atop ours with Ban." He led the way into the room and collapsed into a chair. He tossed Keplan a pear and chose an apple for himself. "Why are you here?"

Keplan turned the fruit in his hands, suddenly without appetite. Azimir didn't know. Brentemir had not told him. For whatever cruel series of reasons, he forced Keplan to tell him himself. *How do you even keep that a secret?*

"We're only here for a week, I heard. You should come back to Mirik with us when we go, though. I'm sure my father will let you."

"I don't think I can." He looked down.

"Of course, the Hare. But surely Firas could spare a day or evening."

The words stung more than Keplan liked, and he paced along the table. "I can't go to Mirik because I have duties here, now, new ones—"

"Keplan?" Brentemir's voice boomed through the foyer, and for a moment Keplan could not tell if it was in anger or fear. The creased brow and finger-tangled hair said it was the latter.

Keplan straightened his shoulders and raised a gloved hand. "Ambassador." He forced his tone to be level. *This is good practice.*

Brentemir's expression changed from confusion to sorrow. His shoulders sagged, and he dipped his head. "Your Majesty."

"What?" Azimir whirled to look at Keplan. "What does he mean? What new duties?"

"I wish it could be different, but my dreams are less important than the safety of a kingdom." He looked over at Azimir. "The queen named my mother's child heir. And I've accepted."

"We were gone just a few weeks. How did all this come to pass?" the ambassador asked.

Azimir waved his father's question away. "But this means you'll stay in the city, right? And we can see each other more often?"

"He'll have a lot of new tasks, planning balls, heading councils, waging wars."

Keplan winced at the bitterness. "Or avoiding them," he corrected. "I didn't give up so much, only to descend into war again." Later he would think on what that meant for Athrolan's relationship with Ban or her alliance with Mirik. Now he just needed to solidify the tentative peace his presence brought. "I might have, at first, but I cannot focus on that now." Keplan looked down at the forgotten fruit in his hand, letting Brentemir process the last few moments in the silence that followed his words.

"Can you give us a minute, Azimir?" Brentemir's frown softened. "We can talk over drinks, as a family. We're still family."

Keplan wondered who Brentemir was trying to convince. "Alright." The silence continued upstairs, interrupted only by the clink of glasses while Bren poured them both a glass of liquor.

Keplan took a wary sniff before tasting. It was acrid and bitter, but grounded his senses. He moved to stare out the window.

Bren leaned on the sill beside him. "I remember my few moments of peace after I chose to take up Mirik during the Gods' War. Am I intruding on yours?"

Keplan glanced at him, shrugged and looked back at the sky. "No. Sometimes the quietest times for me are when someone talks. There are so many voices in my head, I can't even hear my own if I'm alone."

"I've got a fair few in my head too—my father's. Alea's. My captain when I was younger. Kemmer's." His gaze slid over to Keplan and then back to the city. "I know, that's not what you meant. Whatever you feel and hear is vastly different. The thing is, Keplan, that's the case for everyone. No one in this world feels what I do. About some things, perhaps, but we are, none of us, the same. It might be the one thing we all share." He ran a slow hand through his hair, fingers a ponderous echo of the excitement he once had. "How did you get here?" He waved a hand between them. "Standing here beside me about to be King."

"Honestly, I just kept making hard choices. Some didn't even feel like choices, but I guess I could have always run."

"And Blackhouse truly won't take up the throne?"

"He'll be Regent for a year."

"Even still, I'd expect him to retreat to his manor again or take the throne. He's not the man to half-finish a job."

"He has good reasons."

Brentemir's eyes narrowed. "Good enough to thrust an inexperienced boy onto a throne he doesn't want?"

"Shadows follow everyone, Barrackborn. If you want to know more, you can ask him yourself. Besides," Keplan glanced over, letting his carefully maintained façade of earnest kindness fall, "I'm not just any boy, am I?" He felt the burn in his skin, the ice in his veins hinting at his parents' powers.

Brentemir sighed in response. "Then I have some advice for you. Before I took Mirik over, I still wanted to be a soldier, but it killed me watching her fall to ruin. Tzatia herself rebuked me—before the whole Council, to my horror—and said I could not have the glory and power of a king with the responsibility of a soldier." He poured himself another glass and topped off Keplan's. "Stop being the boy. Stop being whatever mess An'thor wants you to be. You're stuck on the edge of so many things—the throne, manhood, sanity, empowerment. Stop waiting. Leap from that edge, and let yourself fly."

Keplan forced speech past the sudden lump in his throat. Brentemir understood more than he expected. The idealism was different, but he forgot the man walked in these same boots twenty years before. "Feels like falling right now."

"And it will. Sometimes I still feel that way. But then you'll look back and realize you haven't smashed on the rocks below."

Keplan nodded. "Thank you."

"The worst part was learning to compromise," Bren confided, peering at some distant point past the horizon. Perhaps it was Mirik.

"The worst part is leaving a life and people I love." Keplan finished off his drink. He was aware of the weight of Brentemir's gaze. "I'm afraid I'm giving up sanity. Being with Firas brings peace I haven't felt in a long while."

"The bartender?"

Keplan glanced over. "Yes."

"I had someone like that during the war. I understand."

"Your Spy Master."

Brentemir's frown was sudden. "Who told you that?"

Keplan shrugged. *Let him think I just heard rumors.* "You had to give up that relationship, though?"

Bren ran a hand over his face with a sigh. "Not because of appearances. She wasn't interested in anything more, and frankly Kemmer was entrancing."

"Right." Keplan rolled his neck. He was not particularly comfortable hearing the details of the ambassador's love affairs. "I was told to end things between us. I've already said goodbye." The words felt strange in his mouth. "I understand, of course, and know the reasons. Doesn't make it easier."

"No, it doesn't." Brentemir drew a shuddering breath. "I don't agree with your choice, but I made the same one. Perhaps that's why it's so hard. But if you need anything in the way of advice, I have a lot of years as uncle to make up for."

For once Keplan's smile felt like a proper one. "I'm sure I'll make use of it."

Brentemir nodded to the lower storey. "Perhaps you ought to talk to your cousin a bit. He's confused, I think."

"Perhaps you should have told him," Keplan countered before finishing his drink and setting the glass aside. "I know this isn't what you wanted."

A shadow flitted across the ambassador's face. "I'm sorry, too."

Keplan pulled the door to and turned. Azimir stood at the top of the stairs. His dark face was hard with bridled hurt. "Did you know, when you befriended me?" Azimir asked.

Keplan's fingers tightened on the banister. This did not sound like a conversation he was interested in having.

Azimir blundered on. "You said I looked interesting when we first met. Me, out of an entire city? I'm flattered, but there are far more interesting people. You said you kept my company because you knew nothing about me. You, who reads secrets like a farmer reads the weather. It's simply not possible." Azimir's voice was low and would have been angry, were it not for the vulnerability. "I want to be your friend because you're funny, if odd. I don't have many friends in the city who aren't over-bred nobles. But I can't understand why you want to be mine. Unless it was because you knew who you were, and you wanted access to the general, to the commander—"

"Azimir, let him be." Brentemir's voice was firm, fatigue replaced with compassion. He stood in the study door, cloak in hand. "I promise he had no idea. I saw the betrayal on his face when he discovered it."

Keplan raised a hand, stopping the rest of the ambassador's words. "I am friends with you because you didn't care where I came from or why I have scars. You are filled with hope that I can't find. You remind me I'm just seventeen, and sometimes I forget that." *And because I wanted Ban to burn.* He offered Azimir his hand. "Besides, now we're family."

Azimir shook it, but his expression remained reserved. Their goodbyes were brief. The evening closed around Keplan as he slipped out. He wished he could be honest with Azimir, but as much as they were cousins, Azimir was not ready for the truth. Keplan's answer was a pleasant thought, and for a while, he would let even himself believe the lie.

Φ

The 20th Day of Lumord, 1272
The City of Ceir Athrolan, Athrolan

Bright colors writhed together, mourning blacks and grays doffed for brilliance, and yet the faces bore the lines and exhaustion from war and uncertainty. The bells were silent. The streets were full, the palace brimmed with guests. An'thor paced another round of the palace before returning to Keplan's room. He nodded at the guards flanking the door. "It's almost time." He stepped through the foyer and into Keplan's chambers. Two serving men offered various adornments while a tailor finished the hem of his breeches. She glanced up at the young man. "I'll be just a moment, Your Majesty. You seem to have grown since we took your measures."

An'thor met Keplan's panicked eyes and waved the servants away. "When you're through, Miss, I need a word in private with His Majesty."

She glanced at Keplan, who nodded. His face was sallow and his lips thin. He stared at some invisible point on the wall until the woman rose and curtsied her way out.

"You look like you're going to vomit."

"I've already done so twice, and I doubt there's anything left in me." He took a tottering step from the dressing stool.

An'thor caught the man's arm and pressed him into a seat before calling for bread and wine. He sat on the edge of the desk.

Keplan's bloodshot eyes roved up to An'thor's black ones. "The words I'm supposed to say, they sound stupid. The promises I'm supposed to make sound hollow."

An'thor shrugged. "And they will be. But starting tomorrow, you will make them not hollow, not stupid. Today just worry about saying them." The bread and wine arrived, and An'thor tore a piece free. "Eat this. Small bite, then a sip. You need food in your gut if you don't want to faint in front of all your new subjects. What are you going to promise?"

"I don't know." Keplan winced as An'thor smeared faint pink makeup on his cheeks.

An'thor stepped back, eyeing his handiwork. "At least you don't look dead." He levered Keplan to his feet. "Whatever you say, mean it. You've told us many pretty things. You stormed in here with ideas and fire and desperation. Don't lose it yet."

"I'm trying. Without burning out, that is."

The general watched Keplan peer into the mirror, remembering a different coronation, a terrified, young woman.

"Now you're the one who looks ill," the boy remarked. The reflection of his colorless eyes met An'thor's. "Regretting your support already?"

An'thor snorted at the wry comment and made a shooing motion. "Take a moment alone, breathe. We'll fetch you shortly."

"You're not afraid I'll escape out the window?"

"Your father did that frequently, but I think the threat of civil war is enough." An'thor backed out of the room, catching Valadai on his way past the foyer. "Quarter of an hour?"

"Yes, general. And the guards?"

"Full guard on the palace, double on the throne room. Entourage has double for the ride into the city." They had gone over the plans four times in the past twenty-four hours, but nothing relieved the knot in his gut. Seven people awaited him outside Keplan's chambers. Fess winked, new Commander's badge glinting over her left breast. "Almost."

He grinned back and took up his place beside her. Keplan would walk behind them, followed by the Heads of the Houses of Nobles and Commons. The whole was surrounded by four guards. *And I hope to the buried gods four's enough.* He already silently gave thanks that coronation finery allowed the carrying of weapons for those within the royal entourage. Fess alone bristled with blades and armor, mail showing through the splits in her sarafan.

The palace shook with the sound of bells. Valadai rapped on the door. "Your Majesty, it's time." He paused, then knocked again.

Keplan burst through the door a moment later. His hair was no longer in a horsetail, but tidy. "Sorry, I'm alright." He slid into place, and An'thor glanced back.

"You have no need to apologize, Your Majesty. Athrolan turns on your clock now." He watched the boy square his shoulders and drop the wide-eyed, nervous expression.

An'thor's chest tightened as they started down the corridor. He watched half a dozen monarchs rise and fall, and Tzatia's reign was the second to break his heart. Now Keplan, young, inspired, and scared, echoed in the halls of those memories.

Φ

Hundreds of strangers turned as the ballroom doors opened. Noise and the warmth of too many people spilled out, thoughts eddying around Keplan's feet. The wine dulled the details, but snippets tangled and tripped his nervous mind.

The fanfare was bold and somber. Mourning ended with the coronation, and the crowd was brilliant blue, purple, and crisp white.

He fought the urge to check whether his embroidered tolstovka still hung straight under his fur-trimmed coat. The throne was a spot of white stone at the end of the aisle, a stone pillar just to the left held the declaration. The usual mutters of the crowd were drowned by horns, and he hoped they covered the thunder of his heart.

Too young…

Poisoned by the general….

No music was loud enough to muffle their thoughts. He tried to pull an appropriate mix of reverence and confidence onto his face. *Don't trip.* He ascended the dais, Daymir a step behind. When he turned, the thoughts crashed against him, and he clenched his hand on the stone.

If only His Highness Blackhouse would take over….

Inhuman spawn….

So, begins Athrolan's new golden age….

He searched the crowd for whoever thought the last. The woman stood at the edge of the aisle where the folding walls of the throne room usually crossed. She offered him a smile, which he returned. Knots in his hunched shoulders loosened.

"Your Majesty," Daymir whispered.

The Head of the House of Commons knelt, opening a heavily jeweled box. The ring within was silver, newly polished, with the jagged tower wrought over of the flat face of the aquamarine. "With this ring you accept your duties as Sovereign of Athrolan, to rule with the lives and dreams of every Athrolani held over your own."

Keplan slid the ring onto his left index finger, then raised his hand. "I accept."

"General, sir." Whispering behind him cut through the reverence.

Keplan glanced back. The master of the palace guard spoke swiftly into An'thor's ear.

Keplan did not catch all the words, but "assassination" and "apprehend" were two. His heart crawled higher in his throat, and the ring bit into his fist. He caught An'thor's eyes. Soldiers' boots thudded in the hall.

An'thor shook his head slightly and jerked his chin at the crowd.

Keplan stepped up the final stair to the throne. Had he been given more time—years like Daymir, perhaps—he would have sat before the stone seat for hours before this, contemplating his future. Instead, this was his first glimpse. It was cold. Fingermarks wore into the arms. Daymir appeared from the left and took a ring from the box the head of the House of Nobles offered. He regarded it for a moment before facing Keplan. "I swear to act as Regent to Your Majesty, to guide and advise until a year's time." His voice rasped with emotion, but his raised left hand was steady. Two guards delivered a chest to the Headmen, and Daymir lifted the crown from the fur mound within.

Thank goodness I'm sitting, elsewise I'd probably faint. Blood rushing in his ears covered Daymir's footsteps and whatever traditional phrase the regent intoned as he held the rough silver over Keplan's loose hair. Keplan wondered if they weighted the crown with lead. It dragged on his skull. Daymir's hands dropped, and he stepped back, falling to his knee. "Long live the King."

Keplan drew a breath, grateful he was expected to sit for a moment. He wondered if it became a tradition after too many monarchs fainted from the nerves of coronation. When the crowd stilled, he raised his hand, heavy with the signet ring. "I swear to prepare myself for every onslaught, every challenge Athrolan will face. I swear she will not face it alone. The weight of the Crown is a heavy one, but precious to me—"

Sharp cracks echoed from the hall, followed by shouts. Keplan rose, ignoring An'thor's hissed command to stay in his seat. *I'm not running, Domariigo; stop your fussing.* He pitched his voice over the concerned mutters. "Athrolan is invaluable to me. From the moment I accepted this duty to stop the war, to keep Athrolan safe, to keep my people from harm." His throat tightened. "I love Athrolan more than I've loved anything, and I swear she will not face these uncertain times alone."

His eyes fixed on the heavy brocade of Athrolan's flag, and knelt, the bow of a peasant before liege. Fabric rustled, swords and jewels clinked as the crowd knelt. The movement swept the hall, flowing into the palace halls. "From this day forth I swear to serve Athrolan, for she is the true sovereign here."

His chest heaved, and his cheeks were abruptly wet but he was smiling. He rose, knees shaking. Daymir gestured to the aisle with a bow.

They fell in around him, escorting him from the room. This time the fanfare sounded brighter, the pace hurried. The moment the doors swung shut behind them, An'thor whirled to Valadai. "Get His Majesty to his chambers. The ride to the city will have to wait until this mess is cleaned up."

"What happened?" Keplan turned to catch An'thor's eye. Guards clogged the hallway, most with weapons drawn. Commander Fess pulled one guard aside, her voice too low to hear. "What was it?"

"An attempt, but not on your life. That's all I can tell you now." An'thor pointed down the hall. "Go rest. I'll be by in an hour to ride to the city, or I'll send a messenger if we need to postpone further."

Keplan jerked his arm from Daymir's hold. "I'm not bowing to rebels my first day."

"Your Majesty, it's not safe—"

"Horseshite, if the attempt wasn't on me, then there's no reason to wait." The scent of leather and canvas, tar and ocean barreled through his mind when he met An'thor's eyes. "Dorcal? Why would they attack their own figurehead?"

Fess raked a hand through her shorn hair. "Your Majesty, there are still two sides to this, even if they no longer war. It was one of your supporters, actually." When An'thor glared at her, she shrugged. "My brother is in the Guard. News travels."

Keplan found it hard to draw breath. Of course, one of his own supporters was capable of murder. His thoughts fell on An'thor and the scent of blood lingering around his hands. *More than one, I'd wager.* He sighed. "Very well, I could use something to eat, and I ought to find my hat."

"All waiting for you, Your Majesty." Daymir offered him a smile. "Court affairs are always late anyway. You can't get that many people organized on time."

Keplan saw the sense and wondered how many of these conversations he would have, being convinced of reasoning, waiting, acting. *"The worst part for me was learning to compromise."* He returned to his chambers, followed by Daymir and his personal guard. The food was welcome, his nerves loosening their hold on his gut for the first time in days. There was more, worse to come, he was sure, but for a moment he could relax.

He left Daymir and his guards in the parlor in favor of the quiet bedroom. His gaze traced the arching line of the aqueduct cutting between the palace and the barracks. Perhaps it was his mood, but the air was clear, the city bright. Black mourning banners were exchanged for brilliant blue or turquoise or white. *I know so little. What possessed me?* A soft knock interrupted his musings.

"The steward tells me fifteen minutes. Guards should have cleared up by then." Daymir's gaze was distant.

"Are you all right?"

"I'm anxious for Her Majesty to meet you. She'll like you, I think."

Lead thudded into Keplan's gut. "Blackhouse, I—"

"Blackhouse? Who is…?" Daymir blinked, then shook his head. "Of course. Forgive me, I was lost in my memory. A different state ride."

"Of course," Keplan echoed. *Please keep your head, just for a few months longer.* Somehow his feet carried him through the doors and into the hall lined with scribes, with servants, with every member of palace staff who managed to slip away from their duties long enough to catch a glimpse of the strange boy suddenly crowned King. A horse waited in the courtyard beside An'thor's gray charger and the various mounts of the Council and two dozen mounted guards. Keplan rested against the horse's flank under the guise of adjusting his reins while the world spun.

An'thor paused beside him. "Breathe, Wardyn."

"Right." A shuddering breath cleared his head. "Through the square and down to the docks?"

"Yes. We'll pause there, and you'll wave, smile. You'll look for all the world like a collected, clever young man." An'thor's thin lips twisted into a wry grin.

"I thought you said my best trait was honesty." Keplan's chuckle was weak, but sincere. He hauled himself into the saddle. "Where's Moly?"

"In her stall in the stables. You can't honestly expect us to let you ride through the city on a scruffy draft pony. This fellow's my re-mount." An'thor shook his head. "You need to look the part, Your Majesty." He jerked his head at the courtyard gates. "On your signal."

Keplan rolled his shoulders back. He found he was smiling and nudged his borrowed horse into a brisk walk. The weather held, despite the clouds. Bells joined the crowd's shouts, and for a moment even the thoughts were quiet. An'thor and Fess's faces were stone, eyes scanning for movement. There were more guards surrounding him than the usual Coronation Ride, but he let himself believe it was due to civil war.

Flowers and rotted fruit were tossed into their path in equal numbers. He remembered the phrase his mother murmured every morning: *Today everything begins.* Not when the crown settled on his head, or the signet ring slipped over his knuckle. Or even that moment in the bar when he watched Daymir admit to his impending madness. *Today, and every day after.* The wind rose, tugging his hair into disarray. He reached to tidy it, then gave up with a rueful grin.

Instead, he waved. "Good morning, Athrolan!"

Φ

The 22nd Day of Lumord, 1272
The City of RoBal, Ban

Maps replaced scrolls of dance patterns. Tea boxes and stylus jars weighed their edges. Rih scanned the parchment, a falcon seeking prey. Brown marked all countries, save for Ban, which was outlined in bright green. Vale was a dark afterthought far to the south, bordering the forest there, tucked between the foothills of the mountains and the older forest the Easterners called the Hartland. It was a military map, unwaxed to allow for additions. She rummaged through a basket until she found a quill and made a tick mark beside Ban for every ten thousand soldiers. She did the same for the Vales, and Mirik.

After a moment's thought, she marked Athrolan. Given their recent civil unrest and close bond with Mirik, their alliance with Ban was uncertain. *Information is important, even if we don't yet know how.* The only rumors of the newly crowned king claimed he was coddled by their general and a former heir regent. She marked the number of officers in Ban. There were more soldiers, of course, but not every woman would rise to the cause, and officers had far more wealth and resources. The Vales added another fifteen thousand. Mirik, while not an ally, could serve as a distraction. *For both our cause and the Emperor's, though. Every woman who dies for him is another woman who cannot join me.*

Ki-elte's hand tapped Ban. When Rih looked up, she smiled. "Planning an invasion?"

Panic burned along Rih's arms. She was not ready to share this with Ki-elte, to tell any one person how far this plan had already gone. *The rebellion has begun, even without my command of it.* It was a wild thing, released from her heart and thundering free. "I'm justing thinking over some news."

"War makes generals of us all. Or we'd think so. We all think we know the officers' careers better than they." Her head tilted as she signed, "What rank were you?"

"The lowest. I couldn't do many tasks they needed for higher ranks, due to my lack of hearing and their lack of accommodation. I proved valuable in other ways, but I suppose they weren't important enough to warrant a promotion."

"Depending on who you marry, you might outrank them all."

Rih shrugged. It bothered her for years, but that passed. Now she simply saw them as allies. "I need to meet with Il-fald, actually, soon."

"I could come if you needed translation."

Rih smiled but shook her head. "She knows my signs. Besides, it's nothing important." She caught Ki-elte's look of disappointment. "If you don't have a visitor this evening, perhaps we could meet and practice then. I have missed our more regular conversations over tea."

Ki-elte's lips quirked. "Why do I feel as if you're the teacher now?"

"Everyone learns from each other. We just take turns." Rih paused. "Thank you, for teaching me so much, for helping me when everything seemed so bleak."

"Thank you for breathing energy back into me." She squeezed Rih's hand and rose. "I'll leave you to your war. Tonight, though, no war, just conversation."

Rih laughed. "Agreed." She began to wrap her robe over her face, but stopped. Blues and purples were her favorite, but inspired calm and peace. *I want to inspire peace, but not yet.* When she emerged from the Hall, purple draped her red kalas, and a pale orange silk covered her head and face from dust.

Though the sun waited until noon to bare her teeth, heat rippled off the baked clay of the buildings, pulsing against her upturned face. In a few weeks, the dry season would end in a deluge. Rih smelled the barracks before she saw them: leather oil for armor, sawdust on the training courts, smoke from one of the city's only metal forges. Rih rounded the corner and jogged up the hill. It was a familiar route, but her thighs burned after disuse. The courtyard churned with activity, and Rih kept to the lee of the wall before slipping up the stairs. Il-fald's office curtain was pushed aside. Rih glanced at the lamp on the desk, lit despite the mid-morning hour. There was a common saying in the army: "War-horns only wake the gods, for no soldier sleeps before battle."

Rih knocked on the doorframe and peered inside.

Yellow sunlight silhouetted Il-fald in the single, narrow window. After a moment she turned. Her gaze was still distant, as if she returned to the room from a thousand leagues or a hundred years. Her expression brightened when she caught sight of her visitor.

"Rih!" The woman's hard arms wrapped around her.

Rih felt the rumble of more words and pulled away with a smile. "What was that? I couldn't see."

Il-fald offered a rueful grin and signed, "I'm sorry. I've been worried." She nodded at the doorway. "Want to pull the curtain? I have an hour before we run drills."

Rih shook her head. "Not here. The meditation rooms."

Il-fald's open expression faded. "Of course." She gestured for Rih to lead the way. The dozen small rooms in the basement were intended for a single person. In the wake of the Gods' War, they were place for introspection rather than actual religious meditation. At mid-morning they were deserted. The room Rih chose was lit only by a smoldering brazier in the center. A censer hung above. The gray-haired woman lit incense and settled into the traditional crouch of meditation.

Rih assumed the same stance, after a brief tussle with her skirts. She caught the mirth crinkling Il-fald's eyes. "I'm still not used to these."

Il-fald's smile bloomed. "Why are you here?"

Rih pulled out her tablet. Il-fald may know many signs, but this was not a time to risk miscommunication. The danger of misreading lips was large enough.

> *I met her. And I need your help. Rather, the help of any woman you trust. There is a message I need sent to the frontlines. I'm told a march is headed there soon. War is beginning.*

The alliance was tucked into a crack in the wood of her desk and nothing was worth the risk of carrying it with her.

"Was she sympathetic? War began a long time ago, ever since Mirik's upheaval." Il-fald often spoke aloud as well as signed.

Rih pressed two fingers to her lips to silence the older woman. She wrote another line and handed her the tablet.

> *She was. I don't speak of our war with Mirik, though I think that has a part to play. If the gods still walked, I would say it was their will. And for all his parading, His Eminence is not a god. Who wins wars?*

Il-fald's writing was careful, the letters simple.

> *The larger army, or so we are taught to believe. Though I believe it is the smarter one. Or the one that comes as a surprise.*

> Rih penned the next line, surprised to see her hands were steady.

> *And how many soldiers do we have compared to officers?*

The training master rocked back on her heels. Her dark eyes fixed on the censer, brows twisting as she put together the meaning of the younger woman's words. Her shaking fingers were clumsy as she signed, "Treason."

Rih shrugged. "We have the larger army. Many may not realize it, but we also have strategists, politicians, spies. We have spies in every man's bed, politicians in every court and brothel of our allies. We have strategists on every street." Her grin bloomed brighter. "And when I'm married off, we will have one more."

Il-fald's head tilted in question.

"I marry Mirik's lord or any other, I'll be out from under the watchful eye of the Emperor. No one listens to us or cares for women's work, women's talk."

The instructor grabbed the wax tablet back.

We can't pass this along, not without being caught, Rih. Why do you think we've never rebelled before? There have been attempts, and I've led the soldiers to cull those insurrections. I'm sure there were many I don't know about too.

Rih shook her head.

Look at my hands. It took you months to learn enough to understand me. More to know enough to respond. We have that time. Time to spread the word to every corner of the empire.

"Rih, this is foolish." At least, now, Il-fald only signed, her lips sealed in a thin, nervous line. There are dozens of men, hundreds in RoBal alone, who speak your signs as well as you."

She cut off Il-fald's sign as she tried to repeat that it was treason. "What are we taught, first and foremost?"

"The Woman's Code."

Rih wrote out the lines, underlining the nation's name.

A woman has a single mind. She wakes for the Empire. She rides for the Empire. Her blood and heart and mind are Ban, breathing and alive. A woman has a single mind.

Her finger tapped the underlined word. "Ban is not our home. We are our home. Each other. We will use phrases they don't know, new signs, and others that mean more to us than to them." She held Il-fald's gaze. "If you won't, I'll find someone else. Think about it." The incense between them was nothing more than ash. She left without another word.

The sun glared from the bleached sky, baleful and sallow. Rih's heart burned brilliant in her chest, crimson as the silk wrapping her skin. She had an hour before Ki-elte returned. She swept her desk clear, save for the maps and her stylus. Then she pried the alliance document from the desk's leg and set it on the map. Usually, she ordered tea, but the energy in her veins begged for an outlet.

Her unused hearth lit quickly, and she slid the shallow black skillet over the flames. A palm-sized ball of thick yellow mare's butter softened there, joined by spicy ginger, sweet honey, sharp pepper, and the bite of coarse, pink salt.

Flat bread and chopped mango arrived a few minutes before Ki-elte, and when her tutor slid the panel aside, she was met with Rih's calm smile.

"I hope you weren't waiting long!"

Rih laughed and shook her head. "Please, sit. I regret to say I lied, though."

Ki-elte voiced a few lines, but the angle and her distraction made it impossible for Rih to see. Her tutor scooped a lump of the mixture into her mug and poured the deep brown tea over it. When she set it aside, Rih asked her to repeat herself. "Oh, I was wondering what the special occasion was, since we usually just order our meals. How did you lie?" She added a few signs to emphasize her voiced words, but it was still uncommon for her to use signs alone.

"I promised not to talk about war." Rih paused to stir her tea. "But I need you to send a message."

"To whom?"

"Every woman you know who is loyal first to her sisters, her daughters, her mother, her friends. We'll create a safe gesture, one we make with hello, when we buy our bread, when we greet our neighbor. Those we trust."

Ki-elte's eyes widened. She set aside her mug and signed, "Rih, this sounds like—"

"Read this." Rih slid the alliance across the desk. She watched anger dissolve into disbelief, into fear.

The other woman's hands shook when she laid the scroll aside. Her gaze settled on Rih's dark eyes.

"This has already begun. I'm sending word to the front lines already. This is real. And I trust you."

The last words melted the daze from the tutor's expression. Something ignited behind the honey of her irises. "Start with those who sign? What if there's a woman who we trust who doesn't know your language."

"We already speak in other languages, a dozen, a hundred, maybe. The language of color, of piercings. Symbols over stores selling herbs, horses, meat, those are languages. We start there, and they can learn enough to get by until they are able to have a private conversation. I'm not saying it will be easy."

Ki-elte's usually expressive face closed, though whether out of determination or fear, Rih did not know. "It'll take some teaching, we can work on that. We need a way to know each other on sight."

Rih's pulse caught Ki-elte's unwavering energy. It would be dangerous to have these conversations, and more dangerous still if they were had before the wrong people. "Colored sashes?"

"It would be too easy to mistrust due to fashion. You said the language of piercings. A type of ring or gem?"

"What about no gem? A simple band." Rih fiddled with the metal of her own rings.

Ki-elte whirled to stare at the door. Her face paled.

Rih grabbed her hand. "What is it?"

"I heard the floor outside creak."

Rih tossed a robe over her desk to hide what she could of the map, then shoved the door open. The hall was dark after the gleam of evening light in her room. A figure blocked the top of the stairwell. "Hello?" A tilt of her head added a question to the sign. If they spoke, she could not hear.

Ki-elte joined her at the door. Rih felt the tremor of the other woman's heartbeat against her shoulder, and the hum of words.

Il-fald staggered into the light. Tears and dirt stained her face. "I'm finished with this life, Rih." Quivering lips almost erased her words.

Rih caught the older woman up in her arms. It was a different embrace than the one they shared just hours ago. Her hand held the back of her head, memories of calluses catching on the newly shorn skin. She pulled away and beckoned her in. "We have tea." Rih prepared a third mug and pressed it into Il-fald's hands. "Why did you leave?"

"I heard someone speaking, and I lost my nerve. Today tried me. I'm not sure why, for it's the same as every other day."

Ki-elte glanced between the two of them. "I could come back another time."

"Stay," Rih insisted. "As long as Il-fald is comfortable."

Il-fald nodded, gaze falling to the mug in her hands.

"You met with someone? Your hair wasn't shaved when we visited earlier."

"I met with the baniol of the Third Arc. About a riding I trained." Her hands were bruised, one wrist swollen, but she managed to sign.

"What happened?"

"The usual—blame for the death of a hundred women who were never ready for actual battle. But this time," she shrugged, "perhaps it was because of our talk, or perhaps I simply had enough. They attacked a caravan with suspicious passengers. Suspected Vale spies. The March was slaughtered." She refused to meet Rih's eyes now. "He said it was my fault as their trainer, that they weren't ready for battle."

"That's rat piss." Rih's hands shook out the curse. "Majilah was here to meet me. And take care of a dozen other things, too, perhaps, but I have a piece of that blame, and the others she met, but not you."

"No, you don't. And neither do they. The Vales defended themselves. Baniol Evem is to blame and no one else." Her lined mouth curled into the echo of a smile. "And that's exactly what I told him."

Rih's stomach clenched. She knew how an officer would remind a subordinate who owned them. Her hand covered Il-fald's for a moment. "What can we do?"

"The tea is good." Il-fald rolled her shoulders and straightened. "And maybe you could tell me the message you wanted me to send."

"Are you sure?"

Il-fald's gray eyes burned into hers. "We're going to die anyway. They punish us, take the cost of our thoughts out on our flesh whether we think them or not."

"He's decided our fate for generations, decided when we live, where and how we die," Ki-elte spat, hastily repeating her vitriol in signs for Rih.

"Our turn." Rih's fingers tightened around both women's hands for a second, long enough to forge solidarity. Then, with Il-fald helping Ki-elte understand more complex signs, she continued, "Ki-elte will spread the word to talk to those we trust, teach them our signs. Those who are sympathetic will wear a plain gold hoop in their ear. No gem, nothing. I don't know what soldiers could wear instead, but we'll think on it. I need you to share that, concisely, to the reinforcements headed northeast. I want them to relay whom among them cannot be trusted. Names. Those who oppose us need to be placed at the forefront of the battles with Mirik. Those who prove their value should be on the roads, the better to pass news."

"You will take the troublesome and put them in a position to be killed?" Ki-elte's cheeks lost their pink for a moment.

"For now, all I want is the movement of information."

"Teaching signs will take some time," Il-fald reminded. "But we can frame it to be about secrecy in the war against Mirik. If we're lucky, the fog of that war will disguise our own."

"Many already know signs. Enough to get by. And when you tell them, you will show them their first word." Ki-elte's grin brightened.

"And what will it be?" Il-fald asked. Her face was lined with pain, but her eyes shone with clarity.

Rih raised her clenched fist between her breasts, her hand curling up and out as it opened, as if she released a bird from the cage of her heart. "Liberty."

The Shadow of Madness

CHAPTER NINETEEN

The 25th Day of Lumord, 1272
The Town of Tut Kunis, Berr

ALEA NEVER KNEW THERE were so many shades of colorless. The land was gray, from the steel of the sky to the iron of the mountainside, to the smoke rising from the cluster of buildings. Even the smallest was built of rough-hewn granite. The road leading up was bare rock, moss and grass clustered along the roadside and the pitiful river were a soft dove.

"Fates, can anything be more dreary?"

"I think it's beautiful."

Arman's scoff stilled in his throat, and he looked over "I suppose you would. But, truly, love, even the grass is gray."

Alea smiled. "At least there's grass at all." Cold blanketed the air and dulled everything but the dusty scent of stone and smoke from peat fires. The mountains plummeted to a plateau made of more scree than grassland. Somewhere a bird croaked. The town clustered in the crook between mountain and plain, distinguishable only by the series of flags flapping from the single post at the entrance. The timelessness crawled up Alea's spine like a chill.

The hillside was not dotted with dead trees, as she first thought, but strange sculptures. She drew up to peer at one erected just at the roadside. *Bones.* The skeleton was not recognizable as a person. Rusted wire bound sun-bleached long bones into a spindly tower. Tarsals fanned over the battered skull in a stark headdress. "Arman," Alea began.

"I know." Wind buffeted his words. His hand tightened on the reins. "We'd best keep going. No sense in staring at this thing longer than needed."

"No, look." She nodded to the skull. "Look at the plates. It's not fossilized. It's a Rakos." Sadness was a dull ache mixed with horror in her chest.

"My suggestion still stands." Arman nudged his horse into a trot. He wore an expression she had not seen since the Gods' War. Ahead, his shoulders rose in a defensive hunch. Acrid smoke and the scent of creosote drifted in his wake.

Their approach seemed to go unnoticed, but eerie quiet made Alea feel watched. They drew up at the walls. These, too, were made of bones. Flags hung in a column flanked the open gate and bore crudely painted portraits. All were plated in stone, all with green eyes. "I can't tell if this is a shrine or a threat."

"It's both." The voice rang from stone and bone. A man in the town's center was the only sign of life. His clothes were as worn as the mountains and sewn in the Berrin fashion. Faded purple of his changsang was the single spot of color. "A shrine to those who made us. A threat to those who would destroy us." He approached, apparently not willing to invite them in yet. "What do you want? No one visits. No one trades. This road only leads to cold and death."

"We're looking for someone," Arman offered. "Someone we were told is here."

"Many people live here." The man's dark eyes were wary, but not accusing.

Alea glanced at the houses, half of which seemed in disrepair or abandoned. "Many is a generous word, Master. I'm looking for the woman."

"Which woman?"

"The woman in my visions." The words clattered in the stillness, and Alea brushed mental fingers over her power. She felt her skin cool and marble. Darkness yawned under the surface. Understanding flickered in the man's face, but also fear. "I've come to learn more of the heritage of my people."

His gaze panned over her face before skittering down to the bare plains on his left. "You're her. The one who stole our ocean."

Φ

The 27th Day of Lumord, 1272
The City of Ceir Athrolan, Athrolan

An'thor peered through the doorway into Keplan's room. "Your Majesty?" Evening's chill sank into the stone. Curtains eddied in the breeze like a shroud. "Keplan?"

A mutter drifted from the dark study. "In here."

The king perched on the broad sill of the study's open window. A long jacket, buttoned at the waist, covered his otherwise bare body. He seemed caught in a staring match with Tzatia's portrait over his desk.

"You were supposed to meet me half an hour ago."

"Why did you want me on the throne?" Keplan did not look from the portrait. "A man ill-made for the throne is worse than no king at all. I was so terrified of war, balancing who I was and who I thought my parents would be in my boots. And everything happened so quickly."

An'thor leaned on the door frame. He wanted a drink, but these were not his rooms and he was not even sure if the boy drank. "You're ill-prepared, not ill-made. When you've burnt the place to the ground, I'll swallow my words." He did not smile. "Athrolan will fall."

The younger man turned, eyes wide into the cavern of his unlit room. "What?"

"Athrolan will fall. The Laen fell. The gods fell. Claimiirn fell. Mirik fell and rose again, changed. I don't know if it will be in a year or in a thousand. I don't know if it'll be by our own hands or another's. All I know is if you're King, she won't fall today."

Keplan stared at him. "No grand sweeping plans? No brilliant dreams?"

"I always have plans, but I change them as much as I make them. It's different, I'll agree, actually being here. During the Gods' War, I traveled so much I missed the intricacies." An'thor traced the lines of Tzatia's face in the portrait.

"It's the only one I let them leave. I can't stand a dozen dead folk staring at me." Keplan swung his leg back into the room and rested his head in his hands. "That war was different. You knew my mother would win."

"I knew the terrible mess war makes and the incredible cost. I didn't understand the sweeping nature of her power, or your father's. I saw it, but couldn't really fathom it." He leaned on the desk. "Tell me, what stories do you know about history?"

"The old ones."

An'thor snorted. "Right. Well, when a kingdom survives war, or uncertainty, who rules? When a nation drags itself from the mud, who is the monarch?"

"Heroes."

"People who didn't study the numbers, or studied them and didn't care."

"You're the legendary hero, Domarriigo. You do it."

"I love Athrolan like a father, but I'm covetous and I think you, listening to all those thoughts you don't own, know why I'm not the man to lead a Golden Age." He watched expressions flit across Keplan's ice-chip eyes. Calculating as An'thor did, but wrapped inside the mania was a shred of hope. An'thor saw shadows of who he had been, who Mel'iend once was. *Who my son could have been.* Perhaps if he saved Keplan from bitterness, every piece of the puzzle An'thor worked at for the last two hundred years would finally fit. "I'm trying to make amends for some stories the legends don't include."

"I'm a king at seventeen. Pretend as we might, this isn't peace, not by a league. Ban and Mirik are breathing at our heels." Keplan glared up at him. "I wish you hadn't roped me into your scheme."

"Your parents' blood roped you in, not me. You couldn't have a normal life no matter what you did, not with that power burning through you." One pale hand fiddled with his shorn, capped horn. "Some of us are born to these roles because we're better suited to them. I was made to protect this world. Your parents were made to mend it. And you, perhaps you're made to rule it."

Keplan pulled a flask out of his coat and took a deep draw before handing it to the general. "You think humans couldn't do it without us?"

"When you've seen as many kingdoms fall as I have." An'thor shrugged and took a gulp. It was fire ale, and cheap at that. *He drinks, but has awful taste.* "I didn't think you were much for drinking."

"I'm not. But it quiets things. Helps me sleep. And I've been tired."

"Watch that habit," the general cautioned.

"Wouldn't want to end up like you."

"You really wouldn't. You ought to have someone teach you meditation. I think it helped your mother." An'thor looked back up to the portrait. "You made good promises to Athrolan, at the coronation. Think you can keep them?"

"I didn't promise anything to Athrolan." Keplan's eyes were fixed on his ungloved hands, nail-bitten and chapped, bleeding from where he worried cracks in the callouses. "I promised it to Firas."

Φ

Cheap wood groaned under the weight of letters and missives on Reka's desk. She shuffled through them again, burning those no longer pertinent. As much as Bren offered an office of her own, she could not bring herself to accept. *It would ingrain me in that house, that kingdom more than I ever want.* She snorted, realizing she thought an office more tethering than sharing children.

Unfurling another missive, she tilted her chair back. It was short and from one of her Border friends. Though Ikel fought in the Gods' War too, she chose to move into the prairie years ago. Now with war brewing, she was more spy than friendly correspondent. Reka bent over the letter. She preferred it this way.

> *Reka,*
>
> *Something is brewing in Ban. A different war than that with Mirik. It centers around the Hall of the Purple Throne, but it's spreading. I think revolution is coming. We've flirted with it before, but this smells different.*
>
> *I see flashes of jewelry, hand signals that have too much of a pattern to be nothing. I fear the country will be torn asunder between two wars. I should clarify – this country needs change, but I fear what it will look like afterward if we are not careful.*
>
> *I know your position in the Mirikin court gives you no peace. Perhaps it's time you returned to your people – our way of life isn't with hierarchy and taking orders.*
>
> *If you ever change your mind about Bren and Mirik, I hope you'll come to us.*
>
> *We miss you,*
> *Ikel*

Reka frowned, read the letter again, then burned it. Another war would be catastrophic. Athrolan was barely recovered from its taste of civil war. Now Ban hovered on the brink and did not even realize it. *It's as if the world rots from within.*

It was not enough to tell Bren, and she wondered if a library's worth of documents would be enough. She had plenty to share with him tonight over drinks. Foregoing her cloak, she stepped into the warm autumn evening.

Bren ushered her up the rear stairs when she arrived. She swore there was another white streak in his beard or hair at each meeting. Now he raked his hands through it. "Can I get you anything? Fireale? Wraith?"

"Wraith is my least favorite of the various habits you adopted from General Domariigo."

Bren rolled his eyes. "I drank it long before I met him. It's Mirikin."

"Doesn't mean it's not swill." She took the glass of wine from him and crossed one knee over the other." How are things in Mirik ?"

"Isn't that what you're supposed to tell me? Famous spy network and so forth."

"I was trying to make conversation. Besides, half of what I do is determining how people think the world looks as much as what actually happens." She took a slow sip.

"I think peace is coming, at least on this side of the ocean."

"You mean for Athrolan. Ban is almost half this continent, and if your wife has her way, they'll certainly not have peace. Whoever thinks peace is on the horizon is simply not paying attention."

Bren looked away. "I'm just being hopeful. Athrolan's more stable with Keplan on the throne. Perhaps once they see Daymir doing so well as Regent, they'll release Keplan of his duties."

"Now you're really not listening. Keplan wouldn't have walked out of there alive if the city didn't want him." She sat back. "Which brings me to our actual conversation for the evening."

"Has there been an attempt on Keplan?"

Reka waved her hand at him. "That would warrant more than a casual talk over drinks, and you are certainly not the first person I would bring that news to. I'm more worried about your sons, and yourself. Azimir in particular. Anyone who aided Keplan has become a target. It was a few street folk at first, people he talked to in the market and were friendly. They were given warnings, bloody ones. Told it was because they 'sided with the usurper.' Most don't even know Keplan's him."

"You're worried they will target us? The Smythesens?"

"The general, your household. Hard to say who. There's little sense involved." She nodded to the window overlooking the garden. "I'd double your guards and tell them there's added threat."

"Consider it done." He followed her gaze to the shadowed garden, but he seemed unseeing. "Any news from Ban?"

"They continue to prepare for war, bolstering their border forts. Part of running a successful empire is always having an army at the ready, whether it's to maintain peace or fight for it during war. Nothing Kemmer's captains couldn't tell her." She paused. "I know war is hard, but sometimes it's necessary. What's more important, Bren: doing the right thing, or peace?"

He shook his head at her with a faint smile. "I've lived through it, Reka. Peace is the right thing. Where do you get these questions?"

She looked away. She loved Mirik, and her position as Spy Master for Brentemir kept her mind and body honed. *But the network could practically run itself.* She knew it was unwise to create a system in which she was unnecessary. *But how can I retire when I'm vital?* She did not see retirement the way Brentemir might, or Daymir even, or Hylier. She did not want to stagnate in an armchair before a hearth for the last twenty years of her life. Any passing interest she had in family was quenched with surrogacy of Kemmer's sons. Her skin itched to move, to travel, to wander and learn. She eyed Brentemir, peering into his glass as if its depths held answers. War was a poor time for one's Spy Master to resign. "I might have to travel soon. Explore some rumors that have surfaced in the west."

"I thought you said nothing was heard from Ban. Are they mobilizing?"

"It wasn't from Ban, exactly, and I don't know enough to relay anything with confidence. At any rate, I received a letter, and I wish to see the evidence for myself."

"Surely you could send Billan or Cas. Or any of the two dozen subordinates I don't know about." The wiry line of Bren's salted auburn brows curled together. "I need you here, especially with threats from Athrolan's resistance."

"You need a go-between to my Athrolani contacts. You don't need me. With all due respect, Bren, Kemmer and this world need me more than you do."

Bren mouthed silently, walking himself through some argument in which he changed her mind, surely. Frustration in his eyes was too close to that of a lover rather than a commanding officer.

"Bren, please understand." She ducked her head to catch his gaze. "I have a few weeks to lay groundwork for my absence. I'll still be in contact with yourself and your wife." She forwent Kemmer's titles, hoping it would remind the ambassador of his loyalties. She stretched and rose. "You wouldn't keep your navy harbored during war, would you?"

"Toar, I know you're right. I just feel like I'm in need of allies."

"Perhaps your allies need of you, instead." She paused at the door to drain her glass before fixing him with a pointed stare. "Double the guard, Brentemir."

"I promise."

She shut the door behind her, listening to the clink of the bottle's mouth on his glass. Already her limbs tingled with the possibility of travel, and her heart ached for change.

Φ

The 29th Day of Lumord, 1272
The City of Ceir Athrolan, Athrolan

"I can't breathe." Keplan clawed blankets from his body, pushing himself upright.

Beside him, something darker than lust shadowed Firas's smirk. "I had to close the windows."

Keplan was aware, in a distant sense, they were not in the Wise Hare. "Are the warehouses burning again?"

"It's the blood, 'Lan." His voice gurgled. Thick, black blood welled under the door, fountaining between the brown stone. It poured from his lover's mouth, his eyes. Acrid smells of sickness and rot joined the sweet tang of fresh blood.

Keplan body dragged as the walls crumbled beneath the wave of gore. Firas reached for him, but not for rescue. His hand clawed, gouging lines down the younger man's forearms. "It's the Gods' Blood. It'll rot us all."

Sweat drenched the sheets tangling his legs. He smelled blood, felt Firas's nails dragging across his skin, his arms were unmarked. He curled into the expanse of thick down and clean linen. *All the larger due to its emptiness.* Instead of Firas, he spoke to the silence in his room and the heavy darkness surrounding his curtained bed. "Do you think I'll ever get used to this? Solitude around the chaos and noise in my skull?"

Exhaustion was lead on his eyes and chest, but he dragged himself upright. The idea of meditation seemed simple, though he had yet to ask about it. His eyes lidded, thin chest rising with each billow of breath. Thrumming of his heart was steady under the thin skin of his throat and wrists, a familiar tap dance between his ribs. Underneath a second pulse thundered, a roar turned whisper by distance. Frowning, he followed the sound through his body, through the rush of his own blood, into a deeper crimson.

Caution screamed in the back of his thoughts, but he pushed on. *I've never explored my mental self the way my parents once did.* Red-brown lines mirrored his veins. Copper laced his arteries. Lines entwined his form, feathering where capillaries lay, through his skin, through the stone, into the groaning earth. *Is everyone connected to the world?* Twisting strands lead to the heaving center of the world, through a burning magma core to the metal sphere grounding the world. To his mind's eyes, it blazed black and copper, shadowed with warm blue and greens. He brushed against it. Pain exploded. Fire seared his skin and throat. Images thundered to the fore, filling his head to brimming. Screams pressed the aching inside of his skull.

All of Athrolan and her neighbors lay below. Instead of a map, he looked upon the rolling hills, grasses and trees waving in a wind he could not feel. Thunder rumbled around his body. Hot rain pelted the ground, each drop red and greasy. It dribbled over rocks and spread through the rivers and lakes.

Blood.

The earth twisted into an ancient face, the bloody tracks turning to frown lines, the tangled trees a mess of snarled hair. It was a woman, and she screamed. "Your blood clots the earth, strangles! Give it back! Give back the Gods' Blood!"

Keplan shoved away, tripping over thoughts and images. He scrambled toward the surface of his mind. His eyes opened on darkness. After a moment he recognized the dim bedroom, the night sky through his open bedroom window, the face of the soldier shaking him.

"Your Majesty!"

"Captain?" His throat ached, and his mouth tasted of blood. "What're you doing here? It's late."

"Early, actually. Almost dawn." She stepped back, hands still out as if ready to soothe or restrain. "We heard you scream."

"We?" Keplan's gaze roved to the three other guards panting in the doorway. Their weapons were drawn, expressions plainly saying he was the most frightening thing in the room. "Right. Thank you. It was just a dream."

"You are bleeding, Your Majesty."

He followed her gaze. Blood drenched the sheets knotted in his hands. "I must have scratched myself. That will be all, thank you, ma'am."

"Yes, Sire. Also, a letter came for you, I've left it in your study." She followed the others out.

Keplan glanced out the window. "I don't even recall falling asleep." *I don't think I ever did.* Stars dimmed in the face of sunrise. He shoved himself from the tangled sheets. The privy tiles were cold, and the eddying wind drew gooseflesh from his sweat-drenched skin. Tepid water filled the washbasin and he braced himself for the sting of new scratches. It never came. Scrubbing the clotted blood from his hands and forearms, he held them to the rising light. No wounds marked his bare body either. But for the pink water and jelly-like clots in the basin, he would have thought it a dream. *So whose blood is on my hands?*

Muttering wind banged shutters against stone and rattled him from his thoughts. It was a council day, though there were few actual issues during the audience earlier that week. Most came to gawk at the new king, not raise complaints. No doubt that would change. A clean tolstovka and loose breeches waited on his wardrobe and he tugged them over still-damp skin. He missed the days when none of his clothing bore embroidery.

As much as he wished to ignore the letter the captain brought, he knew better. *It's probably from Barrackborn. Or Azimir.*

Keplan froze in his study doorway. There was no beige military missive or smooth parchment of noble correspondence. Instead, it was the stiff vellum of a Banis scroll. *Of course.* It made all the sense in the world—an empire reaching out to a new king, clawed fingers scrabbling to gain him as an ally before their enemies did.

Anxiety stuttered his heart. Lighting the lamp on his desk spurred his motivation. Wax sealed ribbons unraveled under his fingers.

> *His Majesty Keplan Wardyn, King of the Nation of Athrolan,*
>
> *We rejoice at the news of your coronation. Athrolan has long been a beacon of strength and progress, and we look forward to our long future as neighbors. We hope, too, we will meet this future as allies.*
>
> *We look forward to your response regarding negotiations and wish you luck and a most smooth transition into what is sure to be a prosperous reign.*

His Eminence Emperor of Ban and the Jade Forest, Jamun-Ilta the Holy Emerald Throne

Keplan's skin crawled with the saccharine tone. He brushed a hand over the signature and seals, ones he recognized.

A door banged and something clattered to the ground. Keplan glanced up. A maid stood in the doorway, eyes wide, hand pressed to her gray-blond hair. "Forgive me, Your Majesty, I thought you already gone."

Keplan waved her concern away. "Who do I call for tea?"

"I'll fetch Jaria for you." She ducked out, returning a moment later with a young woman bearing a tray.

"Fates, that was quick."

"It's our duty to be ready whenever Your Majesty wishes for something."

"Right." He drained the tea and asked for another. The letter joined the stack of economic reports from the past decade.

An'thor arrived with the mid-morning bells. "You were up late, I see."

"Early, actually." Keplan slumped back in his chair. "Is it that obvious? This is my fourth cup of tea since dawn."

The general was dressed for state, eyes as tired as Keplan felt. "The usual preoccupations?"

"Not really, no." *Add some ghostly blood and an alliance with the nation who tortured me.* "I need to ask your advice, actually."

"I thought Blackhouse was for these sorts of things."

"Blackhouse hasn't seen what you have."

"And what is that?"

"War. You've watched cities—Athrolan even—crumble. You saw Azirik drag Mirik into ruin."

"And you're worried you'll do the same?"

Yes. "This is about Ban."

An'thor sat back with a heavy sigh. He fumbled a flask from a small case on his belt. After a slow sip, his gaze returned to Keplan. "You mean to go to war with her as Mirik's ally. Freedom's a noble cause, surely."

"I was considering an alliance, actually."

An'thor's snowy brows rose. "I'd have sworn to the gods you wanted blood from the Empire."

"You're confusing war with revenge."

"Revenge." An'thor peered at Keplan's face. "So your scars are Kisses."

"Did you think I got them from running too quickly through a briar patch?" Keplan fiddled with his gloves.

An'thor looked away. "I just hoped. And when you're King, revenge often looks like war."

"I know it was the Emperor who shed my blood, not his people. But I still want Ban to crumble, want its wealth drained. I want the grasslands burnt to ash." He shook his head. "And I took this throne to avoid war."

"You don't think we'd win?" An'thor asked.

"We've cavalry and navies and fantastic strategists. They've numbers and the cold stones to throw their warriors away. If we won, it wouldn't be worth it."

An'thor hummed, though it was unclear whether he agreed. "I suppose it doesn't matter right now, anyway."

Keplan held up the letter from the emperor. "It does."

Snatching the scroll from the king's hand, An'thor bent over the elegant words. After a moment he tossed it back on the desk. "If you agree, it won't be easy. Politics aside. You'll be no good to us mad."

"I'm already there, Domariigo."

"Not fully, not yet." An'thor's lips were so tight they were almost purple. "You have nightmares about it? What happened?"

"Yes."

"What do you intend to do? Mirik has declared war."

"Well, we aren't Mirik. I'll continue to trade with them, and if they use our goods for war, that's on them. We'll profit, surely." He stared at his hands. In his mind's eye he saw the Banis soldiers who caught him. "I don't want war. I want to negotiate with Ban. I want to take their gold, their gems, their horses. I want to learn them like I know myself."

"And then?"

Keplan did not meet An'thor's gaze. Instead, his eyes were fixed on the city, irises bleached to colorless by the dawn.

CHAPTER TWENTY

The 28th Day of Lumord, 1272
The City of RoBal, Ban

RIH'S DOOR SLAMMED OPEN at dawn. Ceramic shattered when her mug cracked to the ground. Two guards loomed in the narrow doorway. Both were male.

"Rih-elte?"

She nodded once.

"You're summoned to the palace where you will be honored by His Eminence's presence."

She reached for her dropped tea but saw the guard slam the butt of his glaive on the ground. She glanced back to his mouth.

"Now."

A net and shawl were all she grabbed before rushing after them. Burning knotted high in her chest. Surely her heart had stopped. *Not this way, please.* It did not matter that the gods were dead. People prayed before they died, and every step was a blow of the executioner's axe. *I can't even think "rebellion," lest it show on my face.*

Now war loomed. Guards swarmed through the palace. Each level of the pyramid was locked with a different set of keys and passphrases. She stopped memorizing them after the first eight and wondered how often they changed. She remembered the opulence of her last visit. After months of dry, dusty weather, the lush potted plants and indoor garden in the center of the building made her mouth water.

The rebellion can't run without me—there are too many gestures to learn. Another voice, deeper in her heart, promised Ki-elte and Il-fald were enough to keep the movement going. *And what of Majilah Ag?* She signed an alliance. Would she go to war to avenge Rih's death?

Don't think "rebellion," lest it show on your face.

The sloping hall wound up to the fifth floor from the peak. She recognized the dark doors, again, emblazoned with the winged horse. Pale green jade panels flanked the door, visible only when the doors were slid shut. The finery soured her twisting stomach. Clenched teeth bit back her rising bile.

The doors slid apart. It was all she could do to kneel on the mirrored tiles instead of run. Red now accented the usual greens, for war. The emperor himself wore a rusty silk sash. Passed down to each emperor, older than the palace she stood in, it was dyed with the blood of enemy officers. *How many were the foremothers of the Vales?*

Mosil knelt at the emperor's jeweled feet, head bowed, nodding to instructions Rih could not hear. His gaze darted to her, though he did not look up, and the corner of his mouth curled. Perhaps he was no longer angry.

Hard fingers gripped her arm, and the guard levered her to her feet. "He wants to see Mosil-ten-Ebal's handiwork." He twirled his finger, and Rih turned in a circle, eyes fixed on the floor. The guard shoved her back onto her knees.

Don't think "rebellion."

She fixed her gaze on Mosil.

"Yes, Your Eminence. Of course." Most of his words were concealed as he bowed. "I'm glad you think she'll do."

She'll do? This did not feel like an execution, but her pulse still trembled in her throat. Another moment passed, then she was pulled upright and ushered into the hall.

Her cousin met her a minute later and signed, "Come with me." He strode down the ramp, descending to the third level. Subdued decorations told her it was a residential wing. He unlocked a door at the end of a narrow hall, fingertips pressing designs until the wood slid aside. "This is my study," he explained. "Sit." He turned to stare out the window. She sat, toes tapping against the tile. She hated not seeing his face, not knowing if he spoke to himself, knowing she could not hear him.

Finally, he turned and handed a heavy letter and tablet to her, face unreadable. She glanced at the parchment and seals, none of which were Banis, and frowned at him. The tablet bore the translation to the Trade words.

"Just read it."

She tilted the parchment toward the pink light of dawn.

> *Esteemed Excellence, His Eminence Emperor of Ban and the Jade Forest, Jamun-Ilta the Holy Emerald Throne,*
>
> *Athrolan is honored to announce the coronation of His Majesty Keplan Wardyn of the Hartland, son of Lyne'alea ir Suna, Dhoah' Laen and Aud'narman Wardyn, the Earth Shaker Arrowlash. He is supported by His Highness Regent Daymir Blackhouse, and we wish to accept negotiations with your mighty empire.*
>
> *We have learned of your ongoing war with Mirik, and while we are on peaceful terms with the aforementioned nation, we do not wish to engage Ban in warfare. Instead, we hope to seek trade with you. We look forward to*

your response and hope to discuss terms further in person before the month is out.

In friendship,
His Majesty Keplan Wardyn, King of Athrolan and the Hartland
His Highness Regent Daymir Blackhouse
and the Council of Athrolan

Rih placed it carefully back on the desk. Her heart hammered. "*She'll do.*" When Mirik declared war, she thought herself free of the duty of wife, at least for a time. She hoped to be forgotten like so many of the other imperial daughters. "I'm to marry this king? The child of the Rakos and Dhoah' Laen?"

"It is one of the terms of negotiation that His Eminence put forth. Enough resources were invested in your training, and I think His Eminence would rather it not be a waste. I doubt he will let the boy decline the offer."

"Boy?"

"His Majesty is seventeen."

Rih frowned, drawing the letter close again. "I know his name. I've read it before."

"There have been missives regarding his presence in Athrolan for some time, though this is the first official declaration from their own pens."

She could not place the memory. *Hartland. I've read it.* "When will we go?"

"I'll leave in a week. With them." Her cousin's dexterity left much to be desired. He waved to the window. "You'll leave once negotiations are finalized."

"With them?" She went to the window. The palace loomed above the dust-cloaked city. Ebony and silk shaded the room from the worst of the sun. At dawn, however, the brilliance lanced through the slats, spilling red light across the clay and wood.

Golden plains were lost in a haze of dust. Lean yellow flanks flashed through the clouds of dirt as captains trotted along the ranks of soldiers. Soldiers were a dark shadow under the thunderheads of dust. Rih marked the flags of the First March, the Fourth, her eyes counting women she once marched beside. She stopped at thirty-seven Marches, though there were easily twice as many. Her body shook. *The entire First and Second Arcs are out there.* The last time all the armies were called to the capital was for the coronation of the Emperor long before she was born.

If all the women below joined, her rebellion had a chance. *They own us, own our children, our husbands, our bodies. They learn our plans, and they will strike there first.* She jerked her chin at the gathered force. "Is this a display against Mirik?"

Most of his words and signs were lost to his nervous fiddling. She caught the spelling of Athrolan. "Two of those marches are my diplomatic entourage."

"I thought we meant peace with Athrolan. Or did I read a different letter?" She no longer cared about respect or deference.

"The best way to maintain peace is to remind your allies—and your enemies—of war."

Her thoughts paused on the map still on her desk, the tick-marks beside each country. The tick marks beside Athrolan. Adrenaline was a fire in her gut, thunder in her chest.

Rebellion.

"I'm going with you."

"You can't. It's negotiation. Nothing is finalized." He looked back to the army.

She yanked on his sleeve to bring his attention back to her hands. "I'm going with you. If you bring the bride, this boy will know you're serious." She pointed to the army amassed outside. "They remind Athrolan of war. I will be proof that you want peace."

Φ

The 29th Day of Lumord, 1272
The City of Mirik
Kemmer held the long wooden pole she used to arrange her war-pieces, but she did not look at the map inlaid on the table. Instead, her eyes were fixed outside. The ocean was sullen, and the sky seemed to sulk under its flat blanket of clouds. Bren was still gone, and a part of her wondered if he would refuse to return without Keplan in tow. The boy resolutely refused to answer her plea for an alliance. The half-read letter on her desk arrived an hour before and shattered all of her hopes.

She listened to the creak of the balcony encircling the room. "What are we going to do, Al?"

Her son sighed, descending the ladder two rungs at a time. "Damned if I know. That letter from Pa?"

"Keplan."

The young man groaned. "I'm fairly certain he's mad. Like, well and truly."

"But can he lead a country?"

Alleanthus frowned. "You think he can?"

"His decisions are not ones I would make, but they worked. From without he seems reckless, selfish, unstable. Yet nothing crumbled. I am starting to think he's a mastermind."

"You don't sound pleased."

"A Banis march arrives on his doorstep before winter. Not to wage war, but to negotiate a treaty."

Alleanthus groaned and rested his brow against the window. "He's our enemy?"

"Don't be foolish. Politics are far more complicated than 'my enemy's friend is my enemy.' Rather, I fear his choice to ally means I've missed something vital. I fear he sees something I haven't, something none of us have." She scanned the colored tiles marking Ban on the floor. "You said his relationship with Ban was complex."

"Interrogator's Kisses mark his cheeks, though whether he received them officially or at the hands of some zealot mimic, I couldn't say. If he was their victim I can't see why he would negotiate."

Kemmer shrugged. "Perhaps he saw enough violence to wish for no more. Perhaps he has moves yet to make. Perhaps An'thoriend is forcing his hand. There are as many possibilities as there are waking hours in a year."

"So, what is our move?" He leaned on the balcony ladder, dark face tilted.

"Athrolan and Ban are separate problems until they prove they're not." She jerked her head at the map. "I, too, have moves yet to make, and not all of them are kind."

"Does Pa know?" Alleanthus's voice lowered, as if his father could hear the words across the ocean.

"Know what?"

"We might face Athrolan in war."

"Despite his stubbornness, he's not stupid. He can add the digits."

"What side will he choose?"

Her eyes sharpened on her son. "Your father is sentimental and idealistic, but he is no traitor. I don't care who sits on their precious white throne. If you make those accusations, refrain from doing so aloud." She turned back to the window. "Go riding. The forest will do some good for the clutter in your head." When his faltering steps faded, she returned to her perusal of the map.

War hardened her. As stern as she must have sounded to Alleanthus, she was scared. Brentemir always put Alea first. Now, Keplan might take his mother's place in the ambassador's loyalty. *And he might well supplant Mirik.* She loved her husband, and his determination and morality was an inspiration to her more pragmatic mind.

But now she was Hetmir. If forced to choose between her people and her husband, Mirik would win.

Φ

The 30th Day of Lumord, 1272
The City of Ceir Athrolan, Athrolan

The entire room stank of blood. The voices in Keplans's head were as real—sometimes more so—as tolling bells, birds chirping, all the distant city noises drifting on the wind. A loud knock sounded on the study door, and Keplan realized someone had been knocking for a while. He pulled it open to find one of his guards.

"Your Majesty, forgive me for disturbing you, but Captain Hylier is here, claims to have been invited."

"I told him to come after lunch."

"It's midafternoon, Sire." She offered him a faint smile.

Keplan glanced at the sky. "Right, of course, I lost count of the hours. Show him in, please, and would you send for tea and some of those pastries, too?" He cleared his desk and arranged himself in his chair.

"Right away, Sire."

Hylier bowed as he entered, cap in hand. "Your Majesty, good afternoon."

"Captain, have a seat." He propped his elbows on his knees. "Thank you for meeting me."

"It's my pleasure, Sire."

"How do you like your position in the army?"

Hylier frowned. "I like it fine. My commission is up soon, though."

"Do you no longer wish to work for the Crown?" Keplan tilted his head. Hylier struck him as clever, if optimistic. *I need someone who blends in, who people trust.* Mirik's Spy Master set his mind turning, and with a kingdom the size of Athrolan, information was more valuable than coin.

Hylier tilted his head. "I was hoping for something a bit more challenging." He did not elaborate until tea and pastries arrived, and then only after Keplan had doused his food with syrup. "Is there something you needed me to do?"

"When Blackhouse asked, how did you find me?"

"I started with what I knew and asked questions. I've always liked puzzles and people."

"I'd like you to work on another puzzle. You'll be compensated for your time, of course."

"I find my schedule abundantly clear." Hylier grinned, and Keplan was reminded, for a moment, of boyish glee. "I'd like you to look into the networks of the resistance, as well as those who support me. The attempt on Dorcal's life was not an isolated incident, and my reign will not be colored by violence, at least not any more than it has to be."

"Peraan as well?"

"I've heard nothing of him since the ceasefire," Keplan realized. The fact sent a chill down his back. *I've been so wrapped up in ruling and keeping my head I never thought to check.*

Hylier's lips thinned. "You've not been listening then, begging your pardon. He wants you off the throne, and soon."

"I'm not even fully king." Tangles caught around his fingers as he raked a hand through his hair. If only his opposers gave him the chance to make mistakes before blaming him for them.

"As good as. Peraan is dangerous, and surely it looks like peace, sire, but city rumors rarely lie. Well," he risked a wink, "I'll still deny knowing the daughter of the Nel Corner baker if anyone asks."

Keplan offered a grin, but it felt limp on his mouth. "I promise not to tell."

"Peraan's current plot involves those who supported you, or aided your ascension to the throne." Hylier took a second pastry, but refused another cup of tea. "Gives me the winders."

Cold uncurled in Keplan's stomach. *Firas could be on that list.* "Do you have the names?"

"I can acquire them."

Keplan fished a coin purse from his drawer and slid it across the desk. "Find whatever you need. I'll see your commission is renewed, but only as guise. Learn his plan, the names he has. Is a week long enough?" Hissing rose in Keplan's ears, a crackle of burning gore. Red filled his vision, eyes stinging. "What was that?"

"I said I would look into it," Hylier repeated, "and report back in a week or as soon as I have news, whichever is first. Is there anything else?" He paused at the door. "Are you well, Your Majesty?"

"Distracted. Thank you, that'll be all." He did not hear the door close, and when he next glanced at the window it was dusk. When rare sleep came, it brought dreams of blood and writhing earth. He missed the nights wrapped in Firas's arms, tangled in the sheets in the too-hot attic of the Wise Hare.

He turned down the study lamp. Fetching a cheep bottle from his desk, he slipped into the bath waiting in the privy. It did not matter the water tumbling into the copper tub was cold. Metal bit into the nape of his neck when he rested his head back. Exhaustion clogged his thoughts about the kingdom, about Peraan and his plots, about Ban or Mirik's war. *Dorcal was afraid I'd succumb to whatever my parents left in my blood.* Water sloshed around his chin, and he fumbled the faucet closed again.

Magma roiled into life under his thoughts. His eyes flew open. Steam bubbled around him, water rolling into a boil as it deepened to crimson, to burgundy, to the black of clotted blood. Keplan scrambled out, breath heaving. Clear water filled the bath, unmoving, save for gentle sloshing from his escape. He dipped a tentative hand in.

Cold.

He was dashing through the slums before he could think better of it. Adrenaline burned through his limbs. If any guards followed, he lost them in the twisting maze of the market. It was quiet at the Wise Hare, and he heard a storyteller's murmur. He ducked through the front door. Most of the damage from the cannons was repaired, new wood garish and white against the smoke-stained gray beams and boards. *Did Mirrel hire someone or is Firas good at carpentry?* He tucked himself into the farthest barstool.

After a moment Mirrel caught sight of him. Her eyes widened and glanced at the room. Those who noticed his arrival either did not care that the heir was in their midst or had not recognized him. "You shouldn't be here."

"I know, but I need to talk to Firas."

Her lips thinned. "I don't suppose you'd believe he's with someone."

"It's still important."

"If you make a scene, barging in with dramatics to woo my brother, I'll never hear the end of it. We have trusted patrons here, ones that rather us not have such a reputation."

"I'll be discreet, I promise."

"Next time, just come through the back, will you?" She stepped away, grabbing a mug in one hand and a bottle of thick green alcohol in the other.

Keplan took the stairs several at a time, slowing only when he stood before Firas's door. He paused, shifting from foot to foot. Lack of sleep made him reckless. He knocked.

"Mirrel, I've not the energy for your shite. It's quiet, handle it yourself."

"Do you have energy for a friend?"

A bedframe groaned, and the floorboards creaked. The door opened. "'Lan?"

"I'm sorry this is unexpected, but I needed to talk to you."

Firas's beard was shorter, his hair messy. "I can scarcely advise a king."

"It's not about being a fucking king!"

The bartender sighed. "If I let you in will you stop shouting about it?" When Keplan nodded, the older man stepped aside. "What do you need?"

"I haven't slept in days. There's too much noise in my head, too many things in my mind. Every time I try to rest, I simply stare at blood rushing over my kingdom for hours and come to feeling even worse than before."

Firas sat back. "You smell of alcohol."

"It's the only thing that quiets things. I still hear them, but it's less. Garbled almost."

"I can't fix this, 'Lan."

"You did before! Lying next to you, talking to you, listening to your stories, it helped." Pleading twisted his voice brought a tremor to his hands.

"Keplan, you're the ruler of a kingdom. I care for you, but you realize what having you here does to us?"

"Mirrel said I'd give you a bad reputation."

"You aren't loved, not yet and certainly not by all. Someone sees you here, we're in danger. We've been threatened simply for sheltering you. And now you beg to sleep with me because you have nightmares."

"I'm sorry." Keplan sat back. *You were compassionate before.* But the bartender was right. "I didn't know where else to go."

"I can't do this. I can't watch you up on that throne, in your gilded palace, and let you come slum here with us when it could get us killed." The crack in his voice said how much the words pained him.

Keplan nodded, fingers tugging loose threads from his new gloves. "I'm sorry," No matter how many times he said the words, they did not make his heart stop racing. "I hope you have a good evening." When he left, he took the rear door to the alley. The dark crouched over the city, turning pale stone to the bleach of bone. He was abruptly aware he had, in fact, lost his guards.

A second, more desperate, surge of panic carried his numb, stumbling feet back to the lights of the palace. Leaving had been easy. Now ranks of guards on the wall watched the king stumble, weeping, into the courtyard. *"You aren't loved, not yet, and certainly not by all."*

CHAPTER TWENTY-ONE

The 31st Day of Lumord, 1272
The Town of Tut Kunis, Berr

MOANING WIND EDDIED SULLENLY around Alea, lifting grayed locks more from habit than interest. She leaned on the wall, shoulders hunched, staring at the expanse of salt flats. "There's something more going on here." The past weeks gave her face more lines than the twenty years prior.

"Is it the Laen you sense? This is the closest we've come to one of their cities since the war."

Her pupils were blown, the surface knotted with black power. "It's always her." Alea's voice changed, steadied, as she recited the most recent message from a madwoman. "'The Blood flows, clotted and putrid. Blood clogs the city streets. Poisons the trees. Erodes the mountains. We came first, they came second. Blood comes last.'"

Arman sighed, warm breath silent against Alea's icy cheek. "I don't know what it means any more than the last one."

Power drained from her features. "I wish we could get news. I wish we knew what was happening in Athrolan." She stared at her hands, fingers tangled in the tattered hem of her shirt. "The map wasn't wrong."

Arman's gaze flicked to her, though he did not turn from the glint of dusk. Whatever urgency drove Alea into the mountains seemed replaced by patience. It was a patience he did not share and made worse by the avoidant townsfolk. "Daymir's map showed a lake."

"Do you remember when you took the sun in? Just as you opened to the fire of the earth and the sky, I opened to the water, the power of the oceans and the air. I dragged water from all corners of the earth. I could taste where it was from, heavy on the tongue of my mind. Some tasted dusty and spicy from the desert oasis, some hot and sweet from the grasslands. Most tasted of cold salt and ice. And some tasted of blood and bone."

"From here."

"I suppose." Her eyes narrowed on the flats, a general surveying grassland seeded over an ancient battlefield. "They don't trust me."

"Should they?" The words were out before he could bite them back. What honesty their relationship had was not always spoken.

She did not seem offended. Instead, she chewed absently at her lips, chapped to bloody. "No. No one should." The insinuation that even she did not trust herself was too heavy for thin mountain air.

"Dhoah'." The chief's voice cracked from the hooded doorway into the rest of the house. "Supper." He ducked back in, and Arman watched him go.

"Not talkative, eh?"

"Their land is dry and bitter, thus so are their words."

Arman hummed in response, taking her hand for the first time since they entered the town. "We should eat. Who knows what comes tomorrow or the day after." After a gentle tug, she followed him down into the darkness of the house. He imagined her mind stayed perched on the wall, overlooking the bone-white bed of salt.

The houses were the poorly insulated slats of a shanty town, those farther downslope built on stilts for a flood that would never come. Faded colored walls blocked the stark white light lancing off the salt flats.

"Are you going to kill us?" The tiny voice cut through the rattle of wind.

Arman turned, Alea's gaze following his a moment later. A girl, no more than nine, stood in the doorway to the kitchen. "What, little one?" he asked.

She fiddled with the buttons of her blue changsang. "Da said you were Death. You're going to take our souls like you took the ocean."

Arman's shoulders ached with the weight of those words. He caught the scent of damp, sullen ashes as the wind eddied. "No, we're just visiting for a bit. We'll be gone soon."

"Bu, go see your mother." The chief emerged from the kitchen and placed one chapped hand on his daughter's black hair. When she was gone, he handed Arman a large plate. "You can eat out here. I trust you'll be gone once you're through."

Arman thanked him, glancing down at the food. Gray salted meat and beige rice covered anemic lichen. Alea took a distracted bite. If she cared about the flavor, Arman could not tell.

"Sir, when can I see her?" Alea's voice rasped over the bitter air.

"She doesn't want to see you. But she said you will find it in the city." He gestured to the hills in the west.

Arman peered out the window. A narrow track wound up the scree of the mountainside before disappearing into a crevice. The meat was dry and flavorless, save for the bite of mineral salt. He looked back at Alea.

Her unfocused eyes stared through the mountains. "Find what?"

"The question you don't want to ask."

Φ

The 33rd Day of Lumord, 1272
The City of Ceir Athrolan, Athrolan

An'thor's footfalls were a ghost's whisper across the flagstones. Hearth to desk to hearth. Letters crouched on his desk like the monsters in his mind. Unlike monsters, however, letters were not chased away by alcohol. *Not for lack of effort.* He downed the dark liquid and drew a breath through his teeth. It was difficult to let go of all the duties he took over after Tzatia's death. *Besides, nothing good comes of saddling Keplan with everything at once.*

A scroll glowered where he left it on the polished wood. Three lines in and he had downed his drink. By the end, he tossed the offending thing away and started pacing. Dread erased the effects of alcohol.

He tugged on the bell by his door. "Tell His Highness Daymir I need to see him. Now." At the man's startled look he rolled his eyes. "We're not at war, I'm just impatient."

He did a circuit of his room, shoving discarded clothing and disarrayed papers into order. The rumors were bad enough, he did not need to help them with his poor housekeeping.

"General?"

"Ah, Daymir." He took in the regent's training uniform. "I see I did not wake you."

"Indeed not," He gestured to the chairs. "I doubt this is a social call."

"Not at this hour."

"Not from you," Daymir corrected as he took a seat.

An'thor smoothed his frown and handed Daymir the letter. "Tell me what you make of this."

"This is for Keplan."

"I still receive half his mail. Besides, I did not think it wise to bother him with it." An'thor poured them both a glass of wraith.

"You mean, you did not think he was stable enough." Daymir's eyes were clouded with something, exhaustion perhaps, or sorrow.

An'thor's nerves sharpened. "I don't know what you mean."

"Don't be an ass. All the cleverness and blood-power in the world can't counter trauma. We saw it with his grandfather at a distance. Now we are privy to every mood swing."

"I've no patience for lectures, Daymir. I'm tired."

"You're drunk is what." He waved An'thor's retort away and finally turned to the letter, reading it aloud.

> *"Your Majesty King Keplan of Athrolan and the Hartland,*
>
> *We have been blessed with news, and thought, as a show of goodwill, to share it with you.*
>
> *A prophet lives in our village, a woman once like your mother. She tells of a great wave that will wash the world clean of those who do not believe the*

truth. The blood of all that came before will birth a new deity, the One True God.'

"An'thor, this is absurd. We get enough ravings from town idiots and false seers."

"This one isn't false." He pointed at the letter. "Keep reading."

"'The Dhoah' Laen herself has arrived, joining our prophet in the search for the Gods' Blood –' fates *'– soon she will return west bearing the truth on her lips. We tell you this in hopes that you will erect temples to the One True God so your people are not swept away in the approaching storm.*

Respectfully,

Orabon Marum'"

Daymir sank back into the chair, eyes more fogged than before.

"While the bits about Lyne'alea are clearly falsified, the words this madwoman uses are the same Keplan screams in the dreams the guards pretend not to hear."

"What makes this prophet a madwoman when our king sees the same visions?" Daymir still refused to look away from the letter. His hand shook.

An'thor looked away. The words were too close to home. "No sane person calls themselves a prophet. That's for the histories to decide." He took the letter back and ran a finger over the name. "Tut Kunis. It's on the border of the Northlands, and I've never even heard of it."

"What did you say?" Daymir stared at his hands, dark brows almost touching. "The town. What did you say it was called?"

"Tut Kunis?"

"They aren't lying." Daymir finally met An'thor eyes. His face paled. "The second part, about Lyne'alea. They aren't lying, because I sent them there."

"Who?" An'thor's gut churned and soured.

"A few weeks before I rode to meet with Keplan, two riders paid me a visit. I was surprised anyone let them through, but this squall descended –"

"Who were the riders, Daymir?"

"Lyne'alea and Arrowlash. They came seeking the answer to visions she was having. Said the world was rotting, or poisoned, I think. Tut Kunis was once a guard city for a Laen citadel. I forget the name."

"Lymorda." An'thor's gut settled like lead. "The Nenev fought them once, centuries ago. I forgot until now." He leaned forward. "You never managed to tell me? Or Keplan, for that matter."

Something dark flitted across Daymir's features, almost anger, not quite shame. He paced to the hearth. "It slipped my mind."

"The Dhoah' Laen and Earth Shakercame to tea in your manor—while you were exiled—and it slipped your mind." He growled the last three words.

Daymir's hand smacked the mantle. "I was a little preoccupied raising their son to the throne, Domariigo! You think he could handle knowing his parents are traipsing across the country, his mother half-mad with visions?"

An'thor stepped back. Daymir did not shout. Even when Tzatia stripped his titles he had not raised his voice. "What did she say?"

"They've heard nothing from Keplan since he left. I suppose I wouldn't know what to write were I in His Majesty's boots either." Daymir heaved a sigh. "They're looking for answers. Lyne'alea said something is coming, something worse than the gods. Something she caused."

An'thor turned to the window, drink forgotten in his pale hand. "I can smell a storm miles away. I can sense war. This feels like neither, feels worse than both. I just don't know what we can do against something that mighty."

"We already have our weapon."

"If you spout some 'we have each other' nonsense, I swear I'll shoot you where you stand."

"I'd like to think you know me better." Daymir rolled his dark eyes. "I meant Keplan. We have no idea what he is, but I bet my life he can face whatever is coming. It's our duty to see he's ready when it arrives."

"I feel ill."

"I think that's the wraith." Daymir rose. "If that's all, An'thor, I think I'll head to bed. I'm an old man." He paused in the doorway. "I'll think on this letter, and why don't you think on trusting our madman?"

An'thor watched the regent leave before turning back to his window. Dread crouched in his heart. The last time his body felt so much wrongness was watched the girl he thought was the Dhoah' Laen bleed out in his hands.

Something was coming. Alea knew, Keplan knew, even a mountain madwoman knew. Gold lanterns lit the city. The wind was quiet. On the eastern horizon the hills were lost to the night.

Φ

Keplan moved down the rack of bows, testing the weight as he went. In the early morning, the training hall was dim and smelled of sawdust. Azimir always touted the relief he felt after training, and though swords were far beyond Keplan's skill, archery was not. He drew a pale ash hunting bow down and strung it. His muscles protested, but it was faint, and the heat in his forearms was a pleasant, distracting burn. He found the corresponding arrows, tipped with dull metal nubs, and took up position. The first went wide, the second struck the quintain in the gut.

He drew back again, strengthening his stomach and steadying his breath. The straw of the quintain twisted before his eyes. It shrank, gray-streaked black hair lank about its shoulders. Skin marbled white, laced with blue veins. Vacant gray eyes bore into his own. His mother's mouth dripped sea water and clotted blood. "Kill me!"

He shrieked, arrow flying wildly off the mark and shattering against the stone wall.

"What are you doing?" An'thor stood in the doorway, dressed in training gear.

Keplan whirled on the general. "Did you see that?"

"I saw you losing your mind over missing a target." The general tilted his head. "Why, what did you see?"

Lifeless straw once more made up the quintain. Keplan sank to his knees in the sawdust. "I'm losing my mind."

"I thought you already had." An'thor's words were not mocking, but neither were they kind. "What did you see?"

"I saw my ma. She was bleeding, rotting, almost. She begged me to kill her."

An'thor glanced at the quintain. "But you didn't. That arrow flew wide."

"It wasn't a dream. She was there, I could have sworn." He scrubbed his hands on his thighs. "I didn't kill her, but something in my bones told me I should."

An'thor frowned. "What do you mean?"

"Under all the noise, the images, the memories that aren't my own, under all of it there's a voice. It sounds like me, looks like me, but different."

"You said you had dreams. Unpleasant ones." An'thor folded himself cross-legged on the floor beside the boy. "Visions. Let's call them what they are. There's no point in maintaining the pretense."

Keplan sighed. "They come and go. Always, though, there's blood. The smell of copper."

"Have you spoken to anyone else about this?"

"No one."

"Not even Firas?"

Keplan's eyes tightened. "No." He stared out the dark window high on the wall. Under his pounding heart blood and flesh heaved. Roaring was an approaching storm, the changing wind that brought the rain. "Every dream—vision—I have is warning. Blood, the smell of rot. Half the time I wake drenched in sweat and blood, but without wounds." He paced along the benches. "I think they made a mistake."

"Who?"

"My parents. They did what they were born to do, but it's only in hindsight that we see what side we were on and whether it was the right one."

"Keplan, you weren't there," An'thor rebuked. "You didn't live it. It wasn't easy. What your mother did almost destroyed her. There's a reason they disappeared into the woods for twenty years. A person can't live with the things they did, to the world, to themselves, to the gods, to the Laen. The only thing left is to run."

Keplan's bloodshot eyes swiveled to the general. He was angry. Angier than he supposed he ought to be. His mind filled with the face of a young ageless boy, harsh words tossed into icy wind. "Is that why you've gone north all of once since Claimiirn fell? Is that why you sent Mel'iend away?"

"Excuse me?"

"Never mind." Keplan stalked toward the door. "I'll see you tomorrow." His skin writhed on his body, anxiety humming like lightning. *I need to know what my parents did to the world, to the gods.* He broke into a jog.

Like the training court, the library was dark and deserted. The books muttered at him. Histories of the war looked new, compared to the tattered bindings of the older tomes. *Twenty years is just seconds in the life of a book.* He scanned the titles: *Fire and Lightning: How the World Ended, Death of a Deity, A Squire's History of War Volumes 16-19: The Gods' War.* Keplan grabbed the second and another thin tome seemingly unread.

"Kill me!" Dust exploded from the shelves.

Keplan ducked, books tumbling from his arms. Torches guttered and went out. The library was empty and dark as before. Gathering the books again, he tried to ignore his hands shaking around the stiff canvas. Instead of lighting the torches again, he chose a table by a window.

He glanced back at the shadowed shelves. Nothing loomed in the darkness. Nothing whispered in his ear. The bindings creaked as he opened them. His fingers traced the author's name. It was not one he recognized.

> *Nothing survived the war. Our beliefs were shaken to the ground. The creatures we put our faith in, in the absence of the gods themselves, were gone. The world was whole again – and we knew it, like an animal senses a change in the weather. The air was different, fresher. But there was an impermanence to it as well. The sky was brighter, but in turn, cast darker shadows. The world is no longer unraveling. Instead, now, it seems to be suffocating.*

Keplan looked up. "*Your blood is strangling the world.*" He thought they mended the world improperly or made a mistake in killing the gods. Perhaps it was not something they destroyed. What if their powers created something? Together. Something strangling the world, rotting it from within. He turned to the faint image of himself in the window.

What if it's me?

Perhaps it was the old, waving glass, but he swore his reflection grinned.

Φ

The 34th Day of Lumord, 1272
The City of RoBal, Ban

Dusk settled around the wagon train, a protective mother's arm as they prepared for the journey to Athrolan. Anticipation was a cloud over the guards and workers. Rih recognized the emotions before a march to battle. These were at once the same and entirely foreign. Soft scents of leather and the long-horned oxen underscored the tang of sweat and too much perfume.

A dozen of the Banis riahs accompanied the wagons, a gift to Athrolan's new boy king. The fore and rear were made up of ranks of soldiers, more than she expected for peaceful negotiations. Rih both hoped and feared her March would be among them, but saw few familiar faces. *It's better that they aren't. I need them here. I need allies in this city more than in Ceir Athrolan.*

She would have double checked her wagon held her baskets and a thousand gifts she only received now, to look the part of a princess. Instead, she stood at the head of the stairs. The days leading up to this were her chaos. Now was for stillness, the breath before the dart flew.

A hand clasped hers for a moment. She did not have to look to recognize Il-fald's dry, rough palm or the smoky, spicy scent of her muscle rub. "Il-fald."

"Rih." The gesture held a tenderness, a new deference. "I will miss you."

"You too. I'll write. And I'm sure you'll hear enough through servants and guards."

"I'll pass news to you as well when I can." She watched the wagons, but it was clear her mind was far distant. "I worry for you. Alone in a new country, with a strange husband."

"I worry for you, here, in our homeland, with a dangerous emperor." She squeezed her teacher's hand before asking, "Where are you headed next?"

"Baniol Hev ordered us north. To the coast. He fears Mirikin invasion by sea."

They put our women on the front lines. Her heart ached at the thought. "Be careful. I love you." She had never used the gesture for love to Il-fald, but the sorrow in Il-fald's eyes told Rih she understood.

The older woman repeated the gesture, but added another. "I love you, my queen."

Rih found her hands trembled too much to respond. She squeezed Il-fald's fingers hard and turned to the wagons. The layers of silk and netting drew back from the cushions within. They were ready for her. Curtains closed around her and the wagon lurched.

Bricks and wood rafters rolled past. It was rare she simply stared at her home. Soldier's errands distracted her, then fear and fury colored her view. There was still hate aplenty, and she would use it to fuel revolution, but for a moment she laid it aside.

I will miss this. The red of the clay. The black of the teak. The mound of the city, a fist against the colorless sky. She looked back once as they passed under the gate tower. *I'll return.* But it would be at the fore of an army, she promised herself. She would wrest change from the streets, and reap victory from the golden fields.

CHAPTER TWENTY-TWO

The 36th Day of Lumord, 1272
The City of Ceir Athrolan, Athrolan

THE NIGHT'S TEETH GLIMMERED with winter's bite, but Hylier left his thicker, guards' cloak tucked safely in his room. The Lily and Ahonsa was large, but the rooms were mostly let by those staying months, even longer. Coupled with the fact that many of Daymir's supporters chose it, had led him to stay there. Now, however, he could not use the door. Peraan left not long before Hylier made a show of going out for the night. If the barker's schedule held, Hylier had two hours. His fingers found purchase where mortar fell free between the stones of the alley wall.

After a moment's investigation, he hoisted himself up, the soft toes of his boots lighting only long enough for him to find the next hold. Heavy weathered wood of the window frame boosted him high enough to swing a long leg onto the narrow ledge surrounding the third storey. It afforded a view of the backside of a butcher shop and the dingy walk that ran along the wall between the Silver Apron and the Merchant Tier. *Not a pleasant view, for someone who can "hold court" in a place as established as this.* It deserved some thought, but at a later time. Gripping it tightly for silence, he eased open the metal window latch.

The room beyond was dark, but the smell of linen and smoke told him it was a bedchamber rather than a study. He slid his feet along the smooth wood of the floor, pausing to lift them as they brushed against discarded clothing. He suppressed a sneer. Of course, a man as fanatic as Peraan would keep a messy house.

Only then did he realize the window's latch was warm, despite the cold night. The soft sound of air was not from the window, but breath. He raised his face and sniffed softly. *Sandalwood. Musk.* "It Event File 9

K

Event Tag: Mission Compromised

Timestamp: 3:13-2-29-2157/ 10:30-2-29-2157 3:13-2-20-2157

seems our goals are crossing more often, Elang."

The low, familiar laugh was far from friendly. "I'm encouraged. It shows we're on the right paths." She stepped into the faint orange glimmer from the alley's guttering lantern. It was a few years since he last saw her, though that too had been under dim light in morning's early hours. Time did little for the twisted lines on her face or the slick white scars surrounding her eyes. They narrowed on him. The milky blue somehow seemed to see more than the brown. "Why are you here?"

"You think I'll tell?" His scoff was soft. "Neither of us are paid by him, it seems. Enemy of my enemy and all that?"

"Spoken like a child playing war in the street." Her murmur was almost lost in the noise of the common room below.

"We both know politics are more complicated." He shifted his weight carefully off a loose board.

"So, politics brought you here, then," she quipped.

"What, you didn't slip in through the door to leave a perfumed love letter?" he asked with a smile of his own.

Her mouth quirked. "Not this time, no." She brushed past him, lips warm and dry when they grazed his cheek. "I've found what I came for."

He watched her silhouette fade from the doorway then bloom again. "The center of the second rose on the left leg of the desk might be worth a fingering." He could not see her face, but he knew she winked before disappearing. "Good evening, Hylier."

"Evening, Elang."

When the bloom of cold from the window opening faded he began his own exploration. Blades, too expensive for a man of Peraan's background, decorated the shelves. Empty bottles crowded each surface. Their labels looked expensive, but most smelled cheap. The desk held a dozen letters that could warrant an invitation to the gallows in two provinces. Hylier crouched before the desk, thumb tracing the carved wood. It depressed, and a soft click heralded a hidden drawer dropping from underneath. There were several stacks of paper, mostly details of rebel troops and nobles who still did not support Keplan. Hylier copied each name into the tiny booklet in his pocket.

Underneath them all, however, was a letter and a penned list. The handwriting of the first was plain, but legible, and apparently gave the list its final name. Hylier froze at the signature. It was a simple commoner's name, but an old one. One he knew.

Dam Ornsen.

Confusion bloomed in his heart, chased by dread. The penmanship of the list matched the untidy rooms. *Did you find this as well, Reka? Or were you looking for something else?* Though Ambassador Barrackborn might think she was his, heart and pocket, Hylier knew her long enough to realize her loyalty was not always paralleled by her interests.

He scanned the list, chest growing cold. The last two names were both crossed from the list: *Smytheson (Wise Hare, Slummer), A'hane (Azimir, Noble District).*

He shoved it back under the stack of papers and slipped from the room as quickly as silence allowed. He bet gold whatever kept Peraan out had to do with the crisp lines crossing the names. How was he supposed to choose between protecting the son of an ambassador, and the man clearly keeping the king sane? He did not trust Reka, not when it came to lesser goods, not when it came to love or any other emotion beyond contentment. He glanced at the orange glow of the Slummer above the navy dockyards before turning up the street and sprinting toward the noble manors. Firas's death would bring pain, but Azimir's would bring war. Ancient poets and romantics be tossed, some lives were more important than others.

Φ

Had Bren been more sober, he would be concerned wraith no longer burned his throat. The view from his study changed much since his last visit. Even the lanterns were darker. Barkers and marching guards no longer drowned Azimir's boisterous voice as he updated Alleanthus on the past week. The silence was sullen, beaten.

A soft knock interrupted his inebriated observation.

"Father?"

He glanced over his shoulder. "Al, come in. I was just admiring how much better Athrolan looked without the shadow of war."

His son let out a hard breath, as close as he came to a scoff. "Ceir Athrolan looks rough. You can't tell me she's whole, not by a longbow's shot."

Bren scowled. "You never saw Mirik during the war. You never saw her streets filled with trash, her people starving, living in a rats' warren of derelict houses." He smelled the rank, damp corridors even now.

"No. I didn't. But Ceir Athrolan is not Mirik. A city can be broken without being in ruins." Alleanthus moved to the desk, fingers pausing on the bottle of alcohol. "Are you attempting to achieve General Domariigo's level of dependence on this stuff?"

"Just because you don't drink doesn't mean I've become reliant." Bren sighed. The remark took the fight from his words, though. This was the most he drunk in years. "Seeing Athrolan perched on the edge of disaster, and our own country preparing for war.... It hurts my heart."

"Ma sent me with a letter." Alleanthus's words were careful, and he was not a man to change the subject without segue. "It was to the both of us, and I took the liberty of reading it first, on the sail here." Trembling betrayed his nerves as he extended the open parchment.

Bren pinched sobriety into the bridge of his nose. "Ought I read this when I've slept?"

"I think you'll want another glass when you've finished."

Bren groaned and raised the wick of the lamp by his chair.

Brentemir and Alleanthus,

I hope your time in Athrolan is safe. I am glad to hear the city is settling after her time of unrest. I look forward to seeing it myself soon.

I fear I write with business in mind, and not simply to send my wishes. Our warships sail to Ban in a month. You will stay in Ceir Athrolan for a longer time than you both originally planned. I need my ambassadors there to keep an eye on this new king, and hopefully remind him of the need to remain close allies.

I trust you, Bren, to respect my choice in this matter. Alleanthus, I know I can count on you to remind your father of our values should he become blinded by his kind heart.

All my love,
Kemmer

He tossed the letter onto his desk with a sharp sigh. "Toar. This isn't a world I recognize anymore." *I don't recognize my wife anymore, either.*

Alleanthus turned away. "We knew our relationship with Ban could come to this."

"It's not about Ban. It was, originally. But this world, in my lifetime I've seen it rise from darkness. And now I'm afraid she's standing on the edge of this, this chasm, about to plunge down into something deeper and more terrible than before. I keep thinking if we just take a breath and look around, we'd see a bridge, somewhere to the other side." He ran a hand through his gray hair. "I sound like An'thor."

"General Domariigo is a fair bit more bitter than you."

"He did not use to be. He was this mighty force, full of hope and certain about the good in the world. Alea and Arman too. Where did our heroes go?" Bren sank into the chair by the window. "And now my own wife doesn't trust me to think of Mirik without your supervision."

"Ma just knows you lead with your heart. And this isn't the time for that. Hard choices must be weighed carefully in our minds—you taught me that. Adding Keplan to the mix doesn't help."

"I know." He nodded to the door. "Please inform the household we'll stay another few months. I'll need to see the steward, as well, to send for some things I left back home."

Alleanthus paused in the doorway. Worry weighed his dark eyes. "Should I tell Azi when he gets back?"

"I'll do it." Bren listened to his son descend the stairs, heard the steady low tone as he relayed his father's message. Alleanthus was a very different man from Bren. *And he'll make a better ambassador than I ever did.*

The front door banged downstairs, and Alleanthus's tone grew sharp. "What is this?"

"I need to see the Ambassador. It's urgent." The voice rasped with overexertion, but the accent was Athrolani. "It's about his son."

"I am his son," Alleanthus bit back.

Bren went to the doorway and tried to shake the fog of drink from his head. "What happened?"

The man in the foyer below was blond and beaded with sweat. "I'm Captain Hylier. His Majesty asked me to look into those behind the resistance, and I found evidence that your family is in immediate danger. Where is your son? The younger one, Azimir!"

Alleanthus looked up at his father. "He said he was going for a drink. He didn't say where—" A crash outside interrupted the rest of his words.

Panic burnt sobriety into Bren's limbs. "Stable!" He grabbed his sword from the table and dashed down the stairs. Bren motioned for the soldier to circle the stable as they surged into the courtyard. Azimir was on his back, hay matted against the velvet of his tunic. A heavyset woman with shorn hair pinned him to the stable floor. A thick fist had him by the hair, while she pressed a needle-thin blade to a gap between his heaving ribs.

"Let him go!" Bren could not keep the tremble from his voice, but beside him, Alleanthus snarled, hand perfectly steady around his raised blade.

The woman glanced back. It was only a second, but Azimir shoved a booted foot between her breasts and managed to skitter back enough to wrest his hair from her hand.

She scrambled atop him, standing and pulling him with her. The blade now dug into the soft brown flesh between his clavicles. "You aided the Usurper. Treason is punishable by death!"

Azimir glared at the pockmarked face of the woman gripping him. "It's not! We're not Athrolani, so it can't be treason."

Behind, Hylier eased through the partially open door, feet featherlight on the straw. Bren forced himself to not look away from the woman.

A shadow peeled from the darkness of the loft and dropped. In the same moment, Hylier lunged forward. It was a blur of limbs and flashing steel, then a gout of blood doused the fray. Azimir shoved the woman's body off himself and allowed Reka to help him to his feet.

Reka wiped gore from her cheek with a grimace. "Honestly, I've only got the one good eye, Hylier. You could stand to be a bit more careful."

He grinned. "Just imagine how poorly it would have gone without me."

Bren pulled Azimir into his arms. "If it's all the same to you, I'd rather not." He glanced at Alleanthus. "Double guard, around the whole manor, and send a message to the general and Captain of the Guard explaining what happened. They'll want to inspect the body." He squeezed Azimir once more before drawing away. "I've been lenient about your excursions, but as of now they're finished." He glanced up. "Reka, a word?" He watched her eye track the soldier and the others as they filed from the stable. When her gaze returned to him, he caught her up in an embrace. She was warm, and he was drunk. As he pulled away, he found his mouth on hers.

"Fates, Bren, enough." She shoved him away. Her arm wiped her mouth like she cleaned blood from her face.

"What? It's not as if we never have before." He raked a hand through his hair. "I'm sorry. The nerves got to me."

"And drink. We haven't lain together in years, and the last few times included your wife." She pointed to the manor. "You're being a rubbish husband right now. The least you could do is go be a good father."

He mouthed a response he had not formulated, then felt the fight leave his body. "You're right."

"I know I am."

He watched her leave. *I truly don't recognize this world.* He would tell Keplan, and write to Kemmer, but both could wait until morning. He turned back inside, calling for his sons.

Φ

"Can I talk to you?" Hylier's voice cut through the quiet and dark of the alleyway entrance to Reka's rooms.

Reka rested her head against her door. "We're not even on the same side." The words were only an echo of their earlier conversation, but she did not have the strength to think up another excuse. It felt like weeks, not hours had passed since they met in Peraan's rooms.

"We're not on opposite sides either, not yet, at least."

She opened the door, and unloaded her pockets and belt onto her desk. Muffled clunking of weapons on wood was a lullaby to her ears.

"I learned something today and need an opinion." He sank into the chair at the foot of her bed without invitation.

"Please, have a seat," she drawled, unclouded eye rolling. "Can't you process it without a sounding board?"

"Cut the shite." He ran a hand across the booklet in his hand. "Say you spent your whole adulthood fighting for something, for peace, then discover the person you hold in highest regard, whose orders you've followed, who is your friend and supposed confidant, did something terrible."

"Daymir or Keplan?" She crossed her arms, unsurprised. Daymir was noble, and therefore impossible to trust, and Keplan, for all his boyhood, was unfathomable.

"I can't tell. As you said—we're not completely on the same side." He looked at the fire. "What should I do? Do I move against them, or do I trust their actions as I always have?"

She sighed. It was not difficult to figure out of whom he spoke. "We spend all our time concerned with people trusting us, we forget whether or not we trust them. I've forgotten how to trust. You've forgotten how not to, it seems." She ran a finger around her mug's rim. "You go with your gut. That's what I always do."

His frown deepened, but he rose. "All right. Thank you. I won't find you again."

"I won't be here." She did not offer a goodbye as he left, only locked the door behind him. She understood the man's conflicted feelings. She loved Bren.

Not in the conventional sense, but in the sense that people like her depended on people like him, idealistic people too kind and good to see the darkness, the twisted plots that writhed under the surface.

But those plots were necessary to the survival of the world, just as the beauty was necessary for her to hide behind. "Go with your gut." She whispered it to the dark room. She swore an oath to Bren. But before that, all those years ago when the Borderlands were caught between Azirik and Alea, she swore an oath to herself. *Do the hard work, the dirty work, so others won't always have to.* It took a moment to gather her things and clean the room until it seemed disused for days. It took another two hours to find a Banis stall still standing in the battered Thread.

The shopkeep was folding his silks, but the guard outside caught sight of Reka loitering. Leather armor and brown skin gleamed in the low light as she straightened. "Sorry, you can't go in. We just closed for the evening, but you could come back tomorrow."

"I actually hoped to talk to you. I heard a rumor." She made a gesture with her hand, a fist that opened from her chest. "I heard Liberty is coming."

The woman froze, then her face broke into a grin. "Meet me in a quarter of an hour, round back."

Excitement thrummed through her veins, and something bloomed in her gut for the first time in years. *Hope.* Some wars were worth fighting.

And if you won't, Bren, I will.

Φ

The 37th Day of Lumord, 1272
The City of Ceir Athrolan, Athrolan

Firas stumbled downstairs, rubbing rough hands over his arms. It was cold. He hated the mornings Mirrel went to market before getting the fire ready. The kitchen was dark and quiet, and he set about stirring the coals. The smell warmed his heart before his skin. He piled on the logs and nestled the kettle on its hook. Eggs. Today he wanted bread and eggs. It was unlikely they would have much if Mirrel was at the market. He slid open the pantry door and perused his options.

The shelves were well-stocked. Distant bells tolled, marking midmorning. *Hasn't she set about lunch?* He frowned and, kettle forgotten, traipsed back upstairs. Mirrel's focus meant more than once she lost track of time while mending. Fate's knew the common room curtains needed several days' attention. He nudged open her bedroom door. The room was empty, the bed cold and made. Her day's dress was laid across the coverlet. *She never got dressed?* Firas's hangover burned in the wake of dread. "Mirrel?"

He pounded back down the stairs. Every room on the second floor was deserted. "Mirrel!" His search carried him into the common room. He peered under the tables, into the pantry again, as if she could have tucked herself between the wheel of cheese and block of salt.

Then he heard a bump in the courtyard. He shoved open the door, shivering dramatically at the crisp breeze. "Mir, you got water? I couldn't find you—"

Blood splattered the cobblestones. Mirrel's body slumped against the looming gray wall. Red ruined the starched white neck of her underdress. Her head swung against the stable door with soft thumps. He scrambled over to her, fingers fumbling with the rope tangled in the locks of her hair. He pressed her head to its place on her butchered throat as if the ruined flesh would somehow mend itself. His voice broke on her name each time he screamed. He curled around her body, light hair tangling with her bloody, black curls.

His stomach seemed intent on vomiting, but his body was too tense. Gooseflesh peppered bare arms and chest as the cold sun edged toward noon. Disbelief was replaced with horror, then numbness. He did not stir at the distant bang of the inn's front door, and the soft creak of the rear one a moment later.

"Fuck."

Firas glanced up.

A blond soldier stood on the stoop. His pale lips clenched. "Master Smythesen?"

Firas's mind drifted far from his body, unwilling to feel the chill of Mirrel's flesh, or the stickiness of drying blood on his hands. He whispered the first thing he could think of to say. "Can you find a doctor?"

Φ

The knock was urgent. Keplan's drink splashed across his front, staining the pale blue brocade with the black alcohol. "Damn." He patted at the spot, not truly caring about his forced finery. Hylier stood in the hall. The man's head was bowed, his back straight.

"What? You have information?"

"Your Majesty, you're needed in the Slummer."

"Excuse me?"

"The master of the Wise Hare needs to see you."

"Why are you doing his bidding?" Keplan spat the words before finishing off what drink he had not spilled. The thought of seeing Firas twisted his chest, but he could not stomach another rejection. "He said as much that he didn't want to see me."

Fatigue weighed on Hylier's eyes when they met Keplan's. "He didn't send me, Sire. You asked me to check into the threats on your allies from Peraan and his men. I'm afraid to say I was too late for one. Mirrel is dead. Firas needs you."

Keplan's stomach revolted, and he was sick all over Hylier's boots. "Forgive me."

"No need, Your Majesty. I'll send for a horse and guard while you tidy yourself."

"I don't need a guard, dammit!" Keplan snarled as he staggered into the privy.

"You most certainly do." The door clicked shut behind the captain. Keplan stared into the mirror. His belly still heaved, but there seemed to be nothing left to vomit. *I haven't eaten in two days.* He wiped his face and rinsed his mouth twice before changing into his old shirt.

Moly waited in the courtyard. It seemed the stablehands had tried to groom her, but there was little to be done about the scruffy coat or hairy ears and nose. Keplan ignored the two guards who fell in behind him. He did not care about the spectacle he made, a tall man on a too-small horse, racing through the streets of the city at high noon. The Slummer was subdued, and he felt the heavy weight of accusation from the faces peering through the curtains. War was one thing. An assassination of one of their own, a daughter of blood as old as Athrolan, was personal.

Keplan trotted into the courtyard, dismounting before Moly had drawn up. The space reeked of blood. Pink stains marred the plastered walls and white stone. Sawdust scattered across the ground to soak up the worst of the gore. He shoved through the rear door. The common room was dark and cold. He took the stairs two at a time. Firas's room was deserted, but Mirrel's cracked door emitted the faint hitch of weeping.

Firas was curled on the bed, wrapped around a pillow. Keplan faltered in the doorway, but only for a moment. The mattress dipped and creaked under his weight as he tucked himself behind Firas, his knees folded into the hollow of the other man's, nose pressed against the nape of Firas's neck. "I'm so sorry."

"It's not your fault."

Yes, it is. "I'm still sorry." The bed smelled of roses and straw. *Mirrel.*

Firas's voice rasped over the expanse of his grief. "I don't know what to do. She took care of everything. I was a stupid child, through all of it, even when she needed me, I never did enough."

"You loved her."

"That's not enough." He sniffed, shoulder shuddering. "How do I run an inn? How do I look our patrons in the eye? How do I do any of it—live—without her?"

Keplan brushed a kiss across the mess of hair in his face. When faced with Daymir, with Brentemir, with An'thor, he always had the perfect, powerful response. *It's just honesty.* Another person's grief was a far more difficult challenge. He slipped an arm over Firas's chest, lacing their fingers together. "I don't know."

Light crept across the room and faded from the sky. They did not speak. Suppertime came, and Keplan pried the other man from bed. The common room was still dark, still cold, still a void where hard wit and sharp laughter used to be. Keplan dismissed his guards before finding food.

By midnight, the lamps sputtered with too-little oil. Empty plates and two battered mugs decorated the bar between them. Keplan glanced out the window. "It's no longer the worst day of your life, you know."

Firas followed his gaze. "You're right. Perhaps the second worst." His sigh was older than the wind. "What do I do today?"

Keplan traced the old lines of laughter and the new lines of grief on his lover's face. Firas needed purpose, needed strength. *He needs Mirrel.* "We'll start here. We'll tidy everything. You'll set the soup to cook for tomorrow, you'll go through the pantry and make sure you have everything for the week while I deal with the courtyard. We'll clean the common room, we'll scrub every last corner of this place. And then, when you're finally exhausted enough to sleep, you will."

"They left this." He slid a coin across the bar.

Keplan tilted it. The markings were those of an Athrolani mint, but Daymir's profile replaced Tzatia's. "May I keep this?"

"Do what you want." Firas's frown deepened at the mention of the courtyard. "I'll arrange for her burial soon. Maybe in four days, the First Frost was always her favorite festival."

Keplan looked down. Details of a funeral had not occurred to him. "I can ask for a place for her in the memorials."

"No." Firas shook his head. "We've a family plot. It's high up on the hill. We're one of the oldest families in Athrolan, you know." He ran a hand over the bartop. "I appreciate your offer to help and grateful you're here, but I'll want to tidy things alone." He met Keplan's eyes for the first time that night. "Yes, even the courtyard. I'm her brother. I ought to do it."

Keplan felt excluded, then immediate guilt followed. *I've done enough harm.* "Of course. I can help with whatever you need, whenever, just ask."

"You're a king, 'Lan. You've got bigger responsibilities than my grief. I meant what I said the other day. The roots of it, at least. I could have been kinder, but I meant it."

Keplan shook his head. King's responsibilities were nothing in the face of grief. "I want to help, I love you."

Firas's snort was too kind to be a scoff, but only just. "You can't."

"Doesn't matter. And I don't understand, but I'll respect it." Keplan rose, brushing his hand over Firas's. It was a ghost's touch. He wanted to fill his days with the business of the inn, with helping Firas, organizing the Hare's future without Mirrel. None of those were his tasks, after all. He was not family, even if they were his, not in the way that mattered when death arrived. "Could I say goodbye?"

"She's in your room."

Except, when Keplan climbed the stairs of the Wise Hare for the last time, he found it was no longer his room. Walls stood, and the roof stooped, and the window overlooked the city, but something had left the place.

It was the same with the body on the coverlet.

Sheets swaddled her, wrapping all but her face and head. Bloodstains spread from her throat, but her wounds were covered. A faint frown wrinkled her brow, but it was the only expression left, as if she forgot something important, but could not place what.

Hunting and the general brutality of nature prepared him for death. Nothing prepared him for grief. *She protected me. She never even liked me, but she protected me.*

He sank onto the bed beside her. Beetle

"I'm sorry. Firas denies it, but I had a part in this. The minute I shadowed your doorstep your fate was set—" Tears did not come. He wished they would, wished something would release the ache building between his ribs. His brow pressed to her wrapped shoulder. It was the most they ever touched.

Fear, fury, exploded in his mind. Rough hands gripped his shoulders. Ribs cracked against the wall. Pressure seared across his throat. Hot blood pulsed from his body. He lived it twice, thrice, until his pain-blurred eyes fixed on the man standing over Mirrel's body.

Foreign adrenaline jolted sense from his mind, erased his faint control over his emotions. Torrents of pain broke through the floodgate of his mind. *Peraan.* There was another man, but it did not matter. Emptiness came in the wake of grief, of exhaustion, horror, and most of all love.

Stumbling steps took him back across the bloodstained courtyard. Through the kitchen window he heard pans rattling through the too-empty inn as Firas cleaned. Walking to the palace seemed insurmountable and familiar streets only ripped at his grief-cracked heart. Instead, he turned left. Twisting alleys led through leaning, water stained compounds above the naval yards. In the small hours of the morning even torchlight seemed tired, guttering against the ocean air.

A narrow walk jutted between harbor towers, a spider's thread of battered stone over the black waves. Keplan staggered across. White scars marked where the harbor gates scraped closed weeks before. Keplan pressed his cheek to the damp wall. Everything smelled of salt. *Ma.* He understood, now, why she always smelled of storms, of an ocean he never saw. *And Da was woodsmoke and stone.* He wanted to settle on the floor by the fire and listen to his mother's terrible singing.

Small wonder they wanted him to lead a quiet peaceful life. *I should have listened.* Staring down at the darkness of the open ocean only echoed the yawning grief, the horror at every choice he made. He pushed himself upright and wandered down along the wall of the navy barracks. Muttering sailors and creaking rigging drifted over the dockyard.

"I'll see you when I'm next in town." A voice more suited to shouting over crowds cut through the quiet darkness. Peraan shouldered a pack and waved off another question from his companion. "No, errands. It'll be weeks this time."

Keplan no longer needed books to describe a Rakos's rage, or the fathomless cold that overtook the Dhoah' Laen. Frozen fury pulsed through his heart. His feet followed Peraan's steps up the Tzama to the glittering coin-tiled basin of the Fountain of Starflies.

The man paused, and Keplan fell back into the shadow of a brothel.

"I already know you're there, whoever you are."

Keplan pulled his cowl farther and stepped up beside the barker. An empty city square was a terrible place for a king to meet a murderer, but the void where his reason once sat swallowed every instinct. Silence reigned while they stared at water dribbling over the mosaic of silver coins.

Exhaustion. The ache of old joints in winter. Blood washing into a basin. Keplan winced at the last image from the man beside him. *Scare him, make him run and never return to Ceir Athrolan.*

"You one of Luben's boys?" Peraan hazarded. "You can tell him I'll pay him when he takes care of Salt-tongue."

"I'm here about this." Keplan placed the calling coin bearing Daymir's head on the fountain's rim. "We know it was you."

"That was rather the point," Peraan snorted. "And it's scarcely a crime, the bitch was betraying our kingdom, tupping the usurper himself."

Rage melted the ice in his gut. He whirled, one arm cracking across Peraan's shoulders and sending the older man crashing into the fountain.

Sloshing water drenched them both as Peraan rolled onto his back, gasping. Keplan scrambled onto him. One knee ground into the man's groin. The king pinned the barker's hand against the cold coins. His red palm slammed into the man's throat, fingers digging into the fleshy veins. Peraan's free arm pounded against Keplan's face, his shoulders, fingers gouging at the boy's eyes. They scraped down his cheek and Keplan whipped his head, catching the clawing digits between his teeth. His jaw tightened, flesh and gristle grinding, blood spurting into his mouth.

His fingers ripped skin, worming their way behind the choking man's windpipe. Peraan thrashed, trying to buck the thin boy off, but slumped over the fountain's rim was not advantageous. Rage and adrenaline hurtled Keplan beyond the threshold of normal strength. *Let him think this isn't luck. Let him think I have power on my side.*

Let him think I'm a god.

Thrashing subsided. Spasms ceased. Water stilled to a ripple as twitching hands and feet slowed. Keplan gripped tighter for another moment before extricating his fingers from the crushed trachea and bruised wrist. He spat the dead man's gore into the blood-black water.

Peraan's discarded pack tangled his shaking legs as he stepped away. Papers and clothing tumbled out, followed by a bottle of whiskey. Keplan stuffed them back in, glancing at the body in the fountain, bumping against the spout in the center. Nausea writhed up his throat. He grabbed the bag and ran.

Blood's tang filled his mouth, but now it was fresh, and no amount of spitting erased it. He fumbled the bottle out and pried the cork out. Sickening spices of whiskey only set his stomach aflame. *Tell An'thor.* He knew the general had no grounds to judge him for murder, but the moment a confession slipped from his lips it would be real.

Fates, there's a body. The nearest street corner held a closed perfumery and the gleaming front of a Banis bathhouse. Already lantern light bloomed brighter, exposing every shadow as dawn approached. He recognized nothing. Two right turns and a faltering climb up a narrow alley brought him within a block of the fountain. All he needed to do was hide the body, just long enough to give him time to return to the palace and bathe before the crime was discovered.

I've killed a man.

"Murder!" The shout arced over the hard, white stones. "Guards! Someone: call the guard!"

Keplan's pulse stuttered to a halt. Breath hitched and he staggered back. He tossed the dead man's pack away and bolted down the nearest street. Darkness hid his flight through the Thread and back toward the Slummer. Market Square was sinister without its usual stalls. Beggars and prostitutes replaced performers on the corners. Keplan sank against a closed meat vendor to catch his breath. Another swig of whiskey burned through him.

"Boy, you look like you need to forget a fair few things."

Keplan turned. A dust-dealer hunched on a stoop.

"Whatever you're drinking over, it'll be gone from your mind in seconds. You'll forget all your dreams, your thoughts. Copper for a palm, silver for a box."

Keplan crossed the street, where a ladder led up the pillar of an aqueduct. The rusted metal was loud in the darkness before dawn. Cold stone bit through the thin fabric of his finery. His mind tumbled, knocked loose from its tentative moorings. *Something's missing.* Something more than Mirrel's life force, or Peraan's vitriol. The only innocence he still had was in tatters. He should be panicked. He should be horrified.

His mind was silent. Power over another life was intoxicating. No alcohol rivaled extinguishing that spark with his blood-colored palm. It terrified him. It was not for him to decide who lived. It was not for men and women to make that choice for others. An'thor teetered over that line. Already the surge of energy, the sweeping peace of taking a man's life, of revenge, faded. There was no divide between the roaring noise, the churning images in his head and reality. How could he rule with chaos under his skin? How could he focus on war beyond his borders when he cast justice with his own hands? How could he keep the silence without murdering every person who did wrong?

"Whatever you're drinking over, it'll be gone from your mind in seconds. You'll forget all your dreams."

The liquor bottle splintered on the cobblestones below, but Keplan did not flinch. His trembling hands fumbled his way down the ladder. Staggering steps returned him to the stoop. Keplan stared at the tiny leather bags arrayed between them. He wondered if any other kings faced the same fears.

The dust-dealer's rheumy eyes fixed on the king. They were devoid of both recognition and judgement. "Change your mind?"

He would be a good king, he would keep Athrolan from war. *I'll protect them, even if it's from myself.* He jerked a nod at the man.

"All of my dreams, you said?"

END OF BOOK ONE

RESTORED II

THE TRUTH OF GOD

CHAPTER ONE

37th Day of Lumord, 1272
The Eastern Banis Prairie

THE FOURTH NIGHT ON the trail, wolves circled the tents. At the camp's edge, where cookfires burned, they crept even closer. Rih leaned over, peering past the licking flames at the bright eyes blinking at the edge of the firelight. Already the weather was colder, the air carrying teeth as sharp as those glinting several paces away.

"You'd think they'd be frightened, with this many people," she signed to the woman beside her.

The guard spared a glance for the predators. "War makes everyone hungry. It's been centuries since wolves were seen this far west. They've probably come to eat our dead." She turned back to her bowl with a shudder.

Rih winced and looked back to the camp's boundary. The glittering eyes were gone, just a memory lit on her eyes when she closed them. It would take another week to reach Athrolan's capital, more if the river crossing tomorrow went poorly. Even marches as a foot soldier didn't take this long, thousands of pounding feet beating their steady way across the dusty grasslands. It was hard to manage the transition from soldier to dignitary, but the differences in the march made the gulf between the two yawn wider. When she saw that Bimet was through with her food she leaned forward. "I have something to ask of you."

"Are you certain that's a good idea?" Bimet's gaze moved from Rih to the looming tent of the emperor's ambassador. Vi-baln's shadow paced the tent wall, pausing when a runner appeared.

Rih raised the spear beside her. It was mostly decorative, but the blade was sharp. "I'll be quick." Her fingers curled with ease, forcing casual comfort into the conversation to ease her guard's worry.

The guard's shoulders heaved in a sigh and fell into step beside Rih as she set off through the camp. Fire lit the makeshift road between the linen tents.

Once out of eyeline of Vi-baln's tent, Rih ducked between the gently waving fabric walls of the larger barrack tents. Guards paced the edge of camp. Already she caught sight of armbands, caught glimpses of a fist, rising, opening. Liberty. She settled on the outcropping, legs tucked beneath her, and raised her face to the soft air. There was little time to acquaint herself with the surrounding women, but there would be chance enough upon arriving in Athrolan, where they would be watched more but understood less. Bimet found an outcropping still within whistle distance of the camp, but outside the reach of firelight. Of Rih's half-dozen attendants, Bimet was the only one she had known before any of this. Their troops had worked together often, and the red armband she donned on the second day of their march told Rih enough.

"I don't like this," Bimet signed, lips pursed.

Rih shrugged. "There's no other option. I can't trust letters yet, not until I am safely in Athrolan. There're too many eyes on me. And not only Vi-baln's."

"Then I assume it's important?"

"Fourth Riding is being transferred to a nearby town," she said by way of answer. "A little one I can't remember the name of."

Bimet watched the glowing orbs in the trees bob and slink for a moment. "And?"

Beneath Rih's hand the rock was rough, ragged, and gray. Gone was the smooth red of home, the earth stained red by rust or blood. Her fingers curled in the crags, a tether to this changing world. "They're led by Baniol Desfal, of the Third Arc. I don't want him to leave the town alive. I know there are sympathizers there." She fixed Bimet with a pointed expression. "Understood?"

"Understood. I'll get the word out now. It'll go out with the morning progress runners tomorrow at dawn." Bimet rose, hand pressing the small of her back when she straightened. "I'll walk you back to camp."

Rih shook her head. "I can manage myself. The messengers' tent is on the other side of the camp from ours."

When Bimet was gone, Rih's attention drifted to the darkness before her. A small piece of her wished, fleetingly, that she could disappear in the makeshift roads and slip away into the night. She would not, no matter how inviting the dark woods and winding trails might be. But for a few moments, she could pretend. In a fortnight's time she would be in a different type of forest, one of cold white stone and looming duties.

Already she missed Ki-elte. Already her heart ached for home. *A woman will bleed and die for Ban*. She would see them again in a year, perhaps two, on the field of battle. Somehow, she would find a way, find those who would join their cause. In Athrolan, isolation would be their greatest ally. She just hoped she could survive it long enough to see her rebellion through.

Coarse grass pricked her feet through her silken slippers as she wound back to her tent, beside Vi-baln's. She turned the corner and froze. Vi-baln stood in the opening to his tent. Lanterns glowed behind him, gleaming off his broad, bare shoulders. His attention was fixed on her. "You'd best mind your slippers," he called, gray eyes never leaving hers.

She risked a nod, knowing he knew few, if any, of her signs.

"Wolves and all."

It was only after she had ducked into the illusion of safety inside her tent that she let herself shudder. Bimet was right to be cautious. The emperor's reach was long. Even here his ambassador served as sharpened claws. *This is temporary.* He would be gone once she married. Even as Athrolan's bride, however, safety was not guaranteed. Not for the first time, she wondered what His Majesty looked like. How he might act. Would she wish to sew his mouth shut as she wished so often of the baniol? Would he learn her signs? Would he be kind? She drew a long, slow breath. She was a soldier and marriage was war.

Φ

38th Day of Lumord, 1272
The City of Ceir Athrolan

Keplan staggered into his room, rain puddling on the wool carpet from his coat. A void opened in his chest, swallowing his nerves, his terror, the blood staining his hands. He looked down. A shred of tissue, remnants of a trachea perhaps, clung to the edge of a ragged nail. His empty stomach convulsed. His sleeves, too, were black with blood.

His tore the garment off, tossing it into the hearth with shaking hands. It was too damp, however, to do much more than smother the sullen flames. "Toss it!"

Even Azimir's swears felt like an inadequate response. The wooden box weighed in his purse, and he fished it out. He moved through the parlor to his study and sank into the chair without bothering to light a lamp. What he had become? He did not want the weight of his people on his mind. He did not want the grotesque mantle of divinity, nobility, on his shoulders. He wanted only peace and Firas and the distance to escape what he had just done. If holding the world's thoughts in his mind allowed him to end lives, then he would silence them.

All my dreams.

A part of him, the part currently struggling to keep its head above the churning guilt, told him this was not a solution. Not a true one. The box clattered open on the desk's polished top. Inside was a plain waxed pouch, a wide bamboo straw and a slim, sharpened stave the length of his thumb. Once each was arrayed across the king's desk, he leaned back. Firas never tolerated his patrons using drugs—dust or its gentler cousin, black leaf. But it was hard to escape in the Slummer. The beggar had not told him how to use the substance, nor had he bothered to ask or even wonder until this moment. *Fates.* This was a mistake, he was sure, a cliff jump from which he could not recover. Azimir's face flashed through his thoughts, followed by Firas's. His lover's expression morphed from tenderness, however, into the knotted snarl of fury, of grief, the one loneliness Keplan could not comfort. Keplan blinked. Blood. Skin and sinew rending beneath his grasping hands. He reached out, awkward but certain as he tapped the powder onto the gleaming wood. Before Firas's echo could talk him out of it, he bent over and inhaled.

He knew enough to pace himself, to circle his room and lock each door before returning to his study. He hated the portraits on the wall, the looming figures he would never live up to, the exhausted gaze of the queen now reduced to burnt bones in the mausoleum. He paced the balcony, emotions flashing through his chest like cannon fire—immediate and violent and inconsequential.

One after another he tore the portraits down, the hard, ancient wood of their frames clattering together. His gaze was caught by a landscape hanging just above his fireplace, and he paused. A forest. *Like home.* The frantic energy faded, replaced by something bright but too sharp for relief or happiness. He sank back into his chair, lidded eyes picking out each detail of the painted tree trunks. A thousand thoughts crashed through his mind, plans and ideas and fears, but not one lingered. Instead his battered psyche was left in unfamiliar silence.

Φ

38th Day of Lumord, 1272

Fog still clung to the stone, allowing the sleepy night and seedy activity to continue a few hours later than usual. Hylier shrugged into his jacket, wishing, briefly, for the old-fashioned cloaks he grew up wearing. Jackets were more practical, but nothing beat the dampness of the city better than being wrapped in thick wool. In a decade they might have silk-lined coats and horsehair decorations from Ban.

A crowd stalled his hurried steps as he turned a corner to the Lily and Alphonse. Guards swarmed around a fountain—one that was a popular gathering spot for the dandies and flirts of the Silver Apron. Someone had shut the fountain's valve, and the basin looked as if filled with wine.

The sickly smell of sweet blood hit him as he shouldered through the crowd. Murder in the streets was nothing new. One look at the man's face told Hylier this was no murder. This was a message.

"Back! I've had enough of you sick gawkers—"

Hylier flashed the emblem on his chest. "King's Guard." It was not truthful, exactly, but it was the best excuse he and Keplan had chosen for the occasions he would need one.

The man peered at the sigil. "Sorry, sir. Had too many trying to make a name for themselves." He heaved a sigh, pulling a stylus from the damp wrap around his head to make a note on the wax tablet in his hand. "Inspector Greton. Been following Peraan for some time now. Didn't expect to see him bloated in the square this morning."

"Understood." Hylier rolled his shoulders back. He did not have to fake the concern on his face. "This man was connected to crimes against the Crown—private information, of course. I'm just reporting to His Majesty." Hylier wasn't a spy, not in the conventional sense. He just knew people, fell into easy conversations and was forgotten other than a vague sense of friendliness. A journeyman inspector would glean more from the scene than he, but he ought to bring something back, some report. *An enemy of my enemy isn't always my friend.* "You think it was a mugging?"

Greton snorted. "Bag is missing. And he was an affluent man. You have a minute to take a look, just don't disturb anything."

Hylier thanked him and stepped closer to peer at the body. It was hard to tell what would be missing, but Peraan was rarely without his drink, especially in the evening. "Have you any thoughts on the matter?"

"Looks like an argument gone foul—clearly tensions were high. Just look at the man's throat."

Hylier crouched, taking care to touch nothing save the fountain's rim to steady himself. What throat? Windpipe was crushed, gleaming shards of bone jutting from where the thin U-shaped bone ought to be. The rest of the flesh was gnarled and torn free. Several pieces bobbed in the bloody fountain. He had never liked Peraan. The man was not likable even from a fanatic-supporter standpoint. Hylier lifted the edge of the man's coat. Spilled purse. No pack or writing kit. "I think I have all I need. See to it that the Palace Guard gets a writ of everything you find."

Greton seemed to speak in sighs. "I'll have it to you in three days. We're barely through with all the murder and looting that happened during the unrest. But I'll see it done, sir."

"Thank you," Hylier answered, slipping back into the crowd. Unrest. It was a sanitary term for tearing oneself apart. It was how his stomach felt now that danger weighed it, now that murder ran rampant. *And Daymir's involved.* The man had given Peraan names. Was this simply cleaning up after letting the fanatic snip loose ends? How did one break three decades of friendship? Before he knew it, his boots had brought him to Daymir's door rather than Keplan's.

The regent was in his seat by the window, where he had been the day before. Were it not for the different shirt, Hylier would have thought he had not moved.

"Haven't seen you much, though we're just a few city streets away," Daymir remarked, sharp lips becoming a smile.

Hylier returned it and gestured to the couch across from the regent. His hand shook. "May I?"

"Surely. I can call for tea."

"I had breakfast on my way up, though don't let that stop you."

Daymir rose, rang for a server and asked for his breakfast and tea. When he sat again, it was with a groan. "So why are you here?"

"To visit an old friend."

Daymir chuckled. "I'm old, but I fear I have fewer friends here than I did while exiled in Marl Black."

Perhaps you've burned too many bridges. Or murdered them. They had never been close enough for Hylier to voice his true concerns, but he had not come so far without knowing how to twist conversations whichever way he needed. "I'm concerned for His Majesty."

Daymir's gaze hovered somewhere between distant and vacant. Today its focus was on the harbor and the white tips of the waves. Hylier's guilt at choosing Azimir's safety and his confusion over Daymir's apparent betrayal soured his breakfast in his gut. If he were a tea drinker, he would have downed three cups in an attempt to quell the churning. *My job is to trust and obey.*

"Concerned?"

Hylier shrugged. "I heard one of the people he used to stay with while he was in the city was murdered."

"In the city. It's odd, we've always said it that way, for as long as I can remember. But it implies the palace, our barracks, all of this, isn't Ceir Athrolan."

I'm starting to think it isn't. "Odd indeed. But Master—sorry, sir—His Majesty is at risk."

"I was hoping to discuss the new trade routes with you. We'll need more swords on the roads—" His words died when he glanced over. "Ah. Hylier. Forgive me, I've been deep in thought and for a moment I thought you were the general."

Hylier forced a grin onto his face. "Of course. We've all had a long few months. Would you like me to send for the general?"

Daymir shrugged. "I'm sure I can send a note. It ought to be discussed with the House of Commons, I suppose." His voice waned to a mutter. "General Aneral should be back from her inspection of Fort Shadow soon."

"I'm sure." Hylier looked away. Arguing would only make the regent angry, and whatever was left of their relationship in his mind, Hylier wanted to preserve. Besides, there were other names on that list, ones that had yet to be crossed out. "I have a lead on some of the threats against the Crown, from Peraan. I'm going to look into them. Is there anything you might know? He wrote you often enough, even if his prose was unbearable to read." He wondered if Daymir knew of his supporter's death already.

"I know little of the man. I wrote to him once, in the beginning, when I did not know what type of man he was. I did not use my name, of course. He did not need that knowledge."

"Dam Ornsen."

Daymir glanced up, eyes clearing of their fogged memories for a moment. The calculating glint was a knife in Hylier's gut. "You know that name?"

"It was my job to read your correspondence. Even when you took care for us not to know it was yours."

Daymir's gaze lingered on Hylier's, nudging through the soldier's expressions in search of something. Betrayal, perhaps, or honesty. Of course, he would find neither. Hylier did not know where his loyalty lay anymore. After what seemed like a serviceable minute, Hylier rose. "I'd like to look into this, both for you and for His Majesty. If there's nothing else, of course."

"No," Daymir whispered, attention fading from the room and returning to some point between reality and the past. "No, there's nothing."

Hylier sagged against the wall outside the regent's door.

"Captain, is all well?" the regent's door guard asked.

"Well as can be," Hylier responded without thinking.

"His Highness the regent asked for General Aneral earlier, before you visited."

Hylier drew a breath. It was only a matter of time before the entire palace realized Keplan was not the only madman controlling their fate. "I think he's just tired. It's been a long time since he had to shoulder the responsibilities of court. Let him rest for the day, perhaps."

"Of course, Captain."

Hylier wished he could just return to bed. Perhaps if he did, the day would begin with something other than murder and madmen. Instead, he took a moment on the bench between the regent's chambers and Keplan's. A breath and another. Later he would go to the training halls and force his anxiety from his body with sweat and exhaustion. First, however, he had to explain how the Peraan situation had grown suddenly more complicated.

"He awake?" he asked the guard outside the king's door.

"I heard him rattling around early this morning. Shift before mine said he came back late, looking like death. Though it's hard to say if he ever doesn't, begging your pardon."

"I'd keep that thought amongst yourselves," Hylier commented. "I'd like to see him. It's about his safety."

Cold air drifted out when the door swung open. Hylier frowned and shut the door behind him. "Your Majesty? It's Captain Hylier."

"Study," the rasped answer drifted from a half-open door. The walls were bare of every portrait, only the landscapes remaining. The paintings were stacked in a corner, covered by a moldering cloak.

Hylier's hackles rose. The double doors of the king's bedroom were open, as were those to the balcony. He nudged the study door open to see Keplan seated at his desk, bare feet propped on the top, smudging what looked like official Banis scrolls. This was the only hearth that was lit, and the sullen fire did little to counter the early morning draught.

Keplan's hair was lank, the kind of greasy that came from too long in hot water. His clothes were pressed and fresh, but the deep bags under his colorless eyes spoke of a sleepless night. His body trembled, alert despite the clear lines of exhaustion. The guard was right. He looked like death.

"You've not been sleeping?"

"I hired you to listen, not gossip with guards."

"You hired me to help keep you safe, sire." Hylier reminded. It was a stretch of the truth, but not one Keplan could really argue with, he hoped. "There've been some developments with your friend's murder. The network of spies and soldiers who wanted Daymir on the throne is alive and well. Quieted by peace, but not converted. You asked me to find out more, and I found a list. Your cousin's name was on there. Azimir. It's a bold network that would attack an ambassador's son in his own home. And they were very nearly successful. And I'm concerned they'll try for you next."

Keplan barely moved.

"Lord Azimir is safe."

"I would have heard it sooner if he weren't," Keplan noted.

It was callous, even for Keplan. Perhaps shock would rouse the man's concern. "Peraan is dead."

Keplan's gaze wavered, but not to Hylier with curiosity. Instead, his eyes flicked to the hearth and back. Fire smoldered there, reluctant to catch on the damp scrap of fabric.

Hylier bent closer. It was a sleeve, decorated, and Keplan's size. Whatever drenched it was acrid and red. Had Hylier not seen the fountain, he might have thought it wine. "Fates."

Keplan did not respond. His wide eyes were dark, pupils blown from shock or adrenaline or whatever made his whole body shake.

"There's an investigation. I saw it myself this morning. They know it wasn't a robbery. What if they find out?"

Keplan lifted a shoulder. "People won't suspect a king."

"They will if someone saw you. It's the Silver Apron. Someone always sees." He examined the blood-stained sleeve again. "Velvet doesn't burn well."

"I noticed." Keplan's distant gaze rolled to Hylier's. Bloodshot vessels tangled the blue. "I didn't plan to. I meant it, I suppose, but I just—it just happened. You understand?"

Hylier did not understand. He was a soldier, sure, but one during a time of relative peace. Even when the civil war broke out, few were willing to kill their neighbors. But he had never looked at someone the way Keplan looked at Firas. "Of course."

"I can see the Banis camp from here. They'll arrive tomorrow, I suppose. It'll be a distraction from who murdered that pond scum."

"Even for you?" It was pointed and above his station, but Keplan rarely seemed to care about insubordination. "I'll try my best to make this go away, but I can't erase your memories. I'm told it's hard."

Keplan frowned. "You've never killed someone?"

"No. I hope I never have to."

"You're a soldier, isn't that the job?"

"The job is to keep the Athrolani death toll as low as we can. Sometimes that means killing, but lately it hasn't. Hopefully, with you on the throne, that will remain the case."

"It'll be forgotten soon."

"Of course," he whispered again. "I'll see to it this is swept away with distraction. The city does have much to do as it recovers from the crimes during the unrest." Even he heard the strain in his parroted words. *Except I expressly asked them to look into it.*

Keplan hummed indifferently. Despite his lolling head, his thin throat flashed with a pounding pulse.

Hylier hadn't expected the secrets he would manage would be the king's. "There's an inspector, his name is Greton. I don't suppose that means much to you at this point."

Keplan's glazed gaze narrowed a minute before rolling onto his. "Someone of that name frequented the Hare. Usually on nights when a storyteller would bring news from other places. Ban, mostly."

"I imagine so. They've been in the business for generations—even before Her Majesty Tzatia implemented inspectors in Ceir Athrolan—those employed by the city treasury and not the Crown, that is. At any length, sire, they've been in it since the beginning and they breathe lawfulness."

"What does this Greton have to do with the price of wool in Mirik?"

"He's investigating Peraan's murder." He waited until Keplan's eyes seemed fully focused on his. "And he knows it wasn't a simple robbery."

Keplan's face paled further, and his mouth worked as if suddenly dry. "Did you speak to him? What did you say? Can you influence him in any way?"

"I'm clever, but he's just as, if not more, and he's studied this for his entire time in the position. I could do a bit, push his course a bit, but not turn him about. He's tacking against the wind but still a seasoned sailor."

Keplan frowned. "Tacking?"

"Ah, I have a cousin in the navy. It means alternating directions slightly, moving at an angle when the wind is against you. You go back and forth until you've reached your destination." He waved a hand. "It's no matter. I spoke to him just before I came to tell you of Peraan's death. Which, of course, you already knew about. No one seems specifically concerned, but that time will come."

"You think I should confess?"

Hylier drew a long breath. He did not like Keplan. Not as a friend. The man was complicated in the worst ways. But even after a long comradery that bordered on friendship with Daymir, he would never argue that the former exile would make a better monarch. Athrolan was at peace, if tentative, and won on the backs of a dozen lies.

"I think you should do whatever is best for Ceir Athrolan. At this moment, I don't believe that's confessing. And I'm not saying that because you seal my pay. I'm saying it because the most terrible part of the civil war wasn't watching this kingdom attack herself, but seeing the people turn on themselves. I can't stomach watching the people turn on each other, tear one another into pieces." He forced himself to meet those uncanny eyes. "If someone is going to tear themselves apart, even if it's only from guilt, I'd rather it was you and not the city."

Keplan seemed to sink back into the sea of distance between himself and apparently every living thing. After a long moment his attention returned. "When you were there, did you see anything—anything that could point Greton in another direction—any other direction?"

"Nothing comes to mind. Nothing that would help at least, that I'm sure of. There's something, but I—" he sighed. "I need to look into it more."

"Is it something I could help with? Our minds are very different and sometimes that helps."

"I think not." *And tell you your regent may have caused the murder of a dear friend?* He glanced at the tremble in the king's hands and the bloodshot haze over his eyes. "Will this become a habit?"

Keplan frowned. "What?"

"Murdering. Will it become a habit?"

"Hardly. I don't think I have the bones for it. I'm not Domariigo."

The uncertainty was sickening, the distance, the disinterest. It happened once. It might again. Hiding the fact that a serial murderer sat upon Athrolan's throne would not be easy. "I'd hope not."

Something in his voice must have reached Keplan. "I'm not wallowing in apathy over here, Hylier. I'm horrified."

Hylier was abruptly reminded of how much younger the king was than he—a decade separated them, but the shadows in his eyes were darker than Hylier ever feared his own would be.

Φ

41st Day of Lumord, 1272
The Eastern Banis Prairie

The next move was crucial. Her teeth ground on her lip for a moment. Perhaps Bimet spoke, but she didn't look up to check. Her fourteenth tile slid into place beside Bimet's fourth. *Lotus takes all.* She grinned and slid her final one in beside it.

Only then did she look up.

The guard's eyes narrowed on the set, scanning for any error. There was none. "Good game, Your Luminance."

Rih had given up enforcing the use of her name a week ago. The pale tiles rolled in Rih's dark hand. "And you, Bimet. Thank you."

A shadow fell across the tent and Bimet's head turned. She rose and peered out before turning back to Rih. "Someone's come for you—a soldier, said she marched beside you."

Rih gestured for her to enter, sweeping her tiles into their bag at her belt before sitting back. When she glanced up, Kahma stood in the entry. Rih's heart faltered, then burst into an aching flurry. "Kahma!" She surged to her feet, arms around the other woman before she remembered her new station.

"Will you need an interpreter?" Bimet asked.

"Hardly, thank you, though. Would you mind bringing tea for us?"

The guard disappeared and Rih settled back on her cushion. "It's so good to see you!"

"And you, it's been a while." Her hands curled into easy signs, despite missing two of her smallest fingers on her left hand. "Since, when was it, Juniaal?"

"Battle of Nad," Rih corrected with a smile. "Fourth wave. What are you doing here? I thought your Arc was sent north, not east."

"I'm in the Fifth Arc, Jade Riding, now."

Then why are you here? She had not sent word of the rebellion to Kahma. Not yet, at least. And with the loose wrap around her shoulders it was impossible to tell whether she wore an armband at all, let alone what color. "I heard they were riding for a village in the southeast."

A grimace marred Kahma's otherwise delicate features. "That's why I'm here. I got your message."

"Liberty?"

Kahma repeated the word, hand trembling just a bit. "I don't know if it's brilliant or nonsensical to try this. But I think we must."

"If you know—the baniol," she faltered, avoiding the sign for assassination. "What happened?"

"He found out about the plot just hours before. Thought it was coming from Mirik, of course, the villagers were supposedly indoctrinated by Mirikin insurgents. Not a one knew what we were on about, of course. Doesn't matter to the baniol. Had to do the work regardless." Her jaw worked in an effort to keep from shouting, or perhaps from weeping.

The work. Rih knew what that meant, what deeds stained Kahma's hands as deeply as they still did hers. She almost reached out to the other woman, but stopped herself. Maintaining that composure was never easy, and a single touch might shatter it. Comfort came later, when war orders no longer loomed.

"It's a wonder any of us got out alive, when the baniol has his head so far up his shitehole."

Rih rolled her eyes. "It's a wonder any of us survived infancy, frankly." Still, her heart sank. Perhaps she did not have the head for plotting and treason. Surely it was a harried plan, but her nerves were aflame with urgency to do something—anything—to spur her cause onward.

"I hope you know what you're doing. His Eminence sees so much."

"It goes so much further than simply the emperor." Rih's fingers jerked around the words, mouth tightening. "He is a symptom—a dangerous one, one that masks the true illness in our empire, but a symptom. We destroy him another will rise—tumors, one right after the other."

Kahma's expression faded to exhaustion. "I know." She shrugged and her hands dropped to her lap.

Guilt pinched in Rih's chest. Hope was as necessary as honesty. "We need all the allies we can get. Speak to those you trust."

Kahma's smile flashed. "I'll send word if I do." A shadow sank over her features.

"Will you get a chance to go home, soon? See the rest of them? You've been on march for over a year now."

"Bet was my home."

"Bet?"

"The village he made us burn yesterday."

Rih's heart ached. Guilt uncurled that she had not even bothered to learn the town's name. *Bet.* She was no better than the baniol. "I am so sorry, Kahma. If I'd known—"

"This is war. It would have happened regardless, thinking the town housed insurgents. At least your secret is still safe." An echo of strength steeled the woman's frown. "Rih—Your Luminance, I'm sorry—I've got some family on the border. And friends in Mirik, perhaps."

Rih frowned. "In Mirik?"

"My wed-sister has a cousin there. And I'm sure if she spoke to my younger brother, he would support us too. He's a quick-tempered creature but bears no love for His Eminence. We've not always seen on level, but—"

Bimet ducked in, tray in hand, and set the tea between them, hair hiding her speech for a moment before she glanced at Rih directly. "I was apologizing for my tardiness. Fire's a sullen dam with this rain."

Kahma barely glanced at the clay pot and stood. "I should go back to our edge of camp. It was good of you to share your campfires, but you know how little the captain likes us to dawdle. I'll talk to my brother and his wife."

"I hope you find dreams tonight," Rih signed, fingers curling kindness into the words.

Bimet's eyes followed the other woman's exit, then flicked to Rih. Her lips opened, then pursed, but she did not speak.

The soldier's shadow disappeared from the tent wall. Banter and taunts served to distance them a fraction more. But pain surfaced when campfires flickered low across the prairie and stars glimmered in the blackness. In the end, they were all women burning down their own houses, lest they be forced inside the flames.

Φ

43rd Day of Lumord, 1272
The Town of Tut Kunis, Berr

"What does it feel like? For you?" she asked.

Arman glanced up. "I know it looks like sickness, it feels like it too, a bit, but..." He trailed off, eyes fixed out the window of the hut. "It also feels like a relief."

Alea's luminous eyes were steady on his, as attentive as they usually were distant. "I think I know what you mean. It feels right. Familiar."

"It's a relief. But I'm still scared, a bit. Of what it means. I was afraid, years ago during the battle, of what I would become. I saw the Rakos, their twisted forms, their stone flesh, their mania. And I didn't want that. Not for me. Not yet."

"You still became it, though."

"In part. I surrendered. It's odd that we never spoke of this, except in passing. Never processed it. Fates, this has been so lonely. These years, two decades of being alone. Together." His words came faster now. Urgency spurred his tongue. He remembered the Rakos, their stilted words, if they still had them at all, and their calculating animal gaze. If that is where he headed, he needed to speak as much as possible before the power of speech was lost to him entirely. "Before the battle I thought, as your guard, my role was one of fighting. When that didn't work I hiked into the hills behind Athrolan and succumbed. Surrendered. This feels akin to that, just," he faltered. "More. The next step. The final step, perhaps."

Alea's eyes were once again fixed on some point he could not see. "I think there's one more to come. After this. This feels like relief. Coming home. Becoming whole."

"Before I accepted it. This, though," he agreed, "this is closer to welcoming."

The door downstairs banged and her gaze flitted to the ladder leading down. "Speaking of welcoming, I think we're no longer welcome here."

He snorted. "I doubt we ever were."

A small spread was laid out in the front room. Again, outside the windows the town appeared deserted, save for the smoke drifting into the still wind from each chimney. The chief already sat across the table, a steaming mug in one hand.

"You came here seeking a woman—a crone, by your own words."

"Is she ready to speak to me?"

"I was untruthful before. Many have come seeking her, but she never spoke to any. You said she came to you in your dream?"

"It wasn't what I'd call a conversation. A warning. A plea, perhaps, but I could not say whether she knew she'd reached me. Perhaps it was I, and not she, who was trespassing in the dream."

"She was our ward. Since the Gods' War. She arrived wounded and lost twenty-four years ago. Fleeing the Mirikin army. She was unconscious, though her rest was not peaceful. Berrin are devout people, always have been. Many of us worshiped the gods, but many here worshiped the Laen just as much. There was only one place we could think of to bring her, hoping it might make a difference. Heal her or let her pass on to whatever awaited her. Then one morning the wind began to howl. The mountains groaned, weeping boulders. The wind was hot, whipping our skin until it chapped. And the ocean rose, something between a typhoon and a mist. It whipped and howled over the mountain and was gone. When it was gone, she was awake."

"Is she dead?" Alea knew the words were harsh but could not find the energy to care.

"Hardly. The words she used, her premonitions, visions, whatever you wish to call them, entranced many among us, but none more so than Orabon Marum. He was devoted to her. Others were too. Driven by her words and his own determination, he set out to spread her wisdom. First north, then west. I hoped you would leave without bothering us further, but," he shrugged, "like you said, when you dream of her, it's a warning."

Alea leaned forward, her desperation drawing fuel from the faith of this unknown man. "How far behind are we?"

"Months. It was in early spring."

When Keplan left us. Arman glanced at her. If there was any doubt their son bore their power or something even greater, tied to the world itself, the words dashed it to slivers.

"He's from here?" Alea pressed. Lines formed at her eyes from the effort of speaking for so long.

"No, a border town to the west. One that worshiped the gods."

"How did he end up here, a town that worships..." she faltered.

"You?" His dark eyes bored into hers. "He was seeking new faith. When he heard her message, he found it."

"'Gods' Blood?'" Alea quoted.

"There's more to it. Far more. Were she anywhere else, we'd chalk it up to madness. But what she spoke of were legends passed down through generations. Stories we whispered with sanctity in the dark nights of winter. The only faith we could possibly keep through a hundred generations."

"And the citadel—Lymorda—it's still there?"

"Untouched."

She turned to Arman. "Do you think—"

"Perhaps it wasn't her we came to find. Perhaps it was that."

She whirled on the chief. "Will you take me?"

"No." He set down his cup with finality. "But I will show you the trail."

Φ

Lymorda, Citadel of the Laen, Berr

The mountains were not fit for horses, the trail closer to a stone ladder most of the way. Instead they hauled themselves, hand over hand, for the entire afternoon. When they reached the level outcropping, neither could draw full breath from the altitude, and the city below was a smattering of dark spots.

Alea's focus paused on the salt flats far below and the map the chief had handed off before they departed.

"I can't say this is inviting." Arman's hand traced gouges in the stone. A yawning black maw led into the mountain, quickly winding away from sunlight. It was nothing like the smooth metal tunnel that led into the Northlands. Instead it was filled with dust and broken support beams. Alea was certain idealism and misplaced faith were the only things holding the mountains from crushing her. The air inside was different. Cold decay and salt replaced the crisp chill of the slope outside. Despite the damp, not even mold encroached upon the walls. The tunnel stretched on, winding through what must have once been a wining vein. "This wasn't hewn with pickaxes or hammers. It was with hands," Arman whispered as they pressed deeper. "Rakos hands."

Alea nodded. She did not dare to speak yet. A light appeared in the distance and the sound of open air echoed from ahead. She forced her steps to stay measured, though panic screamed for her to run for open air. She stepped eagerly into the light. Rock skittered from the narrow ledge under her boots and she scrabbled at Arman's jerkin. "Fates, if they're not trying to kill us with the crushing rock, then they'll just drop us off a cliff."

Arman nodded absently, his wide eyes scanning the view before them. They were tucked in the shelter of an extinct volcano's yawning mouth. Rippling rock curled up the sides, massive designs carved by Earth Shaker hands. Where Elanal had been quietly somber, this was a testament to titanic power. The citadel itself stood in the center of the caldera. Alea recognized echoes of Le'yne's architecture, but this had been built at the height of the Laen's power, not its end. The city was built in concentric squares, the curling rooftop of the citadel itself rising above, pierced by the black obelisk. Bones decorated the city, save for the central building, but these were the bones of giants. They were of some great animal, bulbous skulls sprouting four tusks twice as long as Alea was tall. Their sloping backs supported the bone columns of the main gate. Pillar-like legs crooked like human elbows and knees, as if poised to charge. "Lymorda. I never thought about the meaning of the name."

"Great Dead."

"You said the Rakos were forgotten, hidden in cities like this. You never came here?"

"I followed the glimmer of their souls, and while they were far flung, none were this far northeast."

"I wonder why. It's beautiful here. Preserved."

"Perhaps the familiarity was too much. Besides, surrounded by wards made of the bones of your own kind is a bit macabre, even for madmen."

They hiked farther. The sound of bone dust under boots and moaning wind were the only greetings. The energy of the place was still but sentient, empty sockets as watchful in death as in life. The citadel loomed closer, great barred doors still impregnable. Alea stopped at the doors. They were unmarked, save for two handprints stamped in the stone. One bore scorch marks. Alea pressed her palm into the right hand, nodding for Arman to do the same. Their hands marbled black and white, ice and fire, wind and earth. The stone groaned, hinges cracking into use after two centuries of stillness.

The room beyond was dark, empty. They entered together, hands brushing but not clasped. The walls writhed with murals, stories picked out in a thousand tiny colors. Alea's throat tightened. Once, the Laen had been as grand as Athrolan. Once they had a rich history, feared and revered by nations. By gods, even. She moved across the room, eyes roving from one scene to the next. Each square panel was as tall as she. Here, among the whispers of ghosts, she might be able to touch her power, mend her connection. She moved deeper into the room, stopping finally before a mighty dais. Instead of an altar like in the other citadels, temples to fallen deities, there were two thrones. She stepped up and settled herself into the seat of black metal. It was unnaturally cold. Her head rested against the hard bowl of the back. She glanced to Arman once before closing her eyes.

She recognized the echo of power, the droplets of black ocean that once brimmed from her veins. They skittered from her grasp, running through her mind like quicksilver. Once, long ago, she had looked on the world through her power, sought the gleam of Arman's golden soul. She sank into the power now, drawing it over her head until everything was black. *I don't have to use it. Just look through it, use it as a spyglass to find the gods' souls.* The latent power in this place promised her there could be another, whispering with the gods' magic.

The world glittered before her, the brown-red of the humans' souls scattered in the town below. She drew back, rising from her body, from the mountains. Athrolan stretched ahead, Ban to her left. Webs of red covered the world, a bloody network of souls and people, impossibly tenuous, impossibly connected. *Blood clogs the city streets.* She had never wondered at the deep color of human souls before, at the richer, brighter color it echoed. Now the curiosity rooted in her mind. Her mental gaze swiveled toward Athrolan, seeking whatever difference that would mark her son's soul. Her vision stung at the brilliant beacon seated in the heart of the great city. It was the burnished copper she recognized. Even from leagues away, through the blanket of Laen power, she could smell the blood. She knew that color, that scent. They were burned in her mind from rending the gods' souls from their bodies.

Her throat ached and the sound of screaming burrowed into her mind. Hot hands gripped her physical shoulders. Her grip on the power faltered and she plummeted back into her body. "Arman!" Her eyes flew open. His brow was pressed to hers. Through her own gasps she heard his sobs.

CHAPTER TWO

46th Day of Lumord, 1272
The City of Ceir Athrolan, Athrolan

GOLDEN NOON LIGHT DAPPLED the silk cover of her carriage. For the past two days it had been awash with the shadows of leaves and branches. Each lurch over the strange, bumpy roads sent another spike of pain up her back. Weeks on the road did no one any favors.

Her long fingers curled around the cup. It might not have been a rough army mug, but it was still far from the delicate glassware of the palace. *What would Athrolan use? Would she be expected to eat as they did? Drink their bitter tea? Or their alcohol?* She shook the nerves away as best she could. Mosil trained her. She knew what dishes they used. Reality, of course, was always shades different. But she was not going into this skirmish with ignorance. *Just apprehension.*

A shadow bloomed across the golden silk and she flinched. In silhouette, Vi-baln's shoulders seemed to span the breadth of her carriage. There must have been wind outside, for his lengths of black hair eddied around the arching headdress he had donned that morning. She watched his shadow hand rise, grasping. Fear flickered through her chest until she realized he must be gesturing at something far ahead. *Athrolan.*

The warm air in the carriage turned cloying. She turned on Bimet. "Roll back the covering. Please."

Bimet ducked out through the back, graceful even in the formal Royal Guard's leathers over billowing cotton. Silk retreated, drawn into precise folds, Rih stood, one hand gripping the naked carriage ribs. Adrenaline was fire in her limbs.

Ocean wind yanked at her clothes, pulling silk taught against the delicate chains. She raised her chin. Vi-baln glanced over, watching for a moment before pointing at the box at her feet. Her own headdress waited inside. It too had feathers, but hers were given by the emperor himself. Vi-baln had plucked his from a falcon he felled earlier. Rih had to step over the thrashing thing that morning. She glanced at the box but made no move to don its contents. *Not yet.*

The wagon lurched beneath her as they descended the foothills to the outer limits. Ceir Athrolan spread below her, glittering and stark.

Black water stains marred the soft marble, and though the gutters were free of refuse, the faint scent of mildew clung to the street sides. Aqueducts arched over the city, water misting through chinks in the ancient stone. They lurched onto the uneven cobbles of the main road. The gates hung open before them, the metal and bolts dark against the massive blocks of the city wall. RoBal's gates served as a demonstration with their spikes and cages against stylized depictions of history. These were plain, though no smaller.

Clusters of musicians and heralds dotted the street corners among the turquoise and gray of the guards. How different was their music? Within her ribs, her heart beat with Banis drums half remembered from her dancing class. It faltered with every wheel-bump on ancient paving stones.

Manors rose to her right, tucked behind their tidy, ivy-hung walls. She glimpsed a dozen flags of various Athrolani noble houses. Mirik's vermillion and green whipped above one of the large houses. Violet draped the Banis ambassador's towers and balconies. The color was garish without the backdrop of rich red clay and black wood. Even more striking was the brilliant turquoise hung from each official building. For an otherwise bland city, the nobles seemed intent on color.

Rih missed the days of entering cities on foot, shoulder to shoulder with her sisters. At least then she could meet people's eyes, she could smell the cooking food and feel the packed clay under her sandals. Here, everything was removed, distant, reaching her through a padding of silks and the scent of horse sweat and leather. Only the sharp bite of ocean salt wound through the haze of her Banis wagon train. She always dreamed of arriving at the head of a march. She never expected it to be as the coddled princess in a wagon.

Vi-baln's fingers gripped her wrist and he jerked his head at the box. He did not need signs when he did not care if she answered.

Her shaking hands fumbled the headdress out. It was a traditional net but covered with hundreds of glass and metal beads. Gemstones dripped from dozens of chains, the end of each finished with smaller, delicate feathers. A few still bore tiny flecks of blood. Jaw clenched, she draped it over her shorn scalp.

Something between fear and anger flamed in her bones, and she forced her chin higher. This would be her city. These would be her people. Whatever the next year brought with war and rebellion, she would learn to find happiness here.

The wagon swayed into an open square filled with onlookers and vendors. A fountain, small by Banis standards, glittered in the center. The rich scent of baking bread was almost akin to the grasslands in summer, but here it was cut by the crisp salt air and the stench of lamp oil. Despite the alien city, the strange pale faces and paler stone, she found dark Banis eyes among the crowd and bright dyed patterns between dark neutrals and eastern embroidery. *I will show them you mean peace.* She did not mean peace, but today she could pretend.

She raised a hand in greeting.

An answering wave rose, then another, then a dozen.

Bimet brushed her arm. "The palace is just ahead."

A swollen bubble of a dome topped the modest, if large building. Rooftops and roads angled down toward the harbor. Every tier was dotted with domes, some flattened, others drawn into a point. Arches cut through each wall, curving stone worn round by rain.

A few dozen nobles and soldiers gathered in the open courtyard. Ivy and ferns clustered in pots and raised marble beds around the fountain. Guards paced the walls, preventing most who tried to climb for a glimpse of the meeting. *Gallants. Their baniols are called gallants.* A thrill shot through her at the sight of a tall, muscled woman in naval garb and an important insignia. A wiry man with gray hair and beard stood dressed in deep blue beside the general. Her gaze lingered on the silver-capped horns of the Ageless warrior, tracing the wrinkled tattoo. Her hackles rose despite the thin arms and paunch under his leather and uniform.

As a child, she and Mosil often snuck into the rear of the smaller palace theater to watch the elaborate wooden puppets portray ancient epics or news from other nations. She knew a puppeteer when she saw one.

Mosil appeared at her elbow, one hand surreptitiously making the sign for "memory."

I rehearsed this, she reminded herself, and stepped from the carriage. The worn marble was cold under the thin soles of her slippers. Vi-baln recited his introductions and flattery, Mosil translating into Trade. Rih dragged her gaze from the general to catch the tail end of Bimet's signs.

"...of the Hartland, King of Athrolan and the Topin Hills." A boy stood a step before the Ageless general, with a modern Athrolani jacket and old-fashioned long hair. Rih swore her pulse stilled. It was not his beaked nose or bloodless face. It wasn't even his obvious youth. *Interrogator's Kisses.*

He swayed. Was he unwell? Drunk? The acrid scent of alcohol underscored that of damp stone. *"He spent some time in Ban, apparently."* Mosil's words during their meeting with Vi-Baln the day before were lead in her churning gut. She did not remember every white traitor or slave her riding took in for questioning, but she remembered the long hair and colorless eyes rolling in the wagon and the muttering of gods and fate and blood.

If he was not already acquainted with madness, interrogation might drive him there. *Does he remember? Does he know my face? Or am I just another brown face to him, just as they are a sea of marble skin?*

Vi-baln's narrow gaze and Mosil's nervous glance nudged her into a faltering curtsy. The king's smile was vacant, and he bowed.

"I look forward to our negotiations and your great empire," he addressed her in Banis, though his accent concealed some of the words. Then it was over.

Vi-baln and Mosil fell into step beside the king, Rih and her entourage following them down the narrow, low halls. Athrolan may have been a few centuries older than the Banis capital, but its corridors were far less opulent. Rih's body demanded she run, urging her to forget her duty, forget her dreams of freedom for her sisters and take to the surrounding hills. Instead, she gripped her hands before her and the tears blurring her vision did not fall.

There was no formal audience or grand entrance. Perhaps that would come later. Mosil had mentioned a ball. Instead, an old man, a steward, perhaps, or serving man, appeared, gesturing down various halls and bowing far too much for Rih's taste.

Her other serving woman, a young girl named Nehla, joined them a moment later as they were escorted down another low, narrow hall. It was dark, despite the pale walls, and decorated with occasional murals.

The door they stopped at was pale wood, lacquered until it shone like glass, and with a heavy lock and handle.

The steward unlocked the door, speaking to Bimet. Rih stepped into the room, scanning the strange architecture. Every door was arched, every window filled with thick glass made wavy with age. Air puffed past her and she turned. The door was shut, and she was alone with her two serving women.

Bimet handed the key to her. "They gave me this," she said, eyes downcast. "His Majesty invites you to explore or rest as you wish today, and requests your presence at the ball honoring your arrival tomorrow evening after negotiations."

Adrenaline trembled in Rih's hands and she sank into one of the parlor chairs. It was plush, but the fabric looked well worn. *How many arses imprinted this thing before now? Where they as scared as I am?* She was beyond even nervous laughter.

Nehla perched next to her. Though she seemed kind, she did not know many signs, relying on Bimet for the majority of their conversations. "Would you like to look around your room? I can help you unpack?"

Rih glanced around, looking for an annex. "Where are your rooms?"

"Below yours. Servants' quarters. But there's a stairwell behind that angled shelf. I guess it's how most ladies in waiting live here."

They were an entire floor away. Her guard and serving woman. Her only voice in this new world. Her stomach pitched. "I think I can unpack tomorrow. I need to rest, I'm not feeling so well."

Nehla searched her eyes, her own pinched with pity. "Are you certain—"

"Please, I'm quite tired. I'll call for you both in the morning." She hesitated, looking around again. "How do I call for you?"

"A bell by our door." Bimet squeezed her hand, but Rih could not find the strength to squeeze back. When she looked up again, save for a dozen trunks, the room was empty.

They tried to decorate it with Ban in mind, it seemed. Landscapes of grasslands hung on two walls of the study, but their craggy outcrops and gray-green slopes belonged to the Felds of southern Athrolan, not the gold Banis prairie. Ban may have boasted ebony wood, but Athrolan's rooms were dark with soot stains from lamp oil and faded blue wallpaper. Instead of a large single chamber divided with screens and built for airflow on hot summer days, her chambers were a series of tight rooms, ending in her bed chamber, which, at least, had two large windows and a balcony door instead of the usual single window.

She drifted from room to room, at a loss. Even the deep sunken bath in her private privy brought nothing but apathy. She would not even have the socialization of a bathhouse, it seemed. A locked door was the only solace when she thought of the king and his young, scarred face.

Though it lacked familiarity, she returned to the privy. Travel—even via a glamorous wagon train—made her reek of sweat and horse and soil. *Sometimes I wish I was born without smell instead of without hearing,* she thought with a small smile.

A minute's fiddling brought water rushing from the metal tap. Two dishes beside the tub held what smelled like soap and something that bubbled delightfully when she mixed it with the water. She left her finery in a pile on the bench by the narrow window and slipped into the water with a grateful sigh. It was not as hot as the thermal pools in Ban, but the day was warm enough she did not mind overmuch. Her eyes lidded and she let herself drift in the lack of sensation. Tomorrow she would attend the exhausting negotiations. Tomorrow she would unpack. Tomorrow the rest of this life of hers would begin. The real work. The framing of her rebellion against the empire she both loved and hated. But that was tomorrow.

Φ

46th Day of Lumord, 1272

A fist banging on Keplan's door disrupted what little sleep he hoped to get that night. He tugged on his robe and padded to the door. Would he ever grow used to having multiple private rooms? He opened the door a crack.

Brentemir stood in the hall, looking as harried as Keplan felt. His hand was raised, ready to unleash another onslaught on the heavy wood. He blinked, bloodshot eyes narrowed in something close to surprise. "Keplan."

"You expected someone else to answer my door?"

"No. Hoping maybe." His gaze roved about the room. "Might I come in?"

Keplan shrugged and gestured to the simple room. It felt odd to have an ambassador, a man of legends, act with deference. "You arrived this evening?" He glanced at the squat clock on his wall, counting the space. "Yesterday evening, I suppose, now."

"I did. Azimir came with me, but I didn't want him here for this."

"And what is this?" Keplan took the seat, watching Bren pace before the fire. "Is this where you beg me to see reason, convince me that all the doubts I've been fighting for the past two weeks are right?"

Bren shook his head. "No. Maybe. I don't understand why you're doing this, why you're throwing your future away. You could come to Mirik, be family, bring your parents, even. Why choose this? Is it because of my sister's promise to Her Majesty all those years ago?" He did not wait for a response, but fell to his knees on the flagging. "Keplan, please. You're all I have left of her. Forget An'thoriend. Forget everything he wants you to be. Those aren't your dreams."

"You want me to give up Domariigo's dreams to acquiesce to yours? Tell me, Bren, when did you decide to take Mirik up?" He slumped back in the chair, wishing there was tea strong enough to ease the pounding in his head and the weakness in his limbs. Apparently dust had a backlash.

"Just before the final battle."

Keplan shook his head. "No, I mean when exactly. In which moment was your mind made up?"

"I saw Athrolan tearing her apart. I saw all of my father's failures and knew that in giving her up to Athrolan, I would be no different."

"Exactly."

Bren's pacing stopped. "She was doing the damage to herself, though. And not because of Arman's failures. And Athrolan isn't your home."

"Isn't it? It's where I sought sanctuary. It's where I've found friendship. It's where the man I love lives. I'm not going to watch it fall to pieces either."

Bren shook his head and looked down. He collapsed into the chair. "I guess I was wrong."

"About what?"

"About who you were. I thought all you wanted was a normal life and family with us in the city. I made the same mistake with your mother. You want the same thing as she—peace and solitude. I thought you sought me out through Azimir because you knew, because you wanted to be welcomed into our home."

"It's a pretty thought."

"Why, then?"

"You won't believe me if I say friendship, I suppose. It's what I told Azimir."

"I might believe it. Azimir's trusting, though, and I think you're a good liar."

Keplan's face smoothed. "I didn't know you were my blood, but I knew you were on the verge of war with Ban, and before I wanted peace, I wanted blood. Part of me still does. I sought out Azimir because I saw him disembark with you in Athrolan and I knew I needed to get to you. You've seen war and don't want it again, but I've seen slavery. I wanted to destroy the Banis and you were my best chance."

"And now?"

"Athrolan is my greatest priority now. But I have not forgotten Ban. And I certainly will not stop your wife's war with them. I may want peace for Athrolan, but all of Ban could burn and I would dance in the light of the flames."

Ice slid down Brentemir's spine. First he had recognized the features of his sister, of Arman. Then he had seen the drive, the intelligence. Now, though, now he saw Arman's determination and Alea's calculation. And in the ice-chip eyes, he saw Azirik's mania. "Are we invited to the ball? Tonight?"

"And the wedding within a few weeks, assuming negotiations are finalized properly today."

"Seems rushed."

"Ban's at war. They have other issues to contend with than a thinly veiled attempt to control a new boy king." The pounding increased in Keplan's temples and he pressed two long fingers against the throb. "Could we discuss this another time, if at all? It's barely dawn and I have a monstrous day before me."

Bren sighed, staring at his boots before rising. "I'm sorry. I'm sorry I didn't understand you better. I'm sorry I couldn't relieve this burden for you."

"I know." Keplan watched him go, watched the wrought bolt fall back into place. Apologies and promises surrounded him, most stemming from pity. He did not want pity. He wanted understanding. He wanted companionship. The bells began their tolling of dawn, and he winced. *I want fucking silence.*

He did not receive silence. Instead, the glaring dawn light crept farther up the walls of his bedroom. Even when he slipped into his study to escape it, sun lanced across the floor and painted the shelves opposite his desk with its brilliance.

Today they would formally ally with Ban. It was already agreed upon, he supposed, but he had read enough history to know nothing was ever as certain as it seemed when it came to nobles. He tried to recall the face of the woman who descended the carriage in the courtyard. He had not thought much on her, save for a few fleeting moments. Frankly, he had thought of little beyond just making it through the day, the minute.

She was tall. Shorn head. He thought he saw dark eyes under the elaborate decorative chains draped over her head. *That could be half the women in Ban.* He longed for someone whose every step and smile and thought he knew like the lines of veins in his own hand.

He was still in his bathrobe staring at the cheap wooden box on his desk when Daymir appeared in the doorway.

Fear and shame shot through his veins.

"We meet in half an hour. You were supposed to see An'thor with me an hour ago to prepare."

"I know." Keplan's voice was a rasp against stone. "I'm sorry, I just—" He shook his head. How could he explain that every time he tried to move, his body seemed too weak to rise, rooted to his chair and the tiny bubble of solitude he still had.

Daymir settled in the seat across the desk, tired eyes all too understanding. "That happens to me too. I'll follow a thought too far, watching the world turn beyond my window until it's nightfall and I've never even had my morning tea."

Keplan blinked. "But you still come back. You can still follow your trail back?"

Daymir frowned, gaze resting on the box.

Keplan glanced between the drug and his regent. If he scrambled to hide it now, all would be lost.

"I do, every time," he finally answered. "But sometimes when I do, it's not to this time. Or this place."

Keplan's nerves settled. "When I visit wherever it is my parents went, that I, too, can see, I'm not worried I won't come back. A bit, perhaps. I'm more worried that when I do, something will follow me."

Daymir nodded, gray hair bobbing. "It helps—when everything seems too heavy—to have something to return to. A reminder of why you're here. Why we need you here. When I was heir I had a shelf on my desk that held my seal, a letter from Her Majesty from decades before, and a few other trinkets. Those were my reminders." He jabbed a finger at the box. "The general keeps his reminders in a box like this too. More ornate, of course."

Keplan flushed. The contents of that box were not why he was here. They were not his reminder. He did not know what was. There was nothing he owned of Firas's, nothing even of his parents. Moly was sweet, but she was happily stabled by the barracks. "I'll try that, then."

Daymir rose with a low groan, wincing as his knees popped in protest. "And try being timely, Your Majesty," he suggested. "State affairs will happen regardless of whether you arrive on time or not, and you might as well get the ordeal over with."

The regent laughed at Keplan's grimace. "I'd hurry, too, if you want to look the part. The Banis are all about the ritual and performance, if I recall."

The door clicked shut behind him and Keplan retreated to the room beside his bedroom and opposite the privy. Brocade, a few silks, and several masses of delicate cotton hung along one side. The other held a dozen boots and shoes with carefully folded jackets and more traditional cloaks. He could not bring himself to look at the two outfits awaiting the ball this evening and the wedding. He rubbed his temples. How could he look a part he did not even feel?

Above, the bell tolled.

Φ

47th Day of Lumord, 1272

Keplan's borrowed euphoria lessened when he turned the corner to the meeting hall and collided with his future bride. She glanced from him to the two women beside her. Both were Banis and dressed in fine silks, but the older of the two wore a leather breastplate over her attire.

His nerves sang through the gentle comfort of dust, but the flickering images in his mind remained mostly peaceful. *I'm safe.* He forced what he hoped was a smile onto his face and bowed. "It appears we're both a bit tardy. Care to walk with me?"

The woman had yet to meet his eyes, her gaze fixed instead on the armored woman. He watched her hands form a flurry of motions. A second later the princess responded with a dozen new ones.

"That would be lovely," the armored woman said. "Thank you."

By the time Keplan formed his question in a way he hoped was neither awkward nor offensive, they had reached the meeting hall in silence. His titles were recited and he found his seat beside An'thoriend.

"How thoughtful of you to join us," the general hissed. "It's not as though our kingdom's future rests upon these discussions."

"It's not as if I can actually contribute," he whispered back under the guise of adjusting the fur hat on his head. "I'm just the mask you all wear to hide your actual faces."

An'thor glared but gave up the argument. "Now that His Majesty is able to join us, shall we begin?"

"Indeed." The heavily muscled man directly across from them leaned forward. "We appreciate you taking the time from your busy day to discuss these matters yourself, Your Majesty."

"Thank you for your patience," Keplan began in Trade. Between the constant drone of translation to and from Banis and the flurry of hands, scratching pens, and whispered conversations, his head was too busy to focus on anything beyond his native language. "As we discussed in our letters to your gracious empire, we are happy to offer an alliance in exchange for peace, trade goods, and continued correspondence and transparency."

"Sealed, of course, with the marriage between yourself and Kajimet Rihelte, chosen daughter of His Esteemed Excellence, His Eminence Emperor of Ban and the Jade Forest, Jamun-Ilta the Holy Emerald Throne, overseen by myself and Hand of the Empire, Vi-baln of RoBal and the Emerald Tier." The man who spoke was an ambassador, Keplan recalled, though the difference between his role and the larger iron-eyed man was lost on him.

Political hostages hidden under the title of marriage. He imaged the woman across the table from him felt as much a victim as he. Keplan faltered, realizing all eyes were on him to respond. None of this was rehearsed, not in the traditional sense, and even if it were, the lines fled his mind at the mettle behind the eyes of the Emperor's Hand. "I hope," he began, his voice emerging as a croak. He cleared his throat, but Daymir's hand pressed against his forearm, stalling any further floundering.

Daymir's smile was a flicker of light in the sea of tense frowns. "Indeed. And this meeting is simply a formality, one that allows us to smooth any issues and sign this alliance together, as a symbol of our nation's lasting friendship."

Vi-baln gestured for a small chest to be brought forward and opened. To Keplan's surprise it did not contain a mass of gems or precious metal, but scrolls.

The Hand drew out each in turn, reading the official words detailing the Banis gifts to the Athrolani crown.

Keplan's thoughts barely focused on the lists of hunting dogs and war cats, of riches and one immaculately bred riah. How could Athrolan possibly compete with such wealth? Though none spoke of it, he knew he traded Athrolan in favor of security and peace. If Ban disliked a single step he took, the might of their empire would fall on his head.

A folded paper slid down the Athrolani side of the table from the Head of the House of Guilds. Keplan unfolded it and skimmed the words.

Correspondence mentioned grain.

Though the hills behind the palace were awash with brilliant leaves, the fields beyond were sullen. When Vi-baln next paused for breath, Keplan spoke up. "Our prior negotiations discussed grain from your fields. We cannot feed our people with gold or your horses—as fine as they are."

"Though we are honored by your generosity," An'thor interjected, shooting a sharp glance at the young king.

Color flamed on Vi-baln's cheeks. The tension around his mouth said it was from anger, not embarrassment. "It was decided that—given that our resources are focused on our army—wealth would suffice as a substitute."

"And the blight?"

Keplan winced. He did not have to be a political mastermind to realize admitting they struggled to feed their own people was a terrible tactic. "Our wheat suffered in the past few years. And I recall the fields of golden grain sweeping across the northern expanse of Ban. This is something we require."

The Banis ambassador whispered some rant in Vi-baln's ear. The Hand's gray eyes leveled on Keplan. Unwavering.

Keplan held the gaze, tilting his head to Admiral Fess. "Perhaps if I tried my hand at flirting with him?"

Fess's lips twitched. "Don't rule out that option. Our kingdom appears to be on the executioner's block."

"We will include a shipment of seed wheat of our strongest stock, on one condition," the man answered when the whispers had died. "Agree to war against Mirik's madwoman of a Hetmir."

No. Keplan's gloved hands curled into fists. He no longer cared about the polite dance or smiles that veiled teeth. "I'm hardly interested in antagonizing one of the oldest kingdoms this side of the continent." Keplan snapped.

Vi-baln's lips thinned. "Mirik may be old, but she is hardly strong. Our empire does not need your aid."

Euphoria fell away, followed by the thrum of energy that was not quite his own. Keplan scoffed. "I spent months embroiled in civil war. No one is interested in diving back into battle. Ban may make her money from bloodshed, but we do not."

"Then we are better at war than you." It was a bald threat, and Keplan bit back his next bitter words.

"We simply focus our economy elsewhere. We have the largest production of wool and timber. We've survived—and won—every war we've joined in the past century." He felt his mouth curl in a smile, but by the pinched expression on the Banis faces, it was not a friendly one. "The most recent of which was against the gods themselves."

"Banis forces joined you in that, and if I recall it was not Athrolan that won that war."

"No. But it was my blood." The room fell silent. Pens no longer scratched parchment. Keplan laced his fingers together and peered at the Hand. "Your emperor may claim divine blood, but I'm the only one who can prove it. Perhaps Athrolan is not what she once was. Perhaps you boast more gold and wheat and bodies and bloodthirsty plots. But there are a thousand terrible truths in my mind alone, and I promise neither you nor your emperor wishes to test them."

The ambassador's jaw worked as he ran figures and tallies in his mind. An appraising look tempered the chill of the Hand's eyes.

The voice was the princess's guard, but the words were Rih's and her eyes pinned him. "I understand you hope to maintain peace for the beginning of your reign. Ban respects that. However, we are at war ourselves. Our war machines need building. Our soldiers need clothing. You mentioned timber and wool."

"I did. Oak would build you machines. Mutton and wool from our flocks would aid your army." Keplan dared not risk a look to An'thor to confirm before barreling onward. "We have access to Nenev technology in the mind of our own general, An'thoriend Domariigo from the ancient legends. Whatever he knows, we may share with you."

"Then we have peace." Vi-baln's deep voice cut off whatever Rih's interpreter began to say. "And an alliance to celebrate. I suggest a wedding at the turning of the month—it is the first day of the raining season in Ban, a time of fertility and health."

Keplan blanched, jaw clenched. "That's in three days."

"Indeed. The match is made, and our alliance secured." Vi-baln's eyes bored into his. "Waiting only gives time for mistakes."

Daymir glanced from the Emperor's Hand to the king. "Perhaps the twenty-fourth of Valemord. If you are able to stay for the next few weeks, I think it would give not only our bride and groom time to acclimate to one another, but our great nations would have time to enjoy each other's culture a bit more before you return. It's the first day of the harvest season here, which carries the same weight as the first day of your rains."

Vi-baln conferred quietly with Mosil, then nodded once. "A fitting day indeed."

The knot in Keplan's gut lessened only a little. Four weeks, three days, it was no matter. In the swell of voices and shuffling scrolls and papers to be signed, Rih caught Keplan's eye, head dipping in a tiny nod. Keplan did not trust

Ban. He barely trusted his own general. But Rih's eyes were as calculating as his own. For whatever reason, she wanted peace as much as he. For the moment, that was enough.

Φ

Rih's door burst open an hour before sundown. Vi-baln's face was tight with rage as he strode across her parlor. Rih scrambled to her feet. Instinct shifted her weight onto her back foot, hidden by her skirts.

"What in the name of all the Holy Emperors were you thinking?" His mouth was wide in a roar, and spittle flew through the air between them. "You were not even supposed to attend negotiations, you were to stay here in your chambers until called for, until the pomp and frivolity of the ball this evening. A wife has no place in matters of state!"

Fear thrummed through her body, but on its tail burned something else. She gripped the back of her chair. If he came closer it would be her first and only defense. She barely understood a shouted word, but dared not take her eyes off his twisted face. In the low light of her room, the faint metallic green and gold paint on his chest and shoulders turned him sickly.

"What do you have to say for yourself?"

Bimet signed a few of his key phrases for her from where she hovered near the servants' entrance. Nehla was nowhere to be seen.

Rih's resolve trembled in her spine. "I was thinking we needed a compromise, and they would accept it better from the woman they will see every day. I was thinking His Eminence sent us here for negotiations," even as she signed her fingers were closer to claws, "and not a declaration of war."

"You presume to know what His Eminence thinks?"

"Was I wrong?" It was not a question, and she prayed the bitterness in her eyes told him as much.

His mouth moved, a hawk panting in the heat. Then his jaw snapped shut, muscles working. When he spoke again it was conversational enough for her to read his lips. "You would do well to remember your station. Even here. Especially here. They may let their common folk cavort with the nobles and let a pauper sit the throne, but that is not how order is maintained. You know that. An empire cannot rule that way."

She saw a glimmer of an excuse and seized it. "I thought if they trusted me, if they saw me as an ally first, then we would be that much closer."

"Closer to what?"

She glanced at Bimet, but her translator's wide eyes were fixed on the Emperor's Hand. "Controlling the boy king. Is that not His Eminence's plan? When we are no longer distracted by Mirik?"

Vi-baln's gaze turned thoughtful, and his finger traced the butt of the decorative atlatl hanging from his sash. "Regardless," he finally stated, "you have been insubordinate and irreverent. To Ambassador Mosil and to me, and therefore by extension, His Eminence."

A chill sank into her bones. Cold control was terrifying compared to shouted rage. She dipped her head. "Forgive me. I only sought to serve."

His hand was hot under her chin as he lifted it, turned her face one way then another. Searching for cracks, perhaps, clues as to what might lie beneath the layers of muscle and skin. "I know your kind. And I've broken countless people like you. You might sit as consort to a king here, but until I return to our capital, I have you in my sights." He stepped away then and paused by the door. "I'll see you at the ball."

When he had left, Rih collapsed into the chair, shaking. *Weeks.* She had hoped to get the wedding over with and send her entourage back to RoBal. Instead they were here for another few weeks. *Weeks under his bitter eyes.*

"That was too close, Your Highness," Bimet signed, fingers flying in her checked panic.

Rih shook her head. "He doesn't know. He thinks he does, but he has no idea. Not truly."

"You can't know that. You ought to focus on your role here for a time. Let the prairie dust settle."

Nehla appeared from the servants' stairs, glancing between the two of them. "What is it?"

"Vi-baln, he came to reprimand me. I think he suspects—" Rih began. A step behind the younger serving woman, Bimet shook her head once, sharply. Rih shrugged. "I spoke out of turn."

Nehla's dark eyes softened and she knelt at Rih's feet. "This isn't an easy time for any of us. Even a glimmer of hope can't be trusted. I often found it hard to navigate different courts' protocols."

What do you mean by hope? Rih forced herself to her feet. "I ought to get ready for this ball."

Nehla's expression brightened and she almost skipped to the dressing room that someone had filled with her trunks' contents during negotiations.

Bimet glanced at Rih, amused. "She just said, 'You must be excited.'"

Rih snorted, following the younger woman. "Hardly. I've never been to one, not since I snuck into them as a child with the other palace children."

Nehla launched into a rapid recounting of her last ball, one in a small city on Ban's western coast. There were hanging glass globes, if Rih understood Bimet's translations, hastily signed between gathering silks and sashes.

A wave of homesickness washed over Rih. Except she did not miss RoBal. She did not miss the barracks, even. She missed Ki-etle's quick wit and determination. She missed Il-fald's faith, and the burgeoning community she had built in the Purple Throne.

Bimet was too cautious. Nehla was too new, not well known enough to trust with anything more trivial than palace gossip. Perhaps her translator was right, and she should keep her head low, stay her course until everything settled. Until Vi-baln's falcon eyes were safely in RoBal and off of her activities.

The bright mirror reflected Bimet's steady hands, her steady eyes, as she looped gemmed rings through Rih's piercings. Rih drew a breath. It would be struggle enough to survive the next few hours of dancing, introductions, and politics without rebellion on her mind. She squeezed her eyes shut. *Do not think the word "rebellion."*

Φ

"I'll never recall these names," Rih lamented. "The man in the alcove by the fountain. He stood beside the king and conferred with him. Is he a consulate?"

Nehla's painted lips curled in a smile. "That's Daymir Blackhouse, regent to the crown and former heir," she explained before taking a long sip of the punch. "Left the court abruptly after being disowned and stripped of all titles following an accusation of swindling and proposing marriage to the Dhoah' Laen."

Rih's brow shot upward at the last piece of information. She knew little about the Dhoah' Laen other than the stories they were all raised with. Still, those stories were not told with the wonder and excitement of legends, but the solemn reservation of a local folktale. It was too real, and those who lived it were still alive—some of them, at least.

"Can you imagine the hubris required to think you could marry Destruction?" She watched the old man's distant gaze follow the dancers about, disinterested, as if watching wind sweep over the prairie. "How was he allowed to return?"

"I heard it was required due to the civil war. It was the only thing that stopped the war."

Bimet's eyes were not following Nehla's colorful descriptions or her waving hands. Instead, they were narrowed on the other woman's face. She did not seem as entertained. A moment later, when Nehla disappeared to retrieve more punch, the translator glanced over at Rih. "Do you know her well?"

"No, hardly at all. Why do you ask?"

"She knows much about Athrolani court."

"That's why Mosil chose her, I believe. He felt she would help me learn these surroundings faster." Rih caught the pinching around Bimet's eyes and turned the question on her. "Do you know her?"

Bimet shook her head. "Only by name. Our herds are from different hills, if you will."

Rih nodded in response but did not press the matter further. Bimet's expression was not one of differing social circles. It was one of distrust. *I need caution as much as I need new allies.*

Bimet's hand pressed to her arm and the interpreter nodded her head in the direction of a young man. Rih turned, frowning. She barely had enough room in her head for remembering the steps to whatever dance she would be required to perform, let alone several dozen Athrolani names with their harsh sounds and arduous length.

"This is Azimir," she introduced.

Azimir offered his hand, a crooked smile adding warmth to his bow. Unlike most of the palace folk, his skin was a light brown and his eyes walnut.

"Just Azimir?"

His smile faltered, but he soldiered on. "Or Azi. Half the time I don't recognize the rest of it."

It was then that she realized he spoke Banis. Well. "I'm Rih-elte."

"Yes, I know. My wishes on your marriage." He nodded to the music. "Would you like to dance? Not sure if you like this tune, but I enjoy the faster ones."

"I'm Deaf," she noted.

His face fell, and his curved lips flapped with what looked like a sincere if halting apology.

She found a smile of her own. "So, I don't know if I like it either. But I'm a bit worried I'm not familiar enough with your dances for a fast one."

"It's easier to hide missteps when your feet skip." He spotted a tray of candied fruit passing and grabbed two from it. "But I'm wholly content to gorge myself if you'd rather wait for another."

She took the proffered food and tried a corner. Two candied kiwi slices sandwiched a spicy cured meat. *Southern Ban.* It was something adopted—or perhaps shared, now knowing their ancestry was one and the same—from the Vales.

"It's slower now, if you'd like," he noted, jerking a thumb at the musicians again.

She finished her food and, bracing herself, nodded.

His hand was light but sure on her ribs; the other found hers. After a moment she realized his twitching finger must be tapping out the song's beat for her.

He babbled on, and she understood an occasional word, but she swore at one point he lapsed into Athrolani. He did not seem to care, however, that she barely responded. And she found neither did she. It allowed her a slow wheel around the ballroom, time to memorize half-remembered names of those they passed. It afforded a moment of peace in the warmth. The thud of feet on marble was faint but echoed in her own steps.

"How much did you actually understand of that?"

"You mentioned the dome once, and seemed very animated about something involving a cow?"

"Toar, I'm sorry!" His head fell back as he laughed, swearing in Trade before returning to Banis. "No, I was curious about your horses. I'm an awful rider. I suppose I should have figured you'd be hard-pressed to understand me with all the moving and bouncing. I'll do better next time, promise you."

Even as he spoke she noticed he held her gaze better. Perhaps not all Athrolani were foul-tempered.

He was younger than her by a few years, but something in his easy smile and warm eyes made him seem both innocent and wise. "I'd offer to dance again, but it'd be selfish on your first night here, keeping you to myself."

She rolled her eyes, gesturing to the ballroom. "I hardly think I have a line awaiting me. But I feel far more on a level battlefield here. Food I can manage without much embarrassment."

"Ah, Your Highness," he fell in beside her, leading the way to the arrayed tables, "food is my specialty."

Φ

"These get worse with age," An'thor confided.

Fess snorted and knocked back another glass. "I disagree. When I was younger I had to work. I'll never miss the long nights as a page trying to sneak food and wine between platter runs." She shuddered. "You people never had pages? Squires?"

"Something similar, but we also never had balls. Requires far too much heat to make large rooms comfortable. Instead, we had game evenings, sporting festivals in the spring, when the snow retreated a bit. And we had hunting parties."

"The idea of sporting festivals—hundreds of you on the tundra—is ominous."

"And I didn't even tell you what our quarry was." It was his turn to snort. "As usual, we were mostly just bloodying up each other."

"The best part," Fess decided, "of having been to many of these is that I know all of the good hiding places and which food is honestly not worth the stomachache." She belched. "Or which drinks. Fates, I cannot stomach the sweet punch the way I used to."

An'thor's lip curled and he looked away. He disliked Fess's jovial nature, the cavalier tone she used even when speaking with her subordinates. She argued it made for better morale. *They won't listen when you give orders they don't agree with.* It was why the army and navy splintered when he and Raven were at odds. And war required distasteful orders. War itself was often a distasteful order.

A flash of royal turquoise caught the edge of his gaze, and his attention shifted from the jesting naval commander to an alcove across the room. Usually, the alcoves held tables and hidden instruments for smaller court proceedings or scribes recording audiences. Now they were filled with seats and cushions. Others were hung with plants he had never seen before. *Something from the Banis, then.* Soon, the delicate vines and fat, moist leaves would wither in Athrolan's crisp, salty air.

The color flashed between the waving fronds of some monstrous potted plant. "I've found our errant king," he interrupted Fess's analysis of her fruit pastry. Ignoring her frown, he shoved from the wall and slipped through the nearest service door.

The narrow servants' passage wound through the palace's thick walls with as many tiny rooms for those awaiting a ring for service as the rest of the palace had mosaics and broad halls. He dodged a frazzled page toting a tray of meat and trying to quickly swallow a bite without being caught. A turn, a set of stairs down, then up, and he found another door, marked with a tarnished plaque:

Xavier's Mount

He nudged it open, emerging between the large plant and a delicate fountain crafted in the shape of the former king's warhorse. The king sat on a bench to the right, almost as hidden as the door itself. "Kind of you to join us, this being your ball."

Keplan shot a glare at the general, but he did not seem taken aback. "It's hardly mine. Hers, maybe." He jerked his sharp chin in the direction of the Banis princess.

An'thor did not follow his gaze. "You need to dance with her. At least once. Others already have and if you wait much longer, the rumors won't cease until Midwinter."

"I'll give them something truly dramatic to whinge about."

An'thor glared. "I don't want to hear it."

"I don't dance."

"Neither did your father, but he took a turn around this very floor with your mother when she asked."

Keplan frowned at the embroidered hat in his hands. "He dances all the time at home. I suppose I did too, there and in the Slummer."

The ache in the boy's voice was contagious, and An'thor settled on the bench beside him. "I know what you mean. It's been decades since I danced. At least, somewhere where people could see."

"Somewhere other than someone's grave, you mean?" Keplan quipped. Perhaps it was the music, or perhaps he was too tired, but the barb lacked its usual bite.

An'thor turned to watch Rih stiffly following Azimir's graceful steps. "Ah, there's the first rumor now. I can already hear the street barkers that your boy-cousin sauntered in, manhood swinging, and claimed your bride's heart before you ever rehearsed your vows."

Keplan made a show of gagging at his choice of words. "I'll dance with her if it means you'll never speak like that again. Small wonder Dorcal turned cannons on you after listening to that for two decades. I doubt I'll last as long."

An'thor watched him edge around the room, stopped every few paces to accept a greeting or avoid another. The boy's tone was as joking as Fess's had been earlier while discussing her ale-sick. *But his eyes are colder than Nenev ice.*

War was familiar to An'thor, and to that end, he preferred it. He recognized it was ridiculous to be dissatisfied with the very peace he worked so hard to forge or with the king he forced upon the throne. *The king I killed for.* The dramatic thought was made ridiculous by the fact that he lost count of how many people he ended. Even with all his touted declarations that he understood madness, even facing Alea's own terrifying stare, his skin crawled when he looked upon her son.

He dumped the rest of his punch in the plant and retreated through the servants' door. This time the path included another two flights of stairs and a few quick strides across the gallants' hall.

"Official business. King's orders," he muttered to the guards flanking the door.

Neither spoke, but one shot the other a skeptical look as he unlocked the heavy oak. The foyer within was dimly lit and the room beyond even darker. An'thor flopped into a worn chair. Silence. He fished out his flask and took a small, slow sip.

"You come here just to brood?" Raven leaned on the bars installed in his former doorway. The only feature hollower than his cheeks were his eyes. "I know we've never been great at conversation, but my parlor seems an odd place to sit in silence."

An'thor chuckled. "Perhaps yours is the only company I can stand anymore."

"Because I know who you are better than any of them."

An'thor shrugged. It was a habit he picked up from Keplan, and not one becoming a legend. He did not care. "I'm worried."

"About what?"

"That you might have been right."

Raven's thick lips curled in a smile, but it did not seem to be a revelation that truly pleased him. "Go on."

"Keplan's clever, he's got the blood, got the vision—no pun intended—but he's unstable. He's young. He's not built to be king. The joy of a monarchy is usually the heir is of middle years by the time the king or queen dies." He glanced over. "Daymir would have been."

Raven sighed. "Don't walk that path, General. It's dangerous and speaks strongly of treason."

"Treason? You turned cannons on your own city. Is this how things will be? Any who speak out against him will be traitor?"

"It's how it's always been, An'thor. Why are you concerned now?"

"He's driving himself too hard. He rarely sleeps. I fear for him," An'thor confessed.

"Is he mad?" Raven's eyes were cold and level.

"He's always claimed that descriptor, surely, for himself."

"But is he truly? I know I hate his mother, his father, they scare the shite right out of me. I would die before I saw either one rule Athrolan. But even I wouldn't argue they were mad."

"I thought it was his power. Lightning and flames aside, his father heard the minds of others. His mother saw the world differently." The general rose, twirling his flask in his hand, eyes fixed on the tooled leather. "But as much as they were strange, we knew what they were. There's never been a creature like Keplan. Not in any history, not in any tale."

"Hasn't there?"

An'thor whirled. "What do you mean?"

Raven ran his blocky hand up the bars of his door then back down. "What other creatures knew men's fates? What other creatures saw the future, saw the past, as we see the present? It's something I've thought on a lot during my weeks in solitude. You might want to as well."

An'thor nodded, though his mind had long since left the conversation and whirled down a dozen dark paths. He let himself out without saying goodbye. The general's gut twisted. Creation and Destruction both had their costs. They all assumed the price would only be taken from Alea and her guard. *When you break the world, mend it again, there are going to be scars, big ones. Ones we didn't plan on.*

The Laen may have been the oldest, the Rakos the strongest. But the gods, the creatures created before humans, they were clever. Conniving. *Gods' Blood.* He locked his door, poured a drink, and knelt to rummage through his desk. The letter had almost been forgotten in the weeks following the coronation and was overshadowed completely by the Banis negotiations. He found the stack of mail from that week and flipped through it. The letter mentioning the One God was distinctive, written on old Berrin vellum. And it was not there. Perhaps he tucked it away in a drawer? Or a chest to not risk Keplan finding it. His glass was all but forgotten as he tore the desk apart. Next came the small box on his bookshelves. Usually it held a flask and a few secret correspondences, along with trinkets from the people whose lives he took in the Crown's name. His last letter from Eras rested in there beside a box of bullets from his revolver. But no fanatic's letter.

Perhaps it had been given to Keplan, perhaps it had been lost. Except An'thor did not lose things. "I'm the general!" His voice pitched off the stone of his room, skittering over the flagging like claws over ice. "I decide what he reads, what he's privy to. I keep him safe!" The iron toe of his boot dented the desk's wood and alcohol splattered over the surface. All the other chapters of his life were written, twisted out of truth decades ago. Athrolan's general was all he was now. He could not lose control, even to a boy. Even to the king he crowned.

CHAPTER THREE

49th Day of Lumord, 1272
The City of Ceir Athrolan, Athrolan

THE CEILING DRIPPED. KEPLAN blinked, watching the rust-stained droplet form, easing from the plaster, cold and fecund. It hovered a moment, then splattered across his brow. He giggled. His skin steamed with fever. The ache of alcohol in his skull had diminished after another small sniff of dust.

I promised myself only once a day. Only when I couldn't sleep. Only when I needed it. He needed it more than he realized. The evening before was a blur of colors and conversation. An'thor's jabs, his spin around the floor late in the evening, Fess as his partner. His laughter bubbled again. Fess was as terrible a dancer as he, especially when drunk. Sea legs made for poor waltzing.

Something else nagged at him, something beyond his fading ale-sick or the part of him screaming in panic that he could never turn back on this addictive path he currently skipped along.

I didn't dance with Rih. An'thor had ordered him to, but that was not the reason. Her eyes picked out every detail of his face. Surely, to try to read his words. It was not a courtier's careful analysis or a future bride's nervous curiosity. *She's sizing me up. A soldier in her ready stance.*

Thunderous knocking interrupted his musing, and he hollered for his guards to open the door. Belatedly, he realized his potential visitors could include the Banis ambassador or the Emperor's Hand. *Or Rih herself.*

Thankfully, the figure that stomped into his chamber was his general instead. "What's got you brooding now?"

Keplan glanced at him but refused to sit up. "I'm not brooding. I'm recovering."

An'thor's dark eyes took in the king's naked sprawl, following the dripping to the crack in the room's ceiling. "I'll have the head of household fetch the masons this afternoon. Kings shouldn't sleep under failing roofs."

Keplan shrugged. "Perhaps if the royal chambers hadn't been host to flies and rot, I'd not have to."

An'thor heaved a sigh. His shaking hands said that if he had begun drinking at all, it had not been enough. "Must you?"

Keplan smiled. "Why are you here? Other than to inspect my chamber walls."

"You're supposed to escort Her Highness Rih-elte about the palace gardens this morning. You have a quarter of an hour to be ready."

"Isn't it raining?" Keplan asked, frowning at the water stain rapidly growing over his ceiling.

An'thor followed his gaze silently, then cleared his throat. "No. And I don't believe that's water, Wardyn."

Keplan sat up with a groan once the man was gone, fingers wiping the liquid from his face. He rubbed it between his fingers. Water was not leaking from his ceiling. It was blood.

He shuddered and paced into the privy. Visions were one thing. Visions he could push aside as figments of his own disturbed imagination. If others saw them he could ignore them no longer. Blood stained his sheets. Leaked from his ceiling. Was it Peraan's? Perhaps, with nowhere left for their spirits to go, the dead stayed close, cluttered the air around the living until they, too, could no longer breathe.

Steaming water eased his muscles and washed away the offending red stains from his skin. Pinked by warmth, even his scars faded. By the time he emerged, his servants had laid out the outfit sewn for the day, made for slow movement and casual walking. He longed for a hike.

Dressed, with his hair tamed into a silver clasp and several colors of face paint on his features, he looked less like a dock urchin. He eyed the ceiling. It no longer dripped, though the crack remained. *Domariigo didn't seem concerned. Or surprised.* He supposed the man had done enough to have more than a few disturbing bloody visions of his own.

Φ

Rih pored over the negotiation transcripts stacked tidily on her desk. There were so many details that went into a simple agreement. An alliance, for all its frills, was nothing more than a wary handshake between travelers lost on the same prairie. *I won't hunt your grouse if you don't eat my gopher.* Except in this version of the metaphor, she noted, she was the grouse.

Nehla's hand slid across the desk, and when Rih looked up, she signed, "You look troubled."

Rih sighed. Was it worth telling her if Bimet did not trust her? She glanced at Bimet, whose steady gaze revealed little. "I'm just tired. Overwhelmed."

"I'd imagine," she answered with a nod. "I hope you'll have time to rest and get to know these halls soon. And surely you've begun to think about who you'll take into your entourage."

"I'm not sure they have the same ideas here. Cliques, it seems, but it seemed that most women in court have only one or two women who attend them," Rih observed. "Though I could use more friends. Perhaps Fess?"

Bimet's brows shot up, signing quickly, "I'm not sure befriending the naval commander is subtle."

Nehla followed the movements, frowning. "I ought to learn your signs, Your Highness. What was that?"

Bimet flashed a tense smile. "Just that perhaps His Eminence wouldn't approve of socializing much with the military."

Nehla sniffed, lips tightening slightly. "Not unless you informed on their every move, I suppose."

Rih appraised her lady in waiting. It was a pointed comment, one that would bring pain if overheard. *She's brave, at least.* Or perhaps, some friendship of Nehla's own gave her enough privilege to not risk punishment. *And that would make her far more dangerous.*

Both women turned to the door, Nehla bouncing up to answer whatever signal had been heard. The king waited in the hall, accompanied by half a dozen lesser nobles and the aforementioned commander. Nehla bowed and glanced back at Rih. "His Majesty is inviting you on a walk. In the gardens."

Rih rose, offering a bow of her own. "Of course, sire. Bimet, would you find my cloak?"

The translator obeyed, appearing a moment later with the garment. The layers of silk and cotton lent the illusion that she wore a sunrise over her shoulders, though the soft peaches and orange hardly accented the purple of her dress. Hoping he did not notice, she wrapped it around herself and took up a place beside him. Bimet walked a step in front, on his other side, so Rih might see her hands.

"I thought you might like to see how different our gardens are from yours. Our land is not as green, but we have some incredible trees." His gaze was distant, eyes seeming to look through her.

Was it she or he who was not quite there? Rih tried a false smile of her own. "I've never seen the Banis gardens either, though I hear they're stunning."

She glanced back at the others. If they listened in on the awkward conversation, they gave no hint, absorbed with some debate. A pang of jealousy shot through Rih's chest as one of the women laughed.

When she looked back, Keplan was watching her. "Can you hear at all?" It was a blunt question and would have been rude without the faint curiosity on his features.

"Not unless the sound is very loud and close. When one of my army sisters blew her whistle beside my ear once, I heard it. Sharp. High." She shrugged, not sure why she tried to describe a sound to someone who could hear it far better than she.

"Army? I thought you were a princess."

Heat flooded her cheeks. Was she supposed to lie? "Any unmarried woman serves the empire, either with her blood or with her body," she demurred.

He looked away but did not seem offended. He seemed not to feel much of anything at all. He seemed content to walk in silence as they stepped through a curved lattice and into a sloped garden. Large chunks of the white stone jutted from the ground, their tops covered with overflowing ivy and mosses. The air had the clear movement of running water. A sweet, biting scent rose with each step. She glanced down, working her slippers deeper into the dense, tiny leaves surrounding the small cobbles of the walkway. White trees with peeling curled bark dotted the slope, delicate branches a mimicry of the massive boles on the hills beyond the city.

They rounded a bend and Keplan whirled. His pale eyes went wide. Rih turned to follow his gaze. Guards and a number of men dressed in brown rushed down the path, arms waving, mouths agape in foreign shouts. Adrenaline ignited in Rih's limbs. She stilled, scanning the landscape. Were they running toward or from something? A snide voice in her mind remarked that this was not RoBal and Athrolan was not at war, but her heart refused to stop hammering.

Bimet's hand gripped her arm as she dragged her out of the way. "It's a dog!" she signed, laughing. "One of the hunting dogs we gifted the king."

Flashing golden fur disrupted the careful, tidy plantings. The animal raced upward toward them, massive paws ripping at the dry earth. Keplan was shouting something at her as he scrambled off the path. Then Rih's legs moved beneath her, skirts lifted in fists as she ran too. A dozen paces, a score, and she was at the nearest gate in the massive wall. Rih glanced back to see the guards gesturing at her, perhaps asking her to catch the creature or beware. She did not care. The animal's eyes were wide and white.

Her fingers found the wrought latch. It was a small door meant for gardeners and groundskeepers, but today, in a time of relative peace, it was unlocked. She pressed and flung the door wide. A rush of golden fur and slaver burst past and then the dog was free.

Rih followed, thighs burning after disuse. Up they ran, past the gouged earth from decades of war, up toward the spindling fingers of white trees. The animal raced in circles, hindquarters bunching as she wove through the grasses, through the trunks. A laugh welled in Rih's throat and she let it free, clapping her hands with each round the dog made. A few more loops and she trotted to a halt. Still the dog's eyes were wide and white. Still Rih's chest heaved, but it was filled with fresh air and, like the dog, her teeth were bared, but now in mirth.

She crouched, hand out. In Ban she often worked with hunting dogs, albeit those trained to hunt people. Still prey was prey, and the commands were the same. "Here," she signaled.

Tail wafting, he approached and sat. Rih ran a gentle hand down the sleek flank and noted absently that the dog had birthed at least one litter within the last year. "Pretty girl," she signed.

Bimet finally caught up to her, eyes crinkled with mirth that she kept, with some success, from becoming an actual smile.

The guards arrived panting a moment later, far less amused. One spoke in Trade, his gestures making it clear he was complaining.

"She was just having fun. We're used to dogs in our city," Bimet explained, signing for Rih's benefit as she spoke in Trade.

"Well she can care after the bitch then, if she's going to let it run about like a wild thing."

Rih's temper frayed. She disliked pulling rank, but if they insisted on speaking over her, she had no interest in manners. "You realize this creature was a gift from me to your king. Dogs are revered in Ban—second only to horses."

The guard, who sported an officer's sigil on his breast, pursed his lips and finally offered a bow. "Forgive me, Your Highness, I didn't think."

"Obviously," Rih retorted, rising. She commanded the dog to follow and moved back to the garden, heart pounding. It was odd to be obeyed, odd to be revered. *Perhaps that's how His Eminence began. A moment of control gone to seed.*

When she returned to them, Vi-baln was glaring but seemed to be unwilling to castigate her in public. Realizing the king might also disapprove of her actions, she turned to find him. Keplan was nowhere to be seen.

Fess's hand brushed her arm, and she mimed having indigestion.

Bimet asked a question, then turned to Rih. "She says His Majesty felt ill and hopes you'll forgive his sudden departure."

Rih frowned, eyes following the path he must have raced down to escape her as she rushed for the hills. "Of course," she answered.

Fess flashed a smile. "I've got to meet for training otherwise I would offer to walk the rest of the way with you. Perhaps another time."

Rih's curiosity flamed. "Training?"

"We've a little group that practices every other afternoon in the officers' hall," Fess explained.

"That sounds lovely!" After a second of biting her lip, she asked, "You said training halls—are they open to anyone? Or are there ones where I might be welcome?"

Fess's heavy shoulders bunched as she crossed her arms in consideration. "Aye. You train?"

"I was a soldier in His Eminence's army until this past year," she repeated, realizing the woman must have been talking over Bimet's translation earlier.

The commander's smile was honest now, and welcoming. "I'll ask the others today, but if they don't mind, why don't you meet us there next time. They're a nice bunch. Mostly. Sometimes our tongues are sharper than our blades nowadays."

Something greater than relief, than desperation burned through Rih's body. She ignored Bimet's signs detailing Vi-baln's protests and bowed to the commander. "I'd be honored."

Φ

The 2nd Day of Valemord, 1272
The Village of Jai, Ban

"Peace!" Reka raised a hand to the guard at the top of the wall. She pushed the braids from her face, letting her take in the old scar and older tattoo. Her outfit was painstakingly devoid of green or vermillion. Still, her heart quickened. A moment passed, then the gate groaned open, just wide enough to permit her. She flashed a smile and slipped through.

A different guard met her on the other side, sliding the bolt home before fixing her with an invasive stare. "What's your business in Jai?"

"My cousin lives here. Ikel." Though not truly related by blood, the two were mistaken for cousins often enough as children. How different they had become that she was unrecognizable.

The guard narrowed his eyes on her tattoo again. "Ah. Border folk. She said you might be by. Monarak something?"

Reka laughed. "Monareka Elang—Reka."

"And you'll be staying how long?"

Until the revolution is won. "For a while. I find myself at a crossroads."

"Where did you ride—" He stopped himself, glancing down the long, dusty but horse-less road behind her. "Where did you travel from?"

"Athrolan, your newest allies. I picked up odd jobs there, but I'm looking for something more fulfilling now. And family."

He frowned at the obvious lines on her face, probably noting that she was well past the years of easy childbearing. "Family?"

"It's been a long time since I saw familiar faces, even in a trade city such as Ceir Athrolan."

"And the Mirikin Hetmir, you know her?"

I bore her children. "Much of what I remember of Mirik is from the Gods' War. I know of the Hetmir a bit—everyone does there, neighbors and all. I couldn't pick her face out of a crowd, though." Reka added a shrug for good measure. "I'm told she's tall."

He did not speak for a moment, eyes inching over her tattoo again.

Reka scratched lazily at the base of one of her braids, inspected her nails, then glanced back at him, unhurried. "Everything all right, sir?"

He nodded, seeming to force the gesture from his distrusting body. "Seems so. Can't be too cautious with the war on. Mirik is everywhere."

How true. Reka made a face. "I'm hoping I can help with that problem, in time."

"Reka?" The voice broke through the guard's questions.

She turned, hand shielding her eyes against the sun-bleached road.

A figure raced through the humble market, people and hens scattering with disgruntled exclamations. Her cousin waved one hand, skirts gripped in the other fist. "Reka!"

Years washed from Reka's heart at the sight. For a moment the street was a mirror, a glimpse into a different life Reka may have led. "Ikel!" The raised hand turned from shield to wave.

Reka's laugh burst like a sob from within her, and her arms locked around her cousin's soft body. *Home.* It was not a sensation she was familiar with, not for a long while yet. "Fates, I missed you. I missed you so much, I forgot what it felt like."

"Oh…" Ikel's voice choked on the emotion and she pulled back, gaze alighting on Reka's scar, her faded tattoo, the myriad lines around her one blazing eye. "We missed you too."

We. In the two decades of her employment with Mirik, her friendship with Bren, there had never been a "we." A "me," surely, with all the complex emotions he could never seem to let go of and all the distance Kemmer forced from her own shame. But there had never been a "we," not since she left her father.

"If she's all through here, I'll sponsor her. In my house, of course," Ikel told the guard, glancing back at Reka. "She's family."

The guard waved them away, mouth a thin line. "Just be sure Jani's here 'fore dark."

"He'll be there early I'm sure, just to escape us two chattering grass squirrels as we recount our decades apart!"

Reka snorted. No matter what paths she took in life, she never thought of herself as a chattering grass squirrel. Her callouses pressed against different ones, but just as weathered, on Ikel's hand as they navigated the market. The lizard tattooed across the dun skin of her left cheek and brow had faded to brown and olive.

She would come back to peruse the wares and listen to gossip, but that would be tomorrow or the next day. "Jani's taken up a guard post? Last you wrote he was still working for the inn. Caravan guard for hire?"

"He was," her cousin agreed, shouldering a basket she must have dropped in her dash to greet Reka. "Not enough caravans to make a proper living. He was home half the days. And mind you, it was nice to have help with the children, but the man makes such a mess being home so much and gets underfoot worse than a litter of puppies."

Reka tried to take the basket to help, laughing at Ikel's determined wave.

"I'm not the one who walked here from another kingdom." The lines of her smile tightened slightly. "Then the matet decreed everyone not a farmer or trader be put on the walls, guarding against Mirikin invasion."

"Fat lot it did. I'm walking right in," Reka muttered, scanning the town as they walked. Guards with non-issued weapons. Old spears, battered bearers. Ankle sandals instead of knee-high armor. Now she regretted not having a moment to find her bearing when she arrived. The signs of war were stark in a town this small. Half of the guards were male, it seemed, but whether that was from proximity to the border or necessity, Reka was not sure.

"Rek?"

She glanced over, realizing she had missed Ikel's last few comments. "I'm sorry, it's been a long walk. All of it, I suppose."

Ikel's fingers squeezed hers. "I'm sure. Let's get you settled." She drew up a moment later at a rel on the corner of a narrower road. Here the street was packed brown earth, not the tidy red cobbles from the marketplace. Poles jutted from the doorway's upper corner, woven grasses provided a sunscreen for the entrance. Someone had woven the fluffy tufts of the grasses into a symbol in the center. Reka tilted her head. It was an antelope. Smile renewed, she stepped down into the kitchen. The windows ringing the portion of the house that stood above ground let in soft, hot sun, filtered through stiff grass curtains. Reka closed her eyes and breathed. Baking. Warm earth. Buzzing insects. A faint crackle rose from the fire in the deep central pit when Ikel shoved a pan into the coals.

When Reka opened her eyes again, a young boy stood in the doorway, tugging on one earlobe. He stopped the moment his mother glanced up from the hearth, hand disappearing into a pocket.

"Who're you?"

"Kas, don't be rude. I told you your aunt would be here soon. This is Reka. Our mothers were sisters."

Reka raised a casual hand. She never knew how to deal with children. They were like horses to her—both too knowing and oblivious at once. "Hello, Kas. Thanks for letting me stay."

He did not respond, so she turned back to the pan. "Haven't had Banis tea in a long while. Though it's becoming more popular in Athrolan now. Trends of fashion and food are subject to alliances as much as anything."

Ikel snorted. "Or perhaps it's just better than that bitter dirty water the Marbleheads drink."

Reka's brows rose at the slur. She loved the Athrolani as much as she loved anyone—that is to say not at all. But not because they were Athrolani. *People are not my favorite.* "Things haven't been easy?"

Ikel's gaze flicked to her son and then back to the tea. "There have been many travelers of late. Ones with information. Others with spears. It's why I wrote to you. Something is coming." She stirred the thick contents of the pan with a broad spoon. "Family ought to be here, lest we fall on different sides of these new walls."

Reka's nerves sparked at the words. She had not walked from Ceir Athrolan and every ally she knew to be on one or the other side of some metaphorical wall. "What have you heard?"

"Kahma wrote me, just a few weeks ago."

"Kahma? Kahma's coming?" Kas asked, bouncing on the balls of his bare feet.

Ikel's lips thinned. "Kahma is in the army, we don't know when we'll see her next. Why don't you go play with your sister?"

"She's weaving and told me I should go eat horseshite—"

"Then go play by yourself," she sighed, frowning as he disappeared deeper into the house. "And don't say that word!"

"Kahma? Someone from Jani's family?"

"His sister. We'll discuss it later, once little ears have gone to bed."

Reka laughed softly. "I don't know how you do that."

"Do what?"

"Deal with them. It's not something that ever interested me, parenthood."

"You never met someone," Ikel answered, as if it was the most obvious thing in the world.

"I've had people whose company I enjoyed more than some. Many even. Pleasure. Conversation. I just never," she shrugged, "fell. Never missed the lack of it, either."

Ikel hummed as if she did not quite believe her cousin, but pressed the matter no further. Instead, she tugged a drawer from the underside of one of the steps leading down to the hearth and pulled out two mugs. A handful of spices went into each, then she poured the pale, thick liquid over each before handing one to Reka.

The Spy Master inhaled the steam. *Lest we fall on different sides.* Had she made a choice against Mirik? Against Athrolan? She combed her fingers through her braids. *I'm not a traitor.* How could one be a traitor if they walked into their employer's study and demanded leave? And he was an ambassador, not the hetmir—he had not been hetmir in decades. *Besdies, I'm not even Mirikin.* She was not sure what she was. The Border nations were all but dissolved, split by the new borders of empires and kingdoms, scattered from past wars, married into a dozen other cultures.

"You all right?"

"Feeling a bit..." She searched for the word. "Lost? Uprooted, I suppose."

"'My blood is the river, carrying my feet across mountains.'" It was an old Border saying, one that spoke to their staunch belief that choice and change were inherent.

"I've let my blood stagnate. I need to remember its pulse and flow."

"Is that why you're here?"

"You wrote me a letter."

"I know why I invited you. Doesn't tell me why you accepted. I thought I'd have to wait a year, two, even, to see your face. You're always speaking of how busy you are, how your jobs take you far and wide."

"Hardly. I mostly roam between cities. Finding people. Losing others." She thought of Hylier and his earnest trust in Daymir, in the order of good and evil. "Making friends."

"And you were able to just leave, you must have high standing."

Reka knew Ikel's verbal fishing was out of love and concern, but Reka disliked being on the receiving side of questioning. Empathy flashed for all the people she wheedled for information. "I suppose. My employer is trusting, sometimes to the point of ignorance. I told him I had a job here, following information. By the time he realizes my reports have stopped, my trail will be long cold."

"What else, then? Beyond work or war?" Ikel settled beside her, hands working on a loaf that must be for their dinner later. Always busy. Always a task. Reka took the bowl of dough from her and began to knead.

Ikel's smile softened and she pulled down dried roots to chop.

Reka had not thought much beyond either work or war in a long while. Five years of living in Mirik, in the small town across the island. Her body, pregnant and full and aching in places she hoped she had not had, was not hers. Meat. "I don't know who I am without work and war."

"You're performing the ruak."

Reka snorted. "Hardly."

"Aren't you though? You've gone so long without yourself, you must reclaim them or declare your new true self. And so long without your people too. You don't recognize it."

"I've never not been me, this sack of bones and blood," Reka protested. She had always been so sure of who she was that the ruak—a rite of transition into a new role or identity—had never seemed necessary.

"What you are changes. New water and stone dust have replaced the blood and bone of you. You're the same—ever changing."

"You're like a library," Reka countered with a smile. "All your thoughts sound pretty but there are many. I don't always agree with them and rarely do they agree with each other." Reka smirked. "That's if I read them at all."

"Just think about it." Ikel swatted at her. "I'm happy you're home."

"I'm happy you're my home."

Φ

The 2nd Day of Valemord, 1272
The City of Ceir Athrolan

The room was large and open, taller than Rih was used to. The variety of weapons was exciting, if only because some were unfamiliar to her. A dozen target quintins lined the back wall, and another room to the left held grappling mats and ropes and walls for climbing. Two men already sparred in there.

Fess's invitation had mentioned a main training hall, but it was unclear which that meant. She glanced back at Bimet, who shrugged.

"I hear women's voices in the next room."

Rih followed her across the sawdusted floor to another broad, open doorway. Fess glanced up from her seat on a bench and waved. When she had finished lacing her soft training boots, she jogged over.

"I'm glad you're joining us." The commander jerked her sharp chin at the men on the mats. "That's Pomodan—the blond—and Jep. Pomo's captain of the guard in the Silver Apron. His partner, there, is the Lord Provost Qaral. Menna and Colonel Curiel are the women by the wrestling rack most interested in drinking their tea."

Rih laughed, and the women glanced over. One raised a hand, the other a skeptical eyebrow. Rih felt heat in her cheeks but steeled herself and went over. "Good morning. Commander Fess was kind enough to invite me to your training session." She offered her arm in the Eastern casual greeting. When they didn't take it, she added a few signs. "You can call me Rih."

The woman who waved took the hand and turned to the translator. "Tell her I say hello and she can call me Curiel."

Bimet smiled patiently. "Just speak to her, like you would anyone else. I'll do the rest."

Curiel's pale cheeks flushed red, and she looked back to Rih. "I'm sorry, that was probably rude. We're not so used to…ah, differences, in the military here."

Rih glanced at the entirely white faces and able bodies and smiled. "I gathered." She turned to the other woman. "You're Menna?"

The woman glanced at Rih's hand as if it was covered in horse dung and turned back to her friend. "Why don't we practice riding? Somewhere where the air is fresh."

Curiel winced. "Maybe later. You can ride alone—I could really stand to practice my grappling. Shoulder's finally feeling better."

All pretense of polite conversation disintegrated. "How can you? How can you practice war with their queen, their figurehead? She's brought nothing but pain to this city!" Menna's gestures flew wildly, composure broken. "She'll bring nothing but death!"

Sawdust puffed in the wake of the door, and no one seemed willing to speak.

Rih's nerves hummed, burning in preparation of violence. *But I was invited.*

Curiel's expression wavered between strained and awkward. "Perhaps just give her time. I know Menna. Her words, though cruel, are often taken back when she's had some time to think."

Rih did not feel particularly charitable. "I will still practice here, as this is my home."

"No one's asking you to leave, Rih," Fess offered. "I'm sorry for Menna. She's a good woman, just hard sometimes."

Rih's hands tightened on the case of her atlatl. "I know many women like that—more concerned with tearing one another down for the coveted favor of men. Most of those I know, those I call my friends, know that's not how we succeed. It's how we lose."

"I think it has more to do with you being Banis," Curiel hazarded, rising to follow them to the benches to don her training vest.

"I wondered. In Ban we have soldiers from all over our empire, all shades of brown and white and black." She flashed a bitter grin, setting her case on the bench. "All equally crushed under the officers' sandals."

Rih knelt to unclip the latches on the wooden box and flipped the lid open. She hoped the conversation would veer from justifying Menna's words in an attempt to comfort her.

Someone knelt in the sawdust beside her. It was Fess. "I've never had the chance to see one up close."

Rih lifted the atlatl from the formed silk and slid away the covering. "This one is new to me. My practice ones were a bit lighter. I admit, I'm far from a master."

"What is your best weapon?"

"The spear. But I promised my teacher I'd practice, so though she might not be watching over my shoulder now, I imagine if I ever see her again it will be the first thing she asks." Rih grinned. "And I've never been good at lying to her."

The atlatl was heavy and smooth, the wood polished rather than worn. The grip was bound with leather, rough side up to help her grip. Copper rings bound each end of the grip, the one at the very base bearing a ring for emblems of luck or prowess. Rih fingered it, wondering what she might bind there. The darts were massive, a hand-span longer than those she was used to. *A proper war dart.* If they only knew they had sent the leader of a rebellion away, unsupervised, with such a weapon. It lessened the sting of Menna's racism.

Curiel's fingers flexed as she observed the beautiful weapon. She glanced at the door where Menna had disappeared. "Perhaps one day you could teach me?"

"I'd like to." Rih bit her lip. "Maybe in turn you could show me the grappling."

Φ

The 13th Day of Valemord, 1272

Incense and the faint odor of tepid tea filled the throne room. The walls were wheeled back into place, shrinking the room to the usual size. Even with the velvet cushions, the throne was dark, and the stone bit into his thin legs until they tingled. He shifted, hoping his expression of vague interest did not slip.

"What can we do, Your Majesty?" the farmer at his feet asked.

Keplan gnawed on his lip. He had not heard the last few lines the man said. *Something about crops and blight.* "Our growing friendship with Ban offers a solution to the blight, Master—" He glanced at the herald standing by the dais's edge.

"Master Wimsen, sire," the boy whispered.

"Master Wimsen. By next spring we will be planting Banis wheat in place of our own weaker crop."

"Banis wheat is fine, sire, but what about this winter—"

"I'm afraid His Majesty can only hear one concern apiece during each audience, Master Wimsen," Daymir interjected. "Please return, and we may have more answers and time to hear your further thoughts."

Keplan did not want further questions, but the man's concern nagged at him. *What about this winter?* He could barely think beyond the next few days, let alone an entire season away. *In that time your kingdom may be on the brink of starvation.* The bright light lancing through the glass dome belied the mercurial weather, but he felt the discord in his bones.

The man was ushered out and the throne room was finally quiet. Keplan pinched the bridge of his nose. His nerves spiraled into the trembling artificial adrenaline as the dust faded from his body. "Is that the last of them?"

Hylier shook his head. "I'm sorry, sire, there's another half hour before your audience ends. Just some discussion left."

"I expected the questions regarding Ban," the consulate noted, "but fates, I hoped they would involve more about what we'd gain and less…" she faltered.

"Blatant hate?" Keplan supplied, flipping through the pages of his personal notes scattered on his lap desk.

Daymir hummed in agreement. "Even if we don't have the knowledge to address the issue now, that last man raised a fair point about winter."

A commotion rose in the hall and Keplan's nerves sang. His memory flashed with images from his coronation, the crown new and heavy on his head. His ears still rang with the sharp smacks. He blinked. His gaze fell to An'thor's hip and the weapon that rested there. The general picked filth from under his cracked yellow nails. Guards still argued in the hall.

The consulates petered into silence, giving up the pretense that nothing happened outside the double doors.

"It's an open audience! I demand my right at audience!"

"Mistress—"

"I'm a 'miss,' you sorry sack of pigshit!"

Keplan bit back a giggle, ignoring Daymir's sharp glare. He enjoyed a good barb.

"Miss, then," even through the door his voice dripped frustration, "you will need to compose yourself prior to going before His Majesty the King—"

The doors slammed open. A woman burst in, face swollen and red from weeping.

Hylier's hand dropped to his sword, stepping down from the dais.

She staggered forward, falling to her knees before Keplan. "Your Majesty, please! My friend, my beautiful patriot of a man, was cut down in cold blood, and you refuse to do a thing. A thing!"

The barmaid. Even through the mask of grief, Keplan recognized her harsh features. Distaste billowed in his gut. "You mean the traitor Peraan?"

"He weren't a traitor!" Her whole body shook.

If dust left Keplan capable of empathy, he might have pitied her. Instead, his pen sketched the frazzled lines of her hair, the wrinkles at the corners of her bloodshot eyes. He added a mole for dramatic effect, though upon glancing up he realized she did indeed sport a beauty mark just below her left eye.

"Why won't you do something? He was an honorable man, one who dreamt of better for us, just as you claim to."

A boot nudged his sharply beneath the table, and he forced himself to focus. "What do you propose we do, miss? We're recovering from a war—a war your Peraan figure-headed, I might add. In war people die. We extend our condolences, but we are in the midst of negotiations and heading into summer with hardly anything to show for our fields' harvest. Your friend's murder is hardly our first priority."

Rih leaned forward, hands flashing several signs. Until that moment, she had been still, learning only. Her translator quickly rose. "Your Majesty, we offer our tracking dogs, skilled in hunting not just game, but human marks as well. Murder on your streets is hardly the way to begin an alliance, let alone a time of peace."

Dogs? Keplan opened his mouth to reply.

"The scent is surely gone," Hylier interjected, "with all the smells in the city. I hope with our continued relationship with Ban, our guards can learn to use tracking dogs, however."

The woman's eyes narrowed on him. "I know you! I know your face!"

"Of course you do, I'm the one Peraan spoke out against. And your king." Panic fanned the flames of Keplan's temper, and he waved for them to escort the woman away.

Daymir leaned forward. "A guard will take your statement, and if we have further news, we will request to see you during our next audience in three days."

"Two days, Your Highness," Hylier whispered.

"Two days from now," he corrected himself.

Keplan watched them escort her out, barely hearing her continued screaming. He could not marry the man she spoke of with the fleshy face he watched life flee from under his own hands. His stomach clenched.

"Sire," Fess leaned forward, "I know she's grief-stricken, but murder in the city is a bit much to ignore—especially someone as influential as Peraan."

Keplan's gaze flicked to her. "He was a pile of horseshite and we all know it. Influence or not. Before I ascended, I had the misfortune of crossing his path not once but twice. Whoever killed the man did us a favor."

"That may be, but retaliation might be a concern." Hylier's voice was low, and the stare he fixed Keplan with was heavy. "The city might be busy investigating other things, and rightfully so, but perhaps a double guard until we determine how far Peraan's influence reached."

"You seem to have a fair idea of his group, Captain," Keplan countered, failing to keep the taunting edge from his voice. "Report back in a week on the Peraan situation—both his actions and the end he very much deserved to meet."

Hylier's bow was sharp, and he did not wait to be dismissed before stalking from the room.

"I'm not certain this meeting is getting us anywhere." The Head of the House of Nobles sighed. "My reports from the Western Provinces aren't good either. Their farmers who were able to plant the Banis seed still struggle. Their fields were slow to sprout. At this rate we'll be harvesting at least two weeks late. More, I fear."

Political intrigue was his bane, but crops and gardening he knew. "Late? I thought the Banis wheat was immune to the blight. Or resistant to it, at the least."

The Consul of Agriculture rubbed a hand over their weary face. "Blight's not the issue now. Banis wheat is used to long, hot days. Little rain. Even in the west, where it's warmer, we've had nothing but clouds and wind since you ascended the throne, sire."

Keplan faltered. *It strangles the world.* "This isn't just an Athrolani problem, is it?"

They shrugged. "I can hardly know. We could ask our allied neighbors, but I would advise against it. While we've enjoyed a few decades of peace with Berr and far longer with Sunam, showing how poor our current hand is would be a dangerous choice when we're already seen as so weak. One more political storm and Athrolan is finished."

Finished. Like most of his thoughts lately, it was fleeting but left fingerprints across his mind. Stains of every idea he no longer dwelled on cluttered his thoughts so thoroughly that nothing was clear. He could forsake love and safety and take a throne to prevent civil war and accept his bloodline and all its burdens to make a kingdom listen. Or he could breathe dust until his mind was quiet for a moment. But no one, save the gods, could change the weather.

"Wardyn!"

He blinked and looked up.

An'thor's black eyes bored into him. "If you're too distracted to focus on your kingdom starving, then perhaps you ought to leave the decisions to us."

"If you're so impatient that you won't allow me to think of a solution, perhaps you're not fit to be a general," Keplan snapped back. Tension rolled over him, and Fess heaved a sigh.

One of the commissioners rolled their eyes.

Honesty. "You can tout my titanic blood all you wish, Dormariigo, but even I can't part the clouds and force the sun. I know our shipment is slated for next year. Did they plant all that was allotted them?"

"Each farmer was given a certain portion, based on their usual yield. It was our hope that in a year or two we could have crossbred the two species, but if we get too little yield, we'll be forced to grind every bit just to survive the winter."

Above the bells rang.

It was all Keplan could do to stay seated while they tolled. Once silence fell again, he rose. "I need to think on this. The Agricultural Guild should research the heartiest varieties—even those our neighbors plant. If keeping our people alive means displaying our poor hand, then so be it. Audience dismissed."

He stalked from the room, gloved hands clenched against the onslaught of other people's worry.

"Sire, we need to talk." Hylier fell in behind him, easily keeping pace with the king's frantic stride.

"I thought I told you to speak with the city guard."

"I thought we were a bit beyond that. She recognized you."

Keplan thanked the guard who opened his chamber door, then flung himself unceremoniously into his desk chair. His boots scattered dust and dirt across his audience notes. "It's not like they're going to believe her. Not against me, against a king." The world's heart thundered in his blood, underscored by his father's fire and his mother's freezing flood.

"You're not a king, not to them, not yet, not by an arrow's shot," Hylier growled. "She's a trusted member of the city, the Silver Apron at that, and she recognizes you—a man who used to frequent a number of ill-patroned bars and, by the way, still does. They're going to listen."

"So what if they do?" Keplan snapped. "I've got guards, an army, a horned psychopath who murdered a dozen people to get me here. I don't know why you needed to discuss this."

Hylier's face lost every ounce of his usual gentleness. "You doodled a portrait of a grieving woman while she wept at your feet, you monster!"

Laughter bubbled up Keplan's throat. It was not funny and he knew it, but his body was no longer his. Now, he only had to worry about gripping the reins of his petulant tongue. He clapped a gloved hand over his mouth. "I am a monster, aren't I? But Athrolan always knew it. Domariigo certainly did."

Hylier lunged across the room, stopping just short of Keplan's shaking body, chest heaving. "I've never wished you weren't king more than I do in this moment."

"So you could strike me?"

"So I thought Athrolan had a chance." He sagged against the desk, rubbing exhausted eyes. "I'm your informant, your captain. I am not your maid to tidy the bloody mess you left in your wake."

"What do I pay you for, then?" Perhaps the buzzing in his blood was not fear but that of flies come to feast on his soul, his empathy long dead, rotting where his heart should be. The buzzing kept him from mirrors, kept him from anything that might expose the truth. *He's right, though.*

When his mouth opened again, he swore the voice was not his. Perhaps the one before had not been his, and this one was the echo of the Slummer bar boy. "Hylier, she's is not the only one grieving. I lost a friend. One of the only ones I've had. I lost someone who took me in not in spite of what I am, but because of it. Even though my sheer presence put her business in danger. Cost her patrons. Cost her life. So forgive me if I can't find a shred of mercy in my heart for someone who sheltered Mirrel's murderer. You know how I knew it was Peraan?"

"Because it's obvious, because you saw the list I left for you?"

"I only saw that when I returned. I knew because I went into that courtyard, pressed my hand into her bloodstains and lived her death until I recognized Peraan's face." Keplan staggered to the bookshelf, hand resting on the box that held the dust. *Fates, the feelings are loud today.* "Now, tell me again that I'm a monster."

Hylier had the grace to blush, though his pale skin turned every change of emotion into pinked cheeks. "I see your point. But mine still stands true. Two truths may be at once, sire. You've ended civil war. You've allied with Ban. You've planned to marry. And you've murdered. All in the name of peace. But, sire, when you're king, peace begins with you."

Keplan looked away. "Have you told anyone? Anyone about this?"

"Fates, no. I gave you his name. I gave you evidence of his intent. I burned your bloody clothes. At this point I'm almost as culpable as you."

Keplan's pale eyes flicked to Hylier's blue ones and he felt a smile flit across his face. "Monster."

Hylier heaved a sigh. "I'm meeting with Daymir this afternoon, and I'll see what others think of the accusation. If I think of something—something other than framing an innocent person or outright murdering the woman—then I'll tell you. Because, sire, neither of those are options."

"Come to me tomorrow night, then. Perhaps both of us can find a solution." Keplan looked away, listening to the door slam behind his informant. Murder was the easiest solution. The shred of himself he still recognized knew it was not an option. But at this moment he could hear nothing over the sound of a thousand thoughts and something he might have called shame.

CHAPTER FOUR

The 20th Day of Valemord, 1272
The City of Ceir Athrolan, Athrolan

"I WAS WONDERING IF I'd have to drag you down from the rooftop myself," Daymir remarked, taking in the king's windblown hair. "Your father liked them too."

Keplan rolled his eyes. "I'll have to find another hiding spot, then."

"Hylier tracked you to the slums, I'm sure he can find you again."

"Except I dole out his purse now." Keplan dropped into one of the chairs at the regent's broad desk. "What's first here?"

"An official notice of investigation from Inspector Greton, a missive from Fort Shadow, a dozen invitations to noble dinners and dances and a request for a private audience," Daymir rattled off.

"Fort Shadow?" Keplan leaned forward to get a better glimpse of the map lacquered to the top of Daymir's desk. "Which one's that?"

Daymir shook his head with a wince. "Ah, Fort Godbane, rather. Built on the site of the Athrolani camp during the siege of Fort Shadow. Old warhorses, new commands and all that."

Keplan did not answer, but something in the regent's gray eyes told him remarking on the slip would be a mistake. "Of course."

He pushed aside the invitations. "Mind looking these over? I'm not as well versed in who has influence here."

"I've been exiled for two decades, Wardyn, you think I know any better? Influence can change overnight. I'm proof of that." Daymir tugged the stack over, glancing at a few names. "I didn't even know Lord Tevon had a daughter."

"She was supposed to take the throne instead of me," Keplan muttered. "Maybe I'll ask her if she'll reconsider over dinner." He skimmed the investigator's report, then folded it into his pocket. They had yet to find the bag Keplan dropped in the gutter. *Some slum-rat probably ran off with it.* If they did find it, however, it could lead them to the dust dealer. Something told him even the man's drug-addled mind would recall a scarred face if enough coin were offered.

"News of that man—Peraan?"

"Little. I guess someone came forward having seen something, testimony scheduled in a few days." Keplan groaned. "I'd hoped to avoid starting my reign with murder."

Godbane's missive stated little else than reports of Mirikin and Banis skirmishes just across the border. They requested more grain, which Keplan denied and signed with a pang. "Is that it?"

"Audience request." Daymir handed it to him without looking up from the invitation he was drafting.

Nena'phe lui Hiral.

Even written in innocuous scribe's script, the name sent a twinge of apprehension up his spine. "It's an asai name."

"I heard they all retreated to the Northlands with their cousins," Daymir remarked. "Other than the general, I met very few. Not the friendliest, I've heard."

"Then let's hope this one's different."

He slit open the seal of the palace heraldry and leaned back to read.

Your Majesty King Keplan Wardyn of the Heartland and the Topin Hills

We were honored at the response from your regent, His Highness Lord Daymir. I now humbly ask for an audience with you to discuss our prophet's news. I know when you hear her words you, too, will understand the might of the One True God's power."

"Fates, what is this?" Keplan whispered. When Daymir glanced up, he repeated the words aloud.

Daymir did not respond. Instead, he drew a thick sheet of vellum from his desk and slid it over to the king. Then he moved to stand before the window, hands clasped before him. His eyes were distant. "This comes at an inconvenient time."

"Inconvenient?" Keplan glanced at the letter but could not bring himself to touch it. "You replied. To a letter I never saw."

"Read it. Then I will ask forgiveness."

Even through the thin silk of his gloves, the vellum irritated his fingers. With the creeping itch came images of a dozen monarchs, warlords, even the Banis emperor himself unfolding similar letters, scanning the same heretical words. Even through the dread, he found himself scoffing at the final paragraph. "'The Dhoah' Laen herself—' they think I won't know where my own mother is?"

Daymir's gaze skittered from the window to the door. "They aren't wrong, Your Majesty."

"You invited heretics into my kingdom!" he bellowed.

"Athrolan needs order, structure, especially following a civil war." Daymir straightened then, an echo of his former presence, but imposing nonetheless. "I hardly think you can call them heretics when their prophets share your visions. Your mother's visions."

"My mother's—" Keplan whirled. "One true god? She ripped the souls from the gods' chests. Only a madman calls himself a prophet, but not even I've stooped so low."

"The general and I discussed it and planned on telling you when it became relevant. After the wedding. After negotiations. How could I explain that Alea crossed the kingdom looking for you and for answers?"

Keplan snarled and, letter gripped in his clammy glove, strode from the room. Daymir's exile years before was based on an attempt at swindling. Was this more of the same? Was this just a symptom of his own particular form of insanity? Daymir's confession of fading memory had been shared in confidence. *This was the only way to unite us. Unite the city.* An'thor was not to be trusted, but if every person in his government held a different secret it was only a matter of time before one brought the whole tremulous thing crashing down.

He pounded on the general's door.

It jerked open, black sclera tinged red with alcoholic bloodshot. "What?"

Keplan's whole body shook, mind torn between his own reality and the half a dozen others rampaging through his consciousness. "Is this a bad time?"

An'thor swayed, wiping spittle and wine from his mouth a moment too late. "Wardyn. I'm beginning to think there is never a good time to see you."

Keplan did not smile. He did not have the patience for An'thor's bitterness. *But no one has seen what he has.* "I need to speak with you. When you're—" he stopped himself from implying there ever was a time the man was sober, "not busy."

An'thor shoved his door open wider but made no other move.

Keplan edged around him. The room was in disarray. Papers and letters littered the floor, and soot from the cold hearth stained the carpet in whatever manic path the general paced. He walked the same route now: hearth to window to desk to hearth.

Keplan settled on the broad window ledge. "I received a request for an audience. From someone who follows Orabon Marum of Tut Kunis."

An'thor glanced up, eyes sharpened but not surprised.

"So, you did know about the letter," Keplan noted. "And when were you thinking of informing me that fanatics were on my stoop? Or that my mother is apparently involved?"

An'thor's pacing slowed. He extended one pale hand. "May I?"

Keplan loosened his fingers, letting the vellum drop to the filthy floor.

If An'thor was bothered by the childish display, he had the fortitude not to comment. He stooped with a groan and scanned the letter.

"I find it absurd that you and Blackhouse conspired to bring these idiots to my kingdom. When did the first letter arrive?"

"A few days before the attempt on Azimir's life."

"Before Mirrel died, you mean," Keplan reminded.

"Exactly. You've not been exactly easy to find or speak with. Since the moment you wore the crown you've done nothing but avoid your duties—"

"Not the point," Keplan spat. "Why did you invite them here?"

An'thor sighed and slumped into his chair. "Honestly, I didn't. This was Daymir. Fates know why." An'thor's black eyes turned on his desk and the disarray across it. "I showed him the first letter. That's all. It was a brief discussion, mostly consisting of me scoffing at the idea of a prophet."

The fight left Keplan but the panic did not. "Why would he do this?"

"Best ask him."

Keplan looked down at his hands, not seeing the delicate fabric but the battered, stained palms beneath. "Were Tzatia's accusations against him true, then?"

"Doubtful, but the queen was scared. Too scared to see what he was actually doing or believe him. He's always been calculating but never cruel."

"And what about sane?" Keplan's words were a whisper.

An'thor stared at him. "That tastes a bit rich, coming from your mouth."

"Humor me."

An'thor shrugged. "He's old."

"Talk about rich—"

"Oh, piss off," An'thor continued. "He's not the same man he was decades ago. Honestly, though, we were never close. When I was in Athrolan before my exile, he was a child. Clever and occasionally petulant, like most children. Our time here during the Gods' War overlapped very briefly, and I was frankly distracted by your mother."

"So was he, if I recall."

An'thor grimaced. "I hardly had the same intentions. Your mother was pretty enough, but I'm not in the habit of courting monsters. Death, perhaps, but not monsters. Regardless of who wanted to tup your mother, Daymir's different. Withdrawn, maybe. I wrote it off to being alone for all those years. Is there something else I should know?"

Keplan was relieved to no longer be discussing his mother's suitors, but this was not a more comfortable turn of conversation. "I assume you remember his grandfather's last years."

"Better than most."

"He told me in confidence, in the bar in Marl Orna. It appears whatever took His Majesty King Xavier also has its claws in Blackhouse."

An'thor rubbed a pale, rough hand over his weathered face. He took a swig from his flask before sucking his teeth. "Well isn't that a fun new delight."

"Have some decency, Domariigo," Keplan muttered. "I wouldn't tell you except I'm afraid he's making choices while not...well."

"Choices including inviting this prophet's followers into Ceir Athrolan?"

"Exactly." Keplan steeled himself. "They mention my mother. Daymir said something about her visions. Last I knew she was still cloistered in the Hartland."

The general's pale hands shook as he found a large bottle under a pile of maps and took a swig. He offered it to Keplan, who shook his head. When it was stoppered again, he drew a breath. "That was the part I scoffed at. And the part Daymir proved right. Before he came here, before he slipped out of Manor Black to meet you, even, he received two visitors. Your parents. They left not long after you, it seemed. Searching for you and for answers. And, apparently, despite what the world feels like, her power hasn't waned. Whatever it is you both sense—and whatever this prophet spouts—is real."

"They're wrong, Domariigo. They have to be." Keplan dropped his head into his hands.

"Then let them come. Let them prove themselves wrong."

The floor trembled under Keplan's stiff boots. His stomach roiled at the thought. His parents had been doting, if protective. Playful, if occasionally preoccupied. Now he knew what tangled their thoughts. The idea of his mother, thin and pale, climbing the mountains between Tut Kunis and Marl Black ate at his heart. Any residual effects of dust were burned in the wake of worry. He finally met An'thor's eyes. "This is too much. How do you do it?"

"Do what?"

"Live. I'm staring down the bolt of this titanic crossbow, finding my own hand on the string more often than not. I don't know what I'm doing, other than I cannot fail. How do you do it?" he asked again. "No one survives as long as you, wins as much as you have, no one becomes a legend without some secret. How do you do it?"

"You don't want to be a legend."

"No, but my parents already made me one. How do you stomach it? I can't sleep. My body hums. My thoughts are quiet, but I can't sleep."

An'thor frowned at the wide eyes, the shaking hands. "You been drinking?"

Keplan's laugh rasped from his throat and he sank onto a bench. An'thor could not know about the dust. Far too many terrible secrets filled the palace. His entire path to the throne was littered with things best left hidden. "A bit."

"That's my secret," An'thor muttered. "But lately not even that helps."

Φ

The 24th of Valemord, 1272

Despite a long bath and Nehla's careful tending to her hands and head, Rih's nerves were raw. Only an hour stood between her and her wedding. She paced, still dressed in her loose dressing gown. With each turn past the door to her parlor, she caught sight of Nehla and Bimet holding some argument. Both had been dressed in their wedding finery for hours, their muted lavender and pink meant to accent the brilliant jewel tones of Rih's own attire.

It was bitterly cold, as if the Athrolani winter decided to wrap her in its arms as a sign of welcome. *Or warning.* Still, on her text trip by her balcony, she flung open the doors, letting the wind bite into her already goosefleshed skin. *Anything. I would give anything to feel something other than dread.*

Bimet's hand was almost hot against her chilled wrist. "Rih, it's time. We'll never get you into your gown if we don't start now."

She cast a pleading look at the interpreter.

"I'm sorry."

Rih glanced back. "Where's Nehla?"

"She's informing the glorious Vi-baln that you'll be ready shortly, but you needed a few more minutes to prepare yourself for the magnitude of marriage," Bimet explained, shutting the doors again.

"The magnitude of this mistake, you mean." She followed her into the dressing room.

"I told her to just wait, but she seemed to think it necessary."

"Is she his ally? Or just oblivious?" Rih dropped her gown, staring at the dress before her with nausea.

"It is hard to say." Bimet's hand was suddenly hard on hers, squeezing for a moment, then releasing to continue. "Don't trust anyone. Even here. Even when he's left. Trust no one."

"Except for you," Rih replied, trying for a smile.

Bimet did not return it, driving home the serious tone of her words. "We are all we have right now."

"I'm terrified after all of this he'll meet me at RoBal's gates in a horrific reveal, like 'blessed baniol' in tiles."

Bimet's face softened at the reference to their beloved game. "I doubt he plays well enough to hide so many moves from you. Even if he plays from the capital. Now, unless you plan on stunning the entire court with your physique, I suggest we get you dressed."

Soon layers of silk swathed her form. Her kalas was a rich plum, woven in a way that shimmered with blood red as she turned. The three wraps over it were varied from deep eggplant to the bright purple of prairie horsetail buds. Nehla reappeared in time to arrange her headdress. Black threads wove between the tiny silver links of her net, and the whole was decorated with garnets, amethysts, and feathers the color of dawn. A crimson sash cut across her waist in a fabric disembowelment.

"The piercings are a mistake," she worried.

Nehla frowned. "Why do you think that?"

"They're hardly Athrolani."

"You're hardly Athrolani," the serving woman replied, kneeling before Rih to help her into her slippers.

Rih searched Nehla's face, wondering whether the woman was just bantering or making an actual point. She so rarely spoke of anything serious, and this conversation was certainly one of the longest they had ever had.

When Rih did not respond, Nehla sat back on her heels. "You're not Athrolani. If you were there'd be no negotiation. There'd be no peace."

"I can't come here flaunting our culture."

"Why not? They have a general who has horns sprouting from his head. A boy king whose blood's hardly human. What does it matter if his bride sports a ring in her nose and wears colored silks?"

Rih wrinkled her nose. Though Bimet and Nehla were meticulous in arranging every fold and drape, it seemed as if the hour passed in a breath-span.

Mosil met her in the parlor. After glancing at her open door, he turned back. "You have conducted yourself with grace," he began. "These are not easy days, and I've been pleased by how well you navigate them. You do me honor. You do yourself honor."

She forced away the urge to respond that he had little to do with it. He was kind more often than he was cruel, and she had enemies enough. Her fingers laced with his for a moment before she stepped away. "Thank you. I've missed your counsel these past weeks, and I am sure I will miss it more when you've returned home."

He flashed a tired smile, and she wondered if the shadow Vi-baln cast over Mosil was as dark as the one over her.

Give me darts, give me a spear. Despite Nehla's reassurance and Mosil's kindness, her nerves were no better. Silks and rings felt as uncomfortable as any Athrolani attire. *Give me armor against whatever tonight brings.*

Φ

Keplan waited in the alcove, head in his hands. Writhing anxiety subsided with the coin-sized pile of dust he breathed an hour before. It did nothing for his churning gut. The throne room door stood open awaiting Rih's wedding procession, but the crowd had yet to settle. Musicians plucked a few strings, tightening others.

He glanced up as Daymir appeared in the alcove's entrance. "If you're going to wear your hair long, you could have pinned it back."

"...for fate's sake, deal with your hair!"

For a breath he pictured Firas stepping through the doors, like so many epic ballads. He would wear flowers in his beard, matching the yellow and green embroidery on his shirt. "Why don't you take my place, since you seem so ready to act without my input," he barked.

Daymir heaved a sigh. "I deserve that. You have to understand, Wardyn, I'm as out of my depth as you now. This is not my Athrolan. She's reeling. Listening to them can't hurt, and I doubt it's wise to anger zealots."

An'thor shot him a pointed look from his place just below the dais, and Keplan forced himself to his feet. "I doubt it's wise to entertain them, either."

He took up his place before the throne, the regent a step behind. A nod to the herald and the music began in earnest. Athrolan's emblem draped every wall, alternated with the gold Banis falcon on red and purple crest. A thick black carpet cut a swath through the crowd. Seemingly, the entire Athrolani court—or what remained of it—had come to witness the union. What space was left had been filled with the lesser nobles in the Banis entourage and the highest officers and wealthiest merchants.

Most had doffed their more somber mourning attire for bright colors—all save Keplan. Other than the cerulean stitching on his kosovorotka, his entire outfit was white. Even the fur trim around his hat was soft ermine.

Each member of the Banis entourage was announced, but it was all Keplan could do not to bolt past them. While he may have been the sole person in white, his future bride was a beacon of magenta.

Daymir spoke first, welcoming them to Athrolan, Keplan echoing his sentiments on behalf of the kingdom.

"We are honored to join Athrolan—a nation almost as old and mighty as our empire—in friendship, a bond symbolized by this union between Your Majesty and one of His Eminence's chosen daughters, the Kajimet Rih-elte."

The ambassador released her, ushering her up the stairs while the tablet bearing their vows was brought forward. The heavy wood bore the Athrolani wedding vows, and a piece of parchment with the Banis translation was pinned to the side.

If Keplan believed in gods—or anything at all—he would have thanked them that tradition decreed Rih make her oath first. It was harder to run when someone was already locked inside the cage they were about to share. She scanned the words, repeating them with steady hands.

Daymir turned to Keplan, tired eyes expectant.

"Today, before both our courts, I swear an oath as—" His voice cracked, dying in his throat. *It's this or war. Anything but war.* "As your king and husband. Our marriage binds our nations together in everlasting fealty and friendship, and so too it binds us, blood and bone, body and mind. I will uphold your honor and your choices, I will regard your duties with sanctity and support. May our joining be a bright point, guiding the union of our kingdoms until we both pass from this world."

Acid burned his throat at the flowery words, so many pretty turns of phrase used to describe imprisonment. He raised his hand, palm out, watching as Rih did the same. If she was as afraid as he, she did not show it. The few glimpses of her mind he caught were building clouds over the grasslands. Not empty, like the landscape seemed, but vast.

"Do you swear to uphold the vows made today?" Daymir glanced sharply at him, whispering, "Your Majesty. Gloves."

Keplan's jaw worked. Oaths were not taken with the shield of fabric. He yanked the offending garment off this left hand and pressed his green palm to hers.

Pain. The acrid stench of burning blood. Smoke as Hi-taln's rel crumbled into coals and ash. Keplan's eyes squeezed shut. Sheer panic and the burn of borrowed willpower rooted him to the throne room, kept his skin touching hers.

Battered consciousness, bright sun on baking grasses. Hands signing something before their owner glanced down and saw he was awake. *It's her.* And again, in the stables, a soldier requesting mounts with signs. There were a dozen, four dozen, people who signed at the stables, more in the city. But he knew her. He knew her bright eyes and fierce, delicate features.

"Your Majesty—" An'thor's voice was incredibly distant, his grip on the king's right wrist iron hard even across the leagues that seemed to separate Keplan from his own body.

He forced his eyes open and met hers. Whatever was written on his face, she saw. Her own gaze widened and she paled under the layers of tasteful paint. His fingers locked around hers when he felt her try to jerk away.

"I do so swear." The words were clotted lifeblood in his throat. Still, he spat them free. Keplan kissed her briefly, turning just enough to only brush the edge of her mouth.

Roaring fire, screaming filled his ears. He turned and realized it was the crowd, cheering for them, cheering for the peace their sacrifice brought.

Rih took his unresponsive arm. Tradition dictated they walk to the throne room doors and receive each guest's blessing. They walked back down the black carpet, Keplan tugging his glove back on with shaking hands. Triumphant music swelled when they flanked the doors. Despite hundreds of hands brushing him, flickering eye contact and curious, distant smiles, his mind was locked in replaying his weeks under the interrogator.

"Your Majesty, are you well?" Rih's interpreter asked.

It took him a moment to realize she was translating Rih's concern.

"Overwhelmed." He forced himself to look at her as the last few courtiers filed out, bobbing bows and curtsies. Whether the blessings took minutes or hours, he did not know. "I just—" Two signs interrupted him and he paused, waiting for the translation.

"Recognized me?"

The hall beyond was almost empty now. "Forgive me, I have to go." He took the hallway at a run, ignoring the startled questions the guards shouted after him. He saw only Hi-taln's body, bleeding into the hearthfire.

Φ

Night fell in silence. Knocks shook his door, An'thor's bitter bark and Daymir's tired coaxing did not sway him. Ballads whined through his open windows, dances picked for his wedding ball. *Who's dancing with her instead of me?*

He stared at the unstained ceiling or watched lights blaze as the city celebrated their king's marriage below. Homesickness was odd, when he could see the very place he missed from his own balcony. Did Firas light candles for fertility and peace in the windows of the Wise Hare or lead patrons in a toast for happiness? Did he grieve a shared life unlived, abandoned and mourned in the tiny attic bedroom just as his sister's had been?

Chest aching, he paced through his chambers to his study, dragging the dust box over and popping the lid open. He froze. It was empty.

His gaze skittered to his double-locked door. He never intended to use it all or have his body beg for more. He barely remembered the logic he twisted that night, hands and mind still stained with blood. None of that changed the fact that here he stood, staring into a void, forced to choose between sobriety or sanity.

Resolve steadied his movements as he ducked into his dressing room. A garish red tolstovka would draw attention from his scars and face. Another layer of powder and rouge hid them further. Plain dark breeches and a black jacket finished the look. He fumbled his plainest boots on and made for the door.

He froze. His guards were paid for their discretion, but nothing replaced loyalty. Instead, he eased open his balcony door and examined the ground below. It was not an easy climb, designed to keep the room's occupant safe, but the burn of urgency erased that of pulled muscles and twisted joints as he let himself drop.

The broad cobbled street led between the palace and the barracks toward the north gate.

A gust of wind threatened his hat's perch, and he shoved his errant hair beneath it before turning south. His steps were unsteady, body weakened from cold and too many ragged emotions.

When he stumbled into a market stall, he relished the scrape of sharp wood against his shoulder. At least the few stares were due to his behavior rather than suspicions at his true identity. In the press of celebration, he was just another drunk. Salt stung his tongue and he paused just above the steep stair down to the rear gate of the Navy compound. In withdrawal's wake, his body trembled and floundered under the waves of thoughts.

He did not realize where his boots dragged him until the stark orange glow of the Wise Hare's lantern hit his aching eyes. He stumbled and stopped. *I can't be here.* He promised Firas he would not shadow the Hare's stoop again. He crumpled into the alley where he first met Mirik's Spy Master, where his world shattered. "Firas," he called, both hoping and fearing his words would break through the ruckus of the Hare's common room. He would do almost anything to see the man again. *Anything but doom our kingdom.* But he did not want Firas to see him now, not like this, covered sweat and the trace of someone else's lips.

As if summoned by the memory of tan hands and dark blond beard, a voice cut through the foggy air from around the corner. "I'm not going to buy anything, but I'll give you a bowl of stew if you budge off our stoop."

Keplan stumbled to a halt in the corner's shadow. His former lover stood on the stair, arms crossed as he frowned at a crumpled figure.

Keplan recognized the rhuemy eyes and shuddering hands of his own dust dealer. He faltered, hands clenched.

"Don't need favors," the dealer hissed.

Firas shrugged. "Then move along."

"Where's the woman? She always let me set up on her nights."

In the low lamp light, Keplan saw Firas's hand curl into a fist. "She's dead and I don't give a shite what you think. Get."

Every ounce of Keplan's blood told him to fall at Firas's feet, beg for the charity he so willingly offered a poor stranger. *I'd give a thousand crowns to have a meal in the Hare, at the bar with you beside me.* He would give the single heavy crown of Athrolan itself if he thought he could. He watched the dealer gather his wares and shuffle a few paces down the road to a dry patch of cobbles. It took his entire will to keep his feet rooted to the ground until Firas had disappeared back inside.

"I'll buy," he offered, crossing the street.

The dealer flashed a smile. "Knew you'd enjoy it. Same amount?"

Keplan nodded, tossing the coin onto the blanket. "That should do fine."

The man's hand were incongruous with his ragged clothes and body, deft as he measured and clipped the box closed. "I'll see you again, then."

"No, you won't," Keplan muttered, wondering if it was a lie or not. He tucked the box away and made for the bars of the Center Teir. Less expensive and more welcoming than the Silver Apron, the bars in the middle of the city were large and varied. Keplan chose the loudest, seediest he could find, a three-story tavern and inn. He barely glanced at the name before finding a small private table.

"Mulled wine," he told the bartender before slumping back. A scan of the room told him this was no place to breathe dust on the tabletop, despite the vulgar banter and obvious brothel in the rear room. Instead, he distracted himself with the innocuous drunken thoughts of the other patrons.

A slight man strode in, dockhand uniform dripping. "Oi, Veska, I'll be down in a moment. Have a fireale waiting, please?"

The bartender snorted and jerked a nod. "Just wipe up your boot prints this time, Rheman, eh?"

The dockhand dashed back to the door, catching the rag tossed to him, and mopped up his tracks. Keplan watched him duck upstairs, envious. The bartender—Veska, apparently—returned a moment later, pouring hot wine into a delicate earthen goblet. Keplan slid a handful of coins across the table. "Leave the bottle, please."

The deep-red wine was thick with spices, something sweet cutting through the rich dry flavor. It made his thoughts fuzzier at the edges, but they still lingered. He turned his attention to the gossip perched on a stool, surrounded by women. *Poorer than a gutter rat but wants a patron for his bardic work. Gave his last coin to look the part.* He recalled Firas's words, that many came to Ceir Athrolan seeking fortune and never left. At the time, he thought it was because they found their fortune on her water-stained streets. He knew better now.

I'm gonna kill him. The thought was so loud, a flash in his mind and Keplan's focus flew to the hulking man across the room. He glowered at another bulkier man at the bar.

Keplan's body hummed with adrenaline, but he did not move. Instead he pressed his mind forward slightly.

If he brings back another mug of that swill claiming you can't taste the difference between gutterwrack and sail's ale, I'm gonna kill him.

Keplan relaxed. He had not realized how often people tossed idle threats until he took a life. Others, it seemed, were so distant from death that it never occurred that others had acted on those same thoughts.

Sashaying brocade and rich rose fabric dragged his attention back to the stairs. The dockhand returned, this time dressed in an elaborately embroidered sarafan, minus the usual billowing long-sleeved shift underneath. A long, wavy blond wig finished the look.

Apparently Keplan's eyes lingered too long: a breath later he no longer sat alone.

"Mind some company?"

Keplan almost refused. But there in those bright black eyes was something he sorely missed. *Compassion.* He gestured to the mulled wine. "Help yourself."

"I'm more a fireale girl, but thank you."

Sure enough, the bartender delivered the promised drink a moment later.

"You're a dockhand?" Keplan asked.

"During the day I'm Rheman, and he's a hand for the merchant docks, specifically Donas's shipping berths. But right now I'm Sha, and she's looking to spend some time with a friendly bar patron, if they've the interest."

"And the money?" Keplan hazarded, hoping it was not rude to ask. He noticed the faint lace edge of the blond wig. It was expensive, he imagined, but appreciated that she did not bother to choose one that looked more natural on her Sunamen skin.

"That's a nice bonus, yes, but I don't mind conversation first," she demurred. "And you are?"

"Lan Guardsen. I, ah…" He licked his dry lips. He could not be a bar hand from the Slummer, not with the rumors that exploded through the lower city upon the discovery of Athrolan's true heir that winter.

Her smile broadened. "You must be a merchant's son."

He grasped the small mercy. People like her were no strangers to truncated truths and altered personal history. "Indeed."

"We get a lot of men like you in this bar, looking to spend their parents' wealth," she murmured, eyes staying on his. "Merchants' sons, that is."

He hummed in response. Thoughts juddered through his mind too loudly for him to even decipher whether they were his. "Did you grow up here?" Her features were Sunamen, but she neither dressed nor spoke like one.

"In the south, border town. But my parents were both troubadours, so I picked up accents well. It makes people more at home."

"I'm not from here either," he blurted. "Well, from Athrolan. Small town in the Felds."

Sha's gaze was just shy of expectant, as if she already knew. He wondered how much of his identity she already deciphered. The hand that brushed his was calloused but warm and delicate.

He twitched but forced his hand to stay under hers.

"Is this all right?"

He nodded. "Just a bit loud in here." She did not need to know he meant his mind, not the common room.

"It gets rowdy but not out of hand. What brought you into Fussy Fat Hen?"

"The fussy what?" A smile eased onto his face, and he thought it just might be real.

She leaned forward, hair wafting perfume toward him. "The bar you're sitting in right now. It's called the Fussy Fat Hen."

He snorted. "It was close. And distracting. It's hard to celebrate a marriage when you miss someone."

"That's scribed truth, Lan." Her gaze softened further. "I've finished my drink if you'd like to come up."

He glanced at the door, then the stairs. Spending the night with Rih was unbearable, but even if he could not be with Firas, he did not want to be alone for his wedding night. "Please."

The narrow hallway was dim but clean. Sha's room was at the very end. She unlocked the door and ushered him in. The double window over the bed let moonlight stream across her thick coverlet. Soft pink light bloomed and he glanced back. Sha had lit a lamp on her dressing table. Keplan's gaze roved over the wig stand, the pallets of paint, the heavy dockhand knapsack, the heaps of rope brought back for repair. Two identities so different, yet fitting.

"How do you do this?"

Sha glanced up, gentle frown in place. "Spend time with people for money?"

"No, that makes sense. I mean, alternate? Do you forget who you are?"

"I'm both. Some days I feel more Sha and others more Rheman, but they're both me."

"It must be freeing." Everything was bright and loud and overwhelming, but in the quiet light of Sha's room, his thoughts were muffled.

"Now it is. It wasn't always, when I thought I had to choose." She drew her curtains and returned to brush a hand over Keplan's cheek. "What are you feeling?"

"Drowning," he whispered.

"Forgive the observation, but I noticed a box in your pocket, and your hands are shaking. Would this be easier if you weren't in dust-drought?"

Withdrawal. He looked down, hating his weakness. How did no one else notice? Was his court that inobservant, or was Sha just familiar with the signs? "It'll just be a moment. If you'd like some—"

"That's not my vice, but thank you," she interjected. "Would you like to tell me about who you're missing?"

Myself, more often than not. He set the dust up on her dressing table. "He's a bartender. Handsome. Roguish, I'd think. Likes to avoid serious conversation until it's dumped in his lap."

"Sounds fun-loving."

"Kinder than any I've met." Keplan leaned forward and breathed relief. It took a moment, then steadiness slipped over him.

"I usually spend the evenings as Sha, but if you'd rather, I can be Rheman tonight." Her hand lingered at the edge of her wig. Even in the grip of dust, the pity in her eyes was agony.

"Sha's fine. You're lovely either way, and I've never cared what body a lover has." He barely remembered he had only had the one lover, truly, but he doubted Sha would ask for written proof of his past experiences.

"I'm the same," she confided. Her hand found his and pulled him toward the bed. He let her unbutton his tolstovka and let his hair loose from the cap. Her hand paused at the gloves.

"It's fine," he rasped. The bed was soft when he fell back onto it, pulling her strong body after him.

"What do you like?"

His vision tunneled on her eyes and he pressed his mouth to hers once, twice. Honesty spilled from him and he blushed. "Oblivion."

Sha had enough curves to not remind him of Firas, but the faint scratch of stubble and the sweet burn of sex was enough to remind him why he was here. He buried his pain in Sha as night fell on his future. He wanted to forget, but not fully. Without those memories he would lose the reason he took the throne altogether. He would not survive forgetting. Neither would Athrolan.

CHAPTER FIVE

The 25th of Valemord, 1272
The City of Ceir Athrolan, Athrolan

RIH MOVED THE GAME piece diagonally, eyes narrowed on the tri-colored board.

Bimet countered immediately and Rih sat back, sighing. "I never lose so often. Not even against you!"

Bimet's dark brows arched and she smiled, returning the pieces to their starting position. "Sore loser, are we?"

"Hardly, I just can't focus on anything," Rih answered. Her mind was filled with the threads she wove into rebellion, with Vi-baln's vicious gaze, or her own isolation. Beyond the carnal, she had not considered all the duties that would begin the moment she became a wife. During their wedding she saw how frail he seemed—thin shoulders, thin face, peaked color. *I came here for a king and his army, not some sickly boy.*

"What is it, exactly?"

"He knows who I am. He recognized me. How can I maintain a happy marriage—or a functional one, if nothing else—when he can't even dance with me on our wedding night?"

"Or do anything else with you," Bimet remarked, shoving a finger into her closed fist crudely.

Rih grimaced. "I'd be happy if he never did that with me, honestly. But the empire is watching me. If this union fails—"

Nehla slipped into the room, holding the door ajar behind her as she bowed. "Your Highness, the Emperor's Hand is here to see you."

Cold washed over her. Now that she was married, she hoped to be done with his overseeing. "Of course."

Vi-baln swept in, scanning the room with an absent gaze. "Good morning, Your Highness. I trust you slept well."

"Well enough, if not long." She prayed he assumed it was because her husband had visited her and not that she had left the ball early and spent the night shivering in her room awaiting Keplan's arrival.

"I suppose that's to be expected." His gaze dropped to the board before her. "I didn't know you played."

She shrugged. "It's a common pastime in the barracks."

His face pinched tight. "I hope you'll give up such nonsense for your duties here, now."

"I've heard the king plays, though, and hoped to entertain him with a game." It was a blatant lie, but she would sell her own teeth to get the man to leave.

"Indeed—I played a round with him myself a few days ago. Perhaps Mosil did well in training you."

She offered a smile and asked if he wished for tea.

"I leave shortly. I came to wish you well and remind you of your loyalty to the Banis empire. Even when you enjoy the liberties of this city."

"A woman has a single mind," she replied.

He stared at her a moment, then his gaze moved to Nehla with a ferocity that made Rih gag. "You have some of the best attendants with you, chosen to support you. Trust them."

Bimet caught Rih's gaze. Apparently she had been right to distrust the other woman.

"I expect I will see you in His Eminence's palace again one day." Vi-baln offered his hand for her to kiss, sharp chin raised. "Until then."

You will. And it will be with my spear tip at your groin. She tapped her lips against his knuckles before rising to escort him to the door. "Travel well," she offered.

When he was a few steps down the hall, he turned back. "Oh, I had a question for you, Your Highness."

Chills spread over her arms at the cold calculation in his eyes. "What's that?"

"I've seen something these past few weeks, something I thought you could answer for me." He paused, then made the gesture for liberty. "Why do I keep seeing this?"

Bile built behind her clenched teeth. "I don't know what you mean."

"Of course you do. I see it between the rows of tents. I see it in the streets, even here. They sign and you answer." His dark gaze fixed hers. "Is there something I should know?"

She forced innocence onto her face, hoping he did not notice how long it took to settle over her features. "It's just a symbol of pride. It started during my last few weeks as a soldier, as things were building between us and Mirik."

"Liberty? We're hardly under their rule."

"I guess it's a sign that we'd like it to stay that way?" Dread rose. She had no idea how many of her signs he knew but refused to use.

"I see." He smiled and made the sign again, eyes never leaving hers. "Best not let the Mirikin see it, then."

"I'll be sure of it." Even when his bright silks disappeared down the hall, she did not feel safe. Panic was a prairie cat crouched in her gut, twitching its tail. She would need to write to the others, tell them the party lie. If she survived this marriage, if she survived this rebellion, the terror of the past few months might age her by decades.

Φ

The 26th Day of Valemord, 1272

"I thought I might find you up here." Azimir plopped down on the gravel beside Keplan with a dramatic sigh. His clothes were clearly from some state event, but he had loosened the neck of his vest and shirt.

"I miss the birds."

Azimir followed his gaze out to the woods beyond the city walls. "I get like that about Mirik sometimes."

"You can always go back," Keplan snapped. "I can't. This is my world now. I'm surrounded by it. The wind in the trees—it whispered or roared. It didn't howl like it does through the streets here. And I miss the creak of the Hare's sign under my bedroom window and the smell of woodsmoke and lamp oil from the docks below." He heaved a sigh of his own. "I'm surrounded by people—guards, mostly, or Domariigo and Blackhouse—but I'm so alone."

Azimir glanced over. "You could talk to your wife."

"She scares me," Keplan confessed, looping his arms around his knees. "She's been training for marriage her whole life—"

"She was a soldier before this, you know."

Keplan winced. "Of course. She told me that, I just forgot." He could barely hold onto a thought for longer than a minute. They slipped through his hands like sand, stream water sluicing from his consciousness. "How'd you know?"

"She told me. At her welcome ball."

Embarrassment flushed his cheeks. "That should have been me."

"It should have, yes. She's interesting. Smart. Something about her just," he shrugged, "makes me want to know more, I suppose."

"You should have married her then. Mirik would be at peace and we could just claim we'd be friends with your friends."

"Almost did, you know."

Keplan glanced over. "You never told me that. That you were promised."

"War happened and then that seemed bigger." He grinned. "Besides, then I'd be deprived of all the beautiful Banis serving women in her entourage. And I'm certain the emperor has more than one daughter."

Keplan grimaced. "I don't know how to be married. I don't know the first thing about it. At least war is something I know what to do with—stop it."

Azimir looked at his hands. "I know I've led a lucky life, but there are casualties with negotiations too. Both of you are sold for this." He raked his hand through his hair, driving the warm black locks into spikes.

Keplan caught sight of the line of scabs across his cousin's throat. *Mirrel wasn't the only one attacked.* "How's that?" He jerked his head at the healing wound.

Azimir shrugged, but his quick smile was gone. "Honestly harder than I thought. Pa's got guards everywhere for me and for Al, but it's hard when you don't feel safe in your own room, you know? I suppose I should be grateful someone killed the man responsible. But I'm not."

"Because you think there's more?"

Azimir frowned at him. "No. Because it doesn't do much good, does it? He's just dead. He won't learn from it. Others won't either. Whatever information you could have gotten from him is colder than he is."

"Right." Keplan stared at his hands. Every other memory and thought might be fleeting, but his hands still recalled the rending of flesh beneath them. "I'm sorry I didn't ask sooner."

"I haven't seen much of you."

"I don't have much time to myself." *And I waste it all getting dust-brained enough to survive the next day.*

"That Captain Hylier's been around a fair bit. You take to him?"

It took Keplan a moment to realize what his cousin meant by the awkward phrasing. "Fates, no. He's for women, I think, and certainly doesn't like me much. And he's not—" His throat tightened at the thought of a rough beard and laughing eyes. "No. I haven't taken to him. And I ought not to take to anyone. Marriage and all that. But, ah," he looked down, scuffing a boot, "I did see someone—a sell-love—on my wedding night."

Azimir's brows arched. "Oh. Man or woman?"

"Depends on when you ask. It's not serious. She's nice though." He longed to tell Azimir about the dust. Truthfully, he longed to tell anyone, to just have the truth out of his mouth and off his shoulders. An'thor would condone it, Daymir would condemn it. Hylier would be further disgusted—the man rarely even became drunk. *But Azimir might understand wishing to escape.* "It's just to stop me from thinking for a little while."

"I never feel like I think too much. Al always says I got Pa's head. I'm too sword-handed for much thinking."

Keplan glanced over at his cousin. He would never consider Azimir simple, but there was a straightforwardness to his speech. The way he spoke about Rih, however, made Keplan wonder if the boy had more insight than he realized. "Thank you for talking to me."

"You're family. Whatever you wear on that tangled mop, be it crown or kitchen soot."

Keplan's chest ached. He longed for the feeling to stay, the sensation of belonging for a moment. Like everything lately, it alighted for a moment, then melted into numbness.

The small palace bell chimed the half-hour. Azimir sighed. "I'm supposed to practice my economics with Al. Are you busy tomorrow evening?"

"Hardly." Keplan paused. This was official Athrolani business. It was not something he ought to share with a dignitary's son from another nation. "I've an audience with some madwoman about a prophet in the afternoon."

Azimir laughed. "Oh, I think my ma got some such letter a few weeks back. Of course, then I was almost assassinated, so she just told them to toss off until after the war with Ban was through. You think there's no truth to it?"

"I think they're a bunch of fools grasping at symbols in an attempt to suss meaning out of this pathetic existence," Keplan spat.

"You know my father was a person of faith."

"I'd argue still is, Azimir."

Azimir frowned. "How's that?"

"He worships my mother. He erected a temple to her in Mirik proper. His faith did not break or end, it simply transferred."

"I suppose you're right. 'When I looked up at her for the first time it was as if she were a star and I was drifting in the black sky.'"

Kepan raised his brows at the flowery language. "What's that from?"

"That's how he describes their first meeting."

"Proving my point." Keplan stood with a groan. "I'll see you when the audience is over with, then? Perhaps we'll have dinner together. Like before."

Azimir nodded, then glanced at the sky. "Toar, looks like snow." With a last wave, he retreated down the tower stairs.

Keplan glanced up at the soft gray clouds. It was too early for snow, but it seemed fitting, with the bite in the air. His steps dragged all the way to his chambers.

He rarely allowed even the maids in and left his parlor and study in disarray. The first empty box of dust went into the flames as soon as the fire in his study caught. A faint sweet smell rising from the cheap wood. He paused, staring at the second. His pulse was thunder, his blood storming in his limbs. He had two minutes.

Fess knocked as he was shutting the lid. "Sire, you asked to see me?"

He hid the box in his desk and called the commander in. Perhaps his nerves would hold on their own. "The door, if you please."

She nudged it shut and settled back in her easy stance. Sawdust and scuffs marred her white training clothes and sweat dampened her hair.

"I need your advice. Particularly on Dorcal."

"You know my thoughts on that, sire. Whatever you need done to keep the crown stable."

"I wanted your thoughts on him as a man, actually. Not as a commander."

"As a man, sire? I'm not sure—"

"As a person, Fess, I'm not being lewd."

Her eyes crinkled with a withheld smile and she dipped her head. "Apologies. I think he's a loyal man. And a proud one. Stubborn. I don't like him socially, but I think he did a fine job."

Keplan pinched the strong bridge of his nose. He was cornered. Watched at every turn. "Then why is he locked in his room and the general's advising me?"

She regarded him a moment, then gestured to the seat. "May I, sire?" When he nodded she settled in, leaning on her knees. "The short answer is, of course, because you put them there. I'm not sure I agree with either the commander or the general's recent methods, if I'm being quite honest."

"You're not the only one," Keplan muttered.

Her brows twitched, but she said nothing.

"He is a wealth of knowledge, but I can't have him in the city."

"Daymir was the figurehead, sire, and you allow him here."

"It was not the regent's cannonball that drove Slummer beams into my shoulder blade, Fess."

"No, I suppose not." She crossed her arms. "I'm not sure what you're aiming for here."

"I don't trust anyone. Not any of them—Dorcal, Domariigo or Blackhouse. For a whole garden of reasons, half of which are only suspicions at this juncture. Domariigo is as wrong as Dorcal, I just happened to be his project at the time. And I can hardly keep the man on house arrest for the rest of my reign. Either way a rebellion could rally around him. He was the strength of Blackhouse's side."

"Use him."

Keplan glanced up. "Use him for what?"

Her jaw worked as she thought about it. "I haven't the faintest. Keeping him as advisor or a lesser officer does not keep you safe. Or on the throne—"

"I don't care about me, I care about Athrolan."

"There're the same now, Your Majesty."

He grimaced. "We've grown stagnant. Look at Ban—they have things our philosophers haven't dreamed of."

"They built those with slave blood and labor. It's easy to dream when you're perched on the broken backs of others."

It was the first time he saw her express much beyond playful respect. "I didn't know you were political."

"Just stating a fact."

Keplan thought for a moment. "They explore. They push outward, in thought as well as land. Athrolan's borders stretch far enough—as it is, the Felds are an entity unto themselves most of the time. But there are places I've seen—on maps," he quickly lied, "—that we've never gone or learned from." He sat back, fiddling with his ostentatious quill.

"You're suggesting you send him afield? Who will keep him from starting a rebellion?"

"Proud. Loyal. That's how you described him. He didn't like it, but he took a knee before me when I asked. I'll give him a choice—explore for the Crown or stay behind bars growing fat. I think if I tell him he'll lose every connection he has with this kingdom if he strays, that will be warning enough."

"That's an awful lot of trust for someone who claims to have none."

"You think it's misplaced?"

Fess stared at him, then looked thoughtfully at the map on his desk. "Not in him, no."

"In who?"

"As your commander and a part of this military, officially, I can't say."

Keplan glanced at the door, then sat back in his seat. "If I were to ask you over ale in the city, what would your answer be? Blackhouse?"

"Daymir, though once a smart and lawful man, is a doddering fool. Your general, however, is not a man I'd invite for dinner no matter how many nasty tasks I required doing. You know ruddy five?" When Keplan shook his head, she sighed. "Tiles, then. He's a tile player, except we're the pieces. I don't know what his goal is, and frankly, I'm beginning to wonder if he does either anymore. I think most of the time he moves us about from boredom."

"That's a studied critique."

"I believe in knowing who your allies are."

"And your enemies."

Her lips curved into a proper smile. "That's just my job."

"That's why I'm bothering with an audience from these zealous prophets. I hate their ideas, but I'd rather know what I'm facing."

"Fathoms beat all, sire," she quoted.

"You've given me much to think on, Fess. Thank you. You may go—I'm sorry to have interrupted your training."

"It's casual, among friends." She hesitated. "Your wife attends too, you know."

"I'm glad she's found something to amuse herself." Even in his own muffled ears it sounded trite and hollow.

Fess rose and bowed. "I know I prattled on about having no one to trust, sire, but I've got Athrolan's interests at heart. You can trust that."

He flashed her a smile of his own. "I know."

"You might want to have someone see to your fireplace. That smell isn't a good sign. Your brickwork might be faulty."

She slipped out the door and Keplan slumped back in his chair, staring at the fire. Her gaze had not wavered as she spoke, and he wondered if it was from sincerity or understanding.

Φ

The 27th of Valemord, 1272

Hylier met him at the garden gates an hour after the noon bells tolled. "Afternoon, sire."

Keplan grimaced. "Afternoon. Guards in place?"

"They are. Are you certain you don't want to meet in a more," he seemed to search for the best word, "traditional place for an audience? The throne room, perhaps."

Keplan shook his head. "I'm not taking this seriously."

"Exactly—"

"I mean it's not worth taking seriously. I'll toss my parents' power in their faces and be done with the matter."

"Very well, sire."

Keplan was quickly learning that his guard's use of the honorific was saved exclusively for when he disagreed with the king.

The gardens were bleak, barely clinging to the green the boasted just a few weeks before. Still, there was stark beauty to the butter-colored leaves and pale trunks. Sun lanced through the looming clouds and between the intricate marble lattice carved over the memorial for the Gods' War. It dappled the broad flagging and scattered cold sunlight across the mosaic. Keplan tilted his head, watching his shadow eclipse the delicate figures picked out in jet and pale chalcedony, coral and lapis.

A set of guards ringed the place, but otherwise the area was deserted. He slipped inside, leaving Hylier to wait by the door. He needed a moment. His chest tightened at the image of his mother, black power spilling over her bony hands, and his father, ignited by the sun. Every child thought their parents gods. He was just the only child who was not far wrong. He did not pace. Instead, he allowed the thoughts to wash over him. His body ached for distance, but this meeting necessitated sobriety.

"Your Majesty, she's here." Hylier stepped aside to allow the woman through. "Sire, this is Nena'phe lui Hiral."

The woman fell into a deep bow. "Swordbearer of the Prophet Hela. I am grateful you chose to speak with me."

Keplan eyed her. "Don't be grateful yet."

She was as tall as he and her auburn hair was cropped at the chin. At her belt hung a hand-and-half sword that explained her broad shoulders and chest. Her features remained unmoved. "Then I am grateful you deigned me the least waste of your time."

His brows rose and he turned to appraise her more fully. "Why are you here?"

"I bring the words of the One True God and the future—"

"Not that bit. That was all in your letter and Marum's. I want to know about you. The bit about why you believe those words at all."

"Ah." She turned, hands loosely clasped behind her back. He saw now the angles of her features and the faint slate tone to her skin.

Asai. At least partly.

"My father taught me so much of their history, but even he couldn't answer what would happen to a world without any of its creators. When I first heard them speak of her I was as skeptical as you. But when I first spoke with her alone, I saw reason. She delivers her prophesies alone, you know, to a single person, rarely the same one. This book is filled with the account of each of us. Together we've found the truth in her visions. And they are terrible and beautiful at once." Her face was lit with hope. "The One God is real."

"Do you know why I asked you to meet here?"

"Because those are your parents and this is a sacred place." She spoke with brazen surety that grated against him.

"No. Because I wanted to remind you what people of my blood did to the last gods that dared to walk this earth."

She stepped back, but her chin rose in defiance. "Your Majesty, that was retaliation, nothing more. They were false gods, seeking control over us."

"Doesn't your god seek the same? He's got you traipsing across the countryside doing his bidding. You know that's how my parents met—caught between the human armies of waring deities." He whirled on her, noting distantly that her eyes were not filled with fear or confusion, but pity. "Best get used to opposition, Nena'phe. You're pitching religion to a generation that saw an entire pantheon massacred. She moseyed up to their throne room and ripped the souls right from their bodies." His gaze snapped from its perusal of the tiles back to hers. "Now that I'm listening to you prattle on, I understand why she didn't have the patience to allow them to die the proper way!"

The calm in the woman's bright brown eyes did not waver. "I came to you to read scripture, not try to convince you of my own faith or prowess in debate."

"Apparently ashen skin isn't the only asai traits you acquired," Keplan quipped. "All right then, read your lady's prophesy."

She bowed, drawing out a small book bound with fine leather. Small illustrations filled some of the pages as she flipped to the center. Though her gaze rested on the page, it did not follow the words as she recited. "'The One True God will rise where the worlds meet, from death and birth, from chaos and order. His blood pools, drowning the world even as it gives it life. Though he will bear the marks of hate, he will be unable to raise its tools."

"You just studied opposites," Keplan noted, picking a loose thread of his gloves. He waved a hand for her to continue. Apprehension flashed up his body as he listened. Earnest certainty overwhelmed his mind. Full of the bite of steel and the nip of ice. Copper flooded his tongue, leaking through his clenched teeth.

Cold sunlight caught in her hair as she tucked it back to read the next lines. "His right hand will be stained bloody with wrath, and his left with the verdant green of life and mercy—"

"Enough!" Annoyance exploded into rage. "You think you can come into my city, into my home, spouting lies? You think you can stand here before the memorial to a woman who massacred the gods and tell me I ought to have a little faith 'or else?'" Blood misted from his mouth with every line. *Wrath. Stained with wrath.* The words spun in his head and clenched his palms to him, as if even through the gloves she might catch a glimpse.

Her beige brows arched and she stepped back, hand falling to her sword hilt. "Sire, it's scripture."

"Then fuck your scripture. And fuck your god." Terror thrummed through his bones. "Next he darkens my walls, I'll show you what I learned from the Godkiller herself!"

She moved back another step, lip lifting in the suggestion of a sneer. She spat on the ground between them. "May The One God grant you mercy, for his Swordbearers will not."

Keplan swayed, eyes still fixed on the bubbles of saliva dripping down the icons of his parents. He found the one thing he hated worse than war: heresy.

"Sire?" Hylier appeared in the doorway, hand resting loosely on the pommel of his sword. When Keplan did not answer, he stepped closer. "Keplan?"

Keplan's mind was a cacophony. He pushed past his guard, motioning for the others to follow him as he strode back through the gardens. Their boots clattered on the marble as they swept into the palace after him. "You," he waved at a squire posted at the door of a meeting hall, "find Domariigo. Admiral Fess too. Ask them to meet me in my study in an hour. And someone ought to inform the Mirikin Embassy I'll not be dining with my cousin tonight."

"Yes, Your Majesty, right away." When the squire disappeared, he glanced at Hylier.

The guard's eyes leveled on him. "Anything else?"

Keplan drew a shaking breath as they turned onto his corridor. "I'm afraid I'm going to need a war council."

Φ

The 29th Day of Valemord, 1272

"Evening, Dorcal."

"Evening, sire."

The neutral tone gave Keplan pause. He expected bitterness. All the fury that rent Athrolan in twain. *I've been spending too many brooding nights with Domariigo.* "I trust you've been comfortable here these past weeks."

"Comfortable enough." Raven rolled a shoulder, the motion unconscious. Isolation looked well on the former commander. His hair was still cropped at the unflattering angle of his thick jaw, but it was clean, and his clothes pressed. "I haven't been drawn to the training courts in my dotage anyway."

"May I sit?"

Raven scoffed and jerked his head at the dusty parlor. "Wherever you want. It's not like I entertain much. There a point to all of this?"

"I can hardly keep you under house arrest for the rest of my reign."

"Her Majesty—peace to her and those she loved—did. With His Highness Blackhouse."

"I'm not Tzatia." Keplan leaned forward, hoping the finality in his voice lent it strength and not a threat. "I have neither her patience nor her fears."

"Or her blood."

Keplan found a smile on his face. He never expected people to like him, and Raven's blatant distaste was refreshingly honest. Nationalism aside, he could grow to respect the man. "Why did you join the navy?"

"My parents were too poor to care after me. Mother's cousin was noble. Noble enough, at least, so I petitioned Her Majesty to let my years as a ship's hand count as page duties. Worked my way up to mariner from there."

"I asked why. Why the navy? Why not the army or going into business as a merchant and have the freedom to come and go as you wish?" Keplan could brush his mind like anyone else's, but it told as much what a person thought or claimed their reasoning to be as their actual motives did. He found, too, the knowledge came harder, jumbled, with dust in his blood.

Raven's dark eyes narrowed on Keplan for a moment, then he rose. Even in his dotage, as he called it, he was a mountain of a man. He moved to the cold hearth, broad hands grasped behind his back. Three portraits hung over the mantle. The first, of course, being of the late queen. On the right was a rendition of the former general, her bright hair a contrast against her ashen skin. *Like the Swordbearer.* His gaze roved over them before fixing on the map on the left. Hearth smoke stained the unwaxed parchment. Tiny red tick marks and Raven's surprisingly delicate handwriting marked its surface. His thick finger jabbed the blank space beyond Mirik. "This. This is why. Seas unconquered. Lands unknown. So many places Athrolan could learn of."

Keplan's smile was in earnest now. "That's what I hoped."

Raven turned back. Now curiosity warmed his reservedness. "Why is that?"

"I don't know what news trickles down through these bars."

"Most of it. Half, perhaps. I heard enough boots and hushed voices to gather we're at war or will be soon. You want me out of your hair so the only people you distrust are outside your walls, not within."

"I'd have to empty the city to do that."

"Smart man."

"First you've said of it."

"I have no doubt that you're clever beyond your years. I just doubt your ability to use that cleverness for good. So, who is it? Mirik? Ban? Yourself?"

Keplan snorted. "I've been at war with that last for the past year." He crossed his arms. "It's with a god."

Raven's full attention settled over Keplan's shoulders. The king was abruptly reminded of why, exactly, the man was revered as a commander. "Excuse me?"

"Some prophet out of the east claims there's a god coming and we all ought to be on our best behavior or he'll kill us."

Raven scoffed. "Your mother killed them."

"Exactly!" Keplan gestured wildly, relieved to finally have someone see the same sense as he. "I've been trying to explain that to everyone, and yet they seem convinced to just hear their side of things. Wouldn't have even listened to the prophet's lackey if Blackhouse hadn't invited them without my knowledge."

Raven frowned. "What does Domariigo think of it all?"

"I think he's curious. But he rarely has only a single horse in a race."

"Ridiculous claims aside, why go to war? Why not pat them on the head and send them back to their prophet?"

"The scripture—it's nonsense! And they claim—" His voice juddered to a halt and his gaze fell to his hands. "They're just wrong. There's no such thing as gods anymore."

Raven's attention moved from the king's face to the gloved palms and back. "Didn't like what they said? I've never claimed to like deities. People having power they shouldn't. Go to war with them if you want but—and I say this from experience—you'd better be certain they're wrong. There are things in this world we might never understand fully."

Keplan seized the change in subject like a lifeline. "That's why I'm here. You joined the navy to explore. We both know there are places and people and things we've never encountered before. If Athrolan is going to survive this new world and all its changes, she'll have to change too." He laughed at Raven's scowl. "She'll have to regain her power, her might. Think of it as a new set of armor, a new sword." He paused. "A new ship. For both of you."

Raven's thick lips twisted in what might have been intended as a smile. "I'm listening."

"Sail beyond the edges of that map, beyond where we've gone before. Map coastlines, document people and places and food. Write a thousand logs on what you find. You come back too soon or come back with an army, you're dead. But I figure exile on the high sea is better than a barred room for a person like you. I can give you time—"

Raven leaned through the bars as if already buffeted by an ocean wind. "When can I leave?"

Φ

The 30th Day of Valemord, 1272

Bitter air buffeted the glass. The sullen gray sky glowered above, close and watchful. Rih sat at the edge of her bed watching the clouds. The sky was so different here. Mercurial and full of so many shades of gray and blue and green and gold. The Banis sky was uniform in its vastness. When red and purple storms rolled across the expanse, her patrol would see them coming hours ahead. Sometimes it still was not enough warning to find shelter in the huge prairie, but they had warning.

Howling wind only now seemed to settle. Rih trusted it as little as she trusted the new court and palace around her. At least in Ban, she knew why she should not believe any of the various nobles and dignitaries.

"Will you go to your training this evening?" Bimet looked up from her place by the window, making sure to face toward Rih. Her hands were occupied with mending a leather pauldron for herself. It was not often they were alone together anymore, but Nehla had requested the afternoon free to visit family in the city.

"I thought I might. I'm used to my time being filled with lessons or training. It's a relief to relax, but I'm at a loss as to what to do most of the time."

"We could explore the city."

Rih cast a horrified glance outside. "Perhaps when we're not at risk of becoming icicles. Besides," she gnawed on one lip, "it doesn't sound safe."

"Safe?"

"A man was murdered just before we arrived—a man important enough to spur a woman to appeal to the king himself. His Majesty may be new to the throne, and perhaps unconventional, but everything seems more precarious than I was led to believe."

Rih paced to her dressing table, laid with the dozens of face paints from her wedding. She had not used them since the ball. Dark bottles of scented oil filled one drawer and she poured a few drops into her hand. Of all the many things she missed of home, the cold weather had her longing for the steam of the bathhouses.

She massaged the oil into her scalp as she turned back to Bimet. "I wouldn't mind meeting Nehla's family—a silk weaver."

Bimet's eyes narrowed and she set aside her work for a moment. "I'm not sure if that's wise, considering."

"She hasn't done anything—other than visit with Vi-baln privately."

"She's his niece, you know. It's why she's so flippant around him. Doesn't have to worry about discipline."

Rih's brows rose. The feeling of being watched had not waned much since the entourage departed. Perhaps Nehla was why. She was humorous and quick, and Rih wished to make her a friend. *But friends don't inform their uncles of your every misstep.* "I didn't know."

"There's hardly a moment away from her—which I'm sure she orchestrates. Hopefully she's close enough with this cousin or sister or whatever she is to visit more often than during the celebrations."

"Such as they were," Rih retorted. "Even still, perhaps I'll go with her one day, meet this family." A Banis silk shop would be a balm on her heart. Her private network had no hierarchy, but her developing friendships with Athrolan should be with nobles, not textile merchants and naval commanders.

Bimet brushed Rih's hand to get her attention. "There's someone knocking."

Rih glanced at the door. Perhaps she could ask the steward to outfit the room with some way to get her attention. The thick wood did not lend itself to renovations, however. As exhausted as she was, her mind begged for something to occupy her. Something other than worry. She changed to a warmer wrap and settled herself on the tall couch in her parlor. "Let them in."

The young man from the ball wavered in the doorway. He flashed a smile and waved an awkward hand. His bow, however, was to an equal. "Afternoon, Princess Rih-elte. I thought you might be needing a visitor, busy as His Majesty is this evening."

She let herself smile in return, wondering at the best way to ask who, exactly, he was. "Then I'm happy to see you. Would you like tea?"

"I wanted to offer to tour you about Athrolan, since I came a lot as a child. But it seems the howling has teeth as well. It'll snow soon, no doubt."

"Another time, perhaps." Rih seized her chance. "What brings you to Ceir Athrolan?"

His broad smile faltered when Bimet finished her translation. "You have no idea who I am, do you?"

Rih felt the flush of embarrassment on her cheeks and looked away for a moment, hoping her dark skin hid the sudden pink. "I've met more strangers in the past two days than in all my years before now combined. My lady Nehla has been indispensable, but I'm afraid she wasn't with us when we first met, and I missed you at the wedding ball."

"It was a long day, I'm sure. I'm not surprised you slipped out early." He gestured to the couch across from them as the Athrolani tea arrived. "May I?" When she nodded, he sat and made himself busy pouring tea. When he had taken a sip, he inclined his head to her. "I'm Azimir A'hane, son of Kemmer A'hane, Military Commissioner of Mirik—"

"And acting Hetmir," Rih finished with him. *And the boy I was supposed to marry to stop his mother's war.* Then he was not Athrolani at all, but Mirikin.

Rih gripped Bimet's wrist even as the other woman brought her weapon to ready. As much as her instincts screamed that they were enemies, his open face was kind and honest. "We ordered that tea, and he's already drunk it. Mirik would be foolish to use their second son as an assassin."

Azimir's dark eyes were wide and fixed on the blade aimed at his gut. "I'm not the most tactful when it comes to these things. My father's the ambassador. I'm just a friendly fool." Hand raised, he leaned back in the couch. "By all means, order your own drinks. I doubt you enjoy Athrolani bitterroot as it is."

His crooked smile was contagious, and after a moment Rih motioned for the woman at the door to request their own tea. "So if you're not here to kill me, what do you want?"

"Politics are funny. My mother wages war against your father, yet leagues away from any bloodshed, we can sit across a—" he peered at the dark, decorated wood of the table between them, " —Berrin captain's table and drink tea."

"And yet, thousands of soldiers still die." She let her teeth add a bite to her smile, to her words. "I was supposed to marry you, you know."

He looked down, mumbling something.

"I know. Considering, I imagine Keplan's more agreeable," Bimet translated.

Rih rolled her eyes but was saved from replying by the arrival of a heavy clay dish of Banis tea. She stirred it absently before pouring the thick liquid into her mug. Their only commonality, as far as she was concerned, was war. It did not bode well for conversation. "Your mother just set sail for our shores, I am told."

"And your father just redirected most of his cavalry and foot soldiers to the beaches."

"He's not my father," she corrected without thinking.

His brows rose. "Forgive me, I just assumed—"

"By blood, I suppose," she explained, brown hands flashing in impatience. "But he never raised me, never acknowledged me. Perhaps this is why I was originally offered to you. Which, I was told, was an insult."

"There's no need to apologize—"

"I wasn't." She lifted her chin, forcing pride she often lacked into her gaze.

He regarded her with narrowed eyes for a moment. Then his smile widened. "No, I don't imagine you would. You remind me of my mother. Clever. Uncompromising. You weren't the insult in the negotiation. Most of Mirik still remembers starving as my grandfather bled her treasury dry in the gods' names. Living in warrens of derelict buildings and eating rotted food sounds a bit like slavery, don't you think?"

She paused in stirring her tea. Under the friendly youth in his face, she caught a glimpse of the woman steering her battleships west. "I think I'd know more about slavery than you might, ambassador's son."

"Probably." His gaze did not waver nor his expression change. After a moment he pointed to the dish between them. "Might I try some of your tea? I've never acquired a taste for the bitter Athrolani stuff."

She finally returned his smile in earnest and poured him a cup. "So, I assume the wedding brought you to Athrolan, to answer my question."

"And the coronation. My father's a bit preoccupied with my cousin. It was all I could do to keep my father from screaming at Kep to change his mind. At least it made the whole thing more interesting."

"I thought Athrolan just avoided civil war. Now I hear of wildfire politics and murders in the streets."

"I wouldn't say avoided. Stopped before it gripped much more than the capital is more accurate." He peered at her. "Was Ban that much safer?"

She shrugged. "I was a soldier, so safety was relative. But the city itself, and others like it, were peaceful in many ways. Peaceful but terrified."

"I've always taken better to battle than politics."

"Do you not agree that negotiations will always be better than war?" she countered. Her tea cooled, almost forgotten on the table in favor of playful verbal sparring.

"Not in all cases—Mirik's war with Ban is a noble one. We're sacrificing some of our own lives so that some of your people are saved."

"That's a poetic way of looking at it," Rih agreed. "Wars take many lives, though. Negotiations only cost one."

"One? I would think none," Azimir said, eyes narrowed in thought. He took a sip and his eyes brightened at the flavor.

"The price of a kingdom's safety is one person's life. Instead of sacrificing the lives of hundreds in a war against Athrolan, I'm just sacrificing mine."

"Perhaps it's just a choice who we sacrifice for peace—the common folk or the aristocracy." He sat back, expression abruptly wistful. "Nothing an ambassador's son would understand, eh?"

"I see your point. Though I will never agree that their suffering is the same."

"Hardly. You've given me a bit to think on." Azimir finished his tea and poured another. "So, what do you think of Athrolan?"

"It's confusing. Disorganized. In RoBal even our leisure time is marked with fear that something we did will have upset the baniol, or fates forbid, His Divine Eminence. And everything is tidy, organized. Traffic in the streets moves smoothly, people keeping to the proper sides. Here it's inefficient. Chaotic, even." She steeled herself. "His Majesty's guards storm from rooms, the general has been drunk every time we speak. The king disregards the protocol of the ball—did you know I studied for weeks to learn that dance?"

Azimir broke into laughter. "I've seen Kep dance with one person only and it was certainly not at a ball. You ought to be counting your luckcharms—he'd have stepped on your foot, likely as not."

Rih sighed dramatically. "I could have been studying something interesting and useful!"

"Well, I appreciated your tutelage." Azimir's shoulders still shook with laughter. "I imagine we'll both need entertainment in the coming months."

Rih's mood sobered. She did have something interesting and useful to occupy her. "I imagine with weather as harsh as this there is little to do."

"Plenty to do around fires—reading, if you're inclined. I struggle being still so I spend much of my time in the training courts."

"I've been training with Admiral Fess and some of her colleagues," Rih confessed. "I'm not certain they appreciate my presence, but they act welcoming enough."

Azimir leaned forward, happily pouring another mug for himself. "Do you know atlatl, then? And those long polearms?"

"Glaives and prairie stars. I'm learning some grappling from another woman there. But I'm surprised at how free my days are."

"Well my offer to show you the city stands." Azimir glanced out the window and his face brightened. "Snow! Mirik doesn't get much of it, island winds sweep it clear."

Rih stared at the snow. It drifted, frozen milkgrass seeds in legion, and settled on every roof and rampart. "It's beautiful."

His smile echoed hers. "I know. Most loathe it, and it mucks up the roads for wagons and mail. Still, there's something freeing about giving up responsibility for a day."

"I expected it to be ugly."

"Snow?"

"Ceir Athrolan. And it's not pretty, not in the way Ban is, with is richness and elaborate details. But it's elegant in a way." She watched the streets fill with snow, ground into wet gray hummocks where wagon wheels churned through. "Perhaps not all of it."

Azimir's chin jerked as he snorted. "Lately I hardly recognize her. I can't imagine what An'thor thinks of how much everything has changed since he first arrived."

Rih's gaze moved from Bimet's hands to the city and back, trying to take everything in. After a moment she frowned, pointing at the dark smudge on the horizon. "Is that more snow?"

Azimir followed her gesture, smile fading. "No. That's the smoke. They're burning the fields, trying to keep blight from spreading."

Half of the gate in the wall eased open, permitting a train of harvest wagons. What should have been overflowing beds were barely stacked past the sideboards. Even the wagoneers looked exhausted.

"I suppose that's one task for the cold months," Rih noted, pulling her wrap closer against the cold. "Try to keep everyone from starving."

Φ

The 31st Day of Valemord, 1272
The Tundra of the Northlands

"At least it's not as bleak as it was last time," Alea offered.

Arman stared at her, incredulous, until his horse stumbled over an icy crag. "Less bleak? Fates, it's a small wonder half the Nenev are monstrous if this is their good day."

Alea chuckled and nudged her mount faster. "We're almost there, if this map's correct."

"I see nothing. And this place is flatter than the sky. Not sure I entirely trust those people either. Didn't tell us the woman had gone at first."

"I think they were protecting her. Last few of our kind, former citadel and so forth. Like Vielrona." Alea glanced up at the clear gray above them. Even at night the light never truly died. "I'll know it when I see it."

Arman hummed noncommittally. It was unlikely they would find her up here. Just another trail to follow. *Why would she even drive them this way?* A glance at Alea told him her face was still set in certainty. It was more than he had seen in weeks.

"There!" Alea's rough voice cut through his musing. One of her water-wrinkled fingers pointed ahead and to the east. A massive iron mile marker jutted, rusty, from the barren hill. She smiled. "We're here."

"There's nothing."

"Look down." She gestured to the base of the hill beyond. A round iron door was set in the earth, ruts from mighty machines softened by several decades of scrubgrass and frost. She pulled up just beside it and dismounted. Her hands tested it, turning it one way, then another, head tilted as if waiting for it to impart some secret. After a few more tries she shook her head. "I don't know the code."

"It's iron, right?"

"Yes. Only thing that survives the seasons up here."

Arman swung himself down and rested a hand on the metal. The sputtering power he could barely access was gone. Rather, the human part of him had burned so much, it was a charred layer barely separating him from his power. Withered conduits between himself and his power trembled and charred as he taxed them too far. Metal was earth. Heat bubbled from his throat. He groaned at the effort. Rust flaked from the surface as it heated, glowing from within. One hand, claws sprouting from the blackened tips of his fingers, made a dragging motion. The hill shuddered. Grasses under his boots wilted and turned black. The skin around his mouth paled to white and cracked over the angry flesh below. Gears squealed beneath the earth. A thud, a thunk, and the door opened.

Alea's cold-tinged lips curled and she handed him his reins. "Perhaps I should have brought you the first time."

He laughed, the sound echoing oddly down the tunnel before them. "I doubt I would have been good company." He dipped his hand into the gutter along the wall digging at the thin residue of fat. It sputtered and ignited.

"Who goes?" The shout echoed from far ahead, made loud by the iron confines.

"An old friend of the Wanderer, riding from Lymorda," Alea answered.

Arman wondered if they could smell the salt from the other end, feel the creeping, unseasonable frost curling down the entrance. Silence, then a second row of flame flickered into being. Arman peered up, blinking at the brightness. A figure limped closer, metal clacking with every other step. The man stopped when he was just a few paces away, leaning on his iron cane. "Dhoah' Lyne'alea. Never thought I'd see you again."

Alea tilted her head, watery eyes peering at the faded burgundy hair and ashen skin. "You're General Aneral's friend."

"Albi'giran. Yes. We never met properly—"

"You fought for us. That's enough," Alea whispered. Were those tears or just the ocean flooding her skin?

"Why don't you come in and rest. We have little in the way of comfort, but if you rode from Berr I doubt you'll snub it," he explained. His chuckle was the rasp of dry grass.

"Old friends are comfort enough," Arman answered. They fell into step behind the asai warrior.

Silence reigned as they walked. A second door opened the same way as the first, though this with a twist of Albi'giran's hand. The tunnel terminated at the base of a circular courtyard. Three stories of rooms circled it, with a dome of bare iron bars making up the open ceiling. Arman glimpsed a crag of rock ringing the opening on the surface. They'd passed a few random clusters of boulders on their journey. How many had hidden the grated ceilings of Nenev houses?

"They're covered with ice blocks in winter, save for the smoke-hole. If you're wondering how we keep winter out."

Arman hummed in response. It felt good to be surrounded by stone and metal and feel the heat of fire beneath his feet. His attention returned to the conversation to hear Alea answering some question.

"It's been months, actually. A bit of a foxhunt across the wilderness, at least for the latter half of it."

"I can't imagine what brings you this far north."

"We're just passing through, I think."

"On your way to where?" His gray-laced brows curled in. "There's nothing north of this. At least, nothing more than ruins and ice. The world's spire is pretty, surely, but you're in the wrong season for malostrii."

"We didn't come for the sky-lights. Just a woman." Alea glanced at the bank of stalls as they stabled their mounts. All but four were empty. "Where is everyone?"

The asai did not meet her eyes. "I'll put some tea and food on. Second floor, third door on the right." He disappeared from view.

Arman leaned on the stall door, running a soothing hand over his horse's neck. He checked over her hooves and sniffed the water in the bucket on her door before joining Alea in the courtyard. She waited for him on a tight grate suspended on chains. She smiled and pulled back a long lever. After a moment gears engaged and they lurched upwards. Arman laughed, watching the ground inch away from under their boots. "I like the Nenev, I think."

She snorted. "Their structures are about the only thing I care to see again."

"We'll have our answers soon, love."

"I don't know," she answered as the platform shuddered to a halt at the second story. "I have more questions now. I want to know the nature of Keplan's—" her voice broke on their son's name, "of his power. Most of me just wants to see him again, power be tossed. I'd sell our last breath to have our answer be here."

Arman followed her into the room Albi'giran had indicated, dumping their bags in an undignified heap. "And if it's not?"

"Then we'll keep looking. Somewhere there's an answer. And if I have to sail to the Gods' Island itself, to Le'yne again, then so be it."

He reached out for her hand, wincing at the clammy chill. "We," he corrected. "This time you won't go alone."

Her brief smile was wan but sincere.

Downstairs, a small, warm room waited, door propped open in welcome. Albi'giran limped to the fireplace, tray of dried meat and kelp in his free hand. "So. What's brought you here?"

Alea seemed transfixed by the fire, so Arman guided her to a seat before answering. "We're looking for an old woman. She had others with her, supporters, of a kind."

"Just a woman? A friend or enemy?"

"Family," Alea interjected, voice breaking through ice on its way from her throat. "Of a kind."

The asai's features showed no surprise. Simply vague interest.

No wonder they're called the Stonefaced, Arman realized. *Calm in the face of the Dhoah' Laen, in the face of her desperate search for the last of her people.*

"You're looking for a book. Not a woman." He jabbed at the coals with the iron tip of his cane.

Alea shook her head. "I've seen her, she keeps talking of blood. Screaming."

"I'm sure. It's all she ever said."

"She was here?" Arman's focus sharpened on the man. They had been quick to trust him, but his flat affect now tightened his nerves. *What do you know?* He took a tentative sip of the tea, winced, and took a larger gulp. "Where did she go? Is she dead?"

"I'd know if she were dead," Alea snapped. The air chilled and the man glanced between them.

"She's not dead, no. She acquired some," he hesitated, glancing at the narrow dim hall outside his open door, "believers."

"Orabon Marum." Alea's hand skimmed the pocket that held their map.

His copper eyes blinked and he reached for another slice of cured bear. "More than him now. Many more. Some from Berr, but some from here as well. They focus not on our past but, like my people, our future. They've heard her teachings, her visions, and have taken them to heart. She speaks of One God who will raise us from this in-between state."

Arman's skin crawled. Alea's visions echoed those words. When she slipped into sleep or away from consciousness, her mouth never ceased moving, whispering whatever messages she heard within. Beside him, Alea's eyes were screwed shut, tears leaking from their corners. "In-between?"

"While you were holed up in your cabin in the forest, this world's been dying. Crops won't grow as fast. Blight strikes harder. Summer here is shorter, colder. I haven't seen the snow geese in four years. Even the ice bears are starving. Perhaps we see it better, up here in the dark north, where even the smallest change would threaten our existence. Something is strangling the world. And they believe he—this One God—will save us."

"God's blood is strangling the world,'" Alea paraphrased.

Albi'giran's face tightened a fraction. "When they arrived I assumed the same as most would—she was a madwomen and they fools. But then I recognized the words. Most of her more coherent babbling matched the histories my people kept. The few of us who remained settled here for a time but then pushed farther north. They felt they had to cast off the shackles of the old ways for hope at a new beginning. So they left our tomes. And the few of us who hindered travel. Suffice to say, I've had plenty of time to read."

Arman felt a flash of pity for the man. Living in the forest had been lonely, surely, but he had Alea and Keplan. Locked in a world of ice and broken machines seemed a terrible fate.

Alea's tearstained face was luminous in the dark. "You said I was looking for a book. You mean your people's history?"

"I mean a book referenced there. It's the history of all of us. You, Earth Shakers, gods, the lot of us."

Her eyes dimmed at his tone. "It's not here, is it?"

"We don't know where it is."

"Neneviir," Arman realized. "It's where you found the Laen Crown. If it's anywhere, it'll be there."

Alea shuddered, face paling further. "I would truly rather not. I've been before and once was more than enough."

"But surely—"

"Where are they headed now?" Alea interrupted him.

Albi'giran's jaw worked and he glared at the fire. "They're marching on Athrolan."

"Keplan's there." Frantic energy lit Alea's features now, looking more alert than she had been in days.

Dread lit Arman's veins, searing his arteries. The food in his hand heated, bear lard dripping down the cracked back of his hand. "Marching?"

"In the name of the One God, they fear if we don't all bow before him then he won't come at all and the world will fall to ruin. So they ride to every city between here and the Banis jungles and see that they have no choice."

"Arman, if Kep's caught in this—" Alea protested.

"Then we had best have all the answers." He reached for her hand, but her fingers were fisted. "No matter where they are. Or what they might be."

Φ

The night air whipped between the bare bars overhead. The low ceiling in the room behind her kept the smoke low, stinging her eyes. Arman had not seemed to notice. Instead, he crouched over the table still holding their barely touched food, making tick marks on the map. She could not stomach planning another journey to Neneviir. It did not matter that Albi'giran claimed it was all but deserted. Neneviir was where she had broken. Cracks from the massacre in Cehn were furthered by pain, by solitude. *And another ally lost faith in me.* If Arman realized how much of herself she left there, his face showed nothing.

Not even the howling wind was loud enough. The screaming never stopped. Each time she closed her eyes to sleep it was there, wavering with the same breath. It hitched when the throat was slit, gurgled over cooling blood. Still it went on. The head in her lap wore a mask of myriad faces, flickering from one to the next once death fell. It was Arman, Ahren, Narier, Bren, that poor man she could not save, the woman who cleaned the manor, the children she helped raise.

Half the time she had no name to pin on the face, but they were familiar as her own blood for the moment they lay there, staring up at her with accusing, puzzled eyes. Their blood pulsed through her hands, entered her flesh and roared through her power. She reached into their chests and parted ribs, parted the wall of souls, ripped the Laen's power open, ripped lungs and hearts open. Then it was Keplan, thin face scarred in a strange pattern. His eyes rolled, pupils blown. The blood spurting from him was brilliant copper, as copper as the gods' had been.

"Is there anything I can do?" Albi'giran's low voice tempered those still muttering in her mind.

She shook her head, glancing back. The smoldering coals of the hearthfire backlit him. Inside, Arman traced some trail Alea's eyes hardened on the asai. "I don't want our path to lead to Neneviir. I know I swore I'd go anywhere for him but," she looked up at the blackness beyond the open roof, "doesn't mean it will be easy."

"Neneviir fell. During the Gods' War, An'thoriend gathered who he could, rallied enough of a force to help. It fractured them, seeing you, I think. Some held faith in the gods or you, others lost it entirely."

"And what about Edrodene?"

"Dead. Years ago. He ruled for a while, clinging to order as they do. There was a bit of a revolt and afterward not much was left of the city. Not enough worth saving." The wind moaned.

"Revolt? Last I heard Athrolan suffers from something similar."

"I heard the same." His copper eyes turned to hers. "You said your son was in their capital? Kap something?"

She nodded. "Keplan. His name is Keplan Wardyn and he's seventeen."

Albi'giran's face softened, the most expression she had seen since they arrived. "I have a daughter, just twenty at the beginning of the month."

"Where is she now?"

"She left with the prophet. Like many of the others her age, they did not know a world with gods in it."

Alea shivered at the thought. "How could you let her go?"

"How could I not? The most I can do is love her and listen. You protect them for too long, the greatest danger becomes themselves."

"I'm realizing that." Alea frowned at him. "Even so, they're fanatics."

"I don't know." His eyes were fixed on the sky. "Read the book and then tell me they're wrong."

CHAPTER SIX

The 32nd Day of Valemord, 1272
The City of Ceir Athrolan, Athrolan

KEPLAN RAN THE LEATHER over the knife again. The library was deserted at dawn. The sharp scent of rich parchment filled the air, bolstered with oil. The leather sank against the steel with a gentle swish. War.

It was all he had been avoiding since he left the Hartland. Perhaps, though, he had not been avoiding it, but rather running from it as it dogged him across the continent. Now it slavered at his sanity and his city. *Swish.* War. It was the only thought in his mind. There was something poetic about it—the only reason he was still in Athrolan, the only reason he married Rih, and the only reason he was still alive was to stop war.

And here I am, starting one over faith. His gaze dropped to his hands, grease-stained and gripping the skin around the blade. *"His right hand will be red with wrath, and his left verdant green of mercy."*

Whatever terrible mistake his parents had made in creating him had come home to roost. It was mighty enough to creep into a madwoman's thoughts, poisoning her mind with lies.

If he feared Athrolan would fall with a pauper king, now he had to see if it could survive a heretic.

An'thor's rasp was grit underfoot. "We need to talk."

"The counsel is in an hour. I'd like to be alone until then."

"Then why aren't you locked in your rooms as usual?"

Keplan gestured to the shelves around him. "Look at these. How many books do you think sit on these shelves?"

"Hundreds. Thousands, perhaps. And in various languages."

"And yet, not a one contains a whisper of what I am. I see so much and understand so little. Now I'm speaking in contradictions too."

"You called a war counsel." The general's hands were too steady for sobriety, but his voice shook with frustration.

"Because we're at war."

"What did you do?"

"I don't think she liked my tone," Keplan whispered. Stillness washed over him, buoyed by a hundred fragments of thoughts rolling off the city. "People have gone to war for less."

An'thor shook his head. "I've been in countless wars, Wardyn. Even started some myself. None of them have been worth it, but this is absurd. And you're sending Dorcal away? Do you wish us to crumble?"

"Dorcal is where I need him to be. We're desiccated. A thousand books and not one written in the last seventeen years. We can barely keep our aqueducts from bursting or running dry. Our crops wither in the field or molder after harvest. We need more. We need to stretch our legs, learn from others. I'll stay here and hold whatever this is at bay. He can bring back hope."

"You trust him?"

"Fates, no," Keplan scoffed, twisting the blade in his hand to send spots of light dancing over the stone walls. "But I don't trust you or Blackhouse either."

"I got you on this cursed throne—"

"That makes me like you less."

"What did she say to you?" An'thor hissed. "You sound as mad as her."

"She read her prophesies. About the god. This woman has been having the same visions I have—earth cracking open, empires rising, falling and blood. Always blood. But she's got it wrong. I think she sees me, watching the same events unfold and mistook me for a piece of it."

"Aren't you? Parents such as yours, you can hardly be irrelevant."

Keplan shook his head. "In the visions something's killing the world. She thinks I'm here to save it."

An'thor's chin rose, his eyes narrowing on the king. "What are you here for, then?"

Keplan flexed his hands, setting aside the knife. "I don't think I'm supposed to be. Whatever my parents were meant to do, it didn't involve me. I interrupted it, broke it somehow. Strangled it. I just have to keep Athrolan whole until something can come along and stop it—stop me."

"Visions. How much of this is because of dust?"

Keplan reared back. "What?"

"I'm not oblivious, boy. You might not be on it now, but you have been. Pacing, chewing on your lips. Your eyes are blacker than mine half the time. You can't focus on anything, or it's all you can think of, just fixating. I'm not for dust, personally, but I've known plenty who are."

"Domariigo, I swear, if you tell," Keplan breathed.

"I'm not telling anyone. It'd be—what was your phrase?—rich coming from a man who hasn't been sober in a decade. I'm not judging you. I don't care enough. But I do care about Athrolan."

"Then give me your firearm."

An'thor's hand dropped to the weapon at his belt. "Why?"

"Because there's something at our door. It's ravaging our fields and laying waste to our people. How many murders have been reported in the past year? We're desperate, frantic. The sky is closing in around us and we can all feel it. Whether it's because of the prophet's lies or mine, I don't know, but I'm going to need everything we have. I promised Ban your knowledge, but I think it's fair I get first choice."

"We can discuss what machines and technology you need after we determine if war is wise."

"I've already decided, General. I'm king here," he leveled his wide eyes on the Nenev, "or have you forgotten that?"

The shelves behind him rattled. Dust drifted from the beams overhead. An'thor's black eyes followed the movement, tracing a phantom trail across the ceiling and down to the window. The glass rattled.

"I told you, Domariigo: something's knocking."

Φ

Roast meat and biscuits cooled on the table. Keplan fiddled with his food as Fess argued with An'thor; it had been going on for the past four minutes and he had long since lost interest.

"I just don't see the sense in arguing with them! Let them erect their temples, let them proselytize on our corners. What harm does it do?"

"Harm?" Fess asked. "They've threatened war if we don't. What happens when this prophet's new scripture decrees her more powerful than His Majesty? What happens when her visions show Athrolan bequeathing half her treasury to their cause? It's a slippery slope, and we're well down it already."

"How is that any different from our alliance with Ban? We married slave traders for peace, I don't see how heretics are any different."

Keplan's frayed patience snapped. "I married them!" he roared. "Not you, Domariigo. And none of you heard what I did, none of you had to stomach that prophet's lies. I've done nothing but avoid war since I ascended, so when I say heresy is worth fighting, I expect you to put down your biscuits and go to war!"

Fess stared at him, her brown eyes wary. "Of course, sire. While General Domariigo seems concerned, I think we all agree this is a threat. And even you, sire, admit it's one we haven't faced before. Perhaps if you tell us what she said we'd be able to ascertain how best to approach them. Do you even know when they'll attack?"

Keplan shook his head. "Has anyone seen Blackhouse? He had first correspondence with them. And," his voice faltered, "he was the last person to speak with my mother."

"The Dhoah' Laen?" an officer asked. "I thought they were gone—hidden in some mountain somewhere."

"The Hartland, actually. And so did I." The king put aside his food and leaned on the table.

"What else did she say? The soldier, that is."

"They call themselves Swordbearers. There's this creature coming, and its existence is smothering the world. That much I can agree on. I've seen it too. But they're wrong. It's not a god. It's a mistake. One my parents made, I think. She said we'd best hope the One True God has mercy on us." He looked up at Fess, then An'thor. "Because their Swordbearers wouldn't."

An'thor's head sank to his pale, ragged hands. "Toss it all."

"I don't think we need to waste any more time discussing whether we should fight them. War's already been declared."

"We don't have the troops. We don't have the grain. We don't have the money," he countered.

"Ban does."

Keplan turned at the new voice. Rih and her translator stood in the doorway to the counsel hall. His wife's hands moved again.

"Forgive me for inviting myself, but I only just learned there was a counsel."

An'thor opened his mouth, but Fess interrupted him. "Her Highness Rihelte is a valuable asset, sire. We train together and I've already learned much."

Keplan waved for a page to produce a chair. He did not want to think of Ban or his marriage, but if she was willing to find a solution, he welcomed her. *I just can't look her in the eye.* "Of course. I apologize for not thinking to invite you."

"How many do they number? Where are they based?" An'thor asked. "Do we even know their allies?"

"Mirik hasn't allied with them," Keplan noted. "Azimir claimed they ignored the letter due to their focus on Ban," he glanced at Rih, "begging your pardon."

A single black brow rose. "It's hardly your fault our nations attack each other," she noted.

"I can hardly beg either of you for support in this, though, when your people are already at war."

"What's one more war?" she quipped.

An'thor's dark gaze bounced between the two of them, narrowing further. "His Majesty has a good point, Your Highness—"

"His Eminence styles himself a god, general," Rih interrupted. "If you think he would tolerate another deity in his empire, you don't know Ban well at all. He is not what one would call tolerant. It's why we win every war we've ever fought."

"I can't ask for help in this, not after we already argued over the wheat we were promised months ago."

"That's negotiations," Fess explained. "Everyone attempts to bring their own costs down."

"You hardly did, offering up our dear general's mind for picking."

An'thor's pale lips thinned and he sat back. "I'm hardly willing to give over that information to Athrolan, let alone a foreign megalomaniac."

Keplan turned on him. "What happened to caring about Athrolan? Or was that just pretty talk this morning?"

An'thor shot him a glare. "If you understood the magnitude of what my people created, you would realize why I can't trust it to humans."

"Then why don't we agree: I'll trust that you'll only give us the technology our pathetic human minds can handle, and you'll trust that what Nena'phe told me is worth going to war over."

Fess cleared her throat. "Let's reach out to other nations to ask what they have heard and their reactions. I'll send scouting ships along the coast to determine the reach of these Swordbearers, if you permit me, of course, sire."

Her deference was pointed in the wake of An'thor's insubordination. Keplan nodded. "Granted. Please see that Dorcal departs tomorrow as well. An escort until he's out of our waters should do, but I trust you'll know best."

"Consider it done."

"Rih," he switched to Banis, "would you write to your friends or cousins in RoBal? Ask if they've heard of these people. Informally if you can."

She nodded, making a note on a wax tablet before her.

"Colonels, send missives to each of your holdings and your neighboring nobles. If they have any force worth fighting, someone will have seen it already."

The officers rose, bowing. Conversation hummed in the hallway beyond as they filed out.

"And you, General," Keplan continued, when just he and Fess were alone with the man. "Give me schematics for your weapon or the weapon itself by the end of this meeting or I'll order bars on your door just as I did with Dorcal."

Fess glanced between them. "Sire, I don't know if that's necessary."

"You can't see what I do when I close my eyes. What lies before us if we succumb to fanatics. We will need every asset moving forward."

An'thor slumped in his chair, knocking back his drink. It smelled of mildew and honey. "I don't agree with this. Any of it."

"Your concern has been noted."

The general unclipped his revolver from its holster and placed the weapon on the table with a *thunk*. His hand did not move from the oiled leather and polished bone. "I've used this a handful of times. Most was in defense of your mother and her people. It's a responsibility. When you take up a weapon like this you must be ready to kill, because unlike blades, bullets can't be blocked."

"Is that how you became general after the war?"

An'thor did not respond, only rose, leaving his weapon on the table, and made for the door. Above bells tolled, echoing balefully from snow-dusted white towers. Riders burst from the stables, their white and turquoise uniforms covered with blood-red cloaks. By week's end, news of war would reach every corner of Athrolan.

Φ

The 34th Day of Valemord, 1272

Raven jerked the door open, blinking against the sudden light from the hall. "Yes?"

An'thor swayed in the doorway, peering up at him. "Your arrest is lifted."

"I know. I leave tomorrow." Raven faltered, realizing the man was not announcing it. "Is this your attempt at amends?"

"Fuck if I know. I'm too drunk to sleep and too tired to fight. You have a minute?"

Raven preferred to sleep. The hours before a journey were meant to be spent in solitude. He opened the door wider and sighed. "A minute."

An'thor lurched into the dark study, slumping into Raven's chair without further invitation. "I think you got the better end of the gamble here."

"I was under house arrest for a month. I've lost my titles. Lost my queen."

"We both lost her, Raven," An'thor muttered. "Everyone lost Tzatia. Eras too. Yet you're leaving their memories here."

"You left Claimiirn. It's hardly different."

"Claimiirn was in ruins."

"Arguably, so is Athrolan." Raven crossed his arms over his bare chest. "I thought you were too tired to fight."

An'thor stared at his hands, sullen. "Do you have any—"

"No. You're not drinking my best liquor like it's brook water. His Majesty gave me a choice—house arrest for the rest of my days or go explore. I wouldn't say it was much of a choice, frankly."

"I suppose you have no ties here, no children, no wife. Just duty."

Raven winced. "There was a child. Once." He rarely spoke of it. Rarely held it in his waking mind.

An'thor looked away. "You never told me."

"Eras hardly told me, either," Raven excused. "I'd make a gutterwash father. I'd have tried, but…" He trailed off and shrugged. An'thor would have made just a mess of parenthood, he was sure, but perhaps half of the man's personality was built upon a father's grief.

"I think I tried, with Mel'iend. Failed him, in the end. But I tried."

"Did he survive the war?"

An'thor looked away and Raven knew to press the issue no further. "When are you due back?"

"When I've found something worth reporting, I suppose."

"Until nothing looks familiar," the general whispered. "Wardyn asked for my revolver."

Raven's gaze dropped to An'thor's belt. Sure enough, a dark splotch marked where the weapon usually hung. His concern flared. "And you gave it to him?"

"I wouldn't say it was much of a choice," An'thor repeated. "What do you think he expects you to find out there?"

"He said we were stagnant. We needed to progress."

"First that, then asking for Nenev machines? It bodes ill."

"Does it?" Raven shrugged. "He's not wrong. But I think there's more. Whatever it is he sees in that mind of his, whether it's real or not, I think he wants it explained."

"You think you'll find the answers?"

Raven sighed, looking down at his packed bags. "Doesn't matter if I do or don't. Athrolan has no place for me. You either, I'd wager. He's changing the face of her. I'm not saying he won't do the kingdom good, I just refuse to believe a human throne should be sat by," he raked a hand through his hair, "by that."

"But Eras was fine."

"Eras never sat the throne, and she was half human."

"So is Keplan," An'thor reminded him.

Raven clenched his teeth, mind flickering back to the colorless, luminous gaze of his king. "You've clearly never looked His Majesty in the eyes. Leastwise, not while sober."

An'thor seemed to debate a response, then shook his head. "I know he's what's best. For the same reasons you think he's a mistake. He knows so much, I have to believe he'll see us through this chaos. But I wonder how much of it is his own making."

"How much is yours, though?"

An'thor met his eyes, expression unreadable. "Tell me about the last time you saw her. Alive. Well."

Raven sighed. He did not have to ask which her An'thor meant. "It was just before she named the new fort in memory of Fort Shadow. She invited me to tea."

By the time the Nenev left, dawn brightened the skyline. Raven scrubbed a hand over his exhausted eyes. His chests were already packed, his uniform—conspicuously lacking his commander's badge—pressed and waiting on the armor stand. He brushed a hand over Eras's portrait and spared a nod to his queen before lifting the map down. It rolled easily and he tucked it into a waterproof pouch in his writing kit. It left a pale spot on the soot-stained wall above the mantle.

"Sir Dorcal!" A woman's voice cut through the quiet study.

"Mariner Jorn?" He looked up to see his first mate in the doorway, burly arms crossed over the bright Athrolani naval uniform. Her wicked grin widened. "See you slept as well as I did."

"Keep chattering and I'll give you night's watch," he snapped. Her smile tugged an answering one from him, however, and he shouldered his bags. "It's been a while since I went farther than a diplomat's run," he mused, pausing at the top of the steep stairs down the naval docks. The city was awash with brilliant white, filth masked by snow, and cold enough that the Slummer stench had yet to permeate. He would even miss that.

The docks were quiet, lacquered wood thunking against the canvas padding in the thick air. Three boats awaited them, prepared to sail, but only one held all they might need for a voyage.

"I see His Majesty provided us an escort in the chance we decide to turn back to port."

Jorn bounced on the balls of her feet. "He hardly knows us at all, it seems. I could smell the salt in my dreams last night."

"Hardly slept," Raven answered before adjusting his bag on his shoulder. He glanced at the palace, then out at the fog-shrouded horizon. Curiosity uncurled in his gut.

Φ

The 36th Day of Valemord, 1272
The Village of Jai, Ban

Jani propped his head on his crossed arms as he peered over the wall. "Anything to do this morning?"

"Nothing I know about yet," Reka responded in Banis.

He grinned. "That's how it often is in this busy house. Come hunting with me?"

She grinned, vaulting over the wall he leaned on and into the garden behind their rel. "Love nothing more."

It was easy to fall into the familiar truncated speech. Ikel spoke Banis better than Jani spoke Border or Trade. Reka spoke enough Banis not to be a concern for the town guards, apparently.

She crept back inside through the rear ladder. Her hammock hung across the narrow hall from the children's, and the last thing she wanted to do was wake them. The quiet hours of morning were precious. She grabbed her bow and the oiled leather hood that kept her head and shoulders dry. By the time she had slipped through the kitchen, grabbed a handful of pressed meat and nut mix, and emerged, Jani already waited in the street.

"You survived," he noted with a nod to the still quiet house. "Took me years to figure out how to get out without waking them."

"Tools of the trade," she joked, falling into stride beside him.

The town was beginning to stir, but just barely. With the rains came gray mornings and the urge to stay inside and weave. Jani whistled up to the guard on duty, tossing a string of beads up.

Reka glanced at him curiously.

"Bribe. Not allowed out during war, but a fair few of us can't survive on rations. I've picked up a few private guard jobs, but nothing big enough to pay for all of us to eat. Can't with the scheduled shifts."

Reka shook her head. "They ought to pay you for your time. Athrolan military does. Extra if you're an officer."

Jani shook his head as they ducked through the small door set in the gate. "We get all our own needs met—food, clothes, housing if we need. It's just our families that suffer. Incentive not to have one," he explained.

Reka grimaced. Ban had so many more resources than Athrolan, though much of it was gleaned on the back of slavery and rarely seen by anyone below the nobles and dignitaries. Athrolan had her own host of issues with corruption and nationalism. *I can't say which I'd choose if I had to.* Sometimes there was a benefit to belonging nowhere.

Rich yellow grasses stretched between copses of broad-branched trees, brilliant green wedged at their roots as they prepared to push new growth. Each step dampened Reka's boots. Hot smells of baking wheat were replaced by the damp earth and rain on the exposed juts of brown stone. Above, the slate-colored sky warned of a wet afternoon. Trails wove between the tender stalks, and it was along one of these they walked. They did not speak, Jani pointing occasionally to where a snare hid in the grass or a print sank particularly deep into the damp earth.

The first string of snares was camouflaged in the dense mat of dead grasses at the roots of the waving green stalks. Jani knelt, checking that the loop was still open. Reka scanned the rise ahead while he adjusted the supports.

"It's unnerving," she murmured. Even with the distant rumble of thunder and the wind, she did not trust her voice not to carry.

He sat back, following her gaze. After a second he nodded. "Most don't last long out here, if they weren't raised on it. So open, makes you feel too small."

Reka hummed. "Anyone could be watching us and we'd never know. Makes me feel like we're being stalked."

"Half of Ban feels like that. Even in the city." Jani rose with a sigh, moving to the next loop.

Reka eyed him. Ikel had yet to speak to her privately, and while Reka was happy to relax, she could not shake the shadow hanging over her visit. "Is that what Ikel meant in her letter? About something brewing?"

Jani paused, fingers cradling the hemp string. This one had been nibbled through and the soil below was stained with flecks of dried blood. "What did she tell you?"

Panic flashed in Reka's veins. Had Ikel told him, even? When she found her way, it was with little guidance, save for her first meeting with the merchant's guard. She chose a neutral phrase. "That Ban was changing."

He did not answer, moving from empty snare to empty snare. Then, among the prairie grass, there was a flutter of frantic movement. He crouched, following the line for another few paces before he found the trapped creature. It was a hare, fat with the wet season's abundance.

Jani crouched and grabbed it by the tethered foot. With practiced efficiency he snapped its neck and loosened the snare. He sat for a moment, staring at the cooling body. Finally he cleared his throat. "This is an insidious country. Always watched, always measured, and always, always, left wanting. It started with the women. A woman, really. Many have carried the idea and even acted upon it, but we'd only hear about it at the end, when they were executed. This time it was different." He flashed a smile as the sky rumbled a prelude to the storm.

"There was nothing to hear," Reka realized. "The word—it's just a typical sign. One half your empire uses."

"Half is a bit optimistic, but yes. You can't just see the sign or hear a word and know its second meaning, the life it lives when prayed and spoken and signed with hope. There's a network, hardly any of it written, but each of us who carries the spark of liberty also carries a piece of the revolution in their bones. My sister brought word first. She's a—"

"The soldier." Reka knelt beside him, pressing forward. "It's reached the military? That's where a rebellion goes to die."

"You just left Athrolan, you know that's not true. It's not where they die if they're born there. We've a general—I don't know her name or her rank or even where she is or how old. I just know that she began this, and with our help—and yours too, I hope—she will win it."

Thunder clapped above them, and rain began in earnest. Jani laughed and tucked the hare into his bag. "There's an outcropping ahead, we'll wait out the worst of it."

Reka nodded, ducking her head to keep the rain from her eyes as they broke into a jog. A boulder topped the next rise, one piece broken and creating a makeshift angled roof. They wedged themselves inside and Jani dropped to a crouch. "Should bag another three hares—the snares on the southern loop are the farthest from the road and often catch something."

"I'll see if those gazelle are still by the lake on our way back," Reka agreed. She did not know how she felt about revolution. Athrolan's attempt at civil war was ugly and clumsy. War was not the Border way. Even with their bands dissolved and absorbed into other cultures as empires spread, she adhered to her moral rule of single combat wherever she could. Thoughtful lines on Jani's calm face told her the discussion of revolution was over the for the time being, but leaving it dangling felt a bit like the hare, tugging on a string as it waited for death.

"Jani, about what you said—"

His fingers were hard on her bicep and he pointed. The grasses waved, the movement almost masked by the wind. Except this angled southwest.

Rih eased herself farther into the rock's cleft, timing her motion with the gusts of wind. The line of horses bore no riders, only the tips of their ears and heads bobbing above the tall grasses in the swale. Still, movement before and after them told her they were flanked by people. "Banis?" she mouthed.

Jani's head shook once and he pointed at her. "Mirikin. Horses."

She glanced back out. Sure enough, the few sets of ears and manes were long and loose, not the upright elegance of riahs. *Toar, what are they doing this far south?* She knew, of course, that the war brought them here, but she had not realized how far Kemmer pressed.

Thankfully the shelter barely fit the two of them, and was of no use to the dozen or so riders. The march moved on through the rain and disappeared to the west.

Jani drew a slow breath. His face was pale and Reka saw the flutter of a pounding pulse in his throat. "I didn't know they were so close."

Reka shook her head. "Neither did I. You going to tell the guards?"

"I'll warn them, but they can't make an official report when we're not allowed outside the village walls. Or permitted to let anyone in." He fiddled with the end of his braid. "I can't keep leaving, not if they're that close. It's only a matter of time before I either get caught or they follow me back. We're on few enough maps that we've been ignored so far, but it won't last."

"Let's finish your snares and head home then," she offered.

Using curtains of rain as cover, they kept to the gullies. It was a death wish to follow streambeds during the wet season, but the steep banks had enough vegetation to hide most of their movement. Reka's heart raced with every particularly active hummock of grass or grouse that took to the sky with their passing. More than once she glanced over her shoulder, expecting to see a line of Mirikin riders bearing down.

The rest of Jani's snares were empty, save one that clearly had been cut with a knife. He grimaced and untied the string, shortening the tether to make a new loop.

"I think your friends there might have taken our supper."

Reka winced. "Not my friends."

The gazelle had gone from the gully just beyond the town, startled by all the traffic in the last few hours. Reka followed Jani back across the deserted prairie and through the gates without comment.

Their house was awake and bustling when they returned. Kas sat at one of the tiers chopping roots while her younger brother attempted to mend his doll's sandal.

"Any luck?" Ikel asked, looking up with a smile.

"Some." Jani retrieved the hare from his bag and brought it over to the basin by the door to clean. He glanced at their children. "Saw some former friends of your cousin while sheltering from the rain."

Ikel paled and her gaze moved from him to Reka and back. "I'm glad you made such good time, then."

Reka sighed. She was not sure she agreed with keeping everything from the children. Innocence was only noticed by its absence and was something she had no interest in preserving. "There were only a few, but I didn't expect them."

Jani hung the hare's feet up to dry to be sold for hunting cats or dogs. Ikel lapsed into quiet, stirring the spices toasting in the broad skillet.

"I spoke with your cousin today," Jani commented, tugging the hare's skin free in one smooth motion. "About my sister."

Ikel did not look up, but her every movement was sharp, its normalcy rehearsed. "Oh? And what did you think, Reka?"

Reka stared at the fire. She may not have agreed with armies or battles, but crouched under red rock as the patrol passed, she had apparently made her choice. "I think she and I would get along. And you're right—I'm ready for the ruak."

Φ

The 38th Day of Valemord, 1272
The City of Ceir Athrolan, Athrolan

Rih drew back, free arm pointed, guiding her sight to the target. She breathed once, twice, then let fly. Her room was stifling. Even her own skin felt too close, too tight. Each throw she hoped would settle her nerves enough to prevent her bones from quaking. Training with the commander and her friends was a diversion, but she rarely let herself sink into practice like she used to. She longed for the training halls in RoBal where she would throw until she settled in a thoughtless trance.

Ragged skin edged her nails from picking in her idle moments. She was not sure whether the insurmountable issues rising before her were real or just shadows cast by other, larger problems. Conversation took weeks when she was so far from any of her allies, and since the failure of Bet, she had not risked anything beyond suggesting movements of her trusted people to safer locations until it was time.

She jogged across the training court to collect her darts. When she turned back she saw Azimir leaning on the doorframe, dressed in training gear.

"Morning, Your Highness," he greeted.

She raised a hand. Knowing the training courts were deserted, she'd offered Bimet the morning off. She returned to the bench, looking through her plain wrap. She missed the pockets and pouches of soldiers' clothes, where she could keep a tablet and stylus at all times.

When she glanced up at a loss, he smiled. "I'll ask yes or no questions. I just finished training. Are you busy?"

She shook her head.

"Would you like to go into the city? It's warmer today."

She smiled and nodded, placing her weapon back in its case and bundling its darts together.

He crouched to catch her eye again. "I'm going to clean up and change into something more suitable. Should I meet you and Bimet at your rooms in an hour?"

Again, she nodded.

He sprang up and made for the door, waving cheerfully.

She waited to ring for Bimet until her bath was done, but even after weeks of practice she could not manage all her piercings and nets with the same ease.

By the time her translator arrived, Rih had draped a wrap over her head and shoulders. Bimet flashed a smile. "Where are we off to, Your Highness?"

"Azimir offered to show me the city," Rih explained before handing her the tray of rings that matched her dark blue outfit. "It's warmer today, he said."

Bimet threaded the wire through Rih's ears and nose, twirling the metal until the onyx and sapphire beads were centered. "You've spent a lot of time with Master A'hane," Bimet noted, surveying her handiwork. "More than with your husband."

Rih scowled, stepping back from Bimet's preening. "He knows where I live. He can visit at any time. I wouldn't want to spend time with the woman who brought me to the interrogators either."

"Of course. But people talk."

"You and Nehla are with us, and surely there will be guards. We're hardly alone. If he doesn't want to see me, His Majesty can suffer the rumors." She raised her head, surveying her reflection in the broad mirror. Her nerves did not show in her expression, thankfully. It was not true, and she knew it. The bravado was false, and whatever repercussions came would fall on her head more than Athrolan's king. *I just want to see the city!*

Nehla arrived a moment later, dressed for the cold city and bearing her usual bright smile. "Morning! I met Master A'hane at the door. He says we're going into the city?"

Rih nodded. "I thought we could also visit your family, if we have time. I wanted to see their silks."

Rih led them through her rooms and out the door where the young man waited with two guards dressed in Mirikin green.

"I don't suppose we should even try a pretense, with half the court following after us," he joked. "My father's been absurd since the attempt."

"I thought you said it was directed at one of Keplan's supporters in the city."

He winced, lively face sobering for a moment. "There was another. On me. On those of us who helped Keplan when he was first in the city, 'fore we knew what he was."

Fear was sharp in her gut. "I'm beginning to think the ordered evil of RoBal is preferable to this mess. I suppose that's what His Eminence bargains on." She stopped as two Banis guards appeared, realizing how bitter, how traitorous her words sounded.

Azimir did not seem to notice, face brightening at Bimet's presence. "I hoped you might join us, Lady Bimet." He bowed to Rih. "As much as I enjoy a challenge, your dialect of Banis is not one I can learn over one excursion."

Rih laughed. "It's not a dialect, which might make it easier. But not that easy."

"It's another language?" he asked, falling in beside her. His guards took up the rear. "Surely it's based in Banis."

"I wouldn't know, really, what Banis sounds like—I know the shapes your mouth makes to speak it, but signing is a different language altogether. The gestures are not in the same order as the words when someone speaks, just as sentences in Trade are structured differently than those in Banis. Signs are different too, in that we put the most important part first, and there are fewer fiddly words that get in the way."

Azimir frowned. "So, like me, you know two languages."

"Yes, but unlike you, here, I am one of the only people who speaks my first language."

He looked down, then back up. "You must be lonely."

The understanding in his eyes sent an ache through her chest. "Truthfully, I have always been, even in Ban. Even in the army. Even surrounded by my sisters who bled for me and for whom I would gladly bleed, I was alone."

His smile was fleeting. "I imagine there are many who feel that way. Your errant husband, for one."

She ducked her head to hide the flush in her cheeks. "He's surrounded by an entourage whose sole purpose is to keep him occupied. I'm sure he's simply busy."

The palace doors opened before them, permitting a biting wind that ushered them into the cold courtyard. Rih shivered, blinking in the bright sunlight.

"You all right?" Azimir asked.

She nodded and tugged her short Athrolani cloak tighter. The deep blue wool had been a gift from Keplan, apparently. Her layers did much to protect her from the worst of the chill, but the wind was insistent. "Just adjusting!"

He strode onto Tzama, heading toward the largest of the roads leading down toward the harbor. "I think you'd have more to talk about if either of you gave it a chance. Though I knew him before he ever ascended the throne, so perhaps I view him differently."

Rih frowned. "But he was always heir."

"Officially, yes, his mother's child was named as heir to the Athrolani throne, but he did not know who his mother was, who she had been to Athrolan, at least, nor that he was heir. He arrived on the back of a fuzzy draft pony and worked for his bed and board in the slums. He lived there longer than he's been crowned, actually." He paused, expression tense. "It's his story, though. Not mine to tell."

He gestured to the frost-covered city before them. "I've got little to do this afternoon, so I am yours to command. Would you like food? What would you like to see?"

"Nehla's cousin owns a silk shop. Perhaps we could go there?"

Azimir turned to Nehla, asking a series of questions Rih did not try to follow. Instead, she took in the view. Cracks in the stone were stained black from decades exposed to the ocean's moisture. It lent depth to the otherwise uniform white. The gray wood of every lamppost bore a coat of frost. Curls of it decorated the southern windows, sheltered from the brunt of the ocean wind.

Now women's fan-shaped embroidered headdresses were replaced with pointed wool felt edged with fur, most with flaps over the ears. Men, too, donned thick fur caps.

Azimir waved to get her attention. "Lady Nehla says it's in the Guildhall courts. Fairly safe there, and we'd cross a fair bit of the city, if you're not well sick of me yet."

Bimet began to protest, but Rih refused to look at her hands. "That sounds lovely."

They set out, Azimir waving exuberantly at the first large state building they passed. "The second-largest city guardhouse, Your Highness. The largest is by the docks, of course, but I prefer the Thorns—the guards from here." He grinned. "They know the best Slummer bars."

They continued, his tirade interrupted only when he spotted something new to explain. It was clear much of the nuance and detail of Azimir's tour were lost in Bimet's efforts to keep up with his rapid words.

While verbose, Azimir seemed harmless, and they were surrounded by her own guards. Rih let herself relax. Recalling the depth in his gaze as they spoke of war, she amended that thought. *Friendly. Not harmless.* Stalls and open store counters lined the main street, scents of cooking meat and sweet bread wafting out on steam and smoke. Her stomach uncurled in interest, and Azimir glanced over.

"Hungry?" Bimet translated, craning to catch Rih's eye.

"Is there anything you can't eat?" he asked.

There was no need to translate Rih's headshake, and after dodging a few larger wagons, Azimir returned from a small tavern bearing a covered woven tray.

"Best in the city," he insisted. Thick dark sauce covered thin strips of shaved, raw mutton. Curling green leaves topped the affair, their sharp scent accenting the heat of the sauce.

Her eyes narrowed with skepticism, half teasing, half serious. To her relief, it was rich and delicious. He laughed as she reached for another before following him farther down the tiers.

The food was gone by the time Azimir stopped outside a broad storefront. "After you, Your Highness."

Rih slipped through the door, eyes fluttering shut. Raw silk. The acrid smell of dye. Warm sandalwood. Tears pricked the edges of her eyes. *Home.*

A woman appeared from the back, mouth moving rapidly in a language Rih did not know. It seemed to bear the wide-mouthed words of Trade, but she knew too few words to pick any out. Some form of lizard decorated her left jawline.

She reached to embrace Nehla, who stepped back quickly and gestured to Rih. "May I introduce Kajimet Rih-elte of RoBal."

The woman paled and dropped into a curtsey. "Forgive me, You Highness—"

"It's nothing," Rih promised. "I just came to look about and give you and Nehla a chance to visit. Please go about your business."

The woman's face brightened and her hands flew into motion. "Mobeka. I'm honored you would grace our humble shop. And it's lovely to see our signs again," she confided, "I've worried I'll forget it from disuse. My father was Deaf too."

Rih grinned, heart thundering with melancholy and comfort at once. "I'm happy to see them too. And to see familiar colors. I didn't know you were Banis, though," she equivocated, eyes lingering on the tattoo. "I haven't seen art like your lizard before. Is it common in Athrolan?"

Mobeka's head flung back in laughter. "Oh, fate's trail, no. I grew up a day's hike from Jai—how I met my husband. My father was Banis, surely, but my mother was Border. Their tradition is to get a tattoo. Salamanders because I'm a child of two worlds. Three now, if you count Athrolan." She pushed her hair away again. "Forgive me, again. I'll let you browse, if you please."

Azimir had already become distracted with a high-collared vest in a blood red. Taking the opportunity to have a moment to herself, Rih stepped away. She slipped down an aisle of massive silk bolts. Several were undyed, but many more bore the brilliant crimson and purples and cerulean of RoBal. One was embroidered like Athrolani brocade but picked out in distinctly Banis colors. Another set of silks beside it were more subdued.

Her attention lingered on a pale-yellow wool cap with a Banis net stitched overtop. The bright white threads were dotted with gold topaz and pearls. Beaded fringe hung from the front like a wealthy woman's kokoshnik.

Nehla's cousin appeared from the other end of the aisle. "Do you see something you like?"

Rih gestured to the hat. "Do you make these in lavender?"

"I would be honored to create something bespoke for Your Highness." Her bright smile faded and she angled her back to the door before confiding, "My brother is a baniol."

"That must bring you honor," Rih replied, uncertain.

The weaver rolled her eyes, hand quickly signing, "Liberty."

Rih's nerves flamed. "Does he know, your brother?"

"Yes. He's an ally. He's been fighting for us for months. Quietly, of course, but he admires you." Mobeka's eyes flicked to something behind them, and Rih whirled.

Azimir leaned against one of the textile racks, watching her curiously.

Now panic flooded her limbs. *Don't react.*

"Your signs," he remarked, mimicking a few. "They're beautiful. I might not learn it in an afternoon, but would it be hard to teach?"

"It's a language, same as any, I suppose."

"I'm good at languages. Perhaps you could teach me."

"I'd love to learn as well," Nehla agreed, emerging with a folded bolt of black cloth over one arm. "What's that one again? I remember Vi-baln asking after it."

"Just a farewell. A sign of solidarity," Rih answered quickly, looking away at her rebellion's calling card as Mobeka translated. The memory of teaching the women in the Purple Throne weighed on her. The wound of losing them was raw, still. "It was lovely to see a small piece of home, but we ought to let Mistress Mobeka have her shop back."

"I'll send my runner with some samples for you to look over," Mobeka offered. When Rih frowned, she smiled, reminding her, "For the cap you admired."

Rih tried a grin of her own, but her nerves were too frayed for it to feel sincere.

Once their goodbyes were said, they emerged again, onto the street. Azimir was as boisterous as before, leading them down to docks. The Guildhalls were beautiful, the elaborate marble filigree edging their rooves containing hints at the trades represented within. Rih's gaze was caught by the new red stripe trimming the Athrolani sigils over each gate and aqueduct. *War.* "What is Mirik's opinion of Athrolan's new war?"

Azimir shrugged. "I don't think my father cares for it. But the whole thing is complex. More complex than we realized. What about yourself?"

"I wasn't invited to the counsel."

Azimir shook his head. "You're a soldier."

She grinned. "I arrived anyway. Suggested His Majesty request aide from Ban. We've enough troops. I doubt he'll consider it, though."

"I don't see why," Azimir scoffed. "If he's concerned enough to wage war on this religion, he should be able to put aside his fears. Send you, in the least."

"Me?" Rih rolled her eyes. "They'd as soon listen to me as an inbred colt. Actually, they'd listen to the colt first, I'd imagine."

Azimir stepped under an awning of the Berrin Trade Guild. A long counter connected the kitchens within to the street. He tossed a couple coins on the counter and ordered before turning back to her. "You're practically queen here."

Rih let that settle in her mind. *Queen.* She doubted Keplan considered her such, or that anyone else did. She wielded about as much clout as any of the lesser noble ladies. "I think you're optimistic."

"You said you went to the war counsel without invitation," the Hetmir's son noted, pressing a hot mug into her hands. At her cautious sniff, he laughed. "It's Berrin *ucal.*"

She took a sip, letting the hot, bitter flavor wash over her tongue. Setting the mug on the counter so she could sign, she responded, "It's good. But I still think you're wrong."

"Maybe." He shrugged. "They didn't tell you to leave, did they?"

"No." She frowned. "They listened."

"You interrupted an Athrolani war counsel and they considered your thoughts. You're closer to queen than me, at least. Perhaps Keplan would consider taking Banis help if you were the one to ask for it." He knocked back a tiny glass of steaming yellow liquor before nursing his own mug of ucal.

When they had finished their drinks, Azimir's face lit up. "We've got guards enough—care to see the Thread?"

Bimet's weapon hand flexed. "Your Highness, it's late. The Emperor's Hand—"

"I'm being diplomatic," Rih interjected. "I need to see the city, we have guards with us, and alienating His Majesty's cousin is a poor idea. They're not at war with one another and Athrolan refuses to be."

"You're not Athrolani," Bimet countered in sign. "I'm just thinking of your safety. You mean too much to take so many risks."

Rih took a moment, hand reaching for Bimet. She needed friends. As much as Azimir was witty and kind, Bimet was her solace. The only woman she could trust. *A reminder of why I'm here.* "Perhaps another time, Azimir. There's another audience tomorrow, and I'd like to study the notes from the last one."

He shrugged and easily turned around. "I'll walk you back to the palace then. My father will be wanting me home for dinner—I swear he'd follow me about himself out of worry if he didn't have duties to attend."

It was a long walk, and the air grew colder. By the time they arrived at the palace courtyard, even Azimir's enthusiasm had slackened.

"Thank you for your company. I fear I may be overwhelming at times. Keplan barely listened the first time I dragged him through the markets and warehouses."

"I enjoyed myself, actually." Exhaustion weighed on her, but she had enjoyed the glimpse of her new home. "I'm just a bit tired and find homesickness is as debilitating as any other illness. I hope to see you again."

"You surely will." He turned, waving as he walked backward. "Good evening, Your Highness!"

Nehla watched him go, eyes appreciative. "Begging your pardon, Your Highness, but I understand why you danced with him."

"He's barely a man—sixteen, I think," Rih argued. Her chest was tight. If the Hetmir had stayed her hand, Rih would have been married to Azimir. She had as much interest in his body as she did in Keplan's, but Azimir's face held nothing of his cousin's mercurial calculation.

"You think his mother set him up for this?" Bimet asked.

Rih scoffed, sweeping into the faint warmth of the drafty palace. "I have no doubt. But is it because I'm His Eminence's daughter, or because we both plan to overthrow him?"

Φ

The 39th Day of Valemord, 1272

The heavy metal projectiles clattered on Keplan's desk. He watched them roll about before gathering them into his hand and lining them upright on the lacquered wood. Schematics in thin, cheap notebooks replaced the audience records and missives of a king's usual study.

He still did not understand what provided the force, and as much as he wished for An'thor's help, he knew his general's temper was far too short to press his luck just yet.

Keplan raked his hand through his hair. With a mechanism of death arrayed before him, his thoughts refused to quiet. He slumped into his chair, eyeing the box on his desk. *I can't keep doing this.* The thought was fleeting, but unless he was mistaken, it was his own.

A servingman appeared at his door. "Your Majesty, Captain Hylier is here to see you. Said you asked for him."

"Show him in, thank you, Gorden."

The captain paused in the doorway. "Am I interrupting?"

Keplan grunted. "How've you been? I haven't seen you lately."

"You sent me away, last I recall." Hylier shook his head. "Been busy."

He pointed to the chair across the desk from the king, and Keplan nodded. "Have you learned anything?"

"I have." Hylier's eyes fixed on the disassembled weapon on Keplan's desk. "Is that what I think it is?"

"I demanded it. The last war Athrolan fought against the gods, she had my parents in her armory. I don't. I don't even know where they are, Hylier." He looked up, noting the captain's usually bright and energetic face was drawn. "What is it?"

The captain shook his head. "I haven't found everything I wanted to. They might have simply let it go if it weren't for Greton spurring the cursed thing on. Our only saving grace is they haven't found his pack."

Keplan lifted a shoulder, suddenly unable to meet the man's eyes. "Did you look under the aqueducts in the Slummer?"

Hylier sighed. "I didn't. I don't know why they would. They put a call out, of course, but nothing specific. That where you left it?"

"Should still be there, unless urchins got to it. But the wine he carried is gone. Tasted like arse anyway."

"I'll see what I can do. It gives us a tiny step above them, though I don't know what I'll do with it yet." He rubbed a hand over his tired face. "There's something else, something I've been keeping from you—not out of malice, but until I knew more, knew for certain. And I didn't know, not until today."

"What is it?"

"I found something the night Mirrel died. It's how I knew to look for her and for Azimir. When I agreed to work for you—in both capacities—I assumed it would complement my work for Daymir. In the very least, it wouldn't interfere."

"What're you aiming for here?"

Hylier's pale brows furrowed. "I'm getting to it. I've worked for Daymir for a long time. And my family before me. He's not always been a kind man, or charitable, but he's never cruel. Never killed. But it seems I have, in advertently, been working for opposing sides."

Keplan's head tilted. His thoughts were tangled. He wished, fleetingly, that he had breathed dust before this meeting. It would make him calmer but perhaps hinder his ability to suss out what his captain possibly meant. "You implying he was more than just a figurehead?"

"I don't know. I found a list and a letter in Peraan's desk. It contained a name—the final name on the list."

"Mirrel's?"

Hylier's voice lost the edge it had borne since learning Keplan had killed. Instead it was weary and full of regret. "I owe you an apology, Keplan. I saw two names on that list and I was forced to choose."

Anger flashed through Keplan's chest, followed by fear and despair. *Mirrel might have lived.* Perhaps Peraan would still have attacked, perhaps he would still have harmed her, harmed the inn, but she would be alive. He forced sense through the emotional miasma. "What's that to do with Blackhouse?"

"The letter with the name—it was signed by Dam Ornsen."

"I don't know that name."

"Few do. It's Daymir's. Like you, most nobles have lay-names, aliases for business that might tarnish or confuse their standing in court. He hasn't used it for business in years—I'd know. We read every letter that passed over Manor Black's threshold."

"But you missed this one?"

"I was hardly the only one on duty. Perhaps someone didn't understand the significance. But I can't suss out what his reasoning would be."

"Daymir has no interest in the throne," Keplan insisted.

"You were screaming at him not so long ago. Inviting zealots into your city."

"I hardly trust him with state affairs, but not because he's malicious. His sense is just misplaced. I can't see how sending Mirrel to her death behooves him. What's left of his mind might be a warren, but it's a fairly honest one."

"I know." Hylier sighed. "I think good men do bad things in the name of what's right. You've done the same. But it doesn't seem to be the case here."

Keplan ignored the vague compliment. "Who else knows about the letter?"

"No one." He bated, fiddling with the badge on his breast. "Someone. One person. Someone who does work like mine." He glanced up. "Not captain's work."

"I followed," Keplan assured. "A spy."

"She works for Mirik, and I assume she was there to protect Azimir."

Keplan snorted. "Spymaster Elang. We've met. I don't care for her."

Hylier smiled. "She's better off duty."

Keplan made a face. "I'd rather not carry that image. What about the name—Dom what?"

"Dam Ornsen."

"I don't know if Reka knows whose name it is. Few did. Daymir rarely used it, honestly."

Keplan's eyes narrowed. "It's his name, but perhaps someone borrowed it."

Hylier leaned forward, eyes narrowed in thought. "If there's someone pretending to be your regent—even in disguise—we've got a larger issue than blaming someone for murder."

CHAPTER SEVEN

The 40th Day of Valemord, 1272
The City of Neneviir

FROST CLUNG TO IRON. Rust dripped bloody stains on the ice. Alea's boots ground against the packed snow as she edged down the street. Last she entered Neneviir it was by steam engine. She pulled her cloak higher around her neck, though she was not truly cold. Her bones did not recognize cold.

"Up here," Arman called. "There's a main road." Even against the wind his voice sounded too loud.

She did not answer, just trudged farther into the city. Here, stone formed the buildings' frames. Ice walls had long since crumbled, weakened with each summer's perpetual days.

Much of the city still teetered atop itself, buildings piled high on permafrost. Like most cities they'd seen, its grandeur was an echo, an underpinning long tattered and faded.

Arman waited at a crossroad, cloak open, sweat dripping down his face. A bead clung to the cracked skin around his mouth. "I think it's up this way. With machines and technology, you'd think they would have designed their streets in squares."

"It's a wheel. Spokes," Alea ground out, one arm lifting in the direction of the palace. Bitter salt water pooled under her tongue. "Hub."

He watched her face for a moment, then followed her gesture with his gaze. "Right. I suppose this will lead right there, then."

I would rather it didn't. Alea followed the swirling heat of his wake as they continued. Already the days were shorter, the sun never reaching near its zenith, even at midday. She was grateful to the faint green curtains that lit the sky each evening. They kept her awake, grounded from all but the darkest of her dreams. With every league farther north, the sky-lights grew brighter, and her thoughts grew more sickening.

"Fates."

She glanced up at Arman's breathed awe. The massive blocks of the palace's dome echoed Athrolan's. Most were still intact, save for the crest of the structure, blown out from within. Towering ridges ran down the curve from the opening where the ice had melted and solidified again. "It wasn't like that before. Something happened."

"Albi'giran said there was a revolt. Perhaps it collapsed then."

Alea shrugged, pushing past him and into the courtyard. The bank of oversized carriage houses for the steam engines stretched from the edge of the palace. All but one had collapsed, the stone scorched and buried in decades of snow. She wondered absently what had happened to the boy who helped her, the boy sent to his death by his own uncle. Tearing herself away from the tangled path of memories, she lurched up the broad stairs. Hoare frost covered most of the rooms, protected from the clawing fingers of the wind or the brief warmth of summer.

The iron doors to the great hall, however, stood open. Snow piled at their foot, drifting like ghosts as the air breathed down the gaping hole in the ceiling.

"Where do we even start?" Arman wondered aloud. "Down here?"

Alea shuddered, dragging her eyes from the yawning door to the prison's entrance. "I doubt it." Truth was, though, the palace was huge, and catacombs were as good a place to hide ugly truths as any. *I never saw the book in the treasury. Though I wasn't looking.*

Arman trotted down the stairs, even the thick soles of his boots slipping on the ice-covered steps. Alea stayed at the foot of the stairs. Every thud of her laboring heart sent droplets misting from her skin, her gasps ice crystals in the air. War followed so quickly on the heels of what she experienced in Neneviir's dungeon and, like so many things, those memories were mostly locked behind iron gates in her mind. But now, with their setting before her, they were too vivid to ignore.

Bren had asked, in passing, if anything had been taken from her. Whether he meant physically or mentally, she was not sure. Of course not, she had replied. What she really meant, though, was how could they not?

Little snow had drifted in through the barred windows, and the interrogation room was untouched. Arman stepped in, lip curled as he winced at the chair and bloodstains. "Places like this make me wonder if the world's worth saving at all. Whose blood do you think it is?"

She spared a single glance for the room where her fingers were ripped out of place, her nose broken, her spirit crushed and hidden behind the mask of a captain named Lenna Grayhill. In many ways she had never removed it. "Some of it's mine."

"Yours? You said you— " His voice faltered into silence. By the time he saw her just before the battle, her bruises were almost faded and the darkness behind her eyes could have been due to any number of wartime horrors.

Rows of cells led deeper under the palace, faint, snow-filtered light creeping through the windows. He paused beside one, bars rent open. Bones littered the floor. Alea crouched, wrinkled fingertips brushing the dome of a horned skull.

"You did this."

She nodded. "Mel'iend arrived just afterward. I couldn't wait. They realized who I was." She wondered at his unreadable stare, what new uncomfortable thoughts drifted through his fevered head.

"I can't believe An'thor sent you into this alone. Makes me trust him less. Though I'm not certain I trusted him since childhood." He looked away.

"He didn't know. Didn't send me, really. I sent myself. Besides, time makes monsters of most heroes." She glanced down at the body. "Even us."

"Especially us." His whisper rasped through the quiet. "Let's keep looking."

She slipped from her prison cell and led the way deeper into the palace's knotted gut. She remembered bolting up the stairs, turning a corner and finding another stairway. She followed the memory, faltering to a halt when a beam twice as thick as her own body barred the way. "I thought this was the way."

"I'm sure there's another," Arman murmured, fingers burning on the sallow skin of her wrist. "Here, a hall beside it. Let's just go around." To the left, thick iron bulkheads lay open, the metal scorched and dimpled. Pipes crowded the ceiling, leading from somewhere farther in. Arman fell in behind her again, but even so, the air was warmer, if only from its stillness. Their steps hissed in heaps piled at the edge of the corridor. "Snow?" she asked.

"Ash," he answered. He turned, scanning the iron plates lining the hall. "Something burned."

Alea turned to look back the way they came, instinct flaring ice across her cheeks. Her boot caught on something in the lee of a pipe's large elbow. She knelt, brushing ash and dust away. Seared sinew mummified over delicate scorched phalanges. Fire, then isolated bitter cold petrified what was left of their body. Alea's eyes picked out another and another, tucked in corners and behind columns of reaching ductwork. "Not something," she whispered. "Someone. Many of them."

"Accident or the revolt?"

Alea did not answer, just continued, each step carefully chosen. After another dozen bulkheads, the hall ended. A cavern yawned ahead, plummeting into a crevasse and reaching up to the lattice of iron that made the foundation of some room far above. Rent metal curved outward, bent by fury and fire. Perhaps it was the throne room's floor. Gears, each the height of a house, filled the space. Some stood vertical, others overlaid one another like interlocking flagging.

If a guardrail ever bordered the platform they now stood upon, it was long rusted or ripped away. Rent metal jutted from each side of the cleft, whatever structure it held blasted to pieces below. More fragments pierced the walls.

"What is this?" Arman's whisper bounced from the walls, skipping downward.

"When I first arrived, the ground hummed. I think this is why. Perhaps this is where they drew the metal to make their steam engines, their lattice, their revolvers. Pipes lay along the roads, too—channeling hot air to the central houses."

"It must have broken. Or overheated." He pointed. "There are boulders wedged in some of the gears."

"Sabotage."

"Something this thorough seems closer to suicide." Arman brushed a hand along the ice-covered wall. Rivulets trickled from the wake of his touch. "We ought to turn back. None of this looks stable—at least not for me. You said it was upstairs?"

Alea followed his gesture. Far above, rising from the iron lattice, was a chimney. Tangled pipes clustered at its entrance. "If we could get there, I imagine some of those pipes lead—"

Grinding metal interrupted her musing. Arman's sweat misted in the air, his clenched fist hardening in plated stone. A ladder below them ripped from its moorings, rising to hover before them. Alea placed a tentative boot on the bottom rung. Arman leaped on beside, one arm looped behind her. Before she could protest further, the ladder lurched upward. Stone crumbled from the walls as they passed, Arman's green eyes squeezed shut with the effort. They flew out, over the abyss, and rose incrementally, until the chimney swallowed them. The cavern shrank into a tiny square beneath their boots.

Hearths passed, their metal grates flashing glimpses of the rooms beyond. More bodies. Bedrooms. Manufacturing halls. Their journey into the bowels of the palace must have delved deeper than Alea realized. Mel'iend's comment that the Nenev built up and not down, seemed ill-founded.

"Stop!" The metal ladder clattered against the side and Alea grabbed at the pipes, panting. "I think I saw it. Storage of some sort."

When Arman turned to her, pale marble plates scabbed his face. The flesh between glowed sickly yellow. Her own power curled out, unbidden. As much as he was her guard, her partner, her companion for this journey and so many before this, he was also a stranger. A touch of his fingers softened the bars of the hearth enough to wrench them free.

It was wide enough to crawl through, but not by much. Alea pushed herself into the square vent, sloughing skin snagging as she wedged herself past the metal grate. She tumbled into the room and lay, panting on the floor for a moment. Black coagulated blood oozed from the torn flesh of her shoulder where the rusted metal peeled it back. Already, the ragged edge grayed, vitality fading with her every shallow breath.

Arman slipped through behind her, body flickering with translucence. He crouched beside her, smoldering fingers hovering over her scrape. "Are you all right?"

"It's just my body," she muttered. And it was. Every day her mind seemed more connected to the power drenching the world and less tethered to its physical cage of meat and bone. She glanced around. "We found it. I remember the smell of the dust."

"Creosote. I think I would have liked this place when it still churned."

She staggered to her feet and took stock. What was left of the finery of a dozen fallen nations had faded, picked over as much as the bones of the bodies below. Alea scanned the chests and shelves, searching for anything that resembled a book or scroll. *Fates, I'd settle for child's scrawl on a tutor's wax tablet.* Arman wandered in the other direction, his steps fading between the stacked furniture. Sealed treaties were shoved beside Athrolani royal lineages. The Kovasit, the Tzoan, the Xain. Somewhere in those pages lay the dead end of An'thor's line, crushed in Claimiirn. What bloodline would rise now that Tzatia had died?

She turned a corner and froze. A blanket draped over a shelf, stretched on a rope in a lean-to. Ragged furs and straw-stuffed pillows piled beneath. That is where she found the shrine.

The images were simple, strange in their style but unmistakable. They were scrawled across the raw wood of the back of a wardrobe. A woman, sooty hair and smoky power radiating from her. Beside her stood another, drawn in chalk and rust.

"Arman," she whispered, as much a recognition as a call.

She knelt on the cold furs of the makeshift bed. Parchment, weathered into spidersilk fragility, disintegrated beneath her knees.

A moment later Arman emerged from around the corner. "Found a handful of weapons, a map of a continent I'm not sure exists, and enough foreign coin to buy a Sunamen oasis two centuries ago. No book, though." When she did not answer, he settled beside her. "It's a shrine, as if someone worshiped you. Us."

Mel'iend. "I'm not something to be worshiped," she protested. "Not even you, with your sacrifice and burning hope."

Arman peered at the wall. "Someone survived the revolt. Someone who saw the mural in Lymorda."

"Or the book." Alea pointed to a fragment of parchment illustrated with a white hand set aflame. Even if they gathered all the pieces, their salt water and scorch would destroy every fragment. "Why is it each victory we have is overwhelmed by defeat?"

"There's more." Arman pointed to the wall, where another image was hidden by the tattered blanket. He lifted the corner.

Above the two figures stood a third, larger and drawn in sharp, violent strokes. He was painted in blood.

"Have you thought about what this means? We keep seeking answers, and all we find is this—icons of us created from priceless tiles and child's chalk. And our son. You were the one who poured over texts before the war, who learned the nature of yourself and our enemies. Tell me this doesn't mean what I think it does."

"Copper power, red blood. Bright brown. The gods." She drew a shuddering breath, the truth weighing on her heart, on her mind. She did not want to believe it either. Her damp fingers hovered over the marks. Corrosion flowed in her fingers' wake, rust knotting the art until it was unrecognizable. "We found our answer in Elanasa. I just refused to see it."

"He's what you saw, what the Laen predicted, then. What these people worship." Arman sat back on his heels. "Do you think An'thor had anything to do with this?"

Alea shook her head. "This is hope. He lost his decades ago—before we ever met him, I think." Her heart ached, every flick of its watery valves sending flashes of electricity through her chest. "It's how he recognized me."

Arman opened his mouth to argue, perhaps, or reassure, but whatever words he thought died, left to atrophy with his tongue. Even now, it wasn't hope that drove them. It was desperation, duty. Love, perhaps. But not hope. "What's next?"

"I don't even know where to look. If he's the blood the prophet means, then why are my dreams so violent? Why is the world dying?"

"What you saw in the Laen book, you said it was more powerful, more beautiful than we could ever be. Perhaps we're just missing one piece, one step we were meant to complete."

"It's not because of him," she snapped. *It can't be.*

Arman's eyes were exhausted, but the reassurance on his face was sincere. "I know. It's not our son's blood that poisons the world." He reached out, as if to brush a lank strand from her face but stopped, hand dropping back to his lap. "We'll figure out our next step in the morning. Though with this light it's anyone's guess when dawn comes."

She flashed a smile, seawater trickling from between pearlescent teeth. As sheltered as the treasury was, she could not bear to sleep beneath her own shrine, no matter how rudimentary. Instead, she borrowed the blankets and pillow and found a few cloaks hung on forms. Half the winding corridors were blocked, but there was no reason to hurry.

A massive iron bar had crashed from the throne room ceiling, protecting the dais from the worst of the weather. Snow drifted at the sides, and Alea cleared a space for their stolen comfort.

"I think I can get some of this straw to light, if you'd like a fire," Arman offered, kicking at the long moldered hay on the floor. "I can't feel the cold."

Alea shrugged, tucked in the fur, eyes fixed on the sky through the gash in the roof. Iron dug into her shoulder as she tucked herself against the stairs. Cold gnawed her bones, dragged at her heart and feet and hands. She did not really mind. "Malonostrii."

Arman frowned, following her gaze. Faint pink and blue curtains drifted across the clear black sky, sending rainbow glimmers through what little ice was still translucent. "You came here just before the war."

"You knew that." Her mind flickered with every terrible dream of blood, every beautiful memory of Keplan.

"I'm just marveling. You rode here all on your own."

"I had help. An'thor. His cousin—no, nephew." She forced the words past the ice in her throat. "I think he's the one who made the shrine."

Fabric rustled and then Arman was beside her, radiated heat rippling the air but never breaching the dense film of cold on her skin. "I've spent so many years protecting you. Somewhere along the way I forgot you didn't need me to. Maybe I never knew." The smoke and stone in him shook his voice, or perhaps it was regret.

"There are a lot of things we both forgot. But mostly it's been each other."

"I'm so sorry, Alea. I'm sorry I never saw you through all my worrying. I've built up this image of who and what you are and I realize now, I was wrong." The straw beneath him smoked. "Fates, I would have loved to see you, see who you were, under all of it."

"Naked. Years ago I told someone that no one had ever seen me naked—my true self bared." She could not meet his eyes, only stare at the marbled white and charred cracks in his face. It was too late for a marriage, too late for a legendary love story.

His fingers found hers. The brush of hard, dry skin sent lightning crackling over her clammy hand. The sullen olive of his irises flamed to emerald, to gold. Black writhed up her flesh. *Warmth.* Her gaze rose to his and ice crystalized in her bones.

Their lips met. Lightning exploded from her flesh, crackling over him, through them both. Arman shuddered under her, but a smile curled his lips on hers.

Like he walked through air, as smoke, echoes of every event they ever lived fluttered between their briefly shared mind. Seawater and crackling ozone overlaid the stench of damp campfires, of burning bone. They shared so much, so little. Everything. Nothing. Death and life and pain.

Clawed hands, barely corporeal, gripped her tangled gray hair, her sloughing skin, and tugged her over him, onto him. Ice melted and froze again. Iron rusted. Far below, massive engines ignited, gears shuddered into waking with Arman's fire before the stone and steel crumbled to ash with her ferocity.

When consciousness, what was left of it, returned to her, they lay in ruins. Overhead the sky flamed with emerald, with azure.

Smoke drifted along the stones, coated in black ice. Cracks juddered across the slick surface, forming and retreating in rhythm, in breath. Hay and crushed Nenev bodies burned in every corner. Arman glanced down at his hands. They were nothing more than twisting smoke, blackened stone dust locked in Alea's ice. "Alea?"

Ice crackled again, louder. Brontide shook the building. Electricity flickered across the floor, concentrating where they lay. Dark water curled around each fork of lightning, coagulating until something barely human crouched on the floor.

Arman smiled, fingers materializing from the writhing smoke long enough to brush stringy black hair from rotted skin. "You're beautiful."

She stared down at herself, at the creature reflected in ice. Whatever form she had was mercurial now, at best. "I didn't want to believe it before. But I understand. The gods' blood I shed is killing us all. Us. Our lives. Whatever I severed, whatever connection you and I opened all those years ago, it's infected."

"Battle triage," he whispered. "Just to keep something alive until it can be properly healed."

"Every image we're together. The three of us. Our little family with mighty power. Maybe we'll find the final part of this mystery when we return to him." Her form melted, skin decaying until she was nothing more than black water trickling toward the door.

Arman's own bones and muscle fading into smoke, following her south. "We were meant to repair the world, return our power to the earth."

Her voice was snapping ice, groaning iron. "Instead we birthed a god."

Φ

The 43rd Day of Valemord, 1272
The City of Ceir Athrolan, Athrolan

Dense clouds hung low over the city. The night's dusting of snow was already packed into sullen gray ruts from wagons and hooves and boots. Keplan stomped on a particularly large chunk, wincing when he discovered it was frozen. Thankfully, his guards said nothing. The vermillion and green draping the Mirikin ambassador's manor was bright against the pale stone and frosty street. Keplan waited at the front door for the footman to announce him. This was hardly an official visit, but kings could scarcely barge in and rap on a man's study door.

"Right this way, Your Majesty."

Keplan waved for his guards to wait in the parlor and trudged upstairs. "Barrackborn?"

Bren jerked the door open. The shadows hanging from the bags under his eyes were darker than Keplan imagined possible. "You came."

"You asked." Keplan stepped in, taking a seat by the window without invitation.

"We'll be heading home soon, before the seas get worse. I thought we ought to talk beforehand. As allies, but as family, too." Bren poured a glass of wine for himself, gesturing with the bottle. "Care for some? We've got some charcuterie left, but it's old."

"It's not my taste." Truthfully his fingers trembled. He wished that like An'thor, like Brentemir, he could soothe his nerves with something so easily accepted. Instead, his peace was found in dark corners and a prostitute's pity.

"Kem's secretary sent me a letter—the one you received as well. About the priests."

Keplan pretended to gag. "They're a lot of fools. Will you respond?"

"I did this morning." Brentemir looked away.

"Thank fates." He peered at the scant offering of a cornucopia on the table between his chair and Brentemir's before choosing a thin slice of dry cheese. Fighting the priests was easier if his allies agreed with him—even if they warred with each other.

Brentemir moved from his desk to the window, looking down at Keplan with an expression unreadable behind his reservedness. Outside the still, foggy air settled lower over the city.

"I wanted to talk to you about something myself, actually."

"I assumed. You haven't seen us outside of state business since you were crowned."

"I've seen Azi. Besides, I'm busy kinging and all." He grimaced at the dry food but continued to nibble. "What happened the night he was attacked?"

"I thought I was going to die of fear. I saw my baby boy with a sword to his throat. Haven't quite recovered from it, though it appears he has."

Keplan grunted. Azimir had a new depth behind his eyes. Whether it was from fear or enlightenment he could never guess, but apparently it was something the boy's own father failed to recognize. "And the assassin—she was killed?"

"One of our swords took her—your captain helped, or tried to. I honestly can't recall much beyond the look in Azi's eyes. You'll understand when you have children. Why do you ask?"

"There's an ongoing investigation into the death of the man who ordered the assassinations. I'm trying to determine who might still be active and whether whoever murdered him was acting politically."

"As opposed to?"

Keplan met the ambassador's eyes. "Vengeance. Azimir was not the only one attacked. There were others on their list, and still more who simply disappeared. Most connected with my ascension, however superficially. But risking war by attacking a visiting ambassador's family is further than I expected. Surely your Spy Master knows something."

Bren glanced up, surprise widening his tired gray eyes. "I didn't realize you knew each other. She's out of the country. Traveling."

"Working for Kemmer, you mean." Keplan sighed. "Surely my people have their own avenues. I was just hoping you knew something."

"My family was attacked on foreign ground. I've tripled my guard, we're leaving Athrolan, and my son is safe," Bren reiterated. "This is not my country. Beyond that I couldn't give a shit what happens."

"I wish I could say the same." Keplan rose in a fluid motion and snatched the wine from the table. It smelled like overripe fruit. "So why did you ask me here? Besides my jovial company."

"You're married now."

Keplan poured some into the empty goblet and knocked it back. The sticky taste would distract him enough for the moment. He leaned on the polished desk. "I'd like to forget that fact."

Brentemir raised his brows. "You made your bed and now you've got to sleep in it—both of you. Azimir mentioned you've barely spoken to her. Have you thought about heirs?"

Keplan twisted the goblet slowly, watching the dark drink coat the thin glass. He had not. "I'm seventeen."

"If you're old enough to sit on the throne, you're old enough to father a child. If you're bedding people—regardless of what sits in their breeches—you'd best be prepared to accept the various consequences, one of which is children. And when you're king, the kingdom expects heirs. Tzatia only had you and look what happened."

"That was hardly the same situation."

"I know it's complicated. Your parents aren't here, and I wanted to let you know it wasn't easy with Kemmer and I—"

"I'm not forcing my friend to bear the children I can't!" Keplan made for the door. "This is a horrific conversation, one I'd rather not have."

"I don't see the Earth Shaker about to have it with you, so I'll have to suffice!"

Keplan whirled. "My father's not here because he and my mother are halfway across the tundra trying to save this pathetic excuse for a world. Again!"

Bren sat back, eyes alight with sudden desperation. "You heard from them?"

Keplan snorted, grateful to have the ambassador off the topic of procreation. "Fates, no. It's all just rumors. Daymir did. And those fanatics. And their prophet, and seemingly everyone but us." His chest ached with homesickness. It was easy to say he longed to return to the Hare. But he missed the forest and simplicity of woodcraft and hunting.

The room fell silent. Below, the guards burst into laughter at some jest. Gongs sounded the call for dinner in the neighboring Berrin ambassador's manor. Bren scrubbed a hand through his gray hair. The gesture was so akin to Azimir's, it made Keplan stare for a moment.

"I miss them too." Bren sighed. "I'm sorry for this, Keplan. For all of it."

The fight left Keplan. He was tired of fighting—fighting religion, fighting Domariigo, fighting Hylier. *Mostly just fighting myself.* He barely remembered how to converse without vitriol. "If I weren't the only one who could fix it, I'd think it was a mistake," Keplan confessed.

"I remember that feeling. The power in it. The dread." Brentemir met his gaze. "The lie. There is always someone who can do it better, wiser. Look at

Kemmer. I don't agree with half her choices but Mirik's military is so much stronger under her than it ever was under me."

"I'm the only one with my parents' blood," the king reminded. "I don't think there's someone else suited. I'd drain my treasury to find them if I thought there were."

The glass rattled in the study window. Their guards fell silent below.

Bren glanced up, frowning. "Wind?"

Keplan shook his head, striding to the window. "Trees are still." It was dusk, but in the sliver of the market he could see at the end of the street, dozens of people had stopped, peering about in confusion. Beneath them, the floor quivered. Cracking stone echoed across the city. *Is Dorcal back?* Keplan pushed aside the fearful first thought. His breath misted the glass as he pressed against it, peering down into the city proper. Water burst from the single aqueduct arching over the walls from the southern hills. Curtains of water obscured half the noble district. The cobblestones disappeared under churning floodwaters.

Dread sank in Keplan's gut. "What is this?"

Bren's frown had not changed. "It happens from time to time. One of the lesser ducts will freeze and weaken, and the stone cracks under the pressure. Your father helped fix one years ago."

"That's not a lesser aqueduct." Keplan peered toward the harbor. Another geyser exploded into the air from the warehouse district, another in the Slummer, in the Silver Apron. "It's all of them."

Fire bloomed, following the slick brown streaks of spilled lamp oil. A moment later the harbor itself ignited. Keplan's guard burst into the room. "Sire—!"

"I can see it, Noren."

The guard gaped, glancing between the two men standing at the window, hands clasped behind their backs as the world seemingly ended outside. Keplan ignored whatever faltering warning or concern his guard babbled behind him. Thousands of thoughts bombarded the king's mind. Fear, his own and his people's. Through them all came one, ferocious and bitter and burning: *wrath.*

Φ

The 44th Day of Valemord, 1272

"Why don't you pick up a hobby?" Bimet asked. "Most queens and noble wives have projects—hopefully charitable, but we can't win every battle."

Rih rolled her eyes, staring out the window for a moment before answering. The streets were still filled with water, though the worst leaks had been repaired during the night. *I never thought the infrastructure would be what I missed most about Ban.* She turned back to her interpreter. "I don't miss being busy—hooves of Faco-il, I'm planning a rebellion against the largest empire in the known world, it's not like I'm bored."

Bimet's dark eyes crinkled in a laugh. "I meant something that soothes you, or delights you, or feeds your heart. You've been training and corresponding when you can, but unless I don't know you very well, I didn't think planning a war fed your heart."

Rih smirked. "Hardly. Though it certainly makes new friends, which I wouldn't have predicted."

"Eh, bloodshed, blood bonds, where's the difference?" Bimet joked. "Have you had a chance to look over the materials from Mobeka?"

Rih shook her head, glancing at the delicate wooden box that held textile samples. "I'm just wistful, which makes me restless. I miss the green and the air and the smell of the baking clay and sunburnt grass."

"You could garden."

Rih laughed in earnest. "I'm on the second story of a drafty building and I haven't touched earth in almost a week."

Bimet shrugged. "I suppose. I'd hardly know how to help either. I kill most things I touch—plant-wise, of course."

"Of course." The princess drew the box toward her and thumbed through the silks and wool. As much as she was drawn to the soft blues and purples, she felt uncomfortable in those colors, as if they no longer complemented her changing image. Her fingers paused on a particularly rich moss green. In Ban it was a color permitted only to the emperor himself. "Maybe I'll choose more reds and pinks to try to brighten this dismal weather."

Nehla burst through the door, already speaking. Rih turned away, wishing the woman would remember how difficult understanding her was normally, let alone when rushed and unable to see half her words.

After a moment Bimet turned to the princess. "Lady Nehla says there's another war council starting in half an hour."

Rih scowled. "I know we arrived at the last one uninvited, but you would think they would invite me out of courtesy alone."

Nehla grinned, this time turning so Rih could read her lips. "They did. I met the king's guard—Hyland something—in the hall. He said to pass the invitation to you from the king himself."

Warmth bloomed in Rih's chest. *I'm invited.* She rushed to her wardrobe, digging through the colored silks. She did not bother with a net or changing her onyx rings to match the peach tone of her nicer wrap. War did not require fashion.

Bimet appeared before her, eyes narrowed on the doorway behind them. "This is not what I meant when I suggested you find a hobby."

Rih frowned. "I'm invited and have little else to do."

"Boredom is no reason to go playing in someone else's war!" Her signs were furtive and sharp, hidden from Nehla by Rih's body.

"This war is as much mine now, and if I intend on borrowing my husband's army, I'll need his trust that I can use it properly. Besides, no harm can come from simply learning what they have to say." She turned, effectively ending the conversation.

Once again, the war council was held in one of the smaller council halls. Judging by the slight warmth emanating from the doorway, they had already started arguing. As much as she hated the imperial rule, she had to admit it was easier to get things done there, than it was with Athrolan's endless debates. *Perhaps that says more about the debaters than iron rules.*

The king was slumped in a chair, colorless eyes unfocused and hands shaking. The food on the table was meager, mostly dried meats. They had not had bread in weeks.

The general's eyes narrowed on Rih as she took her seat.

"Your Highness," he greeted. "I didn't expect you to join us. There's little enough to concern you here."

She felt her brow arch. "Unless more has been decided in the interim, General—which I highly doubt—I imagine there's plenty to discuss."

Keplan glanced between them, gaze absent. "We were just remarking on how this would be a good time to attack, given the weakness of the city. Most of our navy is busy containing the fires in the harbor, and our army has another week of repairs before the masons can properly fix the ducts."

"Have you considered switching to fired clay? RoBal uses pipes for much of their water system, and even under the high heat and pressure from our springs, they rarely break."

Keplan's attention sharpened. "Fewer seams make for fewer weak points?"

"Indeed. I can see if there's a Banis potter in the city who might know more."

Something that almost looked like a smile flitted across his face. "That would be helpful. Consulate, when the head of the Masonry Guild returns, both you and she must reach out to the Kajimet."

The general launched into recounting everything he gleaned from his missives to other cities, most of which had either not heard from the prophet or had seen nothing since the first letter. Rih flipped through her notes from the previous meeting, making tick marks by a few points. *If they boast an army large enough to attack the capital, then where are they hiding them?*

"Honestly, sire, we have little enough proof that they even have an army."

"They threatened the second largest kingdom in the known world. That'd be a whale of a bluff." Fess crossed her arms, leaning back in her chair in a manner far too casual for the king's presence. Keplan did not seem to notice.

Rih waited for the commander to finish the rest of her acerbic rant at the general before raising a hand for attention. "General Domariigo, have you considered that an army of believers may not look like a traditional military? The largest of your cities have indeed heard of this prophet and seen some of her followers. But you simply asked if they had seen Swordbearers. The best invasion isn't one you don't notice, it's one you ignore."

He glared but seemed unable or unwilling to give her a counter-argument.

Keplan's drink spilled as he attempted to drain the last of it. He winced, mopping blood-colored liquor from his embroidered shirt. It already bore old stains. "I'm honestly tempted to ignore it anyway. I can't be worrying about how to fight them off when I can't feed my people and half our harbor is aflame."

That's exactly what they want.

"You could accept Her Highness's offer of troops."

Rih stared at Bimet, wondering if the woman had mistranslated Fess's suggestion.

"You think Mirik would turn a cheek to their enemy's army arriving within jumping distance of their capital? There was no official argument when we allied with the empire, but I fear Banis troops would be a league too far."

The general scoffed. "They value our trade too much. Besides, you're family and Bren won't risk you." He grabbed the last piece of meat, gnawing on it with disinterest.

"Bren isn't Hetmir, and from what I've seen Kemmer is far from gutless," the king argued. "Their family was already attacked on our cobbles."

Rih watched Bimet's hands, her mind bouncing between the opposing verbal volleys. "For the sake of safety, Your Majesty, let's assume they do have an army. The only way to weaken Athrolan further is to separate you from the throne. If you go to Ban to beg for soldiers, the Swordbearers will surely attack."

Keplan frowned, leaning forward. "You just offered aide, now you say it's a poor choice? I don't want to go to Ban. The place disgusts me, but I fear it's the only way to protect my people from this prophet's insanity."

Rih drew a breath and summoned her strength. "Stay in your city. Tend to your people's food, their water. Extinguish these fires. I will go to Ban in your stead and ask my people for aide."

She could not be certain, but she swore the conversation died. Azimir might be idealistic, but he knew Athrolan better than she. She could ask for troops and get a better view of the Banis army for her own machinations.

"You've been married less than a month and you already seek to return home?" the general snapped.

Acting as an ambassador was hardly returning home, but Rih let him have his concerns. Instead, she simply sat back. "I think it's a sound suggestion, but I'm sure you'll have to debate the matter."

Colonel Hamacad rose from the end of the table. "Sire, how do you think that would look, sending your wife to do your bidding? Begging pardon, Your Highness."

Keplan sighed, rubbing a gloved hand over his exhausted face. "I'll think it over. Let's turn our focus to determining where the prophet's strength lies. No matter which troops we use, we'll need a strategy."

Rih glanced at Bimet. The translator's eyes were wide, and it took her a moment to catch up to the others' new arguments.

"I'm sorry," Rih signed to her. "I know you disagree."

"Disagreeing isn't up to me," she answered, but her hands were stiff with forced formality. "But I'm glad you know my reservations." She turned sharply, and Rih felt a puff of air brush her cheek as the door swung open.

Fess paused, the council watching the king's personal guard stride up to Keplan's chair. Hylier bent, whispering something in the man's ear before straightening.

Keplan's face paled and he smacked his hand on the table top. "Something urgent has come up. You have your orders, and for now, I want everyone's focus on bolstering the city or tracking down evidence of this prophet's forces. Dismissed." He hurried from the room, his guard on his heels looking ill.

Φ

Bimet stepped into Rih's study, knocking one of the weights off the bookcase by the door to get her attention. "This came for you. If that's all for the evening, I'll be in my room. Nehla is here finishing some mending if you need anything."

"That'll be all. Have a good night." Rih leaned over her desk to take the scroll. It was plain, with a colorless seal. She cracked the wax and slid the scroll onto a stand to read it better.

> *My dear friend,*
>
> *I hope this finds you well. It was such a delight to see you during your journey to Ceir Athrolan. I know you asked after our mutual sisters-in-arms, and I've finally had a moment to myself.*

Rih's heart thundered into wakefulness. After the endless drama of Athrolan's court and seemingly useless debates, her mind begged for something new.

> *Osak is doing well, though I'm sure she misses home, being on the coast. Of course Sefer, who's there too, with the 17th Arc, loves being so close to the ocean.*

Neither were names Rih recognized. *It's a code!* She drew another paper toward her and began to write. Each name received a dot of colored ink. Blue for best suited for being stationed on the coast, red for on the Athrolani border, and emerald for the capital. Figuring out how best to make use of this would take time, but if nothing else, she had a list of allies. Her eye caught the title of one of the two male names on the list of a dozen. *Powerful allies.*

Her blood pounded with anticipation. She had Bimet, she had Majilah Ag. But this was more. This was the beginnings of a network. She dug a map from her desk next, weighing it with the scroll stand and her discarded wrap. Two marks by the coast. Another four along the Hartland. Five in the capital. And one in a little town just shy of the Athrolani border.

For now, she needed them safe, scattered across the empire so they might spread the word to everyone they could. Her finger paused on the name of an ally far in the south. They were within a few days' march of the edge of the Valen territory. *It's time to write to Majilah Ag.* So much had happened since meeting with the Queen of the Vales, but it could be said her entire course was set by that single handshake in the dark Stytown brothel.

When she glanced up again, Nehla stood in the doorway.

Rih flinched. Her instinct screamed to shove the map and list into her drawers before the other woman could see a single line. *But that would only draw suspicion.* Instead, she shuffled the pages together, as if done with some mundane task. The edges of the parchment trembled with her shaking hands. When she had set it aside, facedown, she looked up expectantly.

It was then that she saw Nehla's rigid body. Her eyes were wide with forced calm and her shoulders were at least a finger-space higher than her usual easy stance. Her jaw bunched, making it almost impossible for Rih to read her lips. "His Majesty Keplan Wardyn."

"What about him?" Rih gave an exaggerated confused look.

"His Majesty is here to see you, Your Highness."

Cold sank over Rih's body. It was late, well past evening. Her hands formed the few signs Nehla knew. "Get Bimet."

She extinguished her lamp and swept from the room to answer the door herself. The gangly figure of the king loomed in the dim hallway. Bile flooded Rih's throat.

"May I?" One gloved hand gestured to her parlor.

She opened the door wider, eyes meeting Bimet's as the interpreter appeared from the servants' stairs.

Bimet glanced from the king to her princess before signing. "What does he want?"

Rih shook her head. There was only one reason a man visited his wife's chambers after dark. Her mind flashed to the box in her chest. Nothing would protect enduring the next few hours. Ki-elte's teas, however, would make them easier. "Would you order tea?" she asked Bimet, words almost lost in a pharyngeal stutter. Would her interpreter stay for the duration, witness to Rih's undoing, or would he request she leave, condemning them to miscommunication? She did not know what to wish for.

Bimet's hand pressed hers and she flinched. "Rih, he asked how your day was."

Rih forced herself to look at the man. "It was uneventful, save for the council."

"Did I interrupt you?"

She followed his gesture to her fist clenched around her pen, hard enough to bleed ink over the lines of her palm. Perhaps that was why her hands seemed unable to sign. She let it fall into her lap, broken. "I was just writing to family. Telling them about the city."

"Have you been able to visit it much?"

"Master A'hane toured us about."

Keplan's head tilted. "Azimir? My cousin?"

Fear flashed up her spine. Would he question their visits, as others had? Would it anger him? "Yes. He visits occasionally to discuss the events between our nations. I think he hopes to forge peace in the future, despite tension now."

The king looked down at his gloved hands. "I didn't know he had an interest in that."

"He seems to just wish everyone would get on well."

"I've been thinking of the same." His jaw clenched, shoulders hunched. She had not realized how tall he was, despite his slender build.

Hot water arrived with an array of teas. Bimet excused herself and returned with a small silk sachet from Rih's ornate box. They were quiet as Keplan poured himself a mug and Rih took a long sip. It scalded her throat, but numbness quickly followed. Her hands and feet tingled.

"Your alliance is appreciated, if a surprise," she began. "Given the circumstances."

His face twitched as if he felt her gaze on his scars. "So you know."

There was an honesty in his terrifying eyes. She recalled his slight smile earlier that day. Perhaps he wanted honesty in return. "I recognized you when I arrived. Could have sworn you wanted Ban to burn."

"I did. A large part of me still does. I would pay dearly, time was I'd die, even, to watch your empire fall to ruin."

"But not anymore?"

Keplan twisted the mug slowly, watching the dark drink coat the clay. "We're married, aren't we?"

She was a league away from her body, it seemed, whether from panic or her drink, she did not know or care.

"I thought I'd hate you. And most of me does, but you still burst into my war council, you still offer help." He surged to his feet.

She flinched, adrenaline, even distant, exploded through her chest.

His thin brows curled together, and for the first time his frigid eyes settled on hers. Seeing. The muscles in one cheek flickered, lamplight gleaming off the scar below. He paled further, gloved hands rising, as if encountering a prairie cat. "Fates. I didn't think—" He looked between the two of them and backed toward the door. "You're going to RoBal for me. You leave in four days."

Rih watched the door close, watched Bimet slide the bolt closed. One hand dragged over her face. Rih's body was aflame, as if every fragment of control, of peace, was burned from her nerves by the flash of colorless irises. Terror that she had displeased him drowned any relief at his absence. "What—" She stopped, shaking, fiddled with the ink on her skirt, and then tried again. "Why did he leave?"

Bimet shook her head. "I don't know. I couldn't know, but I could guess." She crouched before Rih, movements slow, careful not to touch the other woman. "It almost seemed as if he realized what you thought, that he had a moment of empathy, perhaps."

"How could he not have known? A man doesn't appear at his wife's door just before midnight without intending to—" She pushed the woman out of the way and rushed to the privy. Even the acrid taste and stench of vomit did not erase her fear. When her stomach was empty, she still felt no safer, no less afraid.

When she sat back, Bimet's hand appeared holding a damp, warm cloth. She did not sign or attempt to voice anything. Instead, she dabbed at Rih's cheeks, washing away tears and vomit. Another cloth dried her face before the interpreter lifted her off the tiled floor and into her bedroom. A blanket settled over Rih's shoulders, and a mug warmed her palms. *Kava. For trauma.*

Wind eddied and she glanced from the swirling pink depths of the tea to see Bimet had cracked open the door to the balcony. The bedroom door was shut and a heavy chair was pushed against it. Bimet caught Rih's glance from it to her and back.

Her smile was faint but full of feeling. She poured herself a mug of tea and settled at the end of Rih's bed. "I learned signs long before I was sent to become a noble interpreter. It was all I wanted to do. To travel, to speak with people, help them connect. And I was good. My first teacher was one of the scribes in the merchant quarter, a friend of my father's and the only man in his family who voiced. He was a kind man and a good teacher. He was the one who brought me to Vi-baln's attention. He knew my skills were good enough to earn a place in the Hand's entourage. Neither of us knew the price. Naïve. The Emperor's Hand makes sure everyone in his service knows who owns them. My first night in his court I learned he owned my body. I still don't know if this career, the one I wanted more than anything, was worth it."

Rih's heart ached for her, but fear thrummed too loud to let her reach out a hand. She forced her hands into stilted motion. "We're going home. You'll have to see him again."

Bimet must have seen the compassion in her eyes because she smiled, a broader one now. "It was long ago, and I've made my peace."

Bimet leaned against the post of the bed, gaze lost out the window. Rih's nerves still screamed, but there was a spark, deep at the base of her heart. She let it gutter and burn, let her mind wander between dissociation and relief. Outside night deepened, a cosmic burial shroud over her gasping breath.

CHAPTER EIGHT

The 45th Day of Valemord, 1272
The City of Ceir Athrolan, Athrolan

MILDEW BLOOMED IN THE garden. The acrid stench of burning lamp oil clung to the damp stone. Mud squelched under Keplan's leather boots. Beside him, Hylier's strides were almost silent.

"You're quiet this morning."

Keplan shrugged. "I have a lot to think about."

"I thought you avoided such things."

"Usually." Keplan turned his face to the dawn light, seeking the phantom of its warmth. Even on a clear day, cold seemed to seep from the very ground. "I suppose today's problems are ones I feel I can actually solve."

Hylier snorted. "If you have insight into how we're going to solve the issue of Greton's letter, by all means, share."

"He's just asking for an audience with my administration." Keplan shrugged, clasping his hands behind him. It was cold enough to warrant a hat and coat, and for once he was grateful traditional Athrolani style had a penchant for fur.

"An inspector can act on his own. He doesn't need you or His Highness Daymir to arrest anyone. Unless, of course, he's arresting you."

"I doubt he'd arrest me. Accuse, surely, but in what country could a common man march up and dismantle the throne?"

"Arguably, that's what you did."

Keplan glowered. "I don't have time for that nonsense."

"I thought you said you could solve it."

"That wasn't what I meant. I saw Rih last night."

Hylier stared, blue eyes scanning the king's frame as if searching for evidence of how their evening was spent. "And?"

Keplan turned toward the memorials, ducking under a broken arbor. Even here damage from the burst aqueducts was rampant. "In four days she rides to

RoBal to ask for troops on my behalf. What she says or does isn't my concern. But she's going. I think I startled her, though."

"Begging your pardon, Your Majesty, but you're a startling fellow on the best of days."

"And on the worst of them?" Keplan asked wryly.

"Ah, I decline to answer, sire." He cleared his throat. "Speaking of troops, have you spoken to Daymir at all? I noticed he was absent from the war councils."

"I don't trust him."

"You can't wage war without the regent's approval."

"I invited him to the first, he didn't come. His servant said he was ill. I didn't bother telling him about the second. You saw him more often than most while he was exiled. You know his mind is not what it once was."

"He deserves kindness, not exclusion," Hylier argued. Pity and sorrow tinged his voice and Keplan was reminded that the guard's family had served Daymir's for longer than the man had been in exile. "Your family served him from before?"

"My mother's father, Currow, was his steward. He saw the entire house crumble. I was just a boy at the time."

Keplan glanced at the captain. The man was so youthful, it was hard to remember he was at least a decade older than the king. "It must be difficult to see him suffer this way. Reduced to an echo of who he was supposed to be."

"It is. Almost a mockery."

"I'm sorry for my part in it. I don't see another path, and I didn't then, either, but I'm sorry it's this way."

Hylier sighed, lifting his chin a bit. "I'm not the one owed an apology, and you're too young for regrets yet, Wardyn."

Keplan scoffed. "It's not the years you've ridden, but the leagues, I think." They lapsed into silence. The city below was a cacophony of wrenching metal and shouts from bucket brigades as fires began and were extinguished. Somewhere on the docks Fess organized lines of leather bladders to contain the worst of the spilled oil. He wished the city did not look like the chaos and filth of his own mind.

"I found Peraan's bag." Hylier's voice was barely above a murmur, so faint Keplan wondered if it was the wind.

He let the man think over his next words without interruption.

"I looked through it, enough to see it was his. Missing his usual bottle of wine. The parchment is mostly destroyed, but there's a waxed writing kit that might have survived. A signet ring, too. One from Daymir's family that was auctioned off when he was exiled."

They rounded a bend and drew up outside the entrance to the memorials. Ahead, someone was shouting.

"Where is it now?"

"My room in the city. I wrapped it in an old cloak. The sooner we deal with it the better. I dislike being so entangled in this."

"For someone who has such distaste for this work, you're incredibly good at it," Keplan noted.

"Same could be said of you."

"Ruling?"

"I wouldn't go that far." Hylier's tone would have been teasing, were it not for the truth in it. "Influencing people."

"Most of that is wrangling my parents' myths into sense."

"You didn't see them when they were building those myths, though. They weren't people to be wrangled."

"How?" The cry cut through their musing.

Keplan glanced at the memorials. "Grieving?"

Hylier's eyes narrowed. "It's been months since anyone noble died." He loosened his sword in his scabbard and paced up the stairs. "Stay behind me, sire. Just in case."

Keplan did not argue, falling in a few steps behind. Something thumped against stone in the center of the raised lawn.

"How could this happen?"

They crept along the paved walk in the Circuit of Honor. The Xain mausoleum stood in the center, just beside the older, weathered pink granite of the Tzoan.

A crack echoed from between the white marble columns.

Grief flooded Keplan's body. The ache of longing, of regret and burning shame crashed through his senses. He pushed past Hylier.

The mausoleum was dark. There was too little lamp oil for the living to waste it on the dead. The scorched stone table stood empty in the center, ringed by a dozen vaults. All but one was filled. One day Daymir's burnt remains would be sealed behind it. For now, though, he crouched on the floor beside his aunt's grave, sobbing.

"Blackhouse."

The man glanced up, parchment cheeks raw from tears. "Why do you all keep calling me that?"

Frustration crashed into pity in a mental maelstrom. Few things kept him grounded when his own mind spun. *And I'm not about to shove dust up an old man's nostril.* He folded himself onto the floor a few paces from the regent. "This cold weather really sets the bones aching, eh?"

Daymir did not answer, but he watched the king warily.

A moment later Hylier knelt beside his friend. "I know my knees are never pleased in winter."

"You're Dill—Currow's grandson. You look older."

Hylier nodded. "It's been a while indeed. I thought we could visit, maybe over tea?"

Daymir was still fixated by Keplan. "And him, I know his face."

Keplan drew a card from Hylier's deck and tried for vague calmness. "You knew my parents. Hy—ah, Dill—and I have been working together."

Daymir seemed to remember where he was, if not when, and fresh tears leaked from the creases around his fogged eyes. His voice was a distant groan. "Tzatia. Why did no one tell me she passed? No one even fetched me for the funeral. I'm not even across the city. I can't believe I'm king."

Even Hylier seemed uncertain of what to say. "Why don't you come inside? There's so much to discuss. Her memory deserves a bright fire and hot food."

Daymir's hand brushed the inscription on his aunt's vault, gnarled fingers picking out the tiny intricacies that had long since weathered from the older graves. "I never said goodbye. Last we spoke it was a ball, I think, when…" He stopped, looking back up to Keplan. "Did your mother send you?"

He shook his head, at a loss. "She's traveling. Let's get you warm."

Hylier rose, offering the regent an arm to haul himself upright. Together they left the mausoleum, Keplan a step behind. He was an intruder on this moment, witness to vulnerability that should have been sacred, reserved only for family. For those who loved the man. He glanced back at the dark, deserted monument. How soon would it be before Daymir joined them?

They skirted the gardens, entering the palace from a small rear door by the southeast tower. Keplan flagged down a squire as they made their way toward the regent's rooms. "Hot tea, please, and a small lunch—some of that roasted duck, perhaps. To High Highness the Regent's parlor."

"We're clear out of the duck, sire," the squire apologized, ducking her head in a bow. "Our meat and cold storage are low, what with no bread. We could bring some pickled fish."

"Fine, whatever there is, then," he answered, watching her disappear into the servants' hall. *No bread.* His stomach growled in protest. How was the Hare faring, with so little to serve?

"Wardyn."

He glanced ahead, to where Hylier waited by Daymir's open door. The king jogged to catch up. "I ordered something for him."

He glanced into the room from the doorway. The old man sat by the window now. The cold sun glinted off the white stone and shone on pale naked trees.

Daymir's gaze settled somewhere far distant. "I always loved snow, even in exile. It made us equal. At least everyone would be caught in the same storm, unable to leave. No visitors. Sometimes, your mind's the best friend you have when you're left be, left gone to seed."

Keplan knew that feeling well, caught between realities, never certain which one everyone else experienced. "We've ordered you some lunch. Would you like us to leave?"

"I'm surprised you made it up the road in this. Slippery, with fresh fallen—though your parents did. Last they visited." He frowned. "Are they still here?"

Keplan shook his head. "No. They aren't. They went on."

Daymir hummed in response, eyes lidding while his head lolled with exhaustion.

Hylier opened his mouth to speak, but Keplan shook his head. When they left and the heavy wood separated them from Daymir's gentle mutters, the captain turned to him.

"It's as if he sees all of his past and present at once. You were there and so was your mother."

"Seeing moments simultaneously," Keplan reiterated. "Small wonder his mind's lost. I know seeing so much frays mine."

Hylier looked at the king, expression unreadable. "Is that why you didn't you tell him he was in Athrolan? Or that he can go where he pleases? Most people argue with him when he gets confused."

"No sense in it." Keplan trudged down the hall. "Wherever he is, he wants to stay there. He wants to be left alone. There, at least, he isn't mad."

"Sire, the matter we spoke of," Hylier reminded him.

Keplan winced. His nerves were aflame from dealing with Daymir. The amount of himself he saw in the older man terrified him. No matter what glimpses of time he saw, like Daymir, the future was unknowable. Of all the briars in his palm, Greton and his murder investigation were the most irritating. "Have you found anything more about the network?"

Hylier glanced down the hall. "Perhaps elsewhere—"

"It's a legitimate question. No one knows where all these names originated or what anyone would gain from simply removing the people who helped me. Some of them, surely, but not all. All we've got is a piss-stained bag, a man I'm glad is dead, and the alias of a man who, more often than not, doesn't even recall my name." Frustration was a caldera, echoing the mighty seething deep down in his mind.

"I've learned all of that while acting as your guard," Hylier spat. "It's not my issue that you've decided to start a war over disliking someone's faith—"

"Blasphemy!" Keplan roared. His thoughts ignited with panic. "They preach this sickening image composed of contradictions. I'm not some all-knowing creature, and if anyone ought to be worried about wrath, it should be them!"

Hylier stepped back, eyes wide. "Sire, I only meant your actions may have been reactive and could have benefited from more time and thought."

Embarrassment slapped his cheeks. The same concerns overhung most of his conversations lately. "Then you sit the throne! Go ahead," he snarled, ripping the signet ring from his hand. It clattered across the flagging. "Take it, take all of it. Take my fate-cursed life while you're at it and save us all some trouble!"

His captain turned on his heel without another word. The palace guards at the end of the hall pretended not to see, and Keplan wondered whether it was out of disdain or pity. The king crumpled to the floor. He backed into an alcove, relishing the bite of cold tile on the back of his head. He ripped the gloves from his hands and pressed them to the slush-splattered floor. His sanity may have been slipping, but even so, he did not miss the allusions in the prophet's scripture. *Green hand, red hand. Sees all, understands none.* He wished he thought to call after Hylier, apologize, offer to help with the puzzle of who needed his allies in the city removed. Loneliness yawned in his chest, and even the fading effects of dust did nothing to help. His allies in the palace were dwindling too, and he had only himself to blame.

Φ

Hylier strode into the city, boots tromping the path to the narrow apartment tucked between the old inn and a milliner's workshop. The window was dark. Cobwebs were strung between the doorknob and the wood of the door. He had a fraction of the connections Reka did, and half of hers were probably to inform on Athrolan herself. *Or on Ambassador Barrackborn's sister.*

He understood better why she left Brentemir's service. It appeared Azirik's lineage had a penchant for perfection and mercurial temperament. *Or outright illness.* Hylier was almost convinced being a monarch required a certain mental instability. Perhaps it was simply because the unintended casualties were so much greater when madness sat the throne. His steps slowed. Reka was Mirik's Spy Master. She had a network ten times his own. Maybe it was time they shared more than just a bed and bitter conversation.

As much as he disliked the pauper-king, he had made a vow—to Daymir, to Athrolan, and to Keplan himself. *And it's not as if I'm untarnished.* He kept a murder victim's bag in his room, hidden from the city inspectors. He helped cover up the crime. And plotted to blame it on someone else. The most he could do was find out Peraan's motives and make sure whoever took the axe-blow was as guilty as the king himself.

He found his way to a Slummer bar, close enough to the docks to have a variety of clientele. He sank into the seat facing the door, leg crooked outward in a welcoming gesture. Once his drink was ordered, he fished a bag of tiles from his pocket. It was a game that required opposition, and with the new alliance, there were more Banis in the city than ever. Hylier could think of one country, at least, who would benefit from both Athrolani instability and the death of the Mirikin Hetmir's son.

"Looking for a partner?"

His brows rose. Of all the people he expected to see, Lady Nehla was not one. Asking what brought her there, however, might lead her to ask him the same. "You play?"

She smiled, flipping her wrap aside and dropping gracefully into the opposite seat. "Well enough. Buy me a drink?"

"I thought Banis didn't drink."

"Most don't." Her eyes leveled on him. "But I've traveled enough to pick up all manner of things from every map corner."

Warning shot up his spine. Until that moment he swore the Banis princess's handmaiden was charming on her best day, vacuous on her worst. The fire in her eyes now, however, told him he was sorely mistaken. "I enjoy tales of travel," he replied, cautious. "I would love to hear some of yours."

Her head tilted, her dark eyes regarding him a moment. "Perhaps you can tell me some Athrolani gossip in return."

He slid the bag of tiles to her. "What's your drink of choice?"

Φ

The 47th Day of Valemord, 1272

Sha's ceiling was draped with gold silks and delicate netting. After a moment Keplan realized they were tied in the same knots as the fishing nets heaped on the floor during his last visit. These, though, were ties of soft cotton. "Your room is beautiful," he whispered.

She propped herself up on one lean arm. Her wig had been discarded at some point earlier, and her shorn dark hair curled at wild angles. "It's hardly much, but I like it."

"It's yours." He frowned. "Wholly yours. I haven't had a room that was just mine since I left home. My life doesn't even feel like mine."

Her dark eyes softened with empathy. "I've been lucky in that. But I know many—common and noble alike—who feel the same. Most of us are trapped by our fear and our circumstance."

His finger traced the faint curves of her chest and narrow hips. "I think I feel trapped by myself. The choices I've made. They didn't seem like choices, like there were other options when I made them." He swallowed past a sudden lump in his throat. "Recently I realized I've been trapping others too. And that's the bit that nags me."

Sha's gaze flicked to the box on her dressing table, the pale green dust scattered on the smooth surface. "Is that what you're trying to forget? Or is it these?" Her thumb smoothed the pocket of his cheek as if it could wipe the scar from his skin.

"It's just…" He shook his head. Tears erupted and he ducked his head. "Fates, I don't even know anymore! There's just so much pain! Pain I've felt and witnessed, pain I've caused. Sometimes it all feels the same."

"Pain is all the same. Joy too. It's what we do with it that changes us. Believe it or not, as carefree as I am, this life isn't easy. Folks are confused by me, whether they're looking at Sha or Rheman. I don't fit into expectations. Most ignore it, but a few don't." Her fingers tightened around his. "That's why we need friends. Lovers. Family, blood or otherwise."

A frown strained his exhausted face. "Can I tell you something?"

She waited, expectant.

"I'm married. It wasn't what I wanted, but I chose it because I thought it would make things better. The whole thing terrified me. I only just realized she's terrified too."

Sha sat up, drawing his head into her lap. Her fingers combed tangles from his long hair. "In this world marriage is a livelihood. And not just our lives rest on its success, but our families or, if it's political, those of thousands." When he cocked his head, she continued. "The soldiers who die when negotiations fall through. The couriers and clerks and ambassadors who must find excuses for what happened or whose families starve when they can no longer do their job because of war. And, of course," her pointed gaze flicked up to his, "the woman abused because she did not please her husband."

His stomach twisted. Rih's terror when he appeared at her door settled in his mind. Perhaps, if dust hadn't burned away empathy with the errant thoughts, he would have understood the origin of her fear sooner. He was so wrapped up in how painful his own life was, the drama of his journey, his conception, that he failed to see the strength it took to face him. *She's a better king than I.*

"Where do you go when you kick up dust?" Sha asked.

"Kick up dust?"

"That drifting of the thoughts, the spinning without care."

His raised his brows. "I thought you didn't breathe it."

"I don't anymore. It never did much for me. Few things get their claws in me. Some people find it easy, others don't."

He shook his head. "I don't know. Inside, I suppose."

"Sometimes that's the scariest." Sha's head tilted. "Would you like to tell me about your marriage?"

He stared at his bare hands for a breath. "I imagine disinterest is better than cruelty, but these marks and my face make it difficult. Make me difficult." The weight of Firas's rejection settled over his shoulders, his lover's face when he realized what trouble their bar boy brought to the inn. "I'm a difficult man. I wish I weren't."

"You said you didn't have a choice."

"Of course I did. But I wasn't ready for it. I didn't have someone to train me, I didn't have my whole life to prepare."

"Perhaps she had a choice too." Sha sat up straighter, extricating her folded legs from under him. "It's my turn to ask if I can tell you something."

"Whatever you wish."

"Someone's been asking around. An inspector. A good one. Asking after a boy, one with a habit for dust." Her dark eyes flicked to his, steady and full of honesty. "Says he murdered a man."

His thoughts were spinning again. There was no way Sha did not know who he was. It was written under every line she spoke. "That could be anyone."

"Could be."

"Why are you telling me?"

"Because the man who was murdered deserved everything he got and more. I've lived in the shadows of this city for years and many here are those I count among my friends, people I would do anything for. And he took one of them from us."

"Mirrel."

Sorrow tugged at Sha's smile. "I'm just thinking if someone is asking for Lan Guardsen, perhaps it's time he takes a trip. Until this wind changes."

Only I will remain. He straightened and looked about for his shirt. "Surely you have somewhere else to be, instead of me just wasting your time with chatter."

"You've paid for my time. It's up to you how you spend it." She took his hand, pausing his retreat. "Why don't you just rest here."

He settled on the bed, the covers soft against his skin, Sha's large calloused hands working knots from his shoulders. The scent of ale and cooking food drifted from below. Outside, the city sounds were muffled.

"The window, would you mind?"

Sha padded soundlessly across her room and swung opened the casement, letting the night air eddy its news through the room. It carried an infant's furious, hungry wail to the corner by the door. It scattered male laughter by their tray of food, swirling there for a moment before it brought the thoughts to where he sprawled on the bed. It seared him, the hunger, the fear, the hope, but he closed his eyes and bathed in his tiny corner of peace.

Φ

The 10th Day of Glasmord, 1272
The City of RoBal, Ban

Noon sun lanced through the building clouds, beams tracking across the prairie like a guard's search lamp. Despite her lack of sleep, humming energy filled Rih. Her eyes picked out familiar hills, dipping swales that marked her journey home. Threatening rain necessitated keeping the cover raised on her wagon, but she leaned out the front as if able to spur the horses faster simply with the force of her own anticipation. Two dozen Athrolani guards augmented her own retinue, and while they kept to themselves for the first days, now fires, food, and the occasional bedroll were shared each evening. Rih even noted Curiel among the paler faces.

RoBal towered in the distance, and Rih's pulse quickened as the mound grew on the horizon. Even under the slate clouds, it loomed an angry red. Already her skin was invigorated by the absence of salt and raw wind. Glinting spears ahead heralded their waiting imperial escort.

Burning joined the thrumming excitement in her limbs. *Anger.* She had longed for home, for the rich flavors and layers of color, even as she detested the inequality and hatred upon which the entire system was built. Still, it was home.

Damp wind picked up, ushering them forward. A glance at Bimet told her they had already been heralded. Sure enough, their escort fell in around them at the next rise.

Adrenaline spiked again at the red armbands. Surreptitious signs passed between a few of her own retinue and the Banis soldiers. It gave her pause. *I thought Bimet was my only ally in Athrolan.* The interpreter's face was unmoved, dark eyes fixed on the stacks of houses ahead. Did she know how far—and close—their movement reached?

"Are you looking forward to being home?" Rih asked Nehla. She knew Bimet's feelings mirrored her own in their ambivalence.

"I am. Letters from family say much has changed. It's been a long time since war waged here, beyond the usual imperial expansion. Undoubtedly fashions have changed, too." Nehla flashed a smile. Her bright eyes were fixed on the road ahead, her perpetual giddiness tempered only by the fatigue of travel. "I can't wait to add new wraps and jewels to bring back to Athrolan."

"I wonder how many Athrolani trends made their way back already."

"Depends on how many you wear while we're here," Nehla countered. "You're a king's wife, you'll set trends faster than most."

Rih laughed. She had only just mastered the basic traditional attire. Learning something new with each season was more daunting than any rebellion.

The road widened, the packed earth giving way to bricks as the scattered huts and shacks closed in along the riverbanks and roadside. Wooden grating and narrow walls ran along the road to keep guests from witnessing the worst of the poverty that crowded outside the walls, caught between clawing free and pressing in.

One of the Athrolani guards rode up, raising the face of her helm to flash Rih a smile. "You promised to teach me that atlatl, and I've heard your training courts are rivaled only by the emperor's gardens."

Rih's mouth curled. "I'd love to, though I fear once you get a taste of proper tea and fruit it might be impossible to pry you from your rooms."

"I want to taste it all! I was on guard duty the night they brought out that candied stuff, it was gone by the time Jaik took over for me. Hardly blame them."

Rih laughed. "You'll have more than enough to try here, as long as you stay close to our wing. If we've a spare moment I'll gladly show you the courts—I've only used those in the barracks and the Purple Throne, but I've been told those in the palace are stunning."

"Purple Throne? That sounds more like a brothel than a place to train," Curiel joked.

"Essentially. It's where I was trained for marriage," Rih explained. Her gaze wandered past her friend to the building tucked against the palace. "It's there, if you have any interest in such things."

Curiel shook her head. "My evenings are occupied by La-naket lately. Your pretty Banis horses aren't the only thing he can ride—"

Rih rolled her eyes. She might have enjoyed a clever, vulgar joke as much as anyone, but the image Curiel's words evoked was one she would rather not see. "As long as our afternoon is free, then, come find me."

The wagon lurched onto the brick-laid main road and Rih glanced forward. As a soldier, she rode through the smaller military gates of RoBal countless times. Today they entered through the massive front gates.

Steeply sloped double walls ringed the city. Though rain washed much of the surface filth away, black blood and brown fluids still streaked the baked clay, draining from the bodies pinned along the top. Most were accused of theft or treason. Rih suppressed a shudder. She wondered how many were innocent. How many had been members of her rebellion. *Did any confess under the interrogators' blades?* Or were they simply dragged through the streets to die atop the heights?

Even the cold, damp air was rank with refuse. Here, the pervasive scent of fruit and clay veered closer to rot and muck. Opulence was a glimmer of dawn far ahead, over the teetering rooftops and haze of the Rises and Stytown. Steam drifted from vents set into the wall, exhaust from the massive churning spring that provided the force for opening and closing the double gates. For now, however, they stood open.

Bimet nudged her. "The herald says we meet with the Hand of the Emperor tomorrow, midmorning. It's an official audience. He received our message only yesterday."

Rih shifted in her seat. She hoped for more time to acclimate, but at least Vi-baln would be as off-guard as she. This may have been her home, but she had never been here as a dignitary. It was a wholly different city when arriving as a guest. The winding streets were crowded as ever, but there was an edge—even without hearing their shouts, Rih caught new lines of tension on faces. Eyes once pinched with exhaustion were now narrowed in anger. Defiance.

Higher, among the sprawling manors, new bars blocked doors, and extra guards paced walls that once only boasted draping vines. Heady lilies and gardenias scented the air, kept damp from other steam vents and water forced through pipes, weaving through the city until cool enough not to scorch the roots.

They drew up in the courtyard, their military escort traded for a diplomatic one. Guards were ushered into smaller guest accommodations, while the officers and Rih's personal attendants fell in behind the princess herself.

Mosil appeared at her elbow as she descended. His smile was tired but true, and his hand on her arm was gentle. "It's good to see you again, cousin."

She flashed a smile. "I did not expect to see you so soon."

His grin widened. "I had a feeling I might. Come, let's get you settled. I'm sure you could use a proper bed and good food. Tell me," he asked, guiding her up the palace stairs and into the dignitaries' wing, "have the Athrolani cooks learned how to make proper buttered tea yet?"

After the inefficiency and rough accommodations of Ceir Athrolan, Rih relaxed into the lush hospitality of home. Everywhere screens were flung open to welcome the fertile breeze, and every question or need was met with gracious acquiescence.

Her travel clothes were whisked away, replaced with new finery once she had visited the sprawling women's baths. When she retreated to her room just before dusk, however, it was empty, save for Nehla. Bimet had left a note explaining she had gone to visit family but would return that night.

Rih collapsed onto her bed with a sigh. Aches she had not realized she had were erased by hot, sulfurous water and the strong hands of a trained masseuse. She glanced up when Nehla settled in a chair by the window.

After a moment her hands rose in awkward signs. "Would you like some tea?"

Rih's heart leapt. "You're learning?"

"Mobeka has been teaching me during our visits. I've always wanted to learn, but my focus was on the politics of fashion. Politics in general."

"Politics of fashion?" The term reminded Rih of Ki-elte and their discussion of clothing as a communication. Perhaps she would find a moment to see her friend.

"It's like anything with culture or meaning behind it. What someone chooses to wear means as much as what they say—it's how they intend to be seen. Before they ever open their mouths—or raise their hands," she amended.

Some words were out of order, but the whole of her meaning was easy to decipher—easier than trying to read the animated woman's lips, at least. "I'm surprised you haven't practiced with either Bimet or me before now."

Nehla's excitement withdrew again. "I don't think Bimet likes me. I know she doesn't, truthfully. I've spent my life studying people and the connections they make with one another. What influences them. I don't trust her, honestly."

Rih sat back. She was not used to having a large group of friends. Even her training group as a child was now scattered among a handful of different positions and assignments; their time together rarely overlapped. *But outright distrust on both sides is unusual, and for the same reasons—connections.* "What influences Bimet, to your mind?"

Nehla's shoulders lifted in a sigh. "Fear."

Rih scanned Nehla's outfit again, more carefully. The woman was always meticulously styled, and now she knew why. Still, every ring bore a jewel, and nothing could be mistaken for a red band. With the false public meaning behind her sign, Rih could not easily ask if Nehla knew or supported the rebellion. "It must be nice to learn from your cousin. Does she get news from home? You said much had changed."

"I've learned a lot from her. She said to tell you that whatever you need, all you need to do is ask and she'll provide—" The ground trembled and Rih turned to see a weight resting on the ground by the door. The chain attached to it cranked it upward again and she rose before her visitor was forced to knock again.

Curiel waited in the hall, easy smile in place. The loose sleeves of her tolstovka were rolled up, and someone had found a plain cotton wrap to protect her shoulders and head from the rain.

She jerked her thumb down the hall, brows curled in a question.

Rih nodded, ducking back into her room to quickly change. As much as she wanted to stay and learn exactly how much Nehla knew, this was neither the time nor place. Too many ears and eyes were fixed on them, and without fluency, Rih worried how much nuance might be lost.

She set out with Curiel alone. In the press and chaos of the city it did not matter that the colonel did not know Banis or how to sign. They took turns pointing at interesting or colorful sights. Though Curiel might have been little more than a stranger, Rih was delighted to see the other woman enjoyed overhanging ivy and took joy in the curtains of drying silk hanging from a hundred lines overhead when they cut through the servants' wing.

Nerves sang up her back when Curiel gripped her arm. She pointed to where an armored figure jogged toward them, waving one hand. They crossed the cobbled walk and Rih caught sight of the tattoo on the woman's shaved scalp.

"Il-fald!"

"Rih!" The woman was barely done signing before Rih locked her arms around her teacher. They stood that way for a moment before she stepped back. "This is Curiel. She's a colonel of Athrolan. I promised to teach her the atlatl, and we found we had some time before the press of dignitary duties descended."

"I don't envy you," Il-fald joked. "Either duty, frankly. If she's as slow a learner as you, you might be sun-weathered as clay before she masters it."

Rih rolled her eyes. "I've been training when I can," she promised. "How are you? How goes the war?"

"Banis hooves are many and swift," she answered, "though Mirik's forces continue to harry our coastline. It's the skirmishes that bite us most. How is Athrolan?" Her dark eyes flitted to Curiel, then back to Rih. "And your studies?"

"Athrolan is cold and wet. My studies have been difficult, though I have more time than I'd prefer, there are few study partners. And now there's war."

"We heard something was brewing—something about a mad king?"

Rih snorted. "My husband is mad, yes, but I'm not certain this war is entirely his own doing."

Il-fald turned, seemingly hearing a call to join her companions. "I've got a missive to deliver, but I need to speak with you." She drew Rih close again, pressing their brows together for a moment before stepping back to sign. "I've got a message from an old friend. In the south."

Majilah Ag. "I'll call on you before I leave." Rih reached out to squeeze her hand once before her former teacher was lost to the crowd. She led Curiel to the palace training courts, but her mind whirled a thousand leagues a second. RoBal was a hulking thing, dark and bloody. It was lush and violent and layered in beauty and complexity. But still, her heart soared. *Home.*

CHAPTER NINE

The 10th Day of Glasmord, 1272
The City of Ceir Athrolan, Athrolan

MIDDAY BELLS TOLLED AGAIN. Keplan jogged from the throne room, waving a dismissive hand as the herald reminded him of his afternoon obligations. He spent the last weeks wallowing, drowning in the despair of a failing city, failing crop, failing leadership.

When he reached the greenhouse, Fess already waited for him. Her greeting was tired, and her smile did not meet her eyes. "Afternoon, sire."

"Fess," he answered. "Domariigo should be here soon."

A bright ray of light flooded her face for a second and she winced. "Remind me again why we're meeting here instead of your study or the audience chamber. Or anywhere else, frankly."

"I was going to ask the same thing," An'thor remarked, appearing on the path from the greenhouse's other entrance.

"That's where we always meet. I need new perspectives. Outside is doom and snow and chaos, and I need to be reminded more exists than that." He took a seat at one of the small tables tucked into a cluster of broad-leaved plants. He guessed they were the same as those that decorated the ballroom for the Banis welcoming celebrations.

Fess tugged a faded kerchief from her breast pocket and wiped her nose. "Seems I'm allergic to something in here, so grab your inspiration and let's make this brief."

"I wanted to speak to both of you outside a war council. They all have opinions and many are good, but I can't think with that many voices rattling around."

"I don't think anyone can," Fess muttered. "I've reports—official and unofficial. And Dorcal's most recent letter."

"Begin there."

She flipped through her officer's log, finding the relevant page and scanning her notes. "He's along the Northland coast. Says if the weather holds, he'll make near Neneviir soon. He's got another dozen message birds. One of his sailors dabbles in art and included several illustrations of the creatures they've encountered."

Keplan smiled. "I'd like to see those when you have a moment."

She made a note and continued. "Next, we've extinguished the fires and most of the spills are contained, though all the water brought down from the hills before the burst is contaminated."

"We have more?"

"We're well into winter. There will be some, but most is locked in ice in the hills. We usually rely on our cisterns until snowmelt."

Keplan looked down. Snowmelt was months away. "Rations. I'll see if we can ship some from the rivers to the east and west, but it will take a year to build another aqueduct from either." He rubbed the bridge of his nose. "Anyone outside the city is to use snow. If there's not enough snowfall, we'll send soldiers into the towns to rig rain collection."

"Our ships use seawater for tea sometimes," she realized. "Boil it and collect the steam the way you would distill wraith. It's not perfect, but it works well enough. If we can find something to burn other than lamp oil or each other, we might be able to create fresh water from the ocean for other uses."

Other uses. "Bathwater will have to be drawn up from the harbor—where it's cleanest, of course."

"You know what happens to your skin, bathing in seawater?" Fess reminded him.

"You know what happens to a city when they begin to run out of water?" An'thor snapped back.

"Enough. I'll speak to the commissioners about how best to implement these ideas. Surely they'll have more, too." Keplan sighed, wishing he had tea. At least his drug habit gave him energy. "You mentioned other reports? Unofficial ones?"

Fess closed her book. "I have a friend who accompanied Her Highness Rihelte to Ban with the Athrolani guard. They arrived in the city yesterday, if they kept up their pace. But she noticed something—rumors, only—on their journey. They stopped in a few towns briefly, and she said there was something under the surface."

"How so?"

An'thor leaned forward, his black eyes lit with curiosity. "Physical or cultural?"

"Not certain. She just noticed certain people among the Banis retinue speaking with individuals in town. They were signing—"

"Half of them are Deaf," Keplan excused. "Probably just looking for others who know their language."

"It's less than half," Fess corrected, "and they weren't just signing. It seems like something more. She said it looks like a network. A community, in the least."

"I fail to see how that involves me."

"You allied with them. Their business is yours."

"Can you ask her to look further into it?"

"I can. Is there something in particular?"

"No, but when she returns, I'd like to speak with her. There's someone else who might have another piece to the puzzle." He did not know what Hylier gleaned that he kept to himself, but if someone knew more, it would be him. "And speaking of unofficial channels, I've a concern of my own. About the investigation into Peraan's murder."

Fess's brows rose. "They certainly seem to think it's related to your allies. Though honestly, I'd imagine Mirik would be as likely. The man called for the assassination of the Hetmir's son. His known Athrolani victims were just common folk from the slums."

Keplan winced. *Mirrel wasn't "just" anything!* "I imagine his reach was farther than we realized, Fess. A friend in the slums informed me they're looking for an addict, someone who was avenging one of their own. Seems like it might have more to do with class than politics."

"Class is politics, Wardyn." An'thor picked at the peeling lacquer on the table.

"There's hunger out there, and filthy water, and a religious war on the horizon. Vigilantes are part of the bargain," Fess argued. "The most you can do is help the investigation and let the rest of it fall by the wayside. We've got far bigger leviathans to spear here."

"I suppose." Keplan's nerves were raw. He hoped for incredulity or answers as useful as her suggestions about the tainted water. Nonchalance was a surprise.

She sneezed, blinking watering eyes. "If that's all you need of me, sire, I'm going to go before my eyes are raisins."

"Apologies, dismissed." He watched her go before turning back to An'thor.

The general rose with a groan, lurching over to examine a colorful flower that resembled large bobbing genitalia. "Where do these even grow?" he muttered before turning back to the king. "So, rumor has it Peraan's murderer is a mad young man with ties to the Slummer. If that's the case, where were you the night he got his throat ripped out?"

Keplan rolled his eyes. He hoped the warrior's eyes were too bloodshot to pick out the pulse thundering in his throat. "Look at me. From what I recall he was a big man. You think I have the strength to fight, let alone kill him?" An'thor's expression was unwavering, and Keplan threw in a shrug. "I wouldn't have minded being the one and have no doubt he deserved death, but it wasn't me."

"If you insist."

"If my path to the throne is drenched in blood, Domariigo, I'm not the one who should be blamed for it."

An'thor seemed to give up the path of questioning and crossed his arms. "You want to sling blame or listen to my report?"

"Do you have one?"

An'thor heaved a sigh. "If I'd known placing your arse on the throne would be akin to raising a petulant adolescent monster, I'd have let Dorcal sack the place."

"I am a petulant adolescent monster, Domariigo," Keplan flashed a grin with all his father's teeth. "Anyway, where are our fanatics now?"

"Gone. Disappeared. Most we can find is tracks and cold campfires. They move fast, for an army."

Keplan's racing blood chilled. "Army? How many?"

"The group sighted to the southeast was two hundred. More if they aren't the same as those seen camping in Claimiirn. Another from Bodian province was seen just before they disappeared into the Ru'un Felds. Estimated close to a hundred. All moving north."

"We're the capital," Keplan argued. "We can handle a few hundred."

"We're a glorified city with poisoned water, no food, and a child for a king," An'thor snapped, whirling on the boy. Every shred of his drunken apathy evaporated.

"What do you suggest, then?"

"Pull whatever you have to out of your arse, pray your wife does your begging for you, and cut whatever ties you still have to the Slummer. You're a king, not a barkeep's bed-buck." He stalked back down the greenhouse path.

Keplan looked down, picking a loose thread from the dingy cotton of his gloves. He did not like the general. Nor did he care if the man liked him at all in return. But he did not want him as an enemy. *He might be a drunk, might be a sorry remnant of a warrior, but you don't live so long without influence and power.* If An'thor was willing to murder people to get Keplan crowned, he did not doubt the violent lengths he would stretch to remove him if he saw fit.

The winter sun sank lower, disappearing from the glass panes overhead. He straightened and traipsed through the palace. Despite his usual scheduled audience times, the throne room was conspicuously empty. Interest in Banis relations had kept his audiences full weeks before, but the current chaos in the city and barren storehouses had people clamoring at Guild Houses and robbing neighbors instead of petitioning the king. Perhaps they realized the latter did little good.

Even Hylier had yet to appear. An'thor would be holed up with the Captain of the City Guard discussing enforced gate checks against the Swordbearers.

Keplan wandered farther into the palace warren until he stood before what had once been the royal wing. He ducked under the heavy velvet curtains, still colored mourning black and covered in dust. Beyond, the double doors stood shut and barred. *To think, an entire wing of a palace squirreled away like a secret.* Keplan lifted one of the lamps. Its wick was still damp with oil, but the tinderbox no longer hung from the lamp hook. He let the curtain fall shut behind him, darkness settling over him.

The silver inlays on the door glimmered. A shove, and they groaned open. Rolled carpets were stacked over the white and gray flagging. High-backed chairs and long couches stood in one corner, shrouded in sheets like the queen herself had been. Cobwebs draped every corner. Dust softened each surface.

A parlor waited beyond, and a study. The few bits of brocade cushions and embroidered curtains he glimpsed were picked out in lavenders and blues, accented with the royal turquoise.

Keplan had yet to make any part of his chambers his own. He may not have arrived in Athrolan with anything, but neither had he acquired anything he cared enough about to display. *My only connection is Moly, and I hardly ever ride anymore.* He had not even seen her in weeks. Guilt panged in his chest.

His city crumbled around his ignorant ears, and the most he could do was succumb to dust in his empty rooms. Energy flared through his veins. First he yanked the curtains back, dust motes exploding from the heavy fabric. Next came the sheets. The ornate carved wood was perhaps a bit outdated, but he never cared for trends. He paced from room to room, uncovering an entire life of a woman he had never met.

Hairbrushes waited by her mirror. Gowns hung in her dressing room. No face paints were laid out, however, and every washbasin and faucet was dusty. It was closer to a shrine than a home. He did not test the bedroom door. Even for him, some places were sacred.

Dozens of books lined the shelves of her study. Histories and the expected lineages were dotted with a few philosophical texts and folders of old letters. He pulled a sheet from the wall behind the sprawling desk and stood face-to-face with his own mother.

Even caught in canvas, her eyes froze him. It was worlds away from the portrait Brentemir showed him in the Hare. Instead of a tender, laughing moment around a fire, it was a formal portrait, akin to those of monarchs. Cascades of black fabric and embroidery made up her sarafan and delicate silver veils hung below the towering silver spines of her kokoshnik. Beside her stood the Earth Shaker, garbed in brilliant golds and white, coiled whip at his hip. Gilding and pearlescent paint freckled his forearms and face.

Keplan sank back against her desk, shaking. Homesickness overwhelmed him. Their faces were so familiar, if younger. Dressed in finery, heads raised with pride at their blood, at their power, they were a vision of the life he never had. Knowledge he was only now cobbling together. He would give it all up in a heartbeat for some semblance of home.

"No wonder you ran," he whispered. "You might not have known what awaited me here, but fates, you still knew better." Parchment crunched beneath him and he looked down. Notes. Plans. Ideas for a future she was desperately trying to wrench from the failing kingdom. *Inspiration.* He wove back through the rooms, emerging from the hall, blinking in the bright light.

"Sire, are you well?" The steward hovered in the hall, frowning. "One of the maids said you were looking for something in those chambers."

"I'm fine, Valadai, thank you." He glanced at the doors, shut behind him. "It's time those rooms were cleaned. And I would like more desks brought in. And notebooks." He raked a hand through his hair. "Please."

He pictured war machine schematics across each surface. Designs of distillation systems to create water for his people on others. If Athrolan would survive, her path would not be forged between the naked walls of his study.

Φ

The 11th Day of Glasmord, 1272

Muscles Rih forgot she had ached in ways she did not recall they could. Sun cast patterns of light across the ceiling through the carved wood window screen. Nehla was gone. Instead, Bimet sat by the windows looking out. Rain saturated the colors, transforming blues and red into sky and blood.

Rih stretched, popping joints back into place that had been subluxated by travel. Donning a robe over her bare skin, she padded across the room to sit at the other bench beside the window. "How was your family?"

Bimet glanced over long enough to read the signs, then her gaze roved back to the city spilling below. Purple shadows clung to the puffiness beneath her eyes. "I missed them. My brother won't be called to the military. He's younger, wants to be an officer, but his request was denied again."

"Is it political?" Rih asked. "Because of your position with me? The rebellion?" Bimet was all she had sometimes, it seemed, but if she had to leave for family, Rih would never question it.

"It's complicated, Rih." Bimet's shoulders heaved in a sigh. "He's younger and has an incredibly good heart, but you know the rules. He works as a guard at the main gates for now, and can only request thrice. They wanted to discuss the rebellion—"

"Did they know about us, about you helping me?"

"No, and they won't. He won't stand a chance of being promoted if he's connected to it."

"He could be an ally," Rih suggested. "We need them."

"He's a boy and I won't hear of him destroying his future." She rose. "I told Nehla to see her own family today. She'll be back in time for the audience, but not before."

"Did you speak to her at all?"

Bimet frowned. "What would I have to say?"

Rih shrugged. "We just had a nice evening. I'm trying to create stronger friendships, even without the rebellion." Rih stopped, suddenly uncertain. "Are you all right?"

"I'm fine." The signs were sharp, and Bimet's face lined with stress. "Being here, seeing family, it's hard, you know."

"I do. I'm sorry I brought you here, but I'm grateful for your support. Truly."

Sorrow and frustration flitted over the interpreter's face. "I sent a request for someone else to help you dress. I may not like her, but Nehla knows far more about the intricacies of fashion. Hopefully they send someone equally skilled." Her smile was tired and insincere.

"I'm sure. I'm going to the bathhouse, if you'd like to come."

"I've already been. I didn't sleep much last night."

Rih paused by the door. "Is there anything I can do?"

"No, but thank you."

Rih's thoughts churned as she gathered her clothes and slipped down to the bathhouse several stories below. Being home was strange. Her time in Athrolan barely amounted to a month but seemed like eternity. It was almost worth dealing with looming imperial eyes to avoid the disorganization and isolation of her husband's kingdom. *Husband. King's wife.* She tugged her robe closer about her shoulders. Those words still felt as foreign as Trade to her.

Damp heat rolled from the double doors to the women's baths as they opened for her. After the raw ocean air this was ecstasy. Golden glass globes hung from chains, casting everything in a rich warm light. She doffed her robes and slipped into the dark steam room. A fired clay grate made up the floor, and water roiled beneath, billowing steam into the small room on its way to the baths themselves. Bottles of scented oils lined a shelf by the door, and she hesitated before choosing something floral over her usual sandalwood.

She started with her arms. Usually one could hire a masseuse for such work, but after years on the road, she enjoyed the opportunity to take stock of her own body. Now it was as much an exercise in remembering the flesh under her hands was, in fact, hers. The line across her calf from an arrow graze. A gnarled circle on her knee where she fell onto scorched ground when along a fire line. Countless nicks and scratches over her forearms from spear combat.

Her head rocked back onto the leather padded seat and she let her eyes lid. Aromatic wood and jasmine combined in a heady scent that relaxed her iron grip on her thoughts as much as the heat and oil coaxed knots from her muscles.

Air wafted over her skin and she cracked one eye to watch the two women who entered. One was broad and heavy, walking with the deliberate grace of a dancer. The other had her same straight black brows but was a good two handspans taller. Rih was too relaxed to greet them or try to bother with conversation.

"It's been such a week—I've had two performances a night for three days. I wouldn't think anyone from the western jungle would be interested in our art, but the ambassador enjoys it apparently."

"Nothing wrong with being in favor."

"Except my feet might never be the same."

Rih only caught a few words as they continued and was almost drifting off when she glimpsed one of the women's hands move incongruously with her words. "I've heard the general herself plans on coming to the city soon."

Rih kept her eyes almost shut, hoping they looked closed in the dark room.

"So she's a diplomat?"

"I think it's the Valen queen."

"You think she'd risk inciting a rebellion while our countries are finally in peace talks?"

Their innocuous spoken conversation continued, but Rih could not tear her attention from their hands. It took all her will not to leap up and confess that she was the leader, to please tell her everything they knew. They thought her sleeping. They thought her voiced. For now, she would feign ignorance. Their rebellion's strength lay in its anonymity.

"I heard a speaker will be at my meeting tonight, we'll have some orders surely. As it is, half of us are in place already."

The door opened and both women's hands fell into stillness. A third woman entered, and Rih made a show of opening her eyes fully and stretching. Nodding to the others, she slipped out before anyone could try to speak to her.

She wiped sweat and dirt from her skin with the excess oil and dipped into the hot tiled pool. Even a plunge in the cool water afterward barely registered among her whirling thoughts. These rumors were new. Her pride twinged at the thought of Majilah Ag receiving credit for the cause, but for now, it behooved them. The fact that she was negotiating with Ban came as a surprise, but perhaps it made perfect sense—no one enjoyed fighting two different wars, and the easiest way into a city was with an invitation.

A letter awaited her when she returned to her room. Il-fald's handwriting was messy, her words almost hurried.

> *R,*
>
> *I've sorely missed you, but my duties are greater than ever, and I fear I won't see you before you're gone again. If your journey back to Athrolan takes you past Jai, I'm sure our dear friend will find you, for she's visiting as well.*
>
> *May your horse's hooves be swift and your spear strike true.*
>
> *All of my love and hope rides with you.*
>
> *-I*

Rih's heart sank. Seeing Il-fald was a bright point in her time here. Her finger brushed over the final line of the letter. She wondered which ally her teacher meant, and despite her heartache, a tiny thrill of hope thrummed through her. A thought percolated through the fear and excitement, settling to add steel to her strength. *I'll be home again soon, with spears and hooves and fury.*

Φ

Other than her yearly visits as one of the emperor's wards, Rih had rarely seen the man. It took a moment, then, for her to realize the man dressed in swaths of emerald silk beside Vi-baln was His Eminence himself.

She dropped to her knees, eyes sliding anywhere but his face. Dizziness flooded her head and she clenched her teeth to keep terror and breakfast spilling across his silk slippers. He inspected his nails, filed short, save for the longest, which was lacquered in a deep red. Perhaps it was her own blood that dyed it, taken the moment she crossed the border. Did that cause her light-headedness now?

"Welcome home, Rih-elte."

"I'm grateful you took the time to meet with me. It's been lovely to see familiar walls again."

Vi-baln leaned forward from his seat, a step beneath the emperor's. "We did not expect to see your bright face so soon after parting."

Bright face. It belied the anonymity she was reassured of in the baths. Were her own allies the only ones who did not know who she was? Or were Vi-baln's words prophylactic? "I'm honored you both chose to receive me, Your Glory, and at such short notice. Indeed I, too, did not foresee returning so soon, even if just as a favor to my beloved, His Majesty the King of Athrolan." She wondered if her face betrayed how stiff the endearment felt in her fingers.

"I am curious of that, of course, but I'm more curious about the current state of our new allies."

The emperor was perusing a fruit tray, seemingly unaware of her presence.

Rih settled back on her heels, glancing to make sure Bimet was prepared for a longwinded translation. Did she distract them with Athrolan's instability or focus their gaze wholly elsewhere? *How can I convince them fighting a budding religion is even worthwhile?* "Living in Athrolan has been quite an adjustment, and they are so different from us that I urge you to consider these have been issues for decades, and I simply haven't seen them. Their governing is one of debate—pedantic more often than not. Currently they struggle to feed their people, and some accident destroyed an aqueduct shortly before I departed. It's since been repaired, but I've heard there are concerns about filling a cistern." She added a shrug to her feigned uncertainty in the off chance the emperor was watching her and not Bimet.

"I see," Vi-baln answered. "I assume you're here to beg for more grain than we've already sent?"

"To my knowledge those shipments have been sealed away, protected from the blight and in storage until next spring when they can be sowed. I'm here about the war."

The Emperor's Hand's brow arched, and Rih quickly looked back to Bimet, crouched at their feet, to catch his response. "War?"

She seized Keplan's line, tossed aside in the dismissive clamor of common sense. "His Majesty sent me to ask for support against Mirik."

"They would never go to war. Family ties, history, and so forth."

"The Hetmir's son was attacked in Ceir Athrolan—by an Athrolani assassin. They are leaving within the month. Now His Majesty has closed his doors to the prophets, and all his attention is on preventing heresy and keeping his people fed."

Vi-baln rolled his eyes. "Prophets? The nonsense from Kut Tunis, you mean."

"With his eyes elsewhere, he fears Mirik will move against them because of their war with us." It was not a lie, but surely Keplan had not intended her to spout his wandering fears to the Emperor of Ban. Rih paused long enough for his mind to run wild but not enough for him to formulate an opinion of his own yet.

The emperor seemed unmoved by her suggestion. "I am surprised His Majesty sent you in his stead. It bodes poorly for Athrolan's stability that he could not risk visiting our beautiful gardens himself."

"It was only because of your considerate tutelage. You had me trained in diplomacy as well as all other traits so important to marriage. He did ask I send his deepest regrets that he would not see RoBal's beauty again. Athrolan would be grateful for both the show of unity against this annoyance and the aide so they might extend their army to their other cities in preparation for whatever the prophet's Swordbearers bring."

"Again?"

She risked a glance at the Emperor's Hand. Vi-baln ducked his chin, whispering something to the emperor.

One black brow arched. The emperor inspected a particularly plump plum, lips pursed with skepticism, then took a bite.

"And what do you think?"

Rih stared at him, blinking. Warning seared her spine straighter. The emperor was dangerous, incredibly so. But Rih recognized the teeth in the man's smile. Her thoughts did not matter. Her body, her mind, did not matter. *So why is he asking me?* "The prophets are an annoyance, a mosquito bite, but it threatens to become necrotic if let fester. I imagine having soldiers in the Athrolani capital is a position of power in regard to Mirik. False deities undermine authority, both your own and his, as a child of the Dhoah' Laen. Athrolan's army is large, but spread thin and underfed. I think it shows a united force against these heretics and Mirik both by sending two hundred spears to the capital." She hardened her nerves, shoulders stiff. "It's what I would do, were I in your place."

Vi-baln rocked back, nostrils flaring. "An entire baniol?"

The sting of danger skittered up her arms. This was a duel. Words, sharper than steel and far more subtle, cut through the swaddling fabric of pretense and manners. She locked eyes with the man, spreading her hands in deference before demurring, "I'm certain His Eminence will find a suitable solution."

The emperor did not speak for a minute, then his left brow twitched. A serving man bowed out and began issuing rapid orders in the hall. Gooseflesh rippled over Rih's arms. Sheer power was often tremulous at best. But here, surrounded by the might, the systemic terror that you might be next, it seemed impervious. "They will ride out with you in two days."

Rih bowed, pressing her brow to the cold stone. "His Majesty will be delighted when I tell him Athrolan and Ban continue to have a long and fruitful friendship."

The emperor leaned back in dismissal. Food was whisked away, and Bimet shuffled on her knees until she was suitably far enough from the dais to respectfully stand. Rih followed suit, both of them backing from the room. Exhaustion warred with adrenaline and her limbs trembled. Only when the massive double doors were shut again and they were out of sight of the four guards did Rih allow herself to slump against the wall.

"That was too bold, Rih!" Bimet's fingers shook as she signed.

"They listened, didn't they?"

"At what cost? The entire city might know who you are."

Rih shook her head. "I don't think they do. Suspect, perhaps, but nothing more than their usual distrust of everything. It's how they stay safe."

Movement drew her attention to the end of the hall. Mosil approached, hand raised in greeting. When he was closer, Rih saw his smile was tight and his eyes deeply shadowed. "Your Highness, I'd be honored if you joined me in the gardens."

"Excuse me?"

His gaze flicked between her interpreter and the audience room doors. "Surely you won't begrudge a cousin the news from afar. Besides, His Eminence would despair to know a guest was left to their own devices."

Rih did not need Bimet to translate the meaning of those heavy words. *I'm not to be left unattended.* She smiled. The emperor had secrets. The massive emerald mound of the palace was built on them. *And they fear I'll find them.* "I'd be delighted."

"Perhaps your attendant would like time to see family."

Bimet frowned, mouth opening to protest before Rih dismissed her concern. "I'll be fine for the afternoon. I look forward to playing tiles later, though."

Bimet nodded and, with a last distrustful look at the ambassador, disappeared.

Mosil's face relaxed a fraction and he gestured to a long narrow hall angling to the rear of the palace. His signing had improved, though his health was seemingly the price. "It's good to see you."

"And you. Are you sure you can afford the diversion of conversation? Things seem quite busy."

His expression darkened. "RoBal always rides at the forefront." It was an old saying, one that used to speak to progress.

The hall cut right as they rounded to the rear of the palace. Mosil did not speak again until they stepped through double doors and onto a long, covered walk. The outer halls of each palace floor were broad, open balconies, each decorated with a different set of colors accented by flowers and rich foliage.

Here, the building's face was no longer tiered, but a sheer wall dozens of stories in height. Thousands of blossoming plants covered its surface, tucked into nooks and hanging pots, many just perched atop one another without a root to be seen. A single ramp led down into a sea of green below. Rih's stomach lurched. The gardens were half the size of the city itself. "This is incredible. The water they must require—"

"RoBal is the city of springs," Mosil reminded her.

"The six fountains of the city called Seven Springs." It was a common joke, built on the fact that only six were accounted for, the final one long since dried up.

"This is where the seventh went," he confided. "His Eminence allows it to be used for these gardens alone."

Allows. As if the man had any control over the life flowing from the earth. He was better at bloodletting than nurture. An image flashed through her mind—springs, bubbling from the earth, thick and clotted with blood. She shuddered.

"Each section is tended by a devoted gardener who is lucky enough to live in the palace below. Last winter the palace was decorated with imperial purple and some blue as well."

She scanned the planted wall. It was awash with crimson blooms. "Red for war?"

"Or wrath."

She frowned. "His Majesty said something similar. What does it mean?"

"You didn't read the prophet's scripture?"

"No one did, save His Majesty." The ramp was steep but carved with intricate designs for traction. Above the clouds billowed and grew, darkening from dove to slate.

"I was hoping to get your opinion on it, actually."

"Mine? That's the second time my opinion has been asked by those who don't often seek it."

He had the grace to blush. "His Eminence learns as much from what we openly tell him as what he gleans from his thousand insidious avenues." He flashed a smile, gesturing to the lush world engulfing them. "Here, at least, I can hope the very leaves don't boast ears. I'd like to show you His Eminence's world of miniature."

It was only then that she recognized a wheat ear and a falcon's talon were carved into the stone beneath their sandals. "Tiles. The ramp is decorated in tiles."

"It's his favorite game," Mosil signed.

"Is he any good?"

Mosil's lips twitched and his shoulder tensed. "There is no one better. How else would he still be emperor?"

Rih laughed. Though bitter and weak under stress, she had forgotten her cousin was a master of two-sided answers.

A faint summer breeze drifted from the north, and he raised his nose. "I could visit here every day until I die and I'd still not recognize every scent and bloom. That sweetness, it could be any number of a hundred flowers."

Every word seemed to bear unnatural weight. The emperor was an overarching shadow, but not something oft discussed. It was too dangerous. Ban was hardly a place of faith beyond that in their own emperor. If Mosil thought the prophet's words bore consideration, there was more to it than she realized. "What does the prophesy claim?"

Mosil did not answer. Were it not for the set of his jaw, she would have thought he had not seen the signs. Heat grew the farther down they walked. The massive boughs cradled the brief sun from that morning, holding it between their reaching branches as rain approached. Clamor from the city streets and the bustle of the palace faded with each step, replaced by the chatter of birds and the burble of fountains.

The ambassador gazed at the whiskered fish in a pool along the path. "The One True God will rise where the worlds meet, from death and birth, from chaos and order. His blood pools, drowning the world even as it gives it life. Though he will bear the marks of hate, he will be unable to raise its tools. His right hand will be stained bloody with wrath, and his left with the verdant green of life and mercy. Thrice he will die and..."

Rih's blood chilled and she turned away. Moss blanketed the forest floor, a living carpet of a thousand different greens. One mound, at the base of a winding curling tree, boasted tiny white blossoms. She remembered the king's palm, naked and green, pressed to hers. "Not many are pardoned, but they number in the dozens, at least in RoBal," she began. "Many have both tattoos. And those scars."

He fixed her with a stare, his eyes lit with something previously hidden. "So you recognize your husband in the words."

"He's the child of the Dhoah' Laen. His blood carries Earth Shaker power. I'd be a fool not to wonder how it manifests in him. He's not well, though. If he is a god, then he is a mad one. What god doesn't seek worship?"

"And the other line—where two worlds meet. Ban, Athrolan?"

"Perhaps. Our cities are the opposite. Even in their design: RoBal is built up, Ceir Athrolan dug down, both in tiers. Perhaps one would fit around the other."

"They chose to push the cityfolk beneath them, while we just climbed over ours. Wouldn't you agree? And what of the drowning in blood?"

The nerves that sang of danger while she knelt at the emperor's feet piped again, but this time the tone was different. Athrolan's king was scarred and broken at the interrogators hands, perhaps misused by others with power. Still, he could scarcely wield divine power. "I'm not a priestess—I can't interpret scripture."

Mosil gestured deeper into the forest. "The path is this way." Massive boles closed in about them, blocking the fading light and the faint misting rain. Beyond, tucked between the towering boles, was an entire forest in miniature. Rivulets were tiny rivers, gnarled pines and birches and a dozen trees she did not recognize were bent over rocks and curled from tiny cliffs. "How does one make this—are they very young?"

"On the contrary," Mosil answered, "they are very old. His Eminence acquired a Berrin gardener some years ago—during the Gods' War, I believe. She has tended this grove ever since. Each one is formed in a pleasing shape, both artistic and natural. Even the fountain water itself is altered with salts and minerals specific to these trees' needs."

"I think Ceir Athrolan has one like this in the conservatory."

Mosil smiled. "I saw the conservatory during negotiations. It's quaint."

Rih snorted at the gentle condescension. "I'd argue it's a place of restraint rather than," she gestured to the surrounding vibrance, "abundance. Though this is beautiful."

Mosil nodded. "It reminds me of government. Both require decades of planning, pruning, a tiny metaphor for the surrounding world. One is a garden tended, and the other is a king debating the lives of his people or his enemies. A balance between mercy and wrath in itself." He paused, body motionless, save for his hands. "You may not be a priestess, but I've heard you are a general."

Her heart faltered. The forest seemed to spin around her. *No.*

Mosil's gaze pinned her into stillness. "Hi-alan spoke to me when we heard you were returning. She told me the truth. You allied with His Majesty so one day you could bring his army here. You allied with a god," he hesitated, eyes full of fear, of hope, and just a shadow of pride, "in the name of liberty."

She faltered, fear and hope colliding with the shuddering of her own heart. Bimet would insist trusting anyone was dangerous, but Mosil was a far cry safer than Keplan—he understood the grinding attrition of spirit from living under the emperor's eye. Instead of a denial, she simply asked, "And what do you think, cousin?"

"These past few months I've spent more time with Ki-elte. With Hi-alan. You may not need my help; in fact, surely you've planned everything without it, but His Eminence trusts me. Many trust me." His eyes did not leave hers, but he knelt, palms pressed to the gravel path. When he straightened, his eyes glistened. "I say: if His Eminence hoped to reap peace, then he should have sowed seeds, not bones."

Φ

The 14th Day of Glasmord, 1272
The City of Ceir Athrolan, Athrolan

Peace drained from Keplan the moment he opened his bedroom door. "Barrackborn."

"Keplan." Brentemir grabbed him by the shoulders. "What, by Toar, were you're thinking?"

Keplan pried himself away. The touch was cloying. His longing for parents, for approval, for someone to take the weight, did not extend to Azimir's father. *My uncle,* he reminded himself. "What do you want?"

"I want an explanation. Bringing Banis troops here? To our doorstep? I feel like I hardly know you."

"You barely knew me before now!" he retorted. "I've got more than enough people dropping the Dhoah' Laen's duties on my shoulders. I don't need you dropping her personality on me as well. You don't know who I am and, fates, I doubt you'd like me if you did."

"Cut the melodrama," Brentemir muttered. "It was your father's gimmick, and one often accompanied by murder and fire."

Keplan resisted the urge to confess murder often accompanied his, as well. Hylier knew, and that was already too much. The echoes of Peraan's throat snapped through his head. He did not trust himself. The thoughts may never had stayed long, but they only came when his blood sang with dust. They weren't his, he didn't think. But they came from somewhere inside. *Only I will remain.* He shuddered. "I needed their help. I'm not a soldier like you, like my parents were. I'm not a warrior. If this prophesy gets out, we'll have something far more terrifying at our door, and I can't face it alone."

"The Swordbearers." Bren looked away, and this time, Keplan caught the truth behind his shame.

"You couldn't have. You accepted them?"

"Keplan, you can't possibly believe it's a lie. Just listen to the words."

"You inherited your father's thrall? Their god is nothing more than a misunderstanding, but in their hands it becomes a weapon. I can feel the terror. The despair. Tastes like Ban. All of them crying into the abyss and praying for an answer."

Brentemir frowned. "Doesn't matter how hard you pretend, Keplan, your blood doesn't lie. Your father tried that too."

Keplan flung his hands up. "It doesn't matter how true their words might sound, I won't have myself deified! I'm going to war, regardless of your tiny island nation."

Brentemir staggered back. "Keplan, our navy's gone and you brought our enemies within two days of our shores."

"And you brought heretics to ours! I'm not your spy on Ban, I'm not your meek nephew, and I'm surely not your sister. I am king here, despite being gutterwash at it. Believe what you want about me, but it won't change the fact that you're wrong."

He staggered from the room, energy leaving his body in a rush. He locked the bedroom door, ignoring the ambassador's pounding knocks. Keplan's knees cracked on the tiles and he retched. He sought peace with the same dogged ferocity as the emperor sought control. *I've seen his face in dreams and my own stared back.* Nerves danced up his skin, as if his entire skin might leap from his flesh and go dancing down Palace Way.

The knocking had ceased, and when he jerked the door open, it was to an empty study. He needed calm. Peace. Silence. He scrambled through his rooms, checking every box, the top of each shelf. It was gone.

His pulse fluttered, tattered and weak in his arteries. He slumped against his desk and froze. *Of course.* That morning he had slipped it into his trunk for safekeeping when the maid cleaned. Two minutes later the chaos and tang of blood sank beneath the surface again. His body burned with too much energy, and he took off to the training courts.

Three broken arrows and an hour later, his cousin appeared in the doorway. "General Domariigo said you'd be in here."

Keplan barely glanced back as Azimir stepped into the training hall. His cousin's voice buzzed under his skull, both exciting and infuriating at once. "What'd you want? Train?"

Azimir frowned. "I wasn't planning on it, but if you'd like." He moved to the rack of practice swords, testing a few before choosing a falchion.

Keplan watched him, wondering what he measured in each. He mimicked the motions, frowning at one, then rolling his eyes at the next. He finally chose a long, narrow blade.

"Rapier?" Azimir asked, brows arched.

"It's red," Keplan explained, tapping the crimson leather binding the hilt, then wiggling the fingers of his bare right hand. "We match."

Azimir did not answer and instead paced to the center of the training hall. "Pa told me what you said. What he said. I didn't know, but I should have. My grandfather did the same."

Keplan rolled his eyes. "Those gods are gone. And I'm well sick of your father's obsession with my bloodline. With the gods."

"I read it, Keplan. They might be wrong about how much power you wield, but we both agree that description fits you more than a little."

Keplan's body ignited. "She's mistaken—"

"The world is dying. Half the continent is at war. I don't know how you interpret the world drowning, but it seems pretty clear to me. Mirik may have once worshiped, but it isn't faith anymore when you know they're real. Feels more like dread."

Keplan's nerves froze. Was he simply the figurehead of a larger, darker disease? Perhaps whatever rooted in his chest had metastasized farther than Athrolan. Keplan looped his sword in a clumsy circle. The general's voice was a high-pitched whine in the back of his mind telling him that's not how one used a rapier. "I'm just forced to tidy all the messes that were made before me," he snapped.

"Maybe you weren't meant to do both," Azimir suggested. "Maybe inheriting the throne was just the machinations of a scared queen and an elitist general."

Keplan looked down at his hands. "I wish that were true. But I saw what their civil war did to the city. I think I'm the only one who can clean up this chaos."

"People have been tidying up after your parents for decades. After our grandfather. I think we've managed fine, for lowly humans." Azimir shrugged. "I understand you're upset. I hate change—"

"Change?" Anger and something deeper flashed through him, bitter on his tongue. "I'm married to the bitch who imprisoned me, my city is dying, and one of my friends was murdered! By a traitor!"

Azimir winced. He still had not raised his sword, though his stance was ready. "She hardly imprisoned you, Keplan."

"Can you hear her thoughts?" he bellowed. "Can you hear the confession that burst into my head the moment she set eyes on me? *'The foreign spy.'* She knew me somehow. I remember about three painful minutes of the entire march to RoBal, but a piece of it, a piece, is the woman I swore vows to. You think she's the only one terrified in this?" He swung.

His blade clattered against Azimir's as the younger man blocked, wordlessly.

"It's not just memories from Ban or what they did to me. I hear them all, all the time. Feel the pain, of all of it. The only bit I yearn for is the oblivion at the end, but death doesn't even want me. I wish Peraan took me instead of her. I see his face. Mirrel's face."

"Is that why no one's been charged? Do you think he deserved it?" Azimir's voice trailed to a murmur. Each counter was easy, graceful. One arm still tucked casually at his belt for balance.

"And even though he's dead they still won't let me rest. They're hunting his killer, and I wish they'd leave me be. And even though I took this throne, part of me prays they'll find out the truth and accuse me just so I could give up the crown." He was yammering, but the thoughts rushed faster, a deep current under the muffled stillness of his forebrain.

"Accuse..." Azimir shook his head. "Toar, Keplan, you talk like you're the one who killed him."

Keplan's teeth rattled shut, blood welling where his raw cheek caught against incisors. *Are those from you, too, Da? Along with the thoughts?* "I just mean the responsibility."

But Azimir's dark eyes said he knew the truth. His wrist flicked and he stepped easily inside Keplan's guard. The rapier thudded to the sawdusted floor. "You're not right, Lan. Whatever is going on, whatever makes you like this, you need to stop."

Keplan lunged, fist tightening at the last moment. At least he was halfway decent with his hands.

"Keplan!" Azimir's forearms were up, blocking a moment too late.

Mirrel's blood. The interrogator. Bone, or perhaps teeth, crunched under Keplan's knuckles and he suppressed a burble of laughter. Azimir punched his cheek, but even through the haze of dust and pain and despair, Keplan knew his cousin held back. He did not want him to hold back. He wanted to feel everything. And nothing. He dove, toppling them both to the floor. A boot or knee thudded into his gut. Bile welled in his throat, but he had not eaten enough to vomit. Azimir's short hair knotted in his fingers, and he slammed Azimir's head against the flagging.

Firas's tears, burning his shoulder. Peraan's smug face. His hand on Peraan's throat pressing, squeezing, digging –

Pain slammed into the side of Keplan's head. White flashed across his vision and he fell back. His hands were sticky. His vision cleared to show bloodstained sawdust. His cousin rasped on the floor. "Azi – "

"You need help, Keplan." Azimir's voice was hoarse, and a livid bruise already formed on his throat and over one eye. He staggered up, panting. He spat blood on the flagging, but his expression was not contempt. It was not even anger. His mouth was already swollen and bloody. "I'm sorry those things happened. To Mirrel. To you. I'm sorry Firas doesn't love you anymore. But you can't hurt people because of it. You can't hurt me or Rih or Athrolan just because your heart won't stop screaming."

Keplan could not watch his cousin leave. He could barely hear through the panic, through the buzzing. He slumped down, face to the cooling, sticky blood, and closed his eyes.

Φ

Azimir sank onto one of the benches lining the dark hall. Pain throbbed in his head and throat, but his heart hurt worse. He debated telling An'thor or even Fess. But he did not want someone who only knew Keplan as a bitter, foulmouthed man. Last year Keplan replaced the general as his idol. It was his chance at something close to his father's relationship with Alea. At least, that's what he had thought. He wound down the halls, pausing at Rih's door. If she were back, he might rush to her. *She already knows he's been a right arse.*

If he returned home his father would ask, and Azimir certainly did not need idealism and old values. Before he could think better of it, his feet were stomping the path to the Slummer. The high-collared jerkin hid what he imagined was an ugly purple line around his neck, and a handful of water at the courtyard fountain removed most of the blood from his chin. He doubted anyone would care about a blackened eye.

The roads seemed somehow narrower, and he noticed several empty storefronts. The Wise Hare's lanterns cast the street in gold and faint music drifted from within. He stepped in and found the seat at the end of the bar where Keplan had always sat.

A Banis boy was minding the tables and shot him a nod before ducking into the kitchen. Moments later Firas emerged. If ever there was a man haggard enough to look dead on his feet, it was Firas.

Toar. Azimir grimaced. This might have been a poor idea. The bartender stepped up to where Azimir sat, barely spared him a glance. "What'll it be?"

The words slurred, and Azimir looked down. "Just an ale please, Firas."

Recognition flickered across Firas's bloodshot eyes. "Fates, Azi. Didn't recognize you with all the…" He gestured to the boy's face. Without looking he poured a mug and slid it over. "What happened?"

"I was actually hoping you'd have a minute to talk."

Firas's face closed, his beard and mustache meeting as his mouth thinned. "If it's about a certain pauper king, I have nothing to say on the matter."

Azimir took a long, slow sip. "I'm begging here, Firas. Please."

Firas's jaw tightened and he stalked wordlessly away.

This was a mistake. Still, Azimir stayed. There was nowhere better to be, and what little he knew about battle injuries, he ought not to sleep with his head pounding so.

Despite Firas's words and Azimir's refusal of dinner, the boy brought a plate of stew. It tasted of ash. The music was faint, and by morning he could not have named the tunes if his life depended on remembering. An hour later, when the stool beside him was vacated for a final time, he rose with a groan and went to the privy. It was still dark, too dark to see more than the contrast of his skin against the void of the privy depths. His lower back ached. *I'm probably pissing blood.*

"You have a handspan of minutes here," Firas growled across the courtyard as Azimir's swollen fingers messed with the buttons of his trousers. He emerged.

The pain on Firas's face was familiar, and though his eyes were green, the loneliness in them could have made them the king's. "You and I were never close enough for you to come wandering in asking advice on how to tup."

"I don't need advice on—yes, it's about him." Azimir rubbed his face with one hand, hissing as pain sparked through his bruises.

"You never said what happened." Firas passed him the mug he had left inside.

"Keplan. Keplan happened."

"What?" Incredulity laced the words. "He's not a violent man."

"Then you know him less than I thought."

"I just mean...his whole reason for taking the throne was for peace. It's hard to marry that man—" His voice broke on the words. He cleared his throat and tried again. "It's hard to picture that man beating someone senseless. Let alone his own cousin."

"He wants peace, surely, but he can't find any himself. There's something wrong with him, something different. I can't speak with Rih-elte about it, or my father. She'd argue there was never any good in him, and my father would say there was never any evil—"

Firas's snort cut the words. "He's human. For a man descended from ancient titanic power, he's as perfect, perfectly human, as folks are born."

"I'm afraid you and I are the only ones who see it. Especially once this prophesy is loosed upon the world. He needs help but I'm not the one to do it."

"I surely can't. I think it'd do more harm, actually, to see me, to hear how I felt, how I still feel."

Azimir glanced up, startled. "I'm sorry."

"For?"

"I guess I didn't think you had feelings for him. Not anymore, at least. Thought he was a casual dalliance."

"I did too." Firas's whisper cut through the soft summer air. "Fates, I really wish he had been. And sometimes, I wish I'd never met him. Maybe then Mirrel—" He slumped and let out a racking sigh, too exhausted to be a proper sob. "But there are days, more than I'd care to admit, where I think it was worth it. Not her dying, but meeting him. Might have been worth this fucking empty chasm in my chest."

Does he know about Peraan? "Firas, about Mirrel and the man who did it."

Firas snarled, "That bastard, if I found whoever killed him, I'd be so grateful I'd kiss him full on the mouth."

Azimir frowned at his drink. "I think you already have." In the following silence he did not dare look up. "Keplan is a violent man. A tortured one—in his mind I mean, not just the scars. He's killed. Almost did again, with me, tonight. But even I don't think he's evil."

Firas's face was unreadable. His eyes fixed on the city wall towering behind the Hare. "You saying what I think you are? About Peraan? And Keplan? Where he went that night, after Mirrel—?"

"Yes. I am. And I assume that fact will die in this courtyard."

"Seems to be a lot of that." Firas regarded his own ale, then finished it in several slow sips. He placed the mug on the stoop and laced his fingers before speaking. "So why come here? Why, really?"

Azimir scuffed his boots against the stair. It was times like this that he really felt the years between him and most of the men he knew. "What does it look like when someone breathes dust?"

Firas's exhausted body tightened and he turned to look at Azimir. "No. You don't mean that. He can't have, he wouldn't have, why in the name of every dead god..." He trailed off. "'This won't make you forget.'"

Azimir frowned. "What's that?"

"A conversation he and I had. I told him that, ah, sharing intimate time together, if you will, wouldn't make him forget what happened, though he disagreed. I guess in my absence he found something that would." He heaved a sigh. "Azi, if he's breathing dust, I don't know what'll help. I've never, myself, but we're in the Slummer. Folks here have more reasons to forget than most. Once that shite's in your body you…you're not the same." He rose and paced to the privy, then back.

"Firas, I'm sorry, I just don't know who else to turn to."

"I'm trying to keep this inn floating in this putrid sea of bad news. And you've just told me our king is as good as dead."

"He's not dead. I know dust won't kill me, even if my ma said it would—"

"I don't mean physically. The man on the throne isn't the man who stepped up to it. He's not the man who promised to raise Athrolan from stagnation. And he surely isn't the man I—" He growled, kicking the frame of the wagon in the corner. "You should go."

"You think he can get better?"

Firas's eyes were fathomless depths. "It would take a god mightier than we've seen."

Azimir's veins echoed with the blood he shared with Keplan, with the woman who killed the gods his father once worshiped. "If anyone can it's him."

"I pray you're right," Firas shrugged, backlit by the oily lantern at the rear door, "but you and I both know there's no one to listen anymore.

CHAPTER TEN

The 16th Day of Glasmord, 1272
The Icelock, Northern Ilmar Ocean

THE WOOD CREAKED AGAINST the press of icy water, and Raven glanced up. He took pride in his ship working like a single being and, no matter how far from home they may be, he expected the best of his sailors.

Jorn poked her head in. "Thought you might still be up. Midnight shift change."

He rose from his desk with a groan and followed her outside. Sailors shot salutes as he stepped onto the deck. He was respected but rarely liked. Most on board had never been past Athrolani waters and none had been this far north. Storms struck quickly and lasted days before dissipating as swiftly as they had arisen. He tightened his jerkin's hood and stopped beside the fore-shipmen at the helm. "How does she sail?"

"The evening went well, sir. Smooth. We averaged nine knots. Temperature still falls—even with the sun it's past freezing, and the days are ever shorter. We passed more ice an hour ago and should pass Neneviir within the week. Sooner if we unfurled more sail."

Raven eyed the water surrounding them. The depths were black, eerie compared to the gray-green of the waves near Ceir Athrolan. "Not with the ice. We have the moon only for another hour. I'm ordering the bolts and reinforcements to be checked again. I'd hate to discover the hard way that we were unready for ice." He turned to the herald waiting on the decks. "Mek, signal for them to ready the ice-breaks."

As the boy ran up to do his bidding, the former commander watched the ships behind them. He had to admit they made an impressive sight. Once he commanded forty-six runners—fully armed vessels that were smaller than the traditional battleships under Admiral Nellon. Raven's fleet of one was newly outfitted with chevrons of iron-plated hardwood on their bows. The precaution against the massive blocks of ice in the northern-most waters had been raised to keep speed. With temperatures dropping and ice sighted, Raven listened to the tingling instinct that always served him well. The ice-breaks would hopefully not be tested.

The fleet had hugged the land for the first half of the journey, but upon signs of camps on the tundra he had ordered to push into the open ocean. Bergs and other unknown dangers kept the trade routes to the west or by land. While they were unlikely to meet any other vessels, it also meant Fess was sailing with only the most rudimentary maps. Much of their knowledge of the pole had been gleaned from the legends of the Ageless and Claimiirn histories. "Keep pace, Kusen, and wake me if anything changes. Anything on the horizon that isn't ice or water—wake me." He glanced at Jorn. "A word?"

They moved back into his study, weighing a map between them. Black dots marked their progress across the sparsely detailed area through which they sailed. The ship trembled as the ice-break lowered. Raven lifted his mug to keep it from spilling.

The officer leaned against the desk. "We have just over thirty leagues before we reached the pole. What lies between here and there worries me. We'll round the headland tomorrow, if the weather holds."

"That's a gamble this time of year." His gaze slipped back south to the night-shrouded horizon they left weeks before. "Makes me wonder if this was an elaborate execution, sending us in winter. Weather's been worse than ever."

"You think it's him?" Jorn's words were low, but superstition did not tinge her dark eyes. "Or is the world just dying around us?"

"Let's just focus on the headland, eh?"

Jorn's chair creaked as she leaned back, eyes narrowed on him. "You've destroyed men, faced fire and flood in the battle at Claimiirn. You guarded his parents north and turned cannons on your own home to uphold your values. I haven't agreed with you often lately, but I'd never call you a coward."

"I don't stand for creatures thinking they're better than us. I don't think monsters have a place in ruling us. Helping us, surely, but handing down decrees? Forcing us into worship at the foot of a throne meant for one of our own?" He shook his head. "And he arrives, poor and mad and battered and ascends to where she sat."

"I know he's not human by blood, but I can't think of a single person who isn't poor and mad and battered. Noble and commoner alike." Raven ran a finger up the coast they paralleled. He paused at the blank space past the pole. The cartographer had not even bothered to draw little waves. *This is why I became a sailor.*

"You're terrified of him."

"I hate him."

"Same thing, Dorcal." Jorn hunched over her illustrations, glancing up each time ice broke on the bow.

Raven added a few lines to his log, though there was less to say with each passing day. He reread every note they had made for the journey, guttering lantern shedding jumping light on the paper. Nerves set Raven's gut writhing. He paced to the windows to peer at the void beyond. "I've grown soft, sitting state in the city," he confided.

The ship's floor muttered as she crossed the distance between them, hand resting on his for a breath. She did not speak.

Raven looked down at her hand gripping his limp fingers. Fatigue weighed his slumped shoulders. His heart hammered, hollow. He turned, twisting his hand to grasp hers. It had been years since he lay with a woman he didn't have to pay.

"I'm not gonna pretend to be her," she warned.

"I'm not gonna ask you to. I'm not asking anything, if you don't want."

She shrugged, smile tired but sincere. "I think we could both stand to get our minds off tomorrow."

A disused laugh rasped from his throat as he followed her into the bed chamber and shut the door behind. Waves hissed along the lacquered wood as he pulled off his stained coat. He slid a hesitant hand under the waist of her shirt. Her tanned skin and Athrolani dark hair were unfamiliar to his calloused touch, but only the dark, secret part of his heart still cried for Eras's ashen complexion and pale orange hair. The *Endurance* glided, lonely, through black waters.

Φ

The 19th Day of Glasmord, 1272
The Eastern Banis Prairie

Rih took a long sip of tea. The rich flavors that erred on the side of decadence in the cloying heat of Banis summer were comforting in the winter rains. Like the empire itself, every flavor was bright, intense, and fleeting.

They were still days from Athrolan, their progress slowed by the two hundred soldiers marching alongside them. Rih grinned wolfishly. *My army.* It was not strictly true, but for now she could pretend and call it practice.

Oily tea spilled over her lap as the wagon lurched to a halt. *Of all the hoof-trod roads!* Setting the mug aside, she scrambled to peer through the waterproofed carriage cover. The entire train had stopped, horses pawing the road as their riders shifted in their saddles.

"What is it?"

Bimet turned to the driver to relay the princess's question. He shrugged, gesturing at the road ahead and muttering something.

"Says a group of riders blocks the way."

Fear sparked in Rih's chest. "Give me a moment." She grabbed a wrap to hide the fresh greasy stain across her clothes and freed a spear from the rank before jumping down. "Bimet, with me, please."

She strode to the front of the line, edging between snorting horses and uneasy soldiers. Sure enough, twelve riders stretched across the road. Red and orange knots decorated their armor. *Vales.* Despite the Banis spears lowered in their direction, none of their weapons were held at the ready. Rih steeled herself. She did not know most of the soldiers behind her or whether they supported or even knew of her rebellion. Her eyes narrowed on the lead rider. Their features were shadowed, but the masses of black braids spilled from under the heavy leather helm. They dismounted and approached, hands empty and extended.

"I am Kajimet Rih-elte and wife of the Athrolani king, His Majesty Keplan of the Hartland."

The sharp lips curled. "I hardly recognized you, swaddled in silks there."

"Majilah Ag?"

The arms opened farther and she closed the distance between them to clasp Rih's hand, her other clapping the woman on the back. The Valen queen tugged her helm off. "I'm sure you have a long way to ride, but perhaps we could journey together for a stretch."

Rih could not help the bright smile on her face. "I'd be happy to. Why don't you come to my carriage?"

The Valen guards ranged about the royal carriage, watching with wary curiosity as their queen ascended. When Rih joined her a moment later, she caught Nehla's wide-eyed gaze.

"You're friends with the Valen queen?" she signed.

Rih's smile grew tense. Between their brief visit and the close quarters in the carriage, she had not found time to continue their conversation from the Banis capital. Now seemed like a poor time to test the woman's loyalty, however. "It's odd the friends one makes, I suppose."

Majilah Ag scanned both of Rih's attendants. "Would you mind giving us a bit of privacy?"

Nehla glanced at Bimet, then back at Rih before wordlessly retreating to the carriage the attendants shared. Bimet made to followed and a moment later the army swayed back into motion. The queen drew a small notebook from her belt and set about writing.

> *There are too many curious ears to risk speech. Besides, this way there will be no misunderstandings. You may trust your women, but I don't.*

Rih scanned the words as she poured them tea and found a case of dried fruit. She pulled the book toward her.

> *What brings you this far from home? I've heard you're treating with the emperor. It's unexpected.*

Majilah Ag grinned.

We'll never get as far as swearing anything, you have my word on that. It just brokers peace while we get into position. I'm here to investigate a new potential ally – unofficially, for now.

For Vale or our shared interest?

Majilah Ag sipped her tea and chose a dried kiwi.

Your rebellion.

Excitement bloomed in Rih.

And who might that be?

Mirik. There is a woman who joined your cause, according to our informant. She has ties to the island, and there's even rumor she might be a member of their former spy network. Regardless, we plan on meeting with her soon.

Rih hesitated, then moved to answer. Bimet's council focused on secrecy above all else, but more often it seemed to veer toward inaction.

It's something I've considered myself. But not because of any Spy Master.

When Majilah Ag's delicate brow arched in question, Rih continued.

Because of the Hetmir's younger son.

Majilah Ag's eyes widened, lapsing into speech with her surprise. "You're direct. I hadn't realized she had a second child."

He's scarcely out of boyhood – seventeen at most. We were supposed to marry before the war began. Instead, we've become something like friends. He's clever, I think, though he doesn't let on often.

Does he share your bed?

Rih's cheeks flamed and she smoothed her skirts with a firm head shake. No one would share her bed as long as she had any say in the matter.

"Good. It always complicates things."

The queen sat back, eyes distant for a moment while she finished her tea. When her attention returned to Rih, her expression was guarded.

Perhaps I will discuss things with this supposed spy, and you work on the boy. Our meeting is another week away, but we ride fast. I hoped to write you afterward, but considering the circumstances, I decided to delay our journey and meet you in person.

Circumstances?

Perhaps you don't get news, far as you are from home, but things are changing. Armies moving. Every day brings a new patrol or baniol that's redirected. I'd be curious to know your allies in the officers' ranks, for I imagine there's a pattern.

She produced a battered map, marked with movements of various troops. A second paper detailed which baniols or officers were known. Rih's heart dropped. Her every ally was marching north. Despite what her eavesdropping gleaned, many were no longer in place.

How old is this information?

Our most recent report was the day before yesterday, via messenger bird.

Were they avoiding Mirikin ambush? Or did they know? How many people saw the letter delivered before she left Ceir Athrolan? Her thoughts hesitated on Nehla. Keplan had appeared before she could hide the information and her attention had been wholly occupied with terror. She glanced up at Majilah Ag, desperate for direction, for advice. The queen's gaze was grave and reserved. It held no answers.

We need to get into the city. We don't stand a chance if all our allies are outside the walls. You get in regularly despite being an imperial enemy.

Smuggling in twelve Valen warriors in a city where women are inconsequential is far different from hiding hundreds of soldiers. And it will take hundreds.

Rih drew a slow, steady breath.

We have one ally in the palace. My cousin, Mosil, the ambassador to the east. While at war with Mirik many of his duties overlap with the ambassador to Athrolan.

A man? They are quick-tempered and bullheaded.

Contempt settled on the queen's features.

Many might be, in Ban and Vale both, and I understand your hesitancy. I understand your fear. But please know that they are not all evil. They do not all seek to crush us beneath their sandals. We need allies and he is one.

Majilah Ag's lips twisted in scorn and she sat back. "You'll deal with him, then. Ban is built on the bones of a thousand queens, and her rivers still stink of their blood."

I will. And our every movement must be perfect. We'll need a new strategy, one from outside the Banis walls. The Golden Three cities will be the only other threat if we lay our tiles right.

I can handle them easily, though it will draw spears from the assault on the capital.

We'll make up for it. I hoped the war with Mirik would be a distraction. Instead, paranoia is at every corner.

I've lost three allies in as many weeks, not counting Il-fald."

Rih's vision tunneled. "What?"

Majilah Ag's face fell. She did not need to know the signs for the woman's name to recognize grief. "Forgive me, I thought you knew."

"I just saw her. How? When?"

"The twelfth. She was supposed to meet with my man in Stytown. Never showed. He called on her the next morning and found her dead in her bunk. Tongue and hands were cut off."

Rih rushed to the side of the carriage and pushed aside the fabric to vomit onto the muddy road. She lost sisters-in-arms before. She lost her mother. She lost her entire sense of self when she became Keplan's wife. *But none of those were my fault.*

A strong hand rested on her shoulder, long thumb tracing circles. She sat back, accepting the napkin from the Valen queen with a nod of thanks. Dabbing her mouth, she returned to her seat.

We need to act quickly. The longer we wait, the more they'll discover.

The queen nodded in agreement, lapsing back into speech. "I'll be in the capital in a few weeks for negotiations. And again, to sign our official alliance at the end of the year."

Anxiety flooded Rih's body, distant and tingling in the wake of numb grief. That was too soon. Only a general could marshal enough soldiers to besiege a city the size of RoBal in a month and a half. They needed an advantage. A large one. She was certain the answer lay in the grinding gears of the Athrolani general's mind and the weapon he relinquished to Keplan. That was a puzzle for when she returned.

There's much to plan, but we'll be in contact. Keep me apprised of your informant and the woman from Mirik.

Majilah Ag smiled, hand grasping Rih's tightly. She did not have to say anything. Her dark eyes shone with understanding and a dozen sorrows of her own. She rose, steadying herself on the arching supports. "We'd best be off."

She swung onto her mount's back from the swaying carriage, movements effortless. Saluting, she motioned for her guards to fall in about her. "May your horse's hooves be swift and your spear strike true."

The riders wheeled north, aiming for some point concealed by the undulating, stormy horizon. Even in the damp, dust trailed behind as the wagon train inched north. Something burst in Rih's heart, hot with fury and warm with hope. Perhaps wrath's bloody red did not belong solely to one heretical god.

Φ

The 21st Day of Glasmord, 1272
The City of Ceir Athrolan

Wind buffeted the riders, bringing biting hail and roiling thoughts. Keplan shuddered, wishing fashion dictated swaddling cloaks and not crisp wool coats. If he pulled his fur hat any lower it would obscure the road before him. *Perhaps that'd be a boon.*

The slippery stones were no place for a fine mount, even ridden by a king. Instead, he convinced the stable hands to groom and tack up Moly. His boots may have hung below her belly, but her swaying gait and fuzzy ears, pricked forward, were a balm to his raw psyche.

"Your Majesty!"

Keplan glanced to the left, hand raised and false smile affixed to his mouth.

"When will we have water again?"

His body chilled further. "Commander Fess and I've plans for the warehouses beyond. If we outfit them with a distillation system, they'll be—"

"Brief, boy." An'thor growled from behind him, eyes scanning the crowd with distrust.

Keplan turned back to the woman. He saw now her clothes were filthy, her cheeks sunken. "I'm working on it, miss."

"Sire!"

An'thor spurred his charger on, shoving Keplan ahead before he could try to answer another query.

"Questions don't hurt, Domariigo," he hissed to his general.

"One or two, no, but you stand there and it becomes an audience. One on their territory. I've seen riots start from less. And I've never seen a king more deserving of a riot."

"Toss off, old man," he muttered. They rounded the bend and emerged on the broad cobblestones of the docks. Keplan recoiled, his shifted weight bringing Moly to a halt before An'thor's horse collided with her. *I do deserve a riot.*

Fess had insisted he inspect the city himself, probably more for the appearance of caring than wanting his opinion. Still, his heart sank. Despite the driving hail, the stench of burnt lacquered wood clung to the streets. The harbor was clogged with battered ships, their burnt husks jutting from the gnawing waves like bodies after battle.

"Over here, sire!" Fess balanced on a beam between two of the worst warehouses, waving. The one closest to the harbor had all but collapsed into the water, two merchant docks crushed beneath it. The timbers of the other were black with mildew and rot.

Keplan dismounted beside them, looping Moly's reins around a tie-off. "These are the two you meant?"

"Nay, two behind them. I'm trying to figure out a way to destroy the rest of these without making a worse mess."

"This whole place is a mess," Keplan noted, voice low.

She caught the words, flashing a humorless smile. "Welcome to monarchy, sire. If you'll follow me?" She led him into the next bank of warehouses, the two commissioners trailing after.

"Used to make gutterwrack in here. Figured we could pump in seawater to boil it up. Use the equipment we've got." She offered the king a flask.

"No, thank you."

"It's water, sire. Munson over there rigged a small version, just to test. Wouldn't call the water good, but it's drinkable."

Keplan took a hesitant sip. His mouth seemed drier for it, and he still caught the faint acrid taste of lamp oil. Still, his stomach rumbled for more. He took a second taste before handing it back. "Your description was optimistic, Fess."

She laughed, the sound loud in the damp, empty building. "We could stand a bit of hope this winter. Might be all that gets us through, begging your pardon."

He waved away the words. They were honest. He needed that. "How soon? Are the pumps to the cistern repaired?"

The commissioner grimaced, looking over from his low conversation with the man Fess called Munson. "Pumps are fine, one just needed a new wheel. It's the cistern that's the issue now. Cracked sometime last week. Think it was the freeze, sire."

Keplan rubbed a hand over his tired face. "Fates. Can you fix it?"

"It's built into the city's foundations. Dug into the stone. We could line it, I suppose, but we'd have to drain what's left in there."

"Where's an Earth Shaker when you need one?" Keplan whispered. If the commissioner heard, he gave no sign. Clearing his throat, he turned back to the commander. "How many barrels are still useable?"

"For water? Enough, but we'll have to hire wagoneers to transport them up to the higher districts."

"Then hire them." Keplan sighed, exasperated. "I don't care what you do, frankly, or who you have to pay or how much. Get this done."

"Right away, sire." Her playful face was stony. "But may I ask where the money will come from?"

"Fess," An'thor barked. "Not now."

Apprehension weaseled into his blood. He knew the treasury was low. He knew little money was coming in, save for their small allotment from Ban. Though small, Berr was a rich nation, and generous. *But I can't go begging on every stoop.* If he could not raise Athrolan from poverty on his own, then the kingdom would never maintain itself, he feared. Guilt stacked like the unread fiscal reports from his treasurer. Money seemed useless in the face of starvation and thirst. *Until suddenly, it isn't.*

It was as if his every resolution and strength were washed from under him with the flood, eroded like the very stone they stood on. In his mind he saw Ceir Athrolan plummet into a chasm, ocean rushing after the crumbling white towers until nothing was left, save maelstrom and flecks of blue foam. "Consulate?"

The man turned, the sallow light from the dim winter sun glinting on his wan face. "Yes, sire?"

"You said it was cracked. Part of the city's foundation. How deep do those cracks run?"

The commissioner glanced at Munson, at Fess, and to An'thor's boots. "Hard to say, Your Majesty. But deep. They're small yet. And the city is strong. It'll hold for a time."

"But not forever."

The consulate did not speak, but Keplan already knew the answer. He strode from the warehouse. "Anything you need, Fess," he called over his shoulder. "I mean it."

An'thor strode after him, eyes uneasy. "Wardyn, we can't just keep throwing good plans after bad."

"Arguably, the bad ones weren't mine."

"Arguably, you are a bad plan incarnate."

"Agreed." Keplan mounted up, patting Moly's neck. Coarse white hairs dusted his jacket, but he did not care. All that occupied his thoughts was the city collapsing beneath the weight of his misuse and the perfect peace of dust.

They broke into a trot, Keplan's head high. Perhaps their progress would give the illusion of a solution. The streets were full of clamor. Storefronts once boasting the best ale in the house now barked their untainted water, thrice the price of any old-aged wraith. Keplan longed for quiet. Even taverns no longer baked bread. Instead, only the mellow scent of rice drifted over the Berrin section of the market. His heart twinged at the memory of weaving through the market stalls with Azimir. Guilt slipped from his numb fingers, however. *They made their choice.*

"Sire."

Keplan ignored An'thor's low voice. He was tired of the hypocritical judgement tossed from the black eyes. If the city had no faith in him, it was little wonder, with his general sowing bitter words like blight-bitten seeds. He was tired of the breath in his lungs.

"Keplan!" An'thor snarled, "The market!"

An edge to the general's voice cut through Keplan's reverie. The world was suddenly bright and loud before his blown pupils. The crowd was moving, but not in its usual random veins, like an exposed capillary bed. Figures approached from the Slummer. From the docks. From outside the gates. He slowed, scanning the crowd, wondering where they all aimed.

Me. "An'thor—"

"Wrath!" The scream went up from the street corner as he passed. A woman threw back her hood, exposing her cropped hair. It was Nena'phe. And she was dressed as a Mirikin merchant.

Panic exploded in him, and he whirled, yanking Moly's head about. When he called for his general, his voice was a shriek. "Domariigo!"

"Ride, you idiot!"

Moly leapt over the stones, stocky body barreling past the press of people as more and more doffed hoods and hats. Keplan caught the glint of steel.

An'thor's charger broke ahead, cleaving a path.

The half-hearted designs on Keplan's worktable would do nothing to protect them. The war they planned for was here. And Rih would never arrive in time.

Blood spurted across his face. Moly slowed, her whinny a scream over the shouted scripture. She shuddered and sank beneath him, dragging him to the cobbles, one thin leg pinned beneath her heaving flank. It occurred to the king that the hundreds of faces turned toward him in anger were not only Mirikin, but Berrin, Banis, a scattering of other Nenev. And just as many were Athrolani.

The heat in him was no longer panic. It was fury. He was familiar with madness, the kind that piled in the corners of an isolated mind, wriggled in when he was not looking. This was different. It was churning, burning and brittle, bright and almost akin to laughter. He ripped himself free of his decorated saddle, yanking the fur hat from his head, hair coming loose as he did.

"Wardyn!" Domariigo fought to turn back, horse's hooves crushing toes and toppling any who attempted to flee. His hand dropped to the empty holster on his hip and his purple lips knotted in a curse.

In the periphery soldiers clattered onto the walls, helms glinting on rooftops around him. His tendons creaked with their crossbow strings as they drew back and held. An'thor raised his hand to hold fire, at least until the king was out of range. Fanatics' faith bled into his mind, igniting it with fervor. He no longer knew whether his certainty was theirs or his own. Perhaps it did not matter. Perhaps they were the same.

The heretics did not notice the approaching guards or did not heed. Would they pardon the city if he begged? Like him, these people cared for nothing. Nothing beyond their god. The monstrous man rocking at the back of his mind grinned, daring him. Mirth bubbled with spittle from between Keplan's bared teeth. He would give them what they asked for.

"You!" he shouted, gesturing to the asai Swordbearer's ardent face. Beside her a Nenev warrior dropped into a guard stance, pale visage a beacon. The din subsided. Keplan's arms shook with as much adrenaline as dust-drought. Their faith was a heavy ache pressing down on his lungs and fluttering heart.

The crowd eased back a few paces and he staggered toward them.

"You don't even bear a weapon," the Nenev hissed, voice more surprised than scornful. His wiry arms were bare, despite the clawing wind.

"Just the marks of hate." Keplan winked.

"Excuse me?"

Keplan let his gaze rove over the devotees until they settled back on the asai woman. "Read it to me, Nena'phe lui Hiral, Swordbearer of the Seer of Lymorda. You arrived at my door with an army fit for war because I do not worship your god. The least you can do is remind me why."

"You've denied the Truth before."

"Read it!" he roared.

Her voice shook, rattling low over the cobbles toward him. "'Thrice born, the One True God will rise where the worlds meet, from death and birth, from chaos and order. His blood pools, drowning the world even as it gives it life. Though he will bear the marks of hate, he will be unable to raise its tools. His right hand—'"

"That part, yes," he interrupted. He eased the glove from his right hand, praying every Athrolani spyglass trained on him would crack and fog. He fell back into the archaic speech of their doctrines, his blasphemy a mirror of their scripture. "His right hand will be stained bloody with wrath."

He raised the claret palm.

"Blasphemer," Nena'phe whispered, face pinched in defiance.

Keplan went on, yanking his other glove free. "And his left with the verdant green of life and mercy. He will know all, hear all, but listen to none. He will wreak havoc from the sky if you rob him! You've robbed me of peace!" Spittle flew from his mouth, mania flashing through every artery with their every flickering fearful thought. His gaze jumped from one to the next. Terror shimmered over the crowd as the hail returned in earnest.

Keplan's right hand rose, fingers held in the signal to his archers. "You want to spread the truth? Truth is, I am your one god. And I am no longer merciful."

His hand dropped.

Arrows exploded into the ground around him, punctuating his rising laughter. Thrills chased up his spine as he dashed through the deadly rain. Bodies churned around him as panic swept the crowd. An elbow cracked into his cheek. It was joy to just to feel the power. *To feel at all.* For once, the bloody sweet scent was not in his imagination. It was real and fresh and full of hope.

A body collided with him and they crashed to the cobbles. The Nenev warrior staggered back, ghostly hands cupping something silver. A mechanical thunderclap exploded between them.

Heat and cold flashed through Keplan's chest. He chuckled, scrambling upright as the man lowered the weapon. The revolver must have malfunctioned.

"No!" An'thor's voice boomed across the square, and he plunged toward them. His eyes were fixed not on Keplan, but the Nenev boy.

Keplan tried to reach for the general's horse as they clattered past. His hand refused to obey. He glanced down. Blood soaked his left sleeve. *My hand.* Thoughts tumbled out of order now, even the traces of dust unable to keep his mind racing. Cold spread through his shoulder, his arm, and sauntered across the left side of his chest. A glance showed him gnarled flesh and black pulsing blood. *Oh.*

A child stumbled into him screaming, and another spray of blood cascaded over him. This time it was hers. Cold stone rushed to meet him.

THE END OF MERCY

CHAPTER ELEVEN

The 23rd Day of Glasmord, 1272
The Athrolani Coast

RIH'S EYES NARROWED ON the figure approaching from the east. He was riding hard, and poorly. Clods and froth flew behind them as he crested the hill.

Azimir tumbled from his horse, breath heaving. Old bruises colored his eyes and throat. Thin red lines marred his broad cheekbone where it had scraped across something hard. "Your Highness," he gasped, dropping to one knee, swaying at her feet.

Dread chilled her body. "What happened? Are you hurt?"

"Athrolan's occupied. Fanatics. No water." He glanced down at himself. "It's not from battle, mostly. Blood is."

She signaled for them to make camp, drawing Azimir up the stairs into her carriage. She pressed him into one of the seats and set about making tea. He did not speak, head hanging low from his hunched shoulders.

It was only when steaming mugs sat before all three of them that she asked the question again.

"My father accepted the One God's scripture. Before you left, but I didn't know. He left three days ago. I was meant to as well, but I couldn't. Not the way he left things with Keplan. Hardly be a surprise if we had gone to war."

"Mirik and Athrolan?"

He nodded, taking a deep sip of tea. His eyes lidded for a moment, then he shook himself alert. "The Swordbearers came from Mirik. Merchant ships. Two days ago, they attacked. Keplan was riding in the street, trying to give Athrolan water. Just chaos." He shuddered.

"You said it was occupied?"

"They took over, guarding every street. Only way to be allowed out is to accept the One True God and swear fealty."

"Is that how you escaped?"

Azimir's dry lips cracked as he laughed. "I pretended to be their ally—told them I was there on behalf of my father to convince my dear cousin. Said I was going to beg you to consider negotiation just to get you in the walls."

"Why would they negotiate with me?"

"You're his wife, everything falls to you until the heir arrives."

"Heir?" Rih's stomach flipped. "How was he killed? The riot?"

"He's not dead yet, but his doctor says could be any day. Hasn't woken." Azimir's throat bobbed as he swallowed hard. "Shot by a revolver—the Ageless weapon. One of the Swordbearers carried it."

"Athrolan has thousands of people—surely they could organize and overthrow just by sheer numbers."

"It's a bit tricky."

"Planning a rebellion isn't easy but it's surely possible!" she scoffed.

His eyes settled on her, head tilting ever so slightly as if to observe a new angle of her. "Surely, yes. But many are accepting the God. It's easier."

"How can they, after watching their king fall?"

"That's the tricky bit," Azimir elaborated. "Keplan was shot because he revealed himself. Stripped his coat and gloves off in the market and proclaimed he was their One God." The memory of a smile ghosted across his face. "Fairly incredible, really."

"He couldn't be serious," she wondered.

"I don't know. He hated the prophet, her words, hated everything they stood for. Most men would ridicule such prophesies. His loathing was that of a man faced with truth. Not falsehood."

Rih stared at her own hands, wondering if she looked upon them long enough, they would be stained too. "I heard the words in Ban. My cousin told me them. And I, too, was skeptical." Her gaze moved to his.

"But?"

"'In battle we must imagine the worst our enemy could do and plan accordingly.' It's indeed bizarre that I may have married a god, the spawn of two mighty inhuman creatures. But not unlikely."

"Minata Kaz." His smile had life this time. "I'm familiar with her teaching. Read through *Joy in Death* for the second time last summer. You must observe your opponent like a lover, imagining what their body is capable of so you might answer it. Just with a sword instead of ardor."

Rih rolled her eyes. She appreciated the warrior's expertise but had never cared for the sexual metaphors pervading her prose. "I prefer *Waking Blood.*"

"Bit heavy on theory in that one for my tastes. I learn so much from her accounts alone." He ducked his head, then glanced back up. "Funny, sitting here, bruised and half dead joking about dead strategists."

"We'll need her. Once I'm in the city, how do you plan on getting the baniol in to attack?"

Azimir eyed her warily. "Attack? I assumed you'd actually negotiate."

Her brow arched. "My new home is under attack and my husband very well dead. I'm a soldier. I don't negotiate."

He sat back, raking a hand through his matted hair. "What do you need from me?"

"To be rested. You'll have to be our ticket inside those walls. But how to get the soldiers in without being seen?"

"They know you traveled with a retinue."

"Not over two hundred," she countered. I could add a dozen maybe, but any more and they'll question it." She stared at the floor, listening to the horses chomp on their hay just outside. "Wagons."

"They'll search them."

"Then we put just enough on top that it's believable."

Azimir started nodding, leaning forward with eagerness. "Leave anyone who isn't battle-tried behind. Dress a soldier in their stead."

"That's another fifteen."

He swayed in his seat, blinking rapidly. "Do you have water?"

She fished a flagon out and handed it to him.

Half was gone by the time he set it down and wiped his mouth. "Toar, my mind can hardly focus on anything but thirst."

"There's none?"

"Rations. Tight ones. Didn't dare bring any on my ride." He gestured vaguely in the direction of the city. "Anyway, tuck a good four under the canvas in the tent wagons, I'd wager."

"Go rest, Azi," she insisted. "I'll wake you if I need something, but you're no good dead."

He sighed but obeyed, almost falling when he tried to bow and back up at the same time. He paused halfway down the carriage steps. "I hadn't seen it. Battle. Fought, surely, and seen violence. But not battle." For once his head was low, barely meeting her eyes. "You were right when you said I didn't know it."

She watched him go, heart heavy. Azimir was likeable enough, even if she did not trust him. If only the world were kind enough for no one to experience battle. She drew a deep breath, then another, drawing strength into her blood with every billow of her lungs.

When she left her carriage, her resolve was steel. Bimet jogged after her, shouting her signed orders to the gathered troops. "Toss the tents! Dump everything! We can fit enough of you in the wagons to sneak in. The rest will await orders just outside the walls." She jabbed a finger at the camp cook. "Anyone who's more likely to die than kill, stay back, trade with a soldier."

The wagon train writhed with movement. Chests and pans littered the slush-covered roadside. A young squire stripped, trading his gear to a Banis soldier barely a year older. She wrapped her spear in a rag before tethering the Athrolani flag to its end.

Rih whirled, eyes settling on the baniol himself. "And someone find me armor."

Φ

The City of Ceir Athrolan, Athrolan

An'thor slumped in the chair. Blood splattered the floor. Moans drifted from the long infirmary hall outside. The room was dark, empty save for the guard by the door. And the body in the bed, he supposed. Already so much of Keplan's life had fled.

The king's head lolled on the pillow, cracked lips parted. An'thor did not know who dragged the boy from the fray. He recalled only racing after the medics as they flopped Keplan's limp form onto a stretcher. Digging twisted metal from shreds of thin muscle took hours. Now a thick bandage wrapped Keplan's left shoulder and chest. Already the center tinged pink.

"You have a minute?" Fess was silhouetted in the doorway, voice low so as not to disturb the dying.

"Come in."

"What I have to say, he doesn't need to hear."

An'thor watched the carefully folded sheet over the king's sunken chest. If he focused hard, he could see ribs faintly rising. Spiderwebbed veins inched up his exposed skin as life drained from his body. "I don't think he can hear much."

"Last thing to go, and you know it. Don't doom a man not already dead. I'll be in the hall."

An'thor straightened with a groan, nodding to the guard before following the commander. "Been a week now."

"Been four days," she corrected. Biting teeth replaced her gentleness. Her eyes were tired, her face shadowed and pale. "I received a bird from Lady Gella. She'll be here once the roads clear. A week, maybe less."

"The heir? You said he wasn't dead yet."

Fess's hand smacked into the wall beside the general's head. "I don't need to tell you what happens if we wait for him to be cold and withered before calling heirs in. I'm not making your mistakes. We'll speak with Her Grace."

"What about Daymir? I haven't left the infirmary, but I assume someone updated him?"

"He could not recall who Keplan was. Will arrive soon. Until then we have the Kajimet."

"She's hardly useful. The king's wife. A princess. Little more." He leaned on the wall, scratching at the base of one horn. He would have to grind it down soon. The cap was slipping. *Everything's slipping.* "There's still hope. His mother was unconscious for weeks when she bound the worlds—"

"He was shot by some fanatic, not ripping souls from gods."

"Mel'iend is a fool, not a fanatic!"

Fess stepped back, brows arching. Her thick arms crossed over her chest. "So. I was right. You knew that man. That why you went chasing after him, screaming, and left attending your king to the city folk? Some dockhand in a dress dragged him from the chaos."

An'thor shook his head. "I knew him once. My nephew. Thought he was dead."

"It would appear not. Would he listen to you?"

"We ended things poorly. Barrackborn's son has better luck with those zealots than I do, if he ever returns."

"Four days, Domariigo. Give them another three. Regardless, when this is over, whether His Majesty breathes or not, we'll have a mess on our hands. He can't just claim divinity and then sweep it under the nearest rug."

"So you saw that."

"He stood in the city square half naked and proclaimed he was God. Half the city saw it. Coupled with his bloodline, that proclamation is the reason the Swordbearers have been able to subdue us all so easily. We believe him."

An'thor stared at her. "We."

Fess lifted a shoulder in an exhausted shadow of a shrug. "Either he's a madman, or he's right. I know which I'd prefer."

An'thor glowered at her. "I've always known he wasn't human."

"Elitist. I didn't have to meet his parents to know they weren't monarchy material. Sure, they saved us, but humans are meant to rule themselves. It's why the gods rebelled against their creators in the first place—they didn't want to be subjugated. I'd think you'd remember that. All the stories say you were there when the war broke out."

"Only for part of it," he muttered. "Look at this world. Look at your own country. You don't need to have lived half as long as I have to realize you people can't govern yourselves."

Her dark brows arched. "I've always felt the worst rulers are those who think they're better than others. I'm sure our dear Kajimet would agree, having lived under an imperial gaze."

"Not better, as in worth, simply—"

"Keep the rest of those thoughts to yourself. I'm tired of bigotry."

An'thor snarled, but his argument died in his throat when he saw a healer and doctor slipping into Keplan's room. "I'd better see what that's about."

"An'thor."

He turned back to the commander. "Fess."

"Dorcal might have looked away from your myriad indiscretions, but I won't. I won't go to war with you. I won't cow to your archaic ideals. I'd advise you not to even try."

There was nothing he could say that would not sound bitter or childish. He retreated to his vigil over the pauper king. Neither healer nor doctor spoke was they unwrapped the bandages, but their expressions were reserved. The sweet tang of blood and rot hung heavy in the close air.

"He's hardly breathing," An'thor noted.

"He's resting. We gave him something to help with the pain."

"He should have been weaned off that shite a day ago. It's too much."

Neither answered him, and he settled back in his seat as they finished rebandaging the ugly wound. Dread was a deep ache in An'thor's bones. He was so desperate to leave this world in good hands, tended the way it ought to be. If not the Laen, then her offspring. And now that very boy threatened to drift from the world as modestly as he came.

Hold on, you miserable bastard.

Φ

The 24th Day of Glasmord, 1272

It was odd to see the Athrolani gates shut at noon. The wagons drew up at the towering walls, Rih peering up at where guards should stand, far above. The ramparts were deserted.

Azimir cupped his hands about his mouth and shouted something. No response came. Smoke drifted overhead, but it did not smell of cooking and warmth. Azimir was raising his hands to call a second time when the gatehouse door slammed open. A pale man blocked the narrow doorway. Fresh, cheap embroidery emblazoned his dirty shirt with some sigil: a black ring centered on two overlapping handprints. His mouth moved too rapidly for her to decipher which language he used, but both Azimir and Bimet seemed to understand.

"This man's one of the Swordbearers. Says he and his partner will speak with you and Master A'hane alone. The wagons can stay outside."

"We've had a long journey, and I'm eager to put this bloodshed behind us. But please, my people need rest." She looked pointedly at the green palm on his clothes. "Prove you're as interested in upholding the One God's mercy as you are his wrath."

The man shifted, tongue probing the livid void where a tooth sat not long before. His black eyes examined the wagons and riders. Even Rih's carriage had been stripped of its covering. "Fine. But we meet in the market. Neutral ground."

"Agreed."

He eyed her, then Azimir, before retreating. No sooner did the door shut than the whole gate trembled and one-half wrenched open. Azimir nudged his horse forward, glancing back at her once he was through. At Rih's nod, her carriage followed. Every corner was guarded by a pair of Swordbearers. Those Athrolani who moved about the streets did so with furtive steps and a downcast gaze. She did not need to hear to know the city was silent. Hidden by the driver's seat, her hand clenched, white-knuckled, on her atlatl's grip.

Her driver halted at the market. Weapons and viscera littered the streets and bodies piled in the market square. Her teeth clenched. Few belonged to soldiers. Most were children, crushed under panicked, fleeing feet. Scorch marks splashed the pale stone.

Beside her, Bimet's hands moved. "How can they let this go on?"

Rih did not answer. She never understood Athrolan more than she did now. Immobilizing fear was familiar. The Nenev was in conversation with a muscled woman wearing the handprint emblem. The hard lines of the female Swordbearer's muscles did not relax while the pale man fiddled with something. Rih's stare dropped to the holster at his hip. It was empty.

Warning shot up her arms.

Azimir's fingers tightened on his reins.

An arrow burst through the meat of her thigh. Panic was fire in her gut. She tumbled from the carriage, landing in an unsteady crouch.

Hooves pawed above her, and she ducked under the animal's belly. Azimir yanked his mount about, mouth wide in a yell. Another roll brought her to the back of her carriage. Soldiers erupted from her wagons. Bimet appeared at the stairs, belly to the carriage floor. She thrust a fistful of darts at the Kajimet with a nod. Her free hand ripped a delicately curved blade from a sheath under her skirts.

Soldiers erupted from under piled tent poles and supplies. A spear bounced across the cobblestones a hand's breadth from the Nenev man. He whirled, gesturing wildly for his allies to close the gate.

Swordbearers spilled from side streets. A wagoneer whipped his team forward, wedging his wagon in the closing gate. Wood cracked. *Hold,* Rih begged. *Just long enough for the second baniol!* The road beyond the walls was dusty but deserted.

Rih bolted into a deserted stall. She eased backward, wincing as a jug tumbled from a broken shelf and shattered across her face. Spoiled wine stung her eyes and she blinked, wiping a shaking arm across her face. *What are you doing, Rih?* she asked herself. *Cowering?*

Her free hand fingered the wound in her leg. The arrow had passed clear through, leaving two dripping punctures. Tugging her wrap from the armor hidden beneath, she swiped at it with a dart point. The silk ripped easily. It was a scant bandage but would slow the blood. She yanked the quiver over her shoulder and eased weight onto her leg. The pain brought a smile to her face. War. She bathed in the adrenaline. *Finally, something I'm good at.*

A shadow fell across her. The Nenev man loomed in the doorway, strange weapon raised. Rih tucked her shoulder and lunged into his gut. They fell back into the stall, crashing through cheap wood. She tugged her arm free from under him and brought her atlatl around. Blood spurted as the metal spur on the weighted end collided with the side of his head. The blow raced up her arm with a satisfying hum. He stilled beneath her.

Rih dipped her head to the row of whistles on her shoulder. Two short breaths on the smaller one rallied a handful of Banis to her. She pointed toward the docks, then the wealthy upper tier. The officers broke apart, calling for their patrols to strike deeper into the city.

The female Swordbearer bounded across the market toward the trapped wagon, massive sword wheeling. Rih's first tossed dart skittered wide, spinning away from her quarry. The second bounced off the woman's heavy armor. Rih spat in frustration. She had always been better with a spear. She ripped another dart from her quiver but didn't nock it.

Townsfolk leapt from their houses armed with clubs and kitchen knives. She broke into a run, pushing toward where Azimir leaned against a building. She fell against the wall beside him, flashing a bright smile. She jerked her head at the gate. The wagon's sides splintered, the one axle shattering under the weight of the door.

Azimir followed her gaze, pupils huge from excitement or fear. A shaking hand clasped hers tightly. Their fingers laced, sticky with blood. "Gatehouse."

Together they broke into a sprint. Rih's pulse matched her racing stride. Another twenty paces. Another ten. Two. Then she was bolting up the gatehouse stairs, Azimir a step behind. A small clay ball, barely the size of a head, tumbled from above. It rolled, smoking, on the cobbles between them and the gatehouse. A blast knocked them to the ground. Light and heat exploded across her face, tightening her skin. Blinking, she shoved herself upright. The storefronts nearest her were leveled. Another ball rolled across the street. Grabbing Azimir's arm, she dragged them into the shelter of the gatehouse.

Three fanatics crowded in the room, blocking the mechanism and lever. Dodging the first spear thrust, she jabbed the Swordbearer with her dart. His arm cracked beneath her whipping atlatl. She whirled in time to see Azimir kick one Swordbearer down the stairs. The third raised his hands and knelt, murmuring. She shoved him at the mechanism and brandished another dart.

No translation was needed. He dragged the lever up and the walls shook and the gate crept back open.

Azimir jerked his head at the open door, grin feral. "Hear hooves! Go!"

She pushed past him, almost tripping down the stairs. Sure enough, the market swarmed with Banis riders. Spears cut ribbons from the sea air. She grabbed the reins of a bucking Athrolani horse and jerked the spear from its flank before dragging herself into the saddle.

Wind buffeted her as An'thor rushed past, followed by Curiel and all her swords. A baniol wheeled, the Swordbearer's flag trampled into the stone. She punched her weapon in the air, looping it overhead. Allies fell in about her as more and more fanatics were driven into the streets, chased from buildings, cornered in the square.

Beside the broken remains of her carriage, the Nenev man staggered upright. Rih drove her horse forward until her borrowed spear tip rested at the man's throat. A bloody knot marked where she had knocked one horn from his skull. He raised his empty hands, shouting something over his shoulder. Weapons lowered. Blows stilled.

An'thor trotted up beside her, black eyes narrowed. He spat a couple of words; then, realizing she could not understand, looked about for Bimet.

Victory and surprise and joy burned through her. Guards arrived to take the surviving Swordbearers. Every face she recognized was thinner than before and looked as tired as she felt.

After a moment Bimet appeared, limping but otherwise whole. "They'll handle them from here, Kajimet."

Rih fell back with several officers. The courtyard was deserted, most of the guards in the streets. She bent over the fountain after relinquishing her reins. The water sloshed, pinking with blood, light dancing on the lamp oil at the surface.

When she straightened, Azimir swayed beside her, new wounds over his old bruises. He bared bloody teeth in a grin. "Minata Kaz at the fall of Yeth." Their brows pressed together for a breath, then he pulled back, leaving a streak of his sweat and someone else's blood.

Her vision tunneled when she shifted her weight and pain shot down her leg. The world was abruptly real again.

"Infirmary." Azimir waved toward the rear of the palace and looped an arm under hers.

I never realized how long these halls were, she mentally growled. One did not count steps until each one drove fire into her thigh.

There were no beds, not even for the king's wife. Instead, Azimir settled her on a bench in a room off to the side. He unwrapped the matted silk from her flesh and paled. Blood trickled down her leg, puddling on the flagging. Her right arm twitched in reflexive memory of throwing darts.

A healer appeared a moment later and set to work. Bimet slumped on the bench beside Rih, and Azimir leaned against the wall. Rih winced as the wound was cleaned and inflamed flesh was stitched closed.

The healer sat back and bowed, relaying something to Bimet. "She thanks you for bringing the Banis healing kits."

Rih smiled. Banis medicine was prized in the east. Skill in war naturally led to skills in medicine. "I'm glad they can help."

Azimir shook his head when she asked if he was hurt. "Not badly. Most is from before."

"The riot?"

"Kep and I argued."

She stared at the purple ringing his throat. It looked like far more than an argument. "When?"

"Just before. He lost his temper with me. Blamed me for the priests. Can't really fault him there." He looked away at the shadowed bed in the corner of the room.

Cold filled her when she followed his gaze. The bed was not empty.

Keplan's body was sunken, atrophied. His dry skin like pale rawhide. The flickering pulse in the lacework purple veins across his skin was the only sign of vitality. Stinking bloody bandages piled in the corner, forgotten in the chaos of battle.

Air moved and she turned back to the door.

The general loomed in the doorway, bloody and stinking of alcohol as much as gore. His glare fixed on her. "What was that?"

A trace of her fury still burned. "I saved the city, sir."

Azimir pushed off the wall, gaze bouncing between them in frustration. "General, we did what we had to. I told you I was bringing her back, her troops too."

"You can't just storm the city without telling us!"

Rih's temper snapped. "You didn't want my soldiers, but you needed them. You didn't want my help, but you needed it. And now you're furious that once again a human is cleverer than you! Forgive me for undermining your authority, General," she twisted her fingers, adding mockery to the word, "but someone must do your job if you won't. Might as well be me."

"My job?" he retaliated, lip curling, white hand jerking toward Keplan's motionless form. "Your job is to wait for that mad creature to fu—"

"Enough!" Azimir shoved between them. "This isn't the place to debate who failed Athrolan. Argue who's better at saving this piss-ridden excuse for a kingdom in the privy for all I care, but don't do it here."

"His Majesty shouldn't be—" An'thor wheedled.

"Out! Both of you!" Azimir glared at the general. "I'm the only family he's got. If anyone's going sit at his bedside, it'll be me."

Rih staggered upright. The boy was right, and she was exhausted. She longed for a bath, even in the polluted brackish water Athrolan had to offer. Bimet helped her from the room, both watching as An'thor disappeared down the hall.

One corner of the translator's mouth lifted. "Well done, General. Tomorrow RoBal."

Rih offered an exhausted smile. "Perhaps the day after."

Φ

The 25th Day of Glasmord, 1272

Azimir burst into wakefulness. His back ached from sleeping on the bench outside Keplan's door. He shook feeling back into one leg, searching for the source of the shouts that woke him.

"We need help, now!"

He shouldered open the door to the king's infirmary room. His gut clenched at the sight before him. Keplan convulsed, sheets tangled around his emaciated limbs. His pale eyes rolled back, and froth spilled over his blue lips. "What's wrong?"

"I meant a healer, not a boy!" the doctor snarled.

Another healer burst in, eyes wide. She gripped the king's limbs, glancing from the doctor to Azimir. "What's he doing in here?"

"Getting in the way," the man growled, before pressing fingers to Keplan's pulse points. "He's slipping."

Azimir watched them rip sheets and clothes from the lanky, frail body. *No.* His body quaked watching his cousin, his friend spasm into death.

"What did you do?" the healer snarled at the doctor, streaking fluid across her brow as she pushed her hair away.

"Nothing! We lowered the peaceleaf, hoping he might rally, but he's been comatose for days."

"Peaceleaf?" Azimir whispered, heart thudding to a halt.

"For pain." The healer attempted to still Keplan's spasm. Frustration hissed from her as the newly tied bandage dislodged.

"It's made of dust, isn't it?" Azimir's gaze was fixed on his cousin. Cold nausea wormed in his throat. He could not break the confidence of Keplan's snarled implications, but neither could he watch him die.

She rolled her eyes. "Same plant. Hardly the same thing, though."

"But if someone breathed dust, peaceleaf would have less effect, right?"

"This isn't the scholar's debate hall," the doctor ground out. "Unless you have something useful—"

"How much?" the woman interrupted. Her eyes were bitter and steady on Azimir's.

"I don't know. But often. Daily at least."

"He's falling from it. Dust drought." She fumbled in her apron and drew out a gleaming glass tube equipped with a needle and plunger. "You, hold him."

Azimir gripped his cousin's arm, pressing it into stillness against the mattress. "What in Toar's name—"

"Banis medicine is better than ours." The needle slid into Keplan's vein, blood blooming in the clear liquid for a second before she depressed the plunger. The seizing slowed. Color returned to his face. Lines of agony smoothed slightly. He still seemed unresponsive. But alive.

"You. Outside. Now," the healer snapped, ripping her gloves off and dumping them in the bin beside Keplan's door.

Azimir slunk outside after her. Her tone was, for all the world, his mother's. And he was just as chagrined when she turned the weight of her anger on him. "I'm sorry."

"For what?"

He shrugged. "I just think you're expecting an apology."

"Only if you know what you did." She raked a hand through her short black hair. "You could have killed him."

"I wasn't the one who took away the medicine for pain—"

"He fell into dust drought when we weaned him from peaceleaf. We wouldn't have if you'd been honest with us."

Azimir glared. "Honest? In case you didn't notice, he's the Athrolani king. You think he needs rumors like that drifting around?"

"We're doctors. We don't spread rumors," she countered. "And if you hadn't been there, he may well have died."

"You're welcome," Azimir snapped.

"Shut it."

Azimir stepped back. It was not often someone blatantly ignored his perceived rank. Hetmir's son had weight, and Dhoah' Laen's nephew had more. "I'm sorry," he repeated, looking away. "I should have been more honest."

"Is there anything else we ought to know?"

"Not that I know of."

"By the end of this he'll be sober, if he lives. You think he'll stay that way?"

Azimir sighed. "I can hardly guess. I can imagine why he started in the first place, but I don't know."

"Who else knows?"

"No one." *Firas.* "That I'm aware of, at least."

"We'll keep it that way."

"Will he be all right?"

She glanced at the closed door. "Hard to say. Our first priority now is weaning him from the drugs. He can't heal until then, really. His body doesn't know what to do with its resources. But we'll do all we can." She paused, then looked back at him. "It does good, you visiting. He doesn't strike me as someone with many friends. But if he has any, this is where they need to be. We're tending his body, but if he doesn't have a will, there's nothing we can do."

Azimir nodded. "I'll see if anyone else wants to sit with him."

The doctor's hand was warm on his arm. "You're a good man. He gets through this, he'll have you to thank."

Azimir watched her go. If Keplan lived, he wondered what they might say to one another. *Last we spoke his hand was at my throat.*

Φ

Death was different this time. It was silence. It was blackness. It was oblivion. Keplan welcomed it. There was no difference now between his own face and the hideous reflection. Waxy flesh stretched in a grin, sallow cast yellowing.

A voice, thunderous, broke through. "I brought you peace. I'll survive and wrest it from the world. We're a god. Deny all you like, but that prophet spoke true. They'll bow before us, lathe filth from our feet and there will be peace."

"You didn't bring peace. Not to Athrolan. Not to me. Firas did," Keplan bit back.

It was not just Firas that had brought him peace, but the man he allowed himself to be in Firas's arms. A man who hoped. Who laughed. Who saw beauty in the rainbows of oil on the Slummer puddles. He whirled on the mirror. It was just a pane between who he was and who he could be, though he lost sight of who was which. It cracked beneath his fist. "Fuck you," he growled.

The reflection lunged, winding through the cracks in the glass until his almost physical form manifested before Keplan's own. He looked real except at the very corners of Keplan's vision. Hard hands slid over his body, the touch hovering somewhere between lust and loathing. Cracked lips crashed into his, blood and spit mingling until he no longer smelled the rot.

He tasted of dirt and ash. Maybe they both did.

The voice rang in his head now. "Think of how glorious we'd be together, your body, my mind, your monster, my madness tearing violence from the world." Fingers gripped his nape, fumbled at his groin. "Together we'd birth a new pantheon. One deserving of their worship."

Too many days had passed since someone touched him, all of him, even his excuse for a soul. He tilted his chin, mouth parting, and accepted his reflection's cold tongue.

CHAPTER TWELVE

The 28th Day of Glasmord, 1272
The Icelock, Northern Ilmar Ocean

THE WIND HOWLED ACROSS the ice with bitter teeth. Raven stared at the coast, eyes narrowed against the onslaught. *There*. A flash of orange and black against the blue-gray of the snow-blown landscape.

"You see that?"

"See what, sir?"

Raven glanced down at the map without answering. The ink was still wet, the pen strokes lacking details that would come with decades of forays. "Where the fates are we?"

"West of the Ageless city by several leagues, sir. More than that I don't know. Haven't named it yet, thought you might want to."

"Places like this already have names, Jorn." Raven squinted at the paper and then back up to the landscape. "There's something out there."

"Ice bears?"

Shudders ghosted over Raven's shoulders like a lover's taunt. "Haven't yet met a bear that makes the hairs stand on end like this."

"Haven't been to my neck of the world then, sir," she joked, following him from the cabin. A breeze eddied, tugging at his poorly cut hair, snapping lines, almost playful.

He paced along the rail, glancing from his first mate to the men in the rigging. Who would shout it first?

"My ma went out one night to put the sheep in and came face-to-face with a big sow, teeth the size of Metters'—"

"Commander! Wind's a-changing!"

"I know." The affirmation was too quiet for them to hear, but it didn't matter. The breeze billowed, mutters rising into moans through the storm's snapping teeth.

The cold brass of his spyglass bit his fingers. He focused on the massive ice outcropping. Chunks skittered down the surface to splash into the frigid ocean, but there was no judging their exact size. Through the clear blue ice, however, he caught another bloom of light. *Firelight.* He raised his nose, sampling the air whipping about their furled sails. *Stone. Salt. Soot. Decay.*

Above, stars glittered in the cold, cloudless sky. So, not a storm, then. "Hold course!"

Even under the thick wool of his naval coat, hairs stood upright along his arms. He lifted his nose and frowned.

"What is it?"

"We're in the open ocean."

"Aye, and?"

"So why does it smell like low tide?" Dread churned in his gut. The gods were dead, he knew that. He stood on the ramparts of Ceir Athrolan when the world shuddered with their passing. *But those who killed them, they're still here.* His gaze never wavered from the pulsing, flickering glow. "To starboard!" he called.

"Sir, that will bring us within—"

"The Northlands aren't Athrolan. His Majesty won't give a bloody tup how close we come to land. Starboard!"

"Dorcal, it could just be a hunting outpost. Berrin whalers wrecked far afield." The muscles in Jorn's jaw clenched as she attempted to be the voice of reason.

"I doubt Berrin would wreck, even this far north." Raven tugged on another cloak and wrapped gloves over his weather-beaten hands. Something tugged at his chest, like excitement, but underscored with the certainty of dread. "To explore and record, eh, Jorn?"

"Sir?"

"I'm going ashore." He paused and glanced back at Jorn. "And if you mention Metters' crotch again, I'll personally fasten you to the bow and use you as an ice-break."

She cackled and pulled her own cloak tighter. "I'll get the boat."

Waves hissed against the skiff's sides as he rowed, each pull sending a twinge of pain through his right shoulder. Instead of slacking, as he might have done a month ago in the cushioned apathy of his life in the city, he leaned in, let curiosity slip into his belly.

Jorn, perched in aft, scanned the sheer side of the berg, picking out breaking waves that spoke of hazards below. "When His Majesty bundled us off to freeze to death, I don't think this is what he had in mind."

"I think it's exactly this. There's only so much mapping one can do. Last letter we got said he liked your sketches."

"It's not an island. Just a massive berg," she murmured, ignoring the rest of his words. "There's a pull-off ahead."

He slowed and brought the boat alongside the berg, keeping her steady as Jorn slammed a mooring into the ice. Sharp excitement burned in her eyes, belying her skeptical words. One hand loosened his sword in its sheath, damp and salt sticking the steel. She led the way, picks thudding as she hauled herself hand over hand up the undulating face. Raven followed, watching each hold and footing for danger. Breath escaped his mouth in a groan as he rolled over the berg's lip. Fire waited for them.

Flames devoured the wet pile of broken bones. Hanks of dried flesh shuddered under the inferno's might. It was built like a campfire, banked and tended. But campfires were not made the height of the tall commander. Raven's eyes picked out the monstrous curved tusks, the pile of hairy skin stretched over half of a rib cage.

"Fates." Raven's instincts screamed to return to the ship, skitter down the ice, maybe dive into the ocean. Anything but stay. Wind spun around the ice, but where he crouched the air was still. Any snowflake was swept from the ground, bare ice left gleaming under the midmorning stars. Sparks puffed from the fire as bones settled. A shadow loomed from the flames, tibia, humerus, the wing of a scapula that once, perhaps, belonged to a man, ground into articulation.

Raven scrambled backwards, catching himself on the lip of the ice cliff. His breath puffed from between layers of his scarf, freezing a moment later across the mouth of his scarf. Jorn's gasps were eaten by the swirling snow squall.

Blackened skin unrolled across jerked flesh, hunched shoulders straightening into a predator's crouch. Jaundiced eyes blinked and a long ashen nail flicked locks of flame from their face. "Evening, Commander."

"Arrowlash?"

The body unfolded, creosote tumbling from his clothes as he stepped from the fire. The musk of burnt hair and bone wafted across the frigid ice.

"It's just sir now," Raven whispered, though it did not matter. The creature could destroy him whether he were a peasant or a king.

"Demoted. Interesting. And so far north." The voice was rocks cracking in winter's grip. Arman's head tilted slow, entirely reptilian. "Have a seat, kettle's just boiled."

Other than the shelter crafted from some creature's corpse, the camp suffered an utter lack of equipment. Raven recalled passes through the Orn de Galin littered with bones, crags lost to time and haunted by titans. Titans that once were men. "What are you doing?"

The jittering scream of metal against stone set Raven's nerves afire. Arman was laughing. "The usual—looking for allies. Artifacts. World ending. We've been on the road for months now."

We? "Dhoah' Lyne'alea's with you?"

The laugh came again, low. He gestured to the ice beneath him. "You didn't notice? These flames are hotter than any campfire, any inferno lit by war machines. Why hasn't the ice melted, Dorcal?"

Raven found his stomach threatening to revolt. The terror dragged from his bones was the promise in Keplan's eyes brought to fruition. "Dhoah'?" He hoped he forced enough reverence into his voice, but at Jorn's glance, he knew the words sounded closer to horror.

Water trickled across the iceberg, winding between invisible faults in surface, blue and reeking of salt. Droplets congealed, trembling as sullen sparks lit them from within, a rotted tree with lightning boughs. Streaks of black seaweed, of mildew writhed upwards. Fish-pale eyes rolled to focus on him, unmoved, disinterested. Water puddled from her pale, bloated lips, skin slipping from putrefied muscle as she spoke. "How lovely of you to drop by, Raven. What brings you to the skull of the world?"

"Explore," he croaked. Clearing the fear from his throat, he tried again. "We were sent to expand Athrolan's maps. Learn from other places, other people. Found a lot of odd creatures, sea monsters." He gnawed one thick lip. "Didn't think we'd find you."

"No, I imagine not. World's tidier when legends stay quiet."

"Last we all heard you were in the Hartland. Where Keplan left you."

Lightning crackled louder, larger, and her vacant eyes sharpened with interest. "Our son? You've seen him?"

Raven glanced between the two of them. Had she always been taller than he? How could they not know? "Yes, I—"

"Of course, he sent us here. He's king." Jorn's words were out before Raven could stop her. He did not like the creatures before him. He did not trust them, but the one thing he understood was wishing your child was safe. A king was never safe.

"King?" Arman's voice was an avalanche in the mountains.

"His Majesty Keplan of the Hartland and the Topin Hills, king of Athrolan, ascended the throne two months ago. Athrolan was locked in civil war, you might have missed that. Up here. He ended it, in a fashion."

"You don't put him on a throne," she keened. "You don't put something that precious, that beautiful and cut it down, bloody and whimpering to fit on a tidy human throne with a tidy human crown." Alea's voice thundered from every crystal of snow, every droplet of sea air.

Clear blue water bled from cracks rent in centuries-old ice.

"Lyne'alea," Raven protested.

Bones still piled in the flames shuddered and crumbled into white ash, drifting, eddying until they, too, formed pieces of the Earth Shaker's body.

"Dorcal!" Jorn called, voice pitched to carry to him alone.

The iceberg cracked. Raven pitched forward, gloved hands unable to find purchase on the gleaming surface. He scrambled, spiked boots gripping for a moment, then slipping as water trickled past. His hands were drenched, already numbing. Something splashed into the black water below, but he could not crane his neck far enough to see if it was Jorn.

"Milady!" he begged. Tears froze in his stubble. The fluid in his body writhed, agony ripping in his veins as his blood halted, then inched backward, upward. His vision hazed red with puppeteered blood. "Dhoah', I beg you, please!"

The ice inches from his face cracked, reformed into a terrible face with lidless electric eyes. "Why?"

"I didn't want him on the throne. I've never trusted your kind. I wanted human, Xain blood on the Athrolani throne. It was An'thoriend who engineered Keplan's reign." The cowardice tasted like bile on Raven's tongue. Frostbite's black fronds eased up his grasping hands. "Mercy, please."

The storm stilled. Silence pressed on his ears after the slavering wind. "Mercy," the snow hummed. "We gave all of ours to our son."

The iceberg bucked, launching him into the ocean. Aching cold enveloped him. He sank, clawing off his cloak and scarf. Raven had been commander of Athrolan's navy for four decades. Before then, he had been a soldier, running rigging and mending lines. His thick, frostbitten fingers ripped at the buckles of his boots. But before anyone became an Athrolani sailor, they had to dive to the deepest point off the cliffs and bring back a single piece of the hundreds of shipwrecked vessels. Raven clenched his teeth against his final breath bubbling from his body. That air was his ticket to the surface.

Another tug, another kick, and his feet were free. Muscles protested and his chest screamed as he shoved his way to the surface. Waves shoved salt into his gasping mouth. He coughed, choked, then checked the stars. The sky was black, but once more his blood beat forward, not back, and his lungs billowed with air, not ocean.

"Raven!" Jorn's voice was shrill, faint in the dark, but then came the slap of paddles and the groan of weathered wood. Her nose bled, though whether it was from Alea's administrations or her tumble off the berg, he could not guess.

She leaned away, counterbalancing his leaden body as he dragged himself into the skiff. The moment he was he huddled in the bow, she thrust them toward the safety and warmth of their ship.

Jorn shuddered, lips paled by her effort not to vomit. "I understand it now."

Raven raked a hand though his sodden hair. "Understand what?"

"Why you're terrified of Keplan. That blood, that power, on an Athrolani throne? With a Banis army behind him?" She lost her battle and emptied her stomach into the waves.

"They weren't like that, not even in war. Then they were mighty, horrifying, but I knew why folk worshiped them." His gaze followed the roiled stain in the clouds above as the two creatures traveled south. "I ought to warn Athrolan."

"But you won't."

"There's no warning loud enough to prepare them," he whispered. "Our eyes are now fixed north, fixed ahead of us, to lands we've yet to see." He wondered if she heard the shatter of his heart breaking to allow him to speak the next words. "Athrolan has made her choice."

Φ

29th Day of Glasmord, 1272
The City of Ceir Athrolan, Athrolan

The palace was already in mourning, it seemed. Rih drifted through the halls, sometimes with Bimet in tow, but more often alone. She had yet to return to her husband's bedside but did not care whether rumors flew. *I saved their hoof-kicked city. That should be enough.* Neither had she seen An'thor, which was a blessing, save for the fact that she did not trust him. Without her careful gaze, she had no idea what he might do.

Now, however, she dragged her feet toward the infirmary. It was not required of her, but each afternoon she sat vigil, as much to relieve Azimir of the duty as to keep up appearances. With every passing day he seemed more distant, his body more a husk than a living, vital thing.

Rih faced the door to his private room. Illness made her uncomfortable. In the military it was met with death, if one was not deemed useful in another field. But with Athrolan so precarious, even she could not weather the rumors that would arise were she to avoid her husband's bedside.

Her spirits lifted when the guards opened the door and she found Azimir napping in the chair at Keplan's head.

He straightened, wiping his mouth and blinking himself alert. "Ah, Rih. Forgive me, I must have dozed off."

"It's nothing," she offered, belatedly realizing he did not understand. She pointed at the king's still form questioningly.

"I don't know. It seems as if he doesn't have the will," Azimir confessed. "Can't blame him, really."

The sentiment took Rih by surprise, and she found she did not have a response. She had endured as much as he, perhaps, though systemic attrition was different from sudden torture, she knew. Both left lasting marks, physical and otherwise. It was easy to look at a king upon a throne and presume him lucky. In many ways he was, but a cage, however gilded, was nonetheless a cage.

"If you'd like me to stay, I can ask the guard to call for a translator. But if you'd like to be alone, I'd understand. I've been here since dawn anyway."

Rih's brow arched. No one—not even Athrolan's own general—had taken their vigil duties as seriously as the young man before her. *They're family,* she reminded herself. As much as she wanted to speak with him, she was tired of being at the mercy of Bimet's schedule, even if it made conversation easier. She mimed writing and added a quizzical expression.

His face broke into a smile and he fished a notebook from his belt purse. "Da always told me to keep a log—habit left over from his soldier days, I think—

but I rarely find a use, other than to give something else for the cutpurses to grab. Would you prefer I write, or is reading my lips easier?"

She mimed the writing motion again and took his offered notebook and pen.

Lip reading takes much effort, and I often must piece the meaning together based on half the words at most. Writing is nice, for me. It's scary, being dependent on a translator. I can't argue with her or fight. I'm so used to a single step outside meaning death or pain or punishment.

"You're hardly dependent," he voiced.

She scoffed, hastily adding:

Aren't I? Hardly anyone here speaks Banis. Fewer know my signs. Not that the two are related, but surely your Deaf people have their own signs.

He looked down, cheeks flushing with a rare blush before reaching for the log.

I wouldn't know. You're the first I've met. I'm not sure whether it's because fewer of our people are Deaf or that we support them less. Do you wish you could argue with Bimet?

She stared at him, wondering how different her life would have been were she born to Mirik. His question was friendly, if probing.

If she was mad, she could mistranslate – either from simple frustration and confusion or actual malice. And I would never know. She tells me something wrong in negotiations, it means death.

Azimir read her words, pen poised to respond while he ordered his thoughts.

What if others knew your signs? Knew Banis. What if they learned? I'd gladly translate for you.

I taught women before, in RoBal, so they might—

She stopped, heart pounding, hand traitorously close to writing the truth. Minata Kaz's words bloomed in her heart. *"A war is begun by making enemies, but it is won by making allies."* Azimir watched her. Open. Honest. Mirikin. *Not yet.*

So they might have more agency. Men enough know the signs, of course. One in ten Banis are like I am, but it's still fewer. And it cannot be eavesdropped upon. Not as easily.

"That's noble. As much as we tout wanting to free your people, I don't know the first thing about slavery. What it's like." He jerked a thumb at the king, comatose, beside them. "Kep knows Banis."

Rih faltered.

I know. I remember. From before. He was unconscious for most of the ride to RoBal, but the little he did speak was recognizable.

Azimir tilted his head. His bushy brows curled together. Rih was abruptly reminded that he was seventeen. A privileged seventeen. "What happened?"

That's his story.

"No, I mean, it is, and I know as much as he's willing to tell me." He caught himself speaking aloud and extended his hand for the book, taking care with his next words.

I want to know yours.

It would be a lot to write, and she noted as much.

I'm a fast reader. And I'm picking up some of your signs. If you want to try both.

I wasn't always Kajimet.

"What's that one?"

Princess, in your language, but not exactly. Emperor's line, or chosen or favored. Before that I was a soldier, a scout in my arc. I idolized my training master – she was the leader of my troop for the first five years."

"How old were you when you began?" Sure enough, his broad, tan hands curled in a few signs. They were out of order and some wholly nonsense, but his earnest frown warmed her heart.

She corrected him, then held up the appropriate fingers.

"Fourteen? That's young. What about before that?"

We die young.

She sank back in the chair for a moment. How did she tell him of the summer heat in the Purple Throne? Or the imperial concubines' quarters? The cloying silk curtains and perfume that separated the mothers and their work from the children? Of the press of people and parties so loud, even her ears could pick up the vibrations? Food so fine each plate cost more than what was allotted a soldier for a year? And how could she explain to this sweet man—boy, sometimes—that she missed it? Despair welled in her, aching fire, heavy with sun and wind. She let out a sob.

Azimir's calloused fingers were on hers, and he ducked his head so she might see his face through her tears. His dun hands squeezed her brown ones. "I'm sorry."

She shook her head. Ban was homogenous in the way that a stew was—occasionally spicy or sparks of unique flavor, but nothing lasting. She had never been homesick before, even traveling hundreds of leagues. Or felt so homeless. Ban was never so jarring. She wiped her cheek and wrote again.

I've never missed it before. Never expected to. But I realize now I may have missed home for a long time. Even before Athrolan. Even when I was there.

"I love Athrolan but I miss home too. Nothing's the same as I remember it."

What do you miss? You visit often, does so much change for you?

It's something that follows me. I miss my father. He's not the man I remember him being.

Then I'm sorry too.

His smile was sad, and he neither spoke nor wrote any more, but his hand stayed on hers.

It was almost evening when Bimet arrived to ask if they wanted dinner.

"I'll be staying here," Azimir explained. "But thank you."

"I'm tired, I think I'll go for the evening, if you don't mind eating alone."

"I'm not alone." He smiled, patting Keplan's hand. "He's not much of a talker lately, but he rarely was before."

Rih rose and followed Bimet to the door. "Thank you for the conversation. As always, I enjoyed it."

"Any time you wish to talk—well," he hastily corrected himself, "communicate?"

"Talk is fine," Rih signed with a laugh. "It's just a different language is all, same as Trade and Banis. Thankfully you know the latter."

"Then, any time you wish to talk, I'll be here. Have a good evening, Kajimet."

"And you, Azi."

Bimet eyed her as they returned to her rooms. It was only when the door was shut carefully behind them that she launched into questions. "He's the son of your enemy and cousin to your husband. A husband who lies dying."

"He's not dead yet, Bimet," Rih protested, "and it's just conversation. Friendly. As interesting as you are, I'd rather not be beholden to you for all my social activities."

"Beholden?" Bimet's face hardened. "I'm merely advising you to be careful. That was the son of the Hetmir in there, and I don't care what you think, the look in his eyes is far from friendly!"

"I think I have more instinct in me than you, having fought for my life more times than I can recall. He means no harm."

"Harm's not what I was implying, Kajimet," Bimet retorted, signs sharp as blows. "That boy wants you spread on silk for him, and anyone can see it."

Rih stepped back, horrified. She recognized predatory advances easily, it was the only way to survive the Banis court. Azimir had never made her skin crawl or her stomach revolt. He was a friend, as good as Nehla. *He touched my hand. Held it. The city was under attack and his family dying, and the first place he rode was to me.* To her, it was the camaraderie of battle. The bond forged in pain and quenched in blood spilt for a shared cause.

"Sex aside, you need to be careful who you confide in anyway, Rih." Bimet's hands were gentle now, soothing, and her frown eased into concern. "I know you were hoping for more from Nehla, but neither she nor Master A'hane care for our sisters like you do. Like I do."

"I think Nehla is just young and curious," Rih protested. "I didn't want to share this with you when we were in RoBal, since you were so worn by being there, but I did speak with her. She's learning my signs."

Bimet paled. "You know she's niece to the Hand."

"I am daughter to the emperor himself."

Bemit shook her head. "Do you know, when we were in RoBal, she met with him every day."

Rih's stomach clenched. Is that what Nehla had meant when they spoke? Was is not the offer of support as she hoped, but instead a warning from a neutral party or even the enemy themselves?

"You always say I am your caution," Bimet explained, kneeling before Rih. Like Azimir, she took Rih's hands, one thumb circling the webbing of her thumb before continuing. "I want you safe. I want you whole. I want you to keep your position here, in case all else fails."

"If all fails, Bimet, then I will be dragged back to RoBal by the Hand himself, I don't doubt, then raped, beaten, and strung up on the walls." Bemit flinched at her description. "I know the risks, Bimet, and I choose this path anyway. I'll do what I must here, then we'll go west. And take our home back."

"And what about everything here? Have you thought that far ahead?"

Rih rolled her eyes. "There's no point setting down roots here. The grasslands are our home, not these cloying forests and cliffs hemming us in, pinching us between sea and mountain and stone."

"But what if they weren't," Bemit hazarded. The gentle expression on her face looked closer to pity now, and Rih's stomach dropped.

"What do you mean?"

"What if this does have to be our home? If the rebellion falters. It could take a decade to wrest power from the Emerald throne. You are here, even if your heart isn't. I'm here. Your dozen sisters and guards are here too. And while we may be your allies—your most dedicated allies—"

"And friends?"

"And friends," Bimet continued, "we're aware dying here, of age, is as likely as being killed in a bloody revolution."

Rih paced to her windows, shaking with fury and something else, something called forth by her tears earlier. Her breath misted the glass, melting the faint whorls of frost from the evening. The blue night loomed outside. Horses crowded the street below as a dignitary arrived. Rih peered closer. She recognized the livery from her studies with Mosil but could not recall which house it belonged to.

Bimet stepped up beside her, one hand ghosting comfort over her shoulder. "I think that's Lady Gella. They said the Xain heirs were being called forth again as Keplan fades."

Rih realized what emotion weighed on her all afternoon. *Longing*. Longing for freedom, for friendship, and, in the dark part of her mind, for the man in the infirmary to die. "I feel such guilt." The signs were small, a whisper.

"For wishing him gone?" Bimet met her eyes knowingly. "Do you think they'll let you stay if your husband is dead?"

Rih turned away. Her words to Azimir burned in her mind. Arguing with Bimet was dangerous, even as close as they were. Here she was a political prisoner in the guise of a wife. A new fear emerged in her chest. With a new monarch and negotiations to revisit, she was not afraid they would send her home. *I'm afraid they won't let me leave.*

Φ

The 30th Day of Glasmord, 1272

Firas scraped his hair into order again, cursing his decision to cut it short. With his hat doffed, there was no way to hide the wild angle from being pressed under felt and fur for the long walk from the Slummer.

He had been to the palace once before with Mirrel to petition that, despite their youth, they were fit to inherit the inn without anything left in trust.

At the time he had marveled at the striking marble and towering dome. Perhaps it was experience, or perhaps the years had truly been unkind to the building, but he was no longer impressed.

He peered down the hall to the left. A wall of glass stretched at the end, showing towering plants and brilliant blooms. He could not smell the blooms from where he stood, but he could pretend.

"Master Smythesen?"

He whirled, swallowed hard, then nodded. "Aye. Firas Smythesen. Master A'hane wished to speak with me, I believe."

"Indeed." The old man scanned Firas's appearance again before gesturing down another, narrower hall radiating from the entry. "This way. He will receive you in the infirmary."

Dread was sour beer in his gut, and with every step it threatened to overflow his mind as much as his mouth. He could think of one reason, one reason only, that Azimir would summon him to the palace. To the infirmary. The mourning bells had not rung, but surely, they would soon. At least for now he was almost numb.

Azimir met him at the base of the stairs leading down to the infirmary wing. He looked exhausted, thin, like all of them, but not grief-stricken. "Morning, Master Smythesen."

"And you, Master A'hane."

"I'll take him from here, Corporal. Thank you."

When the guard had gone, Azimir gripped the barkeep in a tight embrace. "Thank you for coming."

Firas stepped away, eyes narrowed. "I'm still not exactly sure why you asked for me. You obviously know how to traipse into the Hare at all hours when you need advice." He could not summon any malice to his voice, which was fine. He realized, once the words were out, that he felt none.

Azimir did not answer but set off down the hall. One side held supply rooms, the other private chambers for the wealthy and ailing. At the last door, Azimir nodded to the two guards. "He's with me."

"No one whom General Domariigo himself doesn't permit, Master."

"I'll be there the whole time." When they did not step aside, he sighed. "Captain Hylier and I both know this man."

"Captain Hylier is on assignment elsewhere."

"Bind my hands, if you must." The words were out before Firas thought better of them, but he forced himself not to waver. "Please. For His Majesty."

The female guard seemed to consider the merit of his suggestion but finally stepped aside. "Whatever, just be quick, Azi."

Azimir winked at her and opened the door. "You're a perfect snowdrop, Halfe, thank you."

She rolled her eyes and shut the door behind them.

Firas took in the curtains, the open window, the dry, dusty chamber pot in the corner, and the folded cloth pads for wounds or waste. Anything to avoid looking at the man in the bed. He sniffed, staring at the blanket-covered feet. "I don't know if I can do this."

"You don't have to do anything. I just thought you'd want—"

"I do, it's just... This is hard. After Mirrel, I..." His voice teetered into a whisper and he closed his eyes.

"I'll wait by the window."

Firas sat on the edge of the chair beside the bed. Rough palms scrubbed at the thighs of his breeches. He sucked air in through his teeth and glanced from the motionless shape on the bed to Azimir. The boy was absorbed in a modern scroll that looked like a primer.

He reached out a shaking hand and his weathered fingers laced with Keplan's limp ones. Breath rushed from his lungs when he finally looked at the king's face. "Fates."

Keplan looked both decades older and younger. Frown lines had formed but smile lines faded. His bruise-purple lips were lax and Firas realized that, when awake, Keplan's mouth always held the promise of a smile or a sneer. When he spoke, his voice was a whine. "Hey, Lan. It's good to see you."

He cleared his throat and tried again. "I miss you. I miss when we weren't strangers. When we'd spend the evenings dancing and talking, when you'd come to me in the dark unable to sleep. You always fell asleep by the third line of whatever story I chose to tell you. I've never felt more powerful than when I could bring you peace. I know you're troubled. I know you've been tortured, and not just in Ban. I know you've fallen back on dust and I can imagine why. But please hear me, if you can understand my words or my intent, listen. I know you said not to walk this road, but every day since you left, I realized I already had. Athrolan needs you. I need—"

His voice cracked and his eyes squeezed shut. "I'm so sorry. I'm sorry it came to this. I'm sorry. If I could go back, I'd ask you more, I'd pay more attention, enough that you'd tell me about your foolish plan to take the throne. Maybe then you'd be awake and in the Hare and maybe you'd have woken with Mirrel that morning and—" His other hand fisted in his lap and he squeezed his eyes shut against the wave of grief and fear pummeling his breast. "Neither of us were ready for it. Now that I am, it's too late." The words choked out in a dry sob. "I just can't lose you too."

The bells rang and he jumped. "Guess I ought to be going."

"When you're ready," Azimir answered. The boy's cheeks glistened.

Firas gripped Keplan's unresponsive hand tighter, so tight he hoped he left bruises on both their fingers. "You might be the man who brought peace to Athrolan, but I hope, even for a moment, that I brought peace to you, too."

He was halfway down the infirmary hall when Azimir caught up to him. "Thank you."

Firas turned, anger flaring at this interruption to his private world crumbling. "For what?"

"I don't know if he can hear us, but if anyone's voice could reach him, it'd be yours."

"I wasn't lying." His voice was a rattle over the mountains of his emotion. "I can't handle losing him too."

"None of us can."

"Don't act like your life's mine, boy," he snapped. "The man in there is my light. Bright enough to shed hope on my corner of the Slummer."

Azimir fell silent and stared at their boots, bright and polished, dusty and worn. "I'll let you know when you can visit again."

Firas shook his head. "Next time I hear from you it'll be either because he's awake or he's—" He shook his head. "I suppose I'll know the second one. Rung from the towers and all that."

"I'll find you." Azimir promised.

Firas left without another word. In so many ways it was as if Keplan was already dead. As if he died the night he fled the Hare. What did it matter to Firas if he lived? He was already king. He would always be king. And Firas was history in the biography of Athrolan's most controversial king. *Fates, I wish I was more than a footnote.*

Φ

The 34th Day of Glasmord, 1272
The Village of Jai, Ban

Music pressed on Reka's ears, and smoke hung heavy in the air, stinging her eyes and pinking her rain-raw cheeks. This is what she missed of Athrolan, of Mirik: the weight of people around her, the invisibility of a crowd.

"There's the honored guest!"

Except this party was for her. She cringed at the attention, but stood nonetheless, taking the offered drink and bowing. Banis rarely drank liquor, but tradition dictated every guest buy a drink for the ruakek. Reka was already a bit tired of the grass-wine. It was bitter, tasted mostly of earth, and—as far as she could tell—contained no alcohol whatsoever. Somehow, despite war and death, or perhaps because of it, Ikel had managed to convince the matet to let them commandeer his hall for the gathering.

"I'm happy you let her do this for you," Jani confided. His eyes were bright and warm in the firelight.

Reka laughed. "We both know she'd do it regardless. Any excuse for a celebration."

"If you said no—"

"Oh, it's grand," Reka brushed away the concern. "I'm just happy to feel home around us."

"Have you given any thought to if you'll go to the capital or stay here?"

Reka looked down. "I'm wondering whether I should write to Hetmir A'hane."

His brows arched. "I thought you were for our cause."

"I am, wholly. That's why I think I should. She's a smart woman, and she'll see plain as I have that fighting half the Banis army is better than fighting the whole."

The door banged open, caught by the buffeting wind, and in blew a handful of Banis soldiers and a gust of rain. Most fell into conversation with family, but one caught Reka's eye. His long hair was tied back in a series of bunches, and dark freckles dusted his light brown cheeks. Warmth fluttered in her belly. "What do you know of him?"

Jani followed her gaze. "He's young for his position. My sister said he was an ally, but I've yet to find time to speak to him. Why do you ask? Thinking of following when they go?"

"Thinking of following him to bed, is all."

Jani's brows twitched upward and he followed her gaze to the officer's long, lean legs. "You're not one to settle, eh?"

"Never have been. Doubt the ruak will change that."

"I guess it's silly hoping."

"You want me to stay?" She stared at him, incredulous. "Whyever is that?"

"Because I love my wife more dearly than the stars, and you are a balm to her homesick heart."

"That's poetic."

"It's true. She lights up when she speaks of you, and for the week before you arrived there was no making sense of her, she was so excited. Banis families are so large, with cousins considered siblings and further relations named cousins. It's something I didn't appreciate until she arrived, alone in all the world, her only family scattered like seed."

"I'll stay as long as I can," Reka offered. It was all she had ever offered, but it was the first time she wanted to mean it. She always donned titles and names and faces like a noble donned finery—and discarded them just as easily. None had ever been hers, save for Reka and the scars on her face. But even those belonged more to the person she had been—Border warrior. Spy Master. Surrogate.

"I'm told you will choose a new name."

"I'll keep Reka—it's my skera. My base name. Bone name. The rest of it, I'm not sure." She rubbed her nose, the tattered butterfly tattoo more scar than colored wing. "It's rude to ask, you know."

"I didn't, forgive me."

She grinned. "I don't take offense, just thought you ought to know. Ikel doesn't speak often of our culture?"

"Occasionally, when one of us does something odd to the other. I know lots of the small cultural things. But of the big ceremonies I know nothing. Even weddings."

Reka laughed. "Because we don't have them. The ruak is the only time we really gathered in large groups, and the same ceremony is used for all things because transition is the same—whether for birth, death, childbearing, or a new role. Something old is passing and something new has arrived."

"I look forward to seeing it, then. Ban is progressive with our medicine and war machines and infrastructure. But we are not a culture of ritual."

"It's almost moonrise, are you ready?" Ikel's voice was soft behind her, and Reka nodded. They left, sent with a chorus of goodbyes and well wishes. Reka laughed and shut the door behind them.

Outside the wind rustled in the grasses. Behind the hall stretched a reaching acacia tree and beneath it was a plain fur. By the stripes, Reka guessed it was a gazelle. She stripped and settled onto the fur, legs crossed, hands resting on her knees. The wind sang.

Ikel's face grew shadowed. "Do you ever wonder if they're all truly dead? The gods, I mean. We thought the Laen were all but gone for decades before the Dhoah' herself arose. I miss the prayers, but it seems odd to pray to nothing."

"I always felt prayers were more for us than for them. So rarely were they answered, save for the ruak. And even then, I'd wager a fair few were just theatrics of the ritemaster." She was not accustomed to being celebrated. Not like this. Bren surely doted on her, even long after both his children were born. But like his relationships with all the women in his life, he adored her without truly knowing her at all.

Ikel knelt before her, pulling a thick, sharp needle and a tiny pot of ink from her sash. Blacker than night, Border tattoo ink was made with the ashes of the first Border campfire. Reka suspected this might be from this morning's hearth.

"Who are you?" Ikel asked, her tone focused.

"I am Monareka Elang."

"Why are you here?"

"Because that name and this face no longer sing truth."

"You wish to undergo the ruak?"

Reka nodded, marveling at how much her hands shook.

"Say it, Rek," Ikel murmured gently.

"I wish to undergo the ruak."

"Do you yet know who you will become?"

"I do not, but none who are born ever do."

Her cousin lifted the needle and pressed it into Reka's skin, dipped it in ink, then pressed again. The pinpricks spread over the bridge of her nose, claret blood and crimson ink mingling as her flame-winged butterfly turned wine and burgundy. New curls tapped their way over her cheeks, and delicate feathered antennae unfurled along the arch of her brows. It could have been a minute or an hour later when her cousin sat back. Another pot appeared, this one filled with pale ashes.

Her brows burned as they arched in surprise. Holy ash was hard to find in the wake of the gods' death.

"Eyes closed, fawn." The diminutive name was a balm to her raw identity.

She closed them, relishing in the sharp sensation as ashes and oil were rubbed into her open wound, softening the stark color of the ink. Ikel's hands left her, and the gentle throb of a small drum began.

"We call the lifeblood of the world, we call the spirits who make us, who end us, who guide our arrows. This one has stripped herself before you, asking for guidance. Remind her of her name, of her purpose."

The rain began in earnest, and energy and joy sparked in her veins in the wake of pain and adrenaline. The pain was sweet, scalding her mind until her memory and body were sanitized. She would bear her past like any carefully researched history, but the trauma, the exhaustion, the weight would be left here. *Who am I?* The drum grew louder.

"Who are you?" Ikel asked, wary.

"I am the child of the earth, soothed in the waters of creation, lit with the fires of chaos, gestated in the blood of birth. My bones are stone and my life is light." Across the back of her eyelid, images flickered—Azimir, Alleanthus, Brentemir, Keplan. Male faces, upturned, asked guidance. And a woman, someone she had not seen but knew, knew in her heart, reached out. Smiled.

"Who are you?" Demanding, now disbelieving. "Are you Monareka Elang?"

"No," she whispered. Her painted cheeks were damp, but it did not matter. The symbols were burned into her spirit, into her soul, the core that never changed. Like the landscape, her mind and her body were cut with scars, ridged from collisions, and gouged by flood. But if one looked, the echoes of long-worn mountains were still there, found in the undulating plain. "No. She is my blood, my strength, my endurance. But I am not she."

"Who are you?" This time it was inquisitive, gentle. Welcoming.

"I am Rekajat Monre." Drumming ceased. Her eyes opened. The rain splattered on the roof, filling the air with freshness. Her hair hung loose, long without its binding braids. Her chest was light. Her mind clear.

The space was empty, save for her cousin, silhouetted by the moonlight flickering through the clouds. "I'm honored to greet you."

Ajat released her hold on the bar and shook the tension from her arms. "I'm honored to be here and call you cousin."

"When you are ready." Ikel pressed a kiss to Ajat's forehead, and the reborn woman realized she was not the only one who wept.

She walked naked to the bathhouse, washed with tepid water. She caught her hair up in several thicker braids, the streak of white a braid unto itself now, stark and proud. She twisted them close to her scalp. The side she shaved until the fresh skin gleamed pink and new. Only then did she risk a glance in the mirror at her new face. The scars were livid with the flush of injury, and her butterfly's black wings now spread down, framing her nose and up just under her brows and through.

"Hello."

There were new clothes, altered from her spare traveling set, silk and linen added to the sleeveless leather. It showed more skin but also more muscle. It, like the pale streak in her hair, was proud, she decided.

Once her sandals were laced, she left the bathhouse and returned to the hall. By the soft scent in the air and the fading rain, it was nearly midnight.

Ikel waited in the open doorway and grinned at the sight of her cousin. She gripped Ajat's hand and tugged her inside, holding her arm aloft. "This is my cousin, Rekajat Monre!"

The gathered Banis cheered. They did not need to know the details of the ritual or its weight. All they needed to know was that this was a moment to celebrate. Music began and food appeared, followed by juice and tea.

The freckled man from before grinned and wove through the gathered people.

"I'm told I have you Border women to thank for such a fun party."

"Mostly Ikel," Reka insisted. "I'm just the excuse. It's a rite of passage, of sorts. Been on the road a while."

"So what brought you back home?" A tall young man leaned in, face bright in the light of the fire. Ikel glanced between the two and excused herself.

Reka knew most of the faces, if not their names, but this man was new. "You know how time and life cycle," she lied, "I found myself missing home and family more than I wished to ply my trade. When there's more longing than contentment, it's time."

"And what was your trade again? Jani said you were a tutor, but I've never seen a tutor with shoulders as broad as yours."

Reka's smile was genuine now. Commitment aside, she always enjoyed a good flirt. "Combat tutor. For the children of merchants and lesser nobles. You part of the riding that came last week?"

"What gave it away?"

"Your face."

He put a hand to his faintly freckled cheek in mock embarrassment. "Is there dung on it? Travel-dust?"

"It's new to me," she answered, nudging his sandal with hers. She took a sip. Someone had found a Banis fiddle. "You can call me Ajat."

"Then you can call me Sefer." His hand pressed something cold and hard into her palm. "Lifted this from a Mirikin patrol. Thought you'd appreciate it more than most here."

She glanced down. It was a flask, dented and battered but still full. Unscrewing the top, she sniffed carefully. "Wraith," she noted. "Not my usual, but I'm honored by the gift."

"I'm just happy you took it off my hands. Tell me, do you like dancing?"

Excitement surged stronger than any drug, and she threw herself into the music. Hands brushed over her shoulders, admiring her skin as if new. Often, they belonged to Sefer. Many hours later, though, when she tottered to bed, it was alone, and the sky was not yet light.

Φ

The 35th Day of Glasmord, 1272
The City of Ceir Athrolan

Keplan lay in the grassland, relishing silence. The rocky outcroppings were Athrolani, but the wheat brushing his palms was Banis. Screaming energy from dust no longer coursed through him, but neither did he need it. He floated.

Smoke drifted through the grasses like incense through a censer. He reached out to twist the curl of smoke around his red finger. No matter how much he pleaded with his body, his left shoulder did no more than twitch, limp mold-green hand flopping at the end.

His reflection lounged beside him, one hand trailing through Keplan's hair, humming. The notes slipped past his hearing before he could hear them properly and left him only with the knowledge that music was playing, but not which tune. There was no time here, Keplan realized. So, there could be no music.

His reflection leaned closer, brushing a kiss over the corner of Keplan's mouth. "I want to show you something."

Keplan pushed himself upright, blinking as the dim pink sun hit his eyes. Sunset was continuous here, he realized, but somehow every moment it differed, an unending display of raw, bruised sky.

"There. See?"

Keplan squinted into the sun. A mound rose, earth shuddering as it redistributed itself. It twitched, writhed, until dust settled into a perfect replica of RoBal. No, it was RoBal, as much as they were both Keplan and the grasses under his feet were real. They were not somewhere else, but everywhere and everywhen, always and never. His chest clenched. Opposites.

His reflection flicked its fingers and the earth shuddered again. The walls exploded outward, fire and rubble raining. Geysers burst from the ground, freed after centuries of domesticity. Its mouth opened and out whispered all the screams from the city, close enough so Keplan felt the breath on his neck. When the screaming had finally petered out, the reflection's mouth snapped shut and he smiled. "I made that for you."

Keplan stared at the distant ruins. If he still had a pulse it would be pounding. He could not deny the spectacle had been cathartic. "For me?"

"I wanted to show you what was possible together. What I could do for you if you let me."

"That doesn't look like peace."

His reflection scoffed. "Of course it is."

"People died."

"People die. That's what they do," it snapped. "They'll always burst forth, shining, wither bleating into darkness, and die. It's not war. It's peace—for you and for every Banis slave. Just think." His hand trailed up Keplan's bare thigh, prickling like a spider's legs.

"This is where they end. I end." His thoughts were a jumble, not from the insistent brush of fingers, but the voices.

Voices? *He heard them, drifting from somewhere just past the horizon. Infrequent, unintelligible.*

But these were words he knew.

"We call the lifeblood of the world, spirit who makes us, who ends us, who guides our arrows. Stripped, remember your name, your purpose."

Their legs were tangled, and his reflection's hand combed through his unwashed hair. Let me go. *Revulsion shuddered through him and he pushed away. "Let go."*

The reflection rose, towering over him, stinking breath hot and needful. "I won't stop until God's Blood touches every corner of this world— "

"I don't care if my existence is what's killing the world. This isn't how it ends. This isn't how it's fixed. I made this mess. I'm going to fix it." The reflection's skin glittered as if constructed of countless shattered flecks of glass. Its face flickered between a hundred expressions, some scared, others not.

Keplan lunged, grinding his fist into the sandpaper skin, then again and again, pounding until nothing but glass dust and blood covered the barren earth below him. He blinked and he was in darkness again, alone.

"You think I'm just broken glass?" The voice leapt from his own throat, but it was not his. "I'm inside of you, I'm the burn in your veins, the lust in your groin."

"So be it." Keplan's fingers wrapped around his own throat. His jaw ground, and he refused to close his eyes. He sputtered and the touch of a free hand, invisible but rough, clawed against the grip on his throat. Keplan's green palm twitched with the memory of a fist.

"Mercy! You're the merciful one!" The voice roared in his skull.

His vision flickered as they both fought for air. Thoughts scattered before the battering ram of his resolve. "No. I'm the human one." His chapped lips cracked over his clenched teeth as he grinned. "You're the monster. I'm the madness. Someday I'll be the mercy, but it's not today. You were right. One of us will die. And only I will remain."

His vision flickered. Roaring flames softened to a distant hum. The voices blended into one, the lilting plea of a bartender, then it too faded to a whisper winding around his mind. Keplan smiled and fell into blackness.

Φ

Firas stumbled downstairs, one hand scrubbing wakefulness onto his face. No good news arrived before noon in the Slummer. A second knock, louder, came and he jerked the door open. On his stoop in the dim dawn light stood Azimir, hand raised to knock again.

Firas caught the descending fist with his cupped hand. "Master A'hane."

Shadows underscored the boy's bloodshot eyes, but his face broke into an exhausted smile. "Master Smythesen."

Hope ignited in his gut at the expression. "Is he—"

Overhead a bell tolled, then another. The towers shook, but it was not with a death knell. Firas sank onto the stoop, tears trickling through the shaking fingers over his eyes. "He's awake."

"Yes. At midnight."

"Thank you." Firas shuddered.

"Toar can take all the doctors in the world. You saved Athrolan's king." The younger man nodded once, stepping backward off the steps. "You know what he said, just as he awoke?"

Firas shook his head.

"'You brought me peace.'"

"Tell him…" He fell quiet. Emotions rampaged between his ribs. "Tell him nothing. Please, if he doesn't remember, don't tell him. Athrolan needs his love, his focus, and as much as I do, too, I'm grateful just to know he still breathes. It's enough knowing we're under the same city lamps, even if he's looking down at them and I'm looking up."

CHAPTER THIRTEEN

The 36th Day of Glasmord, 1272
The City of Ceir Athrolan, Athrolan

DAWN CREPT ACROSS THE stone ceiling. Keplan blinked again. Taking stock, he noted his muscles ached from disuse. Screaming or smoke had burned his throat. But pain meant he was alive. An empty chair sat beside him, and a depression on the comforter marked where someone had leaned their hand while holding his. Thoughts scattered as he tore through his mind, searching for the other him, the reflection with too many teeth. There was nothing.

"Kep?" A blurry tan shape by the window stirred, and Azimir's voice came again. "You awake?"

He groaned, throat too raw for proper speech.

"Water?" His cousin poured a mug and pressed it gently to the king's lips, tilting it just enough to drink.

It was cold and tasted stale but not oily. *Are the distillers working then?* Memories of when he first woke were jumbled, doctors excitedly remarking, prodding, Azimir bolting for the door, laughing.

"How do you feel?" Azimir asked when the now-empty glass was set once more beside the bed.

"Throat, body hurts." He tried to push himself farther up on his pillows, but his left arm did not move. Cold weaseled through his chest. Still, he waved his cousin's aid away and managed to sit up on his own. "My arm—what happened?"

Azimir sighed and looked down. "How much do you remember?"

I remember fire and crushing the throat of who I used to be. He doubted Azimir needed to hear that. "Little. Smoke. Priests. An'thor shouting something. Pain. Lots."

Azimir rolled his eyes. "I had to toss General Domariigo from this room—arguing in front of a dying man, can you imagine?" He winced but seemed pleased. "Sorry. Not dying, apparently."

"It's fine. I wasn't sure there, for a while."

"Neither were we." Azimir frowned at the blanket where Keplan's green hand lay until his eyes were less glassy.

"What was he arguing about?"

"With Rih. This city's been a mess since—well you remember that, surely."

"I do. The water and ship and crops—any news?"

"I'm sure your commissioners and officers will have reports," Azimir reassured. "But I don't think you need to be worrying about it just yet."

Keplan sank back against the pillows. He was already exhausted. Apparently, however long he had been unconscious had not counted as sleep. "Why are you still here? I thought you and your father left."

"He did. I didn't." Azimir looked down.

"Why?" His face and neck bore no bruises, but Keplan's hands remembered his cousin's flesh under his fingers. Pain throbbed, and the clear feeling in his veins told him it had been days since he last breathed dust. "Especially after what I—"

"I don't want to talk about that," Azimir interrupted. "I know why you were angry, and why you were scared, and why you lost control."

"What do you mean?"

"You were ill." His dark eyes flicked up to Keplan's. "You went through dust-drought here. They didn't realize, weren't treating you properly."

They can't know. "Dust-drought kills people," Keplan protested, forcing a scoff into his exhausted voice. "I was probably just fevered."

"It almost killed you and would have done if I hadn't explained what was wrong to the nurse."

"I never said I was breathing dust—"

"I'm not arguing, Keplan. I'm telling you I understand. That they're going to help."

Whatever shone in Azimir's eyes looked far too much like empathy for Keplan's comfort. "Tell me about the battle then. After I went down. An'thor rallied the troops?"

"No, actually. An'thor was useless—more interested in having some bloodbath reunion with the Swordbearer who shot you—"

"Right. The Nenev. They know each other?"

"I guess. At any rate they were chasing each other through the city, the guards were at a loss, couldn't get to you or fire on the market without hitting townsfolk or their own. They must have been here for a day or two before, I think. They crawled from the buildings like cockroaches. Started tossing these clay balls, which exploded with fire. Someone finally pulled you free and delivered you to the guards. Then An'thor called a retreat."

"You left the city to their mercy?"

"An'thor did. They didn't kill many afterward. Most casualties were from the panic, honestly."

"I remember a child, and her blood—"

"Be better if you didn't," Azimir suggested, voice low.

"How many dead?"

"A couple hundred. Half as many Swordbearers. They patrolled the streets, hauling people from their homes and demanding fealty to their god."

To me. Keplan's gut heaved and he tossed over just in time to vomit across the flagging. It was dotted with black flecks like soil, and tasted of his reflection's tongue. When he was upright again and had wiped his mouth, he asked, "It's not still like that out there, is it?"

Azimir's face darkened. "I ought to call for them. They're going to want to see you properly alert before they dismiss Lady Gella."

"Poor woman keeps being dragged here for nothing. I'm surprised they weren't all clustered about my feet casting dice and taking wagers." Keplan snorted. "Would you ring for the healers? I want to wash before they all traipse in here."

Azimir leaned around the door, murmuring to the guards outside. When he returned, Keplan asked, "Have you seen Hylier?"

"No. No one has. His fellow guards claim he's still on assignment."

"I'll see what I can find out. There were many favors I asked of him that were not official."

Azimir waggled his brows suggestively and Keplan rolled his eyes.

"Fates, not that. He'd sooner slap me than tup, I'd imagine."

Azimir seemed locked in a brief mental debate but then rose without saying anything more. "I'll talk to the healer and have a maid fetch some loose clothes. Easier with the arm."

The arm. Keplan glanced down at it, at the flaccid green palm. "Right."

Azimir wavered in the doorway a moment longer. "I imagine part of you still wishes for oblivion. And perhaps regrets waking at all. But for what it's worth, I'm glad you're here."

Keplan could not meet his cousin's gaze. He was right, but Keplan made his choice—in the dusty fields of everywhere, everywhen, he chose to live, at least for a little while longer.

Half an hour later Keplan was struggling to put a shirt on. He was half in, tugging at his unyielding arm when the doctor arrived. He looked as if he could use a rest as long as Keplan's.

"Your Majesty." He perched on the chair as he moved Keplan's limp arm. "Injured arm first is easier."

Keplan winced as it was raised. Pain knotted deep in his shoulder. "If I can feel it, why can't I use it?"

"The bullet tore the ligaments and nerves. More superficial ones were missed. If you regain use it will be limited and will take a fair amount of work on your part. One of our healers will visit you daily to help you if you'd like, sire."

Keplan nodded, belly cold. He had so little attachment to his body, his limbs, after his ordeal in RoBal. He stared at the arm; it did not even seem like his anymore. "How long will I stay here? I'm certain there are tasks that need my attention."

The doctor peered outside, as if something might crawl in through the window. "Another few days, then bedrest in your own chambers. You may discuss more with a healer after that."

"Your Majesty, Doctor Kessel?" The guard peered in, glancing between them. "General Domariigo is here with Lady Gella and Master A'hane."

The doctor finished up and bowed himself out while Keplan tried to sit straighter. At least he was properly dressed from the waist up and, as far as he could tell, no longer smelled like the death he so narrowly avoided.

"Wardyn, good to see you didn't leave us." Domariigo's thin pale lips stretched in a smile and the scent of alcohol wafted in with him.

"You'll have to try harder to be rid of me next time," he joked, though neither the woman hovering in the doorway nor Azimir smiled.

Keplan looked over at the woman. "It's good to finally meet you, Lady Gella. I'm surprised you arrived so quickly."

"I'm overjoyed to see you've awoken, sire." She was younger than he expected, and he realized his words about her to Azimir were unfounded. She stood with a back of stone, eyes flashing with enough bite to cow An'thor, in the very least.

"Only because you've no interest in the throne," An'thor muttered.

Her gray glare narrowed on him, but she said nothing in response. "Roads were busy for this time of year—everyone fleeing the war in Ban."

"I'm certain you'd like to be returning home to family, but there are a few matters to tidy before we do so—I'm grateful for your patience."

"It's nothing, Your Majesty."

Realizing she had yet to sit, he gestured to the chair at his bedside. An'thor had already deposited himself by the window, and Azimir seemed content to hover by the door.

"First, I'd like a report on the city, please. Is Fess joining us?"

The general glanced at Azimir accusingly. "I thought you were going to update him."

"It's hardly my job, General."

"If you stopped snapping at each other it could have been done by now," Gella noted.

Keplan's smile broadened. He liked her.

"Commander Fess is at the navy barracks with most of her people and will be until there is safe passage across the city to us."

"Safe passage." Keplan glanced between them. "The Swordbearers won? Where is Rih-elte? She should have arrived home by now—" He frowned. "What day is it?"

"The 36th of Glasmord, sire," Gella offered. "And your wife is indeed safely home. I'm sure she will come visit you as soon as she may."

Keplan waved the sentiment away, remembering his actions before she left, the terror in her eyes, and the steel. He hardly blamed Rih for avoiding him. "She failed to bring troops?"

"Rih saved us, much as she could." Azimir's face broke into a playful grin. He relayed his harrowing journey west to find Rih and their hurried plan to enter the city. "The surprise alone gave the Athrolani army enough advantage to reclaim parts of city—the Noble District, the docks, and naval yards. Keplan—she's magnificent, truly. Fighting beside her was an honor. You're lucky, both as a man and as a king to have her by your side."

An'thor heaved a dramatic sigh. "If you're done spilling seed over it all, A'hane?"

Keplan stared at the general. "Domariigo, you'd do well to mind your tongue, and if you're too drunk to do so, perhaps we could meet another time. If I recall, saving the city from invaders is actually your job, not my wife's."

Gella ducked her head, but the corners of her mouth twitched.

An'thor's black glare inched over Keplan's face and shoulders as if searching for the panicked uncertain boy from a few weeks before.

Don't worry, Domariigo, he's still in here. He's just a bit annoyed. "So, will someone tell me what condition the city is in, please?"

"Least half of it belongs to the Swordbearers still. It started as just the Slummer and Merchant Tier. The swath between them was contested for days, but it's mostly theirs too now.

"So we've the Noble District and the Silver Apron? And some warehouses?"

"Yes, sire," the general bit out.

"And we have you. And Commander Fess. And surely armies coming from the nearest cities. And two Banis baniols awaiting your wife's command." Gella's voice was quiet but demanded attention.

Keplan's skin crawled at the fact that he was first on that list. "So what are we going to do?"

"You're going to sit in here and get better, because we can't risk the throne again. I'll discuss the logistics of routing them out with my officers."

"Perhaps I'm missing something," Keplan interjected, "but why don't you just attack? For fates' sake, this is our city and our people will work with us."

"That's the issue currently, sire," Gella replied, looking up. "They moved door-to-door hauling people out and demanding they swear fealty to the One God or risk death. Claiming the crops, the water, everything was due to following a false god."

"It was under duress—"

"Kep, they believe it." Azimir's face was lined with anguish. "Even in districts they don't control I see red gloves cropping up everywhere. Enough people believe it that those who don't are terrified their neighbors will attack them even if the Swordbearers themselves are held accountable."

The ground trembled, just enough to rattle the panes in the window. Keplan frowned at the glass. "Is that—"

"Earthquakes. Been happening since the battle. Hoped once you woke it'd—"

Keplan's glare stopped Azimir's next words. "And our other cities?"

"Most fare well enough. All the lords have called upon their militias as well as their personal armies to bolster our troops there."

"Right." Keplan cleared his throat with a wince. "Then the next order of business is to deal with the inheritance of the throne so our dear lady can be on her way."

"I doubt the Mirikin boy needs to be here for this," An'thor drawled. "Though I'm sure were he to have a say, he'd advocate dismantling the throne entirely."

Azimir straightened with a snort. "Of course not—peacefully dismantling an existing monarchy in a country of this size would take the work of thousands and at least a few years. Learn your history, General." He shot a wink at Keplan and disappeared.

Silence settled in the corners of the room and under Gella and An'thor's watch, Keplan felt as if he were a child who had misbehaved—or perhaps, more accurately, been injured by doing something ill-planned. "May I ask why Blackhouse isn't the heir? Considering he's regent for another few months. Even if he's got no memory of it."

"His Highness Blackhouse, while regent, was stripped of his titles. His reinstatement at court did not, in fact, reinstate his line of succession. And due to both his concerns and yours, I thought it wise to keep it that way."

Keplan's gut twisted. He suspected An'thor had something to do with that choice in particular. *Don't tell me I have to produce a blood heir. Don't do that to us.* He was already reconsidering Brentemir's offer of advice on surrogacy. "While I know you have duties and a life beyond your lineage, Lady Gella, I hope you'll consider the stability you would lend were something to happen to me again."

"That's a lot of words to say 'please,'" she noted, but it was with a faint smile. "There is still one step between me and the throne—which I knew was a point of debate, which is why I'm here at all, instead of a letter or spokeswoman."

"Rih's not with child. We haven't even—"

She held up her graceful hand. "Begging your pardon, sire, but that's neither what I'm referring to nor any of my business. I'm referring to Her Highness Rih-elte herself."

"She's not queen," An'thor barked.

"Forgive me, General." Her eyes snapped to the man. "But as much as you tout your love for this kingdom and worship the very earth Her Majesty Tzatia walked, you are not Athrolani. I don't care to know how you spent your entire youth, but I am willing to wager it was not studying our court affairs and laws. I did. Every noble did. And Athrolan has no designation between a consort and a queen or king. Surely, we bestow 'Highness' and refrain from the official title until they, too, are crowned upon their partner's passing, but, fate forbid, were something to befall our dear king here, she would become queen. Unless, of course, you write an objection to the traditional line of succession, and it is voted upon by both House of Nobles and House of Guilds."

Something released between Keplan's shoulder blades. Muscles he had not known were tight uncurled a fraction. "There are a hundred better uses of our time. Thank you, Lady Gella. I think, in light of her actions, she has proven her loyalty and her skill. It appears Rih-elte is making a habit of saving Athrolan."

An'thor shoved from his seat and stalked to the door. "As you say, we're busy. If we're through here, I'll be on my way."

"Dismissed," Keplan retorted. When the door slammed, he turned back to the lady. "Thank you. For your counsel. And your candid speech to the general." He frowned. "No offense, but why are you really here? Might not have been as inspiring, but nevertheless, that was nothing a proxy couldn't have said."

Her gentle smile was gone. "Sire, there is a matter I wanted to discuss with you. My cousin is dead. His father died several years after your parents went south." Her bright eyes held his. "Someone is picking off the line of succession and making it look like accidents. I'm not certain whether they kneel to you or to His Highness Blackhouse, or to another altogether, but you need to be on guard."

He stared at her, fitting her words into the pieces of news he caught in the market or from the Hare's patrons. "There were several deaths surrounding the queen's demise as well."

Gella winced. "That was ugly business."

"Indeed. And so is this." He leaned forward, hissing at the pain in his shoulder and disused muscles. "How long can you stay?"

She laid her hands in her lap, fingers held perhaps to hide their shaking. "As long as you need me, sire, you know that."

"Your words are another piece to something I'm already pursuing. Your testimony, should we act, would be invaluable."

"You have me until then. Roads are rough this time of year anyway, and I fear my return to Vale through Ban would be ill-timed."

A distant longing, concern deeper than he had felt, stabbed his chest. "You have children?"

"One, a daughter. She is with my husband."

"You worry for her."

"A parent always worries for their child," she answered. "I can write up details for your investigation, if you'd like."

"Please, when you have a moment. If that's all, you may go. I imagine you have much to tend to, now that you're staying."

She rose and curtsied, low and genuine. "All reigns are perilous, sire. It just depends on how honest we are about it." Her gaze dropped to his green hand. "You have my faith."

Φ

The 40th Day of Glasmord, 1272

Keplan was finally able to walk, though it was only around his chambers. He took full advantage, pacing from his study to door and back. On his third circuit of the day, a knock sounded.

"Yes?" he called from the parlor, easing toward the door.

"It's Captain Hylier, Your Majesty."

Surprise warred with distrust. It had been weeks since they last spoke. Whatever kept the unofficial spy from the king was either treason or danger. "Come in."

The captain entered. His face was thinner and his stance slumped. "Do you have a moment?"

Keplan gestured broadly to the room. "I'm a captive audience, sadly."

"I won't take up too much time," he offered, flashing a smile. "Azimir said he'd be by this afternoon."

"No, please, stay as long as you wish. If I have to sit through one more retelling of something ridiculous he or Al did as boys, I might go properly mad. I think he's trying to keep my spirits up."

Hylier nodded in agreement but did not sit down. "I just came from the south. I hope you'll forgive my absence."

"Honestly, I was unconscious for over half of it."

"I heard. I'm glad to see you're doing better."

"Are you?" The hard words escaped before Keplan could think better of them. He winced and gestured to a chair. "That was uncalled for. I'm sorry. Seems the only thing this arm can do is hurt and it wears on me. Though I suppose I've always been snippy."

The blond captain flashed a grin. "Perhaps. You got my note?"

"I did, though it said precious little. Will you tell me why you were gone? And sit down, I'm tired of looking up at you. Your letter said assignment, though I don't know which you meant."

"I met with Nehla."

"Rih-elte's handmaiden?"

"Just before I left, yes. We traded stories. Her experience in politics makes her as…observant as I am, but about nobles.

"What'd you tell her in return?"

Hylier held his gaze. "That you preferred men, which is why you didn't force yourself on your wife."

"I didn't force myself on her because I could never hurt someone like that, not because I prefer men—which I don't."

Hylier raised a hand. "I was teasing, sire. I just told her gossip from the city, rumors most knew—the water, the priests, so forth. Enough to get Banis news. I could have told her more and gotten more in return, but I don't trust her enough yet."

"What did she say?"

"There's something brewing in Ban. Something big. She's heard of three baniols being rerouted—more I'm sure by now. Officers are juggled like scarves at a fair. Someone is moving pawns, putting trusted people in certain places, removing the distrusted."

"Curiel—the colonel from the army—said something similar."

"I know her, yes. What would she know of Ban?"

"I sent her with Rih-elte's retinue. She mentioned to Admiral Fess, who trains with her, that there was something going on. Does it have to do with Athrolan?"

"I doubt it." Hylier shrugged. "Ban is huge, and to think we're a threat is a bit narcissistic. I do know, though, that war is a good cover for rebellion. And her words got me thinking."

"Of rebelling?"

Hylier's smile was almost back to his usual joking grin. "I'm too comfortable with the purse and my rooms to rebel, sire, and perhaps I've grown used to your acid. Whatever that says about me."

Keplan chuckled and rubbed his shoulder, trying to ease a knot of scar tissue from whatever nerve it seemed to be strangling. "So, rebellion."

"It was more the strategic removal and movement of people. That list of Peraan's contained names that make no sense. If he were getting those names from elsewhere—somewhere he trusted, like His Highness Blackhouse—then he would not question them."

"Even if they made no sense?"

"I met him more than you. He was an ass, puffed up and proud, but not much of a strategist. He left much of that to others, and what he did execute was clumsy at best."

"So this is not his making."

"No, but I still refuse to believe it. I thought of something else—Nehla said she was not sure if the odd movement of their military units was to protect the emperor," Hylier began.

"Or threaten him," Keplan finished. "That list—it was just murders, yes?"

"Yes, and many had yet to be committed. Someone saw to it that he didn't finish the job."

"You're welcome," Keplan quipped. He stared at his red hand. "If we take Peraan's goals out of the puzzle, perhaps the pieces will finally fit. What do all those names have in common?"

Hylier tugged his travel-stained copy of the list from his purse, smoothing it as if somehow the wrinkles hindered his ability to think. "Azimir and Mirrel were your allies. I don't know about one—he was killed in the Swordbearer's attack, I heard."

Keplan peered at the name in question. "You know who he was?"

"Patron of the Hare, I heard, but that's half the Slummer."

"There are noble names on that list. Lesser Athrolani ones."

"Aye, but most are distant relatives to the queen—people I assumed threatened Daymir's claim to the throne. Most are still alive, save for Duke Jaytian."

"And Tzavanir of Ceir Pardelan. He was just in the city before I was crowned." Keplan's stomach dropped. "Hylier, I spoke to Lady Gella earlier this week. She expressed concerns that someone was murdering the line of succession—her cousin and their parents in particular—and making the deaths look accidental. All these people threatened my claim too. Whether because they were heirs or they were a reason to give up the throne."

The guard's face paled. "Whoever was pulling Peraan's strings was trying to help you."

"Killing Mirrel was no favor."

"Maybe not in your eyes, but in theirs." He heaved a sigh. "Perhaps we ought to warn the other heirs while they're in the city."

"How do we explain how we know? And we don't know, honestly. Suspicions are hardly cause for action. If they were, I'd have been imprisoned for murder months ago."

Hylier nodded and sat back. "I'll look into this—and think about expressing your thoughts to Greton, even if it's just under the guise of a passing concern."

"Indeed." Keplan's eyes narrowed on the list. "If this person is clever, and it's safe to assume they are, then Peraan was not their only puppet. Will you look into other notable deaths? See if there's a pattern?"

"Pattern?"

"Manner of death. Time. Who they knew. Where it took place. Was anything missing?" Keplan shrugged, the gesture uneven with his weakened left shoulder. One hand rose to rub a circle on his temple. The voices were different since he awoke, but no less loud. "If I didn't already have a headache this would give me one."

"Keplan, I—" He stopped and corrected himself. "Sire. I owe you an apology. I failed you."

"You're making me nervous," Keplan confessed.

Hylier's words and stance were the most formal he had ever acted toward the king, though he had never been disrespectful. "I saw you every day. It was right before my eyes—the changing moods, the energy—fates, I followed you to the Slummer more than once. But it took your cousin being beaten senseless for us to realize there was anything wrong. We were so convinced you had a proper reason to be vile, that you were simply beyond humanity, that we let you fall so far. It doesn't excuse what you did, the people you—" He drew a breath. "Even if we all agree they deserved it. But I'd be an arse if I didn't acknowledge my part in it."

Embarrassment warmed Keplan's face. "What are you on about?"

"The dust. I heard about what happened—the fight, the priests, so forth. No matter who you are, palaces talk. And I missed it. Holding onto morals too hard sometimes makes me miss the point, I think."

Keplan held a hand up. "I hated you for it, but you were the voice of shame in my head. Shame I needed. I'm going to need allies in the coming months. But I'm going to need friends. You've been a good one, even if I didn't appreciate it at the time. I'd like to make you head of my personal guard. If you're interested."

Hylier's brows rose and he slipped into familiar formality. "That's usually reserved for nobles, sire. A gallant in the least."

"The throne is usually reserved for the same. I think you'll find I've no taste for traditional monarchy." He turned. "Think on it, will you?"

"I don't have to," he answered, taking a knee. "I'd be honored. I assume our unofficial roles will stay?"

"Yes, as before. But your comings and goings will be less questioned. You might have to find other, less recognizable faces to do some of your smaller errands."

"I already have had to."

"And I trust you'll help keep me free of the stuff. At least until this is all over."

"I will." Hylier returned to his seat and leaned on his knees, expression thoughtful. "There's something coming, isn't there? Something dark. Did you see it, wherever you went when you were ill?"

"I saw a lot. Not all of it true, but all of it possible. Often the future looks so like the past it's hard to disentangle them. No wonder we err often. But there is one thing, I could smell it on the wind. I don't know what it is."

"Do you think Athrolan will be changed?"

Keplan found he could not meet the man's eyes. "I think everything will change."

Φ

The 42nd Day of Glasmord, 1272

"I brought something for you," Azimir announced, plopping on to the seat across from Rih and Bimet. She was surprised to see only one of the signs was wrong. He slid a drawing across the table. "You mentioned how many Deaf people were in your country, and I looked into it. Into how your houses are designed, with so many who can't hear. I imagine your room here feels isolating by comparison."

She glanced at the drawing. It was poorly done, but she caught the line of a door jamb and a pulley system very akin to what they used in Ban. She raised her brows. "I find it amusing that it takes you looking at floorplans and schematics to decide for yourself that, yes, it indeed must be isolating."

He cringed. "Ah, well, I've made an arse of myself."

She laughed and held onto the illustration while he tried to tug it out of sight. "It's fine, I'm happy you thought of it at all. May I keep these? Perhaps I'll commission a mason with the king's permission."

Azimir frowned. "You're hardly a prisoner here, you shouldn't need permission to redesign your room."

"No, I shouldn't, but palaces belong to the monarch, and here he is king." She showed the illustration to Bimet, who smiled and tucked it away. "So to what do I owe the honor?"

Azimir snorted. "It's hardly an honor, I'm just the master to your Kajimet."

"Your grandfather was king of Mirik, even if he destroyed the place," Rih pointed out.

"We don't discuss that in our household," Azimir admonished before grinning playfully. "I thought you might like to see something alive, after the winter we've had. Coming back from home must have been difficult. Figured lunch was easier to talk over, than walking." He hesitated. "Was I wrong?"

"Chewing makes lipreading impossible, but walking isn't much easier, since we're not facing one another. Let's just be grateful Bimet is here."

Bimet rolled her eyes, signing and voicing at once. "If you think I'm not ordering the finest meal they've got on Master A'hane's coin, you're fooling yourselves."

Azimir laughed and waved over a footman standing at the fork in one of the paths. The order was simple—distilled water from the warehouses and a plate of meat and cheeses. When they were through, he turned back to Rih. "So, how do Athrolani greenhouses compare to Banis?"

"Regrettably, they can't. Though I have only seen the tops of the trees in ours, I can confirm even those are more lush than the whole of Athrolan." Bimet shot her a warning look and she finishing with an apology.

Azimir crowed. "Don't worry, I've got no horse in that race."

"You did bring us here."

"Well, it's not a slush pile, now is it?"

Rih dipped her head in a warrior's forfeit. "It's lovely, honestly. Just different. Everything is carefully divided. Clear plaques. Tidy branches. Ban's gardens—those I have seen—are overgrown, tumbling, a symphony of life."

Azimir's smile was gentle, almost longing. "I'd love to see that. I love green and growing things."

Rih's brows arched, but she waited to respond until the meager plates of their food arrived. "I didn't take you for one who liked plants. More just swords."

Azimir laughed. "Small wonder. Most folks just think I'm simple and sword-headed. I probably am, most times. But our mother gave us each a potted plant when we were little, said it would teach us patience and care."

"And did it?"

His dark eyes were steady as his hands rose into the perfect signs. "You tell me."

Rih's cheeks warmed, and she was grateful her darker skin hid most of the blush. The benefit of being raised by a courtesan was at least she was familiar with euphemisms.

"Do you wish me to leave?" Bimet asked.

Rih shook her head as discreetly as she could manage.

Azimir's eyes lit with curiosity. "I hadn't said anything just then. What did she say?"

"She asked if we wanted to be alone," Rih explained, still not meeting his eyes. *Please. I so enjoy our friendship.*

"Of course not," Azimir answered, smile still gentle. "I wouldn't want a miscommunication."

She stared at him for several heartbeats. If Bimet was right, the boy exhibited more self-control than most men she had met. "I'm glad. Our conversations are what I enjoy the most."

"Good, me too. Battle wasn't terrible either. What was that club you were using?"

"Atlatl. Not a club, more the handle to a projectile. Those big darts." She bit her lip. "I'm just not nearly as good at shooting as I am at clubbing people, it seems."

"I prefer close combat as well." He pushed the plate toward her, patting his stomach. "I'm stuffed, the rest is for you two."

Rih caught the shadows in his cheeks, fainter than any in the city, she imagined. She felt her stomach answer. "Do you think Athrolan will starve?"

He looked away, brows curling together. "People have already starved. People were killed in the floods. In the fight with the priests. People keep dying."

"Do you think it's his fault?" The words were treason, but she did not care. Treason seemed to be what she was best at.

"I don't think it's because he's king." He fiddled with his napkin. "But perhaps because of what he is."

"You believe it too. Like the Swordbearers."

"Not like the Swordbearers," he countered. "But yes. I do. What about you?"

"I want to believe. I want to think all the terrible things happening in the world have a reason behind them, a reason beyond just human imperfection and malice." She steeled herself. "If I'm married to a god, then surely there's something mighty in store for me."

Azimir's eyes narrowed on her, moved to Bimet, then back to her. "There's not regardless?"

Rih deflected with something coy, but her focus was on his observations, both of Athrolan and her own future. *Perhaps it's time to reach out to his mother.*

Their lunch wound on, despite the obvious lack of food. Rih taught him all the signs for the plants in the greenhouse, though he caught her making up a few that she had never seen before. By the time she and Bimet returned, it was almost evening.

A letter waited on her desk.

She made sure her study door was locked before slitting the seal. It was a plain scroll, decorated with the simple ribbon of a casual friendly correspondence. *For the amount of these I receive, you'd think I'd have more friends.*

> *Dearest R,*
>
> *I'm glad our dear M caught you on the road. In times like these it's good to be reminded of friendship. I've been meaning to write to you since I was posted here (do forgive the reused parchment). My days have been long, and – as you well know – during war the nights always last forever.*
>
> *But I've met a lovely woman who goes by Ajat.*
>
> *I was hoping you would look into her family – I plan to ask her to wed, but I was hoping to know a bit about the family mine would be joining before setting my best tile.*
>
> *Do write if you know anything about her that would shadow my humble honor.*
>
> *Yours, in rain and sun,*
> *Sefer Vam*

Rih slid the scroll onto a stand and peered closer at the thin, battered vellum. Whoever wrote this knew enough of her conversation with Majilah Ag. *So is this Ajat the Mirikin woman she spoke of?* Sefer was a Banis name, one she recognized from her ever-changing list of distant allies. *"Do forgive the reused parchment."* She raised the lamplight and set the scroll just before it. Sure enough, what looked like a shopping list had been inscribed, then rinsed away.

> *Meat*
> *Onions*
> *Nettle tea*
> *Amber rosin*

She frowned. Amber rosin was expensive and rare and used only by imperial musicians. She went down the list again, writing down the first letter of each item. *Monareka Elang.* So whoever now went by Ajat had a previous name. A Border name. And Mirikin ties.

She tucked the information into her drawer of notes, under the stacks of letters from Vi-baln and Mosil. Next, she drew out a blank scroll and clipped it to her writing board.

> *Dearest Mobeka,*

Forgive my lack of correspondence of late. I hope you've fared safe during these times. Your cousin has been a bright spot for me, but I fear we aren't as close as we could be – you know her best – would she be open to friendship, despite our differences?

I have finally chosen which colors I wish for the hat I promised to commission, but I also thought I might send something matching to my cousin back home. I fear for bandits, however, and Mirikin patrols. Do you have a secure route? If you're too busy I do hope you'll refer me to another craftsman.

Her coded deception was hardly as careful as his had been, but this letter had far fewer hands to pass through. She reached for the string to the bell outside her study to call Bimet. Her fingers paused on the silk cord, eyes fixed on the figure in her study doorway.

"Your Majesty." Somehow, her hands did not shake. Whatever it was he wanted, she would face it.

Keplan stepped in. His mouth stretched in what she supposed was meant to be a smile. "I knocked, but I realized you couldn't hear. Would you like me to call for Bimet? I fear I don't know enough of your signs and I doubt they can be used one-handed."

Rih's gaze dropped to the limp arm at his side. His left shoulder hung a bit lower than the right. "Can you write?"

Keplan watched her hands. "You'd like to write?" When she nodded, he smiled. "My penmanship leaves much wanting, but if you'd rather, yes."

Relieved at the excuse, she put away her traitorous letters and found two wax tablets. She slid one across the desk with a stylus. *At least we're still in my study with a heap of polished wood between us.*

He gestured to the chair opposite her questioningly, sitting only after she nodded again. He wrote a few lines, then held the tablet up, smile awkward and expectant.

These past few months must have been bizarre for you. I thought we might start over. I want you to feel at home.

Rih scanned the words. He had not lied—his penmanship was closer to bird-scratch than Banis.

It is hard to feel at home here. I feel as if I have nothing to set roots into.

A royal entourage is hardly nothing, my lady.

She winced. Perhaps her words were too candid, too rude. She recalled his temper and Azimir's bruises. If she could not find the strength to argue with Athrolan's boy king, how would she ever face the emperor?

Surely, I don't have to explain the dangers of a city full of strangers and a temperamental ruler. I might be a princess to you, but I wasn't always. Just as you weren't always the king I see here.

He read the words, then sat back in his seat, face thoughtful. "I rode into Ban with little more than the clothes on my back and the ragged pony beneath me. I entered those gates — the ones hung with your family's colors — in shackles, without friends or family or an understanding of who I was, who I could trust." His lip trembled too much for her to decipher the words, but she suspected he faltered into silence.

She started to write that he forgive her, but he held up his hand, continuing on the tablet:

I realize that, for you, this seems no different. Forced marriage can feel like imprisonment. It did to me, too.

I hope you don't find my query rude, sire, but I saw a man leaving your infirmary. A common man, with dirty boots and a long yellow beard. He spoke with Azimir, and it looked as if he wept for you. Is he why you never came to my bed?

The king read the words, his dark brows knitting like thunderheads over the colorless sky of his eyes. He looked up at her, then back at the words, as if in disbelief.

This man, were his eyes green? And was he just barely taller than Azi?

She had not been close enough to see his eyes, only the redness on his cheeks and the shaking in his wild, gesturing hands.

They are the same height, and I did not see his eyes. But his shirt was blue. Bright, for Athrolani fashion.

Keplan's eyes closed tightly, shoulders heaving in a slow breath. Was he angry? Frustrated?

I have not visited your bed because you seem to have no interest in such things and I'm not a monster.

He cracked a tired smile.

Leastwise, not that kind. But that man is the reason I still draw breath. He is the reason I took the throne to prevent war — however ironic that is now. He is the reason I came back two weeks ago, and not the man who could have.

You speak as if there are two sides to yourself.

Aren't there to all of us? Who we want to be, who we fear we are?

It was her turn to sit back and think. Of course, there were times she was divided, times she questioned her own choices, worried she was not all she wished to be. But never had there been a side of herself she feared.

I suppose in some ways, yes. But I am rarely so divided.

You're lucky, then.

The bitterness in her bones wanted to scowl, wanted to throw every curse at this man lamenting his hardships as she sat before him, as good as shackled by the ring on her finger. She caught the tremble in his hand, though, and the tears in his eyes were just as salty as hers, as the ocean just below. He wanted to start anew, and though she could never trust him, she respected the suffering he endured, so different and yet similar to her own.

I'll prove that you mean peace. It was not something she had believed marching from Ban, not truly. Not with the fire of war burning in her blood. She was quite tired of men's complaints and whims, but it wasn't often she saw them vulnerable. She reached a tentative hand across the desk and pressed it to his before writing again.

I doubt either of us understand, truly, what choices led us here, to this palace, foreign and suddenly home to both of us.

He stared at her hand, then her words, still and silent for several breaths before he responded.

After all you've done for me and my kingdom, I think it's you who should have "mercy" emblazoned on your hand. I'm sorry for the fear and isolation this marriage caused. I caused. I've been told I'm a difficult man. It's a curse, being pawns.

Majilah Ag's gleaming eyes flashed in her mind, and Rih worded her next line carefully. It was an innocent comment, if he was less clever than she assumed.

You mention pawns. I often liken politics to tiles. War, too.

"Do you play?" The gleam in his overly large eyes told her she had not miscalculated.

Quite well. And you?

I've been looking for a partner. Neither of us wants this, but it should not make us enemies.

When she looked up from reading his offer, his eyes rested on hers, and his red palm was extended.

She raised her chin and took his hand.

CHAPTER FOURTEEN

The 47th Day of Glasmord, 1272
The City of Ceir Athrolan, Athrolan

HYLIER ARRIVED JUST BEFORE midnight. Muck coated one of his boots and despite the unseasonably warm evening, he wore a cloak. "Glad to see you're awake," he remarked, by way of greeting.

Keplan emerged from his bedroom, robe trailing after him. "I wish I weren't. What happened?"

"Traipsed across most of the city, got robbed by a street urchin and fell in a puddle trying to get my purse back—my key to my chamber was in there."

Keplan winced. "I'm sorry. We'll put you up if you need it."

Hylier shrugged. "I'll ask the barkeep to let me in. He has a key for emergencies. I was at the Inspector's Guild asking after our dear Greton. That place is a cesspool. Half of them are God-sworn now and attempting to enforce the rule on anyone who so much as sets foot outside without a red glove." Hylier faltered. His exhaustion was clear, shadowing his eyes. "Anyway, I was given this by one of the Swordbearers imprisoned there."

Creases in the cheap parchment made the handwriting almost illegible. Keplan held it to his nearest lamp, one hand working to undo the tightly folded circle. His nose wrinkled in distaste at the salutation.

> *Your esteemed divinity,*
>
> *We now understand why you balk at our words, but we pray you will cast your mercy on us, even for a single evening. Our prophetess wishes to set eyes upon you. In return we will gladly discuss relinquishing our hold on your city.*
>
> *If you agree to these terms, meet us in peace at the alley between Cherry Twist and Widow's Weep.*
>
> *With hope and faith,*
> *Mel Domar*

Keplan glanced up from the sigil scratched at the bottom. "The Swordbearers are requesting an audience."

Hylier scoffed. "They think they're going to come up here and we're not going to imprison them?"

"We wouldn't, if they did—that's poor warmanship, eh?"

Hylier's blue eyes rolled back in mockery. "You're going to fall back on that when they've usurped half the city and blown the other half to fire and back?"

Keplan shook his head. "I think everyone has had plenty of my not obeying etiquette and being a miserable child. Myself most of all. Besides, they invited me, not the other way about. It's just above the naval docks."

"You mean to go? I know you have a friend there, and that's where you used to buy dust—"

Keplan glanced up sharply. His feet yearned to trace those routes again, but this was business, and as much as his heart ached, maintaining his tremulous grip on order in Athrolan took priority over falling into his former lover's arms. "I didn't need the recitation," he replied dryly. "But company would be nice. I'll buy you breakfast in the morning."

"You pay my wage, sire. Technically you buy all my meals."

Keplan grinned, already fishing out his plain attire. "Fair enough."

"Do us both a favor," Hylier suggested when Keplan emerged, dressed in common garb. The guard handed him a poorly dyed glove for his right hand. He already wore a matching one on his own. "And here, I'll tie a sling. Enough folks were injured that no one should spare you a glance."

Neither spoke as they moved through the halls, down the stairs to the higher officers' quarters, and into the street that ran to the south gate. The cold air stank of smoke. The cobbles were more uneven, upset from whatever trembled under the earth.

They rounded a bend and Keplan's weak steps slowed. There was no line drawn in chalk or blood between the districts still controlled by the army and those under Swordbearer rule. There was no need. Warriors in white tunics strolled through the markets, lounged on street corners, played ruddy five and tiles at the mouths of the largest roads. What laughter he heard was sharp, more teeth than tongue.

Keplan longed for familiar night air and the bright sounds of the city at night. Instead, most stalls they passed were boarded up or in ruins. Those that were still open hung a flag with the Swordbearer's sigil. They passed a store selling pastries and Keplan paused to buy one for each of them. It made their progress less suspicious, and his stomach was tired of broth. The price was triple the usual, but it had been weeks since he tasted wheat. *I suppose the Swordbearers brought something useful.*

"It's odd," he confided to Hylier. "They've seen portraits of me, seen me in person enough. None ever recognize me."

"You're not as awkward-looking in person. Close," Hylier joked, "but not quite."

Keplan touched the strong bridge of his nose. If only he could disappear into anonymity's cloak for longer than an evening. Half of him wondered if the people would thank him for the favor. "I always loved these when we ran errands for the Hare," he said, waving his pastry and punctuating the recollection with a large, noisy bite.

Hylier winced at the sound, finishing his own bite before responding. "I love places like that. It's what I miss about Marl Galin. Outside of Manor Black."

"Why are the folk who live there the only ones who don't call the town Marl Black?"

"It's not a badge of honor, hailing from an exile's ward. I don't remember much of when it all happened—my father was Daymir's age and close to him, but he shared little. The man's almost an uncle to me, save for the fancy titles."

"Or lack thereof," Keplan quipped.

Hylier snorted. "Exactly."

"I didn't know you two were so close."

"Not so much of late. I respect him. Deeply. He made hard choices despite his honor and wealth, and I admire that."

"But?"

Hylier drew a long breath. "He holds fast to his ideals. Not what's right. And the man in that room up in the palace is no longer him. Just an echo."

"I'm sure, to him, his ideals are what's right. Very few of us knowingly commit evil. The definitions just vary."

Hylier hummed noncommittally.

"Do you think you'll return home?"

"When?"

"When you're done here."

"I wasn't aware my job was finite. Kings always need information."

But what if Athrolan no longer had a king? What if the Swordbearers won? He shook the thought away, absently wondering if it was his or Hylier's. "Surely you'll retire someday. Family?"

"I'd love a family. And a good house—maybe outside the city, somewhere green and quiet and with good folk." He shrugged. "I enjoy where I am now, aside from the murder."

With every step deeper into the Slummer, Keplan's heart pounded faster. His hands shook, and he was aware of every stray, lingering thought that unwound from the press of overcrowded houses. His body longed for peace, for something to sand down the sharp edge of pain and the chatter in his head.

Hylier raised a hand, pointing to the narrow alley. They were a few streets down from the Wise Hare, a part of the Slummer Keplan knew of but rarely visited. The aqueduct arched over the series of teetering buildings, outdated architecture hidden under decades of repair. Water dripped from overhead, sprayed from chinks in the aqueduct's marble blocks. A lantern flickered at the end of the street, but the alley turned, the golden light truncated by a battered wall roofed with poles and a draped sail pilfered from the docks below.

"Just around this bend, yes?"

Keplan did not answer. Minding his feet and his tongue might make all the difference down here. Hylier seemed to agree, as they both fell into uneasy quiet. He paused at a wall erected from what looked like a pallet. The captain paused and knocked. After a moment a gruff voice muttered something from the other side.

Hylier glanced at Keplan, his usually easygoing features tense. "I've brought He Who Sees All. He wishes to speak with your prophet."

Silence reigned. Water hissed from above, a fine manufactured mist. The puddle around Keplan's boots bore an oily sheen.

The person curled in the lee of the broken wall stirred and blinked up at the two visitors. "You looking for something to ease the night?"

"No, thank you for asking," Hylier replied easily.

Sweat burst across Keplan's neck and chest. *Yes. Please. Something to make the next few months fly past in a blur of distant, unimportant memories.*

"I've got 'whal tear from Berr—hard to come by. How about a pack of leaf, help you do your business and have time to spare? Or a box of dust, folk speak bad of it, but surely you'd enjoy if you tried—"

"I did try and did enjoy, too much!" Keplan snapped. "I'll give you money to leave me be, though."

Hylier grabbed the king's arm before he could hand over the coin, his other hand knocking on the pallet again. "I'm sorry, Master. We'll be through in a moment."

When this was over Keplan would be grateful for Hylier's improvisation and his seamless drop into speaking to Keplan like an equal. Now his mind was occupied with too many thoughts, the majority of which were chanting in the dust-dealer's direction.

The pallet creaked then swung up and out, catching Keplan's left shoulder as he tried to push through into the darkness. He swore.

The man beyond peered at him, black eyes narrowed. It was the Nenev.

Keplan tensed. "You weren't jesting."

"Can we get in?" Hylier asked. "Street's no place for anyone this time of night."

The pale man ushered them in with an exaggerated wave of his hand. "Please, be my guest. The help will be by in a moment with your choice of drink. We have swill, swill, gutterwash and swill."

Keplan cracked a grin. "I've always been partial to gutterwash myself. Hylier? How about you?"

Hylier's blue eyes narrowed on the man. "I'm fine without, thank you. We're here on business."

"You're here 'cause she said you could be, no other reason. You'd have never gotten as far as Welp Street had she not."

"You've changed your tune a bit," Keplan remarked, taking the grungy bottle from the man's hand and pouring himself two fingers. It would take the edge off the gnawing in his mind, and he needed his wits. Between Brentemir, Domariigo, and Daymir, bantering with an acerbic zealot was familiar, at least. "Time was you'd never speak that way to a god."

"Time was," the man quipped, "you'd never admit to being one."

Keplan's grin broadened and he was rewarded by a flash of a mirthless smile on the other man's face. "Is there a required amount of small talk and barbs we must partake in before I see her?"

"Hardly. You'll scarce get anything from her now. It's almost as if since we arrived, since you realized what you were, she's gone quiet." He sighed and settled onto a battered trunk. "She's sleeping."

"We came all this way—" Hylier began.

"You came across the city and it wasn't even raining," the man countered. "Shut up and sit."

In spite of himself, Keplan was beginning to like the man. *Other than the fact that he crippled my arm in an attempt to murder me.* "So. You're Mel Domi?"

"Yeah. Mel'iend before all of this."

A mental echo trailed his words, worming into Keplan's consciousness. He peered closer. White-blond hair, sallow-milk skin. Faded gray ink peeking from a headband dyed red on the right and green on the left. Something else flashed through his mind, a memory, not his, but close. Those features softened by boyhood. Screaming metal and fire. Howling, biting wind. "You helped my mother. Years ago." The math of ages and years faltered at the man's apparent youth. "You were their prince?"

"I'm about as princely as you are a god, in the traditional sense. But yes." His pale lips quirked. "She and I stole a steam engine."

"You trusted her." Keplan allowed himself a grin. "So. I'm here. Are you willing to discuss releasing my city?"

"Discuss, surely. But I think we both realize it's more complicated than that."

Keplan's gaze dropped to the boxes piled everywhere. He could smell the blood and fire through the damp canvas hiding the arsenal. *Bombs.* "Relinquish your war-weapons. Everything but your personal ones. Stop your terrorizing of my people. You can stay, so long as you're peaceful. Believe in me or not, I don't care, just keep it to yourselves."

The Nenev followed his gaze to the boxes of clay spheres. "That's family technology. We don't share it with anyone."

"Then ship it to the palace, care of General Domariigo. Surely you trust your uncle."

He snorted. "He left me for dead. But very well. I'll send it over in a week."

"You'll hand it over to the King's Guard tomorrow."

Mel stared at him, black eyes unblinking. He scratched at the irritated flesh around the stump of his horn. Keplan realized the red on his headband was his own blood, not dye. "Deal."

"Why the change of faith? You believe in me, then you call me a blasphemer and try to kill me."

"I believed in your mother. In our prophet. In you. Now I don't know what to believe."

"What, you had faith in a god until you realized he was real?"

"I believed in god until I realized he was just a man. Just a human."

Keplan sighed. "I'd beg to be 'just' anything."

"Dismount that high horse. We're all just people. In the end. Horns or divinity or fancy titles, in the end we're all just meat waiting to die and praying we matter."

Hylier's eyes widened and he looked away. The man's usual bright mood seemed to have little place in this dark room.

Mel's head tilted, and Keplan caught a trailing mental whisper. "She'll see you now."

When Hylier moved to follow, the Ageless man's arm jerked out. "Nope. Just the god. We'll leave the door open so you know we're not gonna off him. Though, honestly, poisoning the wine would have been easier."

Hylier blanched and stared at Keplan's half-drunk glass, clearly not reassured by Mel's dark chuckle.

"It's fine, Hylier. She can't hurt me." He slipped through the door, blinking as his eyes tried to adjust to further darkness. The room smelled of rosemary. Rags piled in the corner of the otherwise empty room. "My lady?"

The rags shifted, and a gnarled, bony hand slipped out. The finger beckoned. When he knelt before her, a mat of gray hair parted and he caught a glimpse of a moon-pale face folded in a thousand wrinkles. Her chilled hand fumbled at his knee. At the touch her shifting stilled and her wide eyes blinked at his.

Something cold caressed his mind. Not dread or resolve, but something else. The cool of the ocean, of death.

"You poor thing."

"It's nice to meet you," he offered, though the words sounded ridiculous in the dark room, passed between seer and god. "Do you have a name?"

"Oh, I did once. My sisters gave me one, I imagine. Been years since I needed it though."

"Where'd you come from?"

"Berr. Tiny place—"

"Tut Kunis. I saw it in a dream."

"They chased me there, the Mirikin army did. Didn't know about your mother until she stole our sea, left nothing but naked salt."

Despite everything he had seen in his mind, in the space between life and death, the thought of power of that magnitude set his guts writhing.

"But you knew most of that, and the rest doesn't matter. That's not why you're here, why your parents are here."

"They aren't," he corrected.

"Oh, they will be. Time's confusing, the way most people see it as a path. It's not. It's a landscape just like the earth, and we can travel wherever we wish if we've a mind. Most people don't. Makes them dizzy." Her wrinkles rearranged into the topography of a smile. "So tell me why you think you're here."

"Here in this room? I just want to know why," he whispered. "Why I'm alive at all. Why I have these thoughts—why I'm privy to everyone and everything and—fates—if I'm supposed to do something useful with all of this information, why can't I stay sane and sober long enough to do so."

"You already know."

"My parents made a mistake."

She snorted. "Hardly. They gathered the pieces of the world and removed the prototypes from power, set it all up for you, tidy like. Their only mistake was living so long and not telling you how to finish the job."

Keplan frowned. "Finish the job? I'm not the mistake?"

"All the power they gathered, their own and that of the gods your mother ended, it's got to return to the world if any of this is to continue. It's smothering without air, withering without its blood."

"My blood, you mean. The power can't flow back until I'm gone, I die, then?"

She wagged a hand at him, head tilting. Her breath smelled of rotting flowers. "If it were that simple, don't you think I'd have let you by now?"

He sat back. "Let me?"

"Listen to you, parroting my phrases worse than Mel and Nen. I grow so sick of it. You and I exist here, in this world, but also there, in the space between this breath and the next, where time is passable like the mountains. Every time you threatened to stay, I'd kick you out. Nothing so spectacular as your mother's absolute defiance of death. More just keeping the lid on you."

"So if it's not my death—"

"Not just that. You're an artery, clogged with nonsense and too much hubris, clotted like the one they pulled from Jun's heart when it gave out on him."

Keplan had no idea who Jun was, but he realized it probably did not matter. "And I've got to unclog? That's the strangling?"

"You go back to where it all began and rip yourself open, blow wide and release all this power—mine, yours, your parents'—back into the world. There, all fixed." Her gaze was distant. Almost absent, but closer to preoccupied. "You've got all your facts. Now just choose."

"Choose what? Whether to return the power? Either I do and the world goes on or I don't and it doesn't. That's not a choice."

"Just a few moments ago you were wishing for oblivion. I can hardly blame you." Her eyes fluttered shut, and when Keplan opened his mouth to ask another question, Mel shoved the door open. "Out."

Keplan emerged, brows furrowed.

"Not the answers you expected?" Mel quipped, words dissolving into a cackle.

"Those were hardly answers."

"My statement remains."

Keplan shook his head and pointed to the door. "If that's all?"

Mel nodded, wiry arms crossed. "I'll expect your man tomorrow. Make it afternoon, I'll be too ale-sick before noon."

Keplan did not dignify the demand with a response, he merely slipped back out the door and into the damp alley. Hylier did not speak until they had safely left the Slummer. "Did you learn anything?"

"I did. About what I am."

"And what's that?"

"A glorified blood clot in a fat man's heart."

Hylier snorted. "Some prophet."

"She told me how to fix the world. Finish what my mother started."

Hylier's face brightened. "That's more than you've had in weeks."

"She said it's a choice. I just don't see how." Keplan raked a hand through his hair.

"Were you hoping for permission to let the world slip into nothingness?"

Keplan could not bring himself to lie, so he said nothing. Instead, he shrugged deeper into his cloak. It was dawn, but the city streets smelled as foul as they had hours before. Neither spoke again.

Φ

The 49th Day of Glasmord, 1272

Rih's muscles burned with exertion. Another dart embedded itself in the target across the room. The other training hall was crowded as Fess and Curiel did hand combat drills, but the crossbow range was empty. As much as Rih wanted to learn Athrolani hand combat, the battle with the Swordbearers told her exactly how out of practice her atlatl aim was. *Besides, Menna's in there.* She had no doubts the other woman would gladly take the excuse to injure Rih.

Her second dart was closer but still well outside the target's vitals. *"Rih, this could kill you. Doesn't that scare you enough to stop?"* Tears flooded her eyes and her weapon fell from numb fingers. She knelt, gripping the loose sawdust and hay scattered across the floor. In Ban, she could have gone to the funeral gardens. She might have dipped her fingers in oil and walked through the rich flowers and trees, swollen and lush from feeding off the dead. But Il-fald's body would not be there. Instead, it would be tossed into the mud pit that served as Stytown's spring, rotting body folded into the muck for all to see her dishonor.

Il-fald deserved more. Her fingers clenched to fists. Grief shook her jaw and chest in a scream.

A hand brushed her shoulder and she recoiled, arm rising unconsciously to block. Instead of a blow, a gentle hand gripped hers. When she blinked her eyes clear, Menna crouched beside her.

Rih rocked back on her heels, as much to put distance between them as from surprise. "What?"

Though it was clear Menna had no idea what the sign meant, her tense face formed what might have been a smile. Her hair was combed back and braided neatly. They were close enough that Rih caught the sharp scent of the other woman's fresh sweat.

She said a few words, then frowned and tried again in Banis. "You can read my mouth?"

Rih nodded.

"Did you injure yourself?"

Rih shook her head once.

Menna looked at the two darts, then the atlatl itself, cast on the floor. "You don't strike me as someone who'd have a fit because your aim was poor."

Rih glared at her and shook her head again. Whatever the woman was getting at, she wished they would get there soon.

Menna's shoulders heaved in a sigh. "I'll leave you be. I know you do not owe me time or focus, especially after my words. But I would like to make amends."

Exhaustion weighed on Rih. As much as she wanted to turn away and proclaim she owed Menna nothing, she also knew diplomacy mattered, and like most situations, the weight of that fell on her. She was tired of rude people. She was tired of racism and oppression. But she was also tired of lines. She folded her legs so they were kneeling, facing each other.

Menna flashed another nervous smile. "What I said was wrong. Though I thought my reasoning fair, it wasn't. You did not set those fires. And I know the choices soldiers must make, the orders they are forced to carry out. Your people are no more different than mine." She frowned. "Well, you are, but not any lesser, I guess. I wanted you to know that I'm sorry."

Rih did not move for a moment. She wished Menna had chosen to write this instead of the awkward interaction here, but perhaps she never would have read the words. After a breath, she offered her hand.

The other woman's smile was broader this time, and she took Rih's arm before standing. "I hope the rest of your training goes better."

Between grief and Menna's utterly unexpected overture, she was in no headspace to continue practicing. Besides, if the bright noon light filtering through the high, narrow windows was anything to judge by, she had been in the courts for a few hours already.

She put away her weapon and was leaving the courts when a train of porters blocked her passage. Their brows beaded with sweat despite winter's chill as they carted the crates down the hall.

Commander Fess stepped up beside her. "Those are firebombs from the Swordbearers," she explained. "I guess His Majesty reached an agreement, if tentative, with them. Their end was relinquishing all but their personal weapons. And to cease their enforcement of their beliefs."

Rih jerked a thumb at the dimly lit hall and the ornate double doors through which the boxes were carried. It did not look like an armory to her, or even a treasury.

"Old royal quarters," Fess explained. "His Majesty has been using them as a study of sorts, I suppose." She flashed a grin and slung her towel over her shoulder. "I'd best be getting back before my stench fells any of you."

Rih laughed but did not fall into the crowd that streamed from the hall for lunch. Instead, she brought her weapon back to her room. Her nerves were too tight for relaxation or rest, but neither of her handmaids were present. After a quick bath, she slipped on a plain outfit and set out down the hall. On her second circuit of the building, she paused outside the elaborately decorated doors of the former royal wing.

Why does Keplan live in the same wing of suites as we do if he could have these? Rih wavered at the corridor's threshold, curiosity unfurling. There were no guards—the majority had been moved to the palace walls in the wake of the battle. More, still, joined the Banis forces in keeping the peace in the city itself. "I don't suppose they'd begrudge the king's wife a few moments of curiosity."

The door handle was cold under her fingers, but unlocked. The rooms were dark but far from dusty. She expected sheets and curtains covering everything. Instead, four broad desks filled the center of the room. Easels with designs stood beside.

She brushed a hand over the nearest desktop, examining the sketches. They were meticulous depictions of the weapon the general forfeited weeks before. Her memory flashed with the Nenev Swordbearer, finger poised over the trigger that would end her. She shuddered. Dealing death should not be so easy as a single finger.

A notebook lay open, and she paged through. Mostly it held notes on the weapon itself and its history, but another, toward the back, held a list of what the projectiles themselves contained. Her gaze dropped to the stacks of crates along the far wall. She did not have to imagine the destruction. Its evidence was knotted in the king's flesh, the threat hung over her mind whenever she recalled the battle.

An advantage. Rih glanced at the door before lifting the lid of one of the crates. The clay was rough and warm under her palm. Energy thrummed through her at the prospect of raining fire down upon RoBal. Ban never adopted the black powder technology from the east. With an army several times the size of any of their neighbors, they did not need to. The vision was lofty, perhaps. *But in my world, so is liberty.*

The air changed, and she whirled to face the door. Nehla stood in the open doorway, face flushed, smile bright. "I've never been to this side of the palace! Is this an old storage wing?"

Rih froze, trying to flip away from the list without seeming nervous. Nehla was curious, surely, but it was uncanny how often she arrived just in time to interrupt her plotting. *Or glimpse my correspondence.* Realizing the woman expected an answer, she shrugged. "I think it was the old royal wing. The queen's old chambers."

Nehla spun in the large room, mimicking an Athrolani curtsey and the first steps of a traditional dance flawlessly. "Can you imagine living in a room this size? Multiple rooms?"

Rih laughed. "No. Seems like wasted space, most of it."

"These can't be Tzatia's," Nehla commented, tapping the sketches with a graceful hand. "This is His Majesty's hand. I recognize it from all the missives and negotiations."

"You read them?"

"I saw them in Vi-baln's study, when I was tasked with being your handmaid. I thought it odd that a king's penmanship would look so..." her fingers faltered and she looked up, voicing, "common?"

Rih showed her the sign, nodding once Nehla repeated it correctly. "Rumors aside, very little about him seems typical."

"Divine, you mean."

Rih did not answer. Like many in her generation, she was raised without gods, in the shadow of their death. The emperor had been eager to fill that role, and the Banis, terrified, let him. But that did not make Rih devout. "His Majesty asked for the general's weapon during one of the war councils—to study it."

Nehla's eyes widened on the open crate then, and Rih winced. It was too late to flip it shut without the deceit being obvious. "Those are the bombs. I didn't see it, but we heard them from outside the walls while we waited for you. The smell and smoke." She shuddered.

"How can he have these scattered about in here? One was dangerous enough," Nehla remarked. "In the wrong hands—Athrolani or otherwise—they could add to all manner of war machine."

That's exactly what I hope for. Rih made a show of shutting the crate before lying, "I just was curious. As a soldier I'd never seen destruction dealt so easily."

"We ought to go back to your rooms, Kajimet. I don't think they'd appreciate us nosing about in here."

"I saved their capital!" Rih protested.

"So you've stated. Thrice. Today." Nehla sighed. "This is also the kingdom that raised a pauper to the throne and canon-blasted its own people over disliking the heir. Don't mistake gratitude for safety."

Rih laughed, and by Nehla's expression, the sound was too loud for the narrow hall. "Usually Bimet is my caution and you're my fun."

That brought a smile to her handmaid's face, but she spared a final distrustful look for the crates before following Rih out.

When they arrived at Rih's room, Bimet was waiting, thin face lined in concern. "Kajimet, I worried when I couldn't find you." She turned to Nehla, not trying to hide her distaste. "We need to be more careful than ever, Nehla."

The younger woman threw her hands in the air with a smile. "I'm careful. The Swordbearers are loosening their hold as we speak. Besides, holing up in here does no one any good. Speaking of…" She turned to Rih. "I haven't been able to visit my family. Might I have the afternoon off? Now that the curfew and threat is gone—"

"Go," Rih offered. "I'm sure they're worried for you as well."

Rih moved to her privy, grabbing the single jug of wash-water she was permitted a day. She set it on her hearth to warm and caught Bimet staring at her. "Is everything all right?"

Bimet stared at her, expression reserved. She chewed on her lip for a moment before confessing, "There's something I need to tell you. I believe in your cause, in rebellion, in freedom from His Eminence. I do. But I fear you're too optimistic."

Rih rose, uncertain. How could her only true ally lose faith? "You're joking."

"You think Il-fald's death was a joke? Or the town you condemned to burn to death?"

Anger flashed up Rih's spine. "I don't think their deaths were a joke! But this is war. A rebellion is war. That's how it is on the battlefield."

"This is not the battlefield. You're stuck here, above all punishment. Delegating damage."

"Delegating? When was the last time you saw me delegate? I've got to keep an iron fist on this, lest we're discovered."

"None have succeeded in this. For very real reasons. And if you do, what afterward? You anoint yourself as Empress of Ban and start where he left off? You cannot rule it all. Not unless you want to become just like him."

Rih stepped back. The words stung like a smack across the mouth. "I thought we might adopt something akin to Mirik's governing—"

Bimet sneered. "That cock-headed boy got to you after all. I'll leave you to your foolishness, then." She stalked from the room, and a moment later Rih felt a billow of air as the door slammed shut.

Bimet's words soured Rih's excitement at finding the bombs. Without Bimet's help, how could she ever borrow one long enough to study or send to an ally who might reproduce it? She recalled the bright burn of fury at Il-fald's death. The perverse delight that seared her body in battle. Her wash-water bubbled over, steam billowing from her coals, but she was frozen. Perhaps it was not just the emperor's features she inherited, but his ruthless touch.

Φ

The 2nd Day of Vurgmord, 1272

Doctors may have suggested Keplan stay bedridden, or leastwise, comfortably relaxed, but his body surged with restless energy. Another day of staring at the ceiling waiting for someone to visit would drive him back over the brink. Even the fluttering thoughts clustered at the cracks in his window and the gap under his door were not enough of a diversion.

He moved from window to window, tugging curtains back and lighting desk lamps. According to Fess, the distilleries were working well enough for immediate needs, and much of the military was carting snow from the hills beyond. He paused at the nearest mirror, eyes lingering on the reflection there. It did not move, save for when he did. He draped a cloak over it for good measure before continuing his pacing.

What Keplan cared more about now was removing the priests entirely and strengthening Athrolan for whatever storm was coming. Returning power to the world was well and good, but how would they survive until the kingdom was stable enough to continue without him? He did not know how to prepare for a magical onslaught or the impending natural disasters, only war.

A heavy knock startled him from his pondering, and he flinched. Every loud noise was another firebomb exploding. A crack of a revolver blasting his chest open. An aqueduct crumbled above.

When his thoughts cleared, An'thor was standing in from of him. "Easier to find you when you're not perched on the rooftops."

"Considering everyone panicked over my impending demise, I'm amused to see how well everything functions while I'm supposed to be on bedrest."

An'thor snorted. "You know monarchs are figureheads unless they choose to do something with their power."

"And those who do are either revolutionaries like Brentemir or dictators like Jamun-Ilta. And usually it depends on who you ask."

An'thor stared at him, black eyes unblinking.

"What?"

"I was wondering how many people had spoken his name. The emperor."

"He's just a man."

"Is that why you force informality on all of us? 'Domariigo,' 'Barrackborn,' 'Fess.'"

"I think it's foolish to pretend we're anything else." Keplan raised one of the notebooks, waving its pages at the general. "While you're here, I had a question."

"If I answer, will I get my revolver back?"

"Soon. I have to finish a few more schematics." There was nothing about the general he trusted anymore, and relinquishing the only firearm in Athrolan's possession into An'thor's hands made his nerves flame. "This would be easier if you allowed any of your books to be read."

"What'd you want, then?"

"We've put our hands on the Swordbearer's firebombs."

An'thor's features tensed, and he shifted into the memory of a ready stance. "I hope they're locked in the armory where they belong."

"What if I made them larger?" There was a trembling in the floor, faint, almost enough to be imaginary. It shook the blood in his veins and put his every nerve on edge. *Or perhaps that's just Domariigo's attitude.* "I imagine hiding your creations makes it easy to exercise your advantage. So I repeat my question—if I made fireshells large enough for a cannon, what would that look like?"

"Bombs."

"Excuse me?"

"You're asking me how to make bombs." Pride underscored the general's voice.

"Athrolan is at a disadvantage. We can't feed ourselves, half our military is repurposed with bringing wagons of snowmelt down from the hills, and every neighbor is starting to distrust us."

"Not Ban."

"I don't know the last time you trusted someone, General," Keplan remarked, "but that's not what it looks like. That's being manipulated into a tidy place of compliance. Like you did when you put me on the throne."

"So instead you're going to horde yourself atop a pile of weapons you have no right to as warning?" An'thor fell into bitter silence, attention dropping to the notes scattered across Keplan's desk. "What's all this?"

"Notes on my visions. Dreams. Things I saw while I was unconscious."

His albic finger traced the writing, pausing on certain words before trailing down the rest of the page.

Keplan squirmed, mind naked before the general. If An'thor were on the list of people Keplan trusted to know his inner workings, he was at the bottom. "Nonsense, I think, most of it. Nothing the prophet didn't say. Whatever it is that's coming ensnared both our minds, twisting until there's no sense to any of it. I guess we should just count ourselves lucky I'm not spouting divine prophesies."

"Why aren't you?"

Keplan's babbling trailed into uncertain silence. "What?"

"Think of all you could do—reigning as a god-king from his mighty throne."

"It'd be a lie."

"So what if it is. These people can't govern themselves—look at where it's gotten them. You could be leading this kingdom with a fist of iron—I gave you my weapon, gave you the technology, but now your body is broken, your kingdom in shambles, and you're squirrelling threats like a mad old man. Act like you own the place."

"I don't own Athrolan, Domariigo!" Keplan snapped. "I'm a steward to the land and people, like every monarch before me."

"Steward? You believe that? You realize how many people would drop to their knees before you now? After that little display to the Swordbearers? You accepted their scripture. And half the city swore fealty to you while you lay," his black glare dropped to the notes under his hand, "tupping your maniacal twin in some pretty field."

Keplan stepped back, embarrassment and frustration churning his stomach. He sank into the heaving, the heat, the sickly gnawing. "I thought they'd listen. If you wish to talk about displays, let's discuss the fact that you were too busy chasing after some Ageless boy to fetch my body. Or that my wife had to smuggle soldiers through the gates to save our city because you couldn't be arsed. Or that there's a trail of bodies and the boot prints in the blood look suspiciously like yours."

"I don't need to explain myself to you," An'thor rumbled. "I've been here long before you, and if you can't relinquish your silly attachments, then I'll be here long after you're just a colorful paragraph in Athrolan's annals."

Perhaps An'thor did not feel the same pressing certainty that something was coming, perhaps no one in the city did but Keplan. The ground shuddered, books precariously balanced on the surrounding shelves thudded to the floor.

An'thor's eyes narrowed. "Still think they're wrong?"

"That's not me!" he protested. "I can see it, feel it, but it's not me. It's the earth. She bucks and writhes. Death throes, strangled—" His red fist slammed on the table. Panic threatened to overwhelm him. The ground spasmed a last time, glass rattling in the windows, coals spilling onto the flagging from the hearth.

His door slammed open, four guards entering, weapons raised. Hylier stood at their fore, tired eyes shadowed with concern. "Sire, are you all right?"

He glanced between the guards, their weapons, and An'thor's sour face. Fleetingly, he thought of telling them no, the general had threatened him. *Don't tear her asunder again, Wardyn.* He forced a smile. "I'm fine, thank you. Just a bit startled by the earthquake."

"If you insist, sire." Hylier's eyes narrowed on the general. "There's an inspector from the city here to speak with you when you're through."

Keplan fidgeted. *Inspector Greton?* "Of course, show him in. The general was just leaving."

An'thor opened his mouth as if to protest, but instead, slunk sullenly out the door. Were it not for the hard line in the general's neck, he would have looked defeated.

"Show him in, please."

Hylier hovered in the doorway before stepping inside and closing the door.

Keplan dared not flash him a grateful smile or a nervous glance. He sank back into his chair, hoping he still looked imposing without the copious state furs. *Or a working limb.* Longing for dust spread sweat across his skin, and this was not the time to appear nervous, no matter what the inspector had to say.

The man who stepped inside was young, closer to Keplan's age than Hylier's. The king's eyes lingered on the man's broad shoulders, the red blush to his light brown beard. "Your Majesty, thank you for seeing me."

"It's my pleasure," Keplan replied without thinking. Pleasure was perhaps a bit of an exaggeration. It was too late to backtrack. "Your help in keeping my city safe is appreciated, especially in these trying times. I only hope I'm able to return the favor."

"I'm Inspector Greton. His quick gaze darted to the guard at the door. "What I've come to you with is of a very sensitive nature. Perhaps best received alone."

Be polite. Welcoming. Anything but murderous. "Whatever you have to say deserves to be heard by the captain of the King's Guard. Please, sit."

"Very well." The inspector shifted, settling the long black coattails of his uniform behind him as he sat.

"Would you like tea? Wine?" Keplan asked.

"No. I've been entrusted with investigating the murder of one Peraan Goen of Littie's Green. I believe the barmaid Nikola Korier brought the matter to your attention."

"There were larger issues at the time, so I regret I did not follow through with her concerns right away."

"Or at all." The words hardened the air between them, and every nerve in Keplan's body rose to attention. "Do you know why I'm here?"

"I hope it's to inform me that in the process of solving the man's murder, his network has been uncovered. Though I regret the way his life ended, you have to understand anything involving a former enemy to the crown is of interest to us." Words flew from his mouth with a speed just shy of panic. *Easy there.* He forced a smile onto his face. "Forgive me, I've been on bedrest for days and your visit is a welcome diversion."

"Indeed." Greton's brown eyes leveled on Keplan. "Sire, we did uncover some interesting connections—not between Peraan and others, but rather between his death and attacks on notable figures."

Ice pierced Keplan's chest, but he dared not speak. Instead, he schooled his hand into stillness and attempted to put an expression of surprise on his face. Anything other than dread or guilt.

"A dust-dealer I spoke with saw someone dressed in fine clothes in the Slummer the night Paraan died. Said the man was drenched in blood. This is near where, later, Peraan's missing personal effects were found."

Apparently, Sha was not the only one suspecting who visited the Fussy Fat Hen every few weeks.

"Additionally, a palace maid noted that a jacket that matched the description of the murderer's was missing from your wardrobe the week following. Next is your attack on Master Azimir A'hane—the same type of attack as Peraan's. This was, of course, following his country's acceptance of the Swordbearers you decried.

"Lastly," he continued, "there is the matter of the murder of Duke Tzavanir."

"Murder? I thought that was an accident," Keplan finally interjected. "He broke his neck riding at home. A tragic accident, but an accident nonetheless."

"He was visiting Fort Godbane on business, and upon closer investigation, I believe it was an assassination instead. There was bruising in the shape of handprints."

"I see." This time when the floor pitched underneath him, Keplan knew it was only his imagination, the sensation of everything he worked for tilting out of his reach. *If I confessed but told him I couldn't be arrested, I had to keep Athrolan safe, would he believe me?* "You fear there's a murderer in my court?"

"This is not a matter I take lightly. Athrolan was built on honor and tradition, on strength and morals. My family has been inspectors since the position's birth. This is my city as much as it is yours, sire—perhaps more—and I will not have murderers walk free. Even if they're kings." He met Keplan's eyes. "Even if they're divine."

"Excuse me?" A shadow nagged at the back of Keplan's thoughts. Despite the twisting fear in his chest, he never actually thought someone could level the accusation against him. "You're accusing me of murder?"

The inspector scoffed, but it was mirthless. "We can't, not until it's proven, not until we know you're guilty. Let me be perfectly clear." He leaned forward, eyes ripping into Keplan. "I know you're guilty. I've sat across from hundreds of people like you, and I promise each one thinks it was justified, thinks they're above the law. I saw you raise that red palm in the market square and knew without a doubt you had killed."

Keplan sat back, hoping his working jaw looked betrayed, not nervous. "I agree with you."

Hylier gaped at the king, but Keplan refused to so much as blink in his direction.

"I have killed. I grew up killing. Rabbits. Deer. Grouse. Hunted since I could raise a bow." He gestured to his left shoulder. "Won't be able to now, I suppose. Though it wasn't something I enjoyed, I was good at it. But let me be clear, too." He raised his gaze carefully to the inspector's. "I have never killed a person. Yes, I stood in the middle of that market square and spouted scripture deifying me. I raised my bloodstained palm and promised no mercy should they defy me. I stripped myself bare before them, weaponless, asking them to demonstrate the mercy they claimed I'd have. Markedly ill-planned, I'll admit. But do you know why?"

Greton did not speak, and though his forearms bunched with hatred and denial, there was a glimmer in his eyes that spoke to fear.

"Same reason I took the throne. Same reason I raced across the country in the dark to meet an exile in a bar. Same reason I married a woman who brought me to be tortured. I. Want. Peace."

The inspector's head tilted, and he examined the skin about his nails. "I assure you, all avenues are being examined. It's the Silver Apron and the only thing looser than their spending is their lips. Someone saw you. I just have to find them. When rumor of my visit here hits the streets, they will come forward."

"I'm not liked, Inspector. Perhaps you've noticed," Keplan confessed, pitching toward recklessness. There was a relief in this all coming to fruition, even if the fruit were bruised and overripe. "A king is no better than any other man, and if undergoing an investigation, however misled, makes our city safer, I will gladly endure the embarrassment." *Unassuming,* he prayed. *Innocent.*

"If you claim to be innocent, who would you have die in your stead?"

Keplan almost winced at the accuracy of the question. "I haven't trained for years to solve murders, Inspector, but were I looking at someone clearing the path to the throne, I would look first at those who began a civil war over it."

The inspector drew a breath and rose. "You know my thoughts, Your Majesty. I wish we lived in the world you so prettily describe. But I think you and I can agree the world is a far more complex place that that. Good evening, Your Majesty."

Keplan did not watch him go. Instead, his mind fixated on the memory of a tight cell and interrogator's blades. Surely, Athrolan would not treat him the same, if only because he was king. He had long since stopped caring whether anyone knew he was guilty. *But if I'm in prison or executed, who will rule? How will I return the earth's magic to her?*

Neither he nor Hylier spoke while they listened to the fading thump of Greton's receding steps. Somewhere a bell tolled. Evening was an ushering mother, easing the city folk into the end of the day. Waves crashed through him, over him. Blood, slick and dark like the oil clogging his harbor, coated his skin each time he surfaced. The final tile he cast in this murderous game would be ugly and irrevocable.

CHAPTER FIFTEEN

The 2nd Day of Vurgmord, 1272
The City of Ceir Athrolan, Athrolan

KEPLAN PACED HIS ROOM. A small part of him, one currently struggling to keep its head above the churning guilt, told him this was not a solution. Not a true one.

"If you're committed to this, we have to act quickly, sire."

"As if I don't know that," Keplan snapped.

"If you'd like to do this alone, I can come back when you've been arrested," Hylier warned. There were no teeth in the words, however, and he ran a hand through his hair. "Who were you implying? When you said you weren't the one who started a war over the crown?"

"Oh, any number of people."

"I can really only think of two—one of them is somewhere between here and the cold end of the earth, and the other is a terrifying nightmare."

"It just came out," Keplan whispered. "It was something he said earlier today and I—"

"First thing we ought to do is start speaking like we know you're innocent. Even here, even when no one can hear us. It'll make everything more believable." He slumped into the chair the inspector had vacated shortly before. "And we will need to act soon."

Adrenaline rushed through Keplan's body, and he rose to pace his usual route across his parlor. "And do what?"

"We have one advantage still."

"What's that?"

Hylier's long fingers fiddled with his insignia. "I kept the ring. The one Daymir gave to Peraan."

Keplan's focus sharpened. "So we might use it to steer them in another direction? You can't be suggesting we frame a man who's losing his mind. Even I'm not that cruel."

Hylier looked away. "No, I suppose not."

Keplan glared at him in mock annoyance. "I'll ignore the skepticism this once."

"You strangled a man to death, sire, and we're trying to frame someone for it so you'll keep your crown. If I didn't know the details, I'd march you down to the provost at the City Guard this minute." Hylier sighed and leaned his elbows on his knees. "So who did you have in mind?"

"Your confidence is overwhelming. I thought we were going to act like I didn't do any of that," Keplan drawled. His weak legs trembled, and he settled back in his chair. Something had nagged at him since he spoke with An'thor that afternoon. A shadow he was only now recognizing. "When An'thor was here earlier he said something, said if I couldn't let my 'silly attachments' go, then he would be here long after I was just history. What attachments did he mean?"

"You said someone might have borrowed Daymir's common name. Do you think Domariigo would go that far?" Hylier asked.

Keplan's heart faltered. *Would he murder someone I was close to, to keep me in the palace under his careful eye?* "Undoubtably. Whether he actually did remains to be seen."

Hylier pressed his head to his knees as if to stave off rising nausea. "We can't possibly be considering framing the general. The man who has fought more battles and killed more people than most of us combined."

Keplan looked up. "You said they had to deserve it, Hylier. Someone who's murdered at least once to get me on this throne. Someone who would murder again, easily. Someone who has far more blood on his hands than I do, if only we can prove it."

Hylier's brows rose. "You already sent your former commander into the icebound north. You plan on imprisoning the most notorious general Athrolan's had?"

"He's hardly skilled anymore. The man's a drunk. He hid the queen's rotting body for weeks. And I wish that was the worst thing he'd done." Keplan rubbed the bridge of his nose. His head pounded with the press of thoughts, the weight of Hylier's own anxiety and exhaustion. The man was almost as tired as Keplan himself.

"How do you know?" Hylier's pale brows tucked together, two delicate arches over the open gates of his eyes.

He's pretty, Keplan noted. *Not my particular taste, but pretty.* He rubbed his temples again. "I can smell it on him." He was astounded, really, that others did not perceive what he did, the turmoil of thoughts, the cloy of scents. He wondered if others thought the same about Rih and her lack of hearing.

"That testimony won't hold, sire. He's a dangerous man and I need to be careful. If I had known being the captain of the King's Guard might entail breaking into the rooms of one of the most terrifying men I've known, I would have reconsidered."

Keplan's snort was as mirthless as Hylier's barked laugh. They were quiet, neither speaking, just staring—Hylier at his hands, Keplan at the flagging. "I'll call him at tenth bell tomorrow. He'll be well into his drink by then and we'll ramble enough to waste time. Don't know what I'll tell him, but I'll keep him busy for an hour or two. Will you report back afterward?"

Hylier shook his head. "Best not. If we're being watched—and surely, we are—then I'll go home afterward, as if it's a normal evening."

"Your next guard's report is due the day after tomorrow. Unless something goes wrong, I won't see you until then. Is there anything you need?"

When he met Keplan's eyes, his were wide. "Whatever's left of your mercy, sire." He wavered for a moment longer, then nodded and disappeared without another word.

Φ

The 3rd Day of Vurgmord, 1272

In all of his years, Hylier had entered countless houses. Some where he was invited, starched jacket and bitter tea scalding his tongue. Others where he eased into the comfort of a friend's chair, welcomed with laughter. Others, though, he slipped into as a shadow, easing like evening into corners and behind doors.

He had never been so terrified.

Like most raised before the Gods' War, Hylier was weaned on stories of An'thoriend. Most of those stories were epics, sagas where the general was a brilliant light of justice in an unjust history. As a child, he had believed them and steeled his soul with their hope. Now the captain's blood sang with warning. He was no longer a child, and An'thoriend had never been a hero.

He wandered through the gardens, hands laced behind his back. When he reached the arbors, decorated with their full foliage, he ducked into a shadow and pulled his jacket off, balling it under his arm. Next, his cloak flipped to reveal the ragged gray interior. Most captains could afford repairs, and while employed by the king himself, Hylier made more than most captains. Instead of using a tailor, however, he hand-stitched rags and scraps, muddy petticoat scraps or tattered washrags. He fastened the ties, a far cry from the bright buttons on his jacket.

The shades of gray and dingy cream blended into the water-stained marble as he inched up the wall. His strong hands gripped the window sill and he paused, eyes closed. Wind through the trees behind him. Water dripping from the roof onto gravel edging below. A *thunk* followed by creative curses as a maid in the lower levels dropped something heavy. No hobnailed pacing. No popping of a cork or sloshing of liquid into a glass. Hylier levered himself up, elbows locked while he listened again. Still nothing.

He eased over the sill and brought out the thin metal strip he kept tucked in the seam of his cloak, slipping it between the frame and style. A gentle tug of the thread attached to the end bent the flexible metal enough to catch the latch and raise it. The window clicked and he smiled. Like most in the palace, it opened outward, and a minute's shimmying allowed him to slip around the open casement and into the dark room.

The hearth looked like it had not been lit in a decade. A rumpled bearskin lay at the foot of a broad armchair. Two stained, chipped glasses lay beside it, one covered with a layer of dust. The bedroom lamps no longer even had candles, and chests and boxes cluttered the bare flagging, save for a path to the privy. If he had to, he would brave the low stench of stale vomit, but he preferred to start his search in the parlor.

Where would I tuck evidence? Hylier stifled a chuckle. It was like asking a farmer where to place the best copper mine. He lifted a stack of books from a chest and eased the lid open. Officer's logs from the past two decades moldered inside, accompanied by a few sets of training clothes that the captain highly doubted still fit the general. He replaced the lid and arranged the books the way he found them, matching their edges up with the dust.

Turning back toward the study, his heart leapt onto his tongue. A figure stood just by the bedroom door, silhouetted by the dim city light from the window.

Neither he nor the person moved. "General, forgive me, I—" His voice drifted into silence and he peered closer. It was almost enough to pull a proper chuckle from his chest. "I don't know the last time he wore you," he marveled at the stunning armor on the rack. It gleamed in the faint moonlight; he now saw the inlays of turquoise and white lacquer, still bright and bold. He dared not see if the ring fit on one of the gauntlet's fingers. Bringing the thing crashing to the floor was the last thing Hylier needed. Instead, he slipped into the study, turning his attention to the desk and shelves behind.

Beneath a stack of missives and an empty jug that smelled like wraith was a box. Hylier hooked one finger beneath the lid. The velvet interior was faded, worn and eaten by insects in some spots. He tilted it toward the faint residual light from the window. Nausea climbed up his gut. A collection of objects rolled in the bottom. The first was a lock of light gray hair, brittle and wiry from age. The faint scent of decomposition clinging to the velvet interior told him it had probably belonged to the queen. Two rings—one Nenev in style, the other delicate and Athrolani with its filigree and mimic of a kokoshnik. Sure enough, the base was inscribed with the sigil of Felden. Brown dried blood filled the delicate Athrolani filigree. The bottom dropped from his stomach. There were a dozen ornaments in the box—some he recognized, others he did not. Perhaps his concern at having a murderer sit the throne was misplaced.

His skin threatened to jump from his flesh when the bells overhead boomed the time. *Eleventh bell.* He was dawdling. He let silence return in the wake of the bell's toll. He listened to the overloud billow of his own lungs. Floors above creaked as servants moved things about the upper storage levels. And hobnailed boots clicked their way down the hall.

The same boots were used by officers, especially younger ones, but none had that uneven stride, the drunken stumble. And none would pause outside the general's door to fumble with a key. *No.* His grip clenched around the box. Its contents were evidence enough of what would befall him if he were caught. Keplan may have claimed to be a monster, but the general had always been one.

Hylier dropped the ring into the box, shoving it back onto the shelf. He bolted for the bedroom window. An'thor's chamber door banged open and he let out a weary belch. Hylier paused on the sill. There was no time to latch the window behind him. Instead, he tucked his knees and flung himself from the window.

Φ

The 4th Day of Vurgmord, 1272
The Village of Jai, Ban

Thunder did not wake Ajat. Instead, it was the roar of fire and the rumble of hooves. She lunged from bed, back already aching. Sefer stumbled up after her, tugging his tunic over his bare body. Their eyes met in the dark. "I'll check the east gate."

She nodded, pulling her own clothes and boots on. Adrenaline only set her groggy mind in stark relief. One foot braced her crossbow as she drew it back. Beneath the floorboards the earth trembled. She burst from her room and peered through the window at the end of the hall. *Smoke.* Fire. She dunked the towels from over the bath door into the tepid water before ripping them into strips. "Ikel!" she bellowed.

The shout brought her cousin stumbling into the hall. "What?"

"I'll get the children." She shoved the piece of towel over her mouth and pushed Ikel toward the ladder. "Go into the basement. Against the wall. Where's Jani?"

"He had duty, but—"

"Go." She tugged the children's door open and scooped Kas into her arms. "Issa. Up, sprout."

"Ma—?"

"Ma's waiting downstairs. Put this over your mouth and nose."

"Prairie fire or something?" she asked, with all the infinite wisdom of a child.

"Or something," she echoed.

Kas curled against her, barely waking when she tucked the towel between the hard edge of her shoulder and his face. Her other hand tightened on the grip of her crossbow. "Quickly now."

She pushed them down the ladder into the root cellar large enough to shelter a single family from tornados and prairie fires. *Or something.* Ajat emerged from the rel, tying the final strip of fabric over her mouth and nose. The eastern sky glowed orange, flames gnawing at the rain-soaked wood of the gate. Through the smoke—red, then black. She squinted, pulling her hood up. Even over the crackle of fire she caught shouts, whistles. Then a horn blared from the opposite side of the town. *Mirik.*

She swore and sprinted toward the west gate. "Attack!" she called. "West!"

Another five paces and Jani burst from a side road, face pale under streaks of soot and grime. "Ikel—"

"Safe, cellar," Ajat panted. "Gate?"

"Holding." They pounded around the corner together, Banis whistles trilling on every side. At the west gate they skidded to a halt. Grappling hooks wedged in the logs of the walls, and Mirikin soldiers dropped into the town.

Ajat caught sight of one of Kemmer's own agents—Eraka Oland. They knew each other well, their goals often overlapping. Watching the looping swings of the woman's broadsword, Ajat wished that could have been the case this time.

She let out a whistle of her own, high and sharp. "Oland!"

The knight ripped her blade from a Banis soldier's collarbone and whirled. Her green eyes narrowed on Ajat's and she rushed forward, sword rising. "I found her!"

Ajat raised her crossbow and aimed. The bolt thread itself through the meat of the knight's armpit. Ajat slid under the cover of a wagon, searching for Jani while readying her crossbow again. Across the square Oland screamed and ripped the bolt from her flesh.

Blinking through the sting of dust and smoke, she brought her bow up, felling the next soldier who breached the wall. Jani emerged from the town bathhouse behind Oland. His spear blocked her first blow and shattered under the second. Her blade crunched into his head and he fell, limbs twitching as life fled. Bile rushed up Ajat's throat. The gate exploded in a flash of fire and boiling water. Scalding water pelted the ground as the mechanism blasted into the air. The knight staggered from the force but kept hold of her sword.

Ajat fumbled for another bolt, but pain pricked her throat. She slowly looked over to see Sefer crouched beside the wagon, glaive pressed to the sliver of throat between the wet rag on her face and her collar.

"I'm on your side, Sefer. Trying to stop the war."

His expressed did not change. "Up."

A Banis call went up, gurgling into wet silence at another thud of the knight's sword. Shouts became screams and weeping, the crackle of flames from both gates cutting the soft night air. She wriggled from under the wagon, dragging her crossbow in her off-hand.

"Honest, Sefer—"

"Tutor indeed. Oland!" he shouted.

No.

The woman stilled, shoulders relaxing though her weapon did not lower a breath. "Sefer. Finally. Thought you were going to sleep through the whole thing."

Sefer chuckled. "Never miss the fun. East gate guards were better trained than I thought, though." He glanced at the disarmed and dead. His gaze settled on Ajat and his smile dimmed.

"I'm trying to stop this war, same as you," she explained. "This is ridiculous."

The knight shook her head. "We're not trying to stop the war, Elang, we're trying to win it."

"You say shite, I say shit," Ajat ground out. "And it's Rekajat Monre now." She bit her lip, steeling herself for the risk she was about to take. "Kill me if you want, but tell Hetmir A'hane she ought to write to Athrolan's new queen."

"We don't need their lily-white city—"

"Whatever lies you've got, you can spin to her yourself," Oland snapped. "She'll be glad to know where you defected to."

Ajat scanned the blood-soaked ground, picking out familiar features. Her crossbow was jerked from numb fingers. The intimate warmth of the hands tying her wrists told her it was Sefer. Unwilling, her gaze darted to Jani's body heaped at the bathhouse door. His right eye stared, empty. The other half of his skull was gone.

"I'll get them bundled up for the march if you'll torch the rest," Oland suggested.

Sefer looked between the town and Ajat for a second. "No need. We got what we came for. They'll be too busy mending their walls to follow us."

The Mirikin horn blared again. Once briefly, followed by a second trailing note. *Victory*. The rope yanked Ajat forward and she stumbled once before breaking into a slow jog. Behind her, wood cracked and squealed as the east gate fell. She thought of Jani. Of Ikel. Bound behind her, her fingers twitched open, as if releasing a prayer.

Φ

The 6th Day of Vurgmord, 1272
The City of Ceir Athrolan, Athrolan

The scent of clean sawdust warmed the air. Keplan closed his eyes, taking another long breath. Even if his injuries had not kept him penned in his room, he doubted he would have braved the stables before now.

The stall before him lay clean, empty, awaiting its occupant. It was foolish to have ridden Moly into the city. Surely An'thor's remount would have managed the slippery cobbles. His hand brushed the ragged divot on the top of her stall where she had nibbled the wood away.

She was not meant for stabled life. She belonged in the woods, on the Felds. Long, easy rides interrupted only with birdsong.

"It's hard. Losing them."

Keplan glanced up. An'thor leaned on the wall of the next stall. A curry comb dangled from one steady hand. His clothes were plain and dusty. The horse behind him whickered, bobbing his gray head. "How many?"

The general looked down, features surprisingly calm. "I'm a very old man, Keplan. They've all been from the same line. I raised their first grandmother from a foal. She was sweeter than any warhorse had a right. It's funny how much their temperaments mirrored what I needed. Some were runners. Others fighters. More than I'd admit were stubborn and lazy."

"And they were all called Theriim?"

"That's their lineage. Each had a name, of course, but after a while they all become Theriim. Names don't change every time we do." He looped a sinewy arm under his mount's neck. "His dam was the only one ever died from age alone."

"What's that fellow's temperament like?"

An'thor's black eyes flicked up. "Hard to say. Living here, you lose a bit of that relationship. There were times I'd ride every day for a year. Other than drills I'm never in the saddle anymore."

"I miss it too," Keplan noted. He wished he could have spoken to Hylier before now, wished he was not ignorant of what happened the night before last. Surely he would know if something had gone wrong. "What do you say the two of us take off and leave the throne to Blackhouse. Come back in another two decades to see what she looks like."

An'thor's smile was slow, tired. "I think I've missed enough of her years. Plus, it wouldn't feel right leaving her such a mess."

Keplan stared at the hollows of An'thor's cheeks and his drink-blotched nose and brow. Lank hair. *You look like me.* It sent a stab of guilt through him. "Moly was stubborn too. And she loved the outdoors but loved food more. I was just wishing she spent her last weeks in summer fields, but honestly I think she was happy here in these warm walls, fed and cared for."

"Should we all end thusly," An'thor intoned, raising his brush like a goblet. "Heard the inspectors think you killed Peraan."

"Wondering how much else we had in common?"

An'thor snorted. "Just wondering if the rumors were true."

"I didn't do it, but I hope whoever did goes free. I consider it a favor."

"Perhaps. Ends and means and all that." An'thor fixed him with a thoughtful look. No caps covered the raw, sanded stumps of his horns. "You visited the Swordbearers."

"I did."

"The Nenev boy—"

"Mel Domi. Your nephew."

"His name's Mel'iend." Pain flickered over the general's face. "I'll let you return to your musing."

Keplan scanned Moly's stall again, but its emptiness only made him hurt worse. He made his slow way back to the palace. The air was crisp, still, but its bite was tired from weeks of gnawing. Perhaps their months of hunger would soon be at an end. His shoulder ached, as did his back from the stiff way he carried himself now. Still, his mind longed for stimulation, conversation, anything to draw his attention away from the looming information the prophet imparted. Instead of right, he bore left, following the hall around to the royal suites in the palace's rear.

The room was still, hardly touched since he ordered everything set. Stacks of books on religion and philosophy towered around him, waiting for him to delve into what, exactly, he was. That seemed moot now, knowing what he had to do. What he was did not matter. When he first learned who his parents had been, the grandiose childhood he could have had was what stung most.

The life he missed most, though, was the one they worked to give him. Woods. Shelter. Love. Peace. Every move he made seemed compounded with violence. He strode to the stacks of crates, yanking the lid from one. They were clustered in straw, nestled like eggs for the market. He lifted one out by its leather strap and carried it over to his desk before settling into a chair to stare at it.

The door opened and his gaze flicked up. Rih and her translator stood in the doorway. His wife's dark eyes were wide, focused on the object before him.

"It's safe," he promised. "Just don't bring a torch too near."

She approached, head cocked. "They're elegant in a way. Simple."

"Do you like war?" he asked.

She frowned at him, shifting her weight. He could have sworn it was an archer's ready stance. "It's familiar to me. I understand it. How armies move. Why. Where to aim to cause the most damage. Both on a body and tactically. I don't love it, but its intricacies are the only thing I truly trust."

Keplan cracked a smile. "I understand that, in a way. Not war—war is a confusing mess for me—but how people think. Why they act as they do. It's lonely when no one feels something the way you do."

"Or hear it," she countered with a grin. She pointed to the fireshell. "Are you planning on making more?"

"No. wondering what to do with them, actually. Monarchies are like bombs."

"Because they kill?"

"Because they serve one purpose. And once it exists, no matter who lights it, the result is the same."

She stared at him, then looked down at his red hand. "Even if he wants peace?"

"I'm trying to make this kingdom into something it's not, and I keep failing because no matter what I do, I'm still king. There's still a monarch. The whole thing is broken."

"That's how I feel about Ban." Her long fingers reached out, trailing over the hardened clay. A shadow flickered across her features and her lips thinned. *Do not speak the word –*

Keplan leaned forward, as if he could grasp her thought as it slipped from his mental claws. "Do not speak what?"

She stilled and met his eyes. Her gaze was wary but level.

No matter how much candor he requested, this was not home to her. Even the seeming familiarity of her confiding was calculated, a tile flipped and another laid.

"There's something I've been thinking about, since the priests," he confided. "Honestly, even in Ban I noticed it, but I didn't have the context for it, really, until I came here."

Rih leaned back, head jerking to signal him to continue.

"Athrolan is old. And I don't mean she has a rich history and strong foundation or deep roots. I mean she's decrepit. She's wasting away. Like the queen, she's rotting in a stagnant room."

Rih's nose wrinkled in distaste, and he wondered if she knew that ugly piece of how the queen died. "Seems as if the whole world is, too."

Keplan nodded, mind whirling. "I think I'll be glad one of us, at least, understands war before the end."

"Surely General Domariigo is a boon, even if he's only lived half the lifetimes he claims."

Keplan snorted and tapped a fingernail on the clay. "I'm afraid he's a bit like this." A knock sounded and he glanced up. Rih's gaze followed his.

Hylier stood at attention in the doorway. "Afternoon, sire. I have that report whenever you're ready."

"I was just leaving," Rih interjected. "I heard you were no longer on bedrest and thought I would see for myself."

"You're welcome any time," Keplan offered, belatedly realizing it was true. "As I said—I think I'll need your counsel."

She curtsied, and she and Bimet filed out.

Hylier bowed as they left but waited until they were well down the hall before shutting the door. He gestured to the dusty couches, forgotten by the windows. "Mind if we sit somewhere a bit more comfortable? Where that thing isn't staring at us."

Keplan snorted, rising. "It's not a creature, Hylier."

"Don't care." Hylier waited to sit until Keplan had chosen a chair and settled into it. "How have you been?"

Keplan shrugged. "Well enough. I see you survived An'thor's chambers."

"Narrowly, I'll have you know. Came back early—or maybe I'm just slow—and I had to jump. Lay in the gardens covered with moldering leaves while he paced, drunk, above me. Leg's still stiff."

Keplan winced. "I'm sorry. Honestly, you never should have been drawn into this whole mess."

"It can't be helped now." Hylier looked down. "I found something while I was there. Helped me make my peace with our choice."

"What's that?"

"A box. Had some of the queen's hair in it. A ring with the Felden sigil, and a pendant with the duke's. The former still had dried blood in the jewel work. I thought he was knocked from his horse."

"Apparently not."

"At least you never kept tokens," Hylier's eyes flicked to the desks across the room, "that I'm aware of."

Keplan snorted. "I think the nightmares are token enough. But he didn't see you?"

"No, I think he was too distracted by whatever you two spoke about. Kept swearing 'they just made a mess of it.'"

Keplan scowled. "At least Peraan's ring will not seem out of the ordinary with the other two. Eerie."

Hylier winced. "There were more. Other seals I didn't recognize and more basic, common ornaments. Close to a dozen. He's not a man I'd like to cross."

"Too late," Keplan remarked, looking out the window. "I've been trying not to dwell on it ever since. Fates, I'm not made for this."

"Made for what?"

"Intrigue. Ruling. I'm familiar with secrets, but not of this caliber. Give me the gossip of who's tupping whom from the Silver Apron any day."

"That why you were in a staring contest with a fireshell?"

Keplan glanced at the weapon. "Contemplating Athrolan's future. I know it's a disaster, but I can't see a way out."

Hylier rose. "Why don't I put our friend there away and you and I can disappear into the city for distraction."

Keplan shook his head. "Not until the investigation is done. I can't risk someone pointing and shouting that yes, the king was the person they saw ripping that man's throat out."

"Must you speak about murder so flippantly?" Hylier grimaced, cradling the fireshell carefully as he tiptoed over to the crates. He raised the lid and deposited the bomb back in its nest. "Funny that they put all that silk beneath them and not all around. Seems like one could fit more than nine in each. Not that we need more."

"What do you mean?" Keplan craned his neck. "Each one has thirty."

Hylier held up a long length of fabric. Keplan shoved himself up and stumbled over to the crates. Sure enough, the lower layers of fireshells were all replaced with wadded undyed silk.

"Did they come that way?"

Keplan leaned back against the desk. "I wasn't here when they arrived. Haven't opened them until today."

"So either Mel acted like the scum he seems to be, or you've a thief in your castle. Honestly, I can't say which is more likely."

"Either way." Keplan glanced at the door. "I ought to start locking this place."

Hylier paled. "You weren't before? You realize—"

"I do now, Hylier. And that's not what concerns me." His colorless gaze flicked to Hylier's concerned blue one. "A handful of fireshells destroyed my market square. What are they going to do with hundreds?"

Φ

The 7th Day of Vurgmord, 1272

Rih ducked into warmth of the fabric shop, closing her eyes and drawing a deep lungful of acrid dye and clean wool. When she opened them, Mobeka was bustling toward her. "It's lovely to see you again, Kajimet! What a long winter it's been without you gracing our aisles."

Rih laughed, taking the woman's offered hand in both of hers. "I was so glad to hear you were ready for my commission." She glanced back at the two Banis guards. "The rooms are tight here—why don't you find some hot tea and I'll send Bimet for you when we're through?"

After a cautious glance at the seamstress, both guards fell back but did not leave. "We'll wait here, begging your pardon. City's too dangerous for that, Kajimet."

Nehla waved a hand at them. "You know each of us has blades hidden under our skirts—this is my cousin's place and I won't have your filthy armor getting on jade-cost silk." She punctuated the brisk order with a bright smile and handed over a few Athrolani coins. "I promise I'll shout if something happens."

Rih hoped her smile was not overly bright as she turned back to Mobeka. "Might we sit somewhere?"

The seamstress led her over to a long, low sewing table and pulled the padded seat out before taking the plain wooden one opposite. "I was surprised to get your letter, actually. The city has been such chaos the past months."

Nehla dropped a kiss on her cousin's head. "I'll go say hello to the boys. Sewing was never my skill, just the results."

Mobeka chuckled and squeezed her hand. "They'll be glad to see you, I'm sure."

Rih sank onto the cushion, forcing her tense shoulders to relax. Here she could speak freely. Bimet stood a step behind but was hardly needed. As soon as the door to the apartment beyond was shut, Rih answered. "An opportunity arose and I couldn't wait. You said there was a safe route?"

"Of course. All merchants know lesser-used roads. Needs don't stop just because war makes things difficult." She smiled.

Rih shifted, making sure her hands were shielded from anyone entering. "What I have is dangerous. It will need to be packed carefully, each wrapped in silk. That's where I thought of you."

"How dangerous?"

"You heard what happened to the market square?"

Mobeka glanced at Bimet, as if looking for corroboration. "I see. And where do we collect these?"

"I have two armor chests in my chambers and another two in Bimet's. Locked. Packed well enough for a walk across town, but I wouldn't trust a jostling wagon."

"Will there be another?"

"I hope another two—"

"Rih!" Bimet protested. "His Majesty saw us there today. It's only a matter of time before he notices. He may have already!"

"His Majesty?" Mobeka glanced over her shoulder. "You might have mentioned that, begging your pardon. We're here with official papers and all, but our position is still tenuous."

Rih narrowed her eyes on the other woman. She felt for her, but rebellion called for sacrifice, like any war. "Does it change anything?"

She mouthed, hands rising, then falling before forming any discernable sign. "No, I don't suppose so. But it will cost you—there will be guards to bribe."

Rih produced a small purse of Athrolani gold. "And another upon delivery."

"I've got wagons going out in a week and another train at the end of the month, if nothing changes. The latter one is headed to the capital."

"What about a place called Jai?"

She frowned. "You didn't know?"

Rih's heart clenched. "Know what?"

"That was one of our usual stopping points. Just a week ago, half the town burned. Mirik attack. Apparently, there was a deserter there. Now Ban has barred any entering the city until they figure out who's to blame."

The informant. Rih would have bet the finest riah.

"Do you have a friend in another city?"

Rih frowned, examining her hands as if they might jump up and answer her questions on their own. "None that I'd trust with this yet. Unless—" She met Mobeka's warm eyes. "Your wagons go into RoBal itself, yes?"

"Indeed."

"Then these will be delivered to Stytown. The Tower of Jet."

Bimet's hand rested on hers. "Are you certain? The heart of the city is the most dangerous place for such a thing."

"There are so many shipments, no one will notice. We have bribes. Besides, they've got to be there eventually. I'd rather they were waiting for us when we attacked than not at all."

"It just seems so soon."

Rih pushed aside the nagging feeling at the back of her mind. It was too soon, but she could not sit on chests of fireshells for the next year until everything else was in place. The momentum of war was a heady concoction, and she still dreamt of her battle with the Swordbearers. "I've decided."

"To whom will I be sending your commission, Kajimet?" Mobeka asked.

Rih grinned. "Majilah Ag, the Valen Queen."

CHAPTER SIXTEEN

The 9th Day of Vurgmord, 1272
The City of Ceir Athrolan, Athrolan

THE INSPECTORS CAME AT sundown. Keplan sat in his parlor, an untouched dinner plate before him. The letter that morning inviting him to the hearing had indeed said fourth afternoon bell, he just did not expect them to be so punctual. The knock was loud enough for half the hallway to hear, but he took his time folding his napkin. "Yes?"

Hylier was not on duty. Instead, a young woman entered, hand on her pommel. "Sire, two inspectors are waiting outside the throne room. Official business."

"Of course, Corporal." He peered at her face. "Forgive me—"

"It's my first week, sire, no need. It's Kirbe."

"Thank you, Corporal Kirbe. Can you send a runner to your captain, please? Let him know they're here."

"Right away, sire."

Anxiety made sure he was dressed for this occasion hours before, but he still paused to arrange his weak arm in its sleeve and run a shaking hand over his tamed hair. Dressing was more difficult with it covered, but he did not miss his mirror. *Were I the Banis emperor, they'd have to request an audience.* Were he the Banis emperor, everyone would know he was a murderer. He drew helpful thoughts close, the calm curiosity from the guards outside, the steady faith of Azimir across the city. Perhaps this is how he avoided madness. *Not with dust, but with acceptance.* Inspectors were another matter.

His guards fell in around him, escorting him to the large, cold room. Winter filigree of snow and frost settled on the glass dome overhead. Keplan settled himself on the throne, wishing there were cushions for his thin frame. Scribes and guards ranged about, but this was not a court affair, and the room was otherwise empty.

"Show them in."

"District Inspector Hasian and Inspector Greton, Your Majesty."

Both wore the long black jackets cut in a modern style, though he suspected the buttons were not always so shiny. "It's good to see you again, Inspector Greton. Welcome. And District Inspector Hasian, it's good to finally put a face to the woman helping me clean up this mess." He hoped his smile was gentle and did not show his father's teeth.

"Thank you for receiving us, sire, at such short notice. We are here to submit our evidence regarding the murder of Peraan Goen."

"I have been troubled by this case, indeed, and happy to observe my city's workings, but I wasn't aware every murder investigation came before the monarch."

"They don't," Greton snapped, adding a hasty, "sire," to the end when his superior glanced over pointedly.

"When the murderer abides in the palace and is directly under your employ, we thought it prudent."

Keplan's flinch was real, and he made a show of lacing his gloved red fingers through his green. "I'm deeply troubled by that thought. I suppose it's foolish to ask if you're certain." He offered a sad smile. "It's your job to be certain."

"It is, sire. If I may begin?" When the king nodded, the woman turned to Greton. "Your testimony, Inspector."

"When this case was first brought before us it was portrayed as a simple robbery. It is clear now that it was an assassination. Peraan was found dead in the South Fountain of the Silver Apron district of Ceir Athrolan proper in the early morning of 38th of Lumord. His throat had been ripped out, and a bag of his personal effects stolen. His death has uncovered others—ones that were not presumed murder either, at first.

"The damage done to Peraan's flesh indicates a person of great strength who was able-bodied," his gaze flicked up to Keplan's for a breath before returning to his paper, "at the time. Though the Silver Apron is a busy district, the murder took place quickly and in the small hours of the night. No one witnessed the crime itself, but a person was seen, bloodstained, in the Slummer district drinking wine and buying dust shortly after the victim died."

Victim. Peraan did not deserve the word, in Keplan's mind. Mirrel did, torn apart in her own courtyard. Azimir did, blade to his throat in his stables.

"Peraan's bag was found later in the Slummer, having been washed from an alley during the flooding. It was intact, but the time and rain had washed any fabric, handprint, or hair that might have led us to the murderer sooner. Our search continued, however, for one piece of Peraan's personal effects still missing: a ring, of which he was very proud, from the former royal estate of one Daymir Blackhouse."

Keplan leaned forward. This was the part he did not know. He may have scattered the clues, but how they found them and what the inspectors ultimately decided was a mystery. "But you've found it now?"

"Indeed," the district inspector answered. "Between Peraan's connection to the unfortunate attack on Master Azimir A'hane and bruises on Duke Tzavanir, previously thought to have died of a riding accident, we suspected someone within the court, or even a royal themselves, was responsible."

"Me, you mean," Keplan noted. "I don't believe we need to be coy here."

The district inspector stared at Inspector Greton, eyes narrowed. "You went to him?"

"I thought he'd confess. Everyone claimed the man was nervous and rash. Besides, his words led us to the murderer, didn't they?"

Keplan hid his tiny smile of glee with his hand. *Oh, that wasn't a sanctioned visit?* "My unorthodox behavior aside, Greton, you said you've found the murderer?"

"Indeed. During our investigation, we uncovered a witness who claimed to have seen a cloaked rider on a pale horse follow the duke into the woods that day. Upon your own urging, sire, and that testimony, I obtained a writ of search from the Commissioner of Palace Affairs and the Palace Steward himself for both your chambers and those of General Domariigo."

"You searched my things?"

"Indeed, while you were recovering in the infirmary. Of course, there was nothing to find, other than a strange taste in minimalist decoration."

Keplan snorted. "I'm afraid this first year has been a bit too distracting for me to truly sink into the finer aspects of nobility."

Hasian's eyes crinkled in checked humor. "I regret to say, however, that we found this in the general's rooms." She produced a small box and unfolded the wax paper protecting it. Its plain lid hinged upward.

Keplan peered inside. Nestled between the countess's ring and the queen's hair, beside a handful of other gruesome mementos gleamed Peraan's ring. Something shuttered closed on his heart at the image. *I did that.* "I see. And the others?"

"Belonging to other nobles and those associated with the crown. Moreover, letters were discovered in his possession between himself and the victim that implied the general hired him to systematically remove those who might influence you. He was using the alias 'Dam Ornsen,' a known moniker of—"

"Daymir Blackhouse." Keplan dropped his head in his hands. *Even Azimir was an influence?* He knew the general had little interest in the excitable young man, but assassination seemed a bit far. "I admit, I'm stunned. I suspected he did not have my best interests at heart, but to reach this far? Why murder Peraan, then?"

"I believe he was tidying his own loose ends, as it were."

"Of course, we pressed further into the testimony that placed a man of your build and age in the Slummer and were, indeed, able to find a witness as to you own whereabouts that evening. Inspector Greton?"

Lead thudded into Keplan's gut. He was drunk, weaving between houses and clambering aqueducts. There was no end to who might have seen him reckless and guilt-ridden.

The younger inspector ushered in a cloaked man, dressed in his finest common clothes. "State your name for the scribes, please, Master."

He removed his hat and patted his curls into order. "Firas Smythesen, of the Slummer. I own the Wise Hare." His eyes were fixed on the district inspector, hat clenched in his hands.

"And you're here as witness in the case of the murder of one Peraan Goen?" Greton asked. It was a formality, so there could be no misinterpretation.

"I am."

"If you could tell both the district inspector and the scribes what you told me? Surely His Majesty remembers."

"Perhaps not," Firas admitted. "There was a lot of drinking. On the night of the murder—the 38th of Lumord—I was with His Majesty in my inn. My sister was murdered the morning before—a lot of that going about then, it seems."

"And the claims to seeing the king in bloody clothes buying drugs?"

Firas winced. "I said my sister was murdered. His Majesty helped scrub the blood from my courtyard walls himself. She was like a sister to him."

"And he stayed late into the evening, then?"

Firas's cheeks flushed pink, but he raised his chin. "Indeed. And I was grateful. I needed the comfort. Do you need to know which position we preferred that night as well, or—"

"That's enough, Master Smythesen," Hasian interrupted with a sigh. "I hope you forgive us the indignity. And do you swear your words here are true and offered without coercion?"

Firas finally met Keplan's eyes. "I do so swear."

Keplan would have given anything—even his precious, fleeting sanity—to stand beside Firas, palms pressed together, and swear his everlasting devotion. Perhaps a few moments during a murder trial was all fate permitted him.

"Then by the Inspector's Code, I formally accuse General An'thoriend Domariigo of the Northlands of murder in the case of Peraan Goen, murder in the case of Duke Tzavanir of Ceir Pardelan, murder in the case of Countess Fiena of Felden."

Greton's eyes locked on Keplan's as the list wound on. Vehemence blazed in his eyes.

Keplan did not muster feigned betrayal at the verdict placed on the general, but his shock was genuine. His blood thundered in his ears and his body felt more alive than it had in months. Looking at Firas was like looking at the sun after decades of darkness, brilliant and aching and full of tears. Keplan did not blink.

"Sire?"

He turned back to the district inspector. "Forgive me, this is all so sudden."

"I asked if you wished to tell him yourself before we take him."

"What will become of him?" Keplan asked. Libraries could be filled with everything he had yet to learn about the laws and customs of this kingdom.

"He will be imprisoned for a year, after which time a committee—including yourself, as king—will decide his ultimate fate."

He looked down and drew a breath. He did not want to tell the general his fate. He did not want to watch the anger in An'thor's eyes or hear the accusation in his gravelly voice. *I've condemned the man in my place. It's the least I can do.* "I will. And I thank you for the consideration. He was always a confidant, and this momentous betrayal aside, I believe I owe him the dignity."

"If course, sire. We will await your orders to bring him in."

Keplan glanced at the door to the throne room. "How many guards did you bring?"

"A city patrol, sire. Why?"

"I fear you'll need them."

They bowed themselves out, Firas leaving first. By the time Keplan emerged from the throne room, his former lover was lost to the night. He thought of running after him, falling to his knees to beg or thank, or simply stare. *Why did you come to my bedside? Why did you lie before the inspectors for me?*

Instead, the king walked to the general's door alone. The halls were quiet, the last of the evening light fading from the windows.

Hylier met him at the door, panting. "I came as soon as I heard. I can go in with you."

"Stay by the door. I'll call for you and the city guards. This is something I need to do myself."

The captain nodded and stepped aside as Keplan knocked.

After a pregnant silence, the door jerked open. An'thor peered out at him, white brows curling together in a frown. Bloodshot vessels were a faint brown haze over black sclera. "Wardyn?"

Keplan's fist clenched, nails digging into his red-stained palm. He had not woken with the plan to burn every bridge that brought him here, but today was a day for fire. "Evening, Domariigo. May I come in?"

An'thor's frown deepened, but he stepped aside. "You want a drink?"

"I would, thank you."

"Why are you here?"

Keplan perched himself on a chair, not answering until the general produced the offered drink. He took a careful sip before looking up. "Athrolan is changing. I know you hope to bring her back to the glory you remember—the white walls, the towering palaces, the warren of tunnels and armies as far as my gaze reaches. But Athrolan doesn't need gods. She doesn't need the Rakos' fire and the Laen's thunder. If you look at her streets, at the trade in the markets and what little food is on her plates, it's not ours. And it's not from the gods."

"It's from that bloody treaty you signed with Ban."

"Actually, it's not. You've helped raise me this far, given me invaluable opportunities. And for those I am grateful. But I'm in lands you've never navigated. Her golden age is past. Her people don't care about palaces or gods. They care about each other; they care about food and safety. I'm not ruling for you. I'm ruling for them. I need a general who will walk beside me. Not slash a path he thinks is right."

Perhaps it was the steel Keplan borrowed from Rih's spirit. Perhaps it was his old candor. An'thor straightened in his seat and his eyes sobered. "You're asking me to resign."

"It's complicated. But I'm not asking."

"Who will replace me?" Deadly calm froze the general's words.

"I'm not certain yet, but I was thinking Rih. She's got more mercy than I do lately. I haven't asked her yet, but as of now, you no longer have control over the Athrolani army."

An'thor's placidity shattered. "You bastard! I'm what made this city what she was! I forged every alliance, I guided Xavier's hand, Tzatia's hand, even from beyond her borders when Athrolan faltered I was there, in the night, to protect her from her own missteps!" He surged to his feet, hands shaking, cracked, stained nails clawing at the air between them. "I made Athrolan! Not you or any Banis whore. Me!"

Keplan waited until the man sputtered into silence. "When I arrived here, Domariigo, your hand had guided her straight into civil war. Your protection forced one of her most beloved queens to rot alone, disrespected and forgotten, in the soiled bed where she died." He rose. "Athrolan has had enough of your guidance."

"Who carried the Nenev into battle that last time? Who saved your mother from her father's genocide?" An'thor snarled. Spittle flew from his thin chapped lips, flushed purple with anger.

"I believe she did that herself." Keplan's chest clenched. Holding so many contradicting truths, so many lies would take all of Keplan's sanity. He wondered if that was why the general's hands shook. If that was why alcohol was the only peace he could find now. Keplan rose. "You want honors for what you've done? Then accept them for putting me on the throne. You literally killed to have me here, so best not falter now."

An'thor paled, his white skin turning sallow under his faded tattoo. His dark gaze darted to the bookcase, undoubtedly searching for the box. "What?"

"You're being arrested by District Inspector Hasian for the murder of Peraan. And Tzavanir. And Fiena."

"I didn't kill him!" An'thor spun, tossing his glass with a snarl.

It took all of Keplan's willpower not to jump when the glass shattered in the hearth beside him. Keplan's soft voice cut through the rattling as An'thor tore apart his room. "I know."

The frantic rummaging stopped. An'thor's age-yellowed hair swung with each denying shake of his head. His horrified growl wound into a frantic scream. "You don't shed blood! Even the prophesy said you wouldn't!" Hobnails scraped stone as the pale old man turned.

Keplan realized that was, in fact, what An'thor was. Old. Wan. Tired. Ill. Keplan leaned forward, murmuring, "I'm not arresting you for his murder."

When An'thor's tirade did not continue, he elaborated. "Surely the city is, but I'm not. I'm arresting you for Mirrel. For Fiena. For the queen's doctor. For what could have happened to Azimir. For the people whose futures you broke and trinkets you took and everyone who met their end by your hand whether it wielded blade or bullets or pen."

"The city should be terrified of you, terrified you'll see their secrets, see their evil, hopeless ways."

"Enough, Domariigo."

"This is my home—"

"Not really. It's not even mine. It's home to whoever comes after us, whoever treads in these faded, broken boot prints. You know that. I think you've always known. Or feared it. This world isn't for you, hasn't been for a long while now."

An'thor sagged against the doorframe. Something lit in his black eyes, something bright and burning and unfamiliar in the wan, drawn face. "What will happen to me, then?"

"Prison for a year. After I don't know. Perhaps death." Keplan shrugged, wincing at the creaking bones. For a fleeting moment, Keplan felt sorrow.

An'thor's pale hand wiped his mouth. He did not shake. His eyes did not rove, searching escape or retaliation. There was no dignity left in him, nor pride. "Call the guards, then."

Φ

The 11th Day of Vurgmord, 1272

A bubble of warmth and noise burst across Keplan's shoulders. His body trembled with the memory of slipping into another bar, dust bright in his mind.

Hylier jerked a nod at the bar. "Fireale? Gutterwrack?"

"Wine. Dark."

Hylier frowned. "People don't drink wine in a bar—"

"Then water or tea, whatever." He waved at the man and turned to find a table. The tail of his long hair was tucked under his usual felt hat. In the wake of the Swordbearer's attack, many of the city folk began sporting color gloves—even indoors. Whether it was to display their devotion or some societal rule dictating common folk mimic a monarch's idiosyncrasies, he did not care. His were plain, as usual, but unremarkable compared to their bright crimson.

Keplan slid behind a table where he had a good view of the room. *Relax.* He forced his back to loosen until his right shoulder was not located beside his ear. He found a smile slipped onto his face watching Hylier pause to dance a few steps with a pretty brunette on his way back, two drinks held high. It earned him a playful slap on his backside, which the captain answered with a wink.

"Here you are." Hylier settled into a chair across the table and pushed a full mug over. "I know you're not into the strong stuff. It's the house's winter mead. Pretty good, if you don't mind sweet."

"I don't." Keplan sniffed. "Autumn, wheat, wildflower honey."

Hylier's brows rose. "I didn't know your powers extended to drinks. Though I suppose sussing ingredients is easier than delving into people's minds."

"I used my nose," Keplan retorted, and took a long draw. He narrowed his eyes on the man. "You always want to be a soldier?"

"Hardly. I mean, I enjoy it well enough now. I hated training. Instructors did not appreciate my cleverness."

"That's why I was asking. You're quick. And seem unchallenged by most things you take on. Flirting included."

Hylier laughed. "I enjoy fun, is all."

"I don't know if I'd recognize fun if I woke up beside it," Keplan explained.

Hylier's arm swept out to encompass the room. "Well, sire, meet fun. Fun, this is His Maj—"

Keplan made a shushing motion but laughed nonetheless. "I'll go by Lan out here. Always did."

"See, aliases are fun."

"I was under the impression they were for murder."

Hylier's mirth faltered and he drew a breath. "Right. Sometimes yes. Let's not be claiming killing is fun, eh?"

"Agreed," Keplan muttered, taking another sip. "So, will fun begin with a lesson in flirting with pretty girls?"

"Depends what you're looking for."

"Clever wit—just someone to talk with for an hour or two where I'm not pretending." *I'll always be pretending.* He saw it in Hylier's eyes, but the captain refrained from voicing it.

The captain grinned. "I understand that. I like someone who can keep up with me. I've been easily bored before."

Keplan scoffed. "I'd imagine there's a fair few who think you can't keep up with them."

Hylier had the grace to blush and shrugged. "You going to dance, or should I order you another?"

"No dancing. Least for me." He propped his chin in his hand. "There wasn't much dancing back home. Music, yes, and Ma would dance a bit, I suppose, but like me, her voice is closer to wailing gulls than song."

"Cards, then?"

Keplan's memory flashed with Rih's words about tiles, carefully curated and so unassuming. His rash words to An'thor about Rih replacing him as general held more water than he initially thought. "Please."

Hylier ordered a few fingers of a sickly-sweet brown liquor and produced a battered deck of cards from his coat pocket. Over the next hour he proved a far better player than Keplan.

After his third mead, Keplan wondered if he may be drunk. He peered at the mug before him as if he suspected it of stealing his belt purse. "Except no one uses belt purses anymore," he lamented.

"Thieves' Hand: you've got three chances to beat me or I take the pot." Hylier threw down a stack of cards. "What was that about a purse?"

"N'one uses purses anymore," Keplan slurred. "Just pocketfolds. I walked out of the woods with archaic fashion and don't know if I'm embarrassed or annoyed."

"Go with the former."

Keplan frowned at the cards. "I'll never win."

"Three tries," Hylier reminded. "I've seen a game turn in one."

"With someone as unskilled as I am?"

"Can't you just—" The guard wiggled his fingers and a borrowed memory of Brentemir doing just that to his mother two decades before flickered beneath his thoughts.

"No. I can hardly control it on a good day and certainly not in a crowded bar. I'm bombarded. It's why I turned to drugs—you remember the drugs," he reminded conspiratorially.

"I do. You know, I think people like your bad fashion. Returning to your purse dilemma."

"My bad fashion—you're doing a poor job selling that gold rook's egg there, Hylier." He tossed down two cards he hoped added up to seventeen.

Hylier grinned and shook his head. "Two more tries, boy-o."

"Don't 'boy-o' me, I'm a king."

"Not tonight, you aren't. Kings don't lose at ruddy five in a bar."

"Watch me," Keplan muttered. Another two cards.

Hylier did not bother to tell him they neither added up to seventeen nor were valid to play during the contest phase of the game, but his smile said enough.

Keplan glowered, shoved the rest of his cards away, and called for a fourth ale. *Or is it my fifth?* "We're playing tiles next."

"Tiles? I've never played—"

"So it'll be just like ruddy five but you'll be losing instead of me," Keplan countered.

"Pay this round and you've a deal."

"I've paid for every round, as you're technically on duty." He frowned. "Drunk on duty, I might add."

Hylier wagged a hand at him. "I'm just the distraction."

"Evening, boys." A low voice cut through the banter and a tall woman slid onto the bench beside Keplan.

Keplan smiled at Sha's familiar warmth. "Evening, Sha. Didn't think I'd see you in here."

"Are you avoiding me?" She gasped playfully, flicking her bright blond wig over her shoulder.

"Hardly—don't you patronize the Hen?"

Her expression darkened. "Veska's not the tender there anymore. Some cobblehead took over, tossed most of us out for paying too little for our rooms. I tell you—no amount of money will buy you bread if there's no bread to be had."

"I'm sorry to hear—fates, manners. Sha, this is Captain Hylier—"

Hylier dismissed his late introduction. "We go way back, same neighborhood when I first arrived here. Is it Sha or Rheman tonight?"

"Sha if I've got my hair on," she answered with a sly smile. Under the table her leg brushed Keplan's. "So, what's our merchant son forgetting this evening?"

Hylier's eyes flicked to Keplan, drink making his tells more obvious. "Forgetting he's a merchant's son."

Sha snorted into her wine. "Wrong bar for that, though," she continued, voice dropping, "I'm glad to see you're not buying from Jolly Jeck anymore, as much as I miss seeing your face."

He winced. "I think it's best for everyone I'm no longer Jeck's patron."

"Rather," Sha agreed dryly. "Care for a dance, either of you?"

"You know me, won't pay for it."

"I only start charging when the bedroom door closes, Dill, and you've got to be the only soldier who takes that part of the conduct seriously."

"I'm up for a dance, though I promise I'll be terrible," Keplan offered.

"Perfect, you'll make me look charitable." She tugged his hand until he followed her out into the cleared area of the room where a dozen other couples already pranced to the off-tune flute. The song easily rolled into another and she draped one arm over his shoulder.

"My arm, I—"

Before he finished, she tucked his weak hand into the broad Banis belt. "That all right?"

He grinned and laced the fingers of his other hand through hers. "Thank you."

She stood at his eye level, dark gaze roving over his features but never leaving his face. "So does your handsome friend know you're not a merchant's son?"

"He's my personal guard. So yes. How'd you know I wasn't? I never told you—did I?" His times at the Fussy Fat Hen were a haze of saturated images too fast for him to properly untangle.

"I'm a student of disguise and costume, I notice when it doesn't quite fit. Besides, our conversations later were clear enough."

Keplan felt a flush pink his cheeks. "You think others notice?"

"Oh, surely, some. But not enough, and they don't care enough to make a fuss. They might know you don't fit here, but that doesn't mean they've gambled on who you really are. Plenty of folk don a persona for the night. You and I just take it another step."

"Sometimes I wonder which one's the real one. Who I really am."

Sha's smile was sad. Lantern light glanced off the sharp lines of her cheeks. "For most of us, sweetling, they both are and aren't at once. Most never truly fit where we are, no matter the hair and jacket we choose." She hesitated, then leaned forward and ghosted over his mouth with a kiss. Longing tugging his stomach. It wasn't the dizzying lurch caused by Firas's grin. Her lips were soft and invited more, but he pulled away. "Not tonight, Sha, I'm sorry."

"Maybe I'm just having fun."

"Maybe my heart's just too distant," he countered gently. "I understand if you'd rather dance with someone else, given—"

"I'm interested in more'n work, you fool," she teased. "Why don't you play a round of tiles with me, since you were so boastful to Dill, and we'll call it an evening."

"Fair," he agreed with a laugh, and led her back to the game.

Two hours later he rubbed his temple with one long finger and groaned. "Sha, I never would have agreed to this had I known you were a master."

"Master, hardly!" she protested. "Most clients enjoy a game or two, so I've had a lot of practice."

Dill's grin was wicked and he leaned forward. "With tiles, or..."

She batted at him with the sleeve of her jacket, now bundled on the table. "Ladies never tell. Who taught you, anyway? You seem to know half the rules and have made up a dozen others."

Keplan let a grin ease onto his face. "A stunning golden riah in the Banis palace stables."

Sha snorted and rolled her eyes. "Small wonder they made you king—you lie as good as any noble, even if you can't dance worth a Berrin bone."

He laid another tile down, watching as Hylier countered him, and Sha took the pot for the third time in a row. His purse was light, his stomach full, and his heart quiet. Loneliness nagged, but it was a gentle melancholy worth feeling for a while.

A large sailor thumped into the booth beside them, black braids still salt-stained. She waved for a bartender and caught Sha's eye. "Hello again."

Sha's smile brightened tenfold. "Chamon! I thought you were gone another three weeks!"

"King called us in on account of the God-tuppers and the general getting the axe. 'Nother fish-shat barricade, I imagine. I'm tired of bobbing in still waters."

Guilt flashed through Keplan at the woman's words. Knowing his choices had far-reaching consequences was one thing. Hearing it from the candid mouth of one of his subjects drove the point further home than he was used to.

Sha's eyes darkened and her smile was just for the sailor. "I know the feeling." At the sound of Keplan's next tiles hitting the table, she flushed and glanced back. "Lan, Dill, this is an old friend of mine, Captain Chamon Zhe. Chamon, this is Captain Dillane Hylier and his errant drinking partner, Lan Guardsen."

Keplan offered his hand in greeting. "I think we're about ready to totter off to bed, you two ought to catch up."

Hylier made a lewd, if discreet, gesture, and Keplan kicked him under the table.

Sha squeezed Keplan's hand in thanks and helped them gather their playing tiles. "It was lovely to talk tonight, though. If you're ever back in this area—"

"I'll find you. Thanks for the dance." He followed Hylier's weaving way through the clusters of tables and out into the soft air. He tilted his head back, breathing deep the smell of the stone and lantern oil, salt and ale. His city. *Home.* His gaze, unsupervised, wandered to the road leading down to the Slummer. His heart ached with the echo of Sha's words, her expression when she saw Chamon.

"You want to go somewhere else?" Hylier asked, following the path of Keplan's attention.

He lied for me. And if Rih's observation was correct, Firas had been at his bedside. Was it at Firas's urging that no one told him, or out of pity? Keplan heaved a sigh and turned back toward the palace. "Not tonight, no."

Φ

The 13th Day of Vurgmord, 1272
The City of Mirik

The path wound through the thick trunks of the red Mirikin trees. Bren tilted his head back to sniff the air. It was a beautiful morning. Orange backlit the boughs. Somewhere a stream trickled. He hiked upward, toward the center of the island, that sacred place, the navel of the world. A cold finger trailed down his spine and his steps quickened with the knowledge he had somewhere to be.

Rumbling grew behind him. His legs ached and he broke into a run. Rushing water turned into a roar. The hill became a cliff and he was scrambling up, up, palms torn by the rough brown rocks. When he hauled himself over the lip, his hands before him were sunken, wrinkled, and corded with tendons and veins. He shuddered, mesmerized and sickened at the new liver spots dotting his flesh.

Now he realized—he did not race toward something. He was running.

The Gate stood before him, the slab of black rock cracked, worn by rain and moss as he had left it years before. It was little more than a picnic spot, a meeting place for young lovers or thieves.

The sky glowed, the sun must have risen during his flight.

He staggered closer. The slab was not the Gate, instead it was a tombstone, broken, exposing the corpse beneath.

Bren's heart faltered at the familiar black hair. "Alea!"

Instead of pine and soil, sickly-sweet rot drifted on the wind. The brilliant glow through the trees was not dawn. It was an inferno.

He fell to his knees, scrabbling at the earth as if by freeing her it would make her less dead.

Her eyes flew open, silver blazing through black, rot and darkness marbling her skin. She screamed, lunging, and his world turned inside out.

Gasping, Bren flung himself from his bed and staggered down the hall to the ramparts. Sobs heaved his burning lungs. *Breathe,* he commanded himself. Stone bit into Bren's elbows where he leaned on the wall. Bitter air tugged at his sweat-drenched clothes, but even in the chill the air was sticky with salt and rank with the cloy of old cookfires. Below, the harbor sat empty. *How did it come to this?* His wife was leagues away, probably leaning on her ship's rail, staring at the stars on the sea. His Spy Master had all but resigned to fight a war he never foresaw. *And the only piece left of my sister is tethered to a throne I swore Keplan would never see.*

Overhead, clouds gathered. He watched them churn, stomach tight. The weather was wrong. Everything in his bones—the soldier, the reluctant sailor, even the superstitious—told him these were death throes of something mighty. Two decades before he had stood on the ramparts these replaced and watched the world mend. The islands half a dozen leagues away had rumbled and burst into being as his sister dissolved the barriers between worlds.

He still did not pretend to understand. The air smelled so fresh then. Vigor replaced withering. But now something had changed. Or rather, something had not. It was as if the blood flow had not crossed the boundaries, as if by pressing the fragments of the world together, their connection to life, or whatever it was that kept them all desperately clawing forward, had scarred over.

Atrophy.

"You miss her." Alleanthus propped himself on the wall with a soft sigh.

Bren lifted a shoulder in a shrug. He did not know which woman his son spoke of, and admitting that would be more telling than he cared for.

"She's reached the coast by now. Should be a bird any day now," Alleanthus continued.

Kemmer, then. "I suppose you're right. I hope the waters were kind. Storms are more common this time of year."

"Weather's been odd though. Never seen a winter so sullen."

Bren nodded. "I wish she would see my reasoning."

Al heaved a second, deeper sigh. "You know I don't agree with you, not wholly, on this."

"I know, I just—I have this nagging sense that something's coming. Something's wrong, I—" His words died and he peered against the night. A flicker against the clouds. Not lightning but fire. "There, did you see that?"

His son leaned forward, but fatigue, not curiosity, pinched his eyes. "I don't see anything."

"There!" Bren insisted. "The clouds."

"It's snow lightning," Alleanthus protested.

Apprehension tightened Bren's stomach. Despite the hot air, gooseflesh dimpled his arms beneath his shirt. "It's over Le'yne. I dreamt of her. It's why I woke. She was screaming, calling for me—"

"You've dreamt of her every month for as long as I can remember!" he lamented. "I remember Mother pulling you away from the ramparts countless nights. I found you asleep up here half a dozen times. How many times did you take a rowboat and go out there just to bob in the water, staring, until dawn?"

"Al, this is different—"

"How many times?"

Bren looked away.

Alleanthus straightened. "I'm going inside. I've a meeting with the Berrin ambassador tomorrow and I'm exhausted." He paused at the landing just below, jaw clenched. "Don't be a fool, Father. You've spent so much time in the past you've failed to notice the present."

Bren did not answer, and when he finally turned to look, his older son was gone. His focus swiveled back to the dark and distant island. He knew what he saw. Lightning flickered across the sky in cool white. This was fire, writhing through the clouds, winding like wind, like a bird.

Like Arman.

Distant rumbling drifted across the water with the scent of salt—not the fresh ocean smell from just off the harbor. This was something else, a deeper, older note, underscored by stone and fire. "Toar," he whispered. His knees creaked as he rushed down the stairs. He did not bother with a cloak, though he knew once out on the water he would regret the choice.

It took half an hour to navigate to their personal berth on the northern tip of the docks. Without the looming warships, his own schooner looked quite tall. He nodded to the guard and strode up the gangway. By now the guards and dockhands knew better than to ask, than to question. He ignored their pointed glances and set about casting off.

Regardless of his son's accusation, Bren had set foot on Le'yne only once before. Several years after his sister disappeared into the south, he slipped out to the island. There amidst black stone he hoped to find something, anything that might bring her back to him.

Wind hissed through the frozen grasses, gray against the black night. Bren let the boat bob for a moment, listening to the slapping waves against the lacquered wood before pushing the bow onto the gravel strand. The place felt entirely different this time. His boots hit the beach and he paused, listening for an echo, a welcome, perhaps. *I have to be mad to sail this far on a whim and a flicker of light.* His gut told him, though, that more than madness drove him across the waves. Some may have forgotten the oldest deities, those that came before the gods of his childhood. He had not.

"Alea?" His whisper was loud against that of the wind, and just as lonely. He dragged the boat higher before trudging up the narrow path in the ragged black cliffs.

Each bootfall tugged his mind backward into memories. Waving goodbye as Alea embarked for Athrolan. Finding her body on the strand. *Step.* Dancing with her, poorly, in the Athrolani palace. Hunkering under the tents at Fort Shadow, watching the rain. *Step.* Watching her rip lightning from the sky as they sailed across the Iron Sea. *Step.* Looking up at her eyes for the first time as he knelt before her in the woods. He swiped at his cheeks. Somehow, under the pressure of war, their two years together crystalized into something purer than most of his other relationships.

"It's not real!" Kemmer shouted at him. "The only reason why your adoration lasted this long is her absence makes her perfect! You don't have to compromise or get angry like you do with every other relationship. Your love for her replaced your faith in the gods and it's just as ignorant as it was then."

"Faith isn't ignorant!"

"Yours is!"

A stair crumbled beneath his boot and he caught himself on a ledge. Stone ripped the meat of his palm and he spat a curse. *Focus, you brute.* He picked the worst of the grit from the wound and hauled himself the last few paces to the clifftop.

Time ought to have softened the stones, coaxed grasses from the roads, weathered the wood to gray slivers. Le'yne had not changed. Despite the wind, the air was close, stale, as if the breeze circulated but never brought fresh air in. *It's how the rest of the world feels, too.* Strangled. Stagnant. He turned slowly in the central square. Thunderous energy threatened to pluck the taught string of his body.

It was not a human voice that growled through the night, but something bitter and full of change. "Evening, Harvest Pig."

Blood of a Hundred
Queens

CHAPTER SEVENTEEN

The 13th Day of Vurgmord, 1272
The Isle of Le'yne

EVERY HAIR ON BREN'S graying head rose. His boots stilled their turning. Jaundice-gold eyes flickered in a shadow that once belonged to ruins. Then sickening darkness peeled from the black around it and formed familiar shoulders and ragged hair. "Arman?"

"Barrackborn." Coals bloomed with the breath in each word, then faded back into darkness. The air around them flickered with fire. "Wondered if you'd see us."

Us. "She's here too?"

Arman stepped into the square fully. Fire and stone etched the suggestion of a body, but more for the empty space where organs and bones ought to be than for any true corporeal form. With the crackle of firewood settling into embers, he jerked a nod to the hill beyond. "Much as I am."

Bren staggered up the hill, following the cluster of ashes and charred bone that left soot streaks but no footprints. He expected embraces. Remarks about how gray their hair had turned or the lines on their faces.

The hall loomed from the clotted clouds, silhouetted with the shuddering fire flitting through the air. He could not shake the sense that he did not walk behind Arman so much as through him. The hall door stood ajar, and a slick trail of oily water led inside.

The years had not been kind to the building. Mold and mildew's earthy rot clung to every corner, and the stench of low tide lingered in the air. Glowering fire licked at damp lichen, and hunks of peat and frozen grass clustered in the center of the hall. There was ferocity in the sacrilege of building a campfire in a temple. *I guess it's not sacrilege if the temple's yours.* He reached to pull his cloak tighter, belatedly remembering he had not brought one.

A moist heap of mildew and algae bubbled up and out until it took the shape of a hunched boneless back and naked scalp. Finding her took twenty years, but the slumped figure across the fire made him wonder if she was still lost to him.

He eased closer, crouching, then shuffling forward on his knees. The stone under his worn hands was achingly cold. His teeth chattered and hoar frost rimmed his watering eyes. He stopped his advance when his longest finger was a breath from the gleaming black claw sprouting from her mildewed bone. "Sistermine."

Her lidless eyes rolled up with a squelch. *Brentemir.*

His laugh tumbled across the inches between them until, dusty, it resembled a sob. "I looked for you."

I know.

Bren leaned forward, but as much as he longed to touch her, his animal self was repulsed, horrified. Drowning had always terrified him. Hundreds of questions flitted through his mind, but none seemed important anymore. How did you ask a titan gone to seed whether she was happy? How she passed the twenty years since they last spoke? Whether she had found peace? The answer to that last one crouched on the flagging before him.

"Why are you here?" It did not escape him that, after decades of searching, he only found her when she wanted him to. There was no sudden whim that would drag her back into his life. "Is it Keplan?"

Bone crunched and smoke billowed as Arman turned to him. "So you've seen him too, spoken with him?"

Is he all right?

Bren winced at the bellowing in his head between the avalanche and typhoon of their voices. "He's king of Athrolan, though I imagine you knew that."

"Raven told us."

Bren glanced up. "As in the former commander? When did you see him?"

"Before now," Arman answered, frowning. "Time is slippery, like our forms. But we were traveling from Neneviir and he saw our fire. Told us Keplan was king. That your plotting?"

"An'thor's," Bren countered. "I tried to keep him safe, off the throne. Alas, I'm realizing with my boys, too, that they've become their own people when I wasn't looking." *When I was looking for you.*

Boys? Something that tasted of longing dusted the air with snow.

"Two. Sons. Alleanthus and Azimir. Azimir's almost a year younger than Keplan, actually." Every conversation, every shared childhood milestone they never shared, pressed on the space between them. Bren's breath was thin and gasping.

Is he all right? Alea repeated.

How did you explain to a mother that her son was temperamental, married, and accused of murder? That he almost died at the hand of the priest devoted to his existence? *You let him do it like the coward you are.* "Did you come to get him?"

We came because the world is ending and where else do we go but here, where it began?

Bren shuddered at Arman's stone-rattle chuckle. "I imagine you've noticed."

Bren shrugged. "Mirik is at war. Athrolan almost was, twice. Those who aren't starving fear for their lives." He had rehearsed this reunion countless times, yet here he was, discussing politics like he sat opposite any other dignitary. He pounded on the stone with a frustrated rumble. "I'm not telling you news you could hear at any bar!"

The cold sharpened around him, frost turning to icicles. *If you think we could enter any bar and ask the news looking like we do, then these last year haven't been kind to your mind. What aren't you telling me?*

"This is ridiculous, acting like this is fine, like you aren't rotting before my eyes, like you still have bodies, like you're still the people who left twenty-one years before. Like I haven't spent my life praying I'll see you again only to find this! Pretending you'll board a ship and walk up to the palace gates of Athrolan to have tea with your maniac son."

What he could barely call Alea lunged at him. Cold erupted in his chest. Decay writhed in his nostrils and lungs. Lightning exploded in his eyes, dancing across the soft gray of his brain before flickering over his skin and retreating. His body shuddered with intimate condemnation.

Guilt clawed like vomit up his throat. His mouth was too busy screaming to apologize, but her fury lessened a fraction. Stillness held Bren for a moment, an apology in itself. She was a starless sky, and he nothing.

It lasted seconds, surely, but when his vision cleared the fire was low, and neither of them were anywhere to be seen. His spirit was too weak from relief to gather the shards of his broken heart.

Φ

The 17th Day of Vurgmord, 1272
The City of Ceir Athrolan, Athrolan

Rih watched the guards take An'thor from the palace. His shoulders were slumped but his jaw clenched. Age-yellow hair blew away from his face. *Am I missing something, being so young?* How could one have lived so long and not see beauty in humanity's frailty and imperfection? The defiant line of An'thor's back, the certain one of Keplan's in the courtyard, showed her the faint steps the emperor must have taken.

Beyond the walls, a train of wagons rocked east. Two thousand soldiers were scattered across the Banis grasslands, hearts hammering with the same devotion and ferocity as hers. Looking out at Athrolan's harried king, she wondered at their similarities. There was beauty in the undiscerning violence of the king's actions.

Keplan turned and his stare settled on hers through the misted glass. He raised a hand. An'thor was jerked onto the street. Another twenty guards fell in around him, but Keplan's eyes remained on Rih.

She had moved to the orchid alcove when Azimir found her a few minutes later. "That was hard to watch," he began without greeting.

"I didn't know you were there."

Azimir shrugged. "Like you, I didn't brave the wind. Just watched from the stables. I'm honestly not certain how to feel." He paused. "Is this all right, my signing? If you'd rather call Bimet—"

She pressed a hand to his to still the nervous words. "This is fine. Just slowly and with confidence."

Azimir's cautious smile broadened. "I'll try that."

"What's making you feel uncertain?"

"An'thor. He put my name on an assassin's list. Simply because he thought I—or my father, more likely—would influence Keplan against him. Or perhaps temper the monstrosity he hoped Kep would become. But I was raised in the shadow of heroes, and one of them was him."

"I think I'd know how to feel. If someone sentenced me to a life of pain not from hatred, but from indifference."

He glanced up from her hands, eyes dark and soft. "I'm sorry you're here, when you hate it."

"I'm not. Out of all the ill fates, I chose this one. I love home and miss it deeply, but the way it looks now, it's a world where I don't fit. A child of so many things and none of them entire." A wave of grief swept over her, for Ilfald and for everything the woman had symbolized to Rih. *I don't fit here, either.*

"I understand that." When her brows raised in invitation, he continued, "My father—he's entrenched in history. Mostly because of his sister. Toar, there wasn't a month that he didn't bring it up or develop a new attempt to find her. Keplan distracted him, but now that he's on the throne it's almost worse, as if the Dhoah' Laen will drag Keplan off the throne like an errant market boy, and then we'll all be happy."

"He says it a lot—we'll be happy again. But I've been happy, and Al's been happy. And my ma, too. But I look at this world—Mirik, Athrolan, Ban, even—these mighty nations decaying from within, people lost and starving and dying and I don't understand how these men don't see it. They want to bring glory back? Well glory brought us here. I'm tired of glory. Of heroes. None of it's real. Not really. Not to the people who matter. The people left behind." His shoulders slumped with fatigue. "I'm rambling."

"You always ramble." Rih turned away, heart pounding. If he had reached into her mind and drawn out the threads of everything that drove her to start the rebellion, his words would not have been truer. She moved deeper into the alcove. Smoky glass shielded the lamps, and pools of water, heated until they steamed, humidified the air. *People in the city drink boiled seawater and here, orchids have steam baths.*

When she looked back, his dark brows were dipped in a frown.

"Did I say something to offend you? You look sad."

"Thoughtful," she explained. "Your words in this room speak to my heart. I miss Ban. I miss my sisters-in-arms. I miss my rude, arrogant cousin. I miss the bathhouses and the brilliant green of the thousands of gardens. I miss the smell and the heat. My heart aches because the very things I seek to save and protect might be destroyed."

His fingers traced a broad, waxy leaf before he signed. "Destroyed because of our parents' war?"

Aim. Breathe. She thought of Majilah Ag, of Il-fald, of every woman who gasped her last in Rih's arms, every starving child in Stytown. Bimet would say it was too soon, but the wheels of war churned ever on, and Rih would have to move or risk being crushed beneath them. "I fear they will be lost when my rebel army takes RoBal."

Azimir stared at the pool before them, lips motionless, hands still. His steady eyes told her he did not for a moment think she was joking. After the space of several breaths, he voiced, "The network across Ban is yours, then?" When she blinked at him in surprise, he smiled. "I was in the market, caught a couple signs that were unfamiliar. But I pieced enough together to learn that someone is trying to topple Ban. It's the benefit of everyone thinking I'm a yammering blockhead. They think I don't notice."

"It's my network, and I planted the seeds before I ever came here, before I knew about Keplan, when the marriage in question was to you."

"How many allies do you have?" His questions were not mocking, but cautiously curious.

"Majilah Ag, queen of the Vales, for one. And a few thousand of the Banis troops. My cousin Mosil, the Banis ambassador to Mirik." Her instincts burst to life and her hands stilled. Bimet would be furious.

"It would have been so much easier had we married." He looked at the orchids, expression distant. "There'd be no secrecy. I know you have no interest in sex or heirs, but all I want is to talk with you. To sit in silence when the light grows dim. To laugh and debate and stand side by side. It might be incredible hubris when you have no interest in the last god this world will ever see, but—"

"Are you asking me to marry you?"

"I don't think so." He raked a hand through his hair, and she could see him, decades from now, lounging in her study in RoBal, ranting about something inconsequential. "I wish to be useful to you. I wish to help you carry whatever load you'll have, whether you're a refugee or the Banis empress."

Blood thundered in her chest. "Is this an elaborate request to be my ally?"

He dropped to one knee. "An ally, surely. But your friend. Your champion. Whatever path you take won't be a life of peace. But you deserve it, after everything you've done and witnessed. And I find myself wanting nothing more than to give you that. And be beside you for the fleeting tranquility and the sea of blood."

A proposal was something she never thought to see and never particularly wanted. But here was a man, a clever one, one who made her laugh, asking if she kindly would consider him not as a husband, but as a partner. "I accept."

His tan face broke into a bright smile and he rose to embrace her. When he pulled away, though, concern once more laced his features. "Have you told Kep?"

"His entire platform is peace. Even if he's failed in that. He might have allied with Ban in a time of war, but he's pointedly remaining neutral. And he hates Ban. I still can't believe I told you."

"I wouldn't have told me at first either. Yammering blockhead, remember?" His grin faded. "He hates Ban, and when you're done with it, it won't look the same. I imagine he'll appreciate that."

"Azi, this entire movement, it's carefully orchestrated, every move calculated—"

"I won't tell anyone. Not unless you ask me to. I meant what I said about being your champion. Your friend."

"There is one thing." She drew a steadying breath and loosed her mental arrow. "I have an offer for your mother."

Φ

The 19th Day of Vurgmord, 1272
"There's something for you, sire." Hylier poked his head into the study. "From your priests."

Keplan glared, yanking the folded letter out of his captain's hand. "They aren't my anything. I doubt they'd even call themselves that."

Hylier snorted and sat uninvited in the chair.

The parchment was old, dingy, as if previous ink had been blotted out to make room for this message. No greeting, just a line.

She's asking for you.

Keplan's gut growled with dread. "I have to go."

Hylier heaved himself up and reached for his hat.

"Alone."

He frowned. "I don't care if you're the most terrifying thing on those streets. I'm not letting you walk into the Slummer all by your lonesome. I don't have to follow you in, but I'm going too."

It was too much of a hassle to argue, and frankly Keplan did not want to walk into a trap. *Who knows the city's opinion of what happened with Domariigo.* Still, something in the note nagged at him. It was as if the prophet's thoughts were so heavy, so strong, they flavored the paper beneath Mel's pen. He pulled on his jacket, more for comfort than warmth. "Just to the door."

Barkers shouted that the king would dismantle the government next, like Mirik. Others claimed he planned to make Azimir the next general. One argued the king was not innocent, but An'thor had taken the fall to protect him.

Keplan shuddered. Neither spoke as they walked, and he wondered if Hylier felt whatever it was that tainted the letter. Maybe the man had lived a life so full of joy that he did not recognize despair. *Has anyone?*

Mel greeted them again, but this time no drinks awaited. Cheekbones were crags on his sallow face. "That was quick."

Keplan did not answer, just shot Hylier a glance that commanded solitude, and pushed into the room. It was much the same, though there were a few new blankets.

"Hela." Her name sprang unbidden from his lips.

"Gods' Blood."

"Mel said you asked for me." He knelt beside her, reaching.

"A painful life doesn't leave much in the way for kindness, eh? Just look at yourself." One thin hand ran up his own weakened arm.

"The symbolism is a bit heavy. Even for someone as melodramatic as me."

Chipped brown teeth punctuated her smile. She pushed herself up, entire form trembling. Keplan knew better than to help. She settled finally, a few inches higher than before. "There. Do you remember what I told you?"

"About returning the power to the world? I recite it every evening before bed," he whispered. "Not really, not aloud. But I remember."

She shook her head. "What I tried to tell you through Nena'phe. Through Mel, though he's bad at making friends. What I hauled my withered self all the way here to get you to hear."

Keplan sat back. "You went to war over it, which I disagree with."

"They may have gotten carried away, but the world is listening to you now. They think you have a plan. All those pretty dreams in your head," she tapped his temple, "you can let them out now. And they will listen."

"I've never liked scripture." She beckoned, and, with a scowl, he began. "The One True God will rise where the worlds meet, from death and birth, from chaos and order. His blood pools, drowning the world even as it gives it life. Though he will bear the marks of hate, he will be unable to raise its tools. Then the bit about mercy and hands and wrath."

"But there's more. You never let them finish. 'He will cast aside mortality once when death is chosen for him, once when death is begged of him, and once when he chooses death for himself.' She will wither and die without blood. Blood that began you, began us."

"My parents. And you. And me." Certainty slid into his chest and he drew a ragged breath. "We have to end."

"Oblivion."

"Why ask me? Why when you could simply step from a bridge, from the harbor gates, or find a knife, a rope. There are a hundred ways to end your life, if you wished. I know. I've thought of them all in the small hours of the night."

She looked away, then her pale, bulging eyes met his. "There's one last thing. You came to me weeks ago seeking answers. And I gave you what you asked for, if not what you wanted. Now I've had time to think. Time to judge you further. I see what you're doing. You mean to bring peace. Like your errant general begged of you—you will rip it from the world."

"If I have to."

"You wouldn't plan for the future if you were meant to let the world wither."

He smiled. "No."

"How do you hear thoughts best? Touch?"

"It helps with objects. Never tried it much with people. The few I've touched have been in passion—romantic or otherwise."

"Killing, you mean."

"Yes."

"Words don't do it justice, words you won't believe. You have to see it. There are echoes of the Laen's power still in me. I'm offering you the answer you seek about what comes after. What you are. But in return I want you to take my life." He barely felt her paper skin as she pressed her brittle hand to his limp one.

Images exploded in his mind. Everywhere. Everywhen. Life surged in him. Blood burst from the riverbeds, overflowing, hot and rich and healthy. Millions of birdsongs rang in his head, thoughts racing and plunging and full of the frantic madness of simply living. His body flushed and hardened with the vitality of an entire world.

Her fingers clenched, and he spiraled inward, through their skin and wound into the lace of her capillaries. What did his mother's look like? There, in the center, was a silver seed, pulsing with her heart, a forgotten embryo of power. *Ma pulled the souls from the gods.* Hela did not deserve that. No one did. Instead, Keplan tugged the seed. It loosened, tendrils gripping her soul for a moment before loosening further. He tucked it into the weakened flesh of his mental palm, blazing emerald in his mind's eyes.

The sensation of tendons and trachea beneath his grip flashed, but he pushed it away. *Mercy.*

When he opened his eyes, her head was cradled in his lap. Her breath was faint but there. He might not be able to save himself or his parents, so entangled with their titanic power, but he would permit himself this one tiny mercy.

He rose and slipped out before she woke. Mel glowered at him as he shut the door quietly. "She's asleep, thank you."

The Nenev returned to cleaning the barrel of his dismantled revolver. "I want to thank you."

"For?" Keplan asked.

"Seeing my uncle for the monster he really is. Not many look past the shiny legends."

Keplan snorted. *I just recognized myself in him and acted accordingly.* "I guess legends never impressed me all that much."

"Well, whatever the reason, thank you." He spun the revolver's barrel. "I don't expect we'll be seeing much of each other after all this comes crashing down. One way or another."

"No, I don't imagine so." Keplan stuck out his hand on impulse. It did not matter that the man was a fanatic, that he pulled the trigger that cost Keplan his arm. "Luck and love go with you."

Mel's grin was crooked as he took the hand. "You too, God's Blood."

It was only when they were out of the Slummer that Hylier asked, "What did she need?"

Peace. "There's such power that once belonged to the world—my parents'. Mine. Hers. And I'm the one who returns it."

"She returned her Laen powers to you?"

"Not me exactly." Keplan glanced at his hand. He wondered if his flesh looked any different inside, where energy still buzzed. "I'm just carrying them for a while. Safe keeping, you might say. Until the end."

Hylier looked away. "I thought that wasn't going to become a habit."

Keplan stopped, colorless eyes fixing on the captain. "I didn't kill her. She asked me to. It would have been a mercy. But they aren't the same, not by a longbow shot."

"I suppose there's a difference between mercy and murder, in the end."

Keplan's blood hummed, and his skin still flamed with hope. "Just depends on the hand you use."

Φ

The 23rd Day of Vurgmord, 1272

Rih adjusted her new hat and shifted in the saddle. It was not often that she rode, but like every Banis child, she grew up on the back of a riah. Ahead, Azimir bounced along on his cob, trying in vain to have a conversation with Bimet.

Keplan's letters had been unexpected, but the request even more so. *Please meet me at the Tomb of Madness to the south of the city. Noon.* Other than the incident with the dog, she had yet to be outside the walls. The trees pressed in, spindly white trunks like bones jutting from the earth. Even with the bright sun, winter was unwilling to relinquish its hold. At least the soft wool was warm, if a little itchy. Her eyes settled on Bimet. Since their time in RoBal, the woman had changed. Withdrawal into reservations and fear. Rih shared her fears, but somehow Bimet could no longer see the way through them.

Another twist in the road and they emerged on the bare hilltop. Blackened trunks ringed the weathered stone of the monument.

Keplan perched on the top, legs crossed, looking out at the city below. His face was as thin as ever, but there was a light in his eyes she had not seen before. He was smiling. "Morning, Your Highness."

Bimet turned quickly, dropping her horse's reins to translate.

Rih responded before slipping off and tying her mount to a tree. She climbed the rest of the way on foot, pausing at the base of the monument. "Is there room for all of us or are you coming down?"

Keplan dropped, landing clumsily. He settled himself at the base in the same fashion, waiting to say more until both she and Azimir sat alongside him. "I'm sorry for the odd request. I just couldn't think down there anymore. And I knew I needed my wits for this."

Azimir nudged her knee with his. "Go on," he signed.

Bimet caught her eye and shook her head. The woman's lips thinned with displeasure. "Not yet."

Keplan looked between the signs. "Would someone enlighten me?"

"There's been a lot of turmoil lately. But I had a favor to ask of you. As your ally." She swallowed. "As your wife."

"Does this have to do with the missing fireshells?"

Fear pulsed up Rih's spine and she dared not look at Bimet. He was just testing. There was no way he knew. Rih did not move. Not even an eyelid flickered. Her long fingers curled, twisted, then tapped her temple, her lips. "I don't know what you mean."

"Over a hundred are missing and my personal guard noticed several Banis textile workers removing chests from both your rooms and those of Bimet." He placed his red hand over his green, the image of patience. "No one carries bolts of cloth or last year's summer dresses that carefully, Rih. I'm at a bit of a loss—my wife is stealing weapons from me. Orchestrating a rebellion. Might be bedding my cousin while I'm not looking."

Despair sank in her gut, and she fought the urge to shut her eyes and end the conversation. The distant contempt she felt for An'thor, all his plotting laid bare as he was hauled from the palace, now turned on her.

There was no point in pretending anymore. She was a soldier, a warrior. She knew when a new battlefield dictated a change in tactics. "All I knew was you had powerful parents and were seventeen. I gambled on a foolish child king. I thought the isolation here would make me invisible. If nothing else, I thought I might be able to seduce you into my cause. Enough to turn the bloody tides in my favor."

"Keplan, listen to her." Azimir leaned forward, finally interjecting. "We came to ask you to help. She means to topple Ban. And she already has the Vales."

"I'm not bedding Azi," she retorted. "But he swore fealty to my cause. I penned a letter asking his mother's support just two days ago."

Bimet's fingers were hard on her wrist. "You did what?"

Rih turned to her interpreter. "I know you've cautioned me to be careful, not to trust, not to move too quickly, but Bimet, if I don't move, we'll be trapped here forever."

She felt Bimet's gaze on her, but she met Keplan's overlarge colorless eyes. "Half your moves are a disaster, an unplanned but necessary dismantling. I see it because I'm weaving the same thing for my own people. You don't have a general—give me half that power, a quarter, and I'll win every battle Athrolan faces, just let me help my people. Fates!" She waved her arms. "You tolerated Domariigo for far too long, and I can promise I'd make a better general than a drunk murderer."

"Do you know why I asked you here?"

She shook her head.

"Athrolan is too bogged in tradition. It's killing her just as much as my blood is killing the world. I think I'm ready to be done with traditions entirely." His ice-chip eyes flicked to Rih's dark gaze and he lifted his chin. "What happens when you reach RoBal? If you win?"

She had yet to see the vicious and terrified boy she married. It was as if he died on the battlefield, leaving Keplan behind.

"When," she corrected, the sign gentle. "We will win."

"What happens to the Emerald Throne?"

She frowned. "I've brought us this far. I'll see it through."

"In my infinite hubris I thought I was the only one who could fix this mess. I was wrong. My parents' mess is mine, but this one? This is all on Athrolan." His face was unreadable, eyes distant glaciers in the snowfield of his face. "There's another battle coming, one humans can't fight. Like you, I know it's one I can win. But there will be nothing left of me."

Azimir blanched. "You don't know that. You can't. Your father lived through two deaths already—"

"And so did I. Apparently we get three."

Rih set that information aside to ponder later. "That leaves Athrolan without a king. Again."

"I'm not what Athrolan needs. She doesn't need a god on a throne, casting mercy and wrath in turns until the world topples. You saved us from the Swordbearers. From war with Ban. It wasn't my faith, my choice. It was your strength. Your planning. You allied with Mirik when His Eminence couldn't. I brought as much violence to the throne as I did peace. There's a world I can see so brilliantly in my mind."

Tears trickled down his cheeks, pausing in the hollows of his scars. "The plains are golden with grain. Not Banis grain, but not Athrolani. The ocean is filled with fish, clear and dark and treacherous. The Berme's Eye is filled with fishes and kelp. Marshes overflow with life. Writhing with abundance. Of course, there's pain—you can't have life without pain—but it's just the usual ache of existence. Not this clamor, this scrabbling. I can feel the air on my face. The whole world, it teems."

Beside her, Azimir squeezed her hand.

"Is it memory or the future?"

"It's not a memory." Keplan repeated the second sign. "What's that one?"

She did it again. "It's our word for fate, or future. It's closer to the meaning for promise."

"It's a promise." Keplan smiled. "Is fifty thousand enough?"

"Pardon?"

"The entire Athrolani army. The navy too—that's another twenty thousand." He slipped the signet ring from his hand gently and offered it to her. "Take my throne instead of my hand, and wreak fire over every man who ever spilt blood that wasn't his own."

Disbelief swirled in her chest, billowing her heart almost like hope. *He can't be serious.* She did not trust him, but perhaps together, they could carve a suitable world from this dying, poisoned thing. Beside her, Bimet's pinched face paled with resigned horror. "Unite them under one crown, under one woman's rule, one woman's strength."

"You've thought about this," Azimir whispered to her.

"When you appeared on the road that day, begging for help. I know there's a line of heirs, but in that moment it was only us. I knew if Keplan died someone would be forced to wrestle the reins from General Domariigo." Her entire body trembled. Ban was one thing. This was something else entirely.

"You've proven you know what you're doing, certainly more than I have. You see the same future as I do. And you've already begun carving a path. What do you say?"

The ring was cold in her hand, even after resting in his palm. She ran a thumb over the sigil. *Dream bigger.* "I swear to honor her, as long as I reign."

CHAPTER EIGHTEEN

The 23rd Day of Vurgmord, 1272
The City of Ceir Athrolan, Athrolan

KEPLAN'S NEXT WORDS DROWNED in screaming. Beneath them, the ground shook. Every shudder released something in him, a popped joint no longer stiff with disuse.

Loose pebbles jittered across the exposed bedrock. He pressed his hand to it. Magma surged far below, pulsed in an approaching rhythm.

"What is it?" Azimir asked. His blocky hand rubbed at the back of his own neck. Did his muscles feel the tension in the earth? Rih looked between them in concern.

"Someone's screaming." Keplan looked to Rih and tapped his temple. "In here. It just goes on and on."

Trembling came again, stronger. Trees quaked on the surrounding hillside. Dead leaves and seedpods shook from their anchors. To the east, clouds clotted the sky.

The uncertain feeling when he glimpsed a mirror was nothing compared to the uneasiness in his shoulders. Lightning crackled through the black thunderheads and they billowed higher. *Thud.*

"All right, that I heard." Azimir hauled himself up, dropping his weight as if he stood on a ship's deck. He offered Bimet's reins to her, but the translator spat at his feet, jerking the leather from his hands. She did not sign her hissed words, nor could Keplan hear them, but he caught enough to know it was a curse.

Rih's hand was hard on his arm. Her fingers moved rapidly but calmly.

Azimir glanced over, shouting the translation from the tree line. "She said there's more to discuss, we ought to keep this to ourselves for the time being."

Keplan nodded. A roar went up and they all ducked. Gouts of flame lit the roiling clouds from within.

"Toar, what is this? An attack?"

Uneasiness was replaced with certainty, with longing, with a thunderous need to protect. Keplan grimaced. Those were not his feelings, but he knew them. They formed the lace inside his bones, the salt in his blood. "These are the heroes everyone prayed for."

Keplan flung himself onto Theriim's back, grateful he took An'thor's horse that morning. His knees pressed and the charger took off, scattering fallen gold leaves and dry soil as they pelted down the hillside. He bent lower, red hand fisted in the gray's mane. A scan of the aqueducts told him nothing had fallen yet, no towers were toppled.

By the time they burst from the trees and onto the swath of fields surrounding the city, ice crystals filled the bitter air. Another man might think this was judgement, dealt for his disregard of tradition, his condemnation of An'thor, or any number of terrible choices. Salt hung in the air, rank, as if low tide had exposed the decades of sludge and navy trash at the bed of the harbor. On the tail of it came the scent of burned flesh, dead earth. The cloy of scorched hair. Keplan's stomach roiled and he clenched his teeth against a surge of bile. *Thud.*

It was not his voice screaming, he realized. But a voice he knew intimately, a voice that sat in his head more often than not. One that murmured lullabies off-tune when he could not sleep.

Air whipped without any proper direction, uncertain and anxious. Atop the city walls soldiers attempted to wrest rusted weapons from their sheaths. Keplan dragged Theriim's head about. Black oily smoke wound from the eastern tree line, where the road disappeared between twisted boles. Putrid water trickled up from between the road's cobbles, from beneath the palace foundation.

"Something's in the trees!" The cry arched from the ramparts and soldiers massed above. Torches appeared, and arrows were lit. Hylier's bright hair gleamed as he shouted orders. Metal screamed, new rust raining across the cobblestones as the gate groaned shut. Guards milled, faces pinched in fear, eyes vacant. *What's wrong with them?*

"Stop!" Keplan drove Theriim toward the east gate, but no one seemed to hear.

Azimir's cob thundered up beside him. The young man's face was streaked with sweat and his cheeks were bloodless. "Kep, turn back!" A wet splat heralded his cousin losing his lunch.

"It's not an attack!" he insisted.

Azimir wheeled back, motioning for Rih to follow him toward the gates. A Banis whistle sounded. Azimir's voice cut over the clamor, translating as they thundered toward the city. "Open the gates!"

Frustration knotted Keplan's stomach. His bones knew. His blood answered. Through the stench of rot and creosote he caught the comfort of his childhood hearth and his father's cooking. Two figures appeared on the road. Theriim shrieked, shying from them. *Thud.*

The journey from Neneviir on horseback would have taken months, but they did not ride. With each step the man's feet turned to stone, then back to blackened flesh. Every step sent convulsions through the earth. *Thud.* Infection raged where his sallow skin was not burned. Cold cracked stone covered the hand knotted with hers.

Black lines radiated across Alea's frozen skin. Long hair hung lank over her abraded scalp. Horror twisted Keplan's gut, but not because of what he saw approaching. Leastwise, not out of disgust.

"It's not an attack," Keplan whispered, though no one could hear over the moaning wind. It whipped around the figures, ripping features from them as water vapor and smoke, replacing them a second later. He tumbled from Theriim's bucking back and staggered forward on foot.

Keplan met them on the outskirts of the cemetery. His father's too-hot hand gripped the king's limp left wrist, thumb rubbing a circle like it had when he could not sleep as a child. He fell into Alea's arms, heedless of the sickening softness of her body or the magma burbling in the cracks on his father's hand. Saltwater dampened his jacket where his mother's face pressed into his shoulder. Whatever battered organ still served as his heart shuddered and broke. *Ma.*

Φ

The Northern Banis Coast

Ajat wiped sweat from her face. The air was cool, still damp with rain, but the march strained her joints. Fifty years was a bit old for marching, in her mind.

Her eyes bored into Sefer's back. Betrayal did not bother her. Not from an emotional standpoint, at least. Only logistically. *So did Kemmer put a strike on me, or was it Bren?* Either was likely, but for entirely different reasons. Kemmer concerned her more.

They crested a hill and turned west. The Banis coast dropped away to the north, rolling dunes dotted with reeds and flushed with color. She raised her nose and breathed the rich salt. She had missed the ocean.

Beyond, backed by the clouds that would bring that afternoon's rain, was the Mirikin fleet. The few ships made decades before against Berrin attack now numbered several hundred. She squinted, but the haze concealed which bore the brilliant vermillion pennant of the Hetmir.

Noticing her steps had slowed, Oland glanced back at her, brows knit. "You all right?"

She scowled and did not answer, but picked up the pace.

He dropped back to ride beside her. "It's not personal. Promise. Just a job."

She added a bit more venom to her glare. "You torched my cousin's village and crushed her husband's skull to find me. You might not consider it personal, but I will."

"I still enjoyed our time together, our nights—"

"I'd stop, unless you want vomit on your horse's pretty hooves." She spat a dusty glob onto the ground to punctuate her words.

He opened his mouth, then shut it and nudged his horse back into place. Ahead, Oland let out a whistle, and they cut north along a packed trail through the dunes. Below, pulled onto the strand, sat a rowboat.

A plain canvas tent stood beside it, undyed to blend into the white sand.

There's the orange flag. Ajat fixed her hard gaze on the fluttering strip of fabric that denoted who, exactly, waited for her. Sand hissed from around her boots, and the ropes around her wrists bit at her skin when she stumbled over the soft ground. The other handful of prisoners fell into a narrow line as they wound through the dunes.

"For the Hetmir!" Oland called.

"For freedom!" The answer went up from the guards ranging around the tent. A canopy was strung over the tent's entrance, a small cookfire built just outside. A stringy hare was stretched on a spit, fat and juices sizzling onto the tired coals.

Ajat rolled her eyes. She never understood armies. Comradery was one thing, but trusting someone and holding them above others simply for their rank in a fabricated hierarchy would never be logical. They stopped under the awning and she relaxed in the momentary shade. The hot breath of Banis summer was fast approaching. Even the flowers knew it, beginning to crisp under the sun. Another month and the rains would be gone altogether.

Sefer emerged from the tent and beckoned to Ajat before following her inside.

A single low lamp sat on a large camp desk. Fishing nets covered the tent's windows, woven loose enough to permit light and air. The Mirikin Hetmir herself sat at the desk, strong features gripped in concentration as she scanned her maps. Her gray-laced auburn hair was raked into a tight knot at the back of her neck.

She glanced up, then turned to look at her prisoner fully. "Reka, I'm glad to see the Banis wilderness didn't swallow you entirely." Her eyes lingered on the new details of the tattoo. "Took us a fair while to find you."

"Ajat, Ser," Sefer interjected.

"Excuse me?"

"Her name's Ajat. She had a ceremony—"

Kemmer waved his words into silence. "Regardless, you found her."

"Did you come looking for me yourself, or did Bren send you after I told him where to shove his elitist ideals."

Kemmer's gray brows arched and she leaned back. Her sharp lips pursed. "You referring to his opposition of our war?"

"Some causes are worth fighting for," Ajat insisted. "I think he's been locked in your precious tower for a bit too long to remember that, though."

Kemmer heaved a sigh, rubbing her forehead. "You're right, of course. I scarcely recognize the man he's become."

Ajat allowed herself a moment of empathy and a smile. "I miss him too. Who he used to be."

Kemmer glanced up, as if recalling that she had an audience. "So what made you defect?"

"I didn't defect. You're fighting Ban and I'm simply seeking a way to protect the people most at risk of dying needlessly. You know Oland killed my cousin's husband? A man more suited to tracking and laughing with his children than war? I thought you were freeing these people, not making them victims of your bloodlust."

Kemmer did not meet her eyes. "That's regrettable. I'll speak with her. That does not change the fact that you disappeared from all contact, assumed another identity, and began trading Mirikin intelligence with some straw-made movement. I can't overlook the fact that you essentially committed treason, Reka."

She surged to her feet, hands pounding on the folding desk, heedless of the ink and pencil she smudged. "My name is Rekajat Monre. I am cousin to Ikel and ally to Kahma, soldier in the Fifth Arc. Close to three thousand soldiers is not a whim, Kemmer. I am here in Ban not to stop your war, but to topple the Banis empire. If you took a moment to actually listen to me, you'd see our goals aren't in opposition at all!"

Kemmer sat back, long arms folding over her narrow chest. A smile quirked on her face after a moment of silence. "Ajat." One hand rose, opened. "I'm glad we agree."

Ajat stepped back, frowning. "What?"

"I wanted to be sure. While you've always worked for Bren, I know you've often struck out on your own. Had your own agenda. I just wasn't certain what it was this time."

"So you know about the rebellion brewing in Ban?" Skepticism cooled the relief, but she could not help her shoulders dropping from their guarded position.

Kemmer lifted a scroll from a pile at the desk's corner. "I received this a few days ago. I had heard rumors, both from Banis prisoners and from my own agents, like Sefer. But we had to be sure. Such information is dangerous in the wrong hands and can't be unspoken."

Ajat stared at the scroll. "May I?"

"Please."

> *Hetmir Kemmer A'hane*
>
> *It may strike you as odd to receive a letter from the wife of the Athrolani king, but I hope you share your son's patience. We have not met in person, but let this serve as introduction. I am Rih-elte, Kajimet of Ban, and wife of His Majesty Keplan Wardyn.*

I write to you with a proposition. You seek to topple Ban, to end the slavery and inequality upon which the empire has been built. So do I. Over the past year, I have developed a network across my country and extending into Athrolan herself as well. A network of soldiers, of women and our allies, who wish for liberty.

I am lucky to count among my allies Majilah Ag of the Vales, Ambassador Mosil-ten Ebal, a man I know you've dealt with often in the past. And, of course, your own son, Azimir. Truthfully, I now count him among my dearest friends.

Ajat's brows rose. She did not know Azimir well. No better than any distant aunt. But it struck her that the impulsive, optimistic boy had struck such an alliance with the woman who might be the next Banis empress. She scanned the closing remarks and returned the scroll to Kemmer's hand. "Azimir's growing up."

"He takes after you, it seems," Kemmer grinned, rising to her full two-pace height. "I always hoped one of them would."

Ajat grimaced. "Did you respond?"

"I did. And this morning a bird came from Athrolan. An'thoriend has been arrested for murders. As in, more than one."

The bottom dropped from Ajat's gut. She did not particularly like the man, but he was an incredible warrior, and she admired his independence. *I'm not the only one who often had their own agenda, apparently.* "I think Keplan well and truly lost his mind."

Kemmer shook her head. "None of his decisions seem to make any rational sense, I agree, but I just hope he sees some larger picture. God and all."

"Gods are dead." Ajat heard the lie in her voice even as she spoke. She felt something that night, as Ikel carved her skin, as who she had been was stripped away, replaced by the fresh flesh of something entirely new.

"Well, one isn't," Kemmer argued. "His temple is erected in Mirik already, just beside his mother's."

"So who's Athrolan's general now?"

Kemmer's grin was wolfish. "Message bird came from Azi yesterday. Made no mention of a general, but it sounds as if your rebel leader has temporary command. Twenty-eight hundred soldiers aren't much against the Banis army, but fifty thousand will be."

Ajat drew a long breath. "It'll be soon, then. There's no way the emperor won't piece this together now."

"I said as much in my letter. We await her move. And her ally, Majilah Ag, should arrive with the last rains to treat with me. Can I count you among us?"

"Always."

Their strong arms locked around one another, Kemmer's dry lips brushing Ajat's cheek. "Welcome home, Ajat Monre."

Φ

The City of Ceir Athrolan, Athrolan

Ice covered the windows. Across the suite the hearthfire blazed. Keplan eased into the room, delicate boots sliding on the sheer ice glazing the stones. The door clicked shut behind him. "Ma? Da? It's me."

Light bloomed through the doorway as he stepped into the parlor. The hulking shape hunched in the hearth raised its hand in greeting.

The privy door was shoved open by a wave of cold seawater.

"I'm sorry it took me so long—the army's been a mess since An'thor—" He stopped himself. "I guess we all ought to start at the beginning."

"Your face," Alea's voice crackled through his head.

He frowned, one arm brushing his cheek as if to whisk away crumbs. "I always get jam—" Sorrow lurched in his stomach. "Oh. I don't know where to begin. I was mistaken for a Mirikin spy. Something about the nose, I guess." His smile flashed.

Alea's waterlogged bones and cartilage flickered into the echo of her own strong nose. *From Azirik. "I'm so sorry."*

"It doesn't matter." Keplan's body dragged with exhaustion, but there was something else. Finality. A relief of his own. "You're here. This world might end. Or not. And it's up to me."

"We left, searching for answers too, you know. We didn't have them all."

"I wondered. I saw you once in a dream, I think, but a true one. There was snow."

"Neneviir. We went in search of a woman."

Keplan wished they had faces he could memorize as they spoke, wished for a moment they were simply his parents, the way he recalled them, and not fathomless titans. Perhaps, like them, he said goodbye to that in the woods a year before.

"What about your arm?" Alea's low voice pressed into his skull, trickling like she did through stones.

He scowled. "The priests you chased here—Swordbearers. One of them carried a revolver like An'thor's. Shot me when I wouldn't let them erect temples to myself on every corner."

Arman's laugh crackled through the room. "Fools. Religious folk always have been." Water splashed at his coals and steam hissed through the room. "Honest, Alea!"

"You went east and north—what were you hunting?"

"You, at first, and then Alea's vision kept getting worse. We knew it was connected to your power or what you might be. Ended up just leading back here the long way around." Bones settled like logs as he shrugged. "I saw Neneviir though. Fascinating, that."

"Did you find any answers?"

"Some. Mostly where we had to go next. Then we found Raven in the Northlands – you sent him to an icy exile. He told us you were king and we knew we had to come back."

"I'm sorry," Keplan whispered. "I know you didn't want this for me."

"It was foolish. My fault."

Arman's flaming skull turned to the oily puddle. "We both chose to keep him ignorant. Of us. Of what he is."

Keplan waved the impending argument away. There was so little time now, it seemed. It should not be wasted on faults or regret. Whatever choices had brought them all here, back to this palace on these cliffs, were long past. "Whatever I am, my existence is an infection. I had those dreams too. Visions. Violence. My blood choking the world."

"Did the prophet tell you why?"

He nodded, settled onto a chair by his father's warmth. "You joined the world but left scar tissue, almost. Perhaps when you brought Da back. But so much of the world's power is caught up in your life forces that without it, the world is suffocating. And I'm the clot, the pinched artery. We're caught in this place like a sheep's tail bound until it withers and drops. She said once I return your power, life will flourish again. She showed me." He smiled, reaching a hand out. "It's beautiful. Do you want to see?"

Water trickled upwards, lit from within by tiny blooms of lightning. It engulfed his hand, freezing and tickling with energy. A stone grip pressed to his limp hand. He closed his eyes and brought the images to the fore.

"Surely dying isn't the answer," Arman murmured when the vision faded from their minds. "Surely you can just act as a conduit. Step out of the doorway."

"The prophet said I have three deaths. This would be the last one. Both times something dragged me back from the brink." He had not let himself dwell on it.

Alea's cold ghosted his arms with a mother's worry. *"Both? My baby, no."* Saltwater beaded on his scarred cheeks.

"After the battle, with my shoulder. And in RoBal. Before I knew, before I ever came here. Interrogation."

The fire raged, sparks scattering across the floor. "Son –"

"It's over," Keplan promised. "I'm here. I made it here. And I did find happiness for a while. Peace."

"That's all we wanted for you. Peace and happiness and a long, simple life."

Heartache pierced Keplan's smile. "I still dream about it. The low common room at night when the last patron is gone and the fire is low. When the music still drifts in the golden night air and Firas, as exhausted as he is giddy, dances to it. And, in the ways that dreams are timeless, Mirrel's there too. Upstairs or in the kitchen come morning. But there."

"Who's Mirrel?" Arman asked.

Keplan blinked and sat back. Of course, they did not know. "Mirrel, she's—she was—my friend. I suppose."

"A lover?" Alea's form uncurled further at the word.

"More like a sister. When I hear or read about siblings, I think of her. Her brother though—I loved him. Love him still. They owned a bar in the city. It's a small place in the slums, but old, with exquisite carvings on the pillars. I left there after I learned about the throne, but…" He shrugged, then trailed off. He wondered how similar the Hare was to his grandmother's Cockerel.

"It's still home," Arman finished.

"What happened? You speak as if they're gone."

"Mirrel's dead," he stated, but the downcast of his eyes and the softness in his face told her his tone was gentle. "Just after I was crowned. She was murdered. Murdered because I am king."

"And this man – Firas?" Alea faltered. *"Did he love you back?"*

"I think he started to. Wanted to. Their father guarded you, Ma." He looked up, finding the brightest clusters of lightning. "He died guarding you in the final battle. Smythesen."

"Kal Smythesen," Arman rasped. "A friend. He told us his wife was pregnant again just before we rode out."

"Well, that's Firas." Keplan shifted. He thought this would feel odd, but it was simply a relief. Perhaps discussing his romance would have been more awkward had his parents been corporeal. "Someone should tell him."

Alea shuddered. "We don't know you'll die, love. You may yet live."

"When are we going to do this? And where?" How was not a question he was ready for.

"We're in a place beyond time, I think," Arman explained.

"Everywhen," Keplan agreed. "I've seen it. Been there. It's the in-between place. Between here and oblivion."

"When is up to you," Arman promised. "Where I think we know."

Keplan looked up. Chills raced up his body, but it had nothing to do with the power rolling off Alea. "Gods' Blood. Their isle. Beside Le'yne."

"I imagine there are kingly duties you ought to see to." Alea's voice tasted bitter.

"A few. I relinquished the throne yesterday, actually. Just before you arrived. My wife—a political marriage—is the Banis Kajimet. She'll take the throne. And be good at it." He was too tired to explain her rebellion, the details, the thousand intricacies between their parallel lives. "Tell me about the journey. What did you see? And Daymir—what did he say when he first saw you? He's regent, actually."

Arman's chuckle rolled smoke through the room. They spoke long into the night, Keplan perched in the perfect temperature between them, laughing, gasping at all the right moments. After all their months apart, this was the fireside story he missed the most.

Hours later, with the moon setting and dawn closer than dusk, he returned to his rooms. Hylier dozed on the couch in the parlor, and Keplan slipped past to his study.

"How're you doing?"

For a moment Keplan did not recognize Hylier's sleep-scratched voice. "I didn't want to wake you."

"I'd be a terrible guard if I slept through someone sneaking into your rooms."

"You'd be a terrible guard if you fell asleep on duty."

"I'm not on duty," he grumbled, sitting up with a theatrical stretch.

"I know." Keplan's grin faded. "I'm all right, I suppose. Tired. Too much energy."

"And your, ah, parents?"

"I'm not sure. It's hard, I imagine, to find your child has become everything you feared they would. But I think they both realize I always would have. Even if I had stayed. I'm just grateful I lived a bit before."

"Returning the power, you think you won't—"

"I'm tired," Keplan reiterated. "I'm looking forward to sleep."

Hylier did not ask whether the king referred to now or to death. He just rose. "Letter came for you, sire."

Exhaustion dragged at his shoulders, but Keplan shook his head. "If it's more hate, I'll toss it in my glass and drink it down with a splash of wraith. I've given up caring."

"And with that, on the 23rd day of Vurgmord, 1272, a true king was born," Hylier drawled. "I'm going to head home. I'll be here tomorrow. For whatever happens. You know, as chaotic as your reign has been, I see hope in it. And we need that."

Keplan's smile faded as soon as the door shut behind the guard. He lit the lamp by his desk, extinguishing the others until he was cocooned in a ball of light.

Someone—Hylier probably—had laid the cease-fire with the Swordbearers, still unsigned, on the desk beside Mirik's latest missives. Already his eyes ached and if he never read through another doctrine, another missive, another list of supplies, he would die happily. A new envelope perched atop the mound of disregarded duties.

It was plain and stamped with the mark of several runners as well as the Dockyard Postal Guild. The handwriting wasn't any Keplan recognized but lacked the uniform loops and curves of a trained scribe. It almost looked like a youth's. The seal was the cheap colorless wax they sold in beads at most markets and post-houses. It snapped open beneath his fingers.

Lan, I'm sorry we haven't spoken.

Keplan's heart thundered into painful waking. He almost did not dare read further. *I need air.* He slipped from his study, from the bubble of bright orange light, and to his bedroom's balcony. The paper, still acrid from being pressed a few days before, hummed in his pocket.

His hand hovered over the letter, but he forced it away. The longer he waited, the longer he could pretend it was written in love. Written with the tenderness the man's hands had held all those months before. *A year,* he realized. *It's been a year.* Did Firas know, too? Did he count the days?

All of Ceir Athrolan lay below him. White stone shone under fading moonlight. Waves glittered, bobbing the battleships awaiting orders in his harbor. *My harbor.* He could have owned the world, and he would trade it all for the letter tucked in his jacket. He settled on the cold stone and began to read.

Lan, I'm sorry we haven't spoken. I'm sorry I turned you away.

In my grief, I didn't think a man like you could understand this life. The life Mirrel and I led. I was wrong. I see what you're doing – not the meetings and orders and silks that fill your days now. But the ripples. Perhaps you understood even better than I did. It's why I testified.

Mistress Ja-ila on the corner opened her home to teach us Slummer rats Banis. I asked her to teach me to write Trade first. I thought about dictating to her, then about not writing to you at all. But I wanted you to know, from my own words, my own hand, that I miss you every day.

I thought about what you said. You've got to have quite the pair to march in and think I was going to fall into your arms, to think that anyone could overlook your crown. And then I thought about your quiet wit, so sly I'd be surprised every time. And I thought about the way you fell into sex like a starved man, like it was the only thing keeping you tethered to this world. And I thought about how you were the first person besides Mirrel that I let in, that I let see me scared and lost.

I miss your strange, quiet smile. I miss your stubborn dedication. I miss your insight, as if the whole world was before you and you could draw pieces of it at will. I know the knowledge in your mind could fell a nation or raise gods. I know you're sacrificing your mind, your body, to keep this dying world alive. I know you have a thousand worries greater than my heartache.

But I still listen for your footsteps on the stairs.

The rending of Keplan's heart drowned the torrent of thoughts welling from the cityfolk. He wished he had a fraction of the faith in himself that Firas seemed to. Had his mother faltered until his father's faith solidified? A flash of anger, betrayal, the image of her screaming, lightning lancing toward his father's sullen sneer, told him it had never been that simple between them.

He learned to write so he could remind me where I came from. There was another reason, echoed in the promise of the last line, the open ending without signature, but his chest ached too much to hold it.

If he had a lifetime, it wouldn't be enough time to process Firas's words. The air trembled with the peal of bells, marking dawn.

Φ

The 25th Day of Vurgmord, 1272
The City of Ceir Athrolan, Athrolan

An'thor rapped on the bars. Within the cell it was dark. "You know this is a mistake!" he called into the low hallway light. Like his countless previous pleas and bargains, it went unanswered. Drops plinked from the pipes above. He paced, boots clapping against the damp stone. Even the two days in the palace under constant surveillance as he put his affairs in order were preferable to this.

Unintelligible voices drifted from the guard station at the end of the corridor. A clunk as the gate ratcheted open and footsteps. Then a ghost appeared just outside his bars.

One pale horn jutted from white blond curls on one temple, a healing stump knotted the other. He offered a nod, jaw clenched in anger or something else An'thor did not recognize.

He then leaned against the bars. "What the fuck are you doing here, Mel'iend?"

"Thought this would be a suitable place to visit. I'm told you don't get out much anymore."

An'thor growled. "That's how prison works. And that's not what I meant. What're you doing in Athrolan? In the capital? With that pathetic band of fanatics?"

"I thought you'd appreciate my choice to ally with the highest powers. It's very Nenev of me, yes?" He struck a pose.

"Preying on people who are too scared to know better?" An'thor spat. "Cults are hardly the highest power."

"I saw the truth in her words echoed in the world, the dying earth." Mel'iend's shoulder shuddered in a shrug. "No one knows scripture like a zealot, uncle, and our scripture is history. It's time you returned to your studies. He hears thoughts. Sees truth. His blood is the vigor of the world. And every shudder of the earth echoes his pain."

"You don't have to convince me that he's something shiny and special. Convince him if you can. I tried and failed. He refuses to own his power, to bend this kingdom to his will."

Mel chuckled, draping a hand over the bars, black eyes scanning the metal like a lover. "That's the single thread that runs through all your actions, uncle. You're a puppeteer with a twisted sense of good theatre."

An'thor's lip curled. His skin crawled and the boy's words wormed through his too-sober mind. "What I do, I do for Athrolan. I do for these pathetic people who can barely burble without direction!"

Mel snorted. "Uncle, their failures are arguably because other beings kept meddling, using humans for their muddled, selfish ends. You're proof, murdering so you can control a god."

"None of these people were worth being executed over. I've killed hundreds more in battle. So have you, as have most people here. Even his parents. Did you come here to let me out? Tell me you've asked for a pardon?"

"Sure." Mel's face opened in the broken gash of an overly bright smile. "I'll pop open this gate and gesture to the streets. 'Pick any direction,' I'll say." His smile shuttered into a glare. "You sent me to my death two decades ago."

"I told you to—"

"You left me for dead!" he roared. "I was a child!"

An'thor staggered against the bars, unable to look at his nephew. He had taken physical blows that hurt less. "You wrote me often enough for me to know you were too young for war and too much of a coward to trust."

Mel turned to look at him, a handspan between their pale faces. Bloodshot sclera shone at the edge of the fathomless black. "You know what I did? I was invisible in my inadequacy. I read the books left up in the attic, shared stories with the other children too weak to matter. Told them about the Dhoah's power and beauty. And when we'd had enough?" His yellowed teeth bared in a grin. "We blew the whole palace to oblivion. And it was simple and easy and terrible. Froze the whole lot of them in their beds. Shot those we had to."

The Swordbearer lunged, thin, wiry arms wrapping around An'thor's head, pressing his throat against the cold metal bars. His other hand rose and An'thor heard the heavy click of a hammer cranking back.

"Pick a direction," Mel'iend crooned.

"What?" An'thor choked out.

"'I don't care which, as long as it's not ours.' Isn't that what you told that little boy in the snow?"

An'thor winced as he swallowed past the biting iron squeezing his windpipe. "Don't stop until nothing looks familiar," he ground out.

Mel's whisper was in his ear now, just beside the cold front sight nuzzling his temple. "New gods. New kings. New nations. New laws. I don't know about you, uncle, but the world doesn't look very familiar to me."

An'thor squeezed his eyes shut. He was too tired for shame or regret. "Toying was never an attractive trait. Just finish it."

"I spent so many nights planning revenge on you. But honestly?" Mel laughed, then the barrel was gone and the unyielding arm loosened. He eased the hammer forward again, and slipped the revolver back into his holster. "It was way better in my imagination. I get nothing out of tormenting a sad old man stuck behind bars."

"So you're just going to leave me here?"

Mel backed down the hall, winking. "Seems fair to me."

The door rattled shut behind him, and the cell plunged once more into dank silence.

Φ

The 26th Day of Vurgmord, 1272

"You have no idea what you've done!" Bimet's hands flashed wildly, her face set in a horrified snarl. "There are people watching you, people who've watched you from the beginning and who can bring your entire movement crashing to the ground!"

Rih ripped the hat from her head with shaking hands. "I don't understand—this is what we've been working toward. I came here to take his army! I'm just happy I didn't have to seduce the man to get it."

"It's too soon!" Tears streaked Bimet's angry face. "We aren't ready! Ban isn't ready."

The words were like a dart to the chest and Rih staggered back. "I thought you were my ally."

"I believe in everything you are, everything you love, Rih. You are my Kajimet. My empress. But this is a mistake. News will be out before nightfall. You could leave tonight and they'd know you were coming before your horse's hooves hit the cobbles." She clasped her hands before herself for a moment, whether to center her thoughts or keep them from shaking, Rih did not know.

"I'm sorry. You've been my temper for so long. My friend. But I've been so isolated here, finding someone who listens and supports me as well as you was rain after summer." Rih reached out to her interpreter. "Please."

Bimet stepped away, but the movement was calm. "I know. I just need some time to think. To plan. I'll send Nehla up with your supper." Her eyes flashed. "And be careful what you tell her. We don't need them knowing any more than they already will."

"I know, Bi. I hope night brings you peace."

"And you."

The room seemed colder in her absence. Rih brought her long rolled map into her bedroom, laying it across the polished floor by the afternoon light cast through her balcony doors. The ink was faded, but her marks were new. She tugged a dart from her quiver and scattered the tiles she and Bimet used as markers across Ban. One piece for Kemmer. The dart tip slid the tile to where the Hetmir's armada waited off the Arc of Zunu. A second for Majilah Ag, who would be arriving in RoBal in three weeks. Rih pointedly chose the prairie cat, etched in black. Another for Mosil, for Ki-elte and her three hundred students. Soon the map was dotted with allies. She rubbed the final tile, the bright green lacquer filling the carving of the horse's skull. There were only a few moves left to make. She slipped the piece into her pocket and stepped back.

Her bones ached from the trembling earth, and her stomach was tight with the pervasive stench of smoke. She returned to her study and glared at the scroll stand. There were a hundred things to do, but she could not bring herself to act. The entire city seemed caught in her same looping restlessness.

Perhaps it's theirs. She understood the terror of the Dhoah' Laen and the Earth Shaker. But she was not frightened by them. She had stared into the eyes of too many predators to fear them. The might of the ocean, the heat of the earth, those were things she understood the way she understood battle. They were the rolling change of the world, brought to form.

Another letter was due to Majilah Ag, though, and so she sat and drew out ink and paper. *And to those in the capital.* Tomorrow would bring a long, complicated meeting with the king. Her gaze dropped to her hand, the heavy, garish ring on her finger. *Rih-elte. Kajimet and queen of Athrolan.* It did not sit right, not yet, but perhaps it was an acquired taste.

It was dark by the time she had finished all her correspondence. She set the scrolls in the basket by the door for the evening runner and paused. The room was cold. The lamps unlit. Her stomach told her supper should have arrived at least half an hour ago. *Maybe Nehla was busy. Or Bimet forgot to tell her.*

Frayed nerves hummed in her arms and she glanced at the door to the servants' quarters, then at the plain soldier's spear on her weapon rack.

She rolled her eyes and headed through the door. She was being paranoid. The stairs were steep, winding in a spiral down two floors. No lamps were lit, save for the very end of the hall. She peered at the names across the doors.

She drew a breath to clear her throat, then stopped herself. It was early evening. The quarters should be lit and bustling as shifts changed. Feeling the scrape of her slippers on stone, she crept forward. *Go back upstairs and get a weapon.* Il-fald's voice rang in her head and she winced.

A shadow moved in a darkened doorway and she froze. There, something dark on the pale flagging within. She inched forward, hovering in the doorway a moment. Every soldier knew the smell of blood.

Adrenaline flooded her body and she ripped the lamp from its hanger and shoved inside. Clothes littered the floor and the bed curtains were ripped, dragged across the floor. Rih's jaw tightened when she realized they were not dyed red, but bloodstained. She lifted one corner enough to glimpse Nehla's face. Her open mouth was a mess of torn flesh and purple blood. Rih did not have to look to know her hands were missing too. *Imperial Silence.* The ultimate blow from the emperor's men.

She let the curtain fall back into place, fury erasing any caution. A sob wrenched itself from her chest, aching and more familiar than her laughter just a few days before.

She did not know what Nehla might have told them, but Rih had to assume it was everything. But Nehla had not known everything. *Bimet!* Rih dashed down the hall, turning left and scanning the ugly Athrolani letters until she found the familiar Banis name. She kicked the door fully open, lamp held out, as much a weapon as a light.

Bimet's room was empty. A chair was splintered, desk drawers open and in disarray. But there was no body. *They have her.* She wished she could jog through the barracks and find Il-fald at her dimly lit desk in the sly hours of the morning. Perhaps if she closed her eyes, prayed hard enough, sacrificed something to the bitter Athrolani wind, it might carry her home.

Fury faded. A familiar path lay ahead, beaten in the earth by a thousand sandals before her, stained with sweat and blood and tears of failure, of defeat. *What about the women who come after me?*

"A woman is of a single mind." Her breath heaved as she returned to her room and locked the door. Clouds gathered over the ocean, black and snarling. She flung open the lid of her chest, digging until she found the small personal grooming kit. The fire bloomed then flickered into darkness as she dumped the kettle over the coals.

"She wakes for the Empire. She rides for the Empire."

Purple pooled at her feet when she undid her wrap. Her tunic dropped a second later. She swung the double doors wide, letting the layers of silk billow. The wind was biting, bitter and foreign. She knelt before her map.

"Her blood and heart and mind are Ban, breathing and alive."

The wooden handle of the razor was familiar, heavy in her hand. She was not wife to His Majesty Keplan of the Hartland and Athrolan. Tiny shorn curls dusted her shoulders. She was not daughter to the Emperor of Ban and the Jade Forest, Jamun-Ilta the Holy Emerald Throne. The scent of shaving oil and blood from each inevitable nick were bright in the fresh air. She dropped the razor to the pile of clothes and stepped onto her balcony.

"A warrior has a single mind."

Naked, bathed in the rising storm, Rih-elte laughed.

CHAPTER NINETEEN

The 25th Day of Vurgmord, 1272
The City of Ceir Athrolan, Athrolan

AZIMIR HURRIED DOWN THE manor stairs, pulling a robe over his naked body. His steward stood bleary-eyed in the foyer, taking someone's cloak. Instead of Keplan's gangly silhouette, Azimir glimpsed Rih's lean shoulders.

"Master A'hane, she insisted."

"It's fine. She's welcome any time," Azimir promised. "Rih, are you all right? It's midnight."

Low lights gleamed off her hands. They were steady. "You said you would be my peace when I couldn't find any."

He gestured down the hall to the parlor beside the dining room. "Master Illos, would you put a kettle on for tea, please? That's all we'll need." Switching to signing, he turned to Rih. "I'm afraid I don't have the pan or herbs to make Banis tea."

He had seen her wide-eyed expression once before, during battle. "I'll have it soon enough."

Despite the exhaustion dragging at his eyes, warning shot up his spine and he asked again, "Are you all right?"

"Nehla's dead. Bimet captured. As we speak, surely there's a riah bound west for RoBal."

Azimir felt the blood drain from him and he settled onto the seat beside her. "Toar, Rih, I'm sorry. What do you need?"

"I will need everything, every ally, from the mightiest soldier to the smallest child if I'm going to win." She drew a breath and Azimir watched the light gleam from her newly shorn skull.

"You're going soon."

"Majilah Ag will be in the capital for peace talks in three weeks. We will meet her there. And I need the world to be whole."

Azimir sat back, heart hammering. "What?"

"I'm not a person of faith. I'm Banis. We prayed to no one, no one but the false god on an emerald throne. False gods and war seem to be my lot in life now. There are thousands of different ways to lay a board—a philosopher once tried to write them all down, from first tile to last. He died at ninety-seven, work still unfinished. But there is only one way to end a game, and I know the moves when I see them." She held her hand out, dropping a game piece into his palm.

It was still warm from her skin, and he held it a moment before looking at the face. A horse's skull, painted green.

"You think Kep is the final piece?"

"I think we both are. I think all of this is. The three most powerful creatures to walk this earth are all in Athrolan, and I've been handed a crown just before I ride to take another. Those aren't coincidences."

"No, they aren't." His hands shook, but each sign was careful. He voiced occasionally, adding detail where his rudimentary signing vocabulary failed him. "I don't know how I will fill the days enough, so that I'm not consumed with worry. I know you have weeks of marching and planning and meeting my mother."

"I'm used to battle. Not like this, perhaps, but enough."

He rose from his chair, clenched a fist, and seemingly forced himself to sit again. "That's not what I mean. Of course, I worry about you, even though I know you are best equipped to protect yourself. I just feel as if I'm losing the two people I love most. I wish I could go with you."

"You could, if you wanted—"

"I think Keplan needs me more."

"I think so too. But afterward, whatever it is, you'll find me. You'll help me rebuild and I'll help you grieve."

"He might not die."

"But he might. And even if he doesn't, the name Keplan Wardyn will." She reached across the distance. "Mind if I stay? Just to talk, until dawn?"

He let their fingers lace for a moment, a pact, as official and weighty as the one she signed that morning with Keplan. "What else are best friends for?"

It was dawn when Illos stepped into the parlor to wake Azimir. "Master A'hane, His Majesty the King of Athrolan is here to speak with you." The steward's eyes pointedly did not even inch toward where Rih lay asleep on the couch. Her hand was still out, fingers curled in the ghost of a word.

Azimir stretched, hissing in pain at the tension in his neck. He wondered if she signed in her sleep, like so many spoke. He groaned, rubbing his eyes. "I'll see him in the dining hall, and I beg of you, please bring tea before I die."

The steward bowed himself out, a tiny smile in place.

Keplan was already seated when Azimir stepped in. "You look as bad as I feel," he remarked.

"Rih stopped by last night. We were up for most of it."

Keplan's eyes narrowed on his cousin, and after a moment his lips quirked. "I thought you looked at her a lot. She's not mine, if that's what you're worried about."

"She's not anyone's," Azimir whispered. "Though I know what you mean. And we didn't. Don't. We're friends. What did you want?" His heart was too heavy for conversation, but something in the shadows under his cousin's eyes made him force exhaustion from his gaze.

"Just to talk." Keplan shifted. "Have you had breakfast yet?"

"No, but I'll call for two, if you'd like." When his cousin nodded, he sent a message down to the kitchens. He was exactly where he needed to be, but he sorely missed Mirikin food. *Never thought I'd long for a crust of bread.*

"How are you doing?" Keplan asked.

"Oh, well enough." Azimir feigned disinterest. "Been a dull few days. I met with my family's steward about the manor. I think Da's furious I'm essentially in charge. He's worried the place will be in disarray. Oh, and Rih's off to war and the Dhoah' Laen returned as a cloud of lightning."

Keplan's laugh sounded more like a cough.

Azimir snorted. His jaw worked as he tongued his teeth with nervous energy. "So, did you talk to them?"

Keplan's flickering frown told him he did not need to clarify of whom he spoke. "Yeah. Through most of last night. I guess they're resting now. They didn't answer my knocks but I could hear the fire through the door—" His head dropped to his hand, shoulders shaking with sobs. "Part of me honestly thought I'd go back to that little cabin in the woods, and they'd be there. Just as they always were. Fates, I can still see their bodies, their faces when I look at them, but every time it's like a ghost, fading into nothing. And I don't dare take a breath to think about my own end and what'll be afterward, so I just barrel forward. Can't close my eyes. Too many images, thoughts. I think them being here opened something. Or maybe it's the prophet's power."

Azimir glanced up, forcing boyish energy across his face. "Anything useful in those visions? The outcome of the next Slummer iguana match?"

"Iguana?"

"Large Banis lizard from the northern islands. Poisonous and easily irritated. Made twenty on a frilled fellow the other night." A pang went through his chest. "I do feel bad for them."

Keplan rolled his eyes. "No. Nothing like that. Just blood. The future. You know, my usual fare. A world where people do not bear the scars I do. I wish I had time." He heaved a ragged breath. "I want to rescue the people like me. Before they need rescuing. What I wouldn't give for someone to break down that door and drag me bodily from their blades. Or to wake up and have the only thoughts rattling around my brain be mine, and mine alone. The echo in here would be incredible."

Azimir surged forward, panic drumming in his chest. This was the conversation he had been avoiding. "We don't know you'll die, we don't, that's not what the prophet said. It might not have sounded pleasant, with all the violent imagery—"

Keplan looked away. "It sounded fatal. My mother ripped open the soul of the world. I might have to cut it afresh. Flood the wounds with life. Hope when it heals it heals whole. Connected." He shrugged. "But, you know, with magic."

A laugh sprang from Azimir's chest.

Keplan glowered. "I don't think it'll feel that funny."

"Kep, I love you, but sometimes you just ought to see your face. So stoic and weighty, then you say things like that." Azimir let out a last chuckle. "Besides, there's only so much talking about you dying that I can stomach. Gives me the winders."

"I'm sorry. I'm sorry for all of it. My reactions. My panic. Our fight. I could have killed you."

"You're not much of a wrestler." Azimir's smile was weak but genuine. "You heard about Rih going to war?"

"I read her note this morning. It's a nightmare."

"I just feel like it's too soon. Too much. Not her rebellion—well, partly—but both of you. I can't lose you both."

"You sound like your father."

"Toar, I mean it, Kep. You don't even know how you're going to do it. Just wait."

"I hoped to stabilize Athrolan before, but you saw them." Keplan's voice was a low rumble. "They're not even human anymore. We barely survived winter. The other cities are clinging to life. Mending the world is complicated. They started the job, but I've got to finish it. I think I'll know how when I get there."

"I don't know if they make instructions for gods." Azimir had never seen Keplan so still. Without tics or manic pacing.

"I need a favor."

"My sword is yours, you know that. Just ask."

"Not as my ally or the Hetmir's son." His eyes were bleached of feeling as much as color. "As family."

Azimir sank into his chair. Whatever he feared, it seemed worse. He nodded, then repeated. "Just ask."

"When it happens, it'll be on the islands. The gods' island. Whatever began there will end there. And I don't know how it will end. It's not something befitting a grand battleship, and besides, Rih will take half her ships west and you're as good a sailor as any Mirikin—"

"I'll take you." Azimir wondered if the earth quaked under Keplan's boots too or just his own. "I'll row you there."

Keplan lapsed into silence, staring at the fire. Their friendship began with babbling, overbearing questions, uncertainty. There were a score of things

Azimir knew he would wish he said, wish he had asked, a dozen stories he ought to recount to fill their last few days together. But only one thing found its way from his heart to his mouth. "Just ask."

Φ

The 28th Day of Vurgmord, 1272

Rih's body hummed with energy. The hills beyond Athrolan were massed with troops. She waited in the barrack courtyard, bouncing on the balls of her feet. Of course, there were those who balked at her orders. Those who had enough of the changing command. They marched south or stayed in the capital. Many of the Banis soldiers she had brought from the capital were gone as well, and surely more would disappear during the coming march. She wondered if they were the ones marching Bimet home. *Stay strong, Bi. I'm coming for you.* Rih's hands scraped against the cold stone, the only sensation grounding her.

Keplan appeared beside her. He held up a wax tablet with a faint smile.

I came to wish you luck.

She smiled back, but it was as if she already looked at a dead man. He always fit so poorly in the role of king that now, without it, his imprint on the kingdom was already fading. *Except for the starved, the thirsty, and the dead.*

Do they know yet that you're to be queen?

She smudged out his words.

There are rumors. I'm letting them fly. When we win, when the world is whole, then they'll know. I asked Lady Gella to come to rule as steward. We'll see how she feels.

She'll say yes, but not out of joy.

Keplan hazarded.

There are a dozen fewer nobles who would gladly take the duty. I don't want someone ruling if it's what they crave.

Well, no one hates it more than me

She glanced over at him, at the overlarge eyes, the pale moon face in the early light.

You and the emperor have so many similar steps but for opposite reasons. You both thought you were destined for the throne. He because he deserves nothing less, and you because you deserve nothing more. He is a man who thinks he's god. You're a god who wishes to be a man.

She was rewarded with his faint smile.

When do you leave?

I'm waiting until the missive arrives at every city. Azimir's rowing me there in a few days. Ma and Da, they're traveling the way they came. I'm glad, though, in the end. That I met you, that I could help you. And that you found Azimir. Everyone needs a friend so faithful.

A flag rose below, a brilliant green horse racing before a tall white tower. It was her personal sigil for now. Her armor burned on her, and she found a bright grin on her face. She offered her hand, soldier to comrade. He tugged his glove off, and his skin was cool, no warmer than the early spring air around her.

"Love and luck go with you, Rih-elte."

"And with you, Keplan Wardyn."

Φ

The 30th Day of Vurgmord, 1272

Cold air nibbled at Daymir's bare hands, but it was not winter's cold. The bells had been tolling for days. Perhaps longer. He pushed his boots deeper into the soil. He missed having a garden. *And solitude.* The boy had come again that morning. He came every few days. Sometimes they spoke, but more often he settled across the tea table, content with silence. It was a kindness, Daymir knew, but not one he appreciated.

He tipped his face to the overcast sky, relishing the wind as it mussed his hair. Its iron gray had faded to white, though he could not recall when. Footsteps approached from behind him, but he did not turn. Make them look. He was not ready to give up the sea air, for them to remind him of things he would rather they did not.

His name is Keplan. Just as sure as he remembered it now, he knew it would be foreign to him in an hour. He did not really mind anymore. This quiet in-between was more familiar. It's why he slipped out more and more, perhaps, though he rarely recalled deciding to don a cloak and stride from the palace.

Below waves thundered into the cliffs. The air was thick with salt, with a bitter, familiar tang. He had missed that in the mountains. He leaned back against the headstone behind him, the sun-warmed stone seeping warmth through the thin fabric of his housecoat.

"Morning!"

The bright voice was not one he recognized. He rocked his head back on the stone to look. She was old, as old as he, perhaps, though whether he was forty or eighty he was not sure. "Morning, mistress. Am I intruding?"

"No, but I rather imagine I am." She settled in a peasant's squat beside him, skirts of her plain sarafan tucked up. Her wool hose were embroidered with bright blue fishes.

"Not really. I mostly talk to myself these days."

"Hela." She stuck a hand out. Her eyes were gray, though they gleamed as if once, they held a secret.

He took the hand. Someone had called him something. *Blackhouse?* But that did not seem to fit in the space between his tongue and teeth. "Ornsen. Dam Ornsen, I think. Are you from the city?"

"No. Haven't decided where I'm from yet." She jerked her head at the hills behind, at the long road winding and the red swollen buds on the trees, just beginning to think of leafing. "We have a friend in common. Keplan."

Daymir frowned. "I assume he's looking for me?"

"No, but he suggested I ride with you a while, since I was headed east."

He looked back out over the ocean. His bones ached, his back was stiff with the raw ocean air, as much as he loved the scent. "I didn't know I was going anywhere."

"Only if you want. I'm headed toward the mountains. Winters are long, but I'm looking forward to not having to listen to anyone yammering for a long while."

He laughed, and the way mirth burned made him wonder when he last had. "On that we can agree."

"What do you think?"

Athrolan had been home for so long, but when he looked over its towers and streets now, even through the waving glass of his window, they were unrecognizable. He missed his orchard. His study. He missed solitude. Groaning, he rose, thinking a silent apology to the headstone's owner as he used it to lever himself upright. "Tell me—Hela, was it?—how do you feel about a little town called Marl Black?"

Φ

The 35th Day of Vurgmord, 1272,
The Village of Jai, Ban

Soot marred what little of Jai's walls still stood. The grasslands were more Banis than Athrolani, and the weather warm. Rih slipped from the saddle. She hated that this destruction was because of her, because of her allies. Even for a greater good, blundering armies wreaked pain wherever they went.

A familiar figure stood under the broken gates. "Rih!"

"Kahma!" She rushed into her friend's arms, squeezing tight, smelling the warm grasses and sharp sweat. She pulled back to sign, "I didn't know you'd be here."

Kahma's face fell, and it was then that Rih noticed her cheeks were streaked with tears, and her eyes were bloodshot. "My brother died. I was permitted to come here to help his wife—with a full riding, of course, to look into the Mirikin threat."

"Mirikin did this?"

"I guess it was chaos. Mirikin came in to extract an informant and a deserter. The Banis soldiers here took the opportunity to attack those they thought were traitors—whether for your cause or the Mirikin, it's hard to say."

Rih rubbed her face. She was exhausted. The Athrolani army strung out behind her. It would be hours before everyone would even arrive or make camp. *How do we hide something this size in the grasslands?* The Banis never had to hide their soldiers. The threat was often enough.

She shoved the concern aside and nodded toward the village. "What do they need? We have medics. Medicine. Precious little food after the Athrolani winter, but what we have we can share."

"Just rest for now." Kahma smiled, hand resting on Rih's shoulder. "There's someone waiting for you."

On the far side of the village, under the copse of acacia trees, was a cluster of tents. They weren't the elaborate, curtained Banis, but plain, serviceable canvas. The largest bore a vermillion flag.

The flaps were bound open in the warm air, and a handful of Mirikin soldiers clustered about a table. One, a towering woman with bright, brassy armor, glanced up as Rih approached. She dipped her head to the man at her right and met Rih at the tent's opening. "Welcome. I'm Hetmir Kemmer A'hane." Her iron gaze followed the signs for a moment, but she did not ask. "You must be Kajimet Rih-elte."

Rih expected someone like Majilah Ag, as stunning as she was dangerous. Kemmer A'hane looked tired. White streaked her auburn hair, and freckles covered her lined face. She was beautiful the way an old city was—with life written on her streets. "I'm honored to meet you, Hetmir A'hane. It's actually Her Majesty now. Queen of Athrolan."

Kemmer's pale brows arched. "That's news."

Rih nodded, reminded of her own youth, her own inexperience. She would need Kemmer and Majilah Ag in the coming months, perhaps even more than she did now. "It's informal for now. You heard about the Dhoah' Laen and the Earth Shaker?"

"And my nephew. Yes. I wish I could have met him."

The older woman nodded toward the prairie outside the walls. "Well, I'm glad to meet you. I was worried the whole journey here. There are at least half a dozen patrols we've lost the trail of in the past month. The fields are rife with Banis scouts."

"And only half of them are mine." Rih flashed a smile. "If you've the maps we can discuss our plans now over dinner—"

"You must be exhausted. Once your arse hits the chair, you'll feel every league. Please. I'd rather know you first. I like to know who's beside me in battle."

"As do I, but we have little time. Our actions were spurred by the capture of my translator and the death of a handmaiden." The wounds were raw still, and she winced at the pain of opening them again. "Let's speak this evening. It will take all night for my army to arrive anyway."

Kemmer snorted, thin lips quirking. "They always leave the slow plodding out of the epics."

"If they didn't, I doubt we'd listen to them at all."

"I understand it now," Kemmer mused.

"What's that?" Rih looked from her interpreter to the Hetmir.

"My son's devotion to you."

"Devotion?"

"Everyone needs their guard. Their support. Lyne'alea had hers in Arman. Arman had his in the other Rakos. Keplan surely had one. He's yours."

"He wrote you about me? Before, I mean?"

"A month ago, when you first began to trust each other. He was torn. Thinking he had to choose between the two of us. He asked for my permission to marry you."

Rih laughed.

"By your reaction I assume he already asked?" Kemmer held her gaze.

"He didn't, really, in the end."

"No? My son is not often one to back away."

"I'm already married and have no wish to do it again. He changed his mind, I think. He did propose, but it was an offer of friendship. Undying, lasting, simple friendship." She met Kemmer's eyes. "Between queens, I think you'll agree that's harder to come by than romance."

Kemmer's smile was bittersweet but genuine. "Go, bathe, rest if you need it." She reached out, stopping Rih as she turned away. "And welcome home, Your Eminence."

The title did not fit, but Rih wondered if one day she would grow to fit it. She wondered if she wanted to. The bathhouse was hastily repaired, but scented oils and thick steam brought tears to her eyes.

The crowded Athrolani horizon, with its hills and cliffs and pale, unfamiliar faces, crowded her heart and her mind. Perhaps this was how Keplan felt, too, inside the confines of his own skull. Now her sandals beat the packed clay, and the baths were crowded with her kinfolk.

Hot water engulfed her, and fingers stiff from holding reins worked dirt and sweat from her skin. By the time she emerged, she felt weightless and at least a few years younger.

Her tent had been erected beside Kemmer's. The emblem from her first journey to Athrolan was replaced, if hastily, with her more fitting new sigil. *If they didn't know Athrolan would change hands when this march started, they'll know by the end.*

Her hammock was already made up, and all she wanted to do was fall into it and never come out. But revolutions did not run themselves. She was almost dressed when she noticed the red flag by the tent flap that served as a knock.

Draping her wrap over her shoulders, she lifted the fabric.

A Banis courier stepped in, kneeling for a breath before looking up. "Your Highness, I brought—"

"I can't understand you through the panting. Take a moment." She took her own untouched glass of water and pressed it into his hands. They were clammy. Shaking. Even the strength in his face quaked under the weight of nerves.

Rih glanced outside. The skies were still clouded. Dark. She had not realized how often the capital was rocked by weather. When she glanced back, he was already speaking again.

"—I had to. But the roads aren't what they used to be." He raked a hand through his dark hair.

"Where did you come from?"

"Package came from RoBal." He had not touched it since dropping it on the floor in his bow, and he seemed unwilling to hold it for the few seconds to hand it to her. "It's from His Eminence."

A chill flashed through her, despite the soft air and long minutes in the baths. Even gifts were not to be trusted.

It was wrapped in oil cloth, meticulously folded and sealed with the stamp of palace runners. She lifted it, gauging the weight before setting it beside the tea tray and lifting the lid. Acrid perfume seeped from the sawdust and straw packing. Jasmine? No, plumeria from the western coast. She pushed aside the straw enough to glimpse dark flesh gone ashy with blood loss.

Rih recognized hands as well as she recognized faces—she knew how each person used them to speak to her, how long fingers flared, how strong ones curled. Even if she did not recognize the tiny bronze ring and jade sigil on the first finger, she would know Bimet's hands. Left over right. Her tongue felt as if it, too, rested on a bed of salt and sawdust.

There was no letter, no message, no note. Only a tile, cupped in the right palm. She slipped it free. It was from one of the emperor's sets—cast in copper heavy with verdigris. Tiny rubies made up the horse's skull.

"Find me a translator, then rest. It's a long way from RoBal." Rih could not meet his eyes. It was no coincidence to receive this package just days before the attack. The emperor expected her.

She slid the lid back onto the box and cradled it under her arm before slipping from her tent. Whatever relief she felt at arriving in Jai was wiped from her body, erased from her thoughts.

Kemmer was still crouched over maps, though her hair was now loose, and a thin robe covered her loose training clothes. She glanced up just long enough to register who stood in the doorway before launching into a diatribe Rih did not bother to try to decipher. Instead, Rih slid the box onto the Hetmir's desk.

"He knows."

Kemmer frowned, lifting the lid with her smallest finger. Her face paled further, and she let the lid drop shut again. "Whose are these?"

"My translator's."

Kemmer's gray eyes flicked to meet Rih's dark gaze. "I'm sorry."

"He's a fool to think this wouldn't happen. No one's power is absolute," Rih insisted. Her hands shook with rage, with horror, with grief.

Kemmer was careful. Organized. Reserved. Rih longed for Majilah Ag and her calculating viciousness. She forced herself to focus through her fury, catching her interpreter's signs a few moments late.

"Your Eminence, this is Ajat, my informant here in Jai. She's a terrific scout, but her skills shine best on packed earth rather than on the ocean. She'll aid you in RoBal."

Rih looked up. The woman was Border, with long dark hair and light brown skin. Her nose and cheeks were tattooed with a bright red and black butterfly. Other than the scar knotting one eye, her gaze could have been Azimir's. Rih's brows rose, but she extended a hand. "Call me Rih or general, please."

"Ajat Monre. I'm honored to be here."

"I'm grateful you came."

It took a moment for Kemmer's officers to assemble, but soon they were ranged about the long desk. When they had, Kemmer settled in her camp chair, eyes fixed on the unrolled maps. "My armada awaits just off the coast, and my army marches west as we speak. By the time they reach the walls of Zunu, we'll have joined them."

"Our issue with all the cities is the walls," Rih noted.

"How can you think to take down those walls—I've stormed keeps with walls half that made of stone," a narrow-faced woman interrupted.

"I'm sure General Rih-elte was about to explain, Oland," Kemmer admonished.

Cheeks hot, Rih bent over the map, pen poised. A red dot marked the capital. "I brought cases of fireshells for you. Ours await us in the city."

"Fireshells?" Kemmer leaned forward, curiosity lighting her eyes.

Rih grinned. "Black powder, like what's used to fire your cannons. But wrapped in a sphere of clay, with a wick. Light the wick, toss it—"

"No more walls."

"No more gates, at least," Rih offered. "The Swordbearers used them to attack Athrolan and I've rarely seen such quick devastation. When will you attack?"

"Night, at year's end."

"That gives us enough time to arrive and for them to send reinforcements."

"I fear they won't," Rih glanced at the box resting on the desk before her. "They know we're coming."

Kemmer's grin broadened. "Of course they do. They think you've gone rogue, stolen the Athrolani troops, and are marching to help us on the coast. One of our informants has been double-crossing us for weeks. Instead of killing the man, we just told him false information."

"You know there'll be a trap laid at the Arc of Zunu," Rih warned.

"Probably, yes, but we're not the point anymore. Your war is bigger than ours." Her hand rested on Rih's forearm. "We've the entire Mirikin navy. They'll be hard-pressed to end us all. Tell me your strategy for the capital."

"There's no way we'll hide most of the Athrolani army." She glanced up to Curiel. "I managed fine with a few hundred Banis, but there's nothing subtle about sand-white faces in Ban. Some of you we can disguise as slaves brought in through Majilah Ag's contacts, but we'll need enough of us in the city to open both the main gates and the palace gates to allow you in."

"How do you plan to do that?"

"RoBal means 'Seven Springs' in old Banis. It's built over six hot springs—it's why we've a bath house on every corner."

"Why call it seven if there are only six?"

"The seventh spring is devoted solely to watering the imperial gardens. Another is outside the city limits." She pointed to the dot on the map. "Another is beneath the gate and powers the mechanisms. That will be our first target. The piping system is a bit complicated, but the runoff tunnels are large enough for people. Most soldiers have to chase urchins out. We'll go in at night."

"What's the second target?"

"Another group—mine—will get in through the gardens. They're large enough to hide us. Once the main gates blow, we'll attack. Fireshells can get us inside, but they will have to be well placed."

"I know someone who works at the main gates, but he's the head of the fourth guard," a young man responded. She caught the hint of blocky eastern features under his Banis skin.

Rih frowned. "I wanted to attack at night, fourth guard might be too late."

Kemmer moved her hand into Rih's view. When she looked up, the Hetmir smiled. "It'll take all night to get in and for the army to be within charging distance."

"Then we'll attack at dawn." Rih chewed on her lower lip. Momentum pushed her, urged her on fiercer than any baniol's copper spurs. But Kemmer was right. Doing it properly was better than quickly. "Let's say we take advantage of your friend."

"Mu-bat."

"Mu-bat. He plants the bombs on the gate's mechanism. That gives my army our entrance. Majilah will have left the capital by then on her way to attack the third city of the Golden Three. I sent her a letter before we departed. She hasn't answered, but as soon as she free of the capital's confines, I'll surely get her response. The palace gates are next."

Kemmer frowned. "Breaking a few pipes will do that?"

Rih kept her contempt of Mirikin and Athrolani plumbing to herself. "Not just the pipes—the pressure can kill a man. We release it at once and you'll have steam a hundred paces high. The entire city was built around them, dry, then the masons directed the water into its new path. It's akin to bleeding a gazelle."

"Messy," Kahma noted.

"But deadly." Rih tapped the palace. "Once we're into the palace we'll need disguises to find a way upward."

"You can't just storm it?"

"A dozen doors and twice as many keys lie between the entrance level and the Emerald Throne." She sighed. "Mosil is my route in."

More marks were made on the maps, others rubbed out. She might have brought thousands of Athrolani troops, but her rebellion rested on a handful of Banis civilians and soldiers. Tiny rubies pressed into the flesh of her palm as her grip tightened on the emperor's tile.

Midnight came before they laid aside plans and pens. There was nothing more, no amount of planning would confirm victory. *Please, Keplan, don't fail me now.*

Kemmer's broad hand rested on the maps. "Very well. Oland, inform my fleet we'll rejoin them tomorrow and to prepare for the journey west."

Rih glanced at Kahma. "Send word to Majilah Ag, to Mosil, to Ki-elte. Tell them I'll see them soon, tell them it's time." Her hands shook, but it was with fury and certainty, not fear. "Tell them I'm bringing the war home."

Φ

The 41st Day of Vurgmord, 1272
The City of Ceir Athrolan, Athrolan

It was a letter Keplan had composed a thousand times in his head. Emotions picked out in relief against the horror of a billion thoughts. It was not long or flowery. He was certain there were misspellings. Smudges. Written over weeks of fear and bloodshed, faint hope, and a sliver of longing. But every word was wrung from the shuddering blood in his veins. Not the gods' blood. Not the human. Just his. But it was also impossible. When Firas could not read there was a finality, a barrier. It was almost snowmelt. Not even a year ago his feet were tripping northward, bound for pain and glory.

Keplan's hand inched toward the top drawer, but he forced himself to his feet. "No." His fist slammed on the desktop. "Fates. It's a grip, love. It's not even that I want it. Because I don't. But my blood gnaws for it. My mind hungers, worse than anything I felt in Ban. I don't notice and before I know it, I'm leaning over the stuff. Breathing. I could breathe with you. Not these horrible gasping sobs. Actual breath. Actual air. I can't remember the last time the air smelled real."

A tune twined through the open window and he slipped into his bedroom. It was wordless, just something composed on the spot. Unlike his letter. A thought slipped between them, a confession, an invitation. He raised a hand, resting it on the memory of the other man's shoulder. The wish of a hand ghosted over his waist and he smiled. Perhaps it was not the thoughts or the monstrous blood that made him mad.

"Gods can fashion the earth at their will. Heard prayers to them and answered every single one. So tell me why I can't will you here. Not much of a True God, eh?"

The tune died in a flurry of happy greetings. Keplan let his arm drop. "Maybe another night, then."

The letter that slipped from his pen that night was not poetry or even proclamation. He was not even sure it was he who wrote it. Keplan stared at the parchment. Were this a drama or a Banis puppet show, the desk would be littered with crumpled drafts. Instead, his pen had hovered over the blank page for the past hour. How did one simultaneously ask for love and explain they would die in the next week? He wondered, all those years ago, what his mother had said, what she told her friends and family and Arman?

> *I know I've asked too much already. I know stumbling into your bar a year ago begged more mercy than I deserved. I'm begging you to have a little more, and grant me goodbye. I was never meant to be king. I was never meant to sit on this human throne and blunder our way out of war. I did so because I was tired of bloodshed and tired of watching your world crumble. But I didn't do it because I was good at it.*
>
> *I long for the peace of the Hare. I hope that's what death is like. But I can't imagine it without Mirrel's bustling energy. I hope the hearth is still warm. I hope you've found someone to help. I wish it could be me. I'd trade a year of the finery here for a single day sweeping the floors.*
>
> *In a few days I travel across the sea to the Isle of the Gods. What power is left to them will pass to me and then to the world. Returning the power, the life force, to the world may, very well, mean my death. It's a romantic notion, made simple because none of us really understand how it will work or what will happen in those minutes, those hours. All we know is it will end them. And probably me. There's a chance, a small one, but one I'm praying for, that it won't. I guess I can only hope it doesn't hurt.*

Tears blurred the words flowing after his pen, but his heart did not need to see. He just hoped Firas would forgive the handwriting. He hesitated over the last few lines. He saw what the possibility of his mother's life did to Brentemir. That was a prison he wished on no one.

For once the thoughts in his head were not foreign, were not pressing in from the hundreds of people he failed or saved. They were his. He paced his room, breath coming in frantic gasps. Silence. He deserved his last night as a king, as a man, as whatever mess he had become, to be peaceful. Even after all the terrible choices he made, he deserved silence at the end. He tore through his desk, riffling through papers and letters he had forgotten about or never answered. It was as if he searched through a dead man's belongings.

Guilt flashed through him at the thought of how much Rih would have to clean up. *Maybe the palace will topple and it won't even matter anymore.* He supposed when one inherited one nation and sacked another, a dead god's unanswered missives might be the least of her worries.

"Where is it?" he snarled, slamming a drawer shut and narrowly missing his thumb. Surely Azimir had come through and cleaned his chambers, or a maid, perhaps. Someone with his best interests at heart. Everything seemed to come easily to the younger man. Even kindness. Empathy might overwhelm his mind, drive him to numb himself with drugs, but Azimir simply basked in it. *Selflessness.* He hated them for it. If he faced a long, glorious life, it would be different. If he faced decades of ruling Athrolan, this would be a mistake. But these few days ahead were his last, and it no longer mattered whether he were sober.

His bedroom was next. The chest at the bottom of his bed was piled with his common clothes, half still speckled with mud, the others wrinkled beyond repair. There, at the bottom where he had hidden it, was a box of dust. He cracked it open and slumped on the floor, tapping a scoop out onto the wooden chest top. Relief was close, but still his nerves ignited, burning away any peace he gleaned from solitude. Perhaps the closer he came, the further his mind seemed from normalcy.

He dipped his head and inhaled silence. He leaned back, heart thundering in relief. His blood heated and hummed, and he settled in to enjoy the quiet sounds that came with existing in a flesh body. Did his parents miss this?

His mind trundled down Athrolan's muddy streets, through the drifting mist of the Slummer, through the lamp-oil haze that blanketed the naval docks. It was only when he heard the creak of the sign outside the Wise Hare that he realized his feet, unsupervised, had followed his heart. Stink clung to his jacket more in this weather. Loneliness underscored even the scent of Slummer runoff.

Firas's words scorched his heart, burned down his throat like elixir, like medicine. It would be cruel now to stumble in, for his bootfalls to clatter up the attic stairs. He just did not know who it would hurt more. Part of him wished for the pain of it all, for the ache of sex and goodbyes and love, just to say he experienced it, just to know what living felt like before he no longer could.

The door clapped open and a young boy stepped out, emptying wash water into the gutter. Keplan stepped closer, tugging his letter out. "Boy. You work there?"

The boy stepped back, washbasin held between them like a shield. "Who's asking?"

"Give this letter to Master Smythesen, will you?" He added a coin to his palm. "It's from an old friend."

The boy eyed the coin and letter, then grabbed both, retreating inside without another word. Keplan tilted his head up to the spitting sky, breathing the smells for a moment. He could not afford to dawdle, but this was a place he wanted to keep, the place he wanted to think of last. The common room's glow spilled across the cobblestones and flooded Keplan's face.

For a moment his eyes met Firas's.

He sank back into the shadows, heart thrumming in his throat. Maybe he did not care how much it hurt his own heart, but he had done enough damage to Firas to last three lifetimes.

"Who's there?"

Keplan stumbled backward, knees cracking on the stone before he found his footing. By the time the bartender had rounded the corner he was pelting into the mist. Part of him—most of him, if he were honest—wished to run into the street, under the teetering walls of the tall Slummer houses, stacked brick on rotting brick. He would climb the Wise Hare's stairs and wordlessly fall into bed.

"Make me forget it, forget everything."

His racing steps brought him up to the arching towers over the harbor gates. If he woke tomorrow in Firas's arms, he could never cross to the Isle's desolate shore. Given a true taste of what he could have, he would never give it up. Even for the world. Life was a funny thing—he spent so long indifferent, unaware of his mortality and therefore uncaring of its beauty. He had never wished for death, though, other than under interrogators' knives. He had times when he didn't care if he lived, but he never came so far as to seek death. *I will.* Soon he walked, opened armed, into her indifferent maw.

He was too afraid to even run. His hand gripped the moss dotting the stone beneath him, yanking at the tender blades until the green stained his palm.

"I'm the only person who really knows what you're feeling right now."

He didn't look over. The reek of seawater and cold rotted flesh drifted, even with the brisk wind. "I suppose you're right. And Father. Funny, the things you never think you'll inherit."

"You've got my hair and nose, too, don't worry." For a fleeting moment her laugh sounded closer to a mountain stream than a swamp, and Keplan glanced over.

"I love you. My whole life you knew me best, and I never had the chance to truly see you. Not till I left. Not until now. But I still love you, and no matter what I see before me, I'll remember you as my mother. Both sides. Both women."

Her gaze, if it still could be called such, lingered on his blown pupils. She looked away, tears peeling the loose flesh of her cheeks. *"I think, against all odds, we did a lovely job with you."*

"Careful. Boasters soon will meet a bitter end."

She elbowed him, exposed bone digging into his skin for a moment.

"But not tonight." He let his head drop to her shoulder, breathing the scent of sea and decay, of wind and distant rain. The snap of lightning mixed with crushed moss.

Φ

The 49th Day of Vurgmord, 1272
The City of RoBal, Ban

Damp leaves and compost pressed on the slats over Rih. Gooseflesh raced along her arms. The wagons had stopped lurching hours before but her stomach still churned with nerves. There was no turning back. There never had been. Something tapped her wrist twice, paused, then once. The west guard tower had called the hour before dawn. She shifted, fingers seeking the latch underneath her. It clicked under her touch and the wagon's bottom dropped open, spilling her onto the soft earth of the imperial gardens.

She drew her first breath of clean, fresh air with relief. Their journey had stunk with the wagons' cargo and the greasy smell from the celebration dinners of Majilah Ag's peace treaty.

She rolled from under the wagon, scanning the dark woods around her. The wagoneer had parked them along the wall separating the northern gardens from The Jewels. Around her others tumbled from the narrow spaces hidden by the wagon's false bottoms. Kahma was already distributing weapons hidden against buckboards. Rih's blood warmed at the familiar grip of her soldier's spear. A quiver of atlatl darts went across her back and the weapon itself looped onto her belt.

"Kahma, you and I will take another four women up to the imperial sanctum. Kol, you and your group cut through the slave quarters. Free as many as you can, but be on the lookout. Jasetti, you take the rest southeast toward the stables. There's a side door there for the draft horses, where we came in."

"Can't say I'd recognize it from under the manure," she joked.

Rih snorted. "Well it's the only gate out of here, save for the palace entrance. It's flanked by a series of palms. Once through there you'll have to make it to the palace gates. Try to make it before the city gates fall. Before they suspect anything. Remember, if possible, give the sign to those you encounter. Many may yet be our allies. Best not do the emperor's work for him and kill each other." She glanced up. Through the dense branches the sky was a soft purple. "It's time."

Kahma's hand rested on her wrist. "A woman has a single mind."

Impatience nagged at Rih's heels, but she tightened her jaw and nodded. "A woman has a single mind. She wakes for the Empire. She marches for the Empire. Her blood and heart and mind are Ban, breathing and alive. A woman has a single mind." Around her a hundred women whispered or signed the words. A still moment passed at the end, then they sealed the prayer with "Liberty."

Half an hour later, Rih was tucked in the shadows of the bonsai fountain, draped in branches and leaves. Two guards rounded the trail ahead, and Rih clenched her teeth to quiet her breath. These were the last two to make the round before dawn. Her chest ached at the fatigue in their features, at the limp set of their shoulders. War's toll was taken from all sides.

Her hand tightened on her spear shaft as they passed. She slipped from under her camouflage, pausing to be sure they had not heard. She held her stance as another of her soldiers emerged from the path ahead of the guards, raising a hand in greeting. Her hand opened in the sign for rebellion.

One guard's hand tensed on his sword, the other spat on the ground. Three leaping steps and Rih's spear tip drove down into the hollow between his clavicle and shoulder. The other guard jerked as Kahma's blade opened his throat.

They dragged the bodies into the brush, covering them with boughs and leaves. A swipe of her sandals removed most evidence of the scuffle. She slipped to the next bole, watching the flicker of movement as the others followed suit. Sneaking in through Majilah Ag's contacts would have been safer. Easier, even. But this was far more direct. Warning tapped in the back of her mind about why none of them had responded. The double guard surrounding the city, however, was the reason, she chose to believe. *You're being paranoid. Not even the emperor would risk his alliance with the Vales.*

She dropped to a crouch and ducked to the next tree, inching toward the palace. Ahead, the ramp gleamed. Several teams broke off, making for the quarters tucked along the base of the palace walls, where their armor or disguises waited in the shadows.

A flurry of movement broke out at the edge of the trees. *The other guards.* Any moment she expected to feel the ground shudder as the gates crumbled. She paused for a moment to brush a hand over the horsehead tile design on the ramp, but she did not know whether it was for luck or in promise.

The ornate folding wood doors at the top of the ramp were shut, the full story of their elaborate carvings stretched before her dark eyes. *The rise of the empire.* Her gaze lingered on the face of Ban's last empress at the bottom. Her skull was pressed into the ground beneath the new emperor's sandal.

Rih's lips curled in a mirthless smile. *Soon, sister.* She beckoned Kahma forward. The soldier crouched, pressing a clay cup to the wood. Her eyes were unfocused as she listened. Overhead the clouds' bellies were cut bloody with sunrise. The soldier glanced up and nodded once.

Rih rolled the doors aside, leaving them wide. The corridor beyond was deserted. Rolling her neck and shoulders, she slipped into the palace. The others would take care of the lower levels, and once the gates were open, Curiel and her allies in the city would take the rest. *But you, Jamun-Ilta, are for us.*

The corridor turned and her steps slowed. Pressing to the wall, she tugged out the tiny leather-bound mirror tied to her armor. Angling it against the dawn light pouring through the windows, she checked the next hall. "Deserted," she signed to the women behind her. They were several levels below the imperial sanctum, and the halls would usually be crawling with guards, but Mosil must have made good on his promise.

"My cousin will meet us two levels up in the dignitaries' wing," she explained. A glance at their collective armor told her it was too worn, too dusty to pass as palace guards, let alone imperial ones. "Be prepared to fight our way in."

Kahma grinned. "That's what I've been waiting for since you first spoke of liberty."

Tears blurred Rih's vision at the sight of her sign, the sign of freedom, loosed in the palace halls. She rounded the corner and broke into a jog. A glance out the high, narrow windows told her the gate was still shut fast. Concern soured her stomach. Wind eddied across the stone and she breathed the familiar scent of perfumed fountains and damp clay. She slipped up the next set of stairs to the wives' suites.

"Go," she signed to one of her women. "Every door with a red tassel on the lamp outside their door. We'll push ahead. Meet us above with Mosil."

The women took off down the hall, knocking faintly at the first door.

Rih watched her go, longing heavy in her chest. *I wish you could see this, mati. I wish all your sisters could too.* Her limbs throbbed with their blood, though, the blood of every woman whose body made the Banis walls, whose blood dyed the emperor's war sash.

Kahma tugged her hand. Already women and men were emerging from their rooms, faces lit, slim, concealable weapons slipping into sashes and folded silks. Each one who met Rih's eyes steeled her soul. She let herself be pulled away to the smaller private stairway at the end of the hall.

The woman froze, hand in the air to halt. Then two fingers extended. Two guards waited for them at the top. Her free hand slipped a long wooden needle from a box at her belt. It was wickedly sharp, discolored green at the tip. She popped it into a slim tube and pressed herself to the wall, counting silently. On three she whirled around the corner and shot up the stairs. Before her first victim finished falling down the stairs, her second poison dart found its home, and his companion tumbled after.

While others dragged the bodies into one wife's room, Rih followed Kahma up the stairs. The dignitary's wing stretched before them. Now came the difficult part. *The part Bimet's death may have cost us.* They crept through the halls, weaving south, then west until they turned a corner.

Rih's nerves calmed at the sight of Mosil's silhouette at the end of the corridor. "Ally," she told her guards, breaking into a soldier's trot. Her cousin did not turn or even sign a greeting.

Her eyes narrowed on his arms, still by his sides. He jerked, then slumped to the floor as the curved blade of a glaive was pulled from his kidneys. Behind him, Bimet straightened, weapons gripped in her two whole hands. For a breathless moment Rih thought she would put the weapon aside, turn and join them. Instead, she raised the polearm to block the hall.

No. Rih hesitated, then lowered her weapon to sign. "Bi, I don't understand."

Bimet did not lower her glaive. Her body shook, and the shadows under her eyes could have swallowed the city entire. "You never did, Kajimet. You were coddled from the moment you became a soldier—not brought on the worst missions, not forced to march farthest. Permitted to become a wife instead of trampled into the dirt."

"Being excluded is not a privilege!" she argued. Precious time was slipping, and the light through the window screens grew ever brighter.

"Perhaps you had terrible choices, but at least you could choose. Do you know what I'd do for your life?"

"I think I do, now." Rih's heart broke. Not for the betrayal, but for her friend. "Why don't you help me? I know you believe in this, believe in our cause."

"But I don't believe you will win."

It was past dawn, yet the palace was still. Doors were locked. Window screens shut despite the warm breeze. Apprehension shot up Rih's spine. Perhaps Kemmer was not the only one heading into a trap. *She's just the only one who saw it.* "What about the gates? Our network? Where is everyone?"

"Your fireshells didn't even make it to the border. The palace has been locked down for days. The baniol's tunics will be red for years to come. His Eminence's war robe will never need dying again."

"I have allies across the entire city," Rih retorted.

"You're a fool if you think they'll rise up now. You should have seen it, Rih." Awe opened Bimet's features, but it was not made of joy. "Don't you smell it?"

Rih did now, under the heady perfume of lilies. The tang of blood, the slick of rendered lard. She rushed to the nearest window, yanking open the screen. The bodies of hundreds of female soldiers piled in the open square between the palace walls and the barracks. Their hair was long, their clothes Valen. The smoke drifting over RoBal the was not from Majilah Ag's peace supper. It was from the pyre of her slaughtered army.

All Rih's rage at Bimet's assumed death roared to life. "What did you do?"

"I arrived two days before she did. I told Vi-baln everything." Bimet seemed unable to look out at her handiwork, and Rih could barely understand her through her chattering chin. "I'm so sorry, Rih. I had to. I wish—"

Rih would have preferred apathy. She would have preferred cowardice. Anything was better than shame, than guilt she felt compelled to comfort away, even in the heart of an enemy.

"A war is begun by making enemies, but it is won by making allies." Minata Kaz was right. Rih did not survive the army, the Purple Throne, or even Athrolan by dividing.

A door opened down the hall. Vi-baln's golden robes shone in the bright light. He ambled toward them, drawing up beside Bimet, seemingly unconcerned with the soldiers fanning across the hall. He stroked the back of Bimet's neck with one large, smooth hand. She shuddered, the fight leaving her eyes. His thumb circled her throat for just a moment, just enough to remind them both who owned RoBal.

CHAPTER TWENTY

The 49th Day of Vurgmord, 1272
The Isle of the Gods

WAVES CRASHED AGAINST THE garnet beach. Alea watched as two figures disembarked from a rowboat and pulled it above the high-tide mark. The shorter drew his cloak tighter against the wind and moved to wait on a boulder. The other stared into the tangled forest in the heart of the island before turning and making his way along the strand toward them.

"He's here," she called to Arman, the brown stone beneath her already waterworn from her pacing. Her mind existed both in the never and always, but one thought overrode all: her son's face had scars. Her fist clenched. A tower fell somewhere in the ruins beyond. This is how kingdoms ended. Fury and vengeance. The boulders clustered by the tree line reddened, sheaves cleaving off at the inferno in their heart. *"Did you see his face?"*

Flames flashed white, then gold. "I did. I can't imagine—"

"Makes you want to let the world rot. You don't do that to a god. Not to him." The waves roiled, lightning blossoming over the sand in frustration.

"Ma?"

She turned, the seaweed and salt solidifying into a mass capable of embracing. Keplan's jacket mildewed under her touch. She brushed her hand over his cheeks.

"I could fix these," she whispered.

"They don't need fixing, Ma. Certainly not now."

Her head tilted, mirroring his. There was no need to speak. Not in that they understood everything in one blink of Keplan's too-large eyes, but in that it was too much to convey, and the world's sand was running from its glass. *"I wish so many things."*

His smile was filled with more hope than sorrow, and he reached out to both of them. "And they'll be true. Maybe not for me, but for someone. Ever since I knew the truth, I've been trying to save the world, or even just my corner of it. But this, this is the first time I know I can actually do something. That I know my actions have an impact. I feel like I'm actually supposed to exist. That I wasn't a mistake."

She trailed lightning down his face. *"You could never be a mistake. Even if ending the world meant creating you, I'd do it again."*

He pressed a kiss to her cheek. "I love you, Ma."

Unable to speak, she pressed her consciousness against his before pulling back. Heat bloomed behind them and Keplan turned.

Sand melted to glass under Arman's steps. The towering flames around him reduced enough that one hand cooled as it reached out. Gleaming white marble clenched Keplan's shoulder. "There are so many things I wish I had the chance to teach you and to learn from you. So many."

"We just have now. Now has to be enough." Keplan squeezed, seemingly unaffected by the coal of Arman's palm.

"I always had to sink into my power," Arman suggested. "Surrender."

Keplan nodded, then looked up with a frown. "How badly does it hurt? I've come close but never—"

"Much, but it's quick." He flashed a smile to Alea. "But my deaths never lasted as long as they should."

They exchanged another few words, then Arman stepped away, hand out to hers. "Milady, it's time."

And it was. Her ice sizzled against his flame and she backed into the ocean, eyes fixed on her son. Of everything she had done and made and said, she was most proud of the battered man on the beach.

The ocean surged and her feet splatted on the tops of Le'yne's black cliffs. Across the ocean gleamed Mirik's distant lights. Despite the waves, the scuttling clouds, it was as if time stopped. She recalled a different night, a different journey down those stairs.

But this time she would not be alone. Flames exploded beside her and she offered him a smile he surely felt more than saw. *"It's probably silly to ask if you're ready."*

"It is. But I am."

Together, they wound up the path, into the hall and down the spirally stairs. Water flooded after them, stone and ash crumbling in their wake, blocking the way back.

Arman's burning form served as a light, but Alea did not need it. She trickled down the walls, through the earth, between every stone and crack in the foundations of Le'yne, of the world. Finally she could stretch. She shuddered, Arman's echoing shiver shaking the ground.

The cavern was dark and empty, devoid of pool or gleaming bundle of souls. She wondered what happened to them so long ago, loosed with nowhere to go. *"Here's where it began. As good a place as any."*

"I'd argue it began in Vielrona, with your hand on my chest and searing pain."

She settled into the hard stone, fingers laced in Arman's, or rather, entwined in the heated air and writhing dust that served as his bones and flesh. "But how we are now began with your death and a walk across the ocean."

Hot air swirled like his breath on her neck. "What would have happened, I wonder. If you hadn't. If you had left me there. Respectfully buried me. Sent a letter to my mother. Married Daymir."

Alea snorted, rheumy eyes rolling. "We'd have lost the war. Or it'd be harder won. Perhaps another of the Rakos would be tapped to channel that power."

Stone rattled against steel in his laughter. "Nonsense. I am the only Earth Shaker, the most powerful."

It was a flash, a fleeting glimpse to an evening years before. Arman, slumped on the flagging of Fort Stone, giggling and drunk. *Fates, we were so young.* Of all the men surrounding her then, however, not even Arman had seen what she was. How could one go twenty years of living together, raising a child, weathering winter and spring floods, and yet never know a person? Perhaps no one had known her. Perhaps knowing a person, truly, was impossible, even for oneself.

Rock cracked, chucks of ceiling shattering on the cave floor. "How do we do this?"

"I did it once, with the gods. I imagine it's much the same." The feeling of timelessness, of nowhere, grew. Her mind reached deeper into Arman's power, scorching and white and full of sound. Power pulsed as she drew it up, out of herself, tugging twisting magic like threaded roots. Another pull and the branches of power came loose. Blackness curled on the edges of her consciousness.

The whirling, raging constant of him pressed against her now, closer than they ever came when they still possessed physical bodies. *"Thank you for always being here."*

"Thank you for listening. For laughing. For everything you did. I know I didn't always do right by you, but fates, I tried."

"It was enough. This life, it wasn't perfect. But all of it, even the pain, was enough." She yanked a final time. Power exploded in the cavern, black power roiling with gold. Sound and light flared. Then there was nothing.

Φ

The City of RoBal, Ban

Sunbaked walls loomed over Ajat's head. She pushed hair from her eyes, hating how the mud clung to her every inch. She tucked herself farther under the shack roof. Damp burlap scratched at her skin with every motion.

An urchin with Sefer's face tossed a net in, just under the draw bridge. He pulled the net out, glance darting between the top of the wall and Ajat. Two rocks plinked from his hand.

Two guards.

The net cast in again.

Ajat was good at waiting. The sun slunk lower, and she fished out a piece of dried meat to quiet her rumbling stomach.

Sefer scanned the open gate again, caught her eye, then slipped away into the squalor that clustered along the road.

Ajat stretched, rolled her neck, and eased to her feet. She trailed along the moat, peering into the water as if looking for some treasure to sell or food to eat. The minutes between the guard change and the gate rising were few, but she could manage. She slipped down the moat's bank, mud coating her legs, and ducked under the bridge.

Her way into the gatehouse was hidden by dusk and the hulking mass of the bridge, at least for the moment. Under the bridge's shadow was a packed bag. She pulled it out and set off across the moat.

In the legends, Banis moats were filled with crocodiles or snakes. Some on the coast even claimed to stock theirs with sea monsters. The true threat of the RoBal moat was the stench. Tucked at the base of the bridge's hinges was a small culvert. Thick muck from deep within the city spilled through, and Ajat steeled herself.

Banis infrastructure was coveted in most nations, but there was a problem when you no longer cared where your waste and sick pooled. She bound up her hair and, holding her bag above the worst of the scum, pulled out an air bladder and sandals with hooks under the ball of each foot. She filled the air bladder with humid air and slipped the sandals on, wincing at the squelch of fates-knew-what between her toes. Feeling along the base of the wall, her fingers caught on the thick bars of the grate.

The last few wagons for the day trundled overhead and dirt rained onto her. Every movement sent water sloshing against the red clay. It did not matter that she knew no one could hear over the din of the city, she felt eyes on her, knew ears were trained to listen to even the slightest sound. A press of another finger and the latch came loose. Metal clunked and she eased the grate off its latch and opened it.

Drawing her last deep breath of clean air, she pressed the bladder's straw to her mouth and dove into the sewer.

She squeezed through the opening, dragging herself through the mud and scum until she reached the larger pipe that ringed the city. Here, at least, the pipe was large enough for her to stand, even if muck and scum oozed around her waist. She pulled herself upright, her pack with its precious contents going on her back. One hand ghosted over the pipes running along the walls, feeling the heat emanating from some. Others were no warmer than the surrounding clay.

Each hot pipe was marked with stripes of colored paint. Her eyes found the red stripe in the darkness and she forged ahead.

Filthy water dragged at her legs. Her sandals' hooks helped her grip the scum-slick bottom. The stench of waste and trash and mildew brought tears to her eyes, but the thought of opening her mouth to breath flooded her throat with bile.

The red pipe curved right, the others cutting deeper into the city. Another twenty paces and the tunnel arched around a massive pilon. *The gate.* A ladder led from a round door in the floor above. The pipe, too, followed the pilon up into what must house the gate's mechanism. Light filtered through the floor slats, and in the slivers of light she caught the glimmer of teeth jutting from the clay. RoBal's massive walls were cemented with secrets as much as mud.

Water rushed through the surrounding pipes, but she heard no footsteps overhead. By her count she had another two minutes before the new guard shift arrived. *Sixty breaths.* Hand over hand, she hauled herself into the gatehouse. Four breaths to scan the room. Massive gears stretched into the darkness. Pipes led to and from. In the far corner was a valve that was fed by the spring. Her gaze dropped to the empty corner under the valve. *Deershit.*

Mu-bat was meant to have brought the crate from the weavers the night before. *No crates or no Mu-bat?*

She scanned the gears, mind whirling. Perhaps keeping it open would be enough. Grabbing the stool, she broke one leg free. Noise no longer mattered. Thirty-nine breaths left, she clambered up the largest gear and shoved the stool leg into its workings.

Footsteps creaked in the hall. Low Banis voices. Her gaze dropped to the open cover down to the sewers. The broken stool beside it. She could make it, but they would know. *Make it count.* Ajat shifted into a crouch, one hand holding her body taught from the gear. Her body ached with adrenaline. Shadows loomed in the door, then two soldiers entered. She dropped.

He coll with the impact and she used her momentum to slam his head forward into the floor. The lamp he carried shattered, oil and ash and fire spilling across the floor. A warning whistle shrieked through the air. She rolled free and came up, panting, blinking sweat and mud from her eye. The second guard's knife skimmed past her face. She twisted with the blow, hand blocking a breath too slow. The blade bit into the meat of her hand. She snarled, glaring at the two fingers tumbling across the floor. A vicious ache throbbed through her hand. He pressed his spear tip against her throat. "Talk."

There was no time to talk. The room stank of ash and blood, the smell of war, of the ruak. She grinned.

"What?"

"Ash and blood."

He spat, eyes not leaving hers.

"We used to call on gods in times of transformation. We'd use ash and blood. I call the lifeblood of the world, spirit who ends us, who guides our arrows. Stripped." She extended her mangled hand from her chest, opening to the sky. In the space it took for him to frown, she lunged, thrusting her bleeding fingers into the broken lamp. Her world imploded in flames. "Remember your name, he who bleeds the earth."

Φ

The Isle of the Gods

The gods' city was nothing more than ruined brown granite. Keplan trailed through the memory of streets, the suggestion of a market. He expected skeletons. Scorch marks, even. Some evidence of the horror his mother caused. Keplan's tongue filled with ash and the salt of brine and blood.

He hiked farther in, steps carrying him up winding stairs, through crumbled arches. His parents were brontide in his blood. His reflection dragged at his bones, drawing him up, in, until he skittered out onto an open rooftop. It had been an amphitheater once. Or perhaps a throne room. Silver dusted the stone, emanating from a point near the center.

Screaming wormed through the air, his mother's inhumane voice wringing water from the very air. Brilliance burned away his vision. Blackness, hot with blood of the world, surged after. Energy flooded his body, pouring upward from the earth. It was pain, lancing with each image, each memory as his consciousness shifted to accommodate each new piece, new position, a weary body sinking into a clean bed and feeling every ache from the day. *How do you carry it all?*

"The thoughts? Or the duty?" He recognized his reflection's drawl. *"Or just existing?"*

"I knew you weren't gone." Keplan fell to his knees, hands pressing to the warm stone of the gods' world. Their foundations. *"All of it."*

"You can't."

Seawater and electricity crackled over the islands. Fire gorged on his flesh. The earth shuddered, cracked beneath his hands. Magma erupted, flooding between his fingers. Red copper erupted from his skin, not his father's scales or his mother's rot, but something wholly new. Lightning crackled. His body lit with flames.

Life pulsed, a flash, hotter than sun, than lightning, freezing with its intensity. It was a small wonder why the skin of the earth cracked with its own might. *I am he who bleeds the earth.*

Like a spine popping with a stretch, the earth opened. Stone melted, rivers boiled. Chalk dusted from Athrolan's cliffs leagues away. His body ached, power writhing from within, life in a womb he both did and did not have.

Mountains rose and wore to nothing. The Banis plains burned and were once more fertile. In the west, ships rocked against the shore, buffeted by tidal waves under a clear sky. He was the ocean air toying with Kemmer's rogue curls as she loosed another volley on Zunu, teeth bared.

He was the earth churning beneath RoBal's springs, heating the water to steaming as the city shuddered under the footfalls of thousands. Archers drew back, and his back ached against the drag of a thousand strings. In Berr, the sea roiled, fishes from the deep places surfacing, ripping junks in twain.

He was the marble toppling from the aqueducts in Ceir Athrolan, crushing the warehouses, the prison where An'thor awaited doom. Sobbing laughter bubbled from Keplan's mouth, and he surrendered himself to the sensation. Everything fell. Everything rose. Mighty billowing breaths.

Life was too much to bear, too much for a single soul, a single land, delicate stone crusted over the burning might of everything. Alea saw the foretelling of this, and in Mother's hubris, thought it him. He saw the ferocity of his blood, the hideous duty resting on his shoulders, and in his own hubris called himself a god.

I am no more god than she. Than Rih, than Firas. Than any child of humanity. They were right. No creature could carry this power, the weight of life. Not at once. *Not alone.*

Life fled his body, flooding after the pulse of energy, and for a perfect moment, there was oblivion.

Φ

The 1st of Lleume, 1273
The City of RoBal, Ban

Rih's knees stung as she was shoved onto the mosaic floor of Vi-baln's private audience chamber. She scanned the room, counting windows, doors, guards, anything that she could use to turn the game in her favor. There were few playing pieces left, though, and all were in his hands. Bimet fell to her knees by the Hand's dais, narrowed eyes focused only on her own hands clenched in her lap.

I would have sworn those hands were yours.

But if they were not Bimet's, then whose? Rih shoved the grisly mystery aside. Kahma dropped beside her, cheek bleeding from Vi-baln's smack. She cast a furtive look to Rih, seeking orders.

Rih shook her head once. Not yet. They would only get a single chance, so whatever their plan, it would have to be good.

Vi-baln's mustard-gold slippers passed before them, and she looked up.

"I was so flattered that Bimet here thought to include us in your little rebellion party. Hurt, of course, that you didn't think of me yourself, but alas." His smile was broad and full of hate. "From the moment my niece Nehla took interest in you, I knew you were one to watch. She was always too clever, playing the superficial, playful courtier." His lip curled.

Beside her, Kahma signed as much as she could, but Rih understood enough for horror to wash over her. Nehla had never been the one to suspect.

I'm so sorry. You tried. If any of them survived this, she would owe a visit to Mobeka. And an apology.

Kahma's hands were moving again.

"His Eminence will be thrilled to hear we've quelled your ambitious—if poorly executed—plot before he ever stepped into his morning baths. It was close there, for a moment. I'll admit even I believed the Valen bitch for a while." Vi-baln had settled into his seat, crossed slippers inches from Bimet's tight face. "Luckily, Bimet is always happy to oblige me, ever since she was a girl."

Nausea twisted between Rih's ribs. At his feet, Bimet trembled. Air puffed past them, and Rih turned. The door was rolled aside as a veiled woman slipped in, head bowed over a tray set with an array of food. She knelt at the dais, tray raised overhead for him to eat from.

After months within Athrolan's famished city, Rih's stomach awoke with a burn. When she glanced back at Vi-baln, he was laughing.

"Hungry, are you? Best be used to it. I doubt they'll feed you before you're brought to the walls."

Time. They needed time. Curiel would be hard-pressed to storm the walls, but surely fifty thousand Athrolani swords would count for something. Keplan had to count for something. She pulled a smile onto her face. "Kill me if you want. Kill every last one of us. It won't save you."

Kahma broke into faltering translation, eyes darting between Rih's flashing hands and Vi-baln's predatory gaze.

"Empty threats won't save you, Kajimet."

"You recall the scripture, the one that drove me here months ago?"

"Vaguely. I'm not in the business of pandering to false gods."

Rih tilted her head. "Aren't you, though?"

"You think you know anything about the wrath of a god? You're nothing more than a lank-haired nag's dam." His expression soured and he rose, shoving the serving woman aside. He dragged Rih to her feet by the shoulder strap of her armor, fruit-sweet breath wafting across her face. "I can promise, you haven't even tasted a hint of its bite. Bimet knows. Her sister too—she was kind enough to lend us a hand. Both of them, actually."

Rih pulled saliva from her adrenaline-dry throat and spat it across his face. His grip loosened and she hit the hard floor, head cracking against the lowest dais step. Colors exploded across her vision and her world spun. When she could see again, Vi-baln's personal guards at the door were motionless lumps of silk, two of the women from the rooms below standing over them, weapons drawn and bloody.

Vi-baln was once again in his chair, hand pressed to the back of his own head. Fresh blood stained the neck of his robes. Bimet stood before him, body shaking. The blade of her glaive, however, was perfectly still, and pressed to the hollow of his throat.

Her free hand signed for Rih, though her eyes never left the man's face. "Her name was Fedar and she was my world. You promised nothing would harm her—any of them—if I brought you the rebel queen. It felt like dying, losing her. Like gasping, without air. Except, worst of all, I still had to go on living afterward."

The ground trembled. It was faint, nothing close to the quakes in Athrolan, but there. The second lasted longer. Maybe it was even closer. Dust eddied down from the rafters.

"Look, Empress." Bimet's face shone with a lifetime of justified fury. "It feels like you might win after all."

Rih stumbled to her feet, head pounding. "Bimet, I—"

"I'll find you later. I'd like a few minutes." All expression fled her face. She no longer even looked tired. Easing her weight to her other foot, she let the glaive bite through the thin skin over his clavicle. "He always enjoyed our time alone."

Rih backed toward the door, torn between trust and suspicion. But she knew countless women who walked in Bimet's sandals. The same fire screamed within their ribs. She yanked her weapons from a dead guard and shut the door behind herself.

The guards outside were dead too, and a dozen armed courtesans awaited her. The serving woman pulled the silk from her face.

Rih caught one glimpse of Ki-elte's bright brown eyes and collapsed into her tutor's arms. The shudder of laughter or weeping passed between them, then Rih pulled away. "I missed you."

"I've missed you, too," Ki-elte answered. "But you've an empire to overthrow and are a bit behind schedule. The guards all expect you, and they're at every door. But I trust you remember how to dress."

Rih grinned. "You'd be so proud—I even have a favorite hat." Someone handed her a kalas and wrap and she set to work. The clay shuddered, a tiny crack racing across the wall. She paused in tucking the last piece of silk. Rih followed the gazes to the windows opposite the Hand's ornate parlor door. Dust plumed in the air just inside the walls. A twitch of the bedrock followed, then boiling water shot skyward.

A hand dragged her back from where she leaned against the sill. "There's no time," Ki-elte scolded, ripping the silk from her. "You and the rest of your girls, with me." They wound upward through the warren of narrow slaves' tunnels and stairs, her thighs burning with every step. The ground continued to tremble, though perhaps it was the momentum of all surrounding her, all their allies in the streets.

Ki-elte pushed aside a curtain and they emerged in the foyer of the emperor's private bathhouse. Rih's arm whipped, muscles loose until the last moment when the dart thudded into a guard's ribs. His fingers scrabbled at the shaft as if he could extricate himself.

Rih leapt. Air swept her side as a blade brushed past. Another slid cold fire between her fifth and sixth rib. She wondered what they heard when she screamed. Panting, she ripped her dart from the guard. Blood spurted, and his limbs shuddered into stillness. Her shoulder blades ached with the effort.

Beneath them, the earth convulsed. It was a moan Rih felt between her ribs. A stretch after decades of slumber. No one had found her fireshells. She rolled from the guard's body in time to block a descending sword with her spear shaft. She kicked up into his gut and flipped her spear around to drive its tip into his belly. She flopped back, breath shallow. Hot blood bubbled from her side. It was an atlatl's dart, and there was no time.

At the end of the hall sunrise shone through the jade doors. She snarled and snapped the shaft off. She wiped a hand through her blood and smeared it across her brow and up her cheek. This was her battle. She shouldered the door open.

Sunlight shot stars through her vision. She jerked her spear free, chest heaving, blood cooling on her leather armor.

The opposite wall was open to the gardens, and no fewer than five pools were built into the floor. In the largest, along the outer wall, waited Jamun-Ilta the Holy Emerald Throne, Emperor of Ban and the Jade Forest.

Naked, without his face paint and finery, he was unremarkable. Annoyance pinched his broad face. "Rih-elte. I expected to see you at a sunset execution."

Of course he signs. She was never permitted to look upon him, not even his hands so she might understand him. "I'm a bit early. And it's not my execution."

"I gave you everything you could ask for. And this is how you repay me?"

"You gave us everything we needed. You gave us rage. You gave us knowledge. You gave us invisibility. And me? You gave me these things most of all."

Darkness pinched the edges of her vision and her knees locked to keep her upright.

"Honestly, I'm offended this is all you think it would take. Look at you. You're bleeding out where you stand. I can hear your lungs wheezing from here."

She laughed, blood and spittle misting the air between them. She grinned. He did not know she bled with the blood of a thousand queens.

Below, the city rocked. Geyser after geyser exploded into the air. Rubble rained from the billowing clouds of steam.

Uncertainty crept across his face. "We destroyed your little clay bombs."

"Those aren't fireshells, Jamun-Ilta." Steam rose from the pools surrounding him, bubbles rising faster, larger as the water heated from below. Every lamp globe in the throne room crackled and exploded. Shards rained across the room, drawing spider-silk lines of blood from their skin. The bathwater tinged pink.

"What is this?" he asked again, gaze roving between her and the miasma outside.

"You thought you could tame us." She tossed the tile into his bathwater. He watched it sink. "You thought you could crush us like you did our foremothers. Like you did the Vales. And here I am, covered in blood, just like all those before me. You may have been crowned by the gods, but they are dead now. And the new one has decreed your time is over."

The sky blackened, knotted clouds pulling strength from the rising stream. The ceiling overhead shifted, dropping even as the earth cracked beneath their feet. She wished the look on his face was fear. She had to settle for disbelief.

Pain radiated across her back as she ripped the atlatl dart from her side. She dragged a last deep breath from her collapsing lungs. Every step spurred her heart faster. Re-bel. Rebel. *Rebel!* The mantra became the tattoo of her footsteps; she launched from the tub's lip, bloody dart raised high.

They collided. Metal wrenched over bone. Blood sprayed her face. She pushed the dart deeper into the tender place just above his clavicle. Her dark eyes bored into whatever was left, rotting, of his soul. She forced her shaking, bloody hands to sign.

"The One True God chooses me."

CHAPTER TWENTY-ONE

The 2nd Day of Lleume, 1273
The Divine Isle

HOT WATER SLID OVER Keplan's skin. Comforting. Blinking, he found himself on a mound of warm black rock, hardened in whorls and currents. Steam rose from the cleft in the rock just beside him. Pulsing heat emanated from below, but it was soft. Quiet. A few paces away a clear spring bubbled from the earth, and it was in its trickling water that he woke. Nothing grew, but destruction bore fertile soil.

Tender palms raked a hairless, burnt scalp. New. Pink. He rolled over onto his naked belly, muscles protesting at the hard stone beneath them as he pushed himself upright. His body would not obey his command to stand or walk, but he could crawl.

Rough stone scraped his burnt palm as he cupped water to his mouth. He watched the spring trickle across the gnarled scar tissue obscuring the curls of claret and green. Clean. The air in his lungs was clear, but it lacked stillness. Now it had bite, ferocity, mirth. This is what the Laen had seen. *It's alive.* So was he.

A sound arched over the barren landscape from somewhere below, by the strand. A bird, perhaps. He propped himself on his stronger arm, the left still weak. *I guess I have no excuse not to exercise it now.*

"Keplan!" The voice came again, the word clear, if strangled with tears and perhaps more than a little laughter. Azimir appeared over the hill and broke into a sprint.

Keplan offered a weak wave.

His cousin stumbled over the undulating rock, avoiding the warren of steaming cracks. When he came to a halt beside Keplan, he was panting, clothes streaked with dirt and sweat. "Kep."

"Azi." His voice was hoarse, lowered from a thousand screams. "You stayed?"

Azimir sank to his knees and stripped his coat off, tucking it over Keplan's bare body. "I thought you might make it. After all of this. And if you didn't, if there was anything left, I thought I'd bring it back."

Keplan thought the stiffness about his mouth might be a smile and tried to broaden it. "None of us deserve you."

Azimir batted the compliment away. "What happened?"

Keplan looked around at the ruins on the next hilltop of Le'yne. At the Mirikin cliffs, half swallowed with solidified lava. "It worked."

"And your parents—?"

"Don't." Keplan's stomach writhed with grief. "Legends paint pretty enough pictures. Truth needn't be a part of these. They're gone, and that's all." He allowed Azimir's hand under his elbow to lift him. "I feel like I ought to be dead."

"That's how you know you're not," Azimir explained with a faint smile. His dark eyes lingered on Keplan's head, on his face.

"I must look it."

"You don't look like you. That's all. Are you able to walk?"

"I think so, just a bit weak to try." He glanced at the Mirikin palace, tucked between new land and old ocean. He imagined he would recover there for a time before returning to his capital. He and Rih could rule in tandem, perhaps. His chest was tight, though, and his smile felt frayed at the edges.

"What is it?"

"Just thinking of going back. Of all that's left ahead. Returning to the throne. Explaining, after all of that, that I survived."

"What if you didn't?" Azimir's questioning gaze settled on him, and the young man propped an elbow on his bent knee.

Something opened in Keplan's ribs. "What do you mean?"

Azimir looked down. "The night before she left, Rih and I had a talk. About a lot of things, but some of it was you. I knew you might live. Call it whatever bit of intuition I inherited from the powerful side of the family. So we made a contingency. Athrolan doesn't need to know you lived. No one has to. If you realize you do want to rule after all, you want the Athrolani crown, it's in its case in your chambers where you left it. Rih will gladly rule a single empire instead of one conjoined. Go home, take up your kingdom, and rule beside the Banis empress for the rest of your days."

Keplan's mouth was dry, and he drank another handful from the spring before running a hand over his bare head. "And if I don't?"

"Then I stumble back home and tell Athrolan their king is dead. Their gods are dead. Proclaim the world is whole and new and alive again. You take the pack I put together and disappear. Rih left you some things too. They're waiting at the post office on the Athrolani docks, addressed to a Lan Guardsen."

"My parents did the same thing. Running." Shame burned in Keplan's gut. "Why does it feel like cowardice?"

"This time the job is done. Truly," Azimir promised. His face was lined with fatigue, as if the last hours—or days, perhaps—had aged him a year. "In a way it is. But you've admitted you don't want the crown. Admitted you're no good at it. We just thought we'd give you a choice if you survived long enough to make one."

Φ

It was dusk when Azimir climbed the steps to his family's manor in Mirik. Sweat and dirt stained his clothes, and his eyes were tired. He walked alone. Already he spotted riders setting out across their new single island as tentative cartographers.

Victory had been declared in their war with Ban, but the news was murky with talk of the new empress. The adjoining estates of the other commissioners were quiet. Azimir rapped on his father's doorframe. It was ajar, but the ambassador seemed transfixed with his untouched drink. "Da?"

Brentemir blinked and looked up. "Azi? I didn't know you were home."

"Just arrived. May I?" He gestured to the seat across the desk. His father did not answer, but after another quiet moment, he sat. He could still smell the stink of sulfur and seawater on his clothes and the tang of his own nervous sweat.

Bren still had not met his gaze. The little auburn still left in his hair seemed faded, as did his wan face. "I watched it from the harbor gates. Like I did the first time."

"It was incredible."

"You saw it in Ceir Athrolan?"

Azimir winced. Where did he even begin the lies? "No, I actually came to Mirik days before. I was the one who rowed Keplan to the island. He asked me to."

Bren stared at Azimir as if viewing a stranger. "I should have been with them."

"You had no place there, Da."

"And you did?" Bren's rumbling voice was scraped thin on the sharp edges of feelings he never bothered to file down.

"Toar, I cowered under my boat for the better portion of it." Azimir sighed, raking a hand through his hair. "When I was nine, you told me the story about the final battle of the Gods' War. The night before. Do you remember?"

"But this is war, and I'll probably die," he rasped, the notes barely in tune.

"You stayed up most of the night singing and dancing. A defiant vigil in the face of certain death. Well," he drew a long breath, "this was mine. Keplan was my Alea. Hero and mystery in turns. And just like her, now he's gone."

Bren stilled, and his eyes squeezed shut. "Gone."

"When you're a god, I don't think death is a strong enough word."

"Alea?"

Azimir shook his head. "I'm sorry."

Bren's head sank to his blocky battered hands. His shoulders shook. "They were all I had. The only ones who remembered what happened. The only ones who saw it through with me."

Anger flashed in Azimir's heart, but it was old, and he was tired. "Da, an entire world saw it through. All of it that we know of, really. You can't define your life by a single year. Even one as powerful as that." His fist clenched and he thought of a young man, burned and beaten, but miraculously whole, disappearing into the press of people in the city. "Keplan was never ours. None of them were. But Ma's yours. I am, and Al too. Rih's mine, as much as she's anyone's. Say your goodbyes. But let them go."

Bren's shoulders shuddered. "I've spent my whole life saying goodbye to them, and yet I somehow still don't know how."

"I doubt anyone knows how to, in the end." He looked at his own hands, more his than either of his parents'. "The Swordbearers will be going on about this for a while now."

"I imagine so, yes." Bren cleared his throat with a frown, as if trying to remember how to be a man. "Where are you headed next?"

Azimir leaned back, mind already slipping through the window, boarding the ship to Athrolan. "The crown belongs to Rih now. I'll deliver it to RoBal with Commander Fess and Lady Gella." His breath shook as he drew it in, feeling the power in the words. "Athrolan is no more."

Bren looked down, a silent moment offered at someone's passing. Except this time it was an era that died. "Toar, I hardly know my place."

Azimir turned to him, arms crossing over his chest. "Stay home. Ride the new coastline. There's a crack in the earth where you can see its pulse." When his father glanced up, shocked, Azimir smiled. "The magma surely will benefit our fields."

Bren frowned. "Our economy rests on grazing, but with the fertile soils." He trailed off and met his son's eyes. "You're right. I belong at home. And when your mother returns, I'll be here to greet her."

Azimir's lips quirked.

"What?"

"That's the first time you've called her that. My mother."

Bren sat back. "How long did you know?"

"A lot longer than anyone realized. It just didn't matter," Azimir confessed.

Sorrow eased over the ambassador's features. "I'm sorry."

"For what?"

"You became a man when I wasn't looking. I realize how much I've missed chasing people I never..." He sighed.

"We've got years, Da. Decades if you stop drinking like An'thor."

Bren's smile was shaky but genuine. His sword hand retreated from the bottle on the shelf behind him. "I'll try my best. Do you leave tomorrow?"

Azimir nodded, rising from the chair. It was late and he was filthy. "I hope to stay in RoBal for a time. Maybe ride the empire a while. I always wanted to visit the jungles."

"I wish you a safe ride to Ban." His father rose, arms opening.

Azimir stepped into them and squeezed. "And I wish you a fair spring." He slipped upstairs, movements unconscious. He called for bathwater and settled at his desk. The moon rose as he penned his letter to Rih, and in the city below, a man who was once a god slipped into the night.

Φ

The 19th Day of Lleume, 1272
The City of RoBal, Ban

Even after weeks, Rih still did not consider the palace hers. She knew the halls better than most and the gardens better than that, but the hulking building was more a nuisance than a home. The piled rubble still being sorted and repaired was a startling splash of bright broken stone in the gleaming clay steps, garish even from the west guard tower, where she now stood.

The room was windowless, save for a narrow slit near the top by the door. The smoke from the pyres in the fields was stronger here. The door swung open and her focus snapped to the man limping in.

Mosil's face was thin but his color far better than it had been in the days just after battle. He bowed to her and gestured to the man shackled behind him. "Evening, Your Grace. I've the man you requested from Ceir Athrolan."

"Bring him in and unchain him."

Mosil ushered the prisoner forward and settled him in a chair. He unlocked the shackles before removing the hood from the man's head and stepping back.

Rih looked down into An'thor's dull black eyes. "Evening, Domariigo."

The Nenev glanced from her hands to Mosil as her cousin translated for her. "What is this?"

"I couldn't let Athrolan's best military resource crumble with half its streets," she informed him. "And you'll address me as Your Grace while you're our guest here."

"Guest," he stated, voice dropping with skepticism. "Something tells me this is a visit I can't refuse."

"I imagine this is better than your previous accommodations, though." She stared at the crumpled legend. "You'll have almost everything you need and some of what you want."

"And in return," he hazarded, "I'm your…what, strategist?"

Rih snorted. "I'm standing atop a fallen empire and you're in prison. I don't need your strategy." She handed him the leather tube protecting all of Keplan's sketches and schematics. "I need your war-weapons."

She stepped back, gesturing to the cot and clay tub on the far side of the room. "I'm sure your ride was a bumpy one. I'll come again tomorrow so we can discuss what else you might need."

He rose as she turned to go. "Wait. What if I say no?"

"Then I wait until you grow tired of counting the floorboards." She nodded to him and followed Mosil from the room. It was locked, of course, but no one noticed one more prisoner among thousands dragged to the tower on the other side of the gardens.

Rih wanted peace as much as Keplan. She smiled, hurrying down the tower stairs and into the fresh air of the gardens. But she was a soldier, and no one knew better the unrest that came in the wake of war. She had killed a monster, but its brethren were still loose in the world. An'thor and his mechanical mind would secure Ban's new liberty.

Across the city Stytown still flooded with the unchecked springs. RoBal was nothing more than an eye, bruised but still glittering. Rih had no interest in rebuilding the crumbled walls, content to let them gape, bones jutting from the cracked clay. New pipes would be laid, as would new laws. The broken government would die and maybe even the empire, in years to come. Kemmer would have more to teach. Rih drew a deep breath of jasmine and the hot summer night. One thumb rubbed the horse-skull tile in her pocket. There was much to learn, but Rih was of a single mind.

Φ

The 34th Day of Lleume, 1273
The City of Ceir Athrolan, Athrolan

Ceir Athrolan was unrecognizable. Brilliant red banners covered most surfaces, a sharp contrast to the turquoise pennants. When Keplan spared a glance for the swollen dome of the palace, his heart faltered. It was cracked open like a hen's egg, made brighter by the black draping every tower. *Mourning.* Mourning a king. A god. A boy who should never have been, should never have ascended the throne. He stepped off the gangway, wincing at the scrape of rough fabric on still-raw skin. He slipped into the crowd, another scarred man after war, another face tilted up among a sea of desperate, hopeful souls.

After the foreign press of Mirik's Jug End where he stayed the last two weeks, Athrolan's broad streets were almost lonely. Half the buildings no longer stood. The prison had been crushed beneath a toppled aqueduct. The gutters flooded with runoff from the new spring bubbling in the hills to the south.

Despite missing half its roof, the post office bustled with clerks and guards alike. He ducked under the scaffolding and into line. Gazes slid over him, past him, lighting on the new scars, not seeing the old. He found the expression tugging his mouth was a smile.

"And for you, Master?" the postmaster called, beckoning Keplan forward.

"I've a letter waiting for Lan Guardsen." A smile tugged its way onto his face. Aliases were for murder, but this time the victim was who he used to be.

The man frowned and peered at the shelves behind him, muttering the name until he found the appropriate section. "Ah, yes. Been here a while. Traveling, were you?"

"A bit."

"Staying home long?" he asked absently, stamping a few sheets of paper, then sliding them across for the younger man to sign.

"Not sure yet. Depends on the next few days."

The postmaster laughed. "I know that story. Said it myself forty years ago when I applied to be a runner. Been here since." He handed over the thick envelope and waved the next person forward.

The sunlight was brilliant off the water, and Keplan hiked the steep stairs past the naval docks. A new sigil hung from the walkway over the open harbor gates: a tower, half red, half white, crossed by a sheaf of wheat on a black field. *The province of Ceir Athrolan in Ban.* His grin returned. This was not the world he or his parents ever walked. It would be a better one.

His scar-thickened fingers fumbled the heavy seal for a moment before it loosened. Tucked in the waxed envelope was a stack of papers. One, a writ of passage to anywhere in the new empire. The next, a note to a sum of money—insignificant when compared to the Athrolani and Banis treasuries, but large for a common man. Lastly, there was a letter. Each was addressed to Master Lan Guardsen. A thrill thrummed in his limbs at the name.

He opened the letter.

Lan,

It feels odd to write to you, not knowing if you'll read this or if you'll be dead. But I suppose I am not writing to who you used to be, who I knew you as. Rather, I'm writing to who you will become. If you have need of anything, any time, no matter how much time or distance has come between now and then, you need only ask.

As I write this, Azi rides west. He and Commander Fess bring the Athrolani crown to me. I don't know yet what I will do with it. You must know that I meant it when I said I saw the same world you did, when I said I'd help make it. There will be more to come, so much more. I pray we succeed. I write that with a smile, you know. As I'm sure you're smiling now, reading it.

You told me very little about your life in Athrolan before taking the throne. I just know that you wished to return to it. And that there was a man waiting. I hope you're reading this beside him. I hope you found there was a place still set for you.

I know I could have done all this alone. But I also know it would have been harder and taken longer. And I am glad for your help, for your recovery, for your perspective.

We made each other better, in the end.

- *Rih*

He did not weep. At least, not until her final line. Sweeping potential lay before him, a vast untainted field. Perhaps it always had, but the night had been too dark, the storm too loud for him to notice. *"I hope you found there was a place still set for you."*

He tucked everything back and lifted the pack onto one shoulder. The city had changed much, but he did not need to mind his feet on their way to the Slummer. His heart still knew the cobblestones. The building beside the Wise Hare was abandoned now, the windows boarded. In daylight the lantern above the inn's stoop was not lit, but the sign groaned a welcome in the breeze. Smoke drifted from the chimney and it smelled of home.

He pushed the door open and stepped inside. Sunlight spilled over the floorboards, and Keplan shot a glance at the bar. It was deserted, and he remembered abruptly that the common room was only open in the afternoons, save for folks renting chambers above. Keplan doubted if the knots in his stomach would allow him to eat anything. Still, he slid onto a stool and set his bag aside.

"Be with you in a moment!" the deep voice rumbled from the kitchen.

Keplan's heart threatened to stop for good. He loosened the collar of his shirt as if it would somehow lessen the pressure building in his chest.

The Banis boy whirled from the kitchen, one hand gripping the severed neck of a plucked chicken, the other dusted in flour. "Sorry, Master, caught us in the midst of preparing supper." His dark eyes flicked from Keplan's scars to the bag at his feet, then back. He offered the flour-covered hand, then the chicken, then decided against a handshake altogether. "Gillus. What can we do for you?"

"I'd like to speak with Master Smythesen, please."

Gillus made a face. "I wouldn't raise your hopes on a room. Things are changing, Banis money and all that."

Keplan's heart sank. It was almost impossible to think of a home that was not the Wise Hare. "Tell him anyway, please."

Gillus raised his voice. "Firas!" When the bartender called through the kitchen doorway, the boy continued. "There's a man here to see you. Says his name is—"

Keplan shook his head.

"He's a traveler," the boy conceded. His full attention returned to Keplan. "May I get you anything?"

"Privacy."

The boy's curiosity inched over Keplan's face, but he nodded and returned to the kitchen. A breath and an eternity later, Firas emerged. His broad back was to Keplan as he set an armload of clean mugs on the counter and began to hang them.

"You wanted a room? What'd you say your name was?"

"I hadn't. It's Guardsen."

The mug clattered against its hook as Firas turned. There was no recognition in his green eyes.

Guardsen was a common name. Scars changed a person. *Years change them more. Even if it's just one.*

There. A glimmer, maybe of tears, probably of anger. Firas's shaking hands pushed the mugs away. His gaze roved over the mottled burn parting his shorn dark hair and his lanky bare arms, bare hands. It refused to meet his, however, brushing over every inch of him, save his eyes. When he opened his mouth, only a few strangled attempts at words emerged. He looked away and sagged forward, wiry arms bracing him against the bar.

"Firas, I'm sorry," Keplan whispered. "I don't mean to hurt you—though I imagine I've done nothing but. Always have." He smiled, but his body was too exhausted, too nervous, to pull it farther than his mouth.

Firas's shoulders jerked and he sniffed. "Why are you here?"

Keplan faltered. He expected a welcome, an embrace. Not questions. "It seemed the thing to do. So much of my life was fluid. Myself, even." He raked a hand through his hair, belatedly realizing it set it at odd angles. He swore softly and tugged it back into order. "When I was here, Firas, I knew myself. Maybe not all of me, but I could see the foundations." He shrugged. "I'm going about this all wrong."

"Going about what?" Firas scrubbed a hand over his face. The one beside Keplan's remained unmoved.

"Apologizing, I suppose."

"Showing up on my stoop when news of your death was literally rung from every tower, when the palace is decorated in mourning colors—fates!" Firas's fist slammed on the countertop. "You know how hard it is to grieve when everything around you is grieving too? Makes the loneliness deeper, biting. You realize you're dead?"

"Keplan is. But I'm not. Lan Guardsen, former barboy, former stable hand, came here to the Wise Hare, hoping his old job might be available. Or his room."

"Both are Gillus's," Firas countered.

"He said things were changing, something about money?" Keplan tried again.

"Building beside us is up for sale. Trying to scrape enough together to buy it. Expand. Her Grace is offering investments for smaller places such as ours and I'm hoping to apply, but that's not really important."

"If you had help," Keplan started. His mind flickered to the note in his bag. He would rather spend the rest of his night alone on the road than buy Firas's heart instead of earn it. That would be for tomorrow, if his tomorrow included Firas. "I just mean—"

"I thought you were dead. The whole city—world, actually—thinks you're dead."

"That was rather the point."

"Why didn't you tell me? After everything, after every secret I kept for you? You saw what I went through when Mirrel died. I hate it, but part of me wonders if she'll come bustling in after you. If there was some miracle, something your mother did. She brought back the Earth Shaker all those years ago—" He groaned. "I'm too sober for this."

"I'm sorry." Keplan looked down. "This was Rih and Azi's plan, actually. I never believed I'd survive. I had to free you from forever listening for my footsteps on the stairs."

Silence yawned between them, broken by Gillus's muttered Banis swears as something boiled over in the kitchen. Firas's lips trembled and he still refused to look away from some distant point in the street outside. When he spoke again, it was barely a murmur, but there. "'All we know is it will end them. And probably me.'" His gaze slid along the bar, inching toward the other man.

"There's a chance, a small one," Keplan prompted.

"But one I'm praying for," Firas rasped. His eyes fixed now on Keplan's shirt collar.

Keplan eased a shaking hand across the countertop until just a hair's breadth separated them. "That it won't."

Green eyes met blue. The silence billowing between them was softer. Listening. He did not dare break it. Whatever thoughts flashing through the bartender's mind were best left to percolate. Keplan eased himself from the stool and stepped quietly behind the bar. Firas did not move as the younger man took a mug and filled it with water. Keplan leaned on the counter beside Firas, taking a slow sip. The water tasted of stone. When he glanced up, Firas was almost smiling.

"What is it?"

"You. Here. It's familiar. I missed it."

"I missed—" Keplan's voice cracked and he cleared his throat.

"The drink," Firas quipped, laugh nervous.

The space buzzing between them was a lifeline. "I missed the way your brow knots when the first rays of morning light hit your face. I missed the way you dance, with so much enthusiasm that it doesn't matter whether you have skill, though you do. I missed the way you'd go from playful to world-weary then back again in a moment, just at the smell of smoke or the glint of firelight. I missed the way your body curled into mine and the way your hands traced every mark on me like they were your favorite city streets, not scars." He looked up, hoping his eyes were honest, not bloodshot or manic. "Of all the things I've lost since I lost my mind, I've missed you the most."

"Then stay," Firas whispered. "Forever's a long time, but it's yours."

Joy bubbled from Keplan's chest. He fell into the other man's arms, laughter escaping as their lips met. *Home.* When he pulled away, he plucked at the strap of Firas's apron. "I'll be needing one of these."

Firas's fingers curled in the short hairs at the nape of the taller man's neck. "I miss your hair."

Keplan dropped his head to press their brows together. "Give it a year or two. Then enough folk will have forgotten the pauper king."

"A year or two." Firas drew a shaking breath, expression sobering. "So much is going to change. This is a lot to carry."

"We'll figure it out," Keplan promised.

"Together." Firas's grin bloomed. "All right, get to work."

Keplan laughed and crossed the common room. The floor creaked beneath his boots and he swung the door open. Dusk was just beginning, the promise of a storm purpling the sky's edges. He stood, chest open, breathing the new air. With a last glance at the falling night, he lit the lantern and shut the door.

END OF RESTORED

ACKNOWLEDGEMENTS

The end of a book, whether we're writing it, or reading, is always a bittersweet moment. Concluding a series even more so. These characters carried me through so many strange and unsettling times, and it's fitting to set them loose on the world when everything is the most uncertain it's been in a long time.

I'm grateful to all the incredible people who helped see this series and book through, and while I could never name them all, here are a few:

Thank you to Kat, for cheering me on and being my platonic soulmate in so many ways. Thank you to Marissa and Amy for all your feedback and dogged enthusiasm even while I was locked in the doldrums.

Thank you to the Sirens team, past and present, and to the Iceland Writers Retreat, for creating such a welcoming place when I needed it most. Thank you to all the incredible queer communities I've found.

And thank you to Brad, for your unwavering love and understanding, even when I'm hunched in the corner with my computer way past the time we were supposed to start watching a movie together or eat dinner. And thank you for reminding me that I need to take a break, even when I have "a thousand, goddamn" deadlines.

And thank you to my parents, who introduced me to stories and to dreams.

ABOUT THE AUTHOR

V. S. Holmes is an international bestselling author. They created the BLOOD OF TITANS series and the NEL BENTLY BOOKS. *Smoke and Rain*, the award-winning first book in their fantasy quartet, became an international bestseller in 2018. *Travelers* is also included in the Peregrine Moon Lander mission as part of the Writers on the Moon Time Capsule. In addition, they write game content for Stone Blade Entertainment.

As a disabled and non-binary human, they work as an advocate and educator for representation in SFF worlds. When not writing, they work as a contract archaeologist throughout the northeastern U.S. They live with their spouse, a fellow archaeologist, their dog Rory, and own too many books.

www.vsholmes.com

www.ingramcontent.com/pod-product-compliance
Lightning Source LLC
Chambersburg PA
CBHW021624030826
48979CB00038B/2555/J

* 9 7 8 1 9 4 9 6 9 3 3 4 8 *